Artwork by Robert Beer.
Typeset in Adobe Garamond Pro at 10.25 : 12.3+pt.
Editorial input from Dániel Balogh, Ridi Faruque, Chris Gibbons & Tomoyuki Kono.
Printed and Bound in Great Britain by TJ Books Limited, Cornwall on acid free paper

T0339036

THE CLAY SANSKRIT LIBRA

FOUNDED BY JOHN & JENNIFER CLA

GENERAL EDITOR

SHELDON POLLOCK

EDITED BY

ISABELLE ONIANS

WWW.CLAYSANSKRITLIBRARY.ORG
WWW.NYUPRESS.ORG

MAHĀBHĀRATA

BOOK SIX

BHĪṢMA

VOLUME TWO

TRANSLATED BY

Alex Cherniak

NEW YORK UNIVERSITY PRESS

JJC FOUNDATION

2009

First Edition 2009

The Clay Sanskrit Library is co-published by
New York University Press
and the JJC Foundation.

Further information about this volume
and the rest of the Clay Sanskrit Library
is available at the end of this book and
on the following Websites:
www.claysanskritlibrary.org
www.nyupress.org

ISBN 978-0-8147-1705-9

Library of Congress Cataloging-in-Publication Data
Mahābhārata. Bhīṣmaparva. English & Sanskrit.
Mahābhārata. Book six, Bhīṣma /
translated by Alex Cherniak;
with foreword by Ranajit Guha. -- 1st ed.
p. cm. – (The Clay Sanskrit Library)
Epic Poetry.
In English and Sanskrit (romanized) on facing pages;
includes translation from Sanskrit.
Vol. 1.
Includes bibliographical references and index.
ISBN 978-0-8147-1705-9
I. Cherniak, Alex. II. Bhagavadgita. English & Sanskrit. III. Title.
BL1138.242.B55E5 2008
294.5'92304521–dc22
2008014986

CONTENTS

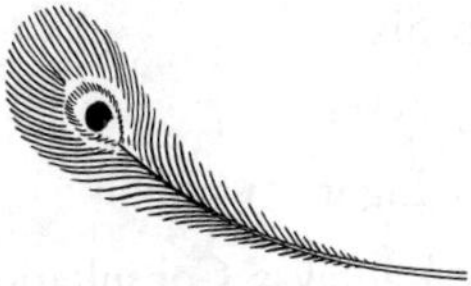

CSL CONVENTIONS

Sanskrit Alphabetical Order

Vowels:	*a ā i ī u ū ṛ ṝ ḷ ḹ e ai o au ṃ ḥ*
Gutturals:	*k kh g gh ṅ*
Palatals:	*c ch j jh ñ*
Retroflex:	*ṭ ṭh ḍ ḍh ṇ*
Dentals:	*t th d dh n*
Labials:	*p ph b bh m*
Semivowels:	*y r l v*
Spirants:	*ś ṣ s h*

Guide to Sanskrit Pronunciation

a	b*u*t
ā, â	f*a*ther
i	s*i*t
ī, î	f*ee*
u	p*u*t
ū, û	b*oo*
ṛ	vocalic *r*, American p*ur*dy or English p*re*tty
ṝ	lengthened *ṛ*
ḷ	vocalic *l*, ab*le*
e, ê, ē	m*a*de, esp. in Welsh pronunciation
ai	b*i*te
o, ô, ō	r*o*pe, esp. Welsh pronunciation; Italian s*o*lo
au	s*ou*nd
ṃ	*anusvāra* nasalizes the preceding vowel
ḥ	*visarga*, a voiceless aspiration (resembling the English *h*), or like Scottish lo*ch*, or an aspiration with a faint echoing of the last element of the preceding vowel so that *taiḥ* is pronounced *taih*[i]
k	lu*ck*
kh	blo*ckh*ead
g	*g*o
gh	bi*gh*ead
ṅ	a*n*ger
c	*ch*ill
ch	mat*chh*ead
j	*j*og
jh	aspirated *j*, he*dgeh*og
ñ	ca*ny*on
ṭ	retroflex *t*, *t*ry (with the tip of tongue turned up to touch the hard palate)
ṭh	same as the preceding but aspirated
ḍ	retroflex *d* (with the tip

	of tongue turned up to touch the hard palate)
ḍh	same as the preceding but aspirated
ṇ	retroflex *n* (with the tip of tongue turned up to touch the hard palate)
t	French *t*out
th	ten*t h*ook
d	*d*inner
dh	guil*dh*all
n	*n*ow
p	*p*ill
ph	u*ph*eaval
b	*b*efore
bh	a*bh*orrent
m	*m*ind
y	*y*es
r	trilled, resembling the Italian pronunciation of *r*
l	*l*inger
v	*w*ord
ś	*sh*ore
ṣ	retroflex *sh* (with the tip of the tongue turned up to touch the hard palate)
s	hi*ss*
h	*h*ood

CSL Punctuation of English

The acute accent on Sanskrit words when they occur outside of the Sanskrit text itself, marks stress, e.g., Ramáyana. It is not part of traditional Sanskrit orthography, transliteration, or transcription, but we supply it here to guide readers in the pronunciation of these unfamiliar words. Since no Sanskrit word is accented on the last syllable it is not necessary to accent disyllables, e.g., Rama.

The second CSL innovation designed to assist the reader in the pronunciation of lengthy unfamiliar words is to insert an unobtrusive middle dot between semantic word breaks in compound names (provided the word break does not fall on a vowel resulting from the fusion of two vowels), e.g., Maha·bhárata, but Ramáyana (not Rama·áyana). Our dot echoes the punctuating middle dot (·) found in the oldest surviving samples of written Indic, the Ashokan inscriptions of the third century BCE.

The deep layering of Sanskrit narrative has also dictated that we use quotation marks only to announce the beginning and end of every direct speech, and not at the beginning of every paragraph.

CSL Punctuation of Sanskrit

The Sanskrit text is also punctuated, in accordance with the punctuation of the English translation. In mid-verse, the punctuation will not alter the sandhi or the scansion. Proper names are capitalized. Most Sanskrit meters have four "feet" (*pāda*); where possible we print the common *śloka* meter on two lines. In the Sanskrit text, we use French *Guillemets* (e.g., *«kva saṃcicīrṣuḥ?»*) instead of English quotation marks (e.g., "Where are you off to?") to avoid confusion with the apostrophes used for vowel elision in sandhi.

SANDHI

Sanskrit presents the learner with a challenge: *sandhi* (euphonic combination). Sandhi means that when two words are joined in connected speech or writing (which in Sanskrit reflects speech), the last letter (or even letters) of the first word often changes; compare the way we pronounce "the" in "the beginning" and "the end."

In Sanskrit the first letter of the second word may also change; and if both the last letter of the first word and the first letter of the second are vowels, they may fuse. This has a parallel in English: a nasal consonant is inserted between two vowels that would otherwise coalesce: "a pear" and "an apple." Sanskrit vowel fusion may produce ambiguity.

The charts on the following pages give the full sandhi system.

Fortunately it is not necessary to know these changes in order to start reading Sanskrit. All that is important to know is the form of the second word without sandhi (pre-sandhi), so that it can be recognized or looked up in a dictionary. Therefore we are printing Sanskrit with a system of punctuation that will indicate, unambiguously, the original form of the second word, i.e., the form without sandhi. Such sandhi mostly concerns the fusion of two vowels.

In Sanskrit, vowels may be short or long and are written differently accordingly. We follow the general convention that a vowel with no mark above it is short. Other books mark a long vowel either with a bar called a macron (*ā*) or with a circumflex (*â*). Our system uses the

VOWEL SANDHI

Initial vowels:	Final vowels: a	ā	i	ī	u	ū	ṛ	e	ai	o	au
a	' â	" â	y a	y a	v a	v a	r a	e '	ā a	o '	āv a
ā	' ā	" ā	y ā	y ā	v ā	v ā	r ā	a ā	ā ā	a ā	āv ā
i	' ê	" ê	' î	" î	v i	v i	r i	a i	ā i	a i	āv i
ī	' ē	" ē	' ī	" ī	v ī	v ī	r ī	a ī	ā ī	a ī	āv ī
u	' ô	" ô	y u	y u	' û	" û	r u	a u	ā u	a u	āv u
ū	' ō	" ō	y ū	y ū	' ū	" ū	r ū	a ū	ā ū	a ū	āv ū
ṛ	a' r	a" r	y ṛ	y ṛ	v ṛ	v ṛ	' ṝ	a ṛ	ā ṛ	a ṛ	āv ṛ
e	' âi	" âi	y e	y e	v e	v e	r e	a e	ā e	a e	āv e
ai	' āi	" āi	y ai	y ai	v ai	v ai	r ai	a ai	ā ai	a ai	āv ai
o	' âu	" âu	y o	y o	v o	v o	r o	a o	ā o	a o	āv o
au	' āu	" āu	y au	y au	v au	v au	r au	a au	ā au	a au	āv au

CONSONANT SANDHI

Permitted finals: k	ṭ	t	p	ṅ	n	m	*(Except āḥ/aḥ)* ḥ/r	āḥ	aḥ	*Initial letters:*
k	ṭ	t	p	ṅ	n	ṃ	ḥ	āḥ	aḥ	k/kh
g	ḍ	d	b	ṅ	n	ṃ	r	ā	o	g/gh
k	ṭ	c	p	ṅ	ṃś	ṃ	ś	āś	aś	c/ch
g	ḍ	j	b	ṅ	ñ	ṃ	r	ā	o	j/jh
k	ṭ	ṭ	p	ṅ	ṃṣ	ṃ	ṣ	āṣ	aṣ	ṭ/ṭh
g	ḍ	ḍ	b	ṅ	ṇ	ṃ	r	ā	o	ḍ/ḍh
k	ṭ	t	p	ṅ	ṃs	ṃ	s	ās	as	t/th
g	ḍ	d	b	ṅ	n	ṃ	r	ā	o	d/dh
k	ṭ	t	p	ṅ	n	ṃ	ḥ	āḥ	aḥ	p/ph
g	ḍ	d	b	ṅ	n	ṃ	r	ā	o	b/bh
ṅ	ṇ	n	m	ṅ	n	ṃ	r	ā	o	*nasals* (n/m)
g	ḍ	d	b	ṅ	n	ṃ	r	ā	o	y/v
g	ḍ	d	b	ṅ	n	ṃ	*zero*[1]	ā	o	r
g	ḍ	l	b	ṅ	l̃[2]	ṃ	r	ā	o	l
k	ṭ	c ch	p	ṅ	ñ ś/ch	ṃ	ḥ	āḥ	aḥ	ś
k	ṭ	t	p	ṅ	n	ṃ	ḥ	āḥ	aḥ	ṣ/s
gg h	ḍḍ h	dd h	bb h	ṅ	n	ṃ	r	ā	o	h
g	ḍ	d	b	ṅ/ṅṅ[3]	n/nn[3]	m	r	ā	a[4]	*vowels*
k	ṭ	t	p	ṅ	n	m	ḥ	āḥ	aḥ	*zero*

[1]ḥ or r disappears, and if a/i/u precedes, this lengthens to ā/ī/ū. [2]e.g. tān+lokān=tāl̃ lokān.
[3]The doubling occurs if the preceding vowel is short. [4]Except: aḥ+a=o '.

macron, except that for initial vowels in sandhi we use a circumflex to indicate that originally the vowel was short, or the shorter of two possibilities (*e* rather than *ai*, *o* rather than *au*).

When we print initial *â*, before sandhi that vowel was *a*

î or *ê*,	*i*
û or *ô*,	*u*
âi,	*e*
âu,	*o*
ā,	*ā*
ī,	*ī*
ū,	*ū*
ē,	*ī*
ō,	*ū*
ai,	*ai*
āu,	*au*

', before sandhi there was a vowel *a*

When a final short vowel (*a*, *i*, or *u*) has merged into a following vowel, we print ' at the end of the word, and when a final long vowel (*ā*, *ī*, or *ū*) has merged into a following vowel we print " at the end of the word. The vast majority of these cases will concern a final *a* or *ā*. See, for instance, the following examples:

What before sandhi was *atra asti* is represented as *atr' âsti*

atra āste	*atr' āste*
kanyā asti	*kany" âsti*
kanyā āste	*kany" āste*
atra iti	*atr' êti*
kanyā iti	*kany" êti*
kanyā īpsitā	*kany" ēpsitā*

Finally, three other points concerning the initial letter of the second word:

(1) A word that before sandhi begins with *ṛ* (vowel), after sandhi begins with *r* followed by a consonant: *yatha" rtu* represents pre-sandhi *yathā ṛtu*.

(2) When before sandhi the previous word ends in *t* and the following word begins with *ś*, after sandhi the last letter of the previous word is *c*

and the following word begins with *ch*: *syāc chāstravit* represents pre-sandhi *syāt śāstravit*.

(3) Where a word begins with *h* and the previous word ends with a double consonant, this is our simplified spelling to show the pre-sandhi form: *tad hasati* is commonly written as *tad dhasati*, but we write *tadd hasati* so that the original initial letter is obvious.

COMPOUNDS

We also punctuate the division of compounds (*samāsa*), simply by inserting a thin vertical line between words. There are words where the decision whether to regard them as compounds is arbitrary. Our principle has been to try to guide readers to the correct dictionary entries.

Exemplar of CSL Style

Where the Devanagari script reads:

कुम्भस्थली रक्षतु वो विकीर्णसिन्धूररेणुर्द्विरदाननस्य ।
प्रशान्तये विघ्नतमश्छटानां निष्ठ्यूतबालातपपल्लवेव ॥

Others would print:

kumbhasthalī rakṣatu vo vikīrṇasindūrareṇur dviradānanasya /
praśāntaye vighnatamaśchaṭānāṃ niṣṭhyūtabālātapapallaveva //

We print:

kumbha|sthalī rakṣatu vo vikīrṇa|sindūra|reṇur dvirad'|ānanasya
praśāntaye vighna|tamaś|chaṭānāṃ niṣṭhyūta|bāl'|ātapa|pallav" êva.

And in English:

May Ganésha's domed forehead protect you! Streaked with vermilion dust, it seems to be emitting the spreading rays of the rising sun to pacify the teeming darkness of obstructions.

("Nava·sáhasanka and the Serpent Princess" I.3)

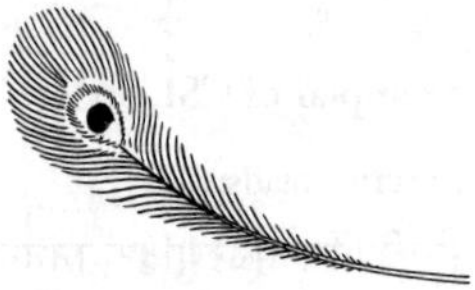

INTRODUCTION

The Book of 'Bhishma' (*Bhīṣmaparvan*), the sixth book of the eighteen-book epic the "Maha·bhárata," narrates the events that occurred during the first ten days of the great battle between the Káuravas and the Pándavas, fought on the vast plain of Kuru·kshetra, the sacrificial ground of their common ancestor Kuru. Books Six through Nine, which cover the eighteen-day war, are named after the four successive generals: Bhishma, Drona, Karna and Shalya, who lead the Káurava forces and are killed in sequence. The present CSL volume contains the second of the two parts of 'Bhishma.'

The Background

The epic recounts the story of the great fratricidal war waged by the descendants of the Bharata lineage for the succession of the kingship. The text views this war as merely an episode in the eternal cosmic struggle between the gods and the demons, transferred to the Earth. The Pándavas are described as the sons of the gods, whereas the Káuravas as incarnate demons. On the earthly plane, the conflicting parties are represented by two groups of cousins, the sons of the royal brothers Dhrita·rashtra and Pandu. Since the former had been born blind, the latter, his junior, rules in his place. Pandu dies, leaving five young sons, the Pándavas, born from his two wives: Yudhi·shthira, Bhima and Árjuna from Kunti, also named Pritha, and twins Nákula and Saha·deva from Madri. Dhrita·rashtra, now regent, has a hundred sons, called the Káuravas. The eldest of them, Duryódhana, is born after Yudhi·shthira who is thus recognized as legitimate heir. Duryódhana envies his cousin and plots against the Pándavas, but the five brothers manage to escape, wander in disguise and marry the Panchála princess Dráupadi. Dhrita·rashtra, attempting to reconcile the rivalry, partitions the kingdom. Yet Duryódhana seeks to deprive his cousins of their share. He challenges Yudhi·shthira to a ritual game of dice, during which, through the trickery of Duryódhana's uncle Shákuni, Yudhi·shthira loses his part of the kingdom. As a penalty, the Pándava brothers, together with their joint wife humiliated by the Káuravas, are exiled to the forest for twelve years, after which, in order to regain their kingdom, they are to spend one year incognito. Upon return from their exile the Pándavas justly claim their share, but Duryódhana rejects their demand. Both sides assemble allies and start preparations for war. 'Bhishma' commences on its very eve.

'Bhishma'

The first half of 'Bhishma' comprises a discourse on traditional cosmology, the famous "Bhagavad Gita" ("Song of the Lord"), and the detailed description of the first four days of the great battle, as related to the blind King Dhrita·rashtra by his divine-sighted messenger the charioteer Sánjaya who acts as a war reporter. The narration of warfare begins with a flash-forward (a pattern common to the four war books) in which Sánjaya suddenly returns from the battlefield to announce to Dhrita·rashtra the fall of general Bhishma and, at the request of the lamenting king, reports to him at length what had happened during the preceding days.

The second half of 'Bhishma' recounts the battle events which take place from the beginning of the fifth day of the war till the end of the tenth. It opens with King Dhrita·rashtra, the father of the Káuravas, asking Sánjaya about the cause of their cousins being invincible. Referring to the same question posed by the eldest of the Káuravas, Duryódhana, before grandfather Bhishma, the patriarch of the family and the commander of the Káurava army, Sánjaya quotes the latter's reply, in which Bhishma explains that the major reason for the Pándavas' invincibility and inevitable victory is that their ally Krishna, the charioteer of Árjuna, is the incarnation of the Lord Vishnu-Naráyana himself, while Árjuna is the incarnation of the god Nara ("Man"). Despite Bhishma's appeal to Duryódhana to conclude peace with the Pándavas, he decides to continue the hostilities.

Formations of troops, heroic feats of arms, bloody massacres, fierce duels, tremendous confusion of routed forces, and scenes of violence and valor are depicted in 'Bhishma' in great detail. Fighting with varying success, the two armies suffer heavy casualties and, after an overnight retreat, driven by Fate and by Time, they resume their horrible fight at the dawn of each following day.

The key role in the strategy and tactics of battle throughout the present book belongs to general Bhishma, the commander of the Káurava forces. Due to his outstanding military skills, he draws up the troops in the most effective way and leads the army in the course of battle. Whenever the Káuravas suffer a reverse, the mighty and heroic warrior Bhishma interferes and always succeeds in improving the situation and inflicting heavy losses on the Pándavas. At the war's outset he promises Duryódhana to kill ten thousand warriors of the Pándava army every single day of battle; and he fulfills his promise.

Nevertheless there is some ambiguity in Bhishma's role. He is obligated to the court of King Dhrita·rashtra for giving him a livelihood and has no choice but to side with his patron. According to his own words, it is his weakness for material wealth that has made him dependent on the Káuravas and compelled him to fight for them. Yet his sympathies are clearly with the Pándavas and he wishes them to win. Bhishma promises Yudhi·shthira to help him with good counsel. After the ninth day of war, when Bhishma has wreaked havoc on their troops, the Pándavas realize that they will be unable to win as long as unconquerable Bhishma is alive, and decide to concentrate all efforts on slaying him. Krishna even expresses his readiness to break his vow of non-engagement in the fight, however Yudhi·shthira rejects that proposal as unrighteous. Instead he offers an alternative plan. He recalls asking Bhishma, on the eve of the great battle, for his blessings, permission to fight against him, and the means to defeat him. Old Bhishma had then blessed the eldest Pándava and, saying that it was not yet the time for his death, invited Yudhi·shthira to come to him on another occasion and inquire again. When the Pándava brothers come now to their old grandfather's tent to take counsel, Bhishma willingly reveals to them the method of killing him, which they will follow.

Bhishma's Past

Bhishma, whose original name is Deva·vrata ("Divine Vow"), is a son of King Shántanu by the goddess Ganga (the river Ganges). He is an incarnation of the god Dyaus who, along with seven other Vasu deities, was cursed by the great celestial sage Vasíshtha to be reborn as a mortal for stealing his wish-granting cow. Unlike the other seven, Dyaus was doomed to dwell for a long time in the human world, to become a law-abiding mortal, expert in all weapons and devoted to his father's well-being, yet to give up the pleasure of being with a woman and the begetting of offspring. The cursed Vasus then came to Ganga and begged her to let them be born of her womb and to release them from the world of mortals at birth. The ever young goddess promised to help them, descended to the earth, went directly to King Pratípa of the Lunar Dynasty, sat down on his lap and told him: "I want you to marry me." The king replied: "Lady, if you wanted me to marry you, you should have sat on my left thigh and not on my right, which belongs to the son or the daughter-in law. Let a son be born to me, and I will have him marry you." Ganga agreed and Pratípa got a son, Shántanu. When the son came of age, Pratípa left the kingdom to him and retired to the forest. Once while hunting on the bank of the Ganges, Shántanu saw a beautiful woman, the goddess Ganga, and fell in love with her. She agreed to become his wife, but set her condition: "Whatever I may do, whether you like it or not, you must neither interfere nor blame me. The day you do that, I will leave you." The infatuated king accepted the terms. Every time a child was born, Ganga would drown him in the Ganges. Shántanu restrained himself, but when she was about to drown their eighth child, the king exclaimed: "At least don't kill this one! What a horrible woman you are!" Ganga spared the child, but immediately vanished with him. One day she reappeared to give Shántanu back his son Deva·vrata, a youth trained in all the arts of the warrior clan. The king took him to the capital and made him the crown prince. Later, however, while out hunting Shántanu saw a fair young maiden Sátyavati and asked for her hand. Her father, a chieftain of fishermen, consented to the marriage provided that her descendants would be heirs to the throne. In order to gratify his old father's desire to marry her, prince Deva·vrata waived his right to succession and took a vow of celibacy. Henceforth, due to his awe-inspiring vow, he is called Bhishma ("Awesome"). Pleased at his son's extraordinary self-sacrifice, Shántanu granted him the boon of being able to choose the time of his death.

Having renounced kingdom and marriage, Bhishma enthroned first his younger brother Chitrángada and, after the latter's death, his youngest, Vichítra·virya. To ensure the continuity of the Kuru lineage, Bhishma abducted for Vichítra·virya the three Kashi princesses, Amba, Ámbika and Ambálika, straight from their *svayaṃvara* (a ceremony in which a bride herself chooses a husband) and won a battle against King Shalva. As soon as Bhishma brought the royal brides to the Kuru capital Hástina·pura, the eldest of them, Amba ("Mother"), told him that she had just chosen King Shalva for her husband and had been betrothed to him. Bhishma immediately sent her back to her bridegroom, but Shalva rejected her on the grounds that she had been won and carried away by another man. Amba returned to Bhishma and said, "Since you have abducted me, you must marry me." Yet because of his oath of celibacy, Bhishma refused to accept her. Dishonored and rejected, Amba sought shelter in a hermitage. There arrived a mighty hero, Rama the son of Jamad·agni, who promised to help her by fighting Bhishma and forcing him to marry her. Close combat ensued between the two equally powerful warriors, ending in victory for neither. After Rama had failed to defeat Bhishma, Amba vowed to kill the offender herself. She undertook harsh penance in order to accumulate the power to take revenge on Bhishma for all her woes. Bhishma's mother, the river Ganges, failed to dissuade Amba and so cursed her to turn into a miserable crooked stream, dried up except in monsoon. Yet through her penance Amba succeeded in retaining one half of her own body and became half-river half-woman. By virtue of her severe austerities she managed to propitiate Rudra/Shiva, who granted her the boon that in her next rebirth she would become a man and bring about Bhishma's death. Thereupon Amba burned herself on a funeral pyre.

In the meantime, the Panchála king Drúpada performed rites begging Shiva for a son, and Shiva replied: "You will have a male child who is a female." In due course the queen gave birth to a daughter Shikhándini, but the parents pretended she was a son and raised the child as a boy, whom they called Shikhándin ("Peacock"). Upon coming of age, "he" married a princess; but when the princess found out that the prince was a female, she was deeply insulted and reported the matter to her father, who immediately declared war on King Drúpada. Shikhándin/Shikhándini fell into despair and left for the forest, intending to commit suicide. There s/he came across a male *yakṣa* goblin named Sthuna who, in response to Shikhándin/Shikhándini's desperate pleas, agreed to a temporary exchange of gender with her, until the hostile army left the city. As soon as the princess's father became convinced of her husband's maleness, he withdrew his troops. When Kubéra, the lord of the *yakṣa*s, learnt of the gender-swap, he punished Sthuna by cursing him to remain female until Shikhándin's death. When the latter returned to the *yakṣa* to give back his manhood, he heard of the curse and was pleased to retain lifelong maleness.

Bhishma's Advice

Bhishma, who had vowed not to "release an arrow at a woman, someone who was previously a woman, someone with a woman's name, or someone who looks like a woman,"[1] adheres to his firm vows and, strictly observing the warrior code, refuses to fight with Shikhándin who was originally born a female. Otherwise unconquerable, Bhishma advises Árjuna to strike him from behind Shikhándin's back. Thus on the tenth day of battle, following the old man's advice, Árjuna, in keeping with his own vow to slay Bhishma, launches an attack against him and, using Bhishma's sworn enemy Shikhándin as a human shield, protecting himself from the enemy forces and enabling him to strike Bhishma, shoots the grandfather with multitudes of arrows without any resistance on Bhishma's part and mortally wounds him. Countless arrows embedded themselves in the old man's body in such a way that "in his entire body there was not even a space two fingers broad that was not pierced with arrows… That mighty-armed hero, the banner of all archers, collapsed to the ground like an uprooted standard of Indra, filling the earth with a great din. Yet Bhishma, pierced all over with hordes of arrows, could not touch the ground" (119.86–91).

Granted the boon of fixing the time of death at his own will, Bhishma postpones his death and remains lying on the battlefield upon his honorable bed of arrows. Choosing to die at an auspicious time, he awaits the winter solstice for fifty days, during which he witnesses the rest of the war and delivers long didactic discourses thereafter, instructing King Yudhi·shthira in *dharma* (his royal duties, law and religion) and *mokṣa* (ways to liberation). Bhishma's wise and insightful teachings form the content of 'Peace' (*Śāntiparvan*) and 'Good Counsel' (*Anuśāsanaparvan*), books Twelve and Thirteen of the great epic.

The text used for the present translation is KINJAWADEKAR's edition of the "Maha·bhárata."

Concordance of Canto Numbers with the Critical Edition

CSL	CE
65–97	61–93
98	94; 95.1–25
99	95.26–53
100–115	96–111
116	112.1–77
117	112.78–138
118–122	113–117

Note

1 "Maha·bhárata," 'Preparations for War,' CSL Edition, v.192.66–67 (tr. GARBUTT 2008: 693); Critical Edition, v.193.62.

Bibliography

SANSKRIT TEXTS

The Mahābhāratam with the Bharata Bhawadeepa Commentary of Nīlakaṇṭha. Edited by RAMACHANDRASHASTRI KINJAWADEKAR. 7 vols. Poona: Chitrashala Press. 1926–36. [CSL]

The Mahābhārata. Critically edited by V.K. SUKTHANKAR, S.K. BELVALKAR, P.L. VAIDYA, et al. 19 vols. Poona: Bhandarkar Oriental Research Institute. 1933–66. [CE]

The Mahābhārata with Nīlakaṇṭha's commentary. Edited by A. KHADILKAR. 8 vols. Bombay: Ganapati Krishnaji Press. 1862–63.

THE "MAHA·BHÁRATA" IN TRANSLATION

CHERNIAK, ALEX (tr.). 2008. *Maha·bhárata, Book Six: Bhishma*, vol. 1. (Clay Sanskrit Library). New York: New York University Press & JJC Foundation.

DUTT, MANMATHA NATH (tr.). 1994. *A Prose English Translation of the Mahābhārata*. 7 vols. Reprint. Delhi: Parimal Publications.

GANGULI, KISARI MOHAN (tr.). 1884–99. *The Mahabharata of Krishna-Dwaipayana Vyasa*. 12 vols. Calcutta: Bharata Press. Reprint by Munshiram Manoharlal. 1993.

GARBUTT, KATHLEEN (tr.). 2008. *Maha·bhárata, Book Five: Preparations for War*, vol. 2. (Clay Sanskrit Library). New York: New York University Press & JJC Foundation.

FITZGERALD, J.L. 2004. *The Mahabharata*, vol.7, Book 11; Book 12, part one. Chicago: University of Chicago Press.

VAN BUITENEN, J.A.B. (tr. and ed.). 1973–78. *The Mahābhārata* [Books 1–5]. 3 vols. Chicago: University of Chicago Press.

WILMOT, PAUL (tr.). 2006. *Maha·bhárata, Book Two: The Great Hall*, (Clay Sanskrit Library). New York: New York University Press & JJC Foundation.

SECONDARY SOURCES

BROCKINGTON, JOHN. 1998. *The Sanskrit Epics*. Leiden: Brill.

BRODBECK S. & BLACK B. (eds.). 2007. *Gender and Narrative in the Mahābhārata*. London & New York: Routledge.

HILTEBEITEL, ALF. 1976. *The Ritual of Battle: Krishna in the Mahābhārata*. Ithaca: Cornell University Press.

———. 2004. *Rethinking the Mahabharata: a reader's guide to the education of the dharma king*. Chicago: University of Chicago Press.

OBERLIES, THOMAS. 2003. *A Grammar of Epic Sanskrit*. New York: Walter de Gruyter.

SHARMA, ARVIND (ed.). 1991. *Essays on the Mahābhārata*. Leiden: Brill.

SØRENSEN, SØREN. 1904–05. *An Index to the Names in the Mahābhārata*. London: Williams and Norgate.

MAHA·BHÁRATA

BOOK SIX

BHISHMA

VOLUME TWO

65–68
KRISHNA'S GLORY

DHṚTARĀṢṬRA uvāca:

65.1 BHAYAṂ ME SU|mahaj jātaṃ vismayaś c' âiva, Sañjaya,
śrutvā Pāṇḍu|kumārāṇāṃ karma devaiḥ su|duṣkaram.
putrāṇāṃ ca parābhāvaṃ śrutvā, Sañjaya, sarvaśaḥ
cintā me mahatī, sūta, bhaviṣyati: kathaṃ tv iti.
dhruvaṃ Vidura|vākyāni dhakṣyanti hṛdayaṃ mama;
yathā hi dṛśyate sarvaṃ daiva|yogena, Sañjaya.
yatra Bhīṣma|mukhāñ śūrān astra|jñān yodha|sattamān
Pāṇḍavānām anīkāni yodhayanti prahāriṇaḥ.
65.5 ken' â|vadhyā mah"|ātmānaḥ Pāṇḍu|putrā mahā|balāḥ?
kena datta|varās, tāta? kiṃ vā jñānaṃ vidanti te
yena kṣayaṃ na gacchanti divi tārā|gaṇā iva?
punaḥ punar na mṛṣyāmi hataṃ sainyaṃ tu Pāṇḍavaiḥ.
mayy eva daṇḍaḥ patati daivāt parama|dāruṇaḥ.
yath"|â|vadhyāḥ Pāṇḍu|sutā, yathā vadhyāś ca me sutāḥ,
etan me sarvam ācakṣva yathā|tattvena, Sañjaya.
na hi pāraṃ prapaśyāmi duḥkhasy' âsya kathaṃ cana,
samudrasy' êva mahato bhujābhyāṃ prataran naraḥ.
putrāṇāṃ vyasanaṃ manye dhruvaṃ prāptaṃ su|dāruṇam.
65.10 ghātayiṣyati me putrān sarvān Bhīmo, na saṃśayaḥ.
na hi paśyāmi taṃ vīraṃ yo me rakṣet sutān raṇe.
dhruvaṃ vināśaḥ saṃprāptaḥ putrāṇāṃ mama, Sañjaya.
tasmān me kāraṇaṃ, sūta, śaktiṃ c' âiva viśeṣataḥ
pṛcchato 'dya yathā|tattvaṃ sarvam ākhyātum arhasi.
Duryodhanaś ca yac cakre dṛṣṭvā svān vimukhān raṇe,

DHRITA·RASHTRA said:

NOW THAT I HAVE heard of the feats accomplished by 65.1
the sons of Pandu, which are difficult even for the
gods to perform, I am filled with great fear and astonishment, Sánjaya. But since I learned of my sons' total defeat, I
am very apprehensive of what the outcome will be, Sánjaya
the charioteer. Vídura's words* will surely burn my heart
out. Everything seems to happen as directed by fate, Sánjaya. The combatants of the Pándava divisions have been
fighting against excellent warriors led by Bhishma, all experts in weaponry. Why can't the great-spirited and mighty 65.5
sons of Pandu be killed? From whom have they obtained
the boon, or what kind of knowledge do they possess, that
they suffer no destruction, like the stars in the sky? I am
unable to bear the news that my troops are being killed by
the Pándavas again and again! It is by fate that this utterly
cruel punishment has befallen me alone—that the Pándavas
are inviolable, whereas my sons are doomed to be slaughtered. Tell me all this as it really is, Sánjaya. I cannot see
the other shore of this sea of sorrow; I am like a man trying to swim across the vast ocean by means of his two
arms. I think that an extremely horrible disaster must have
overcome my sons. Bhima will massacre all my sons, no 65.10
doubt about it! And I do not see any hero who can protect my sons in combat. Surely the time of my sons' destruction has come, Sánjaya. So you should answer all my
questions truthfully, charioteer, especially about the cause
of our defeat and about their secret power. And also, what
did Duryódhana do when he saw his troops fleeing? What
did Bhishma, Drona, Kripa, the son of Súbala, Jayad·ratha,

Bhīṣma|Droṇau, Kṛpaś c' âiva, Saubaleyo, Jayadrathaḥ,
Drauṇir v" âpi mah"|êṣv|āso, Vikarṇo vā mahā|balaḥ.
niścayo v" âpi kas teṣāṃ tadā hy āsīn mah"|ātmanām
vimukheṣu, mahā|prājña, mama putreṣu, Sañjaya?

SAÑJAYA uvāca:

65.15 śṛṇu, rājann, avahitaḥ, śrutvā c' âiv' âvadhāraya.
n' âiva mantra|kṛtaṃ kiṃ cin; n' âiva māyāṃ tathā|vidhām,
na vai vibhīṣikāṃ kāṃ cid, rājan, kurvanti Pāṇḍavāḥ.
yudhyanti te yathā|nyāyaṃ śaktimantaś ca saṃyuge.
dharmeṇa sarva|kāryāṇi jīvit'|ādīni, Bhārata,
ārabhante sadā Pārthāḥ prārthayānā mahad yaśaḥ.
na te yuddhān nivartante dharm'|ôpetā, mahā|balāḥ,
śriyā paramayā yuktā. yato dharmas tato jayaḥ.
ten' â|vadhyā raṇe Pārthā jaya|yuktāś ca, pārthiva.
tava putrā dur|ātmānaḥ, pāpeṣv abhiratāḥ sadā,
65.20 niṣṭhurā, hīna|karmāṇas. tena hīyanti saṃyuge.
su|bahūni nṛśaṃsāni putrais tava, jan'|ēśvara,
nikṛtān' îha Pāṇḍūnāṃ nīcair iva yathā naraiḥ.
sarvaṃ ca tad an|ādṛtya putrāṇāṃ tava kilbiṣam
s'|âpahnavāḥ sad" âiv' āsan Pāṇḍavāḥ, Pāṇḍu|pūrva|ja.
na c' âitān bahu manyante putrās tava, viśāṃ pate.
tasya pāpasya satataṃ kriyamāṇasya karmaṇaḥ
sāmpratam su|mahad ghoraṃ phalaṃ prāptaṃ, jan'|ēśvara.
sa tvaṃ bhuṅkṣva, mahā|rāja, sa|putraḥ sa|suhṛj|janaḥ,
n' âvabudhyasi yad, rājan, vāryamāṇaḥ suhṛj|janaiḥ.
65.25 Vidureṇ', âtha Bhīṣmeṇa, Droṇena ca mah"|ātmanā,
tathā mayā c' âpy a|sakṛd vāryamāṇo na budhyase.

Drona's son the mighty archer, and powerful Vikárna do then? What was the decision of those great-spirited warriors when my sons had taken flight, wise Sánjaya?

SÁNJAYA said:

Listen attentively, Your Majesty, and consider this. The 65.15
Pándavas have not used any mantras, nor any kind of magic, nor any means of terror, Your Majesty. They fight using fair means and are powerful in combat. Seeking to win great renown, the sons of Pritha live and perform all their actions righteously, descendant of Bharata. Endowed with righteousness and great strength, and graced with the highest glory, they never retreat from the battlefield. And wherever righteousness is, there is victory. That is why the sons of Pritha are inviolable and victorious in battle, Your Majesty, whereas your sons are ill-natured and always intent on evil.
They are cruel and vile in their deeds, and that is why they 65.20
suffer losses in combat. Lord of the people, your sons, behaving like villains, have performed countless mean actions against the sons of Pandu. The Pándavas, however, in spite of your sons' wrongdoing, have always been lenient with them, elder brother of Pandu. Yet your sons, ruler of the subjects, do not treat them with due respect. The utterly horrific fruit of that evil activity has now ripened, lord of the people. And you, great king, along with your sons and allies, shall reap it, for you did not heed the warnings of your well-
wishers, Your Majesty. Although repeatedly warned by Ví- 65.25
dura, Bhishma, great-spirited Drona, and myself, you took no heed. Just as a man on the verge of death rejects proper

vākyaṃ hitaṃ ca pathyaṃ ca,
    martyaḥ pathyam iv' âuṣadham,
putrāṇāṃ matam āsthāya
    jitān manyasi Pāṇḍavān.

śṛṇu bhūyo yathā|tattvaṃ yan māṃ tvaṃ paripṛcchasi
kāraṇaṃ, Bharata|śreṣṭha, Pāṇḍavānāṃ jayaṃ prati.
tat te 'haṃ kathayiṣyāmi yathā|śrutam, arin|dama.
Duryodhanena saṃpṛṣṭa etam arthaṃ Pitāmahaḥ
dṛṣṭvā bhrātṝn raṇe sarvān nirjitān su|mahā|rathān
śoka|saṃmūḍha|hṛdayo niśā|kāle sma Kauravaḥ
65.30 pitā|mahaṃ mahā|prājñaṃ vinayen' ôpagamya ha
yad abravīt sutas te 'sau, tan me śṛṇu, jan'|ēśvara.

DURYODHANA uvāca:

Droṇaś ca, tvaṃ ca, Śalyaś ca,
    Kṛpo, Drauṇis tath" âiva ca,
Kṛtavarmā ca, Hārdikyaḥ,
    Kāmbojaś ca Sudakṣiṇaḥ,
Bhūriśravā, Vikarṇaś ca, Bhagadattaś ca vīryavān
mahā|rathāḥ samākhyātāḥ kula|putrās tanu|tyajaḥ
trayāṇām api lokānāṃ paryāptā iti me matiḥ.
Pāṇḍavānāṃ samastāś ca n' âtiṣṭhanta parākrame.
tatra me saṃśayo jātas. tan mam' ācakṣva pṛcchataḥ,
yaṃ samāśritya Kaunteyā jayanty asmān pade pade.

BHĪṢMA uvāca:

65.35 śṛṇu, rājan, vaco mahyaṃ yathā vakṣyāmi, Kaurava.
bahuśaś ca may" ôkto 'si; na ca me tat tvayā kṛtam.
kriyatāṃ Pāṇḍavaiḥ sārdhaṃ śamo, Bharata|sattama.
etat kṣamam ahaṃ manye pṛthivyās tava v", âbhibho.
bhuñj' êmāṃ pṛthivīṃ, rājan, bhrātṛbhiḥ sahitaḥ sukhī,

medicine, you, ignoring our beneficial and appropriate admonitions and sharing the attitude of your sons, have considered the Pándavas already conquered.

Best of the Bharatas, hear more of what you have asked me, about the true reason for the Pándavas' victory. I shall tell you what I have heard, enemy-tamer. Duryódhana asked Bhishma the same thing. Seeing that all his brothers, the great warriors, had been defeated in combat, in the evening the Káurava, his heart overcome by grief, humbly ap- 65.30
proached the grandfather of great wisdom. Listen to what your son said, lord of the people.

DURYÓDHANA said:

Drona, yourself, Shalya, Kripa, Drona's son, Krita·varman the son of Hrídika, Sudákshina the king of the Kambójas, Bhuri·shravas, Vikárna, and mighty Bhaga·datta are known as great warriors from noble families, and are ready to give up their lives. I believe that, when assembled together, you are capable of conquering the three worlds, and yet you did not withstand the Pándavas' attack. So a doubt has arisen in my mind. Please answer my question: On whom do Kunti's sons rely that they can continually vanquish us?

BHISHMA said:

O Káurava king, listen to the words I say to you. I have 65.35
spoken to you many times, but you have never done what I said. Make peace with the Pándavas, best of the Bharatas! In my opinion it would benefit you and the entire earth, my lord. Enjoy this earth happily, Your Majesty, sharing it with your brothers, destroying all your enemies, and delighting

dur|hṛdas tāpayan sarvān, nandayaṃś c' âpi bāndhavān.
na ca me krośatas, tāta śrutavān asi vai purā.
tad idaṃ samanuprāptaṃ yat Pāṇḍūn avamanyase.
yaś ca hetur a|vadhyatve teṣām a|kliṣṭa|karmaṇām,
taṃ śṛṇuṣva, mahā|bāho, mama kīrtayataḥ, prabho.
65.40 n' âsti lokeṣu tad bhūtaṃ, bhavitā no bhaviṣyati,
yo jayet Pāṇḍavān saṃkhye pālitāñ Chārṅga|dhanvanā.
yat tu me kathitaṃ, tāta, munibhir bhāvit'|ātmabhiḥ
purāṇa|gītaṃ, dharma|jña, tac chṛṇuṣva yathā|tatham.
purā kila surāḥ sarve, ṛṣayaś ca samāgatāḥ
Pitāmaham upāseduḥ parvate Gandhamādane.
madhye teṣāṃ samāsīnaḥ Prajāpatir apaśyata
vimānaṃ prajvalad bhāsā, sthitaṃ pravaram ambare.
dhyānen' āvedya taṃ Brahmā, kṛtvā ca niyato 'ñjalim,
namaś|cakāra hṛṣṭ'|ātmā puruṣaṃ param'|ēśvaram.
65.45 ṛṣayas tv atha devāś ca dṛṣṭvā Brahmāṇam utthitam
sthitāḥ prāñjalayaḥ sarve paśyanto mahad adbhutam.
yathāvac ca tam abhyarcya Brahmā brahma|vidāṃ varaḥ
jagāda jagataḥ sraṣṭā paraṃ parama|dharma|vit:
«viśvā|vasur, viśva|mūrtir, viśv'|ēśo,
viṣvak|seno, viśva|karmā, vaśī ca,
viśv'|ēśvaro, Vāsudevo 'si tasmād.
yog'|ātmānaṃ daivataṃ tvām upaimi.
jaya, viśva|mahā|deva! jaya, loka|hite rata!
jaya, yog'|īśvara vibho! jaya, yoga|parāvara!

your kinsmen. I have appealed to you before, but you took no notice. This is the result of your having despised the sons of Pandu.

As for the reason why those heroes, tireless in their deeds, are inviolable, listen, mighty-armed lord, to what I have to say. In all the three worlds there is not, was not, and 65.40
never will be anyone capable of defeating all the Pándavas, protected as they are by the wielder of the Sharnga bow. Sir, expert in what is right, listen to the ancient true story as related to me by the sages accomplished in spirit.

In olden times all the gods and sages together worshipped Grandsire Brahma on Mount Gandha·mádana. Seated in their midst, Praja·pati saw a celestial palace stationed in the sky, blazing with radiance. On ascertaining all about it through contemplation he rejoiced in his heart, and with his hands folded in respect he honored that highest person, the supreme lord. Then all the sages and the gods, seeing 65.45
that Brahma had stood up, rose with their hands folded in reverence, beholding the great miracle. Duly worshipping him, Brahma, the creator of the universe, an expert in the highest virtue and the best of those that know Brahman, praised the Supreme Lord thus:

"You are the all-beneficent lord of the universe, whose form is the entire world, whose power pervades everything: the creator of all, the all-subduing master of the universe, Vásu·deva. Therefore I seek refuge in you, the divinity, whose soul is yoga. Victory to you, O great lord of the universe! Victory to you who are always concerned for the world's welfare! Victory to you, Lord, master of yogins! Victory to you who are cause and effect of yoga! Victory to you,

padma|garbha viśāl'|âkṣa, jaya, lok'|ēśvar'|ēśvara!
bhūta|bhavya|bhavan|nātha, jaya, saumy'|ātma|j'|ātmaja!

65.50 a|saṃkhyeya|guṇ'|ādhāra, jaya, sarva|parāyaṇa!
Nārāyaṇa su|duṣ|pāra, jaya, Śārṅga|dhanur|dhara!

jaya, sarva|guṇ'|ôpeta, viśva|mūrte, nir|āmaya!
viśv'|ēśvara mahā|bāho, jaya, lok'|ârtha|tat|para!

mah"|Ôraga! Varāh'|ādya! Hari|keśa vibho, jaya!
hari|vāsa! diśām|īśa! viśva|vās'! â|mit'|â|vyaya!
vyakt'|â|vyakt', â|mita|sthāna, niyat'|êndriya, sat|kriya!
a|saṃkhyey'|ātma|bhāva|jña! jaya, gambhīra! kāma|da!
an|anta! vidita|prajña! nityaṃ bhūta|vibhāvana!
kṛta|kārya! kṛta|prajña! dharma|jña! vijay'|â|jaya!

65.55 guhy'|ātman! sarva|yog'|ātman!
sphuṭa|saṃbhūta|saṃbhava!
bhūt'|ādya! loka|tattv'|ēśa!
jaya, bhūta|vibhāvana!
ātma|yone! mahā|bhāga! kalpa|saṃkṣepa|tat|para!
udbhāvana! mano|bhāva! jaya, Brahma|jana|priya!
nisarga|sarg'|âbhirata kām'|ēśa, param'|ēśvara!

O source of the primordial lotus, O large-eyed lord of the lords of the world! Victory to you, O lord of the past, the
future, and the present, O son born of a gentle soul! Victory 65.50
to you, O repository of countless attributes, O shelter of all! Victory to you, Naráyana, O wielder of the Sharnga bow, who are extremely difficult to fathom! Victory to you who are taintless and endowed with all virtues, and whose form is the whole universe! Victory to you, O mighty-armed lord of the universe, who are ever intent on the world's benefit!

O great Serpent! O primeval Boar! O primordial lord! O Lion-maned one! O you who are dressed in yellow robes! O lord of the quarters! O abode of the entire world! O boundless one! O imperishable one! Victory to you!* O you who are both manifest and unmanifest, whose abode is limitless, whose senses are restrained, and whose deeds are always virtuous! O knower of the true nature of innumerable souls! O profound one! O granter of desires! Victory to you! O infinite one! O you who are known as Brahman!* O eternal one! O generator of beings! O you all of whose actions have been accomplished! O perfectly wise one! O expert in righteousness! O victorious one!

O mysterious soul! O soul of all yoga! O source of all 65.55
manifest! O primordial being! O master of the true knowledge of the world! O creator of creatures! Victory to you! O self-generated one! O fortunate one! O you intent on the dissolution of an eon! O originator of beings! O generator of thoughts in the mind! O you who are dear to all men of Brahman! Victory to you! O Supreme Lord, lord of desire, naturally engaged in the process of creation! O source of the nectar of immortality! O true reality! O liberated soul! O

amṛt'|ôdbhava! sad|bhāva! mukt'|ātman! vijaya|prada!
Prajāpati|pate! deva padma|nābha mahā|bala!
ātma|bhūta! mahā|bhūta! karm'|ātmañ! jaya, karma|da!

pādau tava dharā devī, diśo bāhur, divaṃ śiraḥ,
mūrtis te 'haṃ, surāḥ kāyaś, candr'|ādityau ca cakṣuṣī.
65.60 balaṃ tapaś ca, satyaṃ ca, karma dharm'|ātmakaṃ tava;
tejo 'gniḥ; pavanaḥ śvāsa; āpas te sveda|saṃbhavāḥ;
Aśvinau śravaṇau nityaṃ; devī jihvā Sarasvatī;
vedāḥ saṃskāra|niṣṭhā hi. tvay' îdaṃ jagad āśritam.
na saṃkhyānaṃ, parīmāṇaṃ, na tejo, na parākramam,
na balaṃ, yoga|yog'|īśa, jānīmas te, na saṃbhavam.
tvad|bhakti|niratā, deva, niyamais tvāṃ samāhitāḥ
arcayāmaḥ sadā, Viṣṇo, param'|ēśaṃ mah"|ēśvaram.

ṛṣayo, deva|gandharvā, yakṣa|rākṣasa|pannagāḥ,
piśācā, mānuṣāś c' âiva, mṛga|pakṣi|sarīsṛpāḥ;
65.65 evam|ādi mayā sṛṣṭaṃ pṛthivyāṃ tvat|prasāda|jam.
padma|nābha, viśāl'|âkṣa, Kṛṣṇa, duḥkha|pranāśana,
tvaṃ gatiḥ sarva|bhūtānāṃ; tvaṃ netā; tvaṃ jagad|guruḥ.
tvat|prasādena, dev'|ēśa, sukhino vibudhāḥ sadā.
pṛthivī nir|bhayā, deva, tvat|prasādāt sad" âbhavat.
tasmād bhava, viśāl'|âkṣa, Yadu|vaṃśa|vivardhanaḥ.
dharma|saṃsthāpan'|ârthāya, daityānāṃ ca vadhāya ca,
jagato dhāraṇ'|ârthāya vijñāpyaṃ kuru me, vibho.
yad etat paramaṃ guhyaṃ tvat|prasādamayaṃ, vibho

granter of victory! O lord of the lords of creatures! O lotus-naveled powerful God!* O self-born one! O great being! O pure-spirited one! May you always be victorious, O giver of duties!

The goddess Earth forms your feet, the quarters are your arms, the sky is your head, I am your form, the gods constitute your body, and the moon and the sun are your eyes.
Austerities and virtuous truth are your power, fire is your 65.60
energy, wind is your breath, and waters arose from your sweat. The twin Ashvins always form your ears, the goddess Sarásvati is your tongue, and the Vedas are your awareness. It is on you that this universe rests. O lord of yoga and master of yogins, we know neither your expanse nor your dimensions, neither your energy nor your prowess, neither your power nor your origin. Engrossed in devotion to you, O God, and resorting to you by keeping our vows, we always worship you, O Supreme Lord, Great God Vishnu.

The gods, sages, *gandhárvas*, *yakshas*, *rákshasas*, serpents,
pisháchas,* humans, animals, birds, and reptiles—all this 65.65
and the rest I created on earth through your grace, O lotus-naveled, large-eyed Krishna, remover of grief. You are the goal of all beings; you are the leader; you are the teacher of the universe. Through your grace, lord of the gods, the deities are ever happy. O god, by your grace the earth has always been fearless. So, large-eyed one, pray be the increaser of the Yadu lineage! Hear my prayer, Lord, for the sake of establishing righteousness, slaughtering demons, and sustaining the universe! O Lord Vásu·deva, I have chanted this
highest mystery of yours as it truly is. After creating yourself 65.70
as divine Sankárshana out of your very self, O Krishna, by

Vāsudeva, tad etat te may" ôdgītaṃ yathā|tatham.
65.70 sṛṣṭvā Saṃkarṣaṇaṃ devaṃ
svayam ātmānam ātmanā,
Kṛṣṇa, tvam ātman" âsrākṣīḥ
Pradyumnaṃ c' ātma|saṃbhavam;
Pradyumnāc c' Âniruddhaṃ tvaṃ,
yaṃ vidur Viṣṇum a|vyayam.
Aniruddho 'sṛjan māṃ vai
Brahmāṇaṃ loka|dhāriṇam.
Vāsudevamayaḥ so 'haṃ tvay" âiv' âsmi vinirmitaḥ.
vibhajya bhāgaśo "tmānaṃ vraja mānuṣatāṃ, vibho.
tatr' âsura|vadhaṃ kṛtvā sarva|loka|sukhāya vai,
dharmaṃ prāpya, yaśaḥ prāpya, yogaṃ prāpsyasi tattvataḥ.
tvāṃ hi brahma'|rṣayo loke, devāś c', â|mita|vikrama,
tais tair hi nāmabhir yuktā gāyanti param'|ātmakam.
65.75 sthitāś ca sarve tvayi bhūta|saṅghāḥ
kṛtv" āśrayaṃ tvāṃ vara|daṃ, su|bāho!
an|ādi|madhy'|ântam, a|pāra|yogaṃ,
lokasya setuṃ pravadanti viprāḥ.»

BHĪṢMA UVĀCA:

66.1 TATAḤ SA BHAGAVĀN devo lokānāṃ īśvar'|ēśvaraḥ
Brahmāṇaṃ pratyuvāc' êdaṃ snigdha|gambhīrayā girā:
«viditaṃ, tāta, yogān me sarvam etat tav' ēpsitam.
tathā tad bhavit"» êty uktvā tatr' âiv' ântar|adhīyata.
tato deva'|rṣi|gandharvā vismayaṃ paramaṃ gatāḥ
kautūhala|parāḥ sarve Pitāmaham ath' âbruvan:
«ko nv ayaṃ yo bhagavatā praṇamya vinayād, vibho,
vāgbhiḥ stuto variṣṭhābhiḥ? śrotum icchāma taṃ vayam.»

yourself you created Pradyúmna, who was born from your own self. From Pradyúmna you created Anirúddha, who is known as imperishable Vishnu. Anirúddha created me, Brahma, as the maintainer of the world. So, created by you, I belong to Vásu·deva's very nature. Dividing yourself into parts, take birth among humans, O lord. When you slaughter demons there for the sake of the entire world's welfare, when you establish virtue and win glory, you will truly attain yoga. O you whose prowess is unlimited, the world's gods and sages praise you, the supreme self, by chanting
your names. All the multitudes of beings, having taken 65.75
refuge in you, dwell in you, the Granter of boons, O fine-armed one! Brahmins call you the world's bridge, without beginning, middle, or end, possessing boundless yoga."

BHISHMA said:

THEN THE VIRTUOUS God of the worlds, the lord of lords, 66.1
responded to Brahma in a soft and deep voice, with these words: "Dear sir, through yoga I am aware of all that you wish for. So be it!" Saying this, he disappeared. Then all the gods, sages, and *gandhárvas*, overwhelmed with great astonishment and driven by curiosity, asked the Grandsire: "Lord, who is he that has been humbly honored and extolled by Your Lordship with the highest words? We are eager to hear about him!"

66.5 evam uktas tu bhagavān pratyuvāca Pitāmahaḥ
deva|brahmarṣi|gandharvān sarvān madhurayā girā:
«yat tat paraṃ bhaviṣyaṃ ca,
bhavitavyaṃ ca yat param,
bhūt'|ātmā yaḥ prabhuś c' âiva,
Brahma yac ca paraṃ padam,
ten' âsmi kṛta|saṃvādaḥ prasannena, sura'|rṣabhāḥ.
jagato 'nugrah'|ârthāya yācito me jagat|patiḥ:
‹mānuṣaṃ lokam ātiṣṭha Vāsudeva iti śrutaḥ,
asurāṇāṃ vadh'|ârthāya saṃbhavasva mahī|tale.›
saṃgrāme nihatā ye te daitya|dānava|rākṣasāḥ,
ta ime nṛṣu saṃbhūtā ghora|rūpā mahā|balāḥ.
66.10 teṣāṃ vadh'|ârthaṃ bhagavān Nareṇa sahito vaśī
mānuṣīṃ yonim āsthāya cariṣyati mahī|tale.
Nara|Nārāyaṇau yau tau purāṇāv ṛṣi|sattamau
sahitau mānuṣe loke saṃbhūtāv a|mita|dyutī.
a|jeyau samare yattau sahitāv a|marair api,
mūḍhās tv etau na jānanti Nara|Nārāyaṇāv ṛṣī.
tasy' âham agra|jaḥ putraḥ sarvasya jagataḥ prabhuḥ,
Vāsudevo 'rcanīyo vaḥ sarva|loka|mah"|ēśvaraḥ.
tathā ‹manuṣyo 'yam› iti kadā cit, sura|sattamāḥ,
n' âvajñeyo mahā|vīryaḥ śaṅkha|cakra|gadā|dharaḥ.
66.15 etat paramakaṃ guhyam; etat paramakaṃ padam;
etat paramakaṃ Brahma; etat paramakaṃ yaśaḥ;
etad a|kṣaram a|vyaktam; etad vai śāśvataṃ mahat;

Addressed in this way, the divine Grandsire replied to all 66.5
the gods, sages, and *gandhárva*s in a sweet voice: "O excellent deities, it is he who is called That, the Supreme, who was, is, and will always be the highest, who is the soul of beings, who is the Lord, who is Brahman, the supreme state. It is with that gracious lord that I have conversed. I have thus requested the lord of the universe to show his mercy to the world: 'Pray enter the human world as the son of Vasu·deva, and take birth on earth in order to slaughter demons!' Those *daityas*, *dánava*s,* and *rákshasa*s of terrifying appearance and immense power were killed in battle but have been
reborn among men. In order to slaughter them, the mighty 66.10
lord will enter a human womb and wander on earth; and so will Nara. Nara and Naráyana,* those primordial and foremost sages of limitless splendor, will be born together in the human world. When engaged in battle they are invincible even by all the gods combined. But the deluded cannot recognize the two divine sages Nara and Naráyana. I, Brahma, the lord of the whole universe, am Vásu·deva's eldest son; and he, the great God of all the worlds, should be worshipped by you. O foremost of deities, you should never ignore him, thinking that this wielder of the conch, the discus, and the mace is a human being endowed with great
power. This is the highest mystery; this is the highest state; 66.15
this is the highest Brahman; this is the highest glory; this is the indestructible and the unmanifest; this is the eternal might. This is eulogized as the Person and yet is unknown. This is the highest energy; this is the highest bliss; this is the highest truth, as spoken by Vishva·karman. So the Lord Vásu·deva of boundless prowess should not be ignored by

yat tat Puruṣa|saṃjñaṃ vai gīyate jñāyate na ca;
etat paramakaṃ teja; etat paramakaṃ sukham;
etat paramakaṃ satyaṃ kīrtitaṃ Viśvakarmaṇā.
tasmāt sarvaiḥ suraiḥ s'|Êndrair lokaiś c' â|mita|vikramaḥ
n' âvajñeyo Vāsudevo ‹mānuṣo 'yam› iti prabhuḥ.
yaś ca ‹mānuṣa|mātro 'yam› iti brūyāt, sa manda|dhīḥ.
Hṛṣīkeśam avajñānāt tam āhuḥ puruṣ|ādhamam.
66.20 yoginaṃ taṃ mah"|ātmānaṃ praviṣṭaṃ mānuṣīṃ tanum
avamanyed Vāsudevaṃ, tam āhus tāmasaṃ janāḥ.
devaṃ car'|â|car'|ātmānaṃ, śrī|vats'|âṅkaṃ, su|varcasam,
padma|nābhaṃ na jānāti, tam āhus tāmasaṃ budhāḥ.
kirīṭa|kaustubha|dharaṃ, mitrāṇām abhayaṅ|karam
avajānan mah"|ātmānaṃ, ghore tamasi majjati.
evaṃ viditvā tattv'|ârthaṃ lokānām īśvar'|ēśvaraḥ
Vāsudevo namas|kāryaḥ sarva|lokaiḥ, sur'|ôttamāḥ.»

BHĪṢMA uvāca:

evam uktvā sa bhagavān sarvān sa'|rṣi|gaṇān purā
visṛjya sarva|lok'|ātmā jagāma bhavanaṃ svakam.
66.25 tato devāḥ sa|gandharvā, munayo, 'psaraso 'pi ca
kathāṃ tāṃ Brahmaṇā gītāṃ śrutvā prītā divaṃ yayuḥ.
etac chrutaṃ mayā, tāta, ṛṣīṇāṃ bhāvit'|ātmanām
Vāsudevaṃ kathayatāṃ samavāye purātanam
Rāmasya Jāmadagnyasya, Mārkaṇḍeyasya dhīmataḥ,
Vyāsa|Nāradayoś c' âpi sakāśād, Bharata'|rṣabha.
etam arthaṃ ca vijñāya, śrutvā ca prabhum a|vyayam
Vāsudevaṃ mah"|ātmānaṃ, lokānām īśvar'|ēśvaram,

Indra and the other gods, or by any men, on the supposition that he is a human being. Dull-witted is he who out of disdain says that Hrishi·kesha is merely a human being. Such a person is called the meanest of men. People say that 66.20
he who ignores Vásu·deva, that great-spirited yogin who has assumed a human body, is ignorant. The wise say that that man is ignorant who does not know the resplendent lotus-naveled God, marked with a curl on his chest, as a favorite of Shri,* containing all moving and unmoving creatures in his soul. A man sinks into a terrible darkness of ignorance if he ignores the great-spirited wearer of the diadem and the Káustubha gem,* who grants safety to his friends. Vásu·deva, the lord of the lords of the worlds, should be honored by all men who know the true reality in this way, foremost of the Gods."

BHISHMA said:

After saying these words to the gods and the hosts of sages in the olden days, and after dismissing them, the Lord Brahma, the soul of all beings, went to his abode. Then the 66.25
gods, *gandhárva*s, sages, and *ápsarase*s,* having listened to that discourse delivered by Brahma, proceeded to heaven, rejoicing.

Sir, I heard this from the sages accomplished in spirit, while they were talking about primordial Vásu·deva in their assembly. O bull-like Bharata, I heard this from Rama the son of Jamad·agni, from wise Markandéya, and also from Vyasa and Nárada. After hearing about the great-spirited, imperishable God Vásu·deva, the lord of the lords of the world, whose son is Brahma the father of the universe, why

66.30 vārito 'si mayā, tāta, munibhir veda|pāra|gaiḥ:
«mā gaccha saṃyugaṃ tena Vāsudevena dhīmatā;
mā Pāṇḍavaiḥ sārdham» iti. tac ca mohān na budhyase.
manye tvāṃ rākṣasaṃ krūraṃ; tathā c' âsi tamo|vṛtaḥ,
yasmād dviṣasi Govindaṃ Pāṇḍavaṃ ca Dhanañjayam.
Nara|Nārāyaṇau devau n' ânyo dviṣyādd hi mānavaḥ.
tasmād bravīmi te, rājann: eṣa vai śāśvato, '|vyayaḥ,
sarva|lokamayo, nityaḥ, śāstā, dhātā, dharo, dhruvaḥ.
lokān dhārayate yas trīṃś car'|â|cara|guruḥ prabhuḥ,
yoddhā jayaś ca jetā ca sarva|prakṛtir īśvaraḥ,
66.35 rājan, sattvamayo hy eṣa tamo|rāga|vivarjitaḥ.
yataḥ Kṛṣṇas tato dharmo; yato dharmas tato jayaḥ.
tasya māhātmya|yogena yogen' ātmana eva ca
dhṛtāḥ Pāṇḍu|sutā, rājañ; jayaś c' âiṣāṃ bhaviṣyati.
śreyo|yuktāṃ sadā buddhiṃ Pāṇḍavānāṃ dadhāti yaḥ,
balaṃ c' âiva raṇe nityaṃ bhayebhyaś c' âiva rakṣati,
sa eṣa śāśvato devaḥ sarva|guhyamayaḥ, śivaḥ,
Vāsudeva iti jñeyo, yan māṃ pṛcchasi, Bhārata.
brāhmaṇaiḥ, kṣatriyair, vaiśyaiḥ, śūdraiś ca kṛta|lakṣaṇaiḥ
sevyate 'bhyarcyate c' âiva nitya|yuktaiḥ sva|karmabhiḥ
66.40 dvāparasya yugasy' ânte, ādau kali|yugasya ca,
sātvataṃ vidhim āsthāya gītaḥ Saṃkarṣaṇena vai.
sa eṣa sarvaṃ sura|martya|lokaṃ,

don't human beings understand this subject and revere and worship that Vásu·deva?

Formerly, sir, you were warned by the sages who are 66.30
perfectly versed in the Vedas, and by myself, saying: "Do not wage war against bow-wielding Vásu·deva and the Pándavas!" But on account of your delusion you failed to understand the warnings. I consider you a cruel demon shrouded in the darkness of ignorance. That is why you hate Go·vinda and the Pándava Dhanan·jaya. What other man would hate the divine Nara and Naráyana? So I am telling you, Your Majesty, that he is everlasting, imperishable, and pervades all worlds; that he is eternal, the ruler, the upholder of the earth, and unchangeable. He is the lord who maintains the three worlds, the teacher of all moving and unmoving creatures; he is the warrior, the victory, and
the victorious; he is the lord, the origin of all. Your Majesty, 66.35
he is permeated with pure goodness and is free from dark ignorance and the stain of passion. Wherever Krishna is, there is righteousness. Wherever righteousness is, there is victory. The sons of Pandu are sustained by the yoga of his great spirit, and by the yoga of his soul. Victory will be on their side, Your Majesty. It is he who always bestows beneficial understanding upon the Pándavas and constantly protects them from dangers. He is the eternal and merciful God known as Vásu·deva, who is hidden everywhere, and about whom you have asked, descendant of Bharata. He is served and worshipped by brahmins, kshatriyas, vaishyas, and shudras, each having their characteristic features, each
always engaged in their respective duties.* At the end of a 66.40
dvápara age and at the beginning of a *kali* age* he is always

samudra|kakṣy"|ântaritāṃ purīṃ ca
yuge yuge mānuṣaṃ c' âiva vāsaṃ
punaḥ punaḥ sṛjate Vāsudevaḥ.

DURYODHANA uvāca:

67.1 VĀSUDEVO MAHAD bhūtaṃ sarva|lokeṣu kathyate.
tasy' āgamaṃ pratiṣṭhāṃ ca jñātum icche, pitā|maha.

BHĪṢMA uvāca:

Vāsudevo mahad bhūtaṃ sarva|daivata|daivatam.
na paraṃ Puṇḍarīkākṣād dṛśyate, Bharata'|ṛṣabha.
Mārkaṇḍeyaś ca Govinde kathayaty adbhutaṃ mahat.
sarva|bhūtāni, bhūt'|ātmā, mah"|ātmā, Puruṣ'|ôttamaḥ.
āpo, vāyuś ca, tejaś ca, trayam etad akalpayat.
sa sṛṣṭvā pṛthivīṃ devaḥ sarva|lok'|ēśvaraḥ prabhuḥ
67.5 apsu vai śayanaṃ cakre mah"|ātmā Puruṣ'|ôttamaḥ.
sarva|tejomayo devo yogāt suṣvāpa tatra ha.
mukhataḥ so 'gnim asṛjat; prāṇād vāyum ath' âpi ca;
Sarasvatīṃ ca vedāṃś ca manasaḥ sasṛje 'cyutaḥ.
eṣa lokān sasarj' ādau, devāṃś c' âpy ṛṣibhiḥ saha,
nidhanaṃ c' âiva mṛtyuṃ ca, prajānāṃ prabhav'|âpyayau.
eṣa dharmaś ca, dharma|jño, vara|daḥ, sarva|kāma|daḥ.
eṣa kartā ca kāryaṃ ca pūrva|devaḥ svayaṃ|prabhuḥ.
bhūtaṃ, bhavyaṃ, bhaviṣyac ca pūrvam etad akalpayat,
ubhe saṃdhye, diśaḥ, khaṃ ca, niyamāṃś ca Janārdanaḥ.
67.10 ṛṣīṃś c' âiva hi Govindas, tapaś c' âiv' âbhyakalpayat,
sraṣṭāraṃ jagataś c' âpi mah"|ātmā prabhur a|vyayaḥ.
agra|jaṃ sarva|bhūtānāṃ Saṃkarṣaṇam akalpayat.

duly extolled, together with Sankárshana. It is Vásu·deva who creates the worlds of the gods and mortals, the city of Dváraka girded by the sea, and the realm of humans, again and again, age after age.

DURYÓDHANA said:

VÁSU·DEVA IS SAID to be the supreme being in all worlds. 67.1
Grandsire, I wish to know of his origin and glory.

BHISHMA said:

Vásu·deva is indeed the supreme being, the deity of all
deities. There is none superior to the Lotus-eyed god, bull
of the Bharatas. Markandéya describes* the great wonder
that is in Go·vinda, as comprising all beings, as the soul of
the existent, as the great-spirited Supreme Person. He created these three elements: water, air, and fire. After creating the goddess Earth, the lord—the ruler of all the worlds,
the great-spirited Supreme Person, the God containing all 67.5
energies—lay down on the waters and there, through yoga,
he lapsed into sleep. Áchyuta created fire from his mouth,
air from his life-breath, and Sarásvati and the Vedas from
his mind. At first He created the worlds, as well as the gods
and sages, and dissolution and death, the birth and decay
of creatures. He is virtue and the virtuous; he is the granter
of boons and the gratifier of all wishes; he is the actor and
the action; he is the primordial, self-powerful God. Janárdana at first created the past, the present, and the future,
the two twilights, the quarters, the sky, and the restraints.
Go·vinda, the great-spirited imperishable lord, also created 67.10
sages, austerities, and the creator of the world. He created
Sankárshana too, the firstborn of all beings.

tasmān Nārāyaṇo jajñe deva|devaḥ sanātanaḥ.
nābhau padmaṃ babhūv' âsya. sarva|lokasya saṃbhavāt
tasmāt Pitāmaho jātas. tasmāj jātās tv imāḥ prajāḥ.
Śeṣaṃ c' âkalpayad devam an|antam viśva|rūpiṇam,
yo dhārayati bhūtāni dharāṃ c' êmāṃ sa|parvatām.
dhyāna|yogena viprāś ca taṃ vadanti mah"|âujasam.
karṇa|srot'|ôdbhavaṃ c' âpi Madhuṃ nāma mah"|âsuram
67.15 tam ugram, ugra|karmāṇam, ugrāṃ buddhiṃ samāsthitam
Brahmaṇo 'pacitiṃ kurvañ jaghāna Puruṣ'|ôttamaḥ.
tasya, tāta, vadhād eva deva|dānava|mānavāḥ
Madhusūdanam ity āhur ṛṣayaś ca Janārdanam.
Varāhaś c' âiva, Siṃhaś ca, Tri|vikrama|gatiḥ prabhuḥ,
eṣa mātā pitā c' âiva sarveṣāṃ prāṇināṃ Hariḥ.
paraṃ hi Puṇḍarīkākṣān na bhūtaṃ, na bhaviṣyati.
mukhato 'sṛjad brāhmaṇān, bāhubhyāṃ kṣatriyāṃs tathā,
vaiśyāṃś c' âpy ūruto, rājañ,
śūdrān padbhyāṃ tath" âiva ca.
tapasā niyato devaṃ
vidhānaṃ sarva|dehinām
67.20 Brahma|bhūtam amā|vāsyāṃ, paurṇa|māsyāṃ tath" âiva ca
yoga|bhūtaṃ paricaran Keśavaṃ mahad āpnuyāt.
Keśavaḥ paramaṃ tejaḥ sarva|loka|pitāmahaḥ.
evam āhur Hṛṣīkeśaṃ munayo vai, nar'|âdhipa.
evam enaṃ vijānīhi ācāryaṃ pitaraṃ gurum.
Kṛṣṇo yasya prasīdeta, lokās ten' â|kṣayā jitāḥ.

From him the eternal God of gods Naráyana was born. A lotus arose from his navel; and since it was the source of the entire world, the Grandsire* came into being, from whom all creatures were born. He created the divine serpent Shesha, also called Anánta, who assumes all forms and supports all beings and this earth with its mountains.

The brahmins come to know that lord endowed with 67.15
intense energy through the yoga of contemplation. Having worshipped Brahma, the Supreme Person slaughtered a mighty and ferocious demon, Madhu, who had arisen from his earwax and, performing fearful deeds, had harbored terrible intentions. Dear sir, after the slaughter of that demon, the gods, *dánava*s, men, and sages began to call Janárdana by the name "Slayer of Madhu." The Boar, the Lion, and the Lord of Three Strides,* Hari is the father and mother of all living beings. There never has been and never will be anyone superior to the Lotus-eyed one, who created brahmins from his mouth, kshatriyas from his arms, vaishyas from his thighs, and shudras from his feet.* Whoever, restrained by austerities, worships the God, the repository of
all embodied beings, the essence of Brahman and of yoga, 67.20
on the days of the new and the full moon, will definitely attain to Késhava. Késhava is the highest energy, the grandsire of all the worlds. Sages call him Hrishi·kesha, lord of men. Realize him as the master, the father, and the teacher. He to whom Krishna is gracious has won the imperishable realms. The man who takes shelter in Krishna when in dire straits, and who recites this hymn, will always be fortunate and happy. Those men who resort to Krishna can never be deluded. Janárdana always protects those who are stricken

yaś c' âiv' âinaṃ bhaya|sthāne Keśavaṃ śaraṇaṃ vrajet
sadā naraḥ paṭhaṃś c' êdaṃ, svastimān sa sukhī bhavet.
ye ca Kṛṣṇaṃ prapadyante, te na muhyanti mānavāḥ.
bhaye mahati ye magnāḥ, pāti nityaṃ Janārdanaḥ.
67.25 etad Yudhiṣṭhiro jñātvā yāthātathyena, Bhārata,
sarv'|ātmanā mah"|ātmānaṃ Keśavaṃ jagad|īśvaram
prapannaḥ śaraṇaṃ, rājan, yogānām prabhum īśvaram.

BHĪṢMA uvāca:

68.1 ŚṚṆU C' ÊDAṂ mahā|rāja Brahma|bhūta|stavaṃ mama
brahma'|rṣibhiś ca devaiś ca yaḥ purā kathito bhuvi.
«sādhyānām api devānāṃ deva|dev'|ēśvaraḥ prabhuḥ,
loka|bhāvana|bhāva|jña, iti tvāṃ Nārado 'bravīt.
bhūtaṃ bhavyaṃ bhaviṣyaṃ ca Mārkaṇḍeyo 'bhyuvāca ha,
yajñaṃ tvāṃ c' âiva yajñānāṃ, tapaś ca tapasām api.
devānām api devaṃ ca tvām āha bhagavān Bhṛguḥ
purāṇaṃ c' âiva paramaṃ Viṣṇo tav' êti ca.
68.5 Vāsudevo Vasūnāṃ tvaṃ, Śakraṃ sthāpayitā tathā,
deva|devo 'si devānām, iti Dvaipāyano 'bravīt.
pūrve prajā|nisargeṣu Dakṣam āhuḥ prajā|patim.
sraṣṭāraṃ sarva|lokānām Aṅgirās tvāṃ tato 'bravīt.
a|vyaktaṃ te śarīr'|ôtthaṃ, vyaktaṃ te manasi sthitam,
devās tvat|saṃbhavāś c' âiva, Devalas tv Asito 'bravīt.
śirasā te divaṃ vyāptaṃ; bāhubhyāṃ pṛthivī dhṛtā;
jaṭharaṃ te trayo lokāḥ. Puruṣo 'si sanātanaḥ.
evaṃ tvām abhijānanti tapasā bhāvitā narāḥ.
ātma|darśana|tṛptānām ṛṣīṇāṃ c' âsi sattamaḥ.
68.10 rāja'|rṣīṇām udārāṇām āhaveṣv a|nivartinām
sarva|dharma|pradhānānāṃ tvaṃ gatir, Madhu|sūdana.»

with great terror. O descendant of Bharata, Yudhi·shthira, 67.25
realizing Késhava completely as the great-spirited lord of the universe, has taken refuge in the Lord who is the master of all yoga.

BHISHMA said:

GREAT KING, hear from me this ancient hymn that was 68.1
chanted on earth in the olden days by the gods and brahminical sages:

"Nárada described you as the lord and master of the god of gods, deities, and saintly *sadhyas*, and the knower of the world's thoughts and feelings. Markandéya characterized you as the past, the present, and the future, the sacrifice of sacrifices and the penance of penances. Virtuous Bhrigu called you the God of gods, saying that yours, Vishnu, is the
supreme *purána*.* Dvaipáyana has said that you are Vásu· 68.5
deva of Vasus, the establisher of Shakra, and the God of gods. At the start, at the time of the creation of living beings, you were called Daksha, the lord of creatures. Ángiras called you the creator of all the worlds. Ásita Dévala said that the unmanifest originated from your body, that the Manifest is in your mind, and that the gods have arisen from you. Heaven is pervaded with your head; the earth is sustained by your two arms; the three worlds are your abdomen. You are the eternal Person. The men accomplished through austerities know you as such. For the sages gratified with the true vision of the self, you are the foremost of all
who really exist. O Slayer of Madhu, you are the shelter of 68.10
the glorious royal sages who never draw back from combats and who excel in all their duties."

iti nityaṃ yoga|vidbhir bhagavān Puruṣ'|ôttamaḥ
Sanatkumāra|pramukhaiḥ stūyate 'bhyarcyate Hariḥ.
eṣa te vistaras, tāta, saṃkṣepaś ca prakīrtitaḥ
Keśavasya yathā|tattvaṃ. su|prīto bhaja Keśavam.

SAÑJAYA uvāca:

puṇyaṃ śrutv" âitad ākhyānaṃ, mahā|rāja, sutas tava
Keśavaṃ bahu mene sa, Pāṇḍavāṃś ca mahārathān.
tam abravīn, mahā|rāja, Bhīṣmaḥ Śāntanavaḥ punaḥ:
«māhātmyaṃ te śrutaṃ, rājan, Keśavasya mah"|ātmanaḥ,
68.15 Narasya ca yathā|tattvaṃ, yan māṃ tvaṃ pṛcchase, nṛ|pa.
yad|arthaṃ nṛṣu saṃbhūtau Nara|Nārāyaṇāv ṛṣī,
a|vadhyau ca yathā vīrau saṃyugeṣv a|parājitau,
yathā ca Pāṇḍavā, rājann, a|gamyā yudhi kasya cit.
prītimān hi dṛḍhaṃ Kṛṣṇaḥ Pāṇḍaveṣu yaśasviṣu.
tasmād bravīmi, rāj'|êndra: śamo bhavatu Pāṇḍavaiḥ.
pṛthivīṃ bhuṅkṣva sahito bhrātṛbhir balibhir vaśī.
Nara|Nārāyaṇau devāv avajñāya naśiṣyasi.»
evam uktvā tava pitā tūṣṇīm āsīd, viśāṃ pate.
vyasarjayac ca rājānaṃ, śayanaṃ ca viveśa ha.
68.20 rājā ca śibiraṃ prāyāt praṇipatya mah"|ātmane,
śiśye ca śayane śubhre tāṃ rātriṃ, Bharata'|rṣabha.

Thus the Lord Hari, the Supreme Person, has been extolled and worshipped by the masters of yoga, starting with Sanat·kumára. Sir, I have related the truth about Késhava to you, at length, and in brief. Revere Késhava with great delight!

SÁNJAYA said:

On hearing this sacred story, great king, your son began to hold Késhava and those great warriors, the sons of Pandu, in high regard. Then Bhishma the son of Shántanu spoke to him again, great king:

"Your Majesty, you have heard about the true glory of great-spirited Késhava and Nara, as requested. You have 68.15
also heard the reason why the two divine sages Nara and Naráyana have taken birth among men, as well as why those two heroes are inviolable and invincible in battle, and why no one can conquer the sons of Pandu, Your Majesty. Krishna is very fond of Pandu's sons. That is why I suggest to you, king of kings, that peace be made with the Pándavas. Restrain yourself and enjoy the earth, sharing it with your mighty brothers. But if you ignore the divine Nara and Naráyana, you will perish."

After saying this, your father* became silent, lord of the
people. He dismissed the king and entered his tent. The 68.20
king, bowing to the great-spirited grandfather, went to his own tent and slept that night on a white bed, descendant of Bharata.

69–74
DAY FIVE

SAÑJAYA UVĀCA:

69.1 VYUṢITĀYĀṂ CA śarvaryām, udite ca divā|kare
ubhe sene, mahā|rāja, yuddhāy' âiva samīyatuḥ.
abhyadhāvanta saṃkruddhāḥ paras|para|jigīṣavaḥ
te sarve sahitā yuddhe samālokya paras|param
Pāṇḍavā Dhārtarāṣṭrāś ca, rājan, dur|mantrite tava,
vyūhau ca vyūhya saṃrabdhāḥ, saṃprahṛṣṭāḥ, prahāriṇaḥ.
arakṣan makara|vyūhaṃ Bhīṣmo, rājan, samantataḥ.
tath" âiva Pāṇḍavā, rājann, arakṣan vyūham ātmanaḥ.
69.5 sa niryayau rath'|ânīkaṃ pitā Devavratas tava
mahatā ratha|vaṃśena saṃvṛto rathināṃ varaḥ.
itar'|êtaram anvīyur yathā|bhāgam avasthitāḥ
rathinaḥ pattayaś c' âiva, dantinaḥ sādinas tathā.

tān dṛṣṭv" âbhyudyatān saṃkhye, Pāṇḍavāś ca yaśasvinaḥ
śyenena vyūha|rājena ten' â|jayyena saṃyuge.
aśobhata mukhe tasya Bhīmaseno mahā|balaḥ,
netre Śikhaṇḍī dur|dharṣo, Dhṛṣṭadyumnaś ca Pārṣataḥ.
śīrṣaṃ tasy' âbhavad vīraḥ Sātyakiḥ satya|vikramaḥ.
vidhunvan Gāṇḍivaṃ Pārtho grīvāyām abhavat tadā.
69.10 akṣauhiṇyā samagrāyā vāma|pakṣo 'bhavat tadā
mah"|ātmā Drupadaḥ śrīmān saha putreṇa saṃyuge.
dakṣiṇaś c' âbhavat pakṣaḥ Kaikeyo 'kṣauhiṇī|patiḥ,
pṛṣṭhato Draupadeyāś ca Saubhadraś c' âpi vīryavān.
pṛṣṭhe samabhavac chrīmān svayaṃ rājā Yudhiṣṭhiraḥ
bhrātṛbhyāṃ sahito dhīmān yamābhyāṃ cāru|vikramaḥ.

SÁNJAYA said:

AFTER THE NIGHT had passed and the sun had risen, great king, the two armies came together to wage war. Because of your bad advice, Your Majesty, your sons and the Pándavas, glaring at each other angrily, drew up their armies, and, all their soldiers being furious and joyous, they advanced against each other, eager to win the battle. Bhishma protected the crocodile formation of his army on every side, Your Majesty, and the Pándavas protected their own formation. Your father Deva·vrata, that best of chariot warriors, advanced, great king, surrounded by a large chariot division. Chariot warriors, foot soldiers, elephants, and horsemen followed each other accordingly, as they were stationed in the array. 69.1

69.5

Watching the hostile troops, the glorious Pándavas drew up their army on the battlefield into the superb hawk formation, which was unconquerable in combat. In its beak shone mighty Bhima·sena. Invincible Shikhándin and Dhrishta·dyumna the son of Príshata formed its eyes. In its head stood valiant Sátyaki, whose power is in truth. In its neck was the son of Pritha, wielding his Gandíva bow. Great-spirited glorious Drúpada with his son formed the left wing of the entire army on the battlefield. The Kékaya army leader stood in its right wing. In its back were the sons of Dráupadi and the mighty son of Subhádra. And in its tail was the glorious and brightly valiant King Yudhi·shthira himself, together with his twin brothers Nákula and Saha·deva. 69.10

praviśya tu raṇe Bhīmo makaraṃ mukhatas tadā,
Bhīṣmam āsādya saṃgrāme chādayām āsa sāyakaiḥ.
tato Bhīṣmo mah"|âstrāṇi pātayām āsa, Bhārata,
mohayan Pāṇḍu|putrāṇāṃ vyūḍhaṃ sainyaṃ mah"|āhave.
69.15 saṃmuhyati tadā sainye tvaramāṇo Dhanañjayaḥ
Bhīṣmaṃ śara|sahasreṇa vivyādha raṇa|mūrdhani.
parisaṃvārya c' âstrāṇi Bhīṣma|muktāni saṃyuge
sven' ânīkena hṛṣṭena yuddhāya samavasthitaḥ.

tato Duryodhano rājā Bhāradvājam abhāṣata
pūrvaṃ dṛṣṭvā vadhaṃ ghoraṃ balasya balināṃ varaḥ,
bhrātṝṇāṃ ca vadhaṃ yuddhe smaramāṇo mahā|rathaḥ:

«ācārya, satataṃ hi tvaṃ hita|kāmo mam', ân|agha.
vayaṃ hi tvāṃ samāśritya, Bhīṣmaṃ c' âiva pitā|maham,
devān api raṇe jetuṃ prārthayāmo, na saṃśayaḥ;
69.20 kim u Pāṇḍu|sutān yuddhe hīna|vīrya|parākramān?
sa tathā kuru, bhadraṃ te, yathā vadhyanti Pāṇḍavāḥ.»

evam uktas tato Droṇas tava putreṇa, māriṣa,
abhinat Pāṇḍav'|ânīkaṃ prekṣamāṇasya Sātyakeḥ.
Sātyakis tu tadā Droṇaṃ vārayām āsa, Bhārata.
tataḥ pravavṛte yuddhaṃ ghora|rūpaṃ bhay'|āvaham.
Śaineyaṃ tu raṇe kruddho Bhāradvājaḥ pratāpavān
avidhyan niśitair bāṇair jatru|deśe hasann iva.
Bhīmasenas tataḥ kruddho Bhāradvājam avidhyata
saṃrakṣan Sātyakiṃ, rājan, Droṇāc chastra|bhṛtāṃ varāt.

Penetrating the crocodile through its mouth on the field of battle, Bhima attacked Bhishma in the fray and enveloped him in arrows. Then Bhishma sent mighty weapons, descendant of Bharata, bewildering the arrayed troops of Pandu's sons in that huge battle. While the troops were 69.15
thus bewildered, Dhanan·jaya, swiftly advancing, wounded Bhishma with a thousand arrows at the front of the battle; and, checking all the weapons launched by Bhishma in that contest, he stood prepared for the combat.

Then King Duryódhana, a great warrior and the champion of mighty men, having witnessed the horrible massacre of his troops, and remembering the slaughter of his brothers in battle on the previous day, spoke to Bharad·vaja's son:

"O faultless teacher, you have always wished me well. Resorting to you and to grandfather Bhishma, we can doubtless seek to defeat even the gods in battle; what then of the 69.20
sons of Pandu, who lack vigor and courage? Blessings be upon you! Please act in such a way that the Pándavas will be slaughtered!"

Addressed by your son in this way, my lord, Drona then broke through the Pándava array under Sátyaki's very eyes. Sátyaki then repelled Drona, descendant of Bharata. And the combat that ensued between them was frightening and terrible to see. The mighty son of Bharad·vaja, filled with battle-fury, wounded the grandson of Shini in the shoulder with sharp arrows, almost laughing as he did so. Then en- 69.25
raged Bhima·sena, in order to protect Sátyaki from Drona, that champion of warriors, struck the son of Bharad·vaja with his shafts; and Drona, Bhishma, and Shalya shrouded

69.25 tato Droṇaś ca, Bhīṣmaś ca, tathā Śalyaś ca, māriṣa,
Bhīmasenaṃ raṇe kruddhāś chādayāṃ cakrire śaraiḥ.
tatr' Âbhimanyuḥ saṃkruddho Draupadeyāś ca, māriṣa,
vivyadhur niśitair bāṇaiḥ sarvāṃs tān udyat'|āyudhān.
Bhīṣma|Droṇau ca saṃkruddhāv āpatantau mahā|balau
pratyudyayau Śikhaṇḍī tu mah"|ēṣv|āso mah"|āhave.
pragṛhya balavad vīro dhanur jalada|nihsvanam
abhyavarṣac charais tūrṇaṃ chādayāno divā|karam.
Śikhaṇḍinaṃ samāsādya Bharatānāṃ pitā|mahaḥ
avarjayata saṃgrāme strītvaṃ tasy' ânusaṃsmaran.
69.30 tato Droṇo, mahā|rāja, abhyadravata taṃ raṇe
rakṣamāṇas tadā Bhīṣmaṃ tava putreṇa coditaḥ.
Śikhaṇḍī tu samāsādya Droṇaṃ śastra|bhṛtāṃ varam
avarjayata saṃtrasto yug'|ânt'|âgnim iv' ôlbaṇam.
tato balena mahatā putras tava, viśāṃ pate,
jugopa Bhīṣmam āsādya prārthayāno mahad yaśaḥ.
tath" âiva Pāṇḍavā, rājan, puras|kṛtya Dhanañjayam
Bhīṣmam ev' âbhyavartanta jaye kṛtvā dṛḍhāṃ matim.
tad yuddham abhavad ghoraṃ devānāṃ dānavair iva,
jayaṃ ca kāṅkṣatāṃ nityaṃ, yaśaś ca param'|âdbhutam.

SAÑJAYA uvāca:

70.1 AKAROT TUMULAṂ yuddhaṃ Bhīṣmaḥ Śāntanavas tadā
Bhīmasena|bhayād icchan putrāṃs tārayituṃ tava.
pūrv|âhṇe tan mahā|raudraṃ rājñāṃ yuddham avartata
Kurūṇāṃ Pāṇḍavānāṃ ca mukhya|śūra|vināśanam.
tasminn ākula|saṃgrāme vartamāne mahā|bhaye

Bhima·sena with arrows on the field of battle, my lord. With sharp arrows Abhimányu and the sons of Dráupadi pierced all those combatants who were brandishing their weapons. Then Shikhándin, the mighty archer, charged against the infuriated and powerful Drona and Bhishma as they were attacking his troops in that huge battle. Forcefully grabbing his bow, which had a twang as thunderous as storm-clouds, the hero swiftly rained down a shower of shafts, enveloping the sun itself. But when confronted by Shikhándin, the grandfather of the Bharatas, mindful of
his female nature, avoided fighting with him. Now Drona, 69.30
urged by your son, charged forward in that combat, great king, in order to protect Bhishma. Shikhándin, however, encountering Drona, that best of weapon-wielding warriors, avoided him, stricken with fear of that warrior who appeared like the dreadful fire at the end of an era. Your son, seeking great fame, advanced with a large host and began to protect Bhishma, lord of the people. And the Pándavas, Your Majesty, headed by Dhanan·jaya, pounced on Bhishma, firmly setting their minds on victory. The combat that ensued between the two armies seeking triumph and glory was as horrific and wonderful as the battle between the gods and the demons.

SÁNJAYA said:

BHISHMA THE SON of Shántanu then waged a tumul- 70.1
tuous battle, desiring to rescue your sons from the danger of Bhima·sena. That immensely terrifying encounter between the Kurus and the Pándavas, during which many foremost of heroes were slaughtered, occurred in the morning. As

abhavat tumulaḥ śabdaḥ saṃspṛśan gaganaṃ mahat.
nadadbhiś ca mahā|nāgair, hreṣamāṇaiś ca vājibhiḥ,
bherī|śaṅkha|ninādaiś ca tumulaḥ samapadyata.
70.5 yuyutsavas te vikrāntā vijayāya mahā|balāḥ
anyonyam abhigarjanto, goṣṭheṣv iva maha"|ṛṣabhāḥ.
śirasāṃ pātyamānānāṃ samare niśitaiḥ śaraiḥ
aśma|vṛṣṭir iv' ākāśe babhūva, Bharata'|ṛṣabha.
kuṇḍal'|ôṣṇīṣa|dhārīṇi jātarūp'|ôjjvalāni ca
patitāni sma dṛśyante śirāṃsi, Bharata'|ṛṣabha.
viśikh'|ônmathitair gātrair, bāhubhiś ca sa|kārmukaiḥ,
sa|hast'|ābharaṇaiś c' ânyair abhavac chāditā mahī.
kavac'|ôpahitair gātrair, hastaiś ca samalaṃkṛtaiḥ,
mukhaiś ca candra|saṃkāśai, rakt'|ânta|nayanaiḥ śubhaiḥ,
70.10 gaja|vāji|manuṣyāṇāṃ sarva|gātraiś ca, bhū|pate,
āsīt sarvā samākīrṇā muhūrtena vasun|dharā.

rajo|meghaiś ca tumulaiḥ śastra|vidyut|prakāśitaiḥ,
āyudhānāṃ ca nirghoṣaḥ stanayitnu|samo 'bhavat.
sa saṃprahāras tumulaḥ, kaṭukaḥ, śoṇit'|ôdakaḥ
prāvartata Kurūṇāṃ ca Pāṇḍavānāṃ ca, Bhārata.

tasmin mahā|bhaye ghore tumule loma|harṣaṇe
vavṛṣuḥ śara|varṣāṇi kṣatriyā yuddha|dur|madāḥ.
akrośan kuñjarās tatra śara|varṣa|pratāpitāḥ
tāvakānāṃ pareṣāṃ ca saṃyuge, Bharata'|ṛṣabha.
70.15 saṃrabdhānāṃ ca vīryāṇāṃ dhīrāṇām a|mit'|âujasām
dhanur|jyā|tala|śabdena na prājñāyata kiṃ cana.
utthiteṣu kabandheṣu sarvataḥ śoṇit'|ôdake

that agitated and utterly horrific clash set in, it made a
tumultuous noise that touched the very sky. That tumult
arose from the trumpeting of huge elephants, the neigh of
horses, the beat of drums, and the blare of conches. Those 70.5
valiant and powerful combatants, eager to win the victory, bellowed at each other like bulls in cowsheds. Heads,
chopped off by sharp arrows in that encounter, were falling
like a downpour of stones from the sky, bull of the Bharatas.
Countless heads, still wearing their earrings and turbans,
were seen lying on the ground, shining like gold, best of the
Bharatas. The ground was covered with ornamented bow-
bearing arms, and with other limbs that had been cut off
with shafts. In an instant the earth was strewn with bodies 70.10
clad in armor, decorated hands, moon-like faces with lovely
red-cornered eyes, and all the limbs of elephants, horses,
and men.

In turbulent dust-clouds where weapons flashed like lightning, the clang of weapons sounded like rumbles of thunder. It was a fierce and dreadful encounter between the Kurus and the Pándavas, and blood flowed in rivers, descendant of Bharata.

In that immensely horrible, frightful, tumultuous, and
hair-raising engagement, warriors, ferocious in battle,
rained showers of arrows. The elephants of your army and
of the enemy's screamed out loud, plagued by torrents of
shafts in battle, bull of the Bharatas. Because of the noise 70.15
made by the bowstrings and palms of those enraged, res-
olute heroes of boundless vigor, nothing could be heard.
While headless bodies stood up on the battlefield where

samare paryadhāvanta nṛ|pā ripu|vadh'|ôdyatāḥ.
śara|śakti|gadābhis te khaḍgaiś c' â|mita|tejasaḥ
nijaghnuḥ samare 'nyonyaṃ śūrāḥ parigha|bāhavaḥ.
babhramuḥ kuñjarāś c' âtra śarair viddhā nir|aṅkuśāḥ;
aśvāś ca paryadhāvanta hat'|ārohā diśo daśa.
utpatya nipatanty anye śara|ghāta|prapīḍitāḥ
tāvakānāṃ pareṣāṃ ca yodhā, Bharata|sattama.
70.20 bāhūnām uttam'|âṅgānāṃ, kārmukāṇāṃ ca, Bhārata,
gadānāṃ, parighāṇāṃ ca, hastānāṃ c' ōrubhiḥ saha,
pādānāṃ, bhūṣaṇānāṃ ca, keyūrāṇāṃ ca saṅghaśaḥ
rāśayas tatra dṛśyante Bhīṣma|Bhīma|samāgame.
aśvānāṃ, kuñjarāṇāṃ ca, rathānāṃ c' â|nivartatām
saṃghātāḥ sma pradṛśyante tatra tatra, viśāṃ pate.
gadābhir, asibhiḥ, prāsair, bāṇaiś ca nata|parvabhiḥ
jaghnuḥ paras|paraṃ tātra kṣatriyāḥ Kāla|coditāḥ.
apare bāhubhir vīrā niyuddha|kuśalā yudhi
bahudhā samasajjanta āyasaiḥ parighair iva.
70.25 muṣṭibhir jānubhiś c' âiva talaiś c' âiva, viśāṃ pate,
anyonyaṃ jaghnire vīrās tāvakāḥ Pāṇḍavaiḥ saha.
patitaiḥ pātyamānaiś ca viceṣṭadbhiś ca bhū|tale
ghoram āyodhanam jajñe tatra tatra, jan'|ēśvara.
vi|rathā rathinaś c' âtra nistriṃśa|vara|dhāriṇaḥ
anyonyam abhyadhāvanta paras|para|vadh'|âiṣiṇaḥ.
tato Duryodhano rājā Kaliṅgair bahubhir vṛtaḥ
puras|kṛtya raṇe Bhīṣmaṃ Pāṇḍavān abhyavartata.
tath" âiva Pāṇḍavāḥ sarve parivārya Vṛkodaram
Bhīṣmam abhyadravan kruddhās. tato yuddham avartata.

blood flowed like water, kings rushed about, intent on slaying their enemies. Heroic combatants of limitless energy, whose arms were like iron bars, slaughtered each other in that battle, with arrows, spears, maces, and swords. Elephants wandered about, wounded with shafts and beyond being curbed by the hook; and horses, deprived of their riders, galloped around in all directions. Many warriors from your army and from the enemy's rose up and fell down, best of the Bharatas, tormented by arrow wounds.

In that combat between Bhishma and Bhima heaps of 70.20
arms, heads, bows, maces, iron clubs, hands, thighs, feet, ornaments and bracelets, descendant of Bharata, were seen piled up all over the field. Hordes of horses, elephants, and warriors who had never fled came into view here and there, lord of the people. Driven on by Time, warriors massacred each other there with maces, swords, lances, and straight shafts. Other heroes skilled in warfare struck one another many blows in that battle, their bare arms like iron bars.
Your heroic soldiers, lord of the people, fought against those 70.25
of the Pándavas, mortally striking each other with fists, knees, and palms. With many warriors fallen, and many others falling or writhing on the ground with pain, that massacre was terrifying indeed, lord of men. Chariot warriors stripped of their chariots, wielding their fine swords, assaulted one another, eager to kill each other. Then, surrounded by the numerous Kalíngas, King Duryódhana, with Bhishma ahead of him, besieged the Pándavas. And the infuriated Pándavas, rallying round Vrikódara, charged against Bhishma. Then a battle ensued!

SAÑJAYA uvāca:

71.1 DṚṢṬVĀ BHĪṢMEṆA saṃsaktān
bhrātṝn anyāṃś ca pārthivān,
samabhyadhāvad Gāṅgeyam
udyat'|âstro Dhanañjayaḥ.
Pāñcajanyasya nirghoṣaṃ, dhanuṣo Gāṇḍīvasya ca,
dhvajaṃ ca dṛṣṭvā Pārthasya sarvān no bhayam āviśat.
siṃha|lāṅgūlam ākāśe, jvalantam iva parvatam,
a|sajjamānaṃ vṛkṣeṣu, dhūma|ketum iv' ôtthitam,
bahu|varṇaṃ vicitraṃ ca, divyaṃ, vānara|lakṣaṇam
apaśyāma, mahā|rāja, dhvajaṃ Gāṇḍīva|dhanvanaḥ.
71.5 vidyutaṃ megha|madhya|sthāṃ bhrājamānām iv' âmbare
dadṛśur Gāṇḍīvaṃ yodhā rukma|pṛṣṭhaṃ mahā|mṛdhe.
aśuśruma bhṛśaṃ c' âsya Śakrasy' êv' âbhigarjataḥ
su|ghoraṃ talayoḥ śabdaṃ nighnatas tava vāhinīm.
caṇḍa|vāto yathā meghaḥ sa|vidyut|stanayitnumān
diśaḥ saṃplāvayan sarvāḥ śara|varṣaiḥ samantataḥ
samabhyadhāvad Gāṅgeyaṃ bhairav'|âstro Dhanañjayaḥ.
diśaṃ prācīṃ pratīcīṃ ca na jānīmo 'stra|mohitāḥ.
kāṃ|dig|bhūtāḥ, śrānta|patrā, hat'|âstrā, hata|cetasaḥ
anyonyam abhisaṃśliṣya yodhās te, Bharata'|rṣabha,
71.10 Bhīṣmam ev' âbhyalīyanta saha sarvais tav' ātma|jaiḥ.
teṣām ārt'|âyanam abhūd Bhīṣmaḥ Śāntanavo raṇe.
samutpatanti vitrastā rathebhyo rathinas tathā,
sādinaś c' âśva|pṛṣṭhebhyo, bhūmau c' âpi padātayaḥ.
śrutvā Gāṇḍīva|nirghoṣaṃ, visphūrjitam iv' âśaneḥ,
sarva|sainyāni bhītāni vyavālīyanta, Bhārata.

SÁNJAYA said:

SEEING HIS BROTHERS and other kings clashing with 71.1
Bhishma, Dhanan·jaya, brandishing his weapons, charged
against the son of Ganga. Fear overtook all the troops as
they heard the blare of the Pancha·janya conch, and the
twang of the Gandíva bow, and saw the Partha's banner. O
great king, we saw the banner of the Gandíva wielder, lion-
tailed, monkey-emblemed, multicolored, wonderful, and
divine, flying in the air like a risen meteor, unobstructed by
trees and resembling a blazing mountain. In that great bat- 71.5
tle the combatants saw the gilded Gandíva bow gleaming
like flashes of lightning between the clouds in the sky. And
as he slaughtered your troops we heard Árjuna's loud shouts
which resembled Indra's roars, and the terrifying sound of
him slapping his arms with his palms. Flooding all the quarters with torrents of shafts, like a storm-driven rain-cloud
charged with lightning and thunder, Dhanan·jaya, armed
with his horrible weapons, attacked the son of Ganga.

Bewildered by his weapons, we could not distinguish the
east from the west. O bull of the Bharatas, your combatants, unable to make out the directions, their animals exhausted, their horses killed, and their hearts lost, huddled
up against each other. Together with all your sons, they 71.10
clustered round Bhishma; and Bhishma the son of Shántanu became their shelter on the field of battle. Struck with
terror, chariot warriors jumped out of their chariots, horsemen leaped down from their horses, and foot soldiers fell
to the ground. On hearing the thunderous twang of the
Gandíva bow, descendant of Bharata, all the troops were
frightened and began to hide.

atha Kāmboja|jair aśvair mahadbhiḥ śīghra|gāmibhiḥ,
go|pānāṃ bahu|sāhasrair balair gopāyanair vṛtaḥ,
Madra|Sauvīra|Gāndhārais, Trigartaiś ca, viśāṃ pate,
sarva|Kāliṅga|mukhyaiś ca Kaliṅg'|âdhipatir vṛtaḥ;
71.15 nānā|nara|gaṇ'|âughaiś ca Duḥśāsana|puraḥ|saraḥ
Jayadrathaś ca nṛ|patiḥ, sahitaḥ sarva|rājabhiḥ;
hay'|āroha|varāś c' âiva tava putreṇa coditāḥ
catur|daśa sahasrāṇi Saubalaṃ paryavārayan.
tatas te sahitāḥ sarve vibhakta|ratha|vāhanāḥ
Pāṇḍavān samare jagmus tāvakā, Bharata'|rṣabha.
rathibhir, vāraṇair, aśvaiḥ, pādātaiś ca samīritam
ghoram āyodhanaṃ cakre mah"|âbhra|sadṛśaṃ rajaḥ.

tomara|prāsa|nārāca|gaj'|âśva|ratha|yodhinām
balena mahatā Bhīṣmaḥ samasajjat Kirīṭinā.
71.20 Āvantyaḥ Kāśi|rājena, Bhīmasenena Saindhavaḥ,
Ajātaśatrur Madrāṇām ṛṣabheṇa yaśasvinā
saha|putraḥ sah'|āmātyaḥ Śalyena samasajjata.
Vikarṇaḥ Sahadevena, Citrasenaḥ Śikhaṇḍinā,
Matsyā Duryodhanaṃ jagmuḥ, Śakuniṃ ca, viśāṃ pate.
Drupadaś, Cekitānaś ca, Sātyakiś ca mahā|rathaḥ
Droṇena samasajjanta sa|putreṇa mah"|ātmanā
Kṛpaś ca, Kṛtavarmā ca Dhṛṣṭaketum abhidrutau.
evaṃ prajavit'|âśvāni bhrānta|nāga|rathāni ca
sainyāni samasajjanta prayuddhāni samantataḥ.

Then the king of the Kalíngas, accompanied by a guard of many thousands of protective forces riding swift and mighty horses of the Kambója breed, lord of the people, and supported by the Madras, the Sauvíras, the Gandháras,
the Tri·gartas, and all the prominent Kalínga warriors; and 71.15
King Jayad·ratha, with hordes of various tribes, joined by all the kings led by Duhshásana; and also fourteen thousand excellent horsemen urged on by your son, all surrounded the son of Súbala. Then all those troops of yours, bull of the Bharatas, joining forces and riding their allotted vehicles, encountered the Pándavas. The dust raised by chariots, elephants, horses, and foot soldiers was like a huge cloud, and it made the battlefield look horrible.

With a large force of elephant riders, horsemen, and chariot warriors, all armed with spears, lances, and arrows,
Bhishma clashed with diadem-decorated Árjuna. The ruler 71.20
of Avánti confronted the king of Kashi, Bhima·sena battled with the ruler of the Sindhus, and Ajáta·shatru with his sons and companions encountered glorious Shalya the mighty king of the Madras. Vikárna fought with Saha·deva, and Chitra·sena with Shikhándin. The Matsyas confronted Duryódhana and Shákuni, lord of the people. Drúpada, Chekitána, and the great warrior Sátyaki clashed with great-spirited Drona and his son. Kripa and Krita·varman charged against Dhrishta·dyumna. So the battling troops were engaged in combat on all sides, their elephants and chariots lurching around, their horses driven onward.

71.25 nir|abhre vidyutas tīvrā, diśaś ca rajas" āvṛtāḥ,
prādur|āsan mah"|ôlkāś ca sa|nirghātā, viśāṃ pate.
pravavau ca mahā|vātaḥ, pāṃsu|varṣaṃ papāta ca.
nabhasy antar|dadhe sūryaḥ sainyena rajas" āvṛtaḥ.
pramohaḥ sarva|sattvānām at'|îva samapadyata
rajasā c' âbhibhūtānām, astra|jālaiś ca tudyatām.
vīra|bāhu|visṛṣṭānāṃ sarv'|āvaraṇa|bhedinām
saṃghātaḥ śara|jālānāṃ tumulaḥ samapadyata.
prakāśaṃ cakrur ākāśam udyatāni bhuj'|ôttamaiḥ
nakṣatra|vimal'|âbhāni śastrāṇi, Bharata'|rṣabha.
71.30 ārṣabhāṇi vicitrāṇi rukma|jāl'|āvṛtāni ca
saṃpetur dikṣu sarvāsu carmāṇi, Bharata'|rṣabha.
sūrya|varṇaiś ca nistriṃśaiḥ pātyamānāni sarvaśaḥ
dikṣu sarvāsv adṛśyanta śarīrāṇi śirāṃsi ca.
bhagna|cakr'|âkṣa|nīḍāś ca, nipātita|mahā|dhvajāḥ,
hat'|âśvāḥ pṛthivīṃ jagmus tatra tatra mahā|rathāḥ.
paripetur hayāś c' âtra ke cic chastra|kṛta|vraṇāḥ
rathān viparikarṣanto hateṣu ratha|yodhiṣu.
śar'|āhatā, bhinna|dehā, baddha|yoktrā hay'|ôttamāḥ
yugāni paryakarṣanta tatra tatra sma, Bhārata.
71.35 adṛśyanta sa|sūtāś ca s'|âśvāḥ sa|ratha|yodhinaḥ
ekena balinā, rājan, vāraṇena vimarditāḥ.
gandha|hasti|mada|srāvam āghrāya bahavo raṇe
saṃnipāte bal'|âughānāṃ vītam ādadire gajāḥ.
sa|tomarair mahā|mātrair nipatadbhir gat'|âsubhiḥ
babhūv' āyodhanaṃ channaṃ nārāc'|âbhihatair gajaiḥ.

Flashes of lightning appeared in the cloudless sky; all the quarters were enveloped in dust. Huge meteors came into view and fell with rumbling sounds, lord of the people. A stormy wind rose, and a downpour of dust fell. The sun in the sky, shrouded by the dust raised by the troops, disappeared from view. All the people were overwhelmed with dust and struck with masses of weapons, and they became completely bewildered. The collision of the swarms of arrows, released by the heroes' arms and able to cut through any obstacle, was tumultuous. Weapons fired by the foremost of arms gleamed like stars and lit up the sky, bull of 71.25
the Bharatas. Various shields, fashioned from bull-hide and 71.30
coated in gold, were scattered in every direction, descendant of Bharata. Bodies and heads, severed by swords radiant like the sun, were seen falling down on all sides. With the wheels, axles, and platforms of their chariots broken and their large banners felled, great warriors, stripped of their horses, fell to the ground here and there. Their charioteers killed, some horses, plagued by the wounds that weapons had inflicted, dragged their chariots along and fell down; the finest horses, injured with arrows, their bodies lacerated, went on dragging their vehicles, descendant of Bharata, still bound by their straps.

Many warriors, along with their drivers, horses, and char- 71.35
iots, were seen smashed by a single mighty elephant. Numerous elephants, smelling the secretions of a rutting elephant in that clash of armies, attacked it even though it was unfit for warfare. The battlefield was strewn with elephants who had been killed with shafts, and with their lance-wielding riders who had also fallen down lifeless. In

saṃnipāte bal'|âughānāṃ preṣitair vara|vāraṇaiḥ
nipetur yudhi saṃbhagnāḥ sa|yodhāḥ sa|dhvajā gajāḥ.
nāga|rāj'|ôpamair hastair nāgair ākṣipya saṃyuge
vyadṛśyanta, mahā|rāja, saṃbhagnā ratha|kūbarāḥ.
71.40 viśīrṇa|ratha|jālāś ca keśeṣv ākṣipya dantibhiḥ
druma|śākhā iv' āvidhya niṣpiṣṭā rathino raṇe.
ratheṣu ca rathān yuddhe saṃsaktān vara|vāraṇāḥ
vikarṣanto diśaḥ sarvāḥ sampetuḥ sarva|śabda|gāḥ.
teṣāṃ tathā karṣatāṃ ca gajānāṃ rūpam ābabhau
saraḥsu nalinī|jālaṃ viṣaktam iva karṣatām.
evaṃ saṃchāditaṃ tatra babhūv' āyodhanaṃ mahat
sādibhiś ca padātaiś ca sa|dhvajaiś ca mahā|rathaiḥ.

SAÑJAYA uvāca:

72.1 ŚIKHAṆḌĪ SAHA Matsyena Virāṭena, viśāṃ pate,
Bhīṣmam āśu mah"|êṣv|āsam āsasāda su|durjayam.
Droṇaṃ, Kṛpaṃ, Vikarṇaṃ ca mah"|êṣv|āsān mahā|balān,
rājñaś c' ânyān raṇe śūrān bahūn ārcchad Dhanañjayaḥ.
Saindhavaṃ ca mah"|êṣv|āsaṃ
s'|âmātyaṃ saha bandhubhiḥ,
prācyāṃś ca dākṣiṇātyāṃś ca
bhūmi|pān, bhūmi|pa'|rṣabha,
putraṃ ca te mah"|êṣv|āsaṃ Duryodhanam a|marṣaṇam
Duḥsahaṃ c' âiva samare Bhīmaseno 'bhyavartata.
72.5 Sahadevas tu Śakunim Ulūkaṃ ca mahā|ratham

that combat between the masses of troops, many elephants collapsed with warriors and banners on their backs, crushed by huge war elephants urged into battle by their riders. The shafts of many chariots, great king, were seen thrown off and broken by elephants with trunks as huge as the king of
serpents. Many warriors whose chariots had been shattered 71.40
in the battle were seized by elephants by the hair, thrown violently like the branches of trees, and smashed against the ground. Huge elephants rushed in every direction, uttering all possible sounds and dragging apart the chariots that had clashed with each other; and as they dragged the vehicles, those elephants looked as if they were pulling out the lotus stalks growing in a lake. Thus the vast field of battle was covered with fallen horsemen, foot soldiers, and great warriors with their banners.

SÁNJAYA said:

O LORD OF THE people, Shikhándin together with Viráta 72.1
the king of the Matsyas quickly charged against Bhishma, that mighty archer who was very difficult to conquer in battle. Dhanan·jaya attacked Drona, Kripa, and the great archer Vikárna endowed with might, and many other kings valiant in battle. In that fight Bhima·sena assaulted that mighty archer the ruler of the Sindhus, along with his companions and relatives, and encountered the Eastern and the Southern kings as well as your intolerant son Duryódhana—the mighty bowman—and Dúhsaha, bull-like
king. Saha·deva charged against Shákuni and the great war- 72.5
rior Ulúka, father and son who were both mighty archers and difficult to vanquish. The great warrior Yudhi·shthira

pitā|putrau mah"|êṣv|āsāv abhyavartata dur|jayau.
Yudhiṣṭhiro, mahā|rāja, gaj'|ânīkaṃ mahā|rathaḥ
samavartata saṃgrāme putreṇa nikṛtas tava.
Mādrī|putras tu Nakulaḥ śūraḥ saṃkrandano yudhi
Trigartānāṃ balaiḥ sārdhaṃ samasajjata Pāṇḍavaḥ.
abhyavartanta dur|dharṣāḥ samare Śālva|Kekayān
Sātyakiś Cekitānaś ca, Saubhadraś ca mahā|rathaḥ.
Dhṛṣṭaketuś ca samare rākṣasaś ca Ghaṭotkacaḥ
putrāṇāṃ te rath'|ânīkaṃ pratyudyātāḥ su|durjayāḥ.
72.10 senā|patir a|mey'|ātmā Dhṛṣṭadyumno mahā|balaḥ
Droṇena samare, rājan, samiyāy' ôgra|karmaṇā.
evam ete mah"|êṣv|āsās tāvakāḥ Pāṇḍavaiḥ saha
sametya samare śūrāḥ saṃprahāraṃ pracakrire.
madhyan|dina|gate sūrye nabhasy ākulatāṃ gate
Kuravaḥ Pāṇḍaveyāś ca nijaghnur itar'|êtaram.
dhvajino hema|citr'|âṅgā vicaranto raṇ'|âjire
sa|patākā rathā rejur vaiyāghra|parivāraṇāḥ.
sametānāṃ ca samare jigīṣūṇāṃ paras|param
babhūva tumulaḥ śabdaḥ siṃhānām iva nardatām.
72.15 tatr' âdbhutam apaśyāma saṃprahāraṃ su|dāruṇam
yad akurvan raṇe vīrāḥ Sṛñjayāḥ Kurubhiḥ saha.
n' âiva khaṃ, na diśo, rājan, na sūryaṃ, śatru|tāpana,
vidiśo v" âpy apaśyāma śarair muktaiḥ samantataḥ.
śaktīnāṃ vimal'|âgrāṇāṃ, tomarāṇāṃ tath" âsyatām,
nistriṃśānāṃ ca pītānāṃ nīl'|ôtpala|nibhāḥ prabhāḥ,
kavacānāṃ vicitrāṇāṃ, bhūṣaṇānāṃ prabhās tathā
khaṃ diśaḥ pradiśaś c' âiva bhāsayām āsur ojasā.

who had been meanly deceived by your son, great king, confronted the enemy's elephant division in battle. Nákula, the Pándava son of Madri, who was able to make hostile heroes weep in combat, clashed with the forces of the Tri·gartas. Sátyaki, Chekitána, and that great warrior the son of Subhádra in their battle-fury attacked the Shalvas and the Kékayas. Dhrishta·ketu, the demon Ghatótkacha, and that bull-like combatant Shataníka, the son of Nákula—all of whom were extremely difficult to defeat—encountered your sons' chariot division on the field of battle. The mighty, 72.10
boundlessly spirited general Dhrishta·dyumna engaged in combat with Drona who was fierce in his feats, Your Majesty.

Thus these great archers of yours, confronting each other, began to fight. The midday sun became agitated in the sky, and the heroic Kurus and Pándavas slaughtered each other.

Chariots moved across the battlefield looking beautiful, with flying banners and flags, with tiger-skin coverings, and with various parts trimmed in gold. A tumultuous noise arose—the noise of fighting warriors roaring like lions, eager to defeat each other in battle. There we watched the 72.15
terrifying but wonderful combat which the valiant Sríñjayas waged against the Kurus. Since everything was enveloped in flying arrows, we could see neither the sky nor the major and minor directions, nor even the sun, enemy-scorching king. The blue-lotus glow that spread from the hurled spears with their gleaming heads, from the lances and copper swords, the armor, and the various ornaments, filled the sky and the major and minor directions with splendor. The battlefield looked majestic, Your Majesty,

vapurbhiś ca nar'|êndrāṇāṃ candra|sūrya|sama|prabhaih
virarāja tadā, rājaṃs, tatra tatra raṇ'|âṅgaṇam.
72.20 ratha|saṅghā nara|vyāghrāḥ samāyāntaś ca saṃyuge
virejuḥ samare, rājan, grahā iva nabhas|tale.

Bhīṣmas tu rathināṃ śreṣṭho Bhīmasenaṃ mahā|balam
avārayata saṃkruddhaḥ sarva|sainyasya paśyataḥ.
tato Bhīṣma|vinirmuktā rukma|puṅkhāḥ śilā|śitāḥ
abhyaghnan samare Bhīmaṃ taila|dhautāḥ su|tejanāḥ.
tasya śaktiṃ mahā|vegāṃ Bhīmaseno mahā|balaḥ
kruddh'|āśīviṣa|saṃkāśāṃ preṣayām āsa, Bhārata.
tām āpatantīṃ sahasā rukma|daṇḍāṃ dur|āsadām
ciccheda samare Bhīṣmaḥ śaraiḥ saṃnata|parvabhiḥ.
72.25 tato 'pareṇa bhallena pītena niśitena ca
kārmukaṃ Bhīmasenasya dvidhā ciccheda, Bhārata.
Sātyakis tu tatas tūrṇaṃ Bhīṣmam āsādya saṃyuge
ā|karṇa|prahitais tīkṣṇair niśitais tigma|tejanaiḥ
śarair bahubhir ānarcchat pitaraṃ te, jan'|ēśvara.

tataḥ saṃdhāya vai tīkṣṇaṃ śaraṃ parama|dāruṇam
Vārṣṇeyasya rathād Bhīṣmaḥ pātayām āsa sārathim.
tasy' âśvāḥ pradrutā, rājan, nihate ratha|sārathau;
tena ten' âiva dhāvanti mano|māruta|raṃhasaḥ.
tataḥ sarvasya sainyasya nisvanas tumulo 'bhavat.
72.30 hā|hā|kāraś ca saṃjajñe Pāṇḍavānāṃ mah"|ātmanām:
«abhidravata! gṛhṇīta! hayān yacchata! dhāvata!»
ity āsīt tumulaḥ śabdo Yuyudhāna|rathaṃ prati.

etasminn eva kāle tu Bhīṣmaḥ Śāntanavas tadā
vyahanat Pāṇḍavīṃ senām āsurīm iva Vṛtra|hā.
te vadhyamānā Bhīṣmeṇa Pāñcālāḥ Somakaiḥ saha
sthirāṃ yuddhe matiṃ kṛtvā Bhīṣmam ev' âbhidudruvuḥ.

with royal bodies scattered here and there, shining like the moon and the sun. Tiger-like warriors, clashing together in 72.20
combat on their fleet of chariots, looked beautiful like the planets in the sky, my lord.

Bhishma, the best of warriors, enraged, repelled powerful Bhima·sena in the sight of the entire army. Bhishma released well-sharpened, gold-nocked, stone-whetted arrows cleansed with oil, and they struck Bhima on the battlefield. Mighty Bhima·sena then sent an immensely swift spear that looked like an irate venomous snake, descendant of Bharata. But as the spear flew forcefully toward him in the battle, Bhishma chopped it down with his straight arrows. Then he split Bhima·sena's bow in two with a sharp, 72.25
copper, spear-headed shaft, descendant of Bharata. In that fight Sátyaki, quickly charging against Bhishma, wounded your father, lord of the people, with many sharp, whetted, scorching arrows, fired from his bow drawn to the ear.

But Bhishma, aiming a sharp and utterly dreadful shaft, struck down the driver of Vrishni's descendant. As soon as the chariot driver was killed, Sátyaki's horses bolted, Your Majesty. Swift as the mind or the wind, the horses careered over the battlefield, raising a tumultuous din from all
the troops. The great-spirited Pándavas screamed out loud 72.30
shouts: "Charge! Catch! Hold the horses! Run!" These cacophonous shouts followed Yuyudhána's chariot.

In the meantime Bhishma the son of Shántanu was crushing the Pándava army like the slayer of Vritra* destroying the *ásura** host. The Panchálas and the Sómakas, bombarded by Bhishma, firmly set their minds on waging combat and charged against him.

Dhṛṣṭadyumna|mukhāś c' âpi Pārthāḥ Śāntanavaṃ raṇe
abhyadhāvañ jigīṣantas tava putrasya vāhinīm.
tath" âiva Kauravā, rājan, Bhīṣma|Droṇa|puro|gamāḥ
abhyadhāvanta vegena. tato yuddham avartata.

SAÑJAYA uvāca:

73.1 VIRĀṬO 'THA tribhir bāṇair
Bhīṣmam ārcchan mahā|ratham
vivyādha turagāṃś c' âsya
tribhir bāṇair mahā|rathaḥ.
taṃ pratyavidhyad daśabhir Bhīṣmaḥ Śāntanavaḥ śaraiḥ
rukma|puṅkhair mah"|êṣv|āsaḥ kṛta|hasto mahā|balaḥ.
Drauṇir Gāṇḍīva|dhanvānaṃ bhīma|dhanvā mahā|rathaḥ
avidhyad iṣubhiḥ ṣaḍbhir dṛḍha|hastaḥ stan'|ântare.
kārmukaṃ tasya ciccheda Phālgunaḥ para|vīra|hā,
avidhyac ca bhṛśaṃ tīkṣṇaiḥ patribhiḥ śatru|karśanaḥ.
73.5 so 'nyat kārmukam ādāya vegavat krodha|mūrchitaḥ,
a|mṛṣyamāṇaḥ Pārthena kārmuka|cchedam āhave,
avidhyat Phālgunaṃ, rājan, navatyā niśitaiḥ śaraiḥ,
Vāsudevaṃ ca saptatyā vivyādha param'|êṣubhiḥ.
tataḥ krodh'|âbhitāmr'|âkṣaḥ Kṛṣṇena saha Phālgunaḥ
dīrgham uṣṇaṃ ca niḥśvasya, cintayitvā punaḥ punaḥ,
dhanuḥ prapīḍya vāmena kareṇ' â|mitra|karśanaḥ,
Gāṇḍīva|dhanvā saṃkruddhaḥ śitān saṃnata|parvaṇaḥ
jīvit'|ânta|karān ghorān samādatta śilīmukhān.
tais tūrṇaṃ samare 'vidhyad Drauṇiṃ balavatāṃ varaḥ.
73.10 tasya te kavacaṃ bhittvā papuḥ śoṇitam āhave,
na vivyathe ca nirbhinno Drauṇir Gāṇḍīva|dhanvanā.

Pritha's sons, led by Dhrishta·dyumna, attacked the son of Shántanu in that encounter, eager to vanquish your son's army. And the Káuravas, led by Bhishma and Drona, violently charged forward, Your Majesty. Then battle ensued!

SÁNJAYA said:

THEN THE GREAT warrior Viráta wounded the great warrior Bhishma with three arrows, and struck his horses with three others. The mighty archer Bhishma the son of Shántanu, who was endowed with great power and dexterity, pierced him with ten gold-nocked arrows in return. Armed with his fierce bow, Drona's son, a mighty archer with steady hands, struck the wielder of the Gandíva bow in the center of his chest with six shafts. But Phálguna, that tormentor of foes and destroyer of hostile heroes, cut through the enemy's bow and wounded him severely with sharp, feathered arrows. In that great combat Drona's son, sense- 73.5
less with fury and unable to bear the Partha's splitting of his bow, swiftly took up another; he injured Phálguna with ninety sharp arrows, Your Majesty, and pierced Vásu·deva with sixty of his best shafts.

Phálguna, his eyes bloodshot with rage, breathed deep and hot sighs and pondered again and again; and so did Krishna. Then, grabbing his bow with his left hand, the wielder of the Gandíva bow, that tormentor of enemies and champion of mighty men, infuriated, drew his sharp, straight, fearful, stone-tipped, death-dealing arrows, and swiftly struck the son of Drona with them in that duel. Those shafts ripped through Drona's son's armor and be- 73.10
gan to drink his blood; but although he was wounded by

tath" âiva ca śarān Drauṇiḥ pravimuñcann a|vihvalaḥ
tasthau sa samare, rājaṃs, trātum icchan mahā|vratam.
tasya tat su|mahat karma śaśaṃsuḥ Kuru|sattamāḥ,
yat Kṛṣṇābhyāṃ sametābhyām abhyāpatata saṃyuge.
sa hi nityam anīkeṣu yudhyate '|bhayam āsthitaḥ
astra|grāmaṃ sa|saṃhāraṃ Droṇāt prāpya su|durlabham.

«mam' âiṣa ācārya|suto Droṇasy' âtipriyaḥ sutaḥ,
brāhmaṇaś ca viśeṣeṇa, mānanīyo mam' êti ca»
73.15 samāsthāya matiṃ vīro Bībhatsuḥ śatru|tāpanaḥ
kṛpāṃ cakre ratha|śreṣṭho Bhāradvāja|sutaṃ prati.
Drauṇiṃ tyaktvā tato yuddhe Kaunteyaḥ śveta|vāhanaḥ
yuyudhe tāvakān nighnaṃs tvaramāṇaḥ parākramī.

Duryodhanas tu daśabhir gārdhra|patraiḥ śilā|śitaiḥ
Bhīmasenaṃ mah"|êṣv|āsaṃ rukma|puṅkhaiḥ samārpayat.
Bhīmasenas tu saṃkruddhaḥ par'|âsu|karaṇaṃ dṛḍham
citraṃ kārmukam ādatta, śarāṃś ca niśitān daśa.
ā|karṇa|prahitais tīkṣṇair vegavadbhir a|jihma|gaiḥ
avidhyat tūrṇam a|vyagraḥ Kuru|rājaṃ mah"|ôrasi.
73.20 tasya kāñcana|sūtra|sthaḥ śaraiḥ saṃchādito maṇiḥ
rarāj' ôrasi vai sūryo grahair iva samāvṛtaḥ.
putras tu tava tejasvī Bhīmasenena tāḍitaḥ
n' âmṛṣyata yathā nāgas tala|śabdaṃ mad'|ôtkaṭaḥ.
tataḥ śarair, mahā|rāja, rukma|puṅkhaiḥ śilā|śitaiḥ
Bhīmaṃ vivyādha saṃkruddhas trāsayāno varūthinīm.

the wielder of the Gandíva bow, he did not waver. The son of Drona stood on the battlefield without flinching, Your Majesty, and kept firing his arrows, intent as he was on protecting Bhishma of great vows. The leaders of the Kurus praised that great feat of his, which he performed by confronting the two Krishnas* together in battle. Having obtained from Drona the rare weaponry and the means of its withdrawal, he fought in your ranks and remained fearless.

"He is the son of my teacher; he is Drona's dear son; being a brahmin, he is especially worthy of my respect." Thinking such things, the great warrior Bibhátsu,* the 73.15
heroic scorcher of enemies, showed mercy to the son of Bharad·vaja's son. And leaving the son of Drona in battle, the valiant son of Kunti, with his white horses, speedily fought on, slaughtering your troops.

Duryódhana pierced the great warrior Bhima·sena with ten vulture-feathered, stone-whetted, gold-nocked shafts. Bhima·sena, immensely enraged, grabbed a strong and splendid bow fit for stripping an enemy of his life, and drew ten sharp arrows; and firing with presence of mind and with his bow drawn back to his ear, he soon wounded the king of the Kurus in his broad chest with sharp, violent, straight-flying arrows. Surrounded by those arrows, 73.20
the gem that hung on his chest by a golden thread gleamed like the sun surrounded by the planets in the sky. But when he was struck by Bhima·sena your vigorous son could not endure it, like a maddened elephant unable to bear a sound of a slap. Filled with fury, great king, he pierced Bhima with gold-nocked and stone-whetted shafts, frightening the enemy troops. Those two immensely powerful

tau yudhyamānau samare bhṛśam anyonya|vikṣatau
putrau te deva|saṃkāśau vyarocetāṃ mahā|balau.

Citrasenaṃ nara|vyāghraṃ Saubhadraḥ para|vīra|hā
avidhyad daśabhir bāṇaiḥ, Purumitraṃ ca saptabhiḥ.
73.25 Satyavrataṃ ca saptatyā viddhvā Śakra|samo yudhi
nṛtyann iva raṇe vīra ārtiṃ naḥ samajījanat.
taṃ pratyavidyad daśabhiś Citrasenaḥ śilīmukhaiḥ,
Satyavrataś ca navabhiḥ, Purumitraś ca saptabhiḥ.
sa viddho vikṣaran raktaṃ śatru|saṃvāraṇaṃ mahat
ciccheda Citrasenasya citraṃ kārmukam Ārjuniḥ;
bhittvā c' âsya tanu|trāṇaṃ śareṇ' ôrasy atāḍayat.

tatas te tāvakā vīrā rāja|putrā mahā|rathāḥ
sametya yudhi saṃrabdhā vivyadhur niśitaiḥ śaraiḥ.
tāṃś ca sarvāñ śarais tīkṣṇair jaghāna param'|âstra|vit.
73.30 tasya dṛṣṭvā tu tat karma parivavruḥ sutās tava
dahantaṃ samare sainyaṃ vane kakṣaṃ yath" ôlbaṇam.
apeta|śiśire kāle samiddham iva pāvakaḥ
atyarocata Saubhadras tava sainyāni nāśayan.

tat tasya caritaṃ dṛṣṭvā pautras tava, viśāṃ pate,
Lakṣmaṇo 'bhyapatat tūrṇaṃ Sātvatī|putram āhave.
Abhimanyus tu saṃkruddho Lakṣmaṇaṃ śubha|lakṣaṇam
vivyādha niśitaiḥ ṣaḍbhiḥ, sārathiṃ ca tribhiḥ śaraiḥ.
tath" âiva Lakṣmaṇo, rājan, Saubhadraṃ niśitaiḥ śaraiḥ
avidhyata, mahā|rāja. tad adbhutam iv' âbhavat.
73.35 tasy' âśvāṃś caturo hatvā, sārathiṃ ca mahā|balaḥ,

sons of yours, fighting on the battlefield and wounding each other severely, looked as beautiful as a pair of gods.

The heroic son of Subhádra, that destroyer of enemy heroes who was equal to Shakra himself in combat, pierced the tiger-like Chitra·sena with ten arrows, Puru·mitra with
seven, and Satya·vrata with seventy; he made us suffer, 73.25
and he seemed to dance on the field of battle. Chitra·sena struck him in return with ten stone-tipped arrows, Satya·vrata with nine, and Puru·mitra with seven. Wounded and bleeding, the son of Árjuna split Chitra·sena's bow—which was large and splendid, a repeller of enemies—and, cutting through his armor, pierced Chitra·sena with an arrow in his chest.

Then your valiant princes, great warriors that they are, united and struck Abhimányu with whetted shafts in their battle-fury; but being an expert in the highest weaponry,
he wounded them all with his sharp arrows. He was scorch- 73.30
ing the hostile troops just as a violent fire, kindled after the winter season, burns lots of dry trees in a forest; and at the sight of that feat of his, your sons encircled him. While destroying your army, Subhádra's son looked very beautiful.

Seeing those heroic deeds of Abhimányu, your grandson Lákshmana, lord of the people, swiftly charged against the son of Sátvati in battle. Enraged, Abhimányu pierced the auspiciously marked Lákshmana with six sharpened arrows, and his chariot driver with three. Lákshmana also pierced the son of Subhádra with whetted shafts, Your Majesty.
That was like a miracle, great king. The powerful son of Su- 73.35
bhádra killed Lákshmana's horses and chariot driver and besieged him with sharp arrows. Lákshmana the destroyer of

abhyadravata Saubhadro Lakṣmaṇaṃ niśitaiḥ śaraiḥ.
hat'|âśve tu rathe tiṣṭhaĪ Lakṣmaṇaḥ para|vīra|hā
śaktiṃ cikṣepa saṃkruddhaḥ Saubhadrasya rathaṃ prati.
tām āpatantīṃ sahasā ghora|rūpāṃ dur|āsadām
Abhimanyuḥ śarais tīkṣṇaiś ciccheda bhujag'|ôpamām.
tataḥ sva|ratham āropya Lakṣmaṇaṃ Gautamas tadā
apovāha rathen' ājau sarva|sainyasya paśyataḥ.

tataḥ samākule tasmin vartamāne mahā|bhaye
abhyadravañ jighāṃsantaḥ paras|para|vadh'|âiṣiṇaḥ.
73.40 tāvakāś ca mah"|êṣv|āsāḥ Pāṇḍavāś ca mahā|rathāḥ
juhvantaḥ samare prāṇān nijaghnur itar'|êtaram.
mukta|keśā, vi|kavacā, vi|rathāś, chinna|kārmukāḥ
bāhubhiḥ samayudhyanta Sṛñjayāḥ Kurubhiḥ saha.
tato Bhīṣmo mahā|bāhuḥ Pāṇḍavānāṃ mah"|ātmanām
senāṃ jaghāna saṃkruddho divyair astrair mahā|balaḥ.
hat'|ēśvarair gajais tatra, narair, aśvaiś ca pātitaiḥ,
rathibhiḥ, sādibhiś c' âiva samāstīryata medinī.

SAÑJAYA uvāca:

74.1 ATHA, RĀJAN mahā|bāhuḥ Sātyakir yuddha|dur|madaḥ
vikṛṣya cāpaṃ samare bhāra|sādhanam uttamam,
prāmuñcat puṅkha|saṃyuktāñ śarān āśīviṣ'|ôpamān,
pragāḍhaṃ laghu citraṃ ca darśayann hasta|lāghavam.
tasya vikṣipataś cāpaṃ, śarān anyāṃś ca muñcataḥ,
ādadānasya bhūyaś ca, saṃdadhānasya c' âparān,
kṣipataś ca śarāṃs tasya, raṇe śatrūn vinighnataḥ
dadṛśe rūpam atyarthaṃ meghasy' êva pravarṣataḥ.

enemy heroes, standing on his horseless chariot filled with fury, hurled a spear, aiming at the chariot of Subhádra'son. But as that terrifying, serpentine, and almost unstoppable spear flew forcefully toward him in battle, Abhimányu split it with sharp arrows. Then the grandson of Gótama lifted Lákshmana onto his chariot and took him away from the battlefield under the eyes of the entire army.

Combatants eager to kill each other assailed one another in that turbulent and terrifying battle, each one seeking the
enemy's death. Sacrificing their lives in that encounter, the 73.40
mighty archers on your side, and the great Pándava warriors, began to slaughter each other. Their hair disheveled and their bows severed, the Srínjayas, stripped of their armor and chariots, fought on with bare hands against the Kurus. Then mighty-armed and powerful Bhishma, infuriated, began to massacre the troops of the great-spirited Pándavas with his divine weapons. And the earth was strewn with slain and injured horses, elephants, foot soldiers, chariot warriors, and horsemen.

SÁNJAYA said:

THEN, YOUR Majesty, mighty-armed Sátyaki, ferocious 74.1
in battle, drawing his unsurpassable bow that was able to bear every strain in combat, displayed his immense and marvelous dexterity and fired feathered arrows like venomous snakes. As he was stretching his bow, firing his arrows, drawing new ones, aiming yet others and slaughtering foes with them in battle, he looked very much like a showering thundercloud. King Duryódhana, seeing him in the 74.5

74.5 tam udīryantam ālokya rājā Duryodhanas tataḥ
rathānām ayutaṃ tasya preṣayām āsa, Bhārata.
tāṃs tu sarvān mah"|êṣv|āsān Sātyakiḥ satya|vikramaḥ
jaghāna param'|êṣv|āso divyen' âstreṇa vīryavān.
sa kṛtvā dāruṇaṃ karma pragṛhīta|śar'|âsanaḥ
āsasāda tato vīro Bhūriśravasam āhave.
sa hi saṃdṛśya senāṃ tāṃ Yuyudhānena pātitām
abhyadhāvata saṃkruddhaḥ Kurūṇāṃ kīrti|vardhanaḥ.
Indr'|āyudha|sa|varṇaṃ tu visphārya su|mahad dhanuḥ
sṛṣṭavān vajra|saṃkāśāñ śarān āśīviṣ'|ôpamān
74.10 sahasraśo, mahā|rāja, darśayan pāṇi|lāghavam.
śarāṃs tān mṛtyu|saṃsparśān Sātyakeś ca pad'|ânugāḥ
na viṣehus tadā, rājan. dudruvus te samantataḥ
vihāya Sātyakiṃ, rājan, samare yuddha|dur|madam.
taṃ dṛṣṭvā Yuyudhānasya sutā daśa mahā|balāḥ,
mahā|rathāḥ samākhyātāś, citra|varm'|āyudha|dhvajāḥ
samāsādya mah"|êṣv|āsaṃ Bhūriśravasam āhave
ūcuḥ sarve su|saṃrabdhā yūpa|ketuṃ mahā|raṇe:
«bho bho Kaurava|dāy'|āda, sah' âsmābhir, mahā|bala,
ehi, yudhyasva saṃgrāme samastaiḥ pṛthag eva vā.
74.15 asmān vā tvaṃ parājitya yaśaḥ prāpnuhi saṃyuge,
vayaṃ vā tvāṃ parājitya prītiṃ dāsyāmahe pituḥ.»
evam uktas tadā śūrais tān uvāca mahā|balaḥ
vīrya|ślāghī nara|śreṣṭhas tān dṛṣṭvā samupasthitān:
«sādhv idaṃ kathyate, vīrā, yady evaṃ matir adya vaḥ.
yudhyadhvaṃ sahitā yattā. nihaniṣyāmi vo raṇe.»

ascendant, dispatched ten thousand chariots against him, descendant of Bharata.

Vigorous Sátyaki, the excellent archer whose power is in truth, killed all those great bowmen with his divine weapon. After performing that fierce feat, the heroic warrior grabbed his bow and fought with Bhuri·shravas in the fray.

Seeing your troops struck down by Yuyudhána, that increaser of the Kurus' fame charged forward in fury. Stretching his massive bow that was multicolored like Indra's rainbow, he shot thousands of shafts like thunderbolts, like venomous snakes; and thus he displayed his dexterity, great 74.10
king. But Sátyaki's followers, Your Majesty, could not endure those arrows whose touch spelled death. They ran away
in all directions, leaving Sátyaki fighting ferociously on the
field of play.

Seeing him alone, Yuyudhána's ten powerful sons, those
famous and mighty warriors with their glistening armor,
weapons, and banners, were all filled with battle-fury, and
they confronted that great archer Bhuri·shravas, whose banner bore the emblem of a sacrificial stake, and spoke to
him: "O mighty kinsman of the Káuravas! Come, fight
with all of us together, or one by one! Either you will win 74.15
glory by defeating us in this combat, or we shall bring joy
to our father by vanquishing you in it." Addressed in this
way by those heroes, that powerful warrior, a supreme king
who was proud of his valor, seeing them intent on fighting,
replied: "Well said, heroes! If such is now your wish, then
fight with me all together, exerting yourselves fully! I will
strike you all down in this encounter!" Hearing this those

evam uktā mah"|êṣv|āsās te vīrāḥ kṣipra|kāriṇaḥ
mahatā śara|varṣeṇa abhyadhāvann arin|damam.
apar'|âhṇe, mahā|rāja, saṃgrāmas tumulo 'bhavat
ekasya ca bahūnāṃ ca sametānāṃ raṇ'|âjire.
74.20 tam ekaṃ rathināṃ śreṣṭhaṃ śarais te samavākiran,
prāvṛṣ' îva yathā Meruṃ siṣicur jala|dā, nṛ|pa.
tais tu muktāñ śarān ghorān Yama|daṇḍ'|âśani|prabhān
a|saṃprāptān a|saṃbhrāntaś cicched' āśu mahā|rathaḥ.
tatr' âdbhutam apaśyāma Saumadatteḥ parākramam,
yad eko bahubhir yuddhe samasajjad a|bhītavat.
visṛjya śara|vṛṣṭiṃ tāṃ daśa, rājan, mahā|rathāḥ
parivārya mahā|bāhuṃ nihantum upacakramuḥ.
Saumadattis tataḥ kruddhas teṣāṃ cāpāni, Bhārata,
ciccheda samare, rājan, yudhyamāno mahā|rathaiḥ.
74.25 ath' âiṣāṃ chinna|dhanuṣāṃ śaraiḥ saṃnata|parvabhiḥ
ciccheda samare, rājañ, śirāṃsi niśitaiḥ śaraiḥ.
te hatā nyapatan bhūmau, vajra|bhagnā iva drumāḥ.
tān dṛṣṭvā nihatān vīrān raṇe putrān mahā|balān
Vārṣṇeyo vinadan, rājan, Bhūriśravasam abhyayāt.
rathaṃ rathena samare pīḍayitvā mahā|balau,
tāv anyonyasya samare nihatya ratha|vājinaḥ,
vi|rathāv abhivalgantau sameyātāṃ mahā|rathau.
pragṛhīta|mahā|khaḍgau tau carma|vara|dhāriṇau
śuśubhāte nara|vyāghrau yuddhāya samavasthitau.

great archers, valiant and dexterous, besieged the enemy-tamer with a huge shower of arrows.

In the afternoon a tumultuous combat occurred on the battlefield between one hero and many warriors united, great king. Those fighters covered the best of chariot war- 74.20
riors with shafts just as clouds pour rain on Mount Meru in the monsoon, Your Majesty. Without flinching, that mighty warrior immediately cut down those terrible arrows they had released, before those arrows like Yama's staff or Indra's thunderbolt could reach him. We witnessed the incredible courage of Soma·datta's son as he fought in battle alone, without fear, against many. The ten great warriors, discharging a downpour of shafts, encircled that mighty-armed hero and tried to slaughter him. The son of Soma·datta, enraged, fought with those great warriors on the battlefield and cut through their bows, royal descendant of Bharata. Then, with his straight arrows, Your Majesty, 74.25
he chopped off the heads of his bowless foes, bull of the Bharatas. So slain, they fell to the ground, like trees smashed by elephants.

Seeing his powerful sons killed in battle, Sátyaki, the hero of the Vrishnis, screaming, charged against Bhuri·shravas, Your Majesty. The two mighty warriors had their chariots driven into each other on the battlefield. Then the two great warriors killed each other's horses, jumped out of their chariots, and attacked each other in unmounted combat. Brandishing their great swords and fine shields, standing there eager to fight, those two tiger-like men looked very beautiful.

74.30 tataḥ Sātyakim abhyetya nistriṃśa|vara|dhāriṇam
Bhīmasenas tvaran, rājan, ratham āropayat tadā.
tav' âpi tanayo, rājan, Bhūriśravasam āhave
āropayad rathaṃ tūrṇaṃ paśyatāṃ sarva|dhanvinām.
tasmiṃs tathā vartamāne raṇe Bhīṣmaṃ mahā|ratham
ayodhayanta saṃrabdhāḥ Pāṇḍavā, Bharata'|rṣabha.
lohitāyati c' āditye tvaramāṇo Dhanañjayaḥ
pañca|viṃśati|sāhasrān nijaghāna mahā|rathān.
te hi Duryodhan'|ādiṣṭās tadā Pārtha|nibarhaṇe
saṃprāpy' âiva gatā nāśaṃ, śalabhā iva pāvakam.
74.35 tato Matsyāḥ Kekayāś ca dhanur|veda|viśāradāḥ
parivavrus tadā Pārthaṃ saha|putraṃ mahā|ratham.
etasminn eva kāle tu sūrye 'stam upagacchati
sarveṣām eva sainyānāṃ pramohaḥ samajāyata.
avahāraṃ tataś cakre pitā Devavratas tava
saṃdhyā|kāle, mahā|rāja, sainyānāṃ śrānta|vāhanaḥ.
Pāṇḍavānāṃ Kurūṇāṃ ca paras|para|samāgame
te sene bhṛśa|saṃvigne yayatuḥ svaṃ niveśanam.
tataḥ sva|śibiraṃ gatvā nyaviśaṃs tatra, Bhārata,
Pāṇḍavāḥ Sṛñjayaiḥ sārdhaṃ, Kuravaś ca yathā|vidhi.

Then Bhima·sena approached Sátyaki and his fine sword in a hurry, Your Majesty, and lifted him onto his chariot. And your son, Your Majesty, quickly lifted Bhuri·shravas onto his chariot in the battle, under the eyes of all the archers. 74.30

Bull of the Bharatas, as the combat raged the infuriated Pándavas fought against that mighty warrior Bhishma. When the sun was growing red, Dhanan·jaya slaughtered twenty-five thousand great enemy warriors in no time at all. They had come at Duryódhana's command to slay Pritha's son Árjuna together with his son, and when they arrived
they perished like moths flying into fire. Then the Matsyas 74.35
and the Kékayas, skilled in archery, surrounded the Partha, that mighty warrior, and his son.

Just then the sun was setting, and all the forces became dazed. In the twilight your father Deva·vrata, whose animals were getting tired, withdrew the troops. After the encounter that occurred between the Pándavas and the Kurus, the troops of both armies retreated to their camps in deep distress. Reaching their camps, the Pándavas and Srínjayas entered their tents for due rest, and so did the Kurus, descendant of Bharata.

75–79
DAY SIX

SAÑJAYA uvāca:

75.1 TE VIŚRAMYA tato rājan sahitāḥ Kuru|Pāṇḍavāḥ
vyatītāyāṃ tu śarvaryāṃ punar yuddhāya niryayuḥ.
tatra śabdo mahān āsīt tava teṣāṃ ca, Bhārata,
yujyatāṃ ratha|mukhyānāṃ, kalpyatāṃ c' âiva dantinām,
saṃnahyatāṃ padātīnāṃ, hayānāṃ c' âiva, Bhārata.
śaṅkha|dundubhi|nādaś ca tumulaḥ sarvato 'bhavat.

tato Yudhiṣṭhiro rājā Dhṛṣṭadyumnam abhāṣata:
«vyūhaṃ vyūha, mahā|bāho, makaraṃ śatru|tāpanam.»
75.5 evam uktas tu Pārthena Dhṛṣṭadyumno mahā|rathaḥ
vyādideśa, mahā|rāja, rathino rathināṃ varaḥ.
śiro 'bhūd Drupadas tasya Pāṇḍavaś ca Dhanañjayaḥ;
cakṣuṣī Sahadevaś ca Nakulaś ca mahā|rathaḥ.
tuṇḍam āsīn, mahā|rāja, Bhīmaseno mahā|balaḥ.
Saubhadro, Draupadeyāś ca, rākṣasaś ca Ghaṭotkacaḥ,
Sātyakir, Dharma|rājaś ca vyūha|grīvāṃ samāsthitāḥ.
pṛṣṭham āsīn, mahā|rāja, Virāṭo vāhinī|patiḥ
Dhṛṣṭadyumnena sahito, mahatyā senayā vṛtaḥ.
Kekayā bhrātaraḥ pañca vāma|pārśvaṃ samāśritāḥ.
75.10 Dhṛṣṭaketur nara|vyāghraḥ Cekitānaś ca vīryavān
dakṣiṇaṃ pakṣam āśritya sthitā vyūhasya rakṣaṇe.
pādayos tu, mahā|rāja, sthitaḥ śrīmān mahā|rathaḥ
Kuntibhojaḥ, Śatānīko mahatyā senayā vṛtaḥ.
Śikhaṇḍī tu mah"|êṣv|āsaḥ Somakaiḥ saṃvṛto balī,
Irāvāṃś ca tataḥ pucche makarasya vyavasthitau.

SÁNJAYA said:

AFTER THE NIGHT had passed, both the Kurus and the 75.1
Pándavas, having rested, got ready once more for battle, Your Majesty. There was a loud din, descendant of Bharata, made by your men and theirs yoking fine chariots, by elephants being equipped for the encounter, by foot soldiers putting on their armor, and by horses being covered with mail. The tumultuous sound of conches and drums spread everywhere, descendant of Bharata.

King Yudhi·shthira then said to Dhrishta·dyumna: "O mighty-armed hero, draw up the army into the enemy-
destroying crocodile formation!" Addressed by the son of 75.5
Pritha in this way, that great warrior Dhrishta·dyumna, the best of chariot fighters, issued the order to the chariot warriors. King Drúpada and the Pándava Dhanan·jaya formed the head of that crocodile. Saha·deva and the great warrior Nákula formed its eyes. Powerful Bhima·sena was its mouth. The son of Subhádra, the sons of Dráupadi, the demon Ghatótkacha, Sátyaki, and the King of Righteousness* were stationed in the neck of that array. Great king, Viráta, the chief of his division, surrounded by a large army, formed its back, together with Dhrishta·dyumna. The five Kékaya
brothers were stationed on its left side. Tiger-like Dhrishta· 75.10
ketu and mighty Chekitána stood on its right side, ready to defend the array. At its feet stood the great glorious warrior Kunti·bhoja, and Shataníka surrounded by a large force, great king. Powerful Shikhándin, that mighty archer, was stationed in the crocodile's tail, supported by the Sómakas and also by Irávat. O great king, descendant of Bharata, the Pándavas at sunrise put their armor on, drew their

evam etan mahā|vyūhaṃ vyūhya, Bhārata, Pāṇḍavāḥ
sūry'|ôdaye, mahā|rāja, punar yuddhāya daṃśitāḥ
Kauravān abhyayus tūrṇaṃ hasty|aśva|ratha|pattibhiḥ
samucchritair dhvajaiś, chatraiḥ, śastraiś ca vimalaiḥ śitaiḥ.
75.15 vyūḍhaṃ dṛṣṭvā tu tat sainyaṃ pitā Devavratas tava
krauñcena mahatā, rājan, pratyavyūhata vāhinīm.
  tasya tuṇḍe mah"|êṣv|āso Bhāradvājo vyarocata.
Aśvatthāmā Kṛpaś c' âiva cakṣur āstāṃ, nar'|ēśvara.
Kṛtavarmā tu sahitaḥ Kāmboja|vara|Bāhlikaiḥ
śirasy āsīn nara|śreṣṭhaḥ śreṣṭhaḥ sarva|dhanuṣmatām.
grīvāyāṃ Śūrasenas tu, tava putraś ca, māriṣa,
Duryodhano, mahā|rāja, rājabhir bahubhir vṛtaḥ.
Prāgjyotiṣas tu sahitaḥ Madra|Sauvīra|Kekayaiḥ
urasy abhūn, nara|śreṣṭha, mahatyā senayā vṛtaḥ.
75.20 sva|senayā ca sahitaḥ su|śarmā Prasthal'|âdhipaḥ
vāma|pakṣaṃ samāśritya daṃśitaḥ samavasthitaḥ.
Tuṣārā, Yavanāś c' âiva, Śakāś ca saha Cūcupaiḥ
dakṣiṇaṃ pakṣam āśritya sthitā vyūhasya, Bhārata.
Śrutāyuś ca, Śatāyuś ca, Saumadattiś ca, māriṣa,
vyūhasya jaghane tasthū rakṣamāṇāḥ paras|param.
tato yuddhāya saṃjagmuḥ Pāṇḍavāḥ Kauravaiḥ saha.
  sūry'|ôdaye, mahā|rāja, tato yuddham abhūn mahat.
pratīyū rathino nāgān, nāgāś ca rathino yayuḥ,
hay'|ārohān rath'|ārohā, rathinaś c' âpi sādinaḥ,
75.25 sādinaś ca hayān, rājan, rathinaś ca mahā|raṇe,
hasty|ārohān hay'|ārohā, rathinaḥ, sādinas tathā.
rathinaḥ pattibhiḥ sārdhaṃ, sādinaś c' âpi pattibhiḥ

army into such a formation, and, ready for battle, with their elephants, horses, chariots, and foot soldiers equipped with banners and parasols and armed with sharp glistening weapons, they immediately charged towards the Káuravas.
Seeing the hostile army in that array, Your Majesty, your 75.15
father Deva·vrata drew up his troops into a counter-array, the great curlew formation.

The mighty archer, the son of Bharad·vaja, stood shining in its beak. Ashva·tthaman and Kripa formed its eyes, lord of men. The best of warriors and of all bowmen Krita·varman, united with the Báhlikas and the foremost heroes of the Kambójas, was stationed in its head. Shura·sena and your son Duryódhana, supported by many kings, great king, stood in its neck, my lord. The ruler of the Prag·jyótishas, joined by the Madras, the Sauvíras, and the Kékayas, and surrounded by a large division, stood in its chest,
best of men. Sushárman the ruler of Prásthala was stationed 75.20
in its left wing, along with his force. The Tusháras, the Yávanas, the Shakas, and the Chúchupas stood on its right wing, descendant of Bharata. Shrutáyus, Shatáyus, and the son of Soma·datta, protecting one another, stood at the back of the formation. Then the Pándavas and the Káuravas confronted each other to wage war.

The battle took place at sunrise, great king. Chariot warriors charged against elephants, and elephants against chariot warriors. Horsemen attacked elephant riders, and chariot warriors assailed cavalry. Cavalry charged against horses 75.25
and chariots in that huge war. Horsemen encountered elephant riders, and chariots rushed against horsemen. Chariot fighters engaged with foot soldiers, and cavalry also con-

anyonyaṃ samare, rājan, pratyadhāvann a|marṣitāḥ.
Bhīmasen'|Ârjuna|yamair guptā c' ânyair mahā|rathaiḥ
śuśubhe Pāṇḍavī senā nakṣatrair iva śarvarī.
tathā Bhīṣma|Kṛpa|Droṇa|Śalya|Duryodhan'|ādibhiḥ
tav' âpi vibabhau senā grahair dyaur iva saṃvṛtā.

Bhīmasenas tu Kaunteyo Droṇaṃ dṛṣṭvā parākramī
abhyayāj javanair aśvair Bhāradvājasya vāhinīm.
75.30 Droṇas tu samare kruddho Bhīmaṃ navabhir āyasaiḥ
vivyādha samara|ślāghī marmāṇy uddiśya vīryavān.
dṛḍh'|āhatas tato Bhīmo Bhāradvājasya saṃyuge
sārathiṃ preṣayām āsa Yamasya sadanaṃ prati.
sa saṃgṛhya svayaṃ vāhān Bhāradvājaḥ pratāpavān
vyadhamat Pāṇḍavīṃ senāṃ, tūla|rāśim iv' ânalaḥ.

te vadhyamānā Droṇena Bhīṣmeṇa ca nar'|ôttamāḥ
Sṛñjayāḥ Kekayaiḥ sārdhaṃ palāyana|par" âbhavan.
tath" âiva tāvakaṃ sainyaṃ Bhīm'|Ârjuna|parikṣatam
muhyate tatra tatr' âiva sa|mad" êva var'|âṅganā.
75.35 abhidyetāṃ tato vyūhau tasmin vīra|vara|kṣaye.
āsīd vyatikaro ghoras tava teṣāṃ ca, Bhārata.

tad adbhutam apaśyāma tāvakānāṃ paraiḥ saha
ek'|âyana|gatāḥ sarve yad ayudhyanta, Bhārata.
pratisaṃvārya c' âstrāṇi te 'nyonyasya, viśāṃ pate,
yuyudhuḥ Pāṇḍavāś c' âiva Kauravāś ca mahā|balāḥ.

fronted infantry. Thus, Your Majesty, they charged against each other in a frenzy in that battle. Protected by Bhima·sena, Árjuna, the twins Nákula and Saha·deva, and by other great warriors, the army of the Pándavas looked beautiful like the night sky studded with stars. And your army too, with Bhishma, Kripa, Drona, Shalya, Duryódhana, and others, shone like the heavens covered with the planets.

At the sight of Drona, mighty Bhima·sena the son of Kunti and his swift horses charged against the division of Bharad·vaja's son. And mighty Drona, proud in combat, 75.30
filled with battle-fury, struck Bhima with nine shafts, aiming them at his vital organs. Bhima, severely wounded, sent the chariot driver of Bharad·vaja's son to the abode of Yama. The powerful son of Bharad·vaja then took the reins of the horses himself, and he began to annihilate the Pándava army like a fire burning a heap of cotton.

The Srínjayas and the Kékayas were excellent men, but struck by Drona and Bhishma they took flight. Like an intoxicated lovely woman, your troops, plagued by Bhima and Árjuna, were giving way in places. In that battle, where 75.35
prominent heroes were slain, there was terrible confusion among your men and theirs, descendant of Bharata.

It was wonderful for us to see how your and the enemy's warriors all fought intent on a single goal, descendant of Bharata. The Pándavas and the Káuravas, endowed with immense strength, lord of the people, battled, repelling each other's weapons.

DHṚTARĀṢṬRA uvāca:

76.1 EVAṂ BAHU|GUṆAṂ sainyam evaṃ bahu|vidhaṃ purā
vyūḍham evaṃ yathā|śāstram a|moghaṃ c' âiva, Sañjaya,
puṣṭam asmākam atyantam, abhikāmaṃ ca naḥ sadā,
prahvam, a|vyasan'|ôpetaṃ, purastād dṛṣṭa|vikramam,
n' âtivṛddham, a|bālaṃ ca, na kṛśaṃ na ca pīvaram,
laghu|vṛtt'|āyata|prāyaṃ, sāra|yodham, an|āmayam
ātta|saṃnāha|śastraṃ ca, bahu|śastra|parigraham;
asi|yuddhe, niyuddhe ca, gadā|yuddhe ca kovidam,
76.5 prāsa'|ṛṣṭi|tomareṣv ājau, parigheṣv āyaseṣu ca,
bhindipāleṣu, śaktīṣu, musaleṣu ca sarvaśaḥ,
kampaneṣu ca, cāpeṣu, kaṇapeṣu ca sarvaśaḥ,
kṣepaṇīṣu citrāṣu, muṣṭi|yuddheṣu ca kṣamam,
a|parokṣaṃ ca vidyāsu, vyāyāmeṣu kṛta|śramam,
śastra|grahaṇa|vidyāsu sarvāsu pariniṣṭhitam,
ārohe, paryavaskande, saraṇe s'|ântara|plute,
samyak praharaṇe, yāne, vyapayāne ca kovidam;
nāg'|âśva|ratha|yāneṣu bahuśaḥ su|parīkṣitam,
parīkṣya ca yathā|nyāyaṃ vetanen' ôpapāditam,
76.10 na goṣṭhyā, n' ôpacāreṇa, na ca bandhu||nimittataḥ,
na sauhṛda|balaiś c' âpi, n' â|kulīna|parigrahaiḥ,
samṛddha|janam, āryaṃ ca, tuṣṭa|saṃbandhi|bāndhavam,
kṛt'|ôpakāra|bhūyiṣṭhaṃ, yaśasvi ca, manasvi ca,
sva|janaiś ca narair mukhyair bahuśo dṛṣṭa|karmabhiḥ
Loka|pāl'|ôpamais, tāta, pālitaṃ, loka|viśrutam,

DHRITA·RASHTRA said:

OUR ARMY, WHICH is endowed with so many virtues, 76.1
comprises various kinds of forces, and is arrayed as the rules
ordain, should be successful, Sánjaya. Our warriors are extremely attached to us, always committed to our interests,
obedient to us, and free from vices; and their prowess has
been tested before. They are neither too old nor too young.
They are neither lean nor fat. They are agile, and mostly
tall, vigorous, and healthy. They are clad in armor and well
armed; they wield many kinds of weapons. They are experts
in fighting with swords, with maces, and with their bare
hands. Our warriors are perfectly skilled in using javelins, 76.5
darts, spears, arrows, iron clubs, short shafts, lances, maces,
pikes, bows, and iron bars, in hurling various missiles, and
also in fisticuffs. They are personally trained in military science and physical exercises, and accomplished in all the
arts of wielding weapons. They are adroit at mounting vehicles, descending from them, riding them, and jumping
from them; and at accurate striking, advancing, and retreating. Our warriors are thoroughly familiar with elephants, 76.10
horses, and chariots, and after being duly examined they have been employed on fair pay, neither through connections nor as a favor, neither for the sake of kinship nor out of friendship or family relation. They are prosperous and respectable, and their kinsmen are content. We have done them many good services. They are glorious and intelligent. Our world-famous troops are protected by our prominent men, who are like the World-guardians* and whose feats have been witnessed by all of us, my friend. Our army is defended by many warriors renowned all over the earth; along

bahubhiḥ kṣatriyair guptaṃ pṛthivyāṃ loka|saṃmataiḥ
asmān abhigataiḥ kāmāt, sa|balaiḥ, sa|pad'|ânugaiḥ;
mah"|ôdadhim iv' āpūrṇam āpagābhiḥ samantataḥ,
a|pakṣaiḥ pakṣa|saṃkāśai rathair nāgaiś ca saṃvṛtam,
76.15 nānā|yodha|jalaṃ, bhīmaṃ, vāhan'|ōrmi|taraṅgiṇam,
kṣepaṇy|asi|gadā|śakti|śara|prāsa|samākulam,
dhvaja|bhūṣaṇa|saṃbādhaṃ, ratna|paṭṭa|su|saṃcitam,
paridhāvadbhir aśvaiś ca vāyu|vega|vikampitam,
a|pāram iva, garjantaṃ sāgara|pratimaṃ mahat;
Droṇa|Bhīṣm'|âbhisaṃguptaṃ, guptaṃ ca Kṛtavarmaṇā,
Kṛpa|Duḥśāsanābhyāṃ ca, Jayadratha|mukhais tathā,
Bhagadatta|Vikarṇābhyāṃ, Drauṇi|Saubala|Bāhlikaiḥ,
guptaṃ pravīrair lokaiś ca sāravadbhir mah"|ātmabhiḥ
yad ahanyata saṃgrāme—daivam etat purātanam.
76.20 n' âitādṛśaṃ samudyogaṃ dṛṣṭavanto hi mānuṣāḥ,
ṛṣayo vā mahā|bhāgāḥ purāṇā bhuvi, Sañjaya.
īdṛśo hi bal'|âughas tu yuktaḥ śastr'|âstra|saṃpadā
vadhyate yatra saṃgrāme, kim anyad bhāga|dheyataḥ?
viparītam idaṃ sarvaṃ pratibhāti sma, Sañjaya,
yatr' ēdṛśaṃ balaṃ ghoraṃ Pāṇḍavān n' âtarad raṇe.
Pāṇḍav'|ârthāya niyataṃ devās tatra samāgatāḥ
yudhyante, māmakaṃ sainyaṃ yath" âvadhyanta, Sañjaya.
ukto hi Vidureṇ' êha hitaṃ pathyaṃ ca, Sañjaya,
na ca jagrāha tan mandaḥ putro Duryodhano mama.

with their forces and followers, they have joined us of their
own accord.

Our host, abounding in elephants and in chariots that
although wingless are as swift as birds, is like a vast ocean
filled with the water of countless rivers falling into it from
every side. Various troops are its waters, and vehicles are 76.15
its waves and billows. This fierce ocean teems with slings,
swords, maces, spears, arrows, and lances. It swarms with
banners and ornaments, and abounds in cloth that's in-
laid with gems. With its rushing horses, our huge oceanic
army, which seems boundless, is raging in a heavy gale,
protected by Drona, Bhishma, Krita·varman, Kripa, and
Duhshásana, by great warriors led by Jayad·ratha, and also
by Bhaga·datta, Vikárna, Drona's son, Súbala's son, and
Báhlika.

If our army, protected by so many heroic, great-spirited,
mighty men, should be slaughtered in battle, it must be
predestined. Neither humans nor even highly virtuous an- 76.20
cient sages ever saw such large-scale preparations for war on
earth, Sánjaya. When such a huge well-armed host is being massacred in battle, what else can this be but fate? It
seems to me quite unnatural, Sánjaya, that such a terrifying
army has not overpowered the Pándavas in combat. Surely
the gods must have assembled together to fight on the Pándavas' side against my host, which is being slaughtered accordingly, Sánjaya. Vídura always gave me appropriate and
beneficial counsels, but my dull-witted son Duryódhana
would not follow them. I believe great-spirited omniscient 76.25
Vídura gave that wise counsel long ago, my friend, because
he had foreseen in advance what is now going on. Sánjaya,

76.25 tasya, manye, matiḥ pūrvaṃ sarva|jñasya mah"|ātmanaḥ
āsīd yathā|gataṃ, tāta, yena dṛṣṭam idaṃ purā.
atha vā bhāvyam evaṃ hi, Sañjay', âitena sarvathā.
purā Dhātrā yathā sṛṣṭaṃ, tat tathā, n' âitad anyathā.

SAÑJAYA uvāca:

77.1 ĀTMA|DOṢĀT tvayā, rājan, prāptaṃ vyasanam īdṛśam.
na hi Duryodhanas tāni paśyate, Bharata'|rṣabha,
yāni tvaṃ dṛṣṭavān, rājan, dharma|saṃkara|kārite.
tava doṣāt purā vṛttaṃ dyūtam etad, viśāṃ pate.
tava doṣeṇa yuddhaṃ ca pravṛttaṃ saha Pāṇḍavaiḥ.
tvam ev' âdya phalaṃ bhuṅkṣva kṛtvā kilbiṣam ātmanā.
ātmanā hi kṛtaṃ karma ātman" âiv' ôpabhujyate.
iha vā pretya vā, rājaṃs, tvayā prāptaṃ yathā|tatham.
77.5 tasmād, rājan, sthiro bhūtvā prāpy' êdaṃ vyasanaṃ mahat
śṛṇu yuddhaṃ yathā|vṛttaṃ śaṃsato me, nar'|âdhipa.

Bhīmasenaḥ su|niśitair bāṇair bhittvā mahā|camūm
āsasāda tato vīraḥ sarvān Duryodhan'|ânujān.
Duḥśāsanaṃ, Durviṣahaṃ,
Duḥsahaṃ, Durmadaṃ, Jayam,
Jayatsenaṃ, Vikarṇaṃ ca,
Citrasenaṃ, Sudarśanam,
Cārucitraṃ, Suvarmāṇaṃ, Duṣkarṇaṃ, Karṇam eva ca—
etān anyāṃś ca su|bahūn samīpa|sthān mahā|rathān
Dhārtarāṣṭrān su|saṃkruddhān dṛṣṭvā Bhīmo mahā|balaḥ
Bhīṣmeṇa samare guptāṃ praviveśa mahā|camūm.
77.10 ath' āhvayanta te 'nyonyam, «ayaṃ prāpto Vṛkodaraḥ!»
ath' ālokya praviṣṭaṃ tam ūcus te sarva eva tu:
«jīva|grāhaṃ nigṛhṇīmo vayam enaṃ, nar'|âdhipāḥ!»

surely all and exactly this is bound to happen as predetermined by the Creator, and it cannot be otherwise.

SÁNJAYA said:

IT IS YOUR OWN fault, Your Majesty, that such a disaster 77.1
has befallen you. You had foreseen what Duryódhana could not: the fateful consequences of his unrighteous conduct, bull of the Bharatas. It was through your fault, lord of the people, that the game of dice took place long ago. And it is through your fault that the war with the Pándavas has broken out. You are now reaping the fruit of the evil to which you committed yourself. One reaps the fruit of one's own actions both here and hereafter. Your Majesty, you have obtained exactly what you sowed. So, Your Majesty, although 77.5
you have met with great misfortune, be strong and listen to me as I tell you, ruler of men, about what happened in the battle.

Heroic Bhima·sena, after breaking through the ranks of your huge army with his well-sharpened arrows, assailed all of Duryódhana's younger brothers. Seeing Duhshásana, Dúrvishaha, Dúhsaha, Dúrmada, Jaya, Jayat·sena, Vikárna, Chitra·sena, Sudárshana, Charu·chitra, Suvárman, Dushkárna, and Karna, and many other great combatants of Dhrita·rashtra's host standing nearby filled with violent rage, the mighty warrior Bhima penetrated the lines of the enemy's large force that was protected by Bhishma in battle.

Seeing that he had entered their ranks, the enemy leaders 77.10
all exclaimed addressing each other: "Kings! Here's Vrikódara! Let's capture him alive!"

sa taiḥ parivṛtaḥ Pārtho bhrātṛbhiḥ kṛta|niścayaiḥ,
prajā|saṃharaṇe sūryaḥ krūrair iva mahā|grahaiḥ.
saṃprāpya madhyaṃ sainyasya na bhīḥ Pāṇḍavam āviśat,
yathā dev'|âsure yuddhe mah"|Êndraṃ prāpya dānavān.
tataḥ śata|sahasrāṇi rathināṃ sarvaśaḥ, prabho,
udyatāni śarais tīvrais tam ekam parivavrire.
sa teṣāṃ pravarān yodhān hasty|aśva|ratha|sādinaḥ
jaghāna samare śūro Dhārtarāṣṭrān a|cintayan.
77.15 teṣāṃ vyavasitaṃ jñātvā Bhīmaseno jighṛkṣatām
samastānāṃ vadhe, rājan, matiṃ cakre mahā|manāḥ.
tato rathaṃ samutsṛjya gadām ādāya Pāṇḍavaḥ
jaghāna Dhārtarāṣṭrāṇāṃ taṃ bal'|âughaṃ mah"|ârṇavam.
Bhīmasene praviṣṭe tu Dhṛṣṭadyumno 'pi Pārṣataḥ
Droṇam utsṛjya tarasā prayayau yatra Saubalaḥ.
nivārya mahatīṃ senāṃ tāvakānāṃ nara'|rṣabhaḥ
āsasāda rathaṃ śūnyaṃ Bhīmasenasya saṃyuge.
dṛṣṭvā Viśokaṃ samare Bhīmasenasya sārathim
Dhṛṣṭadyumno, mahā|rāja, dur|manā, gata|cetanaḥ
77.20 apṛcchad bāṣpa|saṃruddho niḥśvasan, vācam īrayan:
«mama prāṇaiḥ priyatamaḥ kva Bhīma?» iti duḥkhitaḥ.
Viśokas tam uvāc' êdaṃ Dhṛṣṭadyumnaṃ kṛt'|âñjaliḥ:
«saṃsthāpya mām iha balī Pāṇḍaveyaḥ pratāpavān
praviṣṭo Dhārtarāṣṭrāṇām etad bala|mah"|ârṇavam.
mām uktvā puruṣa|vyāghraḥ prīti|yuktam idaṃ vacaḥ:

The son of Pritha, encircled by his cousins who had made this plan, looked like the sun surrounded by the fierce and mighty planets at the time of the world's destruction. Although Bhima was in the very midst of the enemy's host, fear did not overtake him, just as it did not overtake great Indra surrounded by the demonic host during the war between the gods and demons. Hundreds of thousands of chariot warriors, intent on battle and armed with sharp arrows, encircled lone Bhima on every side, my lord. But thinking nothing of your sons, that hero began to slay the foremost among them, who were fighting in battle on elephants, horses, and chariots. Aware of their firm intention 77.15
to kill him, the proud warrior set his mind on slaughtering them all. Grabbing his mace and leaving his chariot, the Pándava started smashing up that oceanic host of your sons.

After Bhima·sena had penetrated the enemy's ranks, Dhrishta·dyumna, the grandson of Príshata, abandoned Drona and swiftly advanced toward the son of Súbala. While repelling your mighty force, that bull-like man came upon Bhima·sena's empty chariot which had been forsaken on the battlefield. Seeing only Bhima·sena's driver Vishóka, Dhrishta·dyumna was deeply distressed and nearly fainted, great king. Overcome by grief, sighing deeply and utter- 77.20
ing words in a voice choked with tears, he asked Vishóka: "Where is Bhima, who is dearer to me than my own life?" Vishóka, his hands folded in respect, replied to Dhrishta·dyumna: "The powerful and courageous Pándava has left me here and plunged into this oceanic host of Dhrita·rashtra's sons. That tiger-like man addressed me with these

‹pratipālaya māṃ, sūta, niyamy' âśvān muhūrtakam.
yāvad etān nihanmy āśu ya ime mad|vadh'|ôdyatāḥ.›
tato dṛṣṭvā pradhāvantaṃ gadā|hastaṃ mahā|balam
sarveṣām eva sainyānāṃ saṃgharṣaḥ samajāyata.
77.25 tasmin su|tumule yuddhe vartamāne bhayānake
bhittvā, rājan, mahā|vyūhaṃ praviveśa Vṛkodaraḥ.»
Viśokasya vacaḥ śrutvā Dhṛṣṭadyumno 'pi Pārṣataḥ
pratyuvāca tataḥ sūtaṃ raṇa|madhye mahā|balaḥ:
«na hi me jīviten' âpi vidyate 'dya prayojanam
Bhīmasenaṃ raṇe hitvā sneham utsṛjya Pāṇḍavaiḥ.
yadi yāmi vinā Bhīmaṃ, kiṃ māṃ kṣatraṃ vadiṣyati,
ek'|âyana|gate Bhīme mayi c' âvasthite yudhi?
a|svasti tasya kurvanti devāḥ s'|Âgni|puro|gamāḥ
yaḥ sahāyān parityajya svastimān āvrajed gṛhān.
77.30 mama Bhīmaḥ sakhā c' âiva saṃbandhī ca mahā|balaḥ;
bhakto 'smān, bhaktimāṃś c' âhaṃ tam apy ari|niṣūdanam.
so 'haṃ tatra gamiṣyāmi yatra yāto Vṛkodaraḥ.
nighnantaṃ mām ripūn paśya dānavān iva Vāsavam.»
evam uktvā tato vīro yayau madhyena, Bhārata,
Bhīmasenasya mārgeṣu gadā|pramathitair gajaiḥ.
sa dadarśa tato Bhīmaṃ dahantaṃ ripu|vāhinīm,
vātaṃ vṛkṣān iva balāt prabhañjantaṃ raṇe ripūn.
te vadhyamānāḥ samare rathinaḥ, sādinas tathā,
pādātā, dantinaś c' âiva cakrur ārta|svaraṃ mahat.
77.35 hā|hā|kāraś ca saṃjajñe tava sainyasya, māriṣa,
vadhyato Bhīmasenena kṛtinā citra|yodhinā.
tataḥ kṛt'|âstrās te sarve parivārya Vṛkodaram

cheerful words: 'Hold the horses still for a moment and wait for me, chariot driver, while I kill these men who are eager to kill me!' All of our troops were delighted to see mighty Bhima charging forward, mace in hand. In the tu- 77.25
multuous and terrifying battle Vrikódara penetrated the enemy's mighty array, Your Majesty."

On hearing Vishóka's words, Dhrishta·dyumna, the powerful grandson of Príshata, responded to the chariot driver on the field of battle: "If I discard my friendship with the Pándavas and give Bhima·sena up in battle today, there will be no meaning to my life! What will the warriors say to me if I return without Bhima, who fought intent on a single goal while I stood idle during the fight? The gods led by Shakra inflict misfortune on the man who comes back home safe and sound after forsaking his companions in trouble. Mighty Bhima is my friend and my relative. The 77.30
slaughterer of foes is devoted to me, and I am full of devotion for him. So I will go where Vrikódara has gone. Watch me strike the enemies down, like Indra slaying demons!"

Having said this, descendant of Bharata, that heroic warrior headed into the breach, following Bhima·sena's tracks that were marked by mace-mangled elephants. Then he saw Bhima scorching the enemy troops, crushing the foes like a stormy wind violently uprooting trees.

Chariot warriors, horsemen, foot soldiers, and elephants were struck in that battle and raised loud cries of pain. Struck by the accomplished warrior Bhima·sena skilled in 77.35
various forms of battle, your warriors screamed out loud cries, my lord. Then all those fighters, skilled in arms, fear-

a|bhītāḥ samavartanta śastra|vṛṣṭyā, paran|tapa.
abhidrutaṃ śastra|bhṛtāṃ variṣṭhaṃ
samantataḥ Pāṇḍavaṃ loka|vīraḥ
sainyena ghoreṇa su|saṃgatena
dṛṣṭvā balī Pārṣato Bhīmasenam,
ath' ôpagacchac chara|vikṣat'|âṅgaṃ,
padātinaṃ, krodha|viṣaṃ vamantam
āśvāsayan Pārṣato Bhīmasenaṃ
gadā|hastaṃ Kālam iv' ânta|kāle.
vi|śalyam enaṃ ca cakāra tūrṇam,
āropayac c' ātma|rathaṃ mah"|ātmā.
bhṛśaṃ pariṣvajya ca Bhīmasenam
āśvāsayām āsa ca śatru|madhye.
77.40 bhrātṝn ath' ôpetya tav' âpi putras
tasmin vimarde mahati pravṛtte:
«ayaṃ dur|ātmā Drupadasya putraḥ
samāgato Bhīmasenena sārdham.
taṃ yāma sarve sahitā nihantuṃ.
mā vo ripuḥ prārthayatām anīkam.»
śrutvā tu vākyaṃ tam a|mṛṣyamāṇā
jyeṣṭh'|ājñayā noditā Dhārtarāṣṭrāḥ
vadhāya niṣpetur ud|āyudhās te,
yuga|kṣaye ketavo yadvad ugrāḥ,
pragṛhya c' âstrāṇi dhanūṃṣi vīrā
jyāṃ nemi|ghoṣaiḥ pravikampayantaḥ.
śarair avarṣan Drupadasya putraṃ
yath" âmbu|dā bhū|dharaṃ vāri|jālaiḥ.
nihatya tāṃś c' âpi śaraiḥ su|tīkṣṇair
na vivyathe samare citra|yodhī.
samabhyudīrṇāṃś ca tav' ātma|jāṃs tathā

lessly enveloped Vrikódara in a downpour of weapons, scorcher of foes.

Príshata's grandson, the mighty and world-famous hero, saw that warrior champion Bhima·sena Pándava besieged on all sides by the serried ranks of that terrible host, fighting on foot though his limbs were mangled by arrows, vomiting the poison of his anger with a mace in his hand, like Time at the hour of the universal destruction; and he advanced towards Bhima·sena and gave him some breathing space. The great-spirited hero quickly took Bhima·sena up onto his chariot and removed the arrows from his body. Then, embracing Bhima, he encouraged him in the very midst of the enemies.

In that fierce fight your son came up to his brothers and 77.40
said: "This wicked son of Drúpada has joined Bhima·sena. We should all attack him with a large force and not let the enemy break our ranks."

Hearing these words Dhrita·rashtra's sons, urged on by the command of their eldest brother, wouldn't stand for it; brandishing their weapons, eager to kill Dhrishta·dyumna, they pounced on him like frightful comets falling at the end of an eon. Holding their bows and other arms, those heroes made the earth quake with the clamor of their chariot wheels. They rained arrows down upon Drúpada's son, just as thunderclouds shower torrents of rain on a mountain.

But that warrior, who was skilled in diverse forms of warfare, did not waver; he even wounded them with well-sharpened arrows in that conflict. Seeing your heroic sons advance and confront him in battle, Drúpada's son, that

niśamya vīrān abhitaḥ sthitān raṇe,
jighāṃsur ugraṃ Drupad'|ātmajo yuvā
pramohan'|âstraṃ yuyuje mahā|rathaḥ.
77.45 kruddho bhṛśaṃ tava putreṣu, rājan,
daityeṣu yadvat samare mah"|Êndraḥ,
tato vyamuhyanta raṇe nṛ|vīrāḥ
pramohan'|âstr'|āhata|buddhi|sattvāḥ.
pradudruvuḥ Kuravaś c' âiva sarve
sa|vāji|nāgāḥ sa|rathāḥ samantāt.
parīta|kālān iva naṣṭa|saṃjñān
moh'|ôpetāṃs tava putrān niśamya.
etasminn eva kāle tu Droṇaḥ śastra|bhṛtāṃ varaḥ
Drupadaṃ tribhir āsādya śarair vivyādha dāruṇaiḥ.
so 'tividdhas tadā, rājan, raṇe Droṇena pārthivaḥ
apāyād Drupado, rājan, pūrva|vairam anusmaran.
jitvā tu Drupadaṃ Droṇaḥ śaṅkhaṃ dadhmau pratāpavān.
tasya śaṅkha|svanaṃ śrutvā vitresuḥ sarva|Somakāḥ.
77.50 atha śuśrāva tejasvī Droṇaḥ śastra|bhṛtāṃ varaḥ
pramohan'|âstreṇa raṇe mohitān ātma|jāṃs tava.
tato Droṇo, mahā|rāja, tvarito 'bhyāyayau raṇāt.
tatr' âpaśyan mah"|êṣv|āso Bhāradvājaḥ pratāpavān
Dhṛṣṭadyumnaṃ ca Bhīmaṃ ca vicarantau mahā|raṇe;
moh'|āviṣṭāṃś ca te putrān apaśyat sa mahā|rathaḥ.
tataḥ prajñ"|âstram ādāya mohan'|âstraṃ vyanāśayat.
atha pratyāgata|prāṇās tava putrā mahā|rathāḥ
punar yuddhāya samare prayayur Bhīma|Pārṣatau.
tato Yudhiṣṭhiraḥ prāha samāhūya sva|sainikān:
77.55 «gacchantu padavīṃ śaktyā Bhīma|Pārṣatayor yudhi
Saubhadra|pramukhā vīrā rathā dvā|daśa daṃśitāḥ.
pravṛttim adhigacchantu. na hi śudhyati me manaḥ.»

mighty young warrior, filled with violent fury and intent on slaughtering them, applied his fearful Stupefying weapon against your sons, Your Majesty, just as great Indra did in 77.45
his fight with the demons. And those valiant men lost their senses, their minds and their energy sapped by that stupefying weapon. And seeing your sons confounded and rendered senseless as if their hour had come, all the Kurus, with their horses, elephants, and chariots, fled in all directions.

Just then, Drona, the best of warriors, charged against Drúpada and struck him with three frightful arrows. Heavily wounded by Drona, that king retreated, thinking about their former enmity. Having defeated Drúpada, mighty Drona blew his conch. Hearing the blare of his conch, all the Sómakas were stricken with fear. Then glorious Drona, 77.50
the champion of warriors, heard that your sons had been struck by the Stupefying weapon and had lost their senses. O great king, the great archer Drona, the mighty son of Bharad·vaja, immediately left his position and went to that place. There the great warrior saw Dhrishta·dyumna and Bhima rampaging across the vast battlefield, and your sons fallen into a swoon. Taking up a weapon named Consciousness, he neutralized the Stupefying weapon. And as soon as your sons regained their senses, those great warriors attacked Bhima and the grandson of Príshata again.

Yudhi·shthira summoned his troops and gave a command: "Let twelve heroic and armored warriors, led by the 77.55
son of Subhádra, follow the trail of Bhima and Príshata's grandson in battle to the best of their power, and gather intelligence about them. My heart is very uneasy."

ta evaṃ samanujñātāḥ śūrā vikrānta|yodhinaḥ
«bāḍham» ity evam uktvā tu sarve puruṣa|māninaḥ
madhyan|dina|gate sūrye prayayuḥ sarva eva hi.
Kekayā, Draupadeyāś ca, Dhṛṣṭaketuś ca vīryavān
Abhimanyuṃ puras|kṛtya mahatyā senayā vṛtāḥ
te kṛtvā samare vyūhaṃ sūcī|mukham arin|damāḥ
bibhidur Dhārtarāṣṭrāṇāṃ tad rath'|ânīkam āhave.
77.60 tān prayātān mah"|êṣv|āsān Abhimanyu|puro|gamān
Bhīmasena|bhay'|āviṣṭā, Dhṛṣṭadyumna|vimohitā
na saṃvārayituṃ śaktā tava senā, jan'|âdhipa,
mada|mūrch"|ânvit'|ātmā vai pramad" êv' âdhvani sthitā.
te 'bhiyātā mah"|êṣv|āsāḥ suvarṇa|vikṛta|dhvajāḥ
parīpsanto 'bhyadhāvanta Dhṛṣṭadyumna|Vṛkodarau.
tau ca dṛṣṭvā mah"|êṣv|āsān Abhimanyu|puro|gamān
babhūvatur mudā yuktau nighnantau tava vāhinīm.
dṛṣṭvā ca sahas" āyāntaṃ Pāñcālyo gurum ātmanaḥ
n' āśaṃsata vadhaṃ vīraḥ putrāṇāṃ tava, Bhārata.
77.65 tato rathaṃ samāropya Kaikeyasya Vṛkodaram
abhyadhāvat su|saṃkruddho Droṇam iṣv|astra|pāra|gam.
tasy' âbhipatatas tūrṇaṃ Bhāradvājaḥ pratāpavān
kruddhaś ciccheda bāṇena dhanuḥ śatru|nibarhaṇaḥ.
anyāṃś ca śataśo bāṇān preṣayām āsa Pārṣate
Duryodhana|hit'|ârthāya bhartṛ|piṇḍam anusmaran.
ath' ânyad dhanur ādāya Pārṣataḥ para|vīra|hā
Droṇaṃ vivyādha saptatyā rukma|puṅkhaiḥ śilā|śitaiḥ.

Thus ordered by the king, all those courageous and heroic combatants, proud of their manliness, exclaimed "Sure!" and advanced under the midday sun. The Kékayas, the sons of Dráupadi, and vigorous Dhrishta·ketu were led by Abhimányu and supported by a great force. Those enemy-tamers drew up their troops into the needle-mouthed formation, and fought and broke through the lines of your sons' chariot division.

Lord of men, your troops, stricken with the fear of Bhima 77.60
and stupefied by Dhrishta·dyumna, were unable to restrain those great archers charging forward with Abhimányu at their head; they stopped in their tracks like an intoxicated desirable young woman in a swoon. And those noble and mighty bowmen with their gilded banners rushed swiftly forward, intent on rescuing Dhrishta·dyumna and Vrikódara. On seeing those warriors led by Abhimányu, the two mighty archers, who were massacring your troops, were filled with joy.

But the heroic king of the Panchálas, seeing his teacher suddenly advancing toward him, did not continue assailing your sons, descendant of Bharata. Putting Vrikódara 77.65
onto the Kékaya ruler's chariot, he furiously charged against Drona, the accomplished master of archery. Enraged, Bharad·vaja's powerful and enemy-destroying son sliced through the bow of the attacking foe with an arrow. And recalling that he had eaten his lord's bread, and so seeking Duryódhana's welfare, Drona shot hundreds of other shafts at the grandson of Príshata. Príshata's grandson, the slayer of hostile heroes, took up another bow and struck Drona with twenty gold-nocked and stone-whetted arrows. But

tasya Droṇaḥ punaś cāpaṃ cicched' â|mitra|karśanaḥ,
hayāṃś ca caturas tūrṇaṃ caturbhiḥ sāyak'|ôttamaiḥ.
77.70 Vaivasvata|kṣayaṃ ghoraṃ preṣayām āsa, Bhārata,
sārathiṃ c' âsya bhallena preṣayām āsa Mṛtyave.
hat'|âśvāt sa rathāt tūrṇam avaplutya mahā|rathaḥ
āruroha mahā|bāhur Abhimanyor mahā|ratham.

tataḥ sa|ratha|nāg'|âśvā samakampata vāhinī
paśyato Bhīmasenasya, Pārṣatasya ca paśyataḥ.
tat prabhagnaṃ balaṃ dṛṣṭvā Droṇen' â|mita|tejasā
n' âśaknuvan vārayituṃ samastās te mahā|rathāḥ.
vadhyamānaṃ tu tat sainyaṃ Droṇena niśitaiḥ śaraiḥ
vyabhramat tatra tatr' âiva kṣobhyamāṇa iv' ârṇavaḥ.
77.75 tathā dṛṣṭvā ca tat sainyaṃ jahṛṣe tāvakaṃ balam.
dṛṣṭv" ācāryaṃ ca saṃkruddhaṃ dahantaṃ ripu|vāhinīm
cukruśuḥ sarvato yodhāḥ «sādhu! sādhv!» iti, Bhārata.

SAÑJAYA uvāca:

78.1 TATO DURYODHANO rājā mohāt pratyāgatas tadā
śara|varṣaiḥ punar Bhīmaṃ pratyavārayad a|cyutam.
ekī|bhūtāḥ punaś c' âiva tava putrā mahā|rathāḥ
sametya samare Bhīmaṃ yodhayām āsur udyatāḥ.
Bhīmaseno 'pi samare saṃprāpya sva|rathaṃ punaḥ
samāruhya mahā|bāhur yayau yena tav' ātma|jaḥ.
pragṛhya ca mahā|vegaṃ par"|âsu|karaṇaṃ dṛḍham
citraṃ śar'|âsanaṃ saṃkhye śarair vivyādha te sutān.
78.5 tato Duryodhano rājā Bhīmasenaṃ mahā|balam

Drona, the tormentor of his foes, split his enemy's new bow,
and with four fine shafts he sent Dhrishta·dyumna's four
horses to the terrible realm of Vivásvat's son, descendant of 77.70
Bharata. And with a spear-headed arrow he also dispatched
the enemy's chariot driver to Death. But the mighty-armed
great warrior hurriedly jumped out of his horseless vehicle
and climbed onto Abhimányu's chariot.

Then, with all its chariots, elephants, and horses, the
army of Bhima·sena and the grandson of Príshata began to
tremble even as they looked on. Seeing their host routed by
Drona of limitless vigor, all those great warriors combined
were unable to control it. As they were massacred by Drona
with his sharpened arrows, the troops rushed around in
confusion, like a raging sea. And seeing the Pándava army in 77.75
such a state, your troops were overjoyed. Seeing the teacher
filled with immense rage and pouncing upon the enemy
host, descendant of Bharata, all your warriors shouted: "Excellent! Excellent!"

SÁNJAYA said:

AFTER REGAINING consciousness, King Duryódhana re- 78.1
pelled indomitable Bhima with rains of arrows. Standing
once more as one, your great warrior sons began to fight
strenuously against Bhima in battle. So mighty-armed
Bhima·sena went back to his own chariot, climbed onto it,
and advanced to where your son was. Grabbing a splendid,
stiff bow of great force—one that was capable of taking the
lives of his enemies—he pierced your son with many arrows
in that fight. Then King Duryódhana severely wounded 78.5
powerful Bhima·sena in his vital organs with a very sharp

nārācena su|tīkṣṇena bhṛśaṃ marmaṇy atāḍayat.
so 'tividdho mah"|êṣv|āsas tava putreṇa dhanvinā
krodha|saṃrakta|nayano vegen' ākṣipya kārmukam
Duryodhanaṃ tribhir bāṇair bāhvor urasi c' ārpayat.
sa tatra śuśubhe rājā śikharair giri|rāḍ iva.

tau dṛṣṭvā samare kruddhau vinighnantau paras|param,
Duryodhan'|ânujāḥ sarve śūrāḥ saṃtyakta|jīvitāḥ
saṃsmṛtya mantritaṃ pūrvaṃ nigrahe bhīma|karmaṇaḥ
niścayaṃ paramaṃ kṛtvā nigrahītuṃ pracakramuḥ.
78.10 tān āpatata ev' ājau Bhīmaseno mahā|balaḥ
pratyudyayau, mahā|rāja, gajaḥ prati|gajān iva.
bhṛśaṃ kruddhaś ca tejasvī nārācena samārpayat
Citrasenaṃ, mahā|rāja, tava putraṃ mahā|yaśāḥ.
tath" êtarāṃs tava sutāṃs tāḍayām āsa, Bhārata,
śarair bahu|vidhaiḥ saṃkhye rukma|puṅkhaiḥ su|tejanaiḥ.

tataḥ saṃsthāpya samare tāny anīkāni sarvaśaḥ
Abhimanyu|prabhṛtayas te dvā|daśa mahā|rathāḥ
preṣitā Dharma|rājena Bhīmasena|pad'|ânugāḥ
pratijagmur, mahā|rāja, tava putrān mahā|balān.
78.15 dṛṣṭvā ratha|sthāṃs tāñ śūrān sūry'|âgni|sama|tejasaḥ,
sarvān eva mah"|êṣv|āsān, bhrājamānāñ, śriyā vṛtān,
mah"|āhave dīpyamānān, suvarṇa|mukuṭ'|ôjjvalān
tatyajuḥ samare Bhīmaṃ tava putrā mahā|balāḥ.
tān n' âmṛṣyata Kaunteyo, «jīvamānā gatā» iti,
anvīya ca punaḥ sarvāṃs tava putrān apīḍayat.
ath' Âbhimanyuṃ samare Bhīmasenena saṃgatam

iron shaft. Badly wounded by your bow-wielding son, that mighty archer, his eyes bloodshot with fury, drew his bow violently and struck Duryódhana with three arrows in his arms and chest. And the king looked beautiful, like the king of the mountains shining with summits.

Seeing the two warriors pounding each other in that
encounter, Duryódhana's heroic younger brothers, all of
whom were ready to give up their lives, keeping in mind
their previous plan to capture Bhima of fearful feats alive,
took a final decision and proceeded to subdue him. As they 78.10
pounced upon him in the fight, mighty Bhima·sena rose
up against them, great king, like an elephant confronting
rival elephants. Immensely furious, that vigorous and glorious warrior struck your son Chitra·sena, great king, with
an iron shaft. Then he afflicted your other sons with gold-
nocked, well-sharpened arrows of various kinds in the fray,
descendant of Bharata.

Now the twelve great warriors led by Abhimányu, who
had been dispatched by the King of Righteousness to follow Bhima·sena's trail, mustered all their troops on the battlefield and attacked your powerful sons, great king. When 78.15
all those heroic and mighty archers came into view, stationed on their chariots, glowing like the fire of the sun,
gleaming with splendor, and shining in that great war with
the radiance of their golden diadems, your powerful sons
turned away from Bhima on the field of battle. But the son
of Kunti could not endure their leaving the encounter alive,
and he chased all your sons and struck them again. When
they saw Abhimányu in concert with Bhima·sena and the
grandson of Príshata, the great warriors of your host, led by

Pārṣatena ca saṃpreksya tava sainye mahā|rathāḥ,
Duryodhana|prabhṛtayaḥ pragṛhīta|śar'|âsanāḥ
bhṛśam aśvaiḥ prajavitaiḥ prayayur yatra te rathāḥ.
78.20 apar'|âhṇe tato, rājan, prāvartata mahā|raṇaḥ
tāvakānāṃ ca balināṃ pareṣāṃ c' âiva, Bhārata.
Abhimanyur Vikarṇasya hayān hatvā mah"|āhave
ath' âinaṃ pañca|viṃśatyā kṣudrakāṇāṃ samārpayat.
hat'|âśvaṃ ratham utsṛjya Vikarṇas tu mahā|rathaḥ
āruroha rathaṃ, rājaṃś, Citrasenasya, Bhārata.
sthitāv eka|rathe tau tu bhrātarau kula|vardhanau
Ārjuniḥ śara|jālena cchādayām āsa, Bhārata.
Citraseno Vikarṇaś ca Kārṣṇiṃ pañcabhir āyasaiḥ
vivyadhatur; na c' âkampat Kārṣṇir Merur iva sthitaḥ.
78.25 Duḥśāsanas tu samare Kekayān pañca, māriṣa,
yodhayām āsa, rāj'|êndra. tad adbhutam iv' âbhavat.
Draupadeyā raṇe kruddhā Duryodhanam avārayan
śarair āśīviṣ'|ākāraiḥ putraṃ tava, viśāṃ pate.
putro 'pi tava Durdharṣo Draupadyās tanayān raṇe
sāyakair niśitai, rājann, ājaghāna pṛthak pṛthak.
taiś c' âpi viddhaḥ śuśubhe rudhireṇa samukṣitaḥ
giriḥ prasravaṇair yadvad gairik'|ādi|vimiśritaiḥ.

Bhīṣmo 'pi samare, rājan, Pāṇḍavānām anīkinīm
kālayām āsa balavān, pālaḥ paśu|gaṇān iva.
78.30 tato Gāṇḍīva|nirghoṣaḥ prādur|āsīd, viśāṃ pate,
dakṣiṇena varūthinyāḥ Pārthasy' ârīn vinighnataḥ.
uttasthuḥ samare tatra kabandhāni samantataḥ
Kurūṇāṃ c' âiva sainyeṣu Pāṇḍavānāṃ ca, Bhārata.

Duryódhana, grabbed their bows and made their way toward them, carried by their immensely swift horses.

In the afternoon, fierce combat ensued between yours and the enemy's forces, great king, descendant of Bharata. 78.20
In that great battle Abhimányu killed Vikárna's horses and wounded him with twenty-five short arrows. Leaving his horseless chariot behind, Your Majesty, the mighty warrior Vikárna climbed onto Chitra·sena's chariot, descendant of Bharata. Árjuna's son shrouded the two brothers—standing on one chariot, the gladdeners of their family—in a web of arrows, descendant of Bharata. Chitra·sena and Vikárna wounded Krishna's nephew with five iron shafts, but he stood his ground without flinching, like Mount Meru. In 78.25
that fight Duhshásana took on the five Kékaya princes, my lord, king of kings. It was like a miracle. In their battle-fury Dráupadi's sons repelled your son Duryódhana with arrows that were like venomous snakes, lord of the people. Then one by one your son Durdhársha struck the sons of Dráupadi with sharpened arrows in the battle, Your Majesty. Wounded by them in return and drenched in blood, he looked beautiful, like a mountain drenched by streams mixed with red chalk and other minerals.

Mighty Bhishma pummeled the Pándava troops, Your Majesty, like a herdsman whipping his herds. Then the 78.30
twang of the Gandíva bow resounded, for the Partha was striking down enemies on your host's right wing, lord of the people. All over that battlefield, in the Kuru and the Pándava armies, headless bodies stood, descendant of Bharata. On boats that were chariots the tiger-like men tried to cross that sea of troops which had blood for its water, arrows for

śoṇit'|ôdaṃ, rath'|āvartaṃ, gaja|dvīpaṃ, hay'|ōrmiṇam
ratha|naubhir nara|vyāghrāḥ prateruḥ sainya|sāgaram.
chinna|hastā, vi|kavacā, vi|dehāś ca nar'|ôttamāḥ
dṛśyante patitās tatra śataśo 'tha sahasraśaḥ.
nihatair matta|mātaṅgaiḥ śoṇit'|âugha|pariplutaiḥ
bhūr bhāti, Bharata|śreṣṭha, parvatair ācitā yathā.
78.35 tatr' âdbhutam apaśyāma tava teṣāṃ ca, Bhārata.
na tatr' āsīt pumān kaś cid yo yoddhuṃ n' âbhikāṅkṣati.
evaṃ yuyudhire vīrāḥ prārthayānā mahad yaśaḥ
tāvakāḥ Pāṇḍavaiḥ sārdhaṃ ākāṅkṣanto jayaṃ yudhi.

SAÑJAYA uvāca:

79.1 TATO DURYODHANO rājā lohitāyati bhāskare
saṃgrāma|rabhaso Bhīmaṃ hantu|kāmo 'bhyadhāvata.
tam āyāntam abhiprekṣya nṛ|vīraṃ dṛḍha|vairiṇam
Bhīmasenaḥ su|saṃkruddha idaṃ vacanam abravīt:
«ayaṃ sa kālaḥ saṃprāpto varṣa|pūg'|âbhikāṅkṣitaḥ.
adya tvāṃ nihaniṣyāmi, yadi n' ôtsṛjase raṇam.
adya Kuntyāḥ parikleśaṃ, vana|vāsaṃ ca kṛtsnaśaḥ,
Draupadyāś ca parikleśaṃ praṇeṣyāmi hate tvayi.
79.5 yat purā matsarī bhūtvā Pāṇḍavān avamanyase,
tasya pāpasya, Gāndhāre, paśya vyasanam āgatam.
Karṇasya matam ājñāya, Saubalasya ca yat purā,
a|cintya Pāṇḍavān kāmād yath"|êṣṭaṃ kṛtavān asi.
yācamānaṃ ca yan mohād Dāśārham avamanyase,
Ulūkasya samādeśaṃ yad dadāsi ca hṛṣṭavat,
adya tvā nihaniṣyāmi s'|ânubandhaṃ sa|bāndhavam.
samī|kariṣye tat pāpaṃ yat purā kṛtavān asi.

its eddies, elephants for its islands, and horses for its waves. Hundreds and thousands of excellent warriors were to be seen lying there with their hands cut off, their armor shattered, and their bodies lacerated. Covered with slain rutting elephants drenched all over in blood, the earth seemed as if
it were covered by mountains, best of the Bharatas. It was 78.35
amazing for us to see, descendant of Bharata, that there was not a single man in either army who didn't want to fight. This is how your heroes, seeking great glory and greedy for the victory, battled on with the Pándavas.

SÁNJAYA said:

As THE SUN grew red, King Duryódhana, eager for com- 79.1
bat, charged against Bhima, wanting to kill him. Seeing that heroic warrior, his avowed enemy, advancing toward him, Bhima·sena was filled with great passion and spoke to him:

"The moment I have been waiting for years has now come. If you don't flee the battle, I will kill you today. By killing you I will completely avenge Kunti's troubles, our sufferings in exile in the forest, and the insult to Dráupadi.
Filled with envy, you humiliated the Pándavas in former 79.5
days. Now, son of Gandhári, face the ruin that comes of the evil you have done. Formerly, following the counsels of Karna and the son of Súbala, you mindlessly mistreated the Pándavas as you pleased. In your delusion, you ignored the chief of the Dashárhas when he begged you for peace. And you gleefully sent us messages through Ulúka. For all that, I will slaughter you along with all your relatives and companions, and I will get even with you for the evil you committed in the past."

evam uktvā dhanur ghoraṃ
vikṛṣy', ôdbhrāmya c' â|sakṛt,
samādhatta śarān ghorān
mah"|âśani|sama|prabhān.
79.10 ṣaḍ|viṃśatim atha kruddho mumoc' āśu Suyodhane
jvalit'|âgni|śikh"|ākārān, vajra|kalpān, a|jihma|gān.
tato 'sya kārmukaṃ dvābhyāṃ,
sūtaṃ dvābhyāṃ ca vivyadhe,
caturbhir aśvāñ javanān
anayad Yama|sādanam.
dvābhyāṃ ca su|vikṛṣṭābhyāṃ śarābhyām ari|mardanaḥ
chatraṃ ciccheda samare rājñas tasya, rath'|ôttama.
tribhiś ca tasya ciccheda jvalantaṃ dhvajam uttamam.
chittvā taṃ ca nanād' ôccais tava putrasya paśyataḥ.
rathāc ca sa dhvajaḥ śrīmān nānā|ratna|vibhūṣitāt
papāta sahasā bhūmau, vidyuj jala|dharād iva.
79.15 jvalantaṃ sūrya|saṃkāśaṃ nāgaṃ maṇimayaṃ śubham
dhvajaṃ Kuru|pateś chinnaṃ dadṛśuḥ sarva|pārthivāḥ.
ath' âinaṃ daśabhir bāṇais tottrair iva mahā|dvipam
ājaghāna raṇe vīraṃ smayann iva mahā|rathaḥ.
tatas tu rājā Sindhūnāṃ ratha|śreṣṭho Jayadrathaḥ
Duryodhanasya jagrāha pārṣṇiṃ sat|puruṣair vṛtaḥ.
Kṛpaś ca rathināṃ śreṣṭhaḥ Kauravyam a|mit'|âujasam
āropayad rathaṃ, rājan, Duryodhanam a|marṣaṇam.
sa gāḍha|viddho, vyathito Bhīmasenena saṃyuge
niṣasāda rath'|ôpasthe rājā Duryodhanas tadā.
79.20 parivārya tato Bhīmaṃ jetu|kāmo Jayadrathaḥ
rathair an|eka|sāhasrair Bhīmasy' âvārayad diśaḥ.

Having said this, Bhima repeatedly brandished his fierce
bow; then he drew it and aimed his terrifying arrows, each
resembling a mighty thunderbolt. In his fury he quickly 79.10
fired at Suyódhana twenty-six straight-flying shafts like
lightning bolts, like flames of glowing fire. Then with two
arrows Bhima cut through his enemy's bow, and with another two he wounded his chariot driver. With four other
arrows he sent his opponent's swift horses to the realm of
Yama. With two well-drawn shafts that enemy-crusher, the
foremost of men cut off the king's parasol in that battle.
With six other arrows he severed Duryódhana's fine and
gleaming banner; and after cutting it down he shouted
out loud in the sight of your son. That resplendent banner, adorned with various gems, collapsed suddenly from
the chariot onto the ground, like lightning striking from a
thundercloud. And all the kings watched as the Kuru ruler's 79.15
radiant banner, blazing like the sun and bearing the emblem of an elephant, fell down severed.

Then the mighty warrior Bhima, almost laughing, wounded the enemy hero in that battle with ten arrows, as if he was hitting a huge elephant with goads. Consequently the king of the Sindhus, the best of chariot fighters and a great warrior, secured Duryódhana's rear, supported by valiant combatants; and the mighty warrior Kripa, the foremost of chariot warriors, took the furious and boundlessly vigorous Kuru chief Duryódhana onto his chariot, Your Majesty. In acute pain, with a deep wound inflicted by

Dhṛṣṭaketus tato, rājann, Abhimanyuś ca vīryavān,
Kekayā, Draupadeyāś ca tava putrān ayodhayan.
Citrasenaḥ, Sucitraś ca, Citrāṅgaś, Citradarśanaḥ,
Cārucitraḥ, Sucāruś ca, tathā Nand'|Ôpanandakau—
aṣṭāv ete mah"|êṣv|āsāḥ su|kumārā yaśasvinaḥ
Abhimanyu|rathaṃ, rājan, samantāt paryavārayan.
ājaghāna tatas tūrṇam Abhimanyur mahā|manāḥ
ek'|âikaṃ pañcabhir viddhvā śaraiḥ saṃnata|parvabhiḥ.
79.25 vajra|mṛtyu|pratīkāśair vicitr'|āyudha|niḥsṛtaiḥ
a|mṛṣyamāṇās te sarve Saubhadraṃ ratha|sattamam
vavṛṣur mārgaṇais tīkṣṇair, giriṃ Merum iv' âmbu|dāḥ.
sa pīḍyamānaḥ samare kṛt'|âstro, yuddha|dur|madaḥ
Abhimanyur, mahā|rāja, tāvakān samakampayat,
yathā dev'|âsure yuddhe vajra|pāṇir mah"|âsurān.
Vikarṇasya tato bhallān preṣayām āsa, Bhārata,
catur|daśa ratha|śreṣṭho ghorān āśīviṣ'|ôpamān.
sa tair Vikarṇasya rathāt pātayām āsa vīryavān
dhvajaṃ, sūtaṃ, hayāṃś c' âsya cchittvā nṛtyann iv' āhave.
79.30 punaś c' ânyāñ śarān pītān a|kuṇṭh'|âgrāñ, śilā|śitān
preṣayām āsa saṃkruddho Vikarṇāya mahā|balaḥ.
te Vikarṇaṃ samāsādya kaṅka|barhiṇa|vāsasaḥ,
bhittvā dehaṃ gatā bhūmiṃ jvalanta iva pannagāḥ.

Bhima·sena in that fight, Duryódhana sank onto the chariot platform, Your Majesty. Then Jayad·ratha, eager to de- 79.20
feat Bhima, encircled him with several thousand chariots, obstructing him on all sides.

Dhrishta·ketu, vigorous Abhimányu, the Kékaya brothers, and the sons of Dráupadi all confronted your sons, Your Majesty. Chitra·sena, Suchítra, Chitránga, Chitra·dárshana, Charu·chitra, Sucháru, Nanda, and Upanánda—these eight young, glorious, and mighty archers surrounded Abhimányu's chariot completely, Your Majesty; but proud Abhimányu immediately wounded them one by one, each with five sharp straight arrows fired from his splendid bow and fright- 79.25
ful like a thunderbolt or death. Unable to tolerate it, they all poured torrents of sharp arrows onto Subhádra's son, that foremost of warriors, just as rain-clouds shower rain upon Mount Meru. Although he was hurt by them in that fight, great king, Abhimányu skilled in weaponry and ferocious in battle made your troops tremble, just as thunderbolt-wielding Indra made the mighty demons tremble during their war against the gods.

O descendant of Bharata, vigorous Abhimányu, that best of warriors, practically dancing in battle, fired fourteen dreadful spear-headed shafts that were like poisonous snakes at Vikárna; and with them he felled Vikárna's banner from his chariot and struck down his driver and horses. Filled 79.30
with fury, the powerful hero shot many sharp-pointed and stone-whetted copper arrows at Vikárna. Striking Vikárna, those heron-feathered shafts cut through his body and went to ground like blazing serpents. Those arrows, their nocks and points finished with gold, were soaked in Vikárna's

te śarā hema|puṅkh'|âgrā vyadṛśyanta mahī|tale
Vikarṇa|rudhira|klinnā, vamanta iva śoṇitam.

Vikarṇaṃ vīkṣya nirbhinnaṃ tasy' âiv' ânye sah'|ôdarāḥ
abhyadravanta samare Saubhadra|pramukhān rathān.
abhiyātvā tath" âiv' āśu
ratha|sthān sūrya|varcasaḥ
avidhyan samare 'nyonyaṃ
saṃrambhād yuddha|dur|madāḥ.

79.35 Durmukhaḥ Śrutakarmāṇaṃ viddhvā saptabhir āśu|gaiḥ
dhvajam ekena ciccheda, sārathiṃ c' âsya saptabhiḥ.
aśvāñ jāmbūnadair jālaiḥ pracchannān vāta|raṃhasaḥ
jaghāna ṣaḍbhir āsādya, sārathiṃ c' âbhyapātayat.
sa hat'|âśve rathe tiṣṭhañ Śrutakarmā mahā|rathaḥ
śaktiṃ cikṣepa saṃkruddho mah"|ôlkāṃ jvalitām iva.
sā Durmukhasya vimalaṃ varma bhittvā yaśasvinaḥ
vidārya prāviśad bhūmiṃ dīpyamānā sva|tejasā.
taṃ dṛṣṭvā vi|rathaṃ tatra Sutasomo mahā|rathaḥ
paśyatāṃ sarva|sainyānāṃ ratham āropayat svakam.

79.40 Śrutakīrtis tathā vīro Jayatsenaṃ sutaṃ tava
abhyayāt samare, rājan, hantu|kāmo yaśasvinam.
tasya vikṣipataś cāpaṃ Śrutakīrter mah"|ātmanaḥ
ciccheda samare, rājañ, Jayatsenaḥ sutas tava
kṣurapreṇa su|tīkṣṇena prahasann iva, Bhārata.

taṃ dṛṣṭvā chinna|dhanvānaṃ Śatānīkaḥ sah'|ôdaram
abhyapadyata tejasvī siṃhavan ninadan muhuḥ.
Śatānīkas tu samare dṛḍhaṃ visphārya kārmukam
vivyādha daśabhis tūrṇaṃ Jayatsenaṃ śilīmukhaiḥ;
nanāda su|mahā|nādaṃ prabhinna iva vāraṇaḥ.

blood and looked as if they were vomiting blood on the ground.

Seeing Vikárna cut through, his brothers charged against the enemy fighters who in that battle were led by Subhádra's son. Radiant like the sun and ferocious in battle, they swiftly attacked the chariot warriors; and in the fight the combatants smote each other in a rage. Dúrmukha pierced 79.35
Shruta·karman with seven shafts, sliced through his banner with one, and wounded his chariot driver with seven more. With six arrows he killed Shruta·karman's horses covered with golden mail that were as swift as the wind, and struck down his driver with seven. Standing on his horseless chariot, the great warrior Shruta·karman, filled with anger, hurled a lance that looked like a blazing meteor. Cutting through and shattering glorious Dúrmukha's glistening armor, the lance, shining with its splendor, entered the earth. The mighty warrior Suta·soma, seeing Shruta·karman stripped of his chariot, took him onto his own within sight of all the troops.

Then heroic Shruta·kirti charged against your glorious 79.40
son Jayat·sena, eager to kill him in battle. As the eminent Shruta·kirti was stretching his bow, your son Jayat·sena severed it in the battle with a very sharp razor-edged arrow, almost laughing as he did so, descendant of Bharata.

Seeing his brother bowless, vigorous Shataníka advanced toward him, roaring again and again like a lion. Forcefully drawing his bow in the fray, Shataníka quickly wounded Jayat·sena with ten shafts and gave a huge roar like a rutting elephant. Then, with an extremely sharp arrow that could 79.45

79.45 ath' ânyena su|tīkṣṇena sarv'|āvaraṇa|bhedinā
Śatānīko Jayatsenaṃ vivyādha hṛdaye bhṛśam.
tathā tasmin vartamāne Duṣkarṇo bhrātur antike
ciccheda samare cāpaṃ Nākuleḥ krodha|mūrchitaḥ.
ath' ânyad dhanur ādāya bhāra|sāham an|uttamam,
samādhatta śitān bāṇāñ Śatānīko mahā|balaḥ.
«tiṣṭha! tiṣṭh'!» êti c' āmantrya Duṣkarṇaṃ bhrātur agrataḥ,
mumoca niśitān bāṇāñ jvalitān pannagān iva.
tato 'sya dhanur ekena, dvābhyāṃ sūtaṃ ca, māriṣa
ciccheda samare tūrṇaṃ, taṃ ca vivyādha saptabhiḥ.
79.50 aśvān mano|javāṃs tasya karburān vāta|raṃhasaḥ
jaghāna niśitais tūrṇaṃ sarvān dvā|daśabhiḥ śaraiḥ.
ath' âpareṇa bhallena su|yukten' āśu|pātinā
Duṣkarṇaṃ su|dṛḍhaṃ kruddho vivyādha hṛdaye bhṛśam.
sa papāta tato bhūmau vajr'|āhata iva drumaḥ.
Duṣkarṇaṃ vyathitaṃ dṛṣṭvā pañca, rājan, mahā|rathāḥ
jighāṃsantaḥ Śatānīkaṃ sarvataḥ paryavārayan.
chādyamānaṃ śara|vrātaiḥ Śatānīkaṃ yaśasvinam
abhyadhāvanta saṃrabdhāḥ Kekayāḥ pañca s'|ôdarāḥ.
tān abhyāpatataḥ prekṣya tava putrā mahā|rathāḥ
79.55 pratyudyayur, mahā|rāja, gajān iva mahā|gajāḥ.
Durmukho, Durjayaś c' âiva, tathā Durmarṣaṇo yuvā,
Śatruñjayaḥ, Śatrusahaḥ—sarve kruddhā yaśasvinaḥ
pratyudyātā, mahā|rāja, Kekayān bhrātaraḥ samam.
rathair nagara|saṃkāśair, hayair yuktair mano|javaiḥ,
nānā|varṇa|vicitrābhiḥ patākābhir alaṃ|kṛtaiḥ,
vara|cāpa|dharā vīrā, vicitra|kavaca|dhvajāḥ

cut through any obstacle, Shataníka severely wounded Jayat·sena in the heart.

At that moment Dushkárna, who was standing near his brother and had become senseless with rage, split the bow of Nákula's son. Taking up another peerless bow that was able to bear great strain, powerful Shataníka aimed some frightful arrows. Stationed before his brother, he challenged Dushkárna, shouting "Stay still! Stay still!" and shot the sharp arrows like blazing serpents at him. Then in that contest he quickly severed Dushkárna's bow with one arrow, and wounded his chariot driver with two. With twelve 79.50
sharpened arrows Shataníka killed all of Dushkárna's dappled horses that were swift as thought and impetuous as the wind; then he wounded Dushkárna badly in the heart with a well-fired, quick-flying, spear-headed shaft. The wounded hero collapsed on the ground like a tree hit by a thunderbolt.

Seeing Dushkárna in trouble, Your Majesty, five great warriors encircled Shataníka on every side, eager to kill him. Glorious Shataníka was shrouded in swarms of arrows; and the five furious Kékaya brothers advanced to rescue him.

Seeing them charging forward, your mighty warrior sons
proceeded against their enemies, great king, just as great 79.55
elephants confront rival elephants. Dúrmukha, Dúrjaya, young Durmárshana, Shatrun·jaya, and Shatru·saha—all those renowned fighters advanced against the Kékayas, great king. Driving chariots which looked like fortified towns adorned with diverse multicolored flags and yoked to horses as swift as thought, your heroic warriors, wielding fine bows,

viviśus te paraṃ sainyaṃ, siṃhā iva vanād vanam.

tesāṃ su|tumulaṃ yuddhaṃ vyatiṣakta|ratha|dvipam
avartata mahā|raudraṃ nighnatām itar'|êtaram.
79.60 anyony'|āgas|kṛtāṃ, rājan, Yama|rāṣṭra|vivardhanam
muhūrt'|âstamite sūrye cakrur yuddhaṃ su|dāruṇam.
rathinaḥ sādinaś c' âiva vyakīryanta sahasraśaḥ.

tataḥ Śāntanavaḥ kruddhaḥ śaraiḥ saṃnata|parvabhiḥ
nāśayām āsa senāṃ tāṃ Bhīṣmas teṣāṃ mah"|ātmanām;
Pāñcālānāṃ ca sainyāni śarair ninye Yama|kṣayam.
evaṃ bhittvā mah"|êṣv|āsaḥ Pāṇḍavānām anīkinīm
kṛtv" âvahāraṃ sainyānāṃ yayau sva|śibiraṃ, nṛ|pa.
Dharma|rājo 'pi saṃprekṣya Dhṛṣṭadyumna|Vṛkodarau,
mūrdhni c' âitāv upāghrāya saṃhṛṣṭaḥ śibiraṃ yayau.

clad in glistening armor, and bearing various banners, penetrated the enemy's ranks like lions rushing from one forest to another.

A tumultuous and immensely terrifying fight then ensued, in which elephants were embroiled with chariots,
and men struck each other down. Doing mischief to one 79.60
another, for a short while before sunset they fought an extremely horrific battle which swelled Yama's kingdom. Thousands of slain chariot warriors and horsemen were scattered over the battlefield.

Then Bhishma the son of Shántanu lost his temper and with straight arrows he began to annihilate the army of the illustrious warriors; and he started sending the Panchálas' troops to Yama's abode. Breaking the Pándavas' ranks in this way, that mighty archer forced the close of play, Your Majesty, and retired to his camp. And the King of Righteousness inspected Dhrishta·dyumna and Vrikódara, smelt their heads, and went to his camp delighted.

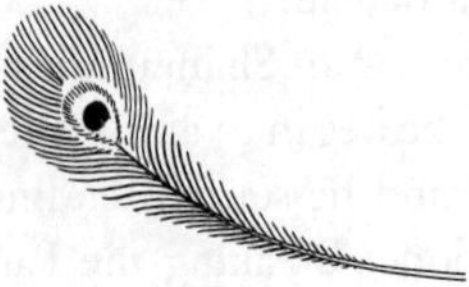

80–86

DAY SEVEN

SAÑJAYA uvāca:

80.1 ATHA ŚŪRĀ, mahā|rāja, paras|para|kṛt'|āgasaḥ
jagmuḥ sva|śibirāṇy eva rudhireṇa samukṣitāḥ.
viśramya ca yathā|nyāyaṃ, pūjayitvā paras|param,
saṃnaddhāḥ samadṛśyanta bhūyo yuddha|cikīrṣayā.
tatas tava suto, rājaṃś, cintay" âbhipariplutaḥ
visravac|choṇit'|âkt'|âṅgaḥ papracch' êdaṃ Pitāmaham.
«sainyāni raudrāṇi bhayānakāni
vyūḍhāni samyag bahula|dhvajāni
vidārya hatvā ca nipīḍya śūrās
te Pāṇḍavānāṃ tvaritā mahā|rathāḥ.
80.5 saṃmohya sarvān yudhi kīrtimanto
vyūhaṃ ca taṃ makaraṃ vajra|kalpam,
praviśya Bhīmena raṇe hato 'smi
ghoraiḥ śarair Mṛtyu|daṇḍa|prakāśaiḥ.
kruddhaṃ tam udvīkṣya bhayena, rājan,
saṃmūrchito na labhe śāntim adya.
icche prasādāt tava, satya|sandha,
prāptuṃ jayaṃ, Pāṇḍaveyāṃś ca hantum.»
ten' âivam uktaḥ prahasan mah"|ātmā
Duryodhanaṃ manyu|gataṃ viditvā,
taṃ pratyuvāc' â|vi|manā manasvī
Gaṅgā|sutaḥ śastra|bhṛtāṃ variṣṭhaḥ:
«pareṇa yatnena vigāhya senāṃ
sarv'|ātman" âhaṃ tava, rāja|putra,
icchāmi dātuṃ vijayaṃ sukhaṃ ca;
na c' ātmānaṃ chādaye 'haṃ tvad|arthe.

SÁNJAYA said:

AND SO, HAVING done wicked things to one another, 80.1
those heroic combatants, drenched in blood, went to
their camps, great king. And having duly rested and paid
homage to each other, they appeared once more, wearing
armor and filled with zeal for the battle.

Your son Duryódhana, Your Majesty, overwhelmed with
anxiety, his limbs stained with blood, questioned grandfather Bhishma. "Our troops are frightful and terrifying;
they are well arrayed and have many banners. And yet those
valiant, swift, and mighty warriors of the Pándavas, shattering our ranks, slaughtering, plaguing, and confusing us all, 80.5
have won glory in combat. Bhima penetrated that crocodile
formation which was fit for a thunderbolt, and wounded
me in battle with fearful arrows that were like staffs of Yama.
Seeing him filled with fury I was overtaken by terror, Your
Majesty, and even now I find no peace. Through your grace,
true to your vows as you are, I seek to attain victory and
slay the Pándavas."

Addressed by him in this way, the wise and great-spirited son of Ganga, the champion of all warriors, knowing that Duryódhana had become indignant, cheerfully replied with a smile. "Your Highness, I wish with all my heart that with my best efforts I could penetrate the enemy's ranks and bring you victory and joy. As far as your objective is concerned, I am not holding myself back.

ete tu raudrā, bahavo, mahā|rathā,
yaśasvinaḥ, śūratamāḥ, kṛt'|âstrāḥ,
ye Pāṇḍavānāṃ samare sahāyā,
jita|klamā roṣa|viṣaṃ vamanti.
80.10 te n' âiva śakyāḥ sahasā vijetuṃ
vīry'|ôddhatāḥ, kṛta|vairās tvayā ca.
ahaṃ senāṃ pratiyotsyāmi, rājan,
sarv'|ātmanā jīvitaṃ tyajya, vīra.
raṇe tav' ârthāya, mah"|ânubhāva,
na jīvitaṃ rakṣyatamaṃ mam' âdya.
sarvāṃs tav' ârthāya sa|deva|daityāl
lokān daheyaṃ; kim u śatru|senām.
tat Pāṇḍavān yodhayiṣyāmi, rājan,
priyaṃ ca te sarvam ahaṃ kariṣye.»
śrutv" âiva c' âitad vacanaṃ tadānīṃ
Duryodhanaḥ prīta|manā babhūva.
sarvāṇi sainyāni tataḥ prahṛṣṭo
«nirgacchat'!» êty āha nṛ|pāṃś ca sarvān.
tad|ājñayā tāni viniryayur drutaṃ
gaj'|âśva|pādāta|rath'|âyutāni.
praharṣa|yuktāni tu tāni, rājan,
mahānti, nānā|vidha|śastravanti,
sthitāni nāg'|âśva|padātimanti
virejur ājau tava, rājan, balāni.
80.15 śastr'|âstra|vidbhir nara|vīra|yodhair
adhiṣṭhitāḥ sainya|gaṇās tvadīyāḥ
rath'|âugha|pādāta|gaj'|âśva|saṅghaiḥ
prayādbhir ājau vidhivat praṇunnaiḥ.
samuddhataṃ vai taruṇ'|ârka|varṇaṃ
rajo babhau, chādayat sūrya|raśmīn.

But these countless, terrifying, glorious, most valiant and mighty warriors, who are skilled in weaponry and allied to the Pándavas in the battle, have conquered their fatigue and
are vomiting the poison of their anger. Endowed with im- 80.10
mense vigor and swearing their hostility to you, they cannot be conquered so easily. I will fight the army, Your Majesty, sparing no efforts and giving up my very life. Illustrious hero, for your sake I will have no regard for my life in the battle today. For your sake I could burn down all the worlds along with the gods and the *daitya*s. What then of the enemy's host? I will fight with those Pándavas, Your Majesty, and do everything you want me to."

And hearing these words Duryódhana became delighted in his heart, and he happily commanded all the troops and kings: "Come out!" And at his command the army, numbering tens of thousands of elephants, horses, foot soldiers, and chariots, came out at once.

Your great force, Your Majesty, abundant in horses, elephants, and foot soldiers, filled with joy and armed with weapons of various kinds, stood on the battlefield looking
splendid. Your troops of soldiers were commanded by war 80.15
heroes—men skilled in weaponry and missiles. Stirred up by the mobilized divisions of chariots, elephants, infantry, and cavalry marching across the field, dust enveloped the rays of the rising sun and took on its color. Mounted on chariots and on the backs of elephants, multicolored flags waved around on the battlefield, fluttering in the wind, Your Majesty, like flashes of lightning in a mass of clouds. The elephants looked brilliant, kitted out properly and standing in great numbers all around.

rejuḥ patākā ratha|danti|saṃsthā
vāt'|ēritā bhrāmyamāṇāḥ samantāt.
nānā|raṅgāḥ samare tatra, rājan,
meghair yuktā vidyutaḥ khe yath" âiva,
vṛndaiḥ sthitāś c' âpi su|saṃprayuktāś
cakāśire danti|gaṇāḥ samantāt.
dhanūṃṣi visphārayatāṃ nṛ|pāṇāṃ
babhūva śabdas tumulo 'tighoraḥ
vimathyato deva|mah"|âsur'|âughair,
yath" ârṇavasy' ādi|yuge tadānīm.
tad ugra|nādaṃ bahu|rūpa|varṇaṃ
tav' ātma|jānāṃ samudīrṇam evam
babhūva sainyaṃ ripu|sainya|hantṛ
yug'|ânta|megh'|âugha|nibhaṃ tadānīm.

SAÑJAYA uvāca:

81.1 ATH' ĀTMA|JAṂ tava punar Gāṅgeyo dhyānam āsthitam
abravīd, Bharata|śreṣṭha, saṃpraharṣa|karaṃ vacaḥ.
«ahaṃ, Droṇaś ca, Śalyaś ca, Kṛtavarmā ca Sātvataḥ,
Aśvatthāmā, Vikarṇaś ca, Bhagadatto, 'tha Saubalaḥ,
Vind'|Ânuvindāv Āvantyau, Bāhlikaḥ saha Bāhlikaiḥ,
Trigarta|rājo balavān, Māgadhaś ca su|durjayaḥ,
Bṛhadbalaś ca Kausalyaś, Citraseno, Viviṃśatiḥ,
rathāś ca bahu|sāhasrāḥ śobhamānā mahā|dhvajāḥ,
81.5 deśa|jāś ca hayā, rājan, sv|ārūḍhā haya|sādibhiḥ,
gaj'|êndrāś ca mad'|ôdvṛttāḥ prabhinna|karaṭā|mukhāḥ,
padātāś ca tathā śūrā nānā|praharaṇ'|āyudhāḥ,
nānā|deśa|samutpannās tvad|arthe yoddhum udyatāḥ.
ete c' ânye ca bahavas tvad|arthe tyakta|jīvitāḥ
devān api raṇe jetuṃ samarthā, iti me matiḥ.
avaśyaṃ tu mayā, rājaṃs, tava vācyaṃ hitaṃ sadā.

Then the kings stretching their bows made a cacophonous and extremely horrific noise like the roar of the foaming ocean being churned up by the hosts of great gods and demons at the start of the age. Your sons' army, diverse in shapes and colors and restless with fierce elephants, was fit to slaughter the enemy army. It looked like a mass of thunderclouds at the end of the age.

SÁNJAYA said:

THEN, BEST OF the Bharatas, the son of Ganga, once 81.1
again addressing your son who was plunged in thought, said these encouraging words to him. "Myself, Drona, Shalya, the Sátvata warrior Krita·varman, Ashva·tthaman, Vikárna, Bhaga·datta, the son of Súbala, Vinda and Anuvínda of Avánti, King Báhlika with the Báhlikas, the powerful king of the Tri·gartas, the Mágadha ruler who is very difficult to defeat, Brihad·bala the king of the Kósalas, Chitra·sena, Vivímshati, many thousands of splendid chariots with tall
banners, numerous country-born horses ridden by skillful 81.5
cavalrymen, many huge maddened rutting elephants secreting juices from their temples and mouths, and countless heroic foot soldiers, bearing various weapons and banners and born in different countries, are all intent on fighting for your sake. I believe that these and many others, all of them ready to sacrifice their lives for your sake, are capable of conquering the very gods in combat. It is my constant duty, Your Majesty, to advise what is beneficial for you. The Pándavas can never be defeated even by the gods

a|śakyāḥ Pāṇḍavā jetuṃ devair api sa|Vāsavaiḥ:
Vāsudeva|sahāyāś ca, mah"|Êndra|sama|vikramāḥ.
sarvath" âhaṃ tu, rāj'|êndra, kariṣye vacanaṃ tava.
81.10 Pāṇḍavān vā raṇe jeṣye, māṃ vā jeṣyanti Pāṇḍavāḥ.»
evam uktvā dadau c' âsmai vi|śalya|karaṇīṃ śubhām
oṣadhīṃ vīrya|saṃpannāṃ. vi|śalyaś c' âbhavat tadā.
tataḥ prabhāte vimale sven' ânīkena vīryavān
avyūhata svayaṃ vyūhaṃ Bhīṣmo vyūha|viśāradaḥ
maṇḍalaṃ manuja|śreṣṭho nānā|śastra|samākulam,
saṃpūrṇaṃ yodha|mukhyaiś ca, tathā danti|padātibhiḥ,
rathair an|eka|sāhasraiḥ samantāt parivāritam,
aśva|vṛndair mahadbhiś ca ṛṣṭi|tomara|dhāribhiḥ.
nāge nāge rathāḥ sapta, sapta c' âśvā rathe rathe,
81.15 anv aśvaṃ daśa dhānuṣkā, dhānuṣke sapta carmiṇaḥ.
evaṃ vyūhaṃ, mahā|rāja, tava sainyaṃ mahā|rathaiḥ
sthitaṃ raṇāya mahate Bhīṣmeṇa yudhi pālitam.
daś' âśvānāṃ sahasrāṇi, dantināṃ ca tath" âiva ca,
rathānām ayutaṃ c' âpi, putrāś ca tava daṃśitāḥ
Citrasen'|ādayaḥ śūrā abhyarakṣan pitā|maham.
rakṣyamāṇaḥ sa taiḥ śūrair, gopyamānāś ca tena te,
saṃnaddhāḥ samadṛśyanta rājānaś ca mahā|balāḥ.

led by Vásava: they have Vásu·deva as their ally, and they are equal to great Indra himself in prowess. Yet I will by all means try to fulfill your command, king of kings. Either I 81.10
shall vanquish the Pándavas in battle, or the Pándavas will vanquish me."

Having said this, Bhishma gave Duryódhana an excellent remedy for healing wounds. Applying that efficient herb, he was cured of his wounds.

And at dawn, when the sky was clear, mighty Bhishma, the best of men and an expert in the arrangement of troops, drew up the army of his warriors into the circular formation teeming with diverse weapons. It was filled with prominent warriors as well as elephants and infantry, and was surrounded on all sides by several thousand chariots and by large divisions of cavalry armed with lances and spears.

By each elephant stood seven chariots, and by each chariot stood seven horsemen. Behind every horseman stood 81.15
ten archers, and by every archer stood ten soldiers with shields. Your host, great king, drawn up in this way by the great warriors and protected in battle by Bhishma, stood ready for the great conflict. Ten thousand horses, ten thousand elephants, ten thousand chariots, and your heroic sons led by Chitra·sena, clad in armor, protected the grandfather. He was under their protection, and those powerful kings were protected by him in turn; and they came into view, ready for the fight.

Duryodhanas tu samare daṃśito ratham āsthitaḥ
vyabhrājata śriyā juṣṭo, yathā Śakras tri|viṣṭape.
81.20 tataḥ śabdo mahān āsīt putrāṇāṃ tava, Bhārata,
ratha|ghoṣaś ca tumulo, vāditrāṇāṃ ca nisvanaḥ.
Bhīṣmeṇa Dhārtarāṣṭrāṇāṃ vyūḍhaḥ pratyaṅ|mukho yudhi
maṇḍalaḥ sa mahā|vyūho dur|bhedyo, '|mitra|ghātanaḥ
sarvataḥ śuśubhe, rājan, raṇe 'rīṇāṃ dur|āsadaḥ.

maṇḍalaṃ tu samālokya vyūhaṃ parama|dur|jayam
svayaṃ Yudhiṣṭhiro rājā vajraṃ vyūhaṃ ath' âkarot.

tathā vyūḍheṣv anīkeṣu yathā|sthānam avasthitāḥ
rathinaḥ sādinaḥ sarve siṃha|nādam ath' ânadan.
bibhitsavas tato vyūhaṃ niryayur yuddha|kāṅkṣiṇaḥ
81.25 itar'|êtarataḥ śūrāḥ
saha|sainyāḥ prahāriṇaḥ.

Bhāradvājo yayau Matsyaṃ,
Drauṇiś c' âpi Shikhaṇḍinam.
svayaṃ Duryodhano rājā Pārṣataṃ samupādravat.
Nakulaḥ Sahadevaś ca Madra|rājam abhīyatuḥ.
Vind'|Ânuvindāv Āvantyāv Irāvantam abhidrutau.
sarve nṛ|pās tu samare Dhanañjayam ayodhayan.
Bhīmaseno raṇe yatto Hārdikyaṃ samavārayat.
Citrasenaṃ, Vikarṇaṃ ca, tathā Durmarṣaṇaṃ vibhuḥ
Ārjuniḥ samare, rājaṃs, tava putrān ayodhayat.
Prāgjyotiṣo mah"|êṣv|āso Haiḍimbaṃ rākṣas'|ôttamam
81.30 abhidudrāva vegena, matto mattam iva dvi|pam.

Duryódhana, wearing his armor, standing resplendent upon his chariot on the battlefield, shone like Shakra in heaven. Loud was the din made by your sons, descendant of 81.20
Bharata, and the rattle of chariots and the sound of musical instruments was deafening. That great and almost impenetrable enemy-destroying circular formation, into which Bhishma had drawn up Dhrita·rashtra's troops for battle, faced west and looked totally beautiful on the battlefield, Your Majesty, difficult as it was for the enemy to attack.

Seeing that almost unbeatable circular array, King Yudhi·shthira in turn drew up his army into the array called thunderbolt.

When the troops had been arrayed in this manner, all the chariot warriors and horsemen, stationed in their proper ranks, shouted a lion-roar. Then, eager for battle, the fierce and heroic combatants in both armies, along with their 81.25
troops, broke ranks and attacked each other.

The son of Bharad·vaja confronted the Matsya king, and the son of Drona confronted Shikhándin. King Duryódhana himself charged against the grandson of Príshata. Nákula and Saha·deva attacked the king of the Madras. Vinda and Anuvínda of Avánti assailed Irávat. All the other kings fought against Dhanan·jaya. Bhima·sena, on his guard, held off the son of Hrídika in the fray. The mighty son of Árjuna fought in battle with your sons Chitra·sena, Vikárna, and Durmárshana, Your Majesty. The Prag·jyótisha ruler, that great archer, violently charged against Hidímba's son, the foremost of demons, like one frenzied elephant 81.30
attacking another. The furious demon Alámbusha assailed war-crazed Sátyaki and his troops. Bhuri·shravas, ready for

Alambuṣas tadā, rājan, Sātyakiṃ yuddha|dur|madam
sa|sainyaṃ samare kruddho rākṣasaḥ samupādravat.
Bhūriśravā raṇe yatto Dhṛṣṭaketum ayodhayat;
Śrutāyuṣaṃ tu rājānaṃ Dharma|putro Yudhiṣṭhiraḥ.
Cekitānas tu samare Kṛpam ev' ânvayodhayat.
śeṣāḥ pratiyayur yattā Bhīṣmam eva mahā|ratham.
tato rāja|sahasrāṇi parivavrur Dhanañjayam
śakti|tomara|nārāca|gadā|parigha|pāṇayaḥ.
Arjuno 'tha bhṛśaṃ kruddho Vārṣṇeyam idam abravīt:
81.35 «paśya, Mādhava, sainyāni Dhārtarāṣṭrasya saṃyuge
vyūḍhāni vyūha|viduṣā Gāṅgeyena mah"|ātmanā.
yuddh'|âbhikāmāñ śūrāṃś ca paśya, Mādhava, daṃśitān.
Trigarta|rājaṃ sahitaṃ bhrātṛbhiḥ paśya, Keśava.
ady' âitān pātayiṣyāmi paśyatas te, Janārdana,
ya ime māṃ, Yadu|śreṣṭha, yoddhu|kāmā raṇ'|âjire.»
evam uktvā tu Kaunteyo dhanur|jyām avamṛjya ca
vavarṣa śara|varṣāṇi nar'|âdhipa|gaṇān prati.
te 'pi taṃ param'|êṣv|āsāḥ śara|varṣair apūrayan,
taḍāgam iva dhārābhir yathā prāvṛṣi toya|dāḥ.
81.40 hā|hā|kāro mahān āsīt tava sainye, viśāṃ pate,
chādyamānau bhṛśaṃ Kṛṣṇau śarair dṛṣṭvā mahā|raṇe.
devā, deva'|rṣayaś c' âiva, gandharvāś ca, mah"|ôragāḥ
vismayaṃ paramaṃ jagmur dṛṣṭvā Kṛṣṇau tathā|gatau.
tataḥ kruddho 'rjuno, rājann, Aindram astram udairayat.
tatr' âdbhutam apaśyāma Vijayasya parākramam.
śastra|vṛṣṭiṃ paraiḥ muktāṃ śar'|âughair yad avārayat,
na ca tatr' âpy a|nirbhinnaḥ kaś cid āsīd, viśāṃ pate.

a fight, clashed with Dhrishta·ketu. In that battle Yudhi·shthira the Son of Righteousness came up against King Shrutáyus; Chekitána confronted Kripa; and the rest of combatants charged with all their might against the mighty warrior Bhishma.

Thousands of kings surrounded Dhanan·jaya with lances, spears, arrows, maces, and iron clubs in their hands; and Árjuna, immensely enraged, addressed the descendant of Vrishni with these words. "Mádhava, look at Dhrita·rashtra's 81.35
army drawn up on the battlefield by Ganga's great-spirited son, the expert in troop formations. Behold these heroes, Mádhava, all clad in armor and eager for battle. Késhava, look at the king of the Tri·gartas and his brothers. O Janárdana, best of the Yadus, today, before your eyes, I will slaughter all those who wish to fight with me on the field of battle!" Saying this the son of Kunti loosed his bowstring and poured showers of arrows on those hosts of kings. And those excellent archers covered him with downpours of shafts, just as rain-clouds fill a tank with floods of water at the time of the monsoon.

Loud shouts rose up amid your troops as they saw the 81.40
two Krishnas* being severely bombarded with arrows in that great encounter. The gods, divine sages, *gandhárvas*, and serpents were filled with the highest wonder when they saw the two Krishnas in such a fix. Then, infuriated, Árjuna invoked Indra's weapon, Your Majesty. We saw Víjaya's marvelous courage as with hordes of his shafts he checked the storm of arrows his enemies had released; and none of his opponents escaped without being wounded, lord of the people. The son of Pritha struck each of those

teṣāṃ rāja|sahasrāṇāṃ, hayānāṃ, dantināṃ tathā
dvābhyāṃ tribhiḥ śaraiś c' ânyān Pārtho vivyādha, māriṣa.
81.45 te hanyamānāḥ Pārthena Bhīṣmaṃ Śāntanavaṃ yayuḥ.
a|gādhe majjamānānāṃ Bhīṣmas trāt" âbhavat tadā.
āpatadbhis tu tais tatra prabhagnaṃ tāvakaṃ balam
saṃcukṣubhe, mahā|rāja, vātair iva mah"|ârṇavaḥ.

SAÑJAYA uvāca:

82.1 TATHĀ PRAVṚTTE saṃgrāme, nivṛtte ca Suśarmaṇi,
bhagneṣu c' âpi vīreṣu Pāṇḍavena mah"|ātmanā,
kṣubhyamāṇe bale tūrṇaṃ sāgara|pratime tava,
pratyudyāte ca Gāṅgeye tvaritaṃ Vijayaṃ prati,
dṛṣṭvā Duryodhano rājā raṇe Pārthasya vikramam,
tvaramāṇaḥ samabhyetya sarvāṃs tān abravīn nṛ|pān,
teṣāṃ ca pramukhe śūraṃ Suśarmāṇaṃ mahā|balam
madhye sarvasya sainyasya bhṛśaṃ saṃharṣayann iva:
82.5 «eṣa Bhīṣmaḥ Śāntanavo yoddhu|kāmo Dhanañjayam
sarv'|ātmanā Kuru|śreṣṭhas, tyaktvā jīvitam ātmanaḥ.
taṃ prayāntaṃ par'|ânīkaṃ sarva|sainyena Bhāratam
saṃyattāḥ samare sarve pālayadhvaṃ pitā|maham.»
«bāḍham» ity evam uktvā tu tāny anīkāni sarvaśaḥ
nar'|êndrāṇāṃ, mahā|rāja, samājagmuḥ pitā|maham.

tataḥ prayātaḥ sahasā Bhīṣmaḥ Śāntanavo 'rjunam,
raṇe Bhāratam āyāntam āsasāda mahā|balaḥ
mahā|śvet'|âśva|yuktena, bhīma|vānara|ketunā,
mahatā, megha|nādena rathen' âtivirājata.
82.10 samare sarva|sainyānām upayāntaṃ Dhanañjayam
abhavat tumulo nādo bhayād dṛṣṭvā Kirīṭinam.

thousands of kings, horses, and elephants with two or three arrows, my lord. Injured by the Partha, they ran to Bhishma 81.45
the son of Shántanu. And Bhishma was the raft for those combatants who were sinking in that fathomless sea. Your army, broken by those fleeing troops, raged in confusion, great king, like the ocean tossed around by stormy winds.

SÁNJAYA said:

DURING THAT battle, when many heroic warriors had 82.1
been routed by the great-spirited son of Pandu, when Sushárman had retreated and before long your host had become agitated like the sea, the son of Ganga hurriedly rose up against Víjaya; and King Duryódhana, seeing the valor of Pritha's son in combat, swiftly approached all those kings with mighty Sushárman standing at their head, and addressed them in the midst of all the troops, encouraging them forcefully. "This Bhishma, the son of Shántanu and 82.5
the foremost of the Kurus, is determined to fight with Dhanan·jaya to the best of his ability, without sparing his own life. All of you, down to the last man, must be ready to protect the Bhárata grandfather as he advances towards the enemy." Voicing their agreement, all the divisions of those lords of men joined the grandfather, great king.

Then greatly powerful Bhishma, the son of Shántanu, suddenly came upon Árjuna, that descendant of Bharata, who was advancing toward him on the battlefield on his shining chariot yoked to mighty white horses, making a thundering rattle and bearing the banner with the emblem of a fierce monkey on it. At the looming sight of Dhanan· 82.10
jaya wearing his diadem, all the troops on the battlefield

abhīṣu|hastaṃ Kṛṣṇaṃ ca dṛṣṭv" ādityam iv' âparam
madhyan|dina|gataṃ saṃkhye na śekuḥ prativīkṣitum.
tathā Śāntanavaṃ Bhīṣmaṃ śvet'|âśvaṃ śveta|kārmukam
na śekuḥ Pāṇḍavā draṣṭuṃ, śveta|graham iv' ôditam.
sa sarvataḥ parivṛtas Trigartaiḥ su|mah"|ātmabhiḥ,
bhrātṛbhis, tava putraiś ca, tath" ânyaiś ca mahā|rathaiḥ.

Bhāradvājas tu samare Matsyaṃ vivyādha patriṇā,
dhvajaṃ c' âsya śareṇ' ājau, dhanuś c' âikena cicchide.
82.15 tad apāsya dhanuś chinnaṃ Virāṭo vāhinī|patiḥ
anyad ādatta vegena dhanur bhāra|sahaṃ dṛḍham,
śarāṃś c' āśīviṣ'|ākārāñ, jvalitān pannagān iva.
Droṇaṃ tribhiḥ pravivyādha, caturbhiś c' âsya vājinaḥ,
dhvajam ekena vivyādha, sārathiṃ c' âsya pañcabhiḥ,
dhanur ek'|êṣuṇ" âvidhyat. tatr' âkrudhyad dvija'|rṣabhaḥ.
tasya Droṇo 'vadhīd aśvāñ śaraiḥ saṃnata|parvabhiḥ
aṣṭābhir, Bharata|śreṣṭha, sūtam ekena patriṇā.

sa hat'|âśvād avaplutya syandanādd hata|sārathiḥ
āruroha rathaṃ tūrṇaṃ putrasya rathināṃ varaḥ.
82.20 tatas tu tau pitā|putrau Bhāradvājaṃ rathe sthitau
mahatā śara|varṣeṇa vārayām āsatur balāt.
Bhāradvājas tataḥ kruddhaḥ śaram āśīviṣ'|ôpamam
cikṣepa samare tūrṇaṃ Śaṅkhaṃ prati, jan'|ēśvara.
sa tasya hṛdayaṃ bhittvā, pītvā śoṇitam āhave,

let out great screams of distress. They saw Krishna with the reins in his hands, but he was dazzling like another midday sun and your warriors were hardly able to look at him in the fray. Nor were the Pándavas able to look at Bhishma the son of Shántanu, who with his white horses and white bow looked like the white planet Shukra, or Venus, rising in the sky. He was surrounded on all sides by the great-spirited Tri·gartas, their brothers and sons, and many other great warriors.

In the meantime the son of Bharad·vaja wounded the Matsya king with a feathered shaft, and cut through his
banner and his bow, each with one arrow. Then Viráta, the 82.15
commander of the division, cast aside his split bow and quickly seized another strong bow that was capable of bearing great strain. Drawing arrows that were like blazing venomous snakes, he hit Drona with three arrows, his horses with four, his banner with one, and his chariot driver with five; and he also struck Drona's bow with one arrow. And Drona, the bull-like brahmin, lost his temper. With eight straight shafts he killed Viráta's horses, and with one feathered arrow he slew his driver, best of Bharatas.

Bereft of his driver, the supreme warrior Viráta quickly jumped out of his horseless vehicle and climbed onto his
son's chariot. Then the father and the son, standing on the 82.20
same chariot and using all their might, held off the son of Bharad·vaja with great downpours of arrows. But in that fight the infuriated son of Bharad·vaja soon shot a shaft at Shankha that was like a poisonous snake, lord of the people; tearing through Shankha's heart, the arrow drank his blood in the fray, and, its fine body soaked in his gore, it

jagāma dharaṇīṃ bāṇo lohit'|ārdra|vara|cchadaḥ.
sa papāta rathāt tūrṇaṃ Bhāradvāja|śar'|āhataḥ
dhanus tyaktvā śarāṃś c' âiva pitur eva samīpataḥ.
hataṃ svam ātma|jaṃ dṛṣṭvā Virāṭaḥ prādravad bhayāt
utsṛjya samare Droṇaṃ, vyātt'|ānanam iv' Ântakam.
82.25 Bhāradvājas tatas tūrṇaṃ Pāṇḍavānāṃ mahā|camūm
dārayām āsa samare śataśo 'tha sahasraśaḥ.

Śikhaṇḍī tu, mahā|rāja, Drauṇim āsādya saṃyuge
ājaghāna bhruvor madhye nārācais tribhir āśu|gaiḥ.
sa babhau ratha|śārdūlo lalāṭe saṃsthitais tribhiḥ
śikharaiḥ kāñcanamayair, Merus tribhir iv' ôcchritaiḥ.
Aśvatthāmā tataḥ kruddho nimeṣ'|ârdhāc Chikhaṇḍinaḥ
dhvajaṃ, sūtam atho, rājaṃs, turagān, āyudhāni ca
śarair bahubhir ācchidya pātayām āsa saṃyuge.
sa hat'|âśvād avaplutya rathād vai rathināṃ varaḥ,
82.30 khaḍgam ādāya su|śitaṃ vimalaṃ ca śar'|āvaram,
śyenavad vyacarat kruddhaḥ Śikhaṇḍī śatru|tāpanaḥ.
sa|khaḍgasya, mahā|rāja, caratas tasya saṃyuge
n' ântaraṃ dadṛśe Drauṇis. tad adbhutam iv' âbhavat.
tataḥ śara|sahasrāṇi bahūni, Bharata'|rṣabha,
preṣayām āsa samare Drauṇiḥ parama|kopanaḥ.
tām āpatantīṃ samare śara|vṛṣṭiṃ su|dāruṇām
asinā tīkṣṇa|dhāreṇa ciccheda balināṃ varaḥ.

stuck in the earth. Hit by Bharad·vaja's son's shaft, Shankha dropped his bow and arrows and fell straight to the ground in his father's presence. Seeing his own son slain, Viráta fled, stricken with terror, leaving Drona who was like Death
with a gaping mouth in battle. Then the son of Bharad·vaja 82.25
shattered one of the Pándavas' large divisions, injuring hundreds and thousands of soldiers.

Meanwhile Shikhándin attacked the son of Drona in the battle, and struck him between the eyebrows with three long and swift-flying arrows, great king. And that tiger-like warrior, with those three long shafts stuck in his forehead, appeared like Mount Meru with its three towering golden peaks. Filled with fury, Your Majesty, with many arrows Ashva·tthaman struck down Shikhándin's banner, chariot driver, horses, and weapons in half the twinkling of an eye. Shikhándin, a superb warrior and the scorcher of his
foes, jumped out of his horseless chariot and, grabbing his 82.30
sharpest sword and his glistening shield, he whirled about in fury, like a hawk. O great king, the son of Drona could not find any weak spots through which to attack Shikhándin who was rampaging, brandishing his sword in the battle. It was like a miracle. Drona's son, filled with immense fury, shot many thousands of arrows at him in that duel, bull of the Bharatas; but Shikhándin, the champion of mighty men, used his sharp-edged sword to check that terrifying downpour of shafts as it fell upon him.

tato 'sya vimalaṃ Drauṇiḥ śata|candraṃ, mano|ramam
carm' âcchinad, asiṃ c' âsya khaṇḍayām āsa saṃyuge;
82.35 śitais tu bahuśo, rājaṃs, taṃ ca vivyādha patribhiḥ.
Śikhaṇḍī tu tataḥ khaḍgaṃ khaṇḍitaṃ tena sāyakaiḥ
āvidhya vyasṛjat tūrṇaṃ jvalantam iva pannagam.
tam āpatantaṃ sahasā kāl'|ânala|sama|prabham
ciccheda samare Drauṇir darśayan pāṇi|lāghavam,
Śikhaṇḍinaṃ ca vivyādha śarair bahubhir āyasaiḥ.
Śikhaṇḍī tu bhṛśaṃ, rājaṃs, tāḍyamānaḥ śitaiḥ śaraiḥ
āruroha rathaṃ tūrṇaṃ Mādhavasya mah"|ātmanaḥ.

Sātyakiś c' âpi saṃkruddho rākṣasaṃ krūram āhave
Alambuṣaṃ śarais tīkṣṇair vivyādha balināṃ varaḥ.
82.40 rākṣas'|êndras tatas tasya dhanuś ciccheda, Bhārata,
ardha|candreṇa samare, taṃ ca vivyādha sāyakaiḥ;
māyāṃ ca rākṣasīṃ kṛtvā śara|varṣair avākirat.

tatr' âdbhutam apaśyāma Śaineyasya parākramam.
a|saṃbhramas tu samare vadhyamānaḥ śitaiḥ śaraiḥ
Aindram astraṃ ca Vārṣṇeyo yojayām āsa, Bhārata,
Vijayād yad anuprāptaṃ Mādhavena yaśasvinā.
tad astraṃ bhasmasāt kṛtvā māyāṃ tāṃ rākṣasīṃ tadā,
Alambuṣaṃ śarair anyair abhyākirata sarvaśaḥ,
parvataṃ vāri|dhārābhiḥ prāvṛṣ' îva balāhakaḥ.
82.45 tat tathā pīḍitaṃ tena Mādhavena yaśasvinā
pradudrāva bhayād rakṣas, tyaktvā Sātyakim āhave.

At length the son of Drona cut through his opponent's
fascinating shield that was adorned with a hundred moons,
crushed his gleaming sword, and wounded him with nu- 82.35
merous feathered arrows, Your Majesty. Shikhándin then
whirled a piece of his sword that had been broken by Drona's
son with his shafts, and hurled it—it looked like a blazing snake. As it speedily flew toward him, looking like the
fire that destroys everything at the end of the age, the son
of Drona cut it down, displaying his dexterity in combat,
and struck Shikhándin with many iron shafts. Shikhándin,
severely wounded with sharp arrows, quickly climbed onto
the chariot of the great-spirited Mádhava, Your Majesty.

Sátyaki, that champion of mighty men, in a fury, pierced
the cruel demon Alámbusha with his whetted shafts in battle. That foremost of demons then split Sátyaki's bow with 82.40
an arrow that had a semicircular head, descendant of Bharata, and struck his enemy in combat with many arrows.
Creating an illusion by means of his demonic power, he
shrouded Sátyaki in torrents of shafts.

Then we witnessed the wonderful prowess of Shini's
grandson. Though he had been wounded with sharp arrows, Bhárata, the descendant of Vrishni did not falter in
that battle; he used Indra's weapon, which the glorious
Mádhava had received from Víjaya. That weapon incinerated the demonic illusion and covered Alámbusha on all
sides with countless arrows, just as a rain-cloud covers a
mountain with torrents of rain during the monsoon. The 82.45
demon, harried by the illustrious Mádhava in this way,
fled in fear, leaving Sátyaki on the battlefield. Having defeated that foremost of demons, who was invincible even

tam a|jeyaṃ rākṣas'|êndraṃ saṃkhye Maghavatā api
Śaineyaḥ prāṇadaj jitvā yodhānāṃ tava paśyatām.
nyahanat tāvakāṃś c' âpi Sātyakiḥ satya|vikramaḥ
niśitair bahubhir bāṇais. te 'dravanta bhay'|ârditāḥ.
etasminn eva kāle tu Drupadasy' ātma|jo balī
Dhṛṣṭadyumno, mahā|rāja, putraṃ tava jan'|ēśvaram
chādayām āsa samare śaraiḥ saṃnata|parvabhiḥ.
sa cchādyamāno viśikhair Dhṛṣṭadyumnena, Bhārata,
82.50 vivyathe na ca, rāj'|êndra, tava putro, jan'|ēśvara.
Dhṛṣṭadyumnaṃ ca samare tūrṇaṃ vivyādha patribhiḥ
ṣaṣṭyā ca triṃśatā c' âiva. tad adbhutam iv' âbhavat.
tasya senā|patiḥ kruddho dhanuś ciccheda, māriṣa,
hayāṃś ca caturaḥ śīghraṃ nijaghāna mahā|balaḥ,
śaraiś c' âinaṃ su|niśitaiḥ kṣipraṃ vivyādha saptabhiḥ.
sa hat'|âśvān mahā|bāhur avaplutya rathād balī
padātir asim udyamya prādravat Pārṣataṃ prati.
Śakunis taṃ samabhyetya rāja|gṛddhī mahā|balaḥ
rājānaṃ sarva|lokasya ratham āropayat svakam.
82.55 tato nṛ|paṃ parājitya Pārṣataḥ para|vīra|hā
nyahanat tāvakaṃ sainyaṃ, vajra|pāṇir iv' âsurān.
Kṛtavarmā raṇe Bhīmaṃ śarair ārcchan mahā|rathaḥ
pracchādayām āsa ca taṃ mahā|megho raviṃ yathā.
tataḥ prahasya samare Bhīmasenaḥ paran|tapaḥ
preṣayām āsa saṃkruddhaḥ sāyakān Kṛtavarmaṇe.
tair ardyamāno 'tirathaḥ Sātvataḥ satya|kovidaḥ
n' âkampata, mahā|rāja, Bhīmaṃ c' ārcchac chitaiḥ śaraiḥ.

by Mághavat in battle, Shini's grandson shouted out loud, while your warriors looked on. Then Sátyaki, whose power is in truth, began to slaughter your troops with numerous whetted arrows. And stricken with terror, they ran away.

In the meantime, great king, Dhrishta·dyumna the powerful son of Drúpada came up against your son, that lord of men, and enveloped him with numerous straight shafts. Bhárata, king of kings and lord of the people, your son,
bombarded by Dhrishta·dyumna with arrows, did not flinch 82.50
in the battle but swiftly hurt Dhrishta·dyumna with feathered arrows, first with sixty and then with thirty. It was like a miracle.

Then the Pándavas' mighty general, filled with anger, severed Duryódhana's bow, felled his four horses in a trice, and quickly wounded the foe with seven well-sharpened shafts. Its horses slain, mighty Duryódhana jumped out of his chariot and rushed on foot toward the grandson of Príshata, sword raised. Shákuni of great strength, wanting to rescue the king, advanced toward him and took that ruler of the entire world onto his chariot.

Príshata's grandson, the destroyer of hostile heroes, hav- 82.55
ing defeated the Kuru king, began to slaughter your troops like the thunderbolt-wielding Indra crushing demons. The great warrior Krita·varman wounded Bhima in battle with many arrows; he shrouded him with shafts, just as a huge mass of clouds envelops the sun. So Bhima·sena the scorcher of his enemies, infuriated and yet laughing, fired numerous arrows at Krita·varman. Suffering on account of them, that superior Sátvata warrior, the knower of the truth, did

tasy' âśvāmś caturo hatvā Bhīmaseno mahā|rathaḥ
sārathiṃ pātayām āsa sa|dhvajaṃ su|pariṣkṛtam.
82.60 śarair bahu|vidhaiś c' âinam ācinot para|vīra|hā,
śakalī|kṛta|sarv'|âṅgo hat'|âśvaḥ pratyadṛśyata.
hat'|âśvaś ca tatas tūrṇam Vṛṣakasya rathaṃ yayau
śyālasya te, mahā|rāja, tava putrasya paśyataḥ.
Bhīmaseno 'pi saṃkruddhas tava sainyam upādravat,
nijaghāna ca saṃkruddho daṇḍa|pāṇir iv' Ântakaḥ.

DHṚTARĀṢṬRA uvāca:

83.1 BAHŪNI HI vicitrāṇi dvairathāni sma, Sañjaya,
Pāṇḍūnāṃ māmakaiḥ sārdham aśrauṣaṃ tava jalpataḥ.
na c' âiva māmakaṃ kaṃ cidd hṛṣṭaṃ śaṃsasi, Sañjaya;
nityaṃ Pāṇḍu|sutān hṛṣṭān a|bhagnān saṃpraśaṃsasi.
jīyamānān, vi|manaso māmakān, vigat'|âujasaḥ
vadase saṃyuge, sūta. diṣṭam etan, na saṃśayaḥ!

SAÑJAYA uvāca:

yathā|śakti, yath"|ôtsāhaṃ yuddhe ceṣṭanti tāvakāḥ
darśayānāḥ paraṃ śaktyā pauruṣaṃ, puruṣa'|rṣabha.
83.5 Gaṅgāyāḥ sura|nadyā vai svādu|bhūtaṃ yath" ôdakam
mah"|ôdadhi|guṇ'|âbhyāsāl lavaṇatvaṃ nigacchati,
tathā tat pauruṣaṃ, rājaṃs, tāvakānāṃ, paran|tapa,
prāpya Pāṇḍu|sutān vīrān vy|arthaṃ bhavati saṃyuge.
ghaṭamānān yathā|śakti, kurvāṇān karma duṣ|karam,

not waver, great king, but hurt Bhima with sharp arrows in return.

The great warrior Bhima·sena killed his enemy's four horses and felled his chariot driver and his well-decorated banner. With arrows of many kinds that crusher of en- 82.60
emy heroes wounded the horseless Krita·varman, whose entire body seemed to be cut to shreds. His horses killed, he quickly climbed onto the chariot of your brother-in-law Vríshaka, great king, in the sight of your son. And wrathful Bhima·sena charged against your troops and began to annihilate them as if he were Death wielding his staff.

DHRITA·RASHTRA said:

I HAVE HEARD you describe many wonderful duels, Sán- 83.1
jaya, fought between the Pándavas and my warriors. But Sánjaya, although you always talk of the sons of Pandu as joyous and never frustrated, you never speak of any of my men being delighted by their duels. And you report, charioteer, that my sons are being defeated and are becoming despondent and devoid of energy in battle. This is fate, no doubt about it!

SÁNJAYA said:

Your warriors, bull-like man, have been striving in combat to the best of their ability and vigor, displaying their
prowess to the utmost. As the water of the divine River 83.5
Ganges, though sweet, becomes salty through contact with the qualities of the ocean, so the prowess of your warriors is in vain when they encounter the heroic sons of Pandu in battle, Your Majesty, scorcher of enemies. O best of the Kurus, you ought not to put the blame on the Káuravas,

na doṣeṇa, Kuru|śreṣṭha, Kauravān gantum arhasi.
tav' âparādhāt su|mahān sa|putrasya, viśāṃ pate,
pṛthivyāḥ prakṣayo ghoro Yama|rāṣṭra|vivardhanaḥ.
ātma|doṣāt samutpannaṃ śocituṃ n' ârhase nṛ|pa.
na hi rakṣanti rājānaḥ sarvath" âtr' âpi jīvitam.
83.10 yuddhe su|kṛtināṃ lokān icchanto vasudh"|âdhipāḥ
camūṃ vigāhya yudhyante nityaṃ svarga|parāyaṇāḥ.

pūrv'|âhṇe tu, mahā|rāja, prāvartata jana|kṣayaḥ.
taṃ tvam eka|manā bhūtvā śṛṇu dev'|âsur'|ôpamam.
Āvantyau tu mah"|êṣv|āsau mahā|senau mahā|balau
Irāvantam abhiprekṣya sameyātāṃ raṇ'|ôtkaṭau.
teṣāṃ pravavṛte yuddhaṃ tumulaṃ, loma|harṣaṇam.
Irāvāṃs tu su|saṃkruddho bhrātarau deva|rūpiṇau
vivyādha niśitais tūrṇaṃ śaraiḥ saṃnata|parvabhiḥ.
tāv enaṃ pratyavidhyetāṃ samare citra|yodhinau.
83.15 yudhyatāṃ hi tathā, rājan, viśeṣo na vyadṛśyata,
yatatāṃ śatru|nāśāya kṛta|pratikṛt'|âiṣiṇām.
Irāvāṃs tu tato, rājann, Anuvindasya sāyakaiḥ
caturbhiś caturo vāhān anayad Yama|sādanam.
bhallābhyāṃ ca su|tīkṣṇābhyāṃ dhanuḥ ketuṃ ca, māriṣa,
ciccheda samare, rājaṃs. tad adbhutam iv' âbhavat.
tyaktv" Ânuvindo 'tha rathaṃ, Vindasya ratham āsthitaḥ
dhanur gṛhītvā navamaṃ bhāra|sādhanam uttamam.

who are struggling to the best of their strength and accom-
plishing feats that are extremely difficult to perform. It is
through your fault and the fault of your son, lord of the
people, that this tremendous and terrible destruction of the
terrestrial world has broken out, increasing the kingdom of
Yama. You should not grieve over that which follows from
your own mistakes, Your Majesty. And in any case, kings
do not at all care to protect their lives in this world; eager 83.10
to attain the realms of the pious in the course of battle, the
rulers of earth, ever intent on winning heaven, fight, penetrating the enemy army.

A great massacre of men took place at the beginning
of that day, great king; it was like the battle between the
gods and the demons. Listen attentively to what happened.
The powerful princes of Avánti, those two mighty archers,
drunk with war, set eyes upon Irávat and charged against
him with their large division. A huge and hair-raising battle
ensued between them. Irávat, enraged, soon wounded the
two brothers of divine appearance with straight and sharpened arrows. And in turn those warriors, skilled in various
forms of battle, shot at Irávat with their shafts in the fight.
As they fought on, Your Majesty, seeking to counter one 83.15
another, either side striving to slay the enemy, it was impossible to distinguish between them. Then Irávat sent Anuvínda's four horses to the realm of Yama with four arrows,
Your Majesty; and with two very sharp, spear-headed shafts
he severed Anuvínda's bow and banner, my lord. It was like
a miracle, Your Majesty. Anuvínda abandoned his vehicle,
climbed onto Vinda's chariot, and seized a superb and peerless bow that was able to bear great strain.

tāv eka|sthau raṇe vīrāv Āvantyau rathināṃ varau
śarān mumucatus tūrṇam Irāvati mah"|ātmani.
83.20 tābhyāṃ muktā mahā|vegāḥ śarāḥ kāñcana|bhūṣaṇāḥ
divā|kara|pathaṃ prāpya cchādayām āsur ambaram.
Irāvāṃs tu tataḥ kruddho bhrātarau tau mahā|rathau
vavarṣa śara|varṣeṇa, sārathiṃ c' âpy apātayat.
tasmin nipatite bhūmau, gata|sattve tu sārathau
rathaḥ pradudrāva diśaḥ samudbhrānta|hayas tataḥ.
tau sa jitvā, mahā|rāja, nāga|rāja|sutā|sutaḥ
pauruṣaṃ khyāpayaṃs tūrṇaṃ vyadhamat tava vāhinīm.
sā vadhyamānā samare Dhārtarāṣṭrī mahā|camūḥ
vegān bahu|vidhāṃś cakre, viṣaṃ pītv" êva mānavaḥ.
83.25 Haiḍimbo rākṣas'|êndras tu Bhagadattaṃ samādravat
rathen' āditya|varṇena sa|dhvajena mahā|balaḥ.
tataḥ Prāgjyotiṣo rājā nāga|rājaṃ samāsthitaḥ,
yathā vajra|dharaḥ pūrvaṃ saṃgrāme Tārakā|maye.
tatra devāḥ sa|gandharvā, ṛṣayaś ca samāgatāḥ
viśeṣaṃ na sma vividur Haiḍimba|Bhagadattayoḥ.
yathā sura|patiḥ Śakras trāsayām āsa dānavān,
tath" âiva samare, rājan, drāvayām āsa Pāṇḍavān.
tena vidrāvyamāṇās te Pāṇḍavāḥ sarvato|diśam
trātāraṃ n' âbhyavindanta sveṣv anīkeṣu, Bhārata.
83.30 Bhaimasenim ratha|sthaṃ tu tatr' âpaśyāma, Bhārata.
śeṣā vi|manaso bhūtvā prādravanta mahā|rathāḥ.
nivṛtteṣu tu Pāṇḍūnāṃ punaḥ sainyeṣu, Bhārata,
āsīn niṣṭānako ghoras tava sainyasya saṃyuge.

Then, standing on the same chariot, the two heroic princes of Avánti, those best of chariot warriors, quickly released their arrows at the great-spirited Irávat in battle. The 83.20
shafts they dispatched were finished with gold, and whizzed with great speed along the path of the sun, obscuring the sky. Irávat in his battle-fury poured a shower of arrows on the two brothers and struck down their chariot driver. As soon as the driver had fallen lifeless to the ground, the chariot was carried off in all directions by the panic-stricken horses. Your Majesty, the son of the serpent king's daughter, having displayed his bravery by vanquishing the two heroes, began to plague your host. Overpowered in combat in this way, your sons' vast army tottered about like a man who has drunk poison.

Hidímba's son, that mighty chief of demons, on his char- 83.25
iot radiant like the sun and furnished with a banner, charged against Bhaga·datta. Riding on his royal elephant, the Prag·jyótisha king looked like thunderbolt-wielding Indra on his heavenly elephant during the battle with the demon Táraka in former times. The gods, *gandhárva*s, and sages gathered there, but they were unable to distinguish between Bhaga·datta and the son of Hidímba. As Shakra, the lord of the gods, made demons tremble with horror, so that king put the Pándavas to flight in that encounter. The Pándavas were being scattered by him in all directions, and they could find
no support within their ranks, descendant of Bharata. We 83.30
saw the son of Bhima·sena standing on his chariot, Bhárata; but the other great warriors lost heart and ran away. But when the Pándavas' troops rallied, a tremendous roar arose among your troops in the battle, descendant of Bharata.

Ghaṭotkacas tato, rājan, Bhagadattaṃ mahā|raṇe
śaraiḥ pracchādayām āsa, Meruṃ girim iv' âmbu|daḥ.
nihatya tāñ śarān rājā rākṣasasya dhanuś|cyutān
Bhaimaseniṃ raṇe tūrṇaṃ sarva|marmasv atāḍayat.
sa tāḍyamāno bahubhiḥ śaraiḥ saṃnata|parvabhiḥ
na vivyathe rākṣas'|êndro bhidyamāna iv' â|calaḥ.
83.35 tasya Prāgjyotiṣaḥ kruddhas tomarān sa catur|daśa
preṣayām āsa samare. tāṃś ciccheda sa rākṣasaḥ.
sa tāṃś chittvā mahā|bāhus tomarān niśitaiḥ śaraiḥ,
Bhagadattaṃ ca vivyādha saptatyā kaṅka|patribhiḥ.
tataḥ Prāgjyotiṣo, rājan, prahasann iva, Bhārata,
tasy' âśvāṃś caturaḥ saṃkhye pātayām āsa sāyakaiḥ.
sa hat'|âśve rathe tiṣṭhan rākṣas'|êndraḥ pratāpavān
śaktiṃ cikṣepa vegena Prāgjyotiṣa|gajaṃ prati.
tām āpatantīṃ sahasā hema|daṇḍāṃ, su|veginīm
tridhā ciccheda nṛ|patiḥ. sā vyakīryata medinīm.
83.40 śaktiṃ vinihatāṃ dṛṣṭvā Haiḍimbaḥ prādravad bhayāt,
yath" Êndrasya raṇāt pūrvaṃ Namucir daitya|sattamaḥ.
taṃ vijitya raṇe śūraṃ vikrāntaṃ, khyāta|pauruṣam,
a|jeyaṃ samare, rājan, Yamena Varuṇena ca,
Pāṇḍavīṃ samare senāṃ sammamarda sa|kuñjaraḥ,
yathā vana|gajo, rājan, mṛdnaṃś carati padminīm.

Then, Your Majesty, Ghatótkacha enveloped Bhaga·datta
with shafts in that fierce encounter, like a rain-cloud pouring showers on Mount Meru. Cutting down those arrows
fired from the demon's bow, the king immediately struck
Bhima·sena's son in all his vital organs; but though he was
wounded by numerous straight shafts, that chief of demons
stood unshaken like a split mountain. Prag·jyótisha, filled 83.35
with anger, hurled fourteen spears at him in the battle, but
the demon cut them all down. After destroying them with
sharpened arrows, mighty-armed Ghatótkacha shot Bhaga·
datta with seventy heron-feathered shafts. Then, with a
smile, the Prag·jyótisha king struck down the demon's four
horses with his arrows in the fight, descendant of Bharata. Standing on his horseless chariot, the mighty chief of
demons hurled a lance at the Prag·jyótisha king's elephant;
but the king split that lance with its golden shaft into three
pieces as it flew toward him with great speed, and the shattered lance fell to the ground. Seeing his lance cut down, 83.40
the son of Hidímba ran away in fright, just as Námuchi the
foremost of demons once fled the battlefield for fear of Indra. In that contest Bhaga·datta had defeated a brave and
vigorous hero renowned for his courage and invincible in
battle even by Yama and Váruna; and now, on his elephant,
he began to crush the Pándava army, Your Majesty, just as
a wild elephant roams around trampling the lotus stalks in
a lake.

Madr'|ēśvaras tu samare yamābhyāṃ samasajjata;
svasrīyau chādayāṃ cakre śar'|âughaiḥ Pāṇḍu|nandanau.
Sahadevas tu samare mātulaṃ dṛśya saṃgatam
avārayac char'|âugheṇa, megho yadvad divā|karam.
83.45 chādyamānaḥ śar'|âugheṇa hṛṣṭarūpataro 'bhavat.
tayoś c' âpy abhavat prītir a|tulā mātṛ|kāraṇāt.
tataḥ prahasya samare Nakulasya mahā|rathaḥ
aśvāñś ca caturo, rājaṃś, caturbhiḥ sāyak'|ôttamaiḥ
preṣayām āsa samare Yamasya sadanaṃ prati.
hat'|âśvāt tu rathāt tūrṇam avaplutya mahā|rathaḥ
āruroha tato yānaṃ bhrātur eva yaśasvinaḥ.
eka|sthau tu raṇe śūrau, dṛḍhe vikṣipya kārmuke,
Madra|rāja|rathaṃ kruddhau chādayām āsatuḥ kṣaṇāt.
sa cchādyamāno bahubhiḥ śaraiḥ saṃnata|parvabhiḥ
83.50 svasrīyābhyāṃ nara|vyāghro n' âkampata, yath" â|calaḥ;
prahasann iva tāṃ c' âpi śara|vṛṣṭiṃ jaghāna ha.
Sahadevas tataḥ kruddhaḥ śaram udgṛhya vīryavān
Madra|rājam abhiprekṣya preṣayām āsa, Bhārata.
sa śaraḥ preṣitas tena, Garuḍ'|ânila iva vegavān,
Madra|rājaṃ vinirbhidya nipapāta mahī|tale.
sa gāḍha|viddho, vyathito rath'|ôpasthe mahā|rathaḥ
niṣasāda, mahā|rāja, kaśmalaṃ ca jagāma ha.
taṃ vi|saṃjñaṃ nipatitaṃ sūtaḥ saṃprekṣya saṃyuge
apovāha rathen' ājau yamābhyām abhipīḍitam.

The king of the Madras began to fight against the twins
Nákula and Saha·deva. He covered his two nephews, the
sons of Pandu, with torrents of shafts. Saha·deva, seeing his
uncle confronting him in battle, veiled him in a swarm of
arrows, like a cloud veiling the sun. Enveloped in a mass 83.45
of arrows, Shalya was thrilled to bits; he became immeasur-
ably pleased for the two of them on their mother's account.
Then, Your Majesty, with four superb arrows the mighty
warrior Shalya sent Nákula's four horses to Yama's lair,
laughing in battle as he did so. Nákula, the great warrior,
quickly jumped out of his horseless chariot and climbed
onto his famous brother's carriage. Standing on the same
chariot in battle, both heroes stretched their strong bows
and started bombarding the Madra king's chariot with
shafts; but though he was shrouded by the numerous
straight arrows his nephews had fired, he stood unshaken 83.50
like a mountain. Then, almost laughing, he checked that
downpour of shafts. So Saha·deva, vigorous and enraged,
seized a shaft and hurled it, Bhárata, aiming at the king of
the Madras. He hurled that shaft with the speed of Gáruda
or the wind; and it cut through the Madra king's body before falling to the ground. Shalya, that mighty warrior, collapsed onto his chariot platform, great king, and passed out.
Seeing that Shalya had been hurt by the twins in the fray
and had fallen unconscious, his driver took the chariot away
from the action.

83.55 dṛṣṭvā Madr'|ēśvara|ratham
Dhārtarāṣṭrāḥ parāṅ|mukham
sarve vi|manaso bhūtvā
«n' êdam ast'» îty acintayan.
nirjitya mātulaṃ saṃkhye Mādrī|putrau mahā|rathau
dadhmatur muditau śaṅkhau, siṃha|nādaṃ ca nedatuḥ.
abhidudruvatur hṛṣṭau tava sainyaṃ viśāṃ pate
yathā daitya|camūṃ, rājann, Indr'|Ôpendrāv iv' â|marau.

SAÑJAYA uvāca:

84.1 TATO YUDHIṢṬHIRO rājā madhyaṃ prāpte divā|kare
Śrutāyuṣam abhiprekṣya codayām āsa vājinaḥ.
abhyadhāvat tato rājā Śrutāyuṣam arin|damam
vinighnan sāyakais tīkṣṇair navabhir nata|parvabhiḥ.
sa saṃvārya raṇe rājā preṣitān Dharma|sūnunā
śarān sapta mah"|êṣv|āsaḥ Kaunteyāya samārpayat.
te tasya kavacaṃ bhittvā papuḥ śoṇitam āhave,
asūn iva vicinvanto dehe tasya mah"|ātmanaḥ.
84.5 Pāṇḍavas tu bhṛśaṃ kruddhas tena rājñā mah"|ātmanā
raṇe varāha|karṇena rājānaṃ hṛdy avidhyata.
ath' âpareṇa bhallena ketuṃ tasya mah"|ātmanaḥ
ratha|śreṣṭho rathāt tūrṇaṃ bhūmau Pārtho nyapātayat.
ketuṃ nipatitaṃ dṛṣṭvā Śrutāyuḥ sa tu pārthivaḥ
Pāṇḍavaṃ viśikhais tīkṣṇai, rājan, vivyādha saptabhiḥ.
tataḥ krodhāt prajajvāla Dharma|putro Yudhiṣṭhiraḥ
yathā yug'|ânte bhūtāni didhakṣur iva pāvakaḥ.
kruddhaṃ tu Pāṇḍavaṃ dṛṣṭvā deva|gandharva|rākṣasāḥ

When they saw the king of the Madras' chariot turn 83.55
back, Dhrita·rashtra's troops thought he was dead, and they
became despondent. And having vanquished their uncle
in battle, the sons of Madri, those great warriors, filled
with joy, blew their conches and shouted a lion-roar. They
charged against your troops in great delight, lord of the people, like the gods Indra and Upéndra charging against the
host of demons.

SÁNJAYA said:

WHEN THE SUN reached the meridian, King Yudhi· 84.1
shthira, seeing Shrutáyus, drove his horses forward and attacked the enemy-tamer, shooting him with nine straight,
sharp arrows. King Shrutáyus, that great archer, thwarted
the arrows sent toward him by the Son of Righteousness,*
and fired seven shafts at Kunti's son. Tearing through his armor as if they were seeking out the breath of life in his body,
they drank the eminent king's blood. And the son of Pandu, 84.5
wounded by his illustrious foe in battle and immensely
irate, shot the king in the heart with an arrow whose tip was
shaped like a boar's ear. With a peerless spear-headed shaft
Pritha's son, that best of warriors, swiftly struck down the
august warrior's banner from his chariot onto the ground.
King Shrutáyus, seeing his banner felled, wounded the son
of Pandu with seven sharp arrows, Your Majesty. Then
Yudhi·shthira the Son of Righteousness blazed up in fury,
like the fire that devours everything at the end of the age.
At the sight of the wrathful Pándava, the gods, *gandhárvas*,
and *rákshasas* trembled, great king, and the whole universe
was thrown into confusion. The thought occurred in the 84.10

pravivyathur, mahā|rāja. vyākulaṃ c' âpy abhūj jagat.
84.10 sarveṣāṃ c' âiva bhūtānām idam āsīn mano|gatam:
«trīl lokān adya saṃkruddho nṛ|po 'yaṃ dhakṣyat'» îti vai.
ṛṣayaś c' âiva devāś ca cakruḥ svasty|ayanaṃ mahat
lokānāṃ, nṛ|pa, śānty|arthaṃ krodhite Pāṇḍave tadā.
sa ca krodha|samāviṣṭaḥ, sṛkkiṇī parilelihan
dadhār' ātma|vapur ghoraṃ yug'|ânt'|āditya|saṃnibham.
tataḥ sarvāṇi sainyāni tāvakāni, viśāṃ pate,
nir|āśāny abhavaṃs tatra jīvitaṃ prati, Bhārata.
sa tu dhairyeṇa taṃ kopaṃ saṃnivārya mahā|yaśāḥ
Śrutāyuṣaḥ praciccheda muṣṭi|deśe mahā|dhanuḥ.
84.15 ath' âinaṃ chinna|dhanvānaṃ nārācena stan'|ântare
nirbibheda raṇe rājā sarva|sainyasya paśyataḥ.
sa|tvaraṃ caraṇe, rājaṃs, tasya vāhān mah"|ātmanaḥ
nijaghāna śaraiḥ kṣipraṃ, sūtaṃ ca su|mahā|balaḥ.
hat'|âśvaṃ tu rathaṃ tyaktvā, dṛṣṭvā rājño 'sya pauruṣam,
vipradudrāva vegena Śrutāyuḥ samare tadā.
tasmiñ jite mah"|êṣv|āse Dharma|putreṇa saṃyuge
Duryodhana|balaṃ, rājan, sarvam āsīt parāṅ|mukham.
etat kṛtvā, mahā|rāja, Dharma|putro Yudhiṣṭhiraḥ
vyātt'|ānano yathā Kālas tava sainyaṃ jaghāna ha.
84.20 Cekitānas tu Vārṣṇeyo Gautamaṃ rathināṃ varam
prekṣatāṃ sarva|sainyānāṃ chādayām āsa sāyakaiḥ.
saṃnivārya śarāṃs tāṃs tu Kṛpaḥ Śāradvato yudhi
Cekitānaṃ raṇe yattaṃ, rājan, vivyādha patribhiḥ.
ath' âpareṇa bhallena dhanuś ciccheda, māriṣa,
sārathiṃ c' âsya samare kṣipra|hasto nyapātayat;
aśvāṃś c' âsy' âvadhīd, rājann, ubhau ca pārṣṇi|sārathī.

mind of every creature: "Today this enraged king will burn down the three worlds!" The son of Pandu was so infuriated that the sages and the gods performed a great benedictory rite for the peace of the worlds, Your Majesty. Filled with anger, and licking the corners of his mouth, the king took on a terrifying appearance and looked like the sun at the end of the age, lord of the people; and all your troops despaired of their lives, descendant of Bharata. But with great fortitude the glorious Pándava mastered his wrath, and he cut
through the large bow of Shrutáyus at the handle. Having 84.15
split his opponent's bow, the king struck him in the center of the chest with an iron arrow while all the troops looked on. Then that enormously strong king quickly killed the august warrior's horses and driver with his arrows in battle. Seeing the king's prowess, Shrutáyus abandoned his horseless chariot, and with great haste he fled from the fight. When that mighty archer was defeated in combat by the Son of Righteousness, Your Majesty, all of Duryódhana's troops turned tail; and having accomplished this feat, great king, Yudhi·shthira the Son of Righteousness began to flay your host like Time with his mouth gaping.

While all the troops were looking on, Chekitána of the 84.20
Vrishnis shrouded Gótama's grandson, that best of chariot warriors, with many arrows. Checking those arrows in that encounter, Kripa the son of Sharádvat wounded Chekitána, who was intent on battle, with feathered shafts, Your Majesty. With a superb spear-headed shaft that agile-handed warrior sliced through Chekitána's bow, my lord, and felled his chariot driver; and then he killed the enemy's horses and outriders, Your Majesty.

so 'vaplutya rathāt tūrṇaṃ gadāṃ jagrāha Sātvataḥ.
sa tayā vīra|ghātinyā gadayā gadināṃ varaḥ
Gautamasya hayān hatvā sārathiṃ ca nyapātayat.
84.25 bhūmi|ṣṭho Gautamas tasya śarāṃś cikṣepa ṣoḍaśa.
śarās te Sātvataṃ bhittvā prāviśan dharaṇī|talam.
Cekitānas tataḥ kruddhaḥ punaś cikṣepa tāṃ gadām
Gautamasya vadh'|ākāṅkṣī, Vṛtrasy' êva Purandaraḥ.
tām āpatantīṃ vimalām, aśma|garbhāṃ mahā|gadām
śarair an|eka|sāhasrair vārayām āsa Gautamaḥ.
Cekitānas tataḥ khaḍgaṃ krodhād uddhṛtya, Bhārata,
lāghavaṃ param āsthāya Gautamaṃ samupādravat.
Gautamo 'pi dhanuṣ tyaktvā pragṛhy' âsiṃ su|saṃyataḥ
vegena mahatā, rājaṃś, Cekitānam upādravat.
84.30 tāv ubhau bala|saṃpannau nistriṃśa|vara|dhāriṇau
nistriṃśābhyāṃ su|tīkṣṇābhyām anyonyaṃ saṃtatakṣatuḥ.
nistriṃśa|veg'|âbhihatau tatas tau puruṣa'|rṣabhau
dharaṇīṃ samanuprāptau sarva|bhūta|niṣevitām
mūrchay" âbhiparīt'|âṅgau, vyāyāmena ca mohitau.
tato 'bhyadhāvad vegena Karakarṣaḥ suhṛttayā,
Cekitānaṃ tathā|bhūtaṃ dṛṣṭvā samara|dur|madam;
ratham āropayac c' âinaṃ sarva|sainyasya paśyataḥ.
tath" âiva Śakuniḥ śūraḥ śyālas tava, viśāṃ pate,
āropayad rathaṃ tūrṇaṃ Gautamaṃ rathināṃ varam.

The Sátvata quickly jumped out of his chariot and grabbed a mace. With that mace that could crush hostile heroes, the best of mace-wielding warriors smote and felled
Gótama's grandson's horses and driver. Standing on the 84.25
ground, the grandson of Gótama fired sixteen arrows at his enemy. Those arrows cut through the Sátvata's body and entered the earth. Then Chekitána, enraged, hurled the mace once again, wanting to slay Gótama's grandson as Indra, the destroyer of strongholds, slew Vritra; but the grandson of Gótama thwarted that huge, gleaming, adamantine mace with several thousand arrows as it flew toward him. Then in his fury Chekitána drew his sword, descendant of Bharata, and with utmost dexterity he charged against Gótama's grandson. The grandson of Gótama also cast aside his bow, seized his sword, and charged against Chekitána
with great force, Your Majesty; and the two mighty war- 84.30
riors, wielding their fine razor-sharp swords, began to lacerate each other with them. After a while those two bull-like men, wounded by the violent blows of their swords, collapsed onto the earth upon which all beings attend. They were dazed by their exertions, their limbs stiff with fatigue. Then Kara·karsha, driven by friendship, proceeded swiftly toward them. Seeing Chekitána in such a state, Kara·karsha, ferocious in battle, lifted him onto his chariot in sight of all the troops. And Shákuni, your valiant brother-in-law, lord of the people, quickly took Gótama's grandson, that best of chariot warriors, onto his chariot.

84.35 Saumadattiṃ tathā kruddho Dhṛṣṭaketur mahā|balaḥ
navatyā sāyakaiḥ kṣipraṃ, rājan, vivyādha vakṣasi.
Saumadattir uraḥ|sthais tair bhṛśaṃ bāṇair aśobhata
madhyan|dine, mahā|rāja, raśmibhis tapano yathā.
Bhūriśravās tu samare Dhṛṣṭaketuṃ mahā|ratham
hata|sūta|hayaṃ cakre vi|rathaṃ sāyak'|ôttamaiḥ.
vi|rathaṃ taṃ samālokya, hat'|âśvaṃ, hata|sārathim
mahatā śara|varṣeṇa cchādayām āsa saṃyuge.
sa ca taṃ ratham utsṛjya Dhṛṣṭaketur mahā|manāḥ
āruroha tato yānaṃ Śatānīkasya, māriṣa.
84.40 Citraseno Vikarṇaś ca, rājan, Durmarṣaṇas tathā
rathino hema|saṃnāhāḥ Saubhadram abhidudruvuḥ.
Abhimanyos tatas tais tu ghoraṃ yuddham avartata
śarīrasya yathā, rājan, vāta|pitta|kaphais tribhiḥ.
vi|rathāṃs tava putrāṃs tu kṛtvā, rājan, mah"|āhave
na jaghāna nara|vyāghraḥ smaran Bhīma|vacas tadā.
tato rājñāṃ bahu|śatair gaj'|âśva|ratha|yāyibhiḥ
saṃvṛtaṃ samare Bhīṣmaṃ devair api dur|āsadam
prayāntaṃ śīghram udvīkṣya, paritrātuṃ sutāṃs tava
Abhimanyuṃ samuddiśya bālam ekaṃ mahā|ratham
84.45 Vāsudevam uvāc' êdaṃ Kaunteyaḥ śveta|vāhanaḥ:

Now powerful Dhrishta·ketu, filled with anger, suddenly struck the son of Soma·datta in the chest with ninety arrows, Your Majesty. And Soma·datta's son looked splendid with those shafts in his chest, great king, like the midday sun with its rays. Bhuri·shravas stripped the great archer Dhrishta·ketu of his chariot by killing his driver and horses with excellent arrows in battle. Seeing his enemy there on the battlefield bereft of his chariot, horses, and driver, Bhuri·shravas enveloped him in a downpour of arrows. Leaving his chariot, proud Dhrishta·ketu climbed onto Shataníka's vehicle, my lord. 84.35

Chitra·sena, Vikárna, and Durmárshana, Your Majesty, riding their chariots and wearing golden armor, attacked the son of Subhádra. A terrible fight ensued between Abhimányu and his opponents; it was like the conflict between the body and its three humors, wind, bile, and phlegm. Abhimányu, that tiger-like man, deprived the enemies of their chariots in that great battle, Your Majesty; but he did not slay them, as he remembered that Bhima had vowed to do so. In order to rescue your sons, Bhishma—who was difficult for even the gods to conquer, and was surrounded in battle by many hundreds of kings riding on elephants, horses, and chariots—quickly advanced toward Abhimányu, who though still a boy was a great warrior fighting alone. Kunti's son Árjuna, the man with the white steeds, watched as Bhishma moved forward, and he said to Vásu·deva: 84.40 84.45

«coday' âśvān, Hṛṣīkeśa, yatr' âite bahulā rathāḥ.
ete hi bahavaḥ śūrāḥ kṛt'|âstrā yuddha|dur|madāḥ
yathā hanyur na naḥ senāṃ, tathā, Mādhava, codaya.»
evam uktaḥ sa Vārṣṇeyaḥ Kaunteyen' â|mit'|âujasā
rathaṃ śveta|hayair yuktaṃ preṣayām āsa saṃyuge.
niṣṭānako mahān āsīt tava sainyasya, māriṣa,
yad Arjuno raṇe kruddhaḥ saṃyātas tāvakān prati.
samāsādya tu Kaunteyo rājñas tān Bhīṣma|rakṣiṇaḥ
Suśarmāṇam atho, rājann, idaṃ vacanam abravīt:
84.50 «jānāmi tvāṃ yudhi śreṣṭham, atyantaṃ pūrva|vairiṇam.
a|nayasy' âdya saṃprāptaṃ phalaṃ paśya su|dāruṇam.
adya te darśayiṣyāmi pūrva|pretān pitā|mahān.»
evaṃ saṃjalpatas tasya Bībhatsoḥ śatru|ghātinaḥ
śrutv" âpi paruṣaṃ vākyaṃ Suśarmā ratha|yūtha|paḥ
na c' âinam abravīt kiṃ cic chubhaṃ vā yadi v" â|śubham.
abhigaty' Ârjunaṃ vīraṃ rājabhir bahubhir vṛtaḥ
purastāt, pṛṣṭhataś c' âiva, pārśvataś c' âiva sarvataḥ
parivāry' Ârjunaṃ saṃkhye tava putrair mahā|rathaḥ
śaraiḥ saṃchādayām āsa, meghair iva divā|karam.
84.55 tataḥ pravṛttaḥ su|mahān saṃgrāmaḥ śoṇit'|ôdakaḥ
tāvakānāṃ ca samare Pāṇḍavānāṃ ca, Bhārata.

SAÑJAYA uvāca:

85.1 SA TUDYAMĀNAS tu śarair Dhanañjayaḥ,
padā hato nāga iva śvasan balī,
bāṇena bāṇena mahā|rathānāṃ
ciccheda cāpāni raṇe prasahya.
saṃchidya cāpāni ca tāni rājñāṃ

"Drive the horses on, Hrishi·kesha, to where those many chariots are. There are so many of those heroes, skilled in weaponry and ferocious in battle. Drive the horses on, Mádhava, so that the enemies might not slaughter our troops!" Addressed in this way by Kunti's boundlessly vigorous son, the descendant of Vrishni drove the chariot and its white steeds into battle. When Árjuna advanced in battle-fury against your host, a loud roar rose among your troops, my lord. Reaching the kings who were protecting Bhishma, the son of Kunti addressed Sushárman with these words, Your Majesty: "I know you as the best in combat and as 84.50
our old and avowed enemy. Now reap the terrible fruit of your evil conduct! Today I will show you your long-dead forefathers!" Hearing the enemy-slayer Bibhátsu utter these harsh words, Sushárman, the commander of a chariot division, said nothing to him in reply, either good or bad. With numerous kings he attacked heroic Árjuna from all sides: from the front, from the rear, and on his flanks. Together with your sons, that great warrior encircled Árjuna in that encounter and enveloped him in arrows, just as clouds envelop the sun. Then a tremendous battle occurred between 84.55
your troops and the Pándavas'; a battle in which blood was shed like water, descendant of Bharata.

SÁNJAYA said:

DHANAN·JAYA, AFFLICTED with arrows, hissing like a 85.1
mighty snake that's been kicked, released shaft after shaft, and in that battle he violently severed the bows of great enemy warriors. Having soon split the bows of those vigorous kings in that encounter, the great-spirited hero, intent

teṣāṃ raṇe vīryavatāṃ kṣaṇena
vivyādha bāṇair yugapan mah"|ātmā
niḥśeṣatāṃ teṣv atha manyamānaḥ.
nipetur ājau rudhira|pradigdhās
te tāḍitāḥ Śakra|sutena, rājan,
vibhinna|gātrāḥ, patit'|ôttam'|âṅgā,
gat'|âsavaś, chinna|tanu|tra|kāyāḥ.
mahīṃ gatāḥ Pārtha|bal'|âbhibhūtā
vicitra|rūpā yugapad vineśuḥ.
dṛṣṭvā hatāṃs tān yudhi rāja|putrāṃs
Trigarta|rājaḥ prayayau rathena.
85.5 teṣāṃ rathānām atha pṛṣṭha|gopā
dvā|triṃśad anye 'bhyapatanta Pārtham.
tath" âiva te saṃparivārya Pārthaṃ,
vikṛṣya cāpāni mahā|ravāṇi,
avīvṛṣan bāṇa|mah"|âugha|vṛṣṭyā
yathā giriṃ toya|dharā jal'|âughaiḥ.
saṃpīḍyamānas tu śar'|âugha|vṛṣṭyā
Dhanañjayas tān yudhi jāta|roṣaḥ
ṣaṣṭyā śaraiḥ saṃyati taila|dhautair
jaghāna tān apy atha pṛṣṭha|gopān.
rathāṃs ca tāṃs tān avajitya saṃkhye
Dhanañjayaḥ prīta|manā yaśasvī
ath' âtvarad Bhīṣma|vadhāya Jiṣṇur,
balāni rājñāṃ samare nihatya.

on their total annihilation, began to shoot all the opponents at once with his arrows. Struck by the son of Shakra* and smeared with blood, they collapsed lifeless on the field of battle, Your Majesty, their limbs lacerated, their heads chopped off, their armor and bodies torn apart. Overpowered by the son of Pritha, they fell to the ground; they looked different, but they all perished together.

Seeing those princes slaughtered in battle, the king of the
Tri·gartas advanced on his chariot; and the thirty-two men 85.5
who had been watching the backs of those slain warriors also pounced on the son of Pritha. Surrounding Pritha's son and stretching their thunderously twanging bows, they showered a downpour of myriads of arrows upon him, just as clouds pour torrents of rain upon a mountain.

Tormented in battle by that heavy rain of shafts, Dhanan·jaya flew into a rage and slaughtered those protectors of the rear with sixty arrows that had been cleansed with oil. On defeating those warriors in the fight, glorious Dhanan·jaya rejoiced in his heart; and having slaughtered those troops in combat, Jishnu sped off to slay Bhishma.

Trigarta|rājo nihatān samīkṣya
mah"|ātmanā tān atha bandhu|vargān,
raṇe puras|kṛtya nar'|âdhipāṃs tāñ
jagāma Pārthaṃ tvarito vadhāya.
abhidrutaṃ c' âstra|bhṛtāṃ variṣṭhaṃ
Dhanañjayaṃ vīkṣya Śikhaṇḍi|mukhyāḥ
85.10 abhyudyayus te śita|śastra|hastā
rirakṣiṣanto ratham Arjunasya.
Pārtho 'pi tān āpatataḥ samīkṣya
Trigarta|rājñā sahitān nṛ|vīrān,
vidhvaṃsayitvā samare dhanuṣmān
Gāṇḍīva|muktair niśitaiḥ pṛṣatkaiḥ,
Bhīṣmaṃ yiyāsur yudhi saṃdadarśa,
Duryodhanaṃ Saindhav'|ādīṃś ca rājñaḥ.
saṃvārayiṣṇūn abhivārayitvā,
muhūrtam āyodhya balena vīraḥ,
utsṛjya rājānam an|anta|vīryo,
Jayadrath'|ādīṃś ca nṛ|pān mah"|âujāḥ,
yayau tato bhīma|balo manasvī
Gāṅgeyam ājau śara|cāpa|pāṇiḥ.
Yudhiṣṭhiraś c' ôgra|balo mah"|ātmā
samāyayau tvarito jāta|kopaḥ,
Madr'|âdhipaṃ samabhityajya saṃkhye,
sva|bhāgam āptaṃ tam an|anta|kīrtiḥ,
sārdhaṃ sa Mādrī|suta|Bhīmasenair
Bhīṣmaṃ yayau Śāntanavaṃ raṇāya.

But at the sight of his many royal friends struck down by their great-spirited opponent, the king of the Tri·gartas placed other kings before him and quickly rushed to exterminate Árjuna. Seeing Dhanan·jaya, the champion bearer of missiles, under attack, mighty warriors led by Shikhándin advanced with sharp weapons in their hands, eager to 85.10
protect Árjuna's chariot.

But Pritha's son, armed with his bow, seeing the heroic men and the king of the Tri·gartas on the attack, smote them down with sharpened arrows released from the Gandíva bow. Wanting to confront Bhishma in battle, he saw Duryódhana and a group of kings led by the ruler of the Sindhus. Fighting with great force for just a moment, heroic Árjuna, endowed with limitless prowess and immense vigor, held off Jayad·ratha and the other kings who were trying to hold him back, and leaving them behind he advanced forward, full of violent strength and great wisdom, with a bow and arrows in his hands, toward the son of Ganga in the fray. And powerful Yudhi·shthira of great spirit and boundless glory, inflamed with anger, left behind the king of the Madras who had been allotted as his share, and together with Madri's sons and Bhima·sena he swiftly proceeded toward Bhishma the son of Shántanu for the fight.

85.15 taiḥ saṃprayuktaiḥ sa mahā|rath'|âgryair
Gaṅgā|sutaḥ samare citra|yodhī
na vivyathe Śāntanavo mah"|ātmā
samāgataiḥ Pāṇḍu|sutaiḥ samastaiḥ.
ath' âitya rājā yudhi satya|sandho
Jayadratho 'tyugra|balo, manasvī,
ciccheda cāpāni mahā|rathānāṃ
prasahya teṣāṃ dhanuṣā vareṇa.
Yudhiṣṭhiraṃ, Bhīmasenaṃ, yamau ca,
Pārthaṃ, Kṛṣṇaṃ yudhi saṃjāta|kopaḥ
Duryodhanaḥ krodha|viṣo mah"|ātmā
jaghāna bāṇair anala|prakāśaiḥ.
Kṛpeṇa, Śalyena, Śalena c' âiva,
tathā, vibho, Citrasenena c' ājau
viddhāḥ śarais te 'tivivṛddha|kopair,
devā yathā daitya|gaṇaiḥ sametaiḥ.
chinn'|āyudhaṃ Śāntanavena rājā
Śikhaṇḍinaṃ prekṣya ca jāta|kopaḥ
Ajātaśatruḥ samare mah"|ātmā
Śikhaṇḍinaṃ kruddha uvāca vākyam:
85.20 «uktvā tathā tvaṃ pitur agrato mām:
‹ahaṃ haniṣyāmi mahā|vrataṃ tam
Bhīṣmaṃ śar'|âughair vimal'|ârka|varṇaiḥ.
satyaṃ vadām'!› îti kṛtā pratijñā
tvayā; na c' âināṃ sa|phalāṃ karoṣi,
Devavrataṃ yan na nihaṃsi yuddhe.
mithyā|pratijño bhava m" âtra, vīra;
rakṣa sva|dharmaṃ sva|kulaṃ yaśaś ca.

The great-spirited son of Ganga and Shántanu, skilled in various forms of battle, did not waver, although he was besieged in that encounter by all the sons of Pandu together with other mighty warriors. Then the wise and extremely powerful King Jayad·ratha, true to his word, violently cut through those great warriors' bows with his own fine bow. Great-spirited Duryódhana, excited with battle-fury and filled with the poison of his anger, struck Yudhi·shthira, Bhima·sena, the twins Nákula and Saha·deva, Pritha's son Árjuna, and Krishna with arrows that gleamed like fire. Wounded by arrows shot by Kripa, Shalya, Shala, and Chitra·sena in that engagement, my lord, the Pándavas were utterly outraged, like the gods afflicted by the united hosts of demons. 85.15

Seeing Shikhándin with his bow split by the son of Shántanu, the great-spirited King Ajáta·shatru, filled with wrath,
spoke to him angrily in the battle: "In your father's pres- 85.20
ence you made a promise by saying these words to me: 'I will slaughter that Bhishma of great vows with hordes of arrows radiant like the sun! I am telling you the truth!' You will not fulfill this promise until you slaughter Deva·vrata in battle. Do not be a man of false promises, hero. Protect your virtue, your family's honor, and your reputation.

prekṣasva Bhīṣmaṃ yudhi bhīma|vegaṃ
sarvāṃs tapantaṃ mama sainya|saṅghān
śar'|âugha|jālair ati|tigma|vegaiḥ,
Kālaṃ yathā Kāla|kṛtaṃ kṣaṇena.
nikṛtta|cāpaḥ samare 'n|apekṣaḥ,
parājitaḥ Śāntanavena c' ājau,
vihāya bandhūn atha s'|ôdarāṃś ca
kva yāsyase? n' ânurūpaṃ tav' êdam.
dṛṣṭvā hi Bhīṣmaṃ tam an|anta|vīryaṃ,
bhagnaṃ ca sainyaṃ dravamāṇam evam,
bhīto 'si nūnaṃ, Drupadasya putra;
tathā hi te mukha|varṇo '|prahṛṣṭaḥ.
85.25 a|jñāyamāne ca Dhanañjaye 'pi
mah|āhave saṃprasakte, nṛ|vīra,
kathaṃ hi Bhīṣmāt prathitaḥ pṛthivyāṃ
bhayaṃ tvam adya prakaroṣi, vīra?»
sa Dharma|rājasya vaco niśamya
rūkṣ'|âkṣaraṃ vipralāp'|ânubaddham,
pratyādeśaṃ manyamāno mah"|ātmā
pratatvare Bhīṣma|vadhāya, rājan.
tam āpatantaṃ mahatā javena
Śikhaṇḍinaṃ Bhīṣmam abhidravantam
āvārayām āsa hi Śalya enaṃ
śastreṇa ghoreṇa su|durjayena.

Look at Bhishma vehemently scorching all the divisions of my troops with hordes of utterly fierce, violent arrows, just as Death, prompted by Time, wipes beings out in an instant. Where are you going with your bow split, indifferent in combat and defeated by the son of Shántanu, abandoning your friends and brothers? This is unseemly of you. Now you have seen Bhishma of limitless vigor, and our army routed and fleeing, you have got frightened, son of
Drúpada, and your expression is downcast. While Dhanan- 85.25
jaya, that heroic man, is engaged in a great battle of which you are unaware, how is it that you, world-famous hero, are afraid of Bhishma?"

Hearing these harsh-sounding and yet reasonable words of the King of Righteousness, and regarding them as a command, the great-spirited warrior sped to slaughter Bhishma, Your Majesty. But as Shikhándin was advancing with great speed, charging against Bhishma, Shalya checked him with a fearful weapon that was extremely difficult to foil.

sa c' âpi dṛṣṭvā samudīryamāṇam
astraṃ yug'|ânt'|âgni|sama|prakāśam,
na saṃmumoha Drupadasya putro,
rājan, mah"|Êndra|pratima|prabhāvaḥ.
tasthau ca tatr' âiva mahā|dhanuṣmāñ
śarais tad astraṃ pratibādhamānaḥ.
ath' ādade Vāruṇam anyad astraṃ
Śikhaṇḍy ath' ôgraṃ pratighātāy' âsya.
85.30 tad astram astreṇa vidāryamāṇaṃ
kha|sthāḥ surā dadṛśuḥ pārthivāś ca.
Bhīṣmas tu, rājan, samare mah"|ātmā,
dhanuś ca citraṃ, dhvajam eva c' âpi
chittv" ânadat Pāṇḍu|sutasya vīro
Yudhiṣṭhirasy' Âjamīḍhasya rājñaḥ.
tataḥ samutsṛjya dhanuḥ sa|bāṇaṃ,
Yudhiṣṭhiraṃ vīkṣya bhay'|âbhibhūtam,
gadāṃ pragṛhy' âbhipapāta saṃkhye
Jayadrathaṃ Bhīmasenaḥ padātiḥ.
tam āpatantaṃ sahasā javena
Jayadrathaḥ sa|gadaṃ Bhīmasenam
vivyādha ghorair Yama|daṇḍa|kalpaiḥ
śitaiḥ śaraiḥ pañca|śataiḥ samantāt.
a|cintayitvā sa śarāṃs tarasvī,
Vṛkodaraḥ krodha|parīta|cetāḥ
jaghāna vāhān samare samastān
pārāvatān Sindhu|rājasya saṃkhye.
tato 'bhivīkṣy' â|pratima|prabhāvas
tav' ātma|jas tvaramāṇo rathena,
85.35 abhyāyayau Bhīmasenaṃ nihantuṃ
samudyat'|âstraḥ sura|rāja|kalpaḥ.

Seeing the discharged weapon that glowed like the fire that appears at the end of an age, Drúpada's son, whose courage was like that of great Indra, was not bewildered, Your Majesty. The mighty bowman stood firm, thwarting that weapon with his shafts. Then Shikhándin took up another weapon—Váruna's terrible weapon—that was capable of warding Shalya's off. The gods in heaven and the 85.30
kings on earth watched as Shalya's weapon was crushed by Váruna's.

Then, Your Majesty, in that fight the great-spirited and valiant Bhishma severed the bow and the variegated banner of Pandu's son King Yudhi·shthira the descendant of Aja·midha, and let out a roar.

Bhima·sena looked over at the fear-stricken Yudhi·shthira, cast aside his bow and arrows, grabbed a mace, and charged on foot against Jayad·ratha in battle. Seeing Bhima·sena suddenly advancing toward him with great speed, brandishing his mace, Jayad·ratha struck him all over with five hundred sharp and frightful arrows, each one resembling Yama's staff. Heedless of the arrows, Vrikódara, his mind overwhelmed with rage, killed all of the Sindhu king's dove-colored horses.

Then your son Chitra·sena—endowed with unmatched
bravery, riding his chariot at great speed, brandishing his 85.35
weapons, and looking like the lord of the gods—charged against Bhima·sena in order to slay him. And Bhima also, with a loud roar, rose powerfully against your son, threat-

Bhīmo 'py ath' âinaṃ sahasā vinadya
pratyudyayau gadayā tarjayānaḥ.
samudyatāṃ tāṃ Yama|daṇḍa|kalpāṃ
dṛṣṭvā gadāṃ te Kuravaḥ samantāt,
vihāya sarve tava putram ugraṃ
pātaṃ gadāyāḥ parihartu|kāmāḥ,
apakrāntās tumule saṃpramarde
su|dāruṇe, Bhārata, mohanīye.
a|mūḍha|cetās tv atha Citraseno
mahā|gadām āpatantīṃ nirīkṣya,
rathaṃ samutsṛjya padātir ājau
pragṛhya khaḍgaṃ, vimalaṃ ca carma,
avaplutaḥ siṃha iv' â|cal'|âgrāj
jagāma c' ânyaṃ bhuvi bhūmi|deśam.
gad" âpi sā prāpya rathaṃ su|citraṃ,
s'|âśvaṃ sa|sūtaṃ vinihatya saṃkhye,
jagāma bhūmiṃ jvalitā mah"|ôlkā
bhraṣṭ" âmbarād gām iva saṃpatantī.
85.40 āścarya|bhūtaṃ su|mahat tvadīyā
dṛṣṭv" âiva tad, Bhārata, saṃprahṛṣṭāḥ
sarve vineduḥ sahitāḥ samantāt;
pupūjire tava putrasya śauryam.

SAÑJAYA uvāca:

86.1 VI|RATHAṂ TAṂ samāsādya Citrasenaṃ yaśasvinam,
ratham āropayām āsa Vikarṇas tanayas tava.
tasmiṃs tathā vartamāne tumule saṃkule bhṛśam
Bhīṣmaḥ Śāntanavas tūrṇaṃ Yudhiṣṭhiram upādravat.
tataḥ sa|ratha|nāg'|âśvāḥ samakampanta Sṛñjayāḥ,
Mṛtyor āsyam anuprāptaṃ menire ca Yudhiṣṭhiram.
Yudhiṣṭhiro 'pi Kauravyo yamābhyāṃ sahitaḥ prabhuḥ

ening him with a mace. Seeing that upraised mace which resembled Yama's staff, all the Kurus, wishing to avoid the mace's fall, forsook your fierce son and retreated. In that tumultuous, terrifying, bewildering clash, Bhárata, Chitra·sena kept his wits about him as he saw that huge mace flying toward him. Seizing a sword and a large shield, he jumped out of his chariot and left it behind like a lion jumping down from the top of a rock, and he proceeded on foot across the battlefield to another spot, Your Majesty.

In the meantime the mace reached that splendid chariot and crushed it along with its horses and driver in the battle, and it fell to the ground like a huge blazing meteor
dropping down from the sky onto the earth. Your troops 85.40
were delighted at the sight of that wondrous feat, descendant of Bharata, and together they all praised your son for his bravery.

SÁNJAYA said:

YOUR SON VIKÁRNA recovered the illustrious Chitra·sena, 86.1
who had been stripped of his chariot, and took him onto his vehicle. While that tumultuous and chaotic battle was raging, Bhishma the son of Shántanu speedily charged against Yudhi·shthira. The Sríñjayas, with their chariots, elephants, and horses, shuddered: they considered Yudhi·shthira to be in the jaws of Death. But lord Yudhi·shthira, the descendant of Kuru, accompanied by the twins Nákula and Saha·

mah"|êṣv|āsaṃ nara|vyāghraṃ Bhīṣmaṃ Śāntanavaṃ yayau.
86.5 tataḥ śara|sahasrāṇi pramuñcan Pāṇḍavo yudhi
Bhīṣmaṃ saṃchādayām āsa, yathā megho divā|karam.
tena samyak praṇītāni śara|jālāni, māriṣa,
patijagrāha Gāṅgeyaḥ śataśo 'tha sahasraśaḥ.
tath" âiva śara|jālāni Bhīṣmeṇ' âstāni, māriṣa,
ākāśe samadṛśyanta kha|gamānāṃ vrajā iva.
nimeṣ'|ârdhena Kaunteyaṃ Bhīṣmaḥ Śāntanavo yudhi
a|dṛśyaṃ samare cakre śara|jālena bhāgaśaḥ.
tato Yudhiṣṭhiro rājā Kauravyasya mah"|ātmanaḥ
nārācaṃ preṣayām āsa kruddha āśīviṣ'|ôpamam.
86.10 a|samprāptaṃ tatas taṃ tu kṣurapreṇa mahā|rathaḥ
ciccheda samare, rājan, Bhīṣmas tasya dhanuś|cyutam.
taṃ tu cchittvā raṇe Bhīṣmo nārācaṃ Kāla|saṃmitam
nijaghne Kaurav'|êndrasya hayān kāñcana|bhūṣaṇān.
hat'|âśvaṃ tu rathaṃ tyaktvā Dharma|putro Yudhiṣṭhiraḥ
āruroha rathaṃ tūrṇaṃ Nakulasya mah"|ātmanaḥ.
yamāv api su|saṃkruddhaḥ samāsādya raṇe tadā
śaraiḥ saṃchādayām āsa Bhīṣmaḥ para|purañ|jayaḥ.
tau tu dṛṣṭvā mahā|rājo Bhīṣma|bāṇa|prapīḍitau
jagām' âtha parāṃ cintāṃ Bhīṣmasya vadha|kāṅkṣayā.
86.15 tato Yudhiṣṭhiro vaśyān rājñas tān samacodayat:
«Bhīṣmaṃ Śāntanavaṃ sarve nihat'!» êti suhṛd|gaṇān.
tatas te pārthivāḥ sarve śrutvā Pārthasya bhāṣitam
mahatā ratha|vaṃśena parivavruḥ pitā|maham.

deva, confronted the tiger-like Bhishma, the mighty archer son of Shántanu. The son of Pandu, firing thousands of arrows, enveloped Bhishma in shafts in that encounter, just as a cloud covers the sun. But the son of Ganga duly thwarted his opponent's myriads of arrows with hundreds and thousands of his own, my lord. 86.5

Then hordes of Bhishma's fired arrows appeared in the air, my lord, like flocks of birds; in half the twinkling of an eye Bhishma the son of Shántanu spun a web of arrows, and piece by piece he turned Kunti's son invisible on the battlefield. King Yudhi·shthira then fired an iron shaft like an irate venomous snake at the great-spirited grandfather of the Kurus. But as soon as it had been released from the 86.10 enemy's bow, and before it reached him, that mighty warrior Bhishma severed it, Your Majesty, with a razor-edged arrow. And when he had severed that Death-like iron shaft, Bhishma felled the horses of the Káurava king, which were decorated with gold. Leaving his horseless vehicle, Yudhi·shthira the Son of Righteousness swiftly climbed onto the chariot of great-spirited Nákula.

Then Bhishma, the conqueror of hostile strongholds, filled with anger, confronted the twins in battle and shrouded them with arrows. Seeing the twins tormented by Bhishma's arrows, the great king, who strove for Bhishma's death, was filled with deep anxiety. Yudhi·shthira roused 86.15 the friends and kings under his command: "All of you together, kill Bhishma!" And hearing the Partha's words, all the kings encircled the grandfather with a huge host of chariots. Surrounded by them, your father Deva·vrata began to play with his bow, Your Majesty, striking down many great

sa samantāt parivṛtaḥ pitā Devavratas tava
cikrīḍa dhanuṣā, rājan, pātayāno mahā|rathān.
taṃ carantaṃ raṇe Pārthā dadṛśuḥ Kauravaṃ yudhi,
mṛga|madhyaṃ praviśy' êva yathā siṃha|śiśuṃ vane.
tarjayānaṃ raṇe vīrāṃs, trāsayānaṃ ca sāyakaiḥ,
dṛṣṭvā tresur, mahā|rāja, siṃhaṃ mṛga|gaṇā iva.
86.20 raṇe Bharata|siṃhasya dadṛśuḥ kṣatriyā gatim,
agner vāyu|sahāyasya yathā kakṣaṃ didhakṣataḥ.
śirāṃsi rathināṃ Bhīṣmaḥ pātayām āsa saṃyuge,
tālebhya iva pakvāni phalāni kuśalo naraḥ.
patadbhiś ca, mahā|rāja, śirobhir dharaṇī|tale
babhūva tumulaḥ śabdaḥ patatām aśmanām iva.

tasmin su|tumule yuddhe vartamāne bhayānake
sarveṣām eva sainyānām āsīd vyatikaro mahān.
bhinneṣu teṣu vyūheṣu kṣatriyā itar'|êtaram
ekam ekaṃ samāhūya yuddhāy' âiv' âvatasthire.
86.25 Śikhaṇḍī tu samāsādya Bharatānāṃ pitā|maham
abhidudrāva vegena, «tiṣṭha! tiṣṭh'!» êti c' âbravīt.
an|ādṛtya tato Bhīṣmas
tam Śikhaṇḍinam āhave
prayayau Sṛñjayān kruddhaḥ,
strītvaṃ cintya Shikhaṇḍinaḥ.
Sṛñjayās tu tato hṛṣṭā dṛṣṭvā Bhīṣmaṃ mahā|raṇe
siṃha|nādān bahu|vidhāṃś cakruḥ śaṅkha|vimiśritān.
tataḥ pravavṛte yuddhaṃ vyatiṣakta|ratha|dvipam
paścimāṃ diśam āsthāya sthite savitari, prabho.

warriors. The sons of Pritha saw the Kuru grandfather rampaging on the battlefield like a young lion in the forest amid a herd of deer. The kings were horrified when they saw him threatening and terrifying the Pándava heroes with his arrows in combat, great king, just as herds of deer are frightened at the sight of a lion. The warriors watched the move- 86.20
ments of that lion of the Bharatas: they were like those of a fire that's just about to burn a heap of dry grass with the help of the wind. In that clash Bhishma chopped off the heads of chariot warriors like a skillful man making ripe coconuts fall from palm trees. The thud of heads falling to the ground made a racket like stones dropping from the sky, great king.

As that terrible and tumultuous battle raged, all the troops lost their positions completely. When the formations were broken, warriors confronted one another, summoning each other for the fight. Shikhándin reached the 86.25
grandfather of the Bharatas and quickly attacked him, shouting: "Stay still! Stay still!" But Bhishma, bearing in mind Shikhándin's female nature and so eschewing him in combat, charged against the Srínjayas. And the Srínjayas, seeing Bhishma cheerful in that great battle, shouted out various lion-roars mixed in with the blare of conches. Then, lord, when the sun was heading into the west, a fierce clash occurred, with elephants becoming enmeshed with chariots.

Dhṛṣṭadyumno 'tha Pāñcālyaḥ Sātyakiś ca mahā|rathaḥ
pīḍayantau bhṛśaṃ sainyaṃ śakti|tomara|vṛṣṭibhiḥ,
86.30 śastraiś ca bahubhī, rājañ, jaghnatus tāvakān raṇe.
te hanyamānāḥ samare tāvakāḥ, puruṣa'|rṣabha,
āryāṃ yuddhe matiṃ kṛtvā na tyajanti sma saṃyugam.
yath"|ôtsāhaṃ ca samare nijaghnus tāvakā raṇe.
tatr' ākrando mahān āsīt tāvakānāṃ mah"|ātmanām
vadhyatāṃ samare, rājan, Pārṣatena mah"|ātmanā.

taṃ śrutvā ninadaṃ ghoraṃ tāvakānāṃ mahā|rathau
Vind'|Ânuvindāv Āvantyau Pārṣataṃ pratyupasthitau.
tau tasya turagān hatvā tvaramāṇau mahā|rathau
chādayām āsatur ubhau śara|varṣeṇa Pārṣatam.
86.35 avapluty' âtha Pāñcālyo rathāt tūrṇaṃ mahā|balaḥ
āruroha rathaṃ tūrṇaṃ Sātyakes tu mah"|ātmanaḥ.
tato Yudhiṣṭhiro rājā mahatyā senayā vṛtaḥ
Āvantyau samare kruddhāv abhyayāt sa paran|tapau.
tath" âiva tava putro 'pi sarv'|ôdyogena, māriṣa,
Vind'|Ânuvindau samare parivāry' ôpatasthivān.

Arjunaś c' âpi saṃkruddhaḥ kṣatriyān, kṣatriya'|rṣabha,
ayodhayata saṃgrāme, vajra|pāṇir iv' âsurān.
Droṇas tu samare kruddhaḥ putrasya priya|kṛt tava
vyadhamat sarva|Pāñcālāṃs, tūla|rāśim iv' ânalaḥ.
86.40 Duryodhana|puro|gās tu putrās tava, viśāṃ pate,
parivārya raṇe Bhīṣmaṃ yuyudhuḥ Pāṇḍavaiḥ saha.
tato Duryodhano rājā lohitāyati bhāskare

The mighty warrior Sátyaki and Dhrishta·dyumna the prince of the Panchálas, greatly plaguing your host with torrents of lances and spears, began to slaughter your troops 86.30
with many weapons in battle, Your Majesty. Though they were being struck down in combat, bull of the Bharatas, your warriors took an honorable decision not to flee from the encounter. And your troops began to pound the foe, fighting with utmost vigor. A loud howl of distress rose among your great-spirited fighters: they were taking punishment from the highly glorious grandson of Príshata in battle.

On hearing your troops' desperate cry, the two mighty warriors of Avánti, Vinda and Anuvínda, rose up against Príshata's grandson. Killing his horses, the two great warriors swiftly enveloped the grandson of Príshata with a downpour of shafts. The powerful prince of the Panchálas 86.35
immediately jumped out of his chariot and had soon climbed onto the vehicle of the great-spirited Sátyaki. Then King Yudhi·shthira, surrounded by a large division, assailed those two furious enemy-scorchers of Avánti in battle. Your son, my lord, surrounded Vinda and Anuvínda and took them on with all his might.

Árjuna, that bull-like warrior, enraged, battled against many warriors, just as thunderbolt-wielding Indra fought against many demons. And Drona, filled with battle-fury, acting to please your son, began to wipe out all the Panchálas like a fire burning down a heap of cotton. Your sons, lord 86.40
of the people, led by Duryódhana, surrounded Bhishma in

abravīt tāvakān sarvāṃs: «tvaradhvam!» iti, Bhārata.
yudhyatāṃ tu tathā teṣāṃ, kurvatāṃ karma duṣ|karam,
astaṃ girim ath' ārūḍhe a|prakāśati bhāskare
prāvartata nadī ghorā śoṇit'|âugha|taraṅgiṇī,
gomāyu|gaṇa|saṃkīrṇā kṣaṇena kṣaṇadā|mukhe.
śivābhir a|śivābhiś ca ruvadbhir bhairavaṃ ravam
ghoram āyodhanaṃ jajñe bhūta|saṅghaiḥ samākulam.
86.45 rākṣasāś ca piśācāś ca tath" ânye piśit'|âśanāḥ
samantato vyadṛśyanta śataśo 'tha sahasraśaḥ.

Arjuno 'tha Suśarm'|ādīn rājñas tān sa|pad'|ânugān
vijitya pṛtanā|madhye yayau sva|śibiraṃ prati.
Yudhiṣṭhiro 'pi Kauravyo bhrātṛbhyāṃ sahitas tathā
yayau sva|śibiraṃ rājā niśāyāṃ senayā vṛtaḥ.
Bhīmaseno 'pi, rāj'|êndra, Duryodhana|mukhān rathān
avajitya tataḥ saṃkhye yayau sva|śibiraṃ prati.
Duryodhano 'pi nṛ|patiḥ parivārya mahā|raṇe
Bhīṣmaṃ Śāntanavaṃ tūrṇaṃ prayātaḥ śibiraṃ prati.
86.50 Droṇo, Drauṇiḥ, Kṛpaḥ, Śalyaḥ, Kṛtavarmā ca Sātvataḥ
parivārya camūṃ sarvāṃ prayayuḥ śibiraṃ prati.
tath" âiva Sātyakī, rājan, Dhṛṣṭadyumnaś ca Pārṣataḥ
parivārya raṇe yodhān yayatuḥ śibiraṃ prati.
evam ete, mahā|rāja, tāvakāḥ Pāṇḍavaiḥ saha
paryavartanta sahitā niśā|kāle, paran|tapa.

the battle, and fought against the Pándavas. Then, descendant of Bharata, when the sun was growing red, King Duryódhana said to all your troops: "Hurry up!" While they battled on, performing difficult feats, the sun reached the western mountain and disappeared from view. As nightfall came on, a frightful river soon began to flow through the battlefield; it had blood for its currents and waves, and it teemed with hordes of jackals. The field of play was a terrible sight, haunted by throngs of ghosts and swarming
with ominous jackals giving out fierce howls. Hundreds and 86.45
thousands of *rákshasas*, *pisháchas*, and other carrion-eating creatures came into view from all sides.

Árjuna, having defeated the kings led by Sushárman along with their followers, proceeded through the ranks toward the camp. Yudhi·shthira, the descendant of Kuru, accompanied by his brothers and surrounded by the troops, also retired to his encampment for the night. Bhima·sena too, after conquering the mighty warriors led by Duryódhana in battle, went to the camp, king of kings. And King Duryódhana, having protected Bhishma the son of Shántanu in that great war, swiftly advanced toward his encampment. Drona, his son, Kripa, Shalya, and the Sátvata 86.50
warrior Krita·varman also proceeded to their tents. Sátyaki and Príshata's grandson Dhrishta·dyumna, Your Majesty, secured their battle-troops and went to their tents as well. Thus, great king, your troops and the Pándavas returned to their encampments at night.

tataḥ sva|śibiraṃ gatvā Pāṇḍavāḥ Kuravas tathā
nyavasanta, mahā|rāja, pūjayantaḥ paras|param.
rakṣāṃ kṛtvā tataḥ śūrā, nyasya gulmān yathā|vidhi,
apanīya ca śalyāṃs te, snātvā ca vividhair jalaiḥ,
86.55 kṛta|svasty|ayanāḥ sarve, saṃstūyantaś ca vandibhiḥ,
gīta|vāditra|śabdena vyakrīḍanta yaśasvinaḥ.
muhūrtam iva tat sarvam abhavat svarga|saṃnibham.
na hi yuddha|kathāṃ kāṃ cit tatr' âkurvan mahā|rathāḥ.
te prasupte bale tatra pariśrānta|jane, nṛ|pa,
hasty|aśva|bahule rātrau prekṣaṇīye babhūvatuḥ.

The Pándavas and the Kurus praised each other, and entered their camps to rest. Those glorious heroes duly posted 86.55
guards to protect their troops, and then they all extracted the arrows from their bodies, bathed in water of various kinds, performed the benedictory rites, and, extolled by the bards, amused themselves with vocal and instrumental music. For a while the whole scene resembled paradise, and the great warriors did not talk about the battle. Both armies, with their numerous elephants, horses, and exhausted men, asleep there at night, Your Majesty, were lovely to behold.

87–96
DAY EIGHT

SAÑJAYA uvāca:

87.1 PARIṆĀMYA NIŚĀṂ tāṃ tu sukhaṃ suptā jan'|ēśvarāḥ
Kuravaḥ Pāṇḍavāś c' âiva punar yuddhāya niryayuḥ.
tataḥ śabdo mahān āsīt senayor ubhayor, nṛ|pa,
nirgacchamānayoḥ saṃkhye sāgara|pratimo mahān.
tato Duryodhano rājā, Citraseno, Viviṃśatiḥ,
Bhīṣmaś ca rathināṃ śreṣṭho, Bhāradvājaś ca vai, nṛ|pa,
ekī|bhūtāḥ, su|saṃyattāḥ Kauravāṇāṃ mahā|camūm
vyūhāya vidadhū, rājan, Pāṇḍavān prati daṃśitāḥ.
87.5 Bhīṣmaḥ kṛtvā mahā|vyūhaṃ pitā tava, viśāṃ pate,
sāgara|pratimaṃ, ghoraṃ, vāhan'|ōrmi|taraṅgiṇam,
agrataḥ sarva|sainyānāṃ Bhīṣmaḥ Śāntanavo yayau
Mālavair, Dākṣiṇātyaiś ca Āvantyaiś ca samanvitaḥ.
tato 'n|antaram ev' āsīd Bhāradvājaḥ pratāpavān
Pulindaiḥ, Pāradaiś c' âiva, tathā Kṣudraka|Mālavaiḥ.
Droṇād an|antaraṃ yatto Bhagadattaḥ pratāpavān
Māgadhaiś ca, Kaliṅgaiś ca, Piśācaiś ca, viśāṃ pate.
Prāgjyotiṣād anu nṛ|paḥ Kausalyo 'tha Bṛhadbalaḥ
Mekalaiḥ, Kuruvindaiś ca, Traipuraiś ca samanvitaḥ.
87.10 Bṛhadbalāt tataḥ śūras Trigartaḥ Prasthal"|âdhipaḥ
Kāmbojair bahubhiḥ sārdhaṃ, Yavanaiś ca sahasraśaḥ.
Drauṇis tu rabhasaḥ śūras Trigartād anu, Bhārata,
prayayau siṃha|nādena nādayāno dharā|talam.
tathā sarveṇa sainyena rājā Duryodhanas tadā
Drauṇer an|antaraṃ prāyāt s'|ôdaryaiḥ parivāritaḥ.
Duryodhanād anu tataḥ Kṛpaḥ Śāradvato yayau.

SÁNJAYA said:

AFTER PASSING THE night and enjoying their restful sleep, 87.1
those lords of men, the Kurus and the Pándavas, advanced into battle once again. A huge oceanic roar rose in the ranks of both armies as they proceeded to the battlefield. Then King Duryódhana, Chitra·sena, Vivímshati, Bhishma the best of all chariot warriors, and the son of Bharad·vaja, Your Majesty, all came together, clad in their armor, and carefully drew up the Káurava army into a battle array
against the Pándavas, lord. Your father Bhishma, lord of the 87.5
people, formed a terrifying and mighty array that had carriages for its waves and billows and thus resembled the surging sea. At the front of all the troops marched Bhishma the son of Shántanu, accompanied by the Málavas, the Southerners, and the Avántis. Right behind him was the mighty son of Bharad·vaja, together with the Pulíndas, the Páradas, and the Kshúdraka-Málavas. After Drona marched powerful Bhaga·datta, intent on battle, along with the Mágadhas, the Kalíngas, and the *pishácha*s, lord of the people. Behind the king of the Prag·jyótishas came Brihad·bala the ruler of the Kósalas, accompanied by the Mékalas, the Kuru·vindas,
and the Tri·puras. After Brihad·bala marched Tri·garta the 87.10
king of Prásthala, supported by numerous Kambójas and by thousands of Yávanas. Behind the ruler of the Tri·gartas came the vigorous son of Drona, making the earth reverberate with his lion-roar. After the son of Drona marched King Duryódhana surrounded by his brothers and all the troops; and behind Duryódhana was Kripa the son of Sharádvat.

evam eṣa mahā|vyūhaḥ prayayau sāgar'|ôpamaḥ.
rejus tatra patākāś ca, śveta|cchatrāṇi c' âbhibho,
aṅgadāny atra citrāṇi, mah"|ârhāṇi dhanūṃṣi ca.
87.15 taṃ tu dṛṣṭvā mahā|vyūhaṃ tāvakānāṃ mahā|rathaḥ
Yudhiṣṭhiro 'bravīt tūrṇam Pārṣatam pṛtanā|patim:
«paśya vyūhaṃ, mah"|êṣv|āsa, nirmitaṃ sāgar'|ôpamam.
prati|vyūhaṃ tvam api hi kuru, Pārṣata, sa|tvaram.»
tataḥ sa Pārṣataḥ śūro vyūhaṃ cakre su|dāruṇam
śṛṅgāṭakaṃ, mahā|rāja, para|vyūha|vināśanam.
śṛṅgābhyāṃ Bhīmasenaś ca Sātyakiś ca mahā|rathaḥ
rathair an|eka|sāhasrais, tathā haya|padātibhiḥ.
tābhyām babhau nara|śreṣṭhaḥ śvet'|âśvo kṛṣṇa|sārathiḥ
madhye Yudhiṣṭhiro rājā, Mādrī|putrau ca Pāṇḍavau.
87.20 ath' ôttare mah"|êṣv|āsāḥ saha|sainyā nar'|âdhipāḥ
vyūhaṃ taṃ pūrayām āsur vyūha|śāstra|viśāradāḥ.
Abhimanyus tataḥ paścād, Virāṭaś ca mahā|rathaḥ,
Draupadeyāś ca saṃhṛṣṭā, rākṣasaś ca Ghaṭotkacaḥ.
evam etaṃ mahā|vyūhaṃ vyūhya, Bhārata, Pāṇḍavāḥ
atiṣṭhan samare śūrā yoddhu|kāmā jay'|âiṣiṇaḥ.
bherī|śabdāś ca tumulā vimiśrāḥ śaṅkha|niḥsvanaiḥ,
kṣveḍit'|āsphoṭit'|ôtkruṣṭair nāditāḥ sarvato diśaḥ.
tataḥ śūrāḥ samāsādya samare te paras|param
netrair a|nimiṣai, rājann, avaikṣanta paras|param.
87.25 nāmabhis te, manuṣy'|êndra, pūrvaṃ yodhāḥ paras|param
yuddhāya samavartanta samāhūy' êtar'|êtaram.

Thus this mighty and oceanic array advanced; and its flags, white parasols, fine bracelets, and precious bows looked splendid, lord.

At the sight of your troops' mighty array, the great war- 87.15
rior Yudhi·shthira immediately said to Príshata's grandson, the general of his army: "Great archer, look at that oceanic array they have formed! Quickly, draw our troops up into a counter-formation, grandson of Príshata!" Then Príshata's fierce grandson formed the triangular array, great king, which is terrible and is capable of breaking through the hostile ranks. On two of its corners stood Bhima·sena and the great warrior Sátyaki, accompanied by several thousand chariots, cavalry, and infantry. Between them stood the best of men, Árjuna with his white horses and dark charioteer.* Yudhi·shthira and the two Pándava sons of Madri were stationed in the middle. Other kings, the great archers, and 87.20
the experts in the science of forming arrays filled up the formation, along with their troops. Abhimányu, the mighty warrior Viráta, the joyous sons of Dráupadi, and the demon Ghatótkacha stood in the rear.

Arranging their formation in this way, descendant of Bharata, the valiant Pándavas stationed themselves on the battlefield eager for battle and desirous of victory. All the quarters resounded with the beat of drums mixed with the blare of conches, the slapping of arms, and the loud shouts of troops. Then those heroes, confronting each other on the battlefield, glared at one another with unblinking eyes,
Your Majesty. The combatants first summoned each other 87.25

tataḥ pravavṛte yuddhaṃ ghora|rūpaṃ bhay'|āvaham
tāvakānāṃ pareṣāṃ ca nighnatām itar'|êtaram.

nārācā niśitāḥ saṃkhye saṃpatanti sma, Bhārata,
vyātt'|ānanā, bhaya|karā uragā iva saṅghaśaḥ.
niṣpetur vimalāḥ śaktyas taila|dhautāḥ, su|tejanāḥ,
ambudebhyo yathā, rājan, bhrājamānāḥ śata|hradāḥ.
gadāś ca vimalaiḥ paṭṭaiḥ pinaddhāḥ svarṇa|bhūṣitaiḥ
patantyas tatra dṛśyante giri|śṛṅg'|ôpamāḥ śubhāḥ.
87.30 nistriṃśāś ca vyarājanta vimal'|âmbara|saṃnibhāḥ,
ārṣabhāṇi ca carmāṇi śata|candrāṇi, Bhārata,
aśobhanta raṇe, rājan, pātyamānāni sarvaśaḥ.

te 'nyonyaṃ samare sene yudhyamāne, nar'|âdhipa,
aśobhetāṃ yathā deva|daitya|sene samudyate.
abhyadravanta samare te 'nyonyaṃ vai samantataḥ.
rathās tu rathibhis tūrṇaṃ preṣitāḥ param'|āhave
yugair yugāni saṃśliṣya yuyudhuḥ pārthiva'|rṣabhāḥ.
dantināṃ yudhyamānānāṃ saṃgharṣāt pāvako 'bhavat
danteṣu, Bharata|śreṣṭha, sa|dhūmaḥ sarvato|diśam.
87.35 prāsair abhihatāḥ ke cid gaja|yodhāḥ samantataḥ
patamānāḥ sma dṛśyante giri|śṛṅgān nagā iva.
pādātāś c' âpy adṛśyanta nighnanto 'tha paras|param
citra|rūpa|dharāḥ śūrā nakhara|prāsa|yodhinaḥ.
anyonyaṃ te samāsādya Kuru|Pāṇḍava|sainikāḥ
astrair nānā|vidhair ghorai raṇe ninyur Yama|kṣayam.
tataḥ Śāntanavo Bhīṣmo ratha|ghoṣeṇa nādayan

for battle by name, lord of men, and then they started fighting. And a fierce and terrifying battle ensued between your troops and the enemies as they struck each other down.

Sharpened iron shafts flew in that encounter, descendant of Bharata, like hordes of frightful serpents with gaping mouths. Lances, gleaming, well whetted, and cleansed with oil, fell like radiant flashes of lightning from thunderclouds, Your Majesty. Maces were seen flying, wrapped in glittering pieces of gold cloth, looking like sparkling mountain peaks.
Various swords were visible there, brilliant like the clear sky, 87.30
descendant of Bharata; and shields made of bull-hide and adorned with hundreds of moons shone beautifully in the battle, Your Majesty.

O lord of men, both of the armies that were engaged in that battle looked splendid, like the hosts of the gods and demons clashing together. In that contest they charged against each other from every side. In that tremendous battle, charioteers threw their chariots around at great speeds; some bull-like kings fought after their chariots' horses had collided. Fire was kindled from the friction of the fighting elephants' tusks, and it spread with smoke in all directions,
best of the Bharatas. Some elephant warriors, falling to the 87.35
ground, struck by javelins, looked like trees felled from a mountain peak. Brave foot soldiers of various kinds could be seen slaughtering each other with curved knives and with darts. The warriors of the Kurus and the Pándavas encountered one another in combat and dispatched each other to Yama's abode with terrible weapons of various kinds. Then

abhyāgamad raṇe Pārthān dhanuḥ|śabdena mohayan.
Pāṇḍavānāṃ rathāś c' âpi nadanto bhairavaṃ svanam
abhyadravanta saṃyattā Dhṛṣṭadyumna|puro|gamāḥ.
87.40 tataḥ pravavṛte yuddhaṃ tava teṣāṃ ca, Bhārata,
nar'|âśva|ratha|nāgānāṃ vyatiṣaktaṃ paras|param.

SAÑJAYA uvāca:

88.1 BHĪṢMAṂ TU samare kruddhaṃ pratapantaṃ samantataḥ
na śekuḥ Pāṇḍavā draṣṭuṃ, tapantam iva bhās|karam.
tataḥ sarvāṇi sainyāni Dharma|putrasya śāsanāt
abhyadravanta Gāṅgeyaṃ mardayantaṃ śitaiḥ śaraiḥ.
sa tu Bhīṣmo raṇa|ślāghī Somakān saha|Sṛñjayān,
Pāñcālāṃś ca mah"|êṣv|āsān pātayām āsa sāyakaiḥ.
te vadhyamānā Bhīṣmeṇa
Pāñcālāḥ Somakaiḥ saha
Bhīṣmam ev' âbhyayus tūrṇaṃ,
tyaktvā mṛtyu|kṛtaṃ bhayam.
88.5 sa teṣāṃ rathināṃ vīro Bhīṣmaḥ Śāntanavo yudhi
ciccheda sahasā, rājan, bāhūn atha śirāṃsi ca.
vi|rathān rathinaś cakre pitā Devavratas tava;
patitāny uttam'|âṅgāni hayebhyo haya|sādinām.
nir|manuṣyāṃś ca mātaṅgāñ śayānān parvat'|ôpamān
apaśyāma, mahā|rāja, Bhīṣm'|âstreṇa pramohitān.
na tatr' āsīt pumān kaś cit Pāṇḍavānāṃ, viśāṃ pate,
anyatra rathināṃ śreṣṭhād Bhīmasenān mahā|balāt.
sa hi Bhīṣmaṃ samāsādya tāḍayām āsa saṃyuge.
tato niṣṭānako ghoro Bhīṣma|Bhīma|samāgame

Bhishma the son of Shántanu, filling the air with the rumble of his chariot, charged against the sons of Pritha in battle, bewildering them with the twang of his bow. And the Pándava warriors led by Dhrishta·dyumna charged forward too, shouting out frightful roars and firmly resolved to fight.
Then a battle took place, descendant of Bharata, between 87.40
your troops and theirs, with men, horses, chariots, and elephants taking each other on.

SÁNJAYA said:

THE PÁNDAVAS were unable to gaze at Bhishma: inflamed 88.1
with anger, he scorched all around like the burning sun. Then, at the command of the Son of Righteousness, all the troops charged against the son of Ganga who was pounding them with sharp arrows. But Bhishma, proud in battle, struck down the great warriors of the Sómakas, the Srínjayas, and the Panchálas with his arrows. Though they were being hit by Bhishma, the Panchálas and the Sómakas abandoned their fear of death and still charged against Bhishma.
Bhishma the son of Shántanu, that hero among chariot war- 88.5
riors, soon chopped off their arms and heads in that conflict, Your Majesty. Your father Deva·vrata stripped the hostile chariot warriors of their chariots; and the heads of riding horsemen fell down from the horses' backs. Great king, we also saw elephants lying on the ground like mountains, bereft of their riders and paralyzed by Bhishma's weapons.

Not one of the Pándavas' men could hold his ground, lord of the people, except mighty Bhima·sena, that best of warriors. Confronting Bhishma, he began to bombard him in battle. During the encounter between Bhishma and

88.10 babhūva sarva|sainyānāṃ ghora|rūpo bhayānakaḥ.
tath" âiva Pāṇḍavā hṛṣṭāḥ siṃha|nādam ath' ânadan.
tato Duryodhano rājā s'|ôdaryaiḥ parivāritaḥ
Bhīṣmaṃ jugopa samare vartamāne jana|kṣaye.
Bhīmas tu sārathiṃ hatvā Bhīṣmasya rathināṃ varaḥ,
pradrut'|âśve rathe tasmin dravamāṇe samantataḥ,
cacāra yudhi, rāj'|êndra, Bhīmo bhīma|parākramaḥ.
Sunābhasya śareṇ' āśu śiraś ciccheda, Bhārata;
kṣurapreṇa su|tīkṣṇena sa hato nyapatad bhuvi.
hate tasmin, mahā|rāja, tava putre mahā|rathe
n' âmṛṣyanta raṇe śūrāḥ s'|ôdarāḥ sapta saṃyuge:
88.15 Ādityaketur, Bahvāśī, Kuṇḍadhāro, Mahodaraḥ,
Aparājitaḥ, Paṇḍitako, Viśālākṣaḥ su|durjayaḥ.
Pāṇḍavaṃ citra|saṃnāhā, vicitra|kavaca|dhvajāḥ
abhyadravanta saṃgrāme yoddhu|kām" âri|mardanāḥ.
Mahodaras tu samare Bhīmaṃ vivyādha patribhiḥ
navabhir vajra|saṃkāśair, Namuciṃ Vṛtra|hā yathā;
Ādityaketuḥ saptatyā, Bahvāśī c' âpi pañcabhiḥ,
navatyā Kuṇḍadhāras tu, Viśālākṣaś ca saptabhiḥ.
Aparājito, mahā|rāja, parājiṣṇur mahā|ratham
śarair bahubhir ānarcchad Bhīmasenaṃ mahā|balam.
88.20 raṇe Paṇḍitakaś c' âinaṃ tribhir bāṇaiḥ samardayat.
sa tan na mamṛṣe Bhīmaḥ śatrubhir vadham āhave.
dhanuḥ prapīḍya vāmena kareṇ' â|mitra|karśanaḥ
śiraś ciccheda samare śareṇa nata|parvaṇā
Aparājitasya su|nasaṃ tava putrasya saṃyuge;
parājitasya Bhīmena nipapāta śiro mahīm.

Bhima·sena a horrific and terrifying din rose up from all the troops; and the delighted Pándavas shouted a lion-roar too. 88.10
Then, supported by his brothers, King Duryódhana started to protect Bhishma in that fight, while the massacre of men continued. Bhima, that champion of chariot warriors, killed Bhishma's driver. While Bhishma's horses careered around, dragging the chariot, Bhima rampaged in battle with fearsome power. Using an arrow whose point was as sharp as a razor, he quickly cut off Sunábha's head, descendant of Bharata, and the slain warrior fell to the ground.

When that great warrior son of yours was killed in that clash, great king, seven of his valiant brothers could not bear it: Adítya·ketu, Bahváshin, Kunda·dhara, Mahódara, 88.15
Aparájita, Pánditaka, and Vishaláksha so hard to beat. Enemy-crushers all, eager to fight and clad in glistening armor with their mail and banners glittering, they charged into battle against the son of Pandu. Mahódara pierced Bhima in that encounter with nine feathered shafts each resembling a thunderbolt, just as the slayer of Vritra pierced the demon Námuchi. Adítya·ketu struck Bhima with seventy arrows, Bahváshin with five, Kunda·dhara with seven, and Vishaláksha with five. Aparájita the victorious wounded mighty Bhima·sena with numerous shafts. Pánditaka 88.20
pierced Bhima with three arrows in that contest.

But Bhima did not tolerate the wounds inflicted by his adversaries in that great combat. Squeezing his bow with his left hand in the fray, with a straight arrow that tormentor of enemies chopped off your son Aparájita's head, graced with its beautiful nose; defeated by Bhima, that warrior's head fell to the ground. With a peerless spear-headed shaft he

ath' âpareṇa bhallena Kuṇḍadhāraṃ mahā|ratham
prāhiṇon Mṛtyu|lokāya sarva|lokasya paśyataḥ.
tataḥ punar a|mey'|ātmā prasaṃdhāya śilīmukham
preṣayām āsa samare Paṇḍitaṃ prati, Bhārata.
88.25 sa śaraḥ Paṇḍitaṃ hatvā viveśa dharaṇī|talam,
yathā naraṃ nihaty' āśu bhujagaḥ Kāla|coditaḥ.
Viśālākṣa|śiraś chittvā pātayām āsa bhū|tale
tribhiḥ śarair a|dīn'|ātmā, smaran kleśaṃ purātanam.
Mahodaraṃ mah"|êṣv|āsaṃ nārācena stan'|ântare
vivyādha samare, rājan. sa hato nyapatad bhuvi.
Ādityaketoḥ ketuṃ ca cchittvā bāṇena saṃyuge
bhallena bhṛśa|tīkṣṇena śiraś ciccheda, Bhārata.
Bahvāśinaṃ tato Bhīmaḥ śareṇa nata|parvaṇā
preṣayām āsa saṃkruddho Yamasya sadanaṃ prati.
88.30 pradudruvus tatas te 'nye putrās tava, viśāṃ pate,
manyamānā hi tat satyaṃ sabhāyāṃ tasya bhāṣitam.
tato Duryodhano rājā bhrātṛ|vyasana|karśitaḥ
abravīt tāvakān yodhān: «Bhīmo 'yaṃ yudhi vadhyatām.»
evam ete mah"|êṣv|āsāḥ putrās tava, viśāṃ pate,
bhrātṝn saṃdṛśya nihatān prāsmaraṃs te hi tad vacaḥ,
yad uktavān mahā|prājñaḥ Kṣattā hitam, an|āmayam,
tad idaṃ samanuprāptaṃ vacanaṃ divya|darśinaḥ.
lobha|moha|samāviṣṭaḥ putra|prītyā, jan'|âdhipa,
na budhyase purā yat, tat tathyam uktaṃ vaco mahat.
88.35 tath" âiva ca vadh'|ârthāya putrāṇāṃ Pāṇḍavo balī
nūnaṃ jāto mahā|bāhur, yathā hanti sma Kauravān.

sent the great warrior Kunda·dhara to the abode of Death
while everyone looked on. Then the boundlessly spirited
Bhima aimed a stone-whetted arrow and shot it at Pánditaka in battle, descendant of Bharata. The arrow killed Pán- 88.25
ditaka and entered the earth, just as a snake, prompted by
Time, bites a man to death and quickly escapes to its hole.
Recalling former misfortunes but keeping his spirits up,
Bhima cut off Vishaláksha's head with three arrows, felling
it to the ground. In that contest he then struck Mahódara in
the center of his chest with an iron arrow, Your Majesty; and
the fighter collapsed onto the ground, slain. Bhima sliced
through Adítya·ketu's banner in battle with an immensely
sharp, spear-headed shaft, and then he chopped off that opponent's head, descendant of Bharata. Then Bhima in his
fury sent Bahváshin to Yama's realm with a straight arrow.

After that, lord of the people, some of your other sons 88.30
fled, believing that what Bhima had said in the assembly-
hall was coming true.* And King Duryódhana, pained by
the disaster that had befallen his brothers, said to his fighters: "This Bhima must be slain in battle!" So your sons,
the mighty archers, lord of the people, seeing their brothers
struck down, recalled the beneficial and wholesome words
that Kshattri Vídura, endowed with great wisdom and divine vision, had spoken,* and which are now being fulfilled.
The great words which you did not heed in the past—you
were overcome by greed and delusion on account of your
affection for your sons—now prove to be true. The power- 88.35
ful and strong-armed Pándava was surely born to exterminate your sons; or so it appears from the way he has been
slaughtering the Káuravas.

tato Duryodhano rājā Bhīṣmam āsādya saṃyuge
duḥkhena mahat" āviṣṭo vilalāpa su|duḥkhitaḥ:
«nihatā bhrātaraḥ śūrā Bhīmasenena me yudhi.
yatamānās tath" ânye 'pi hanyante sarva|sainikāḥ.
bhavāṃś ca madhyasthatayā nityam asmān upekṣate.
so 'haṃ ku|patham ārūḍhaḥ. paśya daivam idaṃ mama.»
etac chrutvā vacaḥ krūraṃ pitā Devavratas tava
Duryodhanam idaṃ vākyam abravīt s'|âśru|locanam:
88.40 «uktam etan mayā pūrvaṃ, Droṇena, Vidureṇa ca,
Gāndhāryā ca yaśasvinyā. tat tvaṃ, tāta, na buddhavān.
samayaś ca mayā pūrvaṃ kṛto vaḥ, śatru|karśana.
n' âhaṃ yudhi niyoktavyo, n' âpy ācāryaḥ kathaṃ cana.
yaṃ yaṃ hi Dhārtarāṣṭrāṇāṃ Bhīmo drakṣyati saṃyuge,
haniṣyati raṇe taṃ taṃ. satyam etad bravīmi te.
sa tvaṃ, rājan, sthiro bhūtvā raṇe kṛtvā dṛḍhāṃ matim
yodhayasva raṇe Pārthān, svargaṃ kṛtvā parāyaṇam.
na śakyāḥ Pāṇḍavā jetuṃ s'|Êndrair api sur'|âsuraiḥ.
tasmād yuddhe sthirāṃ kṛtvā matiṃ, yudhyasva, Bhārata.»

DHṚTARĀṢṬRA uvāca:

89.1 DṚṢṬVĀ ME nihatān putrān bahūn ekena, Sañjaya,
Bhīṣmo, Droṇaḥ, Kṛpaś c' âiva kim akurvata saṃyuge?
ahany ahani me putrāḥ kṣayaṃ gacchanti, Sañjaya.
manye 'haṃ, sarvathā, sūta, daiven' ôpahatā bhṛśam.
yatra me tanayāḥ sarve jīyante, na jayanty uta;
yatra Bhīṣmasya, Droṇasya, Kṛpasya ca mah"|ātmanaḥ,
Saumadatteś ca vīrasya, Bhagadattasya c' ôbhayoḥ,

Then King Duryódhana, overwhelmed with grief, came up to Bhishma on the battlefield and lamented in great distress: "My heroic brothers have been slaughtered in combat by Bhima·sena. And all the other warriors are also being massacred no matter how hard they try. You are indifferent; you always neglect us. What a bad path I have taken! Look at this ill fate!" And on hearing these cruel words, your father Deva·vrata replied to Duryódhana with tears in his eyes: "I told you about this before, and so did Drona, Ví- 88.40
dura, and the famous Gandhári; yet you took no notice, sir. O tormentor of enemies, formerly I set the condition that neither me nor the teacher Drona should be appointed as leaders in battle; not by any means. In this war Bhima will surely kill any of Dhrita·rashtra's warriors whom he may catch sight of. I am telling you the truth; so be firm, Your Majesty, and, firm in your resolve, fight with the sons of Pritha in battle, making heaven your final goal. The sons of Pandu can never be defeated even by the gods led by Indra himself; so set your mind firmly on battle, descendant of Bharata, and fight."

DHRITA·RASHTRA said:

WHAT DID BHISHMA, Drona, and Kripa do in that battle, 89.1
Sánjaya, when they saw so many of my sons slaughtered by one man? Day by day my sons perish, Sánjaya. I consider them to be struck forcibly by fate alone, charioteer. Since all my sons are always conquered and never conquer, and since they are still being killed despite being amid heroes such as Bhishma, Drona, great-spirited Kripa, the valiant son of Soma·datta, Bhaga·datta, Ashva·tthaman, and others 89.5

Aśvatthāmnas tathā, tāta, śūrāṇāṃ a|nivartinām,
89.5 anyeṣāṃ c' âiva śūrāṇāṃ madhya|gās tanayā mama,
yad ahanyanta saṃgrāme—kim anyad bhāga|dheyataḥ?
na hi Duryodhano mandaḥ purā proktam abudhyata.
vāryamāṇo mayā, tāta, Bhīṣmeṇa, Vidureṇa ca,
Gāndhāryā c' âiva dur|medhāḥ satataṃ hita|kāmyayā,
n' âbudhyata purā mohāt. tasya prāptam idaṃ phalam,
yad Bhīmasenaḥ samare putrān mama vi|cetasaḥ
ahany ahani saṃkruddho nayate Yama|sādanam.

SAÑJAYA uvāca:

idaṃ tat samanuprāptaṃ Kṣattur vacanam uttamam.
na buddhavān asi, vibho, procyamānaṃ hitaṃ tadā:
89.10 «nivāraya sutān dyūtāt. Pāṇḍavān mā druh'!» êti ca.
su|hṛdāṃ hita|kāmānāṃ bruvatāṃ tat tad eva ca
na śuśrūṣasi yad vākyaṃ, martyaḥ pathyam iv' âuṣadham,
tad eva tvām anuprāptaṃ vacanaṃ sādhu|bhāṣitam.
Vidura|Droṇa|Bhīṣmāṇāṃ tath" ânyeṣāṃ hit'|âiṣiṇām
a|kṛtvā vacanaṃ pathyaṃ, kṣayaṃ gacchanti Kauravāḥ.
tad etat samanuprāptaṃ pūrvam eva, viśāṃ pate.
tasmān tvaṃ śṛṇu tattvena, yathā yuddham avartata.
madhy'|âhne su|mahā|raudraḥ saṃgrāmaḥ samapadyata
loka|kṣaya|karo, rājaṃs. tan me nigadataḥ śṛṇu.
89.15 tataḥ sarvāṇi sainyāni Dharma|putrasya śāsanāt
saṃrabdhāny abhyavartanta Bhīṣmam eva jighāṃsayā.
Dhṛṣṭadyumnaḥ, Śikhaṇḍī ca, Sātyakiś ca mahā|rathaḥ
yukt'|ânīkā, mahā|rāja, Bhīṣmam eva samabhyayuḥ.
Virāṭo Drupadaś c' âiva sahitāḥ sarva|Somakaiḥ

who never turn their backs on battle, my friend, what else can it be but fate? In the past, dull-witted and evil-minded Duryódhana paid no heed to our counsels, even though he was warned by myself, Bhishma, Vídura, and Gandhári, who always wished for his good. Because of his delusion he failed to understand the advice we used to give him, my friend; and the result of his misconduct is that day by day the infuriated Bhima·sena sends my ignorant sons to the realm of Yama in this war.

SÁNJAYA said:

The Kshattri's excellent and salutary words have now come true. But you, lord, did not heed them as such when
he said, "Prevent your sons from playing dice! Do not plot 89.10
against the Pándavas!" You would not listen to your well-wishing friends who reiterated those words, just as a man on his deathbed rejects wholesome medicine. Now the words of the virtuous have got through to you. Since you neglected the beneficial counsels of Vídura, Drona, Bhishma, and other well-wishers, the Káuravas are now being destroyed. What's happening now was set up back then, lord of the people. So listen to the true account of the battle's events. An immensely terrifying combat, fraught with great massacre, broke out at midday, Your Majesty. Listen to my report.

At the command of the Son of Righteousness, all the 89.15
troops, enraged, charged against Bhishma in their eagerness to kill him. Dhrishta·dyumna, Shikhándin, and the great warrior Sátyaki, unifying their divisions, great king, advanced against Bhishma. Viráta and Drúpada together with

abhyadravanta saṃgrāme Bhīṣmam eva mahā|ratham.
Kekayā, Dhṛṣṭaketuś ca, Kuntibhojaś ca daṃśitāḥ
yukt'|ânīkā, mahā|rāja, Bhīṣmam eva samabhyayuḥ.
Arjuno, Draupadeyāś ca, Cekitānaś ca vīryavān
Duryodhana|samādiṣṭān rājñaḥ sarvān samabhyayuḥ.
89.20 Abhimanyus tathā vīro, Haiḍimbaś ca mahā|rathaḥ,
Bhīmasenaś ca saṃkruddhas te 'bhyadhāvanta Kauravān.
tridhā|bhūtair avadhyanta Pāṇḍavaiḥ Kauravā yudhi.
tath" âiva Kauravai, rājann, avadhyanta pare raṇe.

Droṇas tu rathināṃ śreṣthaḥ Somakān Sṛñjayaiḥ saha
abhyadhāvata saṃkruddhaḥ, preṣayiṣyan Yama|kṣayam.
tatr' ākrando mahān āsīt Sṛñjayānāṃ mah"|ātmanām
vadhyatāṃ samare, rājan, Bhāradvājena dhanvinā.
Droṇena nihatās tatra kṣatriyā bahavo raṇe
viceṣṭanto hy adṛśyanta vyādhi|kliṣṭā narā iva.
89.25 kūjatāṃ, krandatāṃ c' âiva, stanatāṃ c' âiva, Bhārata,
a|niśaṃ śrūyate śabdaḥ kṣut|kliṣṭānāṃ nṛṇām iva.
tath" âiva Kauraveyāṇāṃ Bhīmaseno mahā|balaḥ
cakāra kadanaṃ ghoraṃ, kruddhaḥ Kāla iv' âparaḥ.
vadhyatāṃ tatra sainyānām anyonyena mahā|raṇe
prāvartata nadī ghorā rudhir'|âugha|pravāhinī.
sa saṃgrāmo, mahā|rāja, ghora|rūpo 'bhavan mahān
Kurūṇāṃ Pāṇḍavānāṃ ca Yama|rāṣṭra|vivardhanaḥ.

tato Bhīmo raṇe kruddho rabhasaś ca viśeṣataḥ
gaj'|ânīkaṃ samāsādya preṣayām āsa Mṛtyave.
89.30 tatra, Bhārata, Bhīmena nārāc'|âbhihatā gajāḥ
petuḥ, seduś ca, neduś ca, diśaś ca paribabhramuḥ.
chinna|hastā mahā|nāgāś, chinna|gātrāś ca, māriṣa,

all the Sómakas also attacked the mighty warrior Bhishma; and Dhrishta·ketu, Kunti·bhoja, and the Kékayas charged against him, great king, wearing their armor. Árjuna, the sons of Dráupadi, and vigorous Chekitána assailed all the
kings under Duryódhana's command. Heroic Abhimányu, 89.20
Hidímba's mighty warrior son, and furious Bhima·sena charged against the Káuravas. Split into three divisions, the Pándavas, when they fired, began to make hits on the Káuravas. And the Káuravas, when they fired, began to make hits on their enemies too, Your Majesty.

Drona, that best of chariot warriors, besieged the Sómakas and the Srínjayas, intent on sending them to the realm of Yama. There was lots of screaming from the great-spirited Srínjayas who were slain in that fight, Your Majesty, by that great archer the son of Bharad·vaja. Many warriors struck down in that fight were seen convulsing like people
struck by famine. They moaned, shrieked, and groaned like 89.25
people struck by famine, making a din that carried on and on. In his turn powerful and furious Bhima·sena, like another god of death, wreaked a terrible massacre of the Káurava host. As the troops slaughtered each other, a dreadful river of streaming blood sprung up on the battlefield. That battle between the Kurus and the Pándavas, great king, was huge and frightful, and swelled Yama's domain.

Bhima in his battle-fury assaulted the elephant division
with blistering force and sent it to Death. O descendant 89.30
of Bharata, elephants, wounded by Bhima's iron shafts, collapsed, screamed, sank, or rampaged in all directions. Their trunks chopped off and their bodies lacerated, the elephants fell to the ground screeching with terror like curlews,

krauñcavad vyanadan bhītāḥ, pṛthivīm adhiśiśyire.
Nakulaḥ Sahadevaś ca hay'|ânīkam abhidrutau.
te hayāḥ kāñcan'|āpīḍā, rukma|bhāṇḍa|paricchadāḥ,
vadhyamānā vyadṛśyanta śataśo 'tha sahasraśaḥ.
patadbhis turagai, rājan, samāstīryata medinī.
nir|jihvaiś ca, śvasadbhiś ca, kūjadbhiś ca, gat'|âsubhiḥ
hayair babhau, nara|śreṣṭha, nānā|rūpa|dharair dharā.
89.35 Arjunena hataiḥ saṃkhye tathā, Bhārata, rājabhiḥ
prababhau vasu|dhā ghorā tatra tatra, viśāṃ pate.
rathair bhagnair, dhvajaiś chinnair,
  nikṛttaiś ca mah"|āyudhaiḥ,
cāmarair, vyajanaiś c' âiva,
  cchatraiś ca su|mahā|prabhaiḥ,
hārair, niṣkaiḥ sa|keyūraiḥ, śirobhiś ca sa|kuṇḍalaiḥ,
uṣṇīṣair apaviddhaiś ca, patākābhiś ca sarvaṣaḥ,
anukarṣaiḥ śubhai, rājan, yoktraiś c' âiva sa|raśmibhiḥ
saṃkīrṇā vasu|dhā bhāti vasante kusumair iva.
evam eṣa kṣayo vṛttaḥ Pāṇḍūnām api, Bhārata,
kruddhe Śāntanave Bhīṣme, Droṇe ca ratha|sattame,
89.40 Aśvatthāmni, Kṛpe c' âiva, tath" âiva Kṛtavarmaṇi,
tath" êtareṣu kruddheṣu tāvakānām api kṣayaḥ.

SAÑJAYA uvāca:

90.1 VARTAMĀNE TATHĀ raudre, rājan, vīra|vara|kṣaye
Śakuniḥ Saubalaḥ śrīmān Pāṇḍavān samupādravat.
tath" âiva Sātvato, rājan, Hārdikyaḥ para|vīra|hā
abhyadravata saṃgrāme Pāṇḍavānām varūthinīm.
tataḥ Kāmboja|mukhyānāṃ, nadī|jānāṃ ca vājinām,
Āraṭṭānāṃ, Mahī|jānāṃ, Sindhu|jānāṃ ca sarvaśaḥ,
Vanāyu|jānāṃ śubhrāṇāṃ, tathā parvata|vāsinām

my lord. Nákula and Saha·deva attacked the cavalry division. Those gold-crested horses, adorned with golden trappings and caparisons, were seen killed in their hundreds and thousands, Your Majesty; the earth was strewn with fallen horses. The earth covered with horses of diverse appearance with tongues drooping out of their mouths, gasping
for breath, moaning, and lifeless, looked amazing. Bhárata, 89.35
the earth was a horrific sight, covered with the bodies of kings killed in combat by Árjuna, lord of the people. With crushed chariots, rent banners, mighty weapons broken in bits, torn yak tails and fans, superb shining parasols, golden chains and necklaces, bracelets, heads adorned with earrings, fallen turbans, flags, fine axle-sets, straps, and reins scattered all over, the earth looked beautiful as if carpeted with flowers in spring. Such was the destruction of the Pándava host, descendant of Bharata, when Shántanu's son
Bhishma, supreme warrior Drona, Ashva·tthaman, Kripa, 89.40
and Krita·varman raged in their fury; and your troops suffered a similar destruction when the other side's warriors were provoked.

SÁNJAYA said:

DURING THAT TERRIBLE battle, in which superb heroes 90.1
were slaughtered, Your Majesty, illustrious Shákuni the son of Súbala charged against the Pándavas. And Hrídika's son the Sátvata warrior, that slayer of hostile heroes, advanced in combat against the Pándava army. Then, encircling the hostile troops on every side with a division of numerous fine horses of the Kambója breed, with those of the riverine area, of Arátta, Mahi, and Sindhu, with the white horses of

vājināṃ bahubhiḥ saṃkhye samantāt parivārayan,
90.5 ye c' âpare Tittira|jā javanā, vāta|raṃhasaḥ,
suvarṇ'|âlaṃ|kṛtair etair varmavadbhiḥ, su|kalpitaiḥ
hayair vāta|javair mukhyaiḥ Pāṇḍavasya suto balī
abhyavartata tat sainyaṃ hṛṣṭa|rūpaḥ paran|tapaḥ.
Arjunasy' âtha dāy'|āda Irāvān nāma vīryavān
sutāyāṃ nāga|rājasya jātaḥ Pārthena dhīmatā.
Airāvatena sā dattā an|apatyā mah"|ātmanā,
patyau hate Suparṇena kṛpaṇā, dīna|cetanā.
bhāry"|ârthaṃ tāṃ ca jagrāha Pārthaḥ kāma|vaś'|ânugām.
evam eṣa samutpannaḥ para|pakṣe 'rjun'|ātmajaḥ.
90.10 sa nāga|loke saṃvṛddho, mātrā ca parirakṣitaḥ,
pitṛvyeṇa parityaktaḥ Pārtha|dveṣād dur|ātmanā.
rūpavān, bala|saṃpanno, guṇavān, satya|vikramaḥ
Indra|lokaṃ jagām' āśu śrutvā tatr' Ârjunaṃ gatam.
so 'bhigamya mah"|ātmānaṃ pitaraṃ satya|vikramam
abhyavādayad a|vyagro vinayena kṛt'|âñjaliḥ,
nyavedayata c' ātmānam Arjunasya mah"|ātmanaḥ:
«Irāvān asmi. bhadraṃ te! putraś c' âhaṃ tava, prabho.»
mātuḥ samāgamo yaś ca, tat sarvaṃ pratyavedayat,
tac ca sarvaṃ yathā|vṛttam anusasmāra Pāṇḍavaḥ.
90.15 pariṣvajya sutam api so "tmanaḥ sadṛśaṃ guṇaiḥ,
prītimān anayat Pārtho deva|rāja|niveśane.
so 'rjunena samājñapto deva|loke tadā, nṛ|pa,
prīti|pūrvaṃ mahā|bāhuḥ sva|kāryaṃ prati, Bhārata,

Vanáyu, the horses of the mountainous regions, and those 90.5
of the Títtira breed that are swift as the wind—all those excellent horses being adorned with gold, armored, fully kitted out, and as fleet as the wind—the mighty enemy-taming son of a Pándava, looking delighted, charged against the Káurava host.

He was Árjuna's glorious and vigorous son Irávat, born from the wise son of Pritha by the *naga* king's daughter. Her husband had been killed by fine-feathered Supárna, and, being childless, pitiable, and dejected, she was given in marriage to Árjuna by the great-spirited Airávata. Pritha's son, overcome with desire, took her as his wife. That is how that
son of Árjuna was born from another's wife. Forsaken by his 90.10
wicked paternal uncle out of hatred for the son of Pritha, he grew up in the realm of the *naga*s, protected by his mother.

Handsome and endowed with strength and virtues, his power lay in his truth, and he quickly went to the realm of Indra as soon as he heard that Árjuna had gone there. That mighty-armed hero whose power was in his truth went up to his father, made his obeisance, and, with his hands folded in respect, calmly and humbly introduced himself to great-spirited Árjuna. "I am Irávat. Blessings be to you! I am your son, my lord." When he reminded Árjuna how the latter had met his mother, the Pándava remembered everything
just so. Embracing his son, who was equal to him in virtues, 90.15
the Partha, filled with joy, took him to the palace of the king of the gods. In the realm of the gods Árjuna affectionately informed mighty-armed Irávat of his duties, Your Majesty, descendant of Bharata. He said: "When it's time for war you must give us your support, my son." Irávat replied to

«yuddha|kāle tvay" âsmākaṃ sāhyaṃ deyam» iti, prabho.
«bāḍham!» ity evam uktvā ca yuddha|kāla upāgataḥ
kāma|varṇa|javair aśvair bahubhiḥ saṃvṛto, nṛ|pa.
te hayāḥ kāñcan'|āpīḍā, nānā|varṇā, mano|javāḥ
utpetuḥ sahasā, rājan, haṃsā iva mah"|ôdadhau.
te tvadīyān samāsādya haya|saṅghān mahā|javān,
90.20 kroḍaiḥ kroḍān abhighnanto ghoṇābhiś ca paras|param,
nipetuḥ sahasā, rājan, su|veg'|âbhihatā bhuvi.
nipatadbhis tathā taiś ca haya|saṅghaiḥ paras|param
śuśruve dāruṇaḥ śabdaḥ Suparṇa|patane yathā.
tath" âiva ca, mahā|rāja, samety' ânyonyam āhave
paras|para|vadhaṃ ghoraṃ cakrus te haya|sādinaḥ.
tasmiṃs tathā vartamāne saṃkule tumule bhṛśam
ubhayor api saṃśāntā haya|saṅghāḥ samantataḥ.
prakṣīṇa|sāyakāḥ śūrā nihat'|âśvāḥ, śram'|āturāḥ
vilayaṃ samanuprāptās takṣamāṇāḥ paras|param.
90.25 tataḥ kṣīṇe hay'|ânīke kiṃ|cic|cheṣe ca, Bhārata,
Saubalasy' ātma|jāḥ śūrā nirgatā raṇa|mūrdhani.
vāyu|vega|sama|sparśāñ, jave vāyu|samāṃs tathā
āruhya śīla|saṃpannān, vayaḥ|sthāṃs turag'|ôttamān,
Gajo, Gavākṣo, Vṛṣabhaś, Carmavān, Ārjavaḥ, Śukaḥ—
ṣaḍ ete bala|sampannā niryayur mahato balāt,
vāryamāṇāḥ Śakuninā, taiś ca yodhair mahā|balaiḥ,
saṃnaddhā yuddha|kuśalā, raudra|rūpā, mahā|balāḥ.
tad anīkaṃ, mahā|bāho, bhittvā parama|dur|jayam,
balena mahatā yuktāḥ, svargāya vijay'|âiṣiṇaḥ

him: "Sure!" And so, when it was time for war, he arrived surrounded by a great number of horses of enviable colors and swiftness, Your Majesty.

Those gold-crested, multicolored horses, swift as thought, suddenly appeared on the battlefield like geese on the sea, Your Majesty. They confronted your hordes of horses, who
were also running at great speed. The horses smacked into 90.20
each other forcefully with their noses and chests, and started falling to the ground willy-nilly, Your Majesty, toppled by their immense force. When those hosts of horses clashed together and fell tumbling a terrifying noise was heard, like the sound of a swoop of fine-feathered Gáruda. Your horsemen and those of the enemy, Your Majesty, met each other in that great battle and engaged in mutual carnage. During that immensely chaotic and tumultuous conflict, hosts of horses were completely destroyed, on both sides. Heroic warriors ran out of arrows; stripped of their horses and exhausted with fatigue, they perished lacerating each other.

After the cavalry division had been destroyed with very 90.25
few survivors, Súbala's son's courageous younger brothers rode out to the forefront of the battle, descendant of Bharata. Riding the finest horses—young, strong, and dashing with the force and the speed of the wind—the six powerful heroes Gaja, Gaváksha, Vríshabha, Chármavat, Árjava, and Shuka rode out of their mighty ranks. Shákuni and other mighty warriors tried to restrain them, but they advanced forward, clad in armor, skilled in battle, fierce in appearance, and immensely strong. Possessed of great power, in- 90.30
tent on heaven, and eager for victory, mighty-armed hero, those Gandhára warriors, ferocious in battle, broke through

90.30 viviśus te tadā hṛṣṭā Gāndhārā yuddha|dur|madāḥ.
tān praviṣṭāṃs tadā dṛṣṭvā Irāvān api vīryavān
abravīt samare yodhān vicitrān, dāruṇ'|āyudhān:
«yath" âite Dhārtarāṣṭrasya yodhāḥ s'|ânuga|vāhanāḥ
hanyante samare sarve, tathā nītir vidhīyatām.»
«bāḍham!» ity evam uktvā te sarve yodhā Irāvataḥ
jaghnus teṣāṃ bal'|ânīkaṃ dur|jayaṃ samare paraiḥ.
tad anīkam anīkena samare vīkṣya pātitam,
a|mṛṣyamāṇās te sarve Subalasy' ātma|jā raṇe
Irāvantam abhidrutya sarvataḥ paryavārayan.
90.35 tāḍayantaḥ śitaiḥ prāsaiś, codayantaḥ paras|param
te śūrāḥ paryadhāvanta, kurvanto mahad ākulam.
Irāvān atha nirbhinnaḥ prāsais tīkṣṇair mah"|ātmabhiḥ,
sravatā rudhireṇ' âktas, tottrair viddha iva dvi|paḥ,
purato 'pi ca, pṛṣṭhe ca, pārśvayoś ca bhṛś'|āhataḥ
eko bahubhir atyarthaṃ dhairyād, rājan, na vivyathe.
Irāvān atha saṃkruddhaḥ sarvāṃs tān niśitaiḥ śaraiḥ
mohayām āsa samare, viddhvā para|purañ|jayaḥ.
prāsān uddhṛtya sarvāṃś ca sva|śarīrād arin|damaḥ,
tair eva tāḍayām āsa Subalasy' ātma|jān raṇe.
90.40 vikṛṣya ca śitaṃ khaḍgaṃ, gṛhītvā ca śar'|āvaram,
padātir drutam āgacchaj jighāṃsuḥ Saubalān yudhi.
tataḥ pratyāgata|prāṇāḥ sarve te Subal'|ātmajāḥ
bhūyaḥ krodha|samāviṣṭā Irāvantam abhidrutāḥ.
Irāvān api khaḍgena darśayan pāṇi|lāghavam
abhyavartata tān sarvān Saubalān bala|darpitaḥ.

the enemy ranks, a feat of great difficulty; and it gave them great joy to do so.

Seeing that they had penetrated his lines, vigorous Irávat addressed his splendid warriors, who were armed for battle with frightful weapons: "Devise tactics such that all these combatants of Dhrita·rashtra's son, with their followers and vehicles, will be killed in this fight!" Irávat's entire troops replied: "Sure!" and destroyed that hostile force so difficult for enemies to defeat in battle. Seeing their force struck down by Irávat's troops, all those sons of Súbala charged against Irávat and surrounded him on every side.
Striking Irávat with sharp javelins and urging each other 90.35
on, those heroes rampaged around creating great confusion. And Irávat, afflicted by those great-spirited warriors with their sharp javelins, was drenched in oozing blood, like an elephant tormented by goads. But though he was severely wounded in his chest, back, and both sides, he did not waver; he fought with sterling resolve, one against many. Filled with anger, Irávat, that conqueror of hostile strongholds, shot his enemies with sharpened arrows in that conflict, and stunned them. Swiftly extracting the javelins from his body, that enemy-tamer pierced Súbala's sons with them as
he fought. And drawing his sharp sword and grasping his 90.40
shield, he quickly ran up to Súbala's sons on foot, intent on slaughtering them in battle.

Coming to their senses, all those sons of Súbala, filled with immense fury, charged against Irávat. And Irávat, proud of his strength, displaying his dexterity in wielding a sword, pounced on all those sons of Súbala. As he rampaged around on foot with great agility, all those sons of Súbala,

lāghaven' âtha carataḥ sarve te Subal'|ātmajāḥ
antaraṃ n' âdhyagacchanta carantaḥ śīghra|gair hayaiḥ.
bhūmi|ṣṭham atha taṃ saṃkhye saṃpradṛśya tataḥ punaḥ,
parivārya bhṛśaṃ sarve grahītum upacakramuḥ.
90.45 ath' âbhyāśa|gatānāṃ sa khaḍgen' â|mitra|karśanaḥ
asi|hast'|âpahastābhyāṃ teṣāṃ gātrāṇy akṛntata,
āyudhāni ca sarveṣāṃ, bāhūn api vibhūṣitān.
apatanta nikṛtt'|âṅgā gatā bhūmiṃ gat'|âsavaḥ.
Vṛṣabhas tu, mahā|rāja, bahudhā viparikṣataḥ
amucyata mahā|raudrāt tasmād vīr'|âvakartanāt.
tān sarvān patitān dṛṣṭvā bhīto Duryodhanas tataḥ
abhyabhāṣata saṃkruddho rākṣasaṃ ghora|darśanam
Ārṣyaśṛṅgiṃ mah"|êṣv|āsaṃ, māyāvinam, arin|damam,
vairiṇaṃ Bhīmasenasya pūrvaṃ Baka|vadhena vai:
90.50 «paśya, vīra, yathā hy eṣa Phālgunasya suto balī
māyāvī vi|priyaṃ ghoram akārṣīn me bala|kṣayam.
tvaṃ ca kāma|gamas, tāta, māy"|âstre ca viśāradaḥ,
kṛta|vairaś ca Pārthena. tasmād enaṃ raṇe jahi!»
«bāḍham!» ity evam uktvā tu rākṣaso ghora|darśanaḥ
prayayau siṃha|nādena, yatr' Ârjuna|suto yuvā,
ārūḍhair, yuddha|kuśalair, vimala|prāsa|yodhibhiḥ
vīraiḥ prahāribhir yuktaḥ, svair anīkaiḥ samāvṛtaḥ
hata|śeṣair, mahā|rāja, dvi|sāhasrair hay'|ôttamaiḥ,
nihantu|kāmaḥ samare Irāvantaṃ mahā|balam.

even though they were careering on their swift horses, could not find an opportunity to strike him. Then, when they saw him holding his ground, they encircled him closely once again, and tried to capture him.

But as soon as they came close, Irávat, that tormentor 90.45
of foes, began to slice at their bodies, wielding his sword by turns with his right and left hands and cutting off all the opponents' weapons and their decorated arms. Bereft of life, their bodies mutilated, they fell to the ground dead. Only Vríshabha escaped alive, great king, from that utterly horrible slaughter of heroes—though with many wounds inflicted upon him.

Seeing all of them fallen, Duryódhana became frightened and furious, and he addressed the fierce-looking demon Alámbusha, Rishya·shringa's son, a tamer of his enemies and a great archer possessing the powers of illusion, who had previously become Bhima·sena's avowed enemy after the latter's slaying of the demon Baka. "Hero, look how 90.50
this mighty son of Phálguna has managed to do me grave harm by destroying my force through his powers of illusion. You also are able to move everywhere at will, my friend, and are skilled in the use of magical weapons. You are feuding with the son of Pritha. So kill this one in battle!"

"Sure!" said the fierce-looking demon, and proceeded with a lion-roar to the place where Árjuna's young son was. Alámbusha was surrounded by the well-mounted and heroic combatants of his contingent, who were skilled in battle, accomplished in launching attacks, and fought with gleaming lances. Followed by the two thousand excellent cavalry that had survived, he advanced, great king, eager to

90.55 Irāvān api saṃkruddhas tvaramāṇaḥ parākramī
hantu|kāmam amitra|ghno rākṣasaṃ pratyavārayat.
tam āpatantaṃ saṃpreksya rākṣasaḥ su|mahā|balaḥ
tvaramāṇas tato māyāṃ prayoktum upacakrame.
tena māyāmayāḥ sṛṣṭā hayās tāvanta eva hi,
sv|ārūḍhā rākṣasair ghoraiḥ śūla|paṭṭiśa|dhāribhiḥ.
te saṃrabdhāḥ samāgamya dvi|sāhasrāḥ prahāriṇaḥ
a|cirād gamayām āsuḥ preta|lokaṃ paras|param.
tasmiṃs tu nihate sainye tāv ubhau yuddha|dur|madau
saṃgrāme samatiṣṭhetāṃ, yathā vai Vṛtra|Vāsavau.
90.60 ādravantam abhipreksya rākṣasaṃ yuddha|dur|madam,
Irāvān atha saṃrabdhaḥ pratyadhāvan mahā|balaḥ.
samabhyāśa|gatasy' ājau tasya khaḍgena dur|mateḥ
ciccheda kārmukaṃ dīptaṃ, śar'|āvāpaṃ ca sa|tvaram.
sa nikṛttaṃ dhanur dṛṣṭvā khaṃ javena samāviśat,
Irāvantam abhikruddhaṃ mohayann iva māyayā.
tato 'ntarikṣam utpatya Irāvān api rākṣasam
vimohayitvā māyābhis, tasya gātrāṇi sāyakaiḥ
ciccheda sarva|marma|jñaḥ, kāma|rūpo, dur|āsadaḥ.
tathā sa rākṣasa|śreṣṭhaḥ śaraiḥ kṛttaḥ punaḥ punaḥ,
90.65 saṃbabhūva, mahā|rāja, samavāpa ca yauvanam.
māyā hi saha|jā teṣāṃ; vayo rūpaṃ ca kāma|jam.
evaṃ tad rākṣasasy' âṅgaṃ chinnaṃ chinnaṃ babhūva ha.

slaughter mighty Irávat in battle. And the powerful enemy-slayer Irávat, infuriated, quickly proceeded to restrain the demon who was trying to kill him. 90.55

Seeing the enemy advance, the immensely mighty demon soon began to use his powers of illusion. He created as many horses as the opponent had; and they were ridden by frightful demons brandishing pikes and sharp-pointed spears. Those two thousand enraged combatants from either side confronted each other, and they soon sent one another to the abode of the dead.

When both hosts had been destroyed, the two heroes, ferocious in battle, clashed together in that contest like Vásava and Vritra. Seeing the demon rushing toward him 90.60
in a battle-frenzy, mighty Irávat, enraged, rose up against him. When the wicked demon came close to him in the fray, with a sword Irávat quickly severed Alámbusha's resplendent bow and quiver.

Seeing his bow cut down, the demon immediately flew up into the sky, as if to bewilder the angry Irávat with his powers of illusion. Irávat—who knew all about the body's vulnerable spots, could assume any form at will, and was difficult to conquer—jumped into the sky; he bewildered the demon with his magical powers, and lacerated his limbs with arrows. But though he was cut up again and again, that foremost of demons regenerated his body into the form of 90.65
a youth. For magic is innate in them, and they can assume any age and form at will. And the demon's body did this as it was cut over and over.

Irāvān api saṃkruddho rākṣasaṃ taṃ mahā|balam
paraśvadhena tīkṣṇena ciccheda ca punaḥ punaḥ.
sa tena balinā vīraś chidyamāna Irāvatā
rākṣaso vyanadad ghoraṃ. sa śabdas tumulo 'bhavat.
paraśvadha|kṣataṃ rakṣaḥ susrāva bahu śoṇitam.

tataś cukrodha balavāṃś, cakre vegaṃ ca saṃyuge
Ārṣyaśṛṅgis tato dṛṣṭvā samare śatrum ūrjitam.
90.70 kṛtvā ghoraṃ mahad rūpaṃ grahītum upacakrame
Arjunasya sutaṃ vīraṃ Irāvantaṃ yaśasvinam.
saṃgrāma|śiraso madhye sarveṣāṃ tatra paśyatām,
tāṃ dṛṣṭvā tādṛśīṃ māyāṃ rākṣasasya dur|ātmanaḥ,
Irāvān api saṃkruddho māyāṃ sraṣṭuṃ pracakrame.
tasya krodh'|âbhibhūtasya samareṣv a|nivartinaḥ
yo 'nvayo mātṛkas tasya, sa enam abhipedivān.

sa nāgair bahubhī, rājann, Irāvān saṃvṛto raṇe
dadhāra su|mahad rūpam, Ananta iva bhogavān.
tato bahu|vidhair nāgaiś chādayām āsa rākṣasam.
90.75 chādyamānas tu nāgaiḥ sa dhyātvā rākṣasa|puṅgavaḥ
sauparṇaṃ rūpam āsthāya bhakṣayām āsa pannagān.
māyayā bhakṣite tasminn anvaye tasya mātṛke,
vimohitam Irāvantam nyahanat rākṣaso 'sinā.
sa|kuṇḍalaṃ, sa|mukuṭaṃ, padm'|êndu|sadṛśa|prabham
Irāvataḥ śiro rakṣaḥ pātayām āsa bhū|tale.

So Irávat started furiously cutting the mighty demon over and over again with a sharp battle axe. The heroic demon, lacerated by powerful Irávat, uttered a terrible roar. What a monstrous din that was! Blood kept on gushing from the demon's limbs as they were chopped by the battle axe.

Then the mighty son of Rishya·shringa, seeing the enemy's energy, became excited with rage and showed his mettle in combat. He assumed a hideous form and tried to 90.70
capture Árjuna's valiant and glorious son Irávat. Seeing that illusion produced by the wicked demon in the forefront of battle with everyone looking on, Irávat became angry, and he also began to create illusions. When that hero, who would never retreat from battle, was overwhelmed with fury, his serpentine *naga* kin from his mother's side came to his aid.

Your Majesty, Irávat, surrounded in battle by numerous serpents, assumed a stupendous form like that of the primordial serpent Anánta himself; and then he shrouded the demon in snakes of various kinds. Enveloped in serpents, 90.75
that demon, mighty as a bull, assumed the form of fine-feathered Gáruda and devoured those snakes. His maternal relatives thus devoured through magic, Irávat became distracted, and the demon killed him with a sword. The demon struck off Irávat's head; adorned with earrings and a diadem, it fell to the ground.

tasmiṃs tu vihate vīre rākṣasen' Ârjun'|âtmaje
vi|śokāḥ samapadyanta Dhārtarāṣṭrāḥ sa|rājakāḥ.
tasmin mahati saṃgrāme tādṛśe bhairave punaḥ
mahān vyatikaro ghoraḥ senayoḥ samapadyata.
90.80 gajā, hayāḥ, padātāś ca vimiśrā dantibhir hatāḥ;
rath'|âśva|dantinaś c' âiva pattibhis tatra sūditāḥ.
tathā patti|rath|aughāś ca, hayāś ca bahavo raṇe
rathibhir nihatā, rājaṃs, tava teṣāṃ ca saṃkule.

a|jānann Arjunaś c' âpi nihataṃ putram aurasam,
jaghāna samare śūrān rājñas tān Bhīṣma|rakṣiṇaḥ.
tath" âiva tāvakā, rājan, Sṛñjayāś ca sahasraśaḥ
juhvataḥ samare prāṇān nijaghnur itar'|êtaram.
mukta|keśā, vi|kavacā, vi|rathāś, chinna|kārmukāḥ
bāhubhiḥ samayudhyanta samavetāḥ paras|param.
90.85 tathā marm'|âtigair Bhīṣmo nijaghāna mahā|rathān
kampayan samare senāṃ Pāṇḍavānāṃ paran|tapaḥ.
tena Yaudhiṣṭhire sainye bahavo mānavā hatāḥ,
dantinaḥ, sādinaś c' âiva, rathino, 'tha hayās tathā.

tatra, Bhārata, Bhīṣmasya raṇe dṛṣṭvā parākramam
atyadbhutam apaśyāma Śakrasy' êva parākramam.
tath" âiva Bhīmasenasya Pārṣatasya ca, Bhārata,
raudram āsīt tadā yuddhaṃ, Sātyakasya ca dhanvinaḥ.
dṛṣṭvā Droṇasya vikrāntaṃ Pāṇḍavān bhayam āviśat.
«eka eva raṇe śakto nihantum sarva|sainikān.

When that heroic son of Árjuna had been slain by the demon, Dhrita·rashtra's sons and their kings were freed from their misery. And the tremendous, horrific engagement between the two hosts continued, with everyone getting completely mixed up. Elephants, horses, and foot soldiers tan- 90.80
gled with each other and got crushed by tusked elephants. Many chariot warriors, horses, and elephants were killed by infantry. And hordes of infantry, chariot warriors, and cavalry, from your army and from the enemy's, Your Majesty, were struck down by chariot warriors in that chaotic fight.

Unaware that his own son had been slain, Árjuna smote the brave kings who were protecting Bhishma. Your Majesty, the Srínjayas and thousands of your combatants massacred each other, sacrificing their lives in battle. Stripped of their armor and chariots, their bows severed, their hair disheveled, they fought on hand-to-hand, battling against each other in the fray. And Bhishma, that scorcher of en- 90.85
emies, slaughtered great warriors with his arrows that were able to penetrate the vital organs; he made the Pándava army tremble in that encounter. In Yudhi·shthira's host, many infantrymen, elephants with their riders, chariot warriors, and cavalrymen were slaughtered by Bhishma.

In that conflict, descendant of Bharata, we then witnessed Bhishma's extremely wonderful prowess, which was like that of Shakra himself. And the fighting that was done on the battlefield by Bhima·sena, by Príshata's grandson, and by the mighty archer Sátyaki was fierce indeed, Bhárata. But at the sight of Drona's vigor, fear overwhelmed the Pándavas. "Even alone he could slaughter all our troops in

90.90 kiṃ punaḥ pṛthivī|śūrair yodha|vrātaiḥ samāvṛtaḥ?»
ity abruvan, mahā|rāja, raṇe Droṇena pīḍitāḥ.
vartamāne tathā raudre saṃgrāme, Bharata'|rṣabha,
ubhayoḥ senayoḥ śūrā n' âmṛṣyanta paras|param.
āviṣṭā iva yudhyante rakṣo|bhūtair mahā|balāḥ
tāvakāḥ Pāṇḍaveyāś ca saṃrabdhās, tāta, dhanvinaḥ.
na sma paśyāmahe kaṃ cid, yaḥ prāṇān parirakṣati
saṃgrāme daitya|saṃkāśe tasmin vīra|vara|kṣaye.

DHṚTARĀṢṬRA uvāca:

91.1 IRĀVANTAṂ TU nihataṃ dṛṣṭvā Pārthā mahā|rathāḥ
saṃgrāme kim akurvanta? tan mam' ācakṣva, Sañjaya.

SAÑJAYA uvāca:

Irāvantaṃ tu nihataṃ saṃgrāme vīkṣya rākṣasaḥ
vyanadat su|mahā|nādaṃ Bhaimasenir Ghaṭotkacaḥ.
nadatas tasya śabdena pṛthivī sāgar'|âmbarā
sa|parvata|vanā, rājaṃś, cacāla su|bhṛśaṃ tadā,
antarikṣaṃ, diśaś c' âiva, sarvāś ca pradiśas tathā.
taṃ śrutvā su|mahā|nādaṃ tava sainyasya, Bhārata,
91.5 ūru|stambhaḥ samabhavad, vepathuḥ, sveda eva ca.
sarva eva, mahā|rāja, tāvakā dīna|cetasaḥ
sarvataḥ samaceṣṭanta siṃha|bhītā gajā iva.

narditvā su|mahā|nādaṃ nirghātam iva rākṣasaḥ
jvalitaṃ śūlam udyamya, rūpaṃ kṛtvā vibhīṣaṇam,
nānā|rūpa|praharaṇair vṛto rākṣasa|puṅgavaiḥ

battle. What then if he is surrounded by a large number of the world's bravest combatants?" That's what the Pándavas said when they were plagued by Drona in that engagement, great king. During that terrible battle, bull of the Bharatas, the heroic warriors of both armies were implacable toward each other. The mighty combatants of your army and that of the Pándavas, wielding their bows filled with fury, fought as if they were possessed by demons, my lord. In that conflict that was like a clash between demons, and in which many excellent heroes were slain, we saw no one who cared about his life. 90.90

DHRITA·RASHTRA said:

WHAT DID PRITHA's mighty warrior sons do when they saw Irávat slaughtered, Sánjaya? 91.1

SÁNJAYA said:

Seeing Irávat struck down in battle, the demon Ghatót-kacha, the son of Bhima·sena, uttered a tremendous roar. As he roared, the ocean-clothed earth with all its mountains and forests shook tremendously, Your Majesty. The sky and both the major and minor directions trembled
as well. When your soldiers heard that terrible roar their 91.5
thighs grew numb; they were seized with shuddering and broke into sweats. All your troops, dispirited, scattered in all directions, great king, like elephants frightened by the roar of a lion.

Shouting out with his horrific and thunderous roar, the demon assumed a terrifying form, and, brandishing his pike and surrounded by mighty demons armed with weapons of various kinds, he furiously pounced on your host. He ap-

ājagāma su|saṃkruddhaḥ kāl'|ântaka|Yam'|ôpamaḥ.
tam āpatantaṃ saṃprekṣya saṃkruddhaṃ bhīma|darśanam
sva|balaṃ ca bhayāt tasya prāyaśo vimukhī|kṛtam.

tato Duryodhano rājā Ghaṭotkacam upādravat,
91.10 pragṛhya vipulaṃ cāpaṃ, siṃhavad vinadan muhuḥ.
pṛṣṭhato 'nuyayau c' âinaṃ sravadbhiḥ parvat'|ôpamaiḥ
kuñjarair daśa|sāhasrair Vaṅgānām adhipaḥ svayam.
tam āpatantaṃ saṃprekṣya gaj'|ânīkena saṃvṛtam
putraṃ tava, mahā|rāja, cukopa sa niśā|caraḥ.

tataḥ pravavṛte yuddhaṃ tumulaṃ, loma|harṣaṇam
rākṣasānāṃ ca, rāj'|êndra, Duryodhana|balasya ca.
gaj'|ânīkaṃ ca saṃprekṣya megha|vṛndam iv' ôditam
abhyadhāvanta saṃkruddhā rākṣasāḥ śastra|pāṇayaḥ.
nadanto vividhān nādān meghā iva sa|vidyutaḥ,
91.15 śara|śakty|ṛṣṭi|nārācair nighnanto gaja|yodhinaḥ,
bhindipālais, tathā śūlair, mudgaraiḥ sa|paraśvadhaiḥ,
parvat'|âgraiś ca, vṛkṣaiś ca nijaghnus te mahā|gajān.
bhinna|kumbhān, vi|rudhirān, bhinna|gātrāṃś ca vāraṇān
apaśyāma, mahā|rāja, vadhyamānān niśā|caraiḥ.

teṣu prakṣīyamāṇeṣu bhagneṣu gaja|yodhiṣu
Duryodhano, mahā|rāja, rākṣasān samupādravat
a|marṣa|vaśam āpannas, tyaktvā jīvitam ātmanaḥ.
mumoca niśitān bāṇān rākṣaseṣu mahā|balaḥ,
jaghāna ca mah"|êṣv|āsaḥ pradhānāṃs tatra rākṣasān.
91.20 saṃkruddho, Bharata|śreṣṭha, putro Duryodhanas tava
Vegavantaṃ, Mahāraudraṃ, Vidyujjihvaṃ, Pramāthinam

peared like Yama, the Destroyer, at the time of dissolution.
Seeing that fierce-looking demon advancing, almost all our
troops turned their backs for fear of him.

Then King Duryódhana, seizing a large bow and roaring 91.10
again and again like a lion, charged against Ghatótkacha.
Behind him came the ruler of the Vangas himself, with ten
thousand mountainous elephants that were secreting their
juices. At the sight of your son advancing, surrounded by an
elephant division, O great king, the night-ranging demon
got excited with rage.

Then a tumultuous and hair-raising battle took place between the demons and Duryódhana's force, king of kings.
Seeing the elephant division rising like a mass of clouds, the
infuriated demons rushed forward with weapons in their
hands, roaring various roars, like thunderclouds charged
with lightning. They started to smash up the elephant war- 91.15
riors with arrows, lances, spears, iron shafts, javelins, spikes,
mallets, and battle axes, and to crush the elephants with
rocks and trees. We saw elephants that were drained of
blood, their foreheads split open, their limbs severed, massacred by the night-ranging demons, great king.

When that elephant division was routed and destroyed,
Duryódhana, overcome by anger and ready to sacrifice his
life, charged against the demons, great king. That great
archer fired sharpened arrows at the demons, scorcher of
enemies, and killed their chiefs. O best of the Bharatas, 91.20
with four arrows your mighty son Duryódhana, enraged,
killed four demons: Végavat, Maha·raudra, Vidyuj·jihva,

śaraiś caturbhiś caturo nijaghāna mahā|balaḥ.
tataḥ punar a|mey'|ātmā śara|varṣaṃ dur|āsadam
mumoca Bharata|śreṣṭho niśā|cara|balaṃ prati.

tat tu dṛṣṭvā mahat karma putrasya tava, māriṣa,
krodhen' âbhiprajajvāla Bhaimasenir mahā|balaḥ.
sa visphārya mahac cāpam Indr'|âśani|sama|svanam,
abhidudrāva vegena Duryodhanam arin|damam.
tam āpatantam udvīkṣya Kāla|sṛṣṭam iv' Ântakam,
91.25 na vivyathe, mahā|rāja, putro Duryodhanas tava.
ath' âinam abravīt kruddhaḥ krūraḥ saṃrakta|locanaḥ:

«ady' ānṛṇyaṃ gamiṣyāmi pitṝṇāṃ mātur eva ca,
ye tvayā su|nṛśaṃsena dīrgha|kālaṃ pravāsitāḥ!
yac ca te Pāṇḍavā, rājaṃś, chala|dyūte parājitāḥ,
yac c' âiva Draupadī Kṛṣṇā eka|vastrā, rajasvalā
sabhām ānīya, dur|buddhe, bahudhā kleśitā tvayā,
tava ca priya|kāmena āśrama|sthā dur|ātmanā
Saindhavena parāmṛṣṭā paribhūya pitṝn mama—
eteṣām apamānānām anyeṣāṃ ca, kul'|âdhama,
91.30 antam adya gamiṣyāmi, yadi n' ôtsṛjase raṇam!»

evam uktvā tu Haiḍimbo mahad visphārya kārmukam,
saṃdaśya daśanair oṣṭhaṃ, sṛkkiṇī parisaṃlihan,
śara|varṣeṇa mahatā Duryodhanam avākirat,
parvataṃ vāri|dhārābhiḥ prāvṛṣ' îva balāhakaḥ.

and Pramáthin. Then that foremost of the Bharatas, endowed with limitless spirit, again discharged an irresistible downpour of shafts at the host of the night-ranging demons.

Seeing your son's great feat, my lord, the immensely powerful son of Bhima·sena blazed up with fury. Stretching his mighty bow that was as resplendent as Indra's thunderbolt, he charged forcefully against the enemy-taming Duryódhana. Seeing the demon advancing toward him like Death
created by Time, your son Duryódhana did not flinch, great 91.25
king. The cruel demon, his eyes bloodshot with fury, said to him:

"You, sinner! Today I will pay the debt I owe to my fathers and mother, who spent a long time in exile, banished by you, most wicked man! King, it is through your roguery that the sons of Pandu lost the game of dice! It was at your command that Krishná the daughter of Drúpada, in her menses and wearing a single cloth, was brought into the assembly hall and wronged there, you evil-minded wretch! It was in order to please you that the malicious ruler of the Sindhus, disregarding my fathers, abducted Dráupadi when
she dwelled at the hermitage! For these and other insults I 91.30
will take revenge on you today, disgrace to the family, unless you flee from battle!"

After saying these words, the son of Hidímba drew a mighty bow, bit his lip with his teeth, licked the corners of his mouth, and enveloped Duryódhana in a heavy downpour of arrows just as a rain-cloud covers a mountain with torrents of rain in the monsoon.

SAÑJAYA uvāca:

92.1 TATAS TAD BĀṆA|varṣaṃ tu duḥ|sahaṃ dānavair api
dadhāra yudhi rāj'|êndro yathā varṣaṃ mahā|dvipaḥ;
tataḥ krodha|samāviṣṭo, niḥśvasann iva pannagaḥ,
saṃśayaṃ paramaṃ prāptaḥ putras te, Bharata'|rṣabha,
mumoca niśitāṃs tīkṣṇān nārācān pañca|viṃśatim.
te 'patan sahasā, rājaṃs, tasmin rākṣasa|puṅgave,
āśīviṣā iva kruddhāḥ parvate Gandhamādane.
sa tair viddhaḥ, sravan raktaṃ, prabhinna iva kuñjaraḥ,
92.5 dadhre matiṃ vināśāya rājñaḥ sa piśit'|âśanaḥ,
jagrāha ca mahā|śaktiṃ girīṇām api dāraṇīm,
saṃpradīptāṃ, mah"|ôlk|ābhām, aśaniṃ jvalitām iva
samudyacchan mahā|bāhur jighāṃsus tanayaṃ tava.
tām udyatām abhiprekṣya Vaṅgānām adhipas tvaran
kuñjaraṃ giri|saṃkāśaṃ rākṣasaṃ pratyacodayat.
sa nāga|pravareṇ' ājau balinā śīghra|gāminā
yato Duryodhana|rathas, taṃ mārgaṃ pratyapadyata
rathaṃ ca vārayām āsa kuñjareṇa sutasya te.
mārgam āvāritaṃ dṛṣṭvā rājñā Vaṅgena dhīmatā,
92.10 Ghaṭotkaco, mahā|rāja, krodha|saṃrakta|locanaḥ
udyatāṃ tāṃ mahā|śaktiṃ tasmiṃś cikṣepa vāraṇe.
sa tay" âbhihato, rājaṃs, tena bāhu|pramuktayā
saṃjāta|rudhir'|ôtpīḍaḥ papāta ca mamāra ca.
pataty atha gaje c' âpi Vaṅgānām īśvaro balī
javena samabhidrutya jagāma dharaṇī|talam.
Duryodhano 'pi saṃprekṣya pātitaṃ vara|vāraṇam,

SÁNJAYA said:

IN THAT BATTLE, the king of kings withstood that down- 92.1
pour of arrows that would have been difficult even for the gods to endure, just as a mighty elephant bears a rainstorm. Then, filled with fury and hissing like a snake, bull of the Bharatas, your son, having braved that serious danger, fired twenty-five whetted iron arrows with sharp heads. They fell onto that bull of a demon just as irate venomous snakes rush to Mount Gandha·mádana.

Wounded by them, and shedding blood as a rutting elephant secretes juices, the flesh-eater set his mind on destroy- 92.5
ing the king. So he grabbed a huge spear that could even cut through rocks. The mighty-armed demon, wanting to slay your son, raised that spear: it was as resplendent as a large meteor, it glowed with light and looked like flashes of lightning. Seeing it raised, the king of the Vangas quickly urged his elephant on, toward that mountain-like demon. Riding his superb, mighty, and swift elephant, he stationed himself in the line of Duryódhana's chariot, screening your son's chariot with his elephant.

Seeing the way blocked by that wise king of the Vangas,
O great king, Ghatótkacha, his eyes bloodshot with rage, 92.10
hurled that huge upraised spear at the elephant. Struck by that spear hurled from Ghatótkacha's arm, Your Majesty, the elephant, bleeding profusely, collapsed and died. As the elephant was collapsing, the mighty king of the Vangas quickly leaped to the ground. Duryódhana, having seen his army broken and that excellent elephant struck down, was overcome with grave anxiety. But honoring the warrior code and out of self-respect, King Duryódhana, though

prabhagnaṃ ca balaṃ dṛṣṭvā jagāma paramāṃ vyathām.
kṣatra|dharmaṃ puras|kṛtya, ātmanaś c' âbhimānitām,
prāpte 'pakramaṇe rājā tasthau girir iv' â|calaḥ.
92.15 saṃdhāya ca śitaṃ bāṇaṃ Kāl'|âgni|sama|tejasam
mumoca parama|kruddhas tasmin ghore niśā|care.
tam āpatantaṃ saṃprekṣya bāṇam Indr'|âśani|prabham,
lāghavān mocayām āsa mah"|ātmā vai Ghaṭotkacaḥ.
bhūya eva nanād' ôgraḥ krodha|saṃrakta|locanaḥ;
trāsayām āsa sainyāni yug'|ânte jala|do yathā.

taṃ śrutvā ninadaṃ ghoraṃ tasya bhīmasya rakṣasaḥ
ācāryam upasaṃgamya Bhīṣmaḥ Śāntanavo 'bravīt:
«yath" âiṣa ninado ghoraḥ śrūyate rākṣas'|ēritaḥ,
Haiḍimbo yudhyate nūnaṃ rājñā Duryodhanena ha.
92.20 n' âiṣa śakyo hi saṃgrāme jetuṃ bhūtena kena cit.
tatra gacchata, bhadraṃ vo, rājānaṃ parirakṣata.
abhidruto mahā|bhāgo rākṣasena mah"|ātmanā.
etadd hi paramaṃ kṛtyaṃ sarveṣāṃ naḥ paran|tapāḥ.»
pitā|maha|vacaḥ śrutvā tvaramāṇā mahā|rathāḥ
uttamaṃ javam āsthāya prayayur, yatra Kauravaḥ.
Droṇaś ca, Somadattaś ca, Bāhliko, 'tha Jayadrathaḥ,
Kṛpo, Bhūriśravāḥ, Śalya, Āvantyaḥ sa|Bṛhadbalaḥ,
Aśvatthāmā, Vikarṇaś ca, Citraseno, Viviṃśatiḥ,
rathāś c' ân|eka|sāhasrā ye teṣām anuyāyinaḥ
92.25 abhidrutaṃ parīpsantaḥ putraṃ Duryodhanaṃ tava.

he could have fled, stood still like an immovable mountain; he aimed a sharp arrow that blazed like the fire of 92.15
Time, and filled with a violent rage he fired it at the terrible night-ranger. Seeing that arrow resplendent like Indra's thunderbolt flying toward him, great-spirited Ghatótkacha deprived it of its momentum. Then, his eyes bloodshot with fury, he roared fiercely once again like a cloud at the end of the age, and made the troops tremble.

Hearing the hideous roar of that terrifying demon, Bhishma the son of Shántanu approached the teacher Drona and said: "This frightful roar that is being sounded is uttered by a demon, and suggests that the son of Hidímba is now fighting with King Duryódhana. That demon cannot be de- 92.20
feated in combat by any creature. So go there and protect the king. Blessings be to you! The glorious hero has been assailed by the great-spirited demon. Rescuing the king is your foremost duty and that of us all, scorcher of enemies." When they heard the grandfather's words, the mighty warriors immediately advanced with the utmost speed to the place where the Káurava king was. Drona, Soma·datta, Báhlika, Jayad·ratha, Kripa, Bhuri·shravas, Shalya, the Avánti prince, Brihad·bala, Ashva·tthaman, Vikárna, Chitra·sena, Vivímshati, and several thousand combatants who followed them were all eager to rescue your son Duryódhana who 92.25
was under attack.

tad anīkam an|ādhṛṣyaṃ, pālitaṃ tu mahā|rathaiḥ,
ātatāyinam āyāntaṃ prekṣya rākṣasa|sattamaḥ
n' âkampata mahā|bāhur, Maināka iva parvataḥ,
pragṛhya vipulaṃ cāpaṃ, jñātibhiḥ parivāritaḥ
śūla|mudgara|hastaiś ca, nānā|praharaṇair api.
tataḥ samabhavad yuddhaṃ tumulaṃ, loma|harṣaṇam
rākṣasānāṃ ca mukhyasya Duryodhana|balasya ca.
dhanuṣāṃ kūjatāṃ śabdaḥ sarvatas tumulo raṇe
aśrūyata, mahā|rāja, vaṃśānāṃ dahyatām iva.
92.30 astrāṇāṃ pātyamānānāṃ kavaceṣu śarīriṇām
śabdaḥ samabhavad, rājann, giriṇām iva bhidyatām.
vīra|bāhu|visṛṣṭānāṃ tomarāṇāṃ, viśāṃ pate,
rūpam āsīd viyat|sthānāṃ sarpāṇām iva sarpatām.
tataḥ parama|saṃkruddho visphārya su|mahad dhanuḥ,
rākṣas'|êndro mahā|bāhur vinadan bhairavaṃ ravam,
ācāryasy' ârdha|candreṇa kruddhaś ciccheda kārmukam,
Somadattasya bhallena dhvajam unmathya c' ânadat.
Bāhlikaṃ ca tribhir bāṇair abhyavidhyat stan'|ântare;
Kṛpam ekena vivyādha; Citrasenaṃ tribhiḥ śaraiḥ.
92.35 pūrṇ'|āyata|visṛṣṭena samyak praṇihitena ca
jatru|deśe samāsādya Vikarṇaṃ samatāḍayat.
nyaṣīdat sa rath'|ôpasthe śoṇitena pariplutaḥ.
tataḥ punar a|mey'|ātmā nārācān daśa pañca ca
Bhūriśravasi saṃkruddhaḥ prāhiṇod, Bharata'|rṣabha.
te varma bhittvā tasy' āśu prāviśan medinī|talam.

Seeing that unconquerable host that was protected by great warriors and was advancing, bows drawn, toward him, that supreme mighty-armed demon stood immovable like Mount Mainráka, holding a huge bow and surrounded by his kinsmen with pikes, mallets, and various other weapons in their hands.

Then a tumultuous and hair-raising battle ensued between the demons and Duryódhana's main force. A howling din of twanging bows could be heard from all sides in that battle, great king, like the crackling of burning bamboo. The noise of weapons striking against men's ar- 92.30
mor, Your Majesty, was like the sound of mountains splitting. O lord of the people, the lances hurled by the heroes' arms looked like serpents flying through the sky. Then the mighty-armed demon king, filled with intense fury, stretched his enormous bow, uttered a fierce roar, and angrily severed the teacher Drona's bow with an arrow that had a semicircular head. The demon felled Soma·datta's banner with a spear-headed shaft and gave a loud shout. He wounded Báhlika in the center of his chest with three arrows, pierced Kripa with one shaft, and Chitra·sena with three. He then attacked Vikárna and struck him in the 92.35
shoulder with a well-aimed arrow fired from his bow at full stretch; and Vikárna, drenched in blood, collapsed onto his chariot platform. After that the boundlessly spirited demon, enraged, shot fifteen iron shafts at Bhuri·shravas, descendant of Bharata. Tearing through his armor, they swiftly entered the earth. Then he injured the drivers of Vivímshati and of Drona's son; and they fell onto their chariot platforms, letting go of the horses' reins. Firing an

Viviṃśateś ca Drauṇeś ca yantārau samatāḍayat.
tau petatū rath|ôpasthe raśmīn utsṛjya vājinām.
Sindhu|rājño 'rdha|candreṇa vārāhaṃ svarṇa|bhūṣitam
unmamātha, mahā|rāja; dvitīyen' âcchinad dhanuḥ.
92.40 caturbhir atha nārācair Āvantyasya mah"|ātmanaḥ
jaghāna caturo vāhān krodha|saṃrakta|locanaḥ.
pūrṇ'|āyata|visṛṣṭena, pītena, niśitena ca
nirbibheda, mahā|rāja, rāja|putraṃ Bṛhadbalam.
sa gāḍha|viddho, vyathito rath'|ôpastha upāviśat.
bhṛśaṃ krodhena c' āviṣṭo ratha|stho rākṣas'|âdhipaḥ
cikṣepa niśitāṃs tīkṣṇāñ śarān āśīviṣ'|ôpamān.
bibhidus te, mahā|rāja, Śalyaṃ yuddha|viśāradam.

SAÑJAYA uvāca:

93.1 VIMUKHĪ|KṚTYA tān sarvāṃs tāvakān yudhi rākṣasaḥ
jighāṃsur, Bharata|śreṣṭha, Duryodhanam upādravat.
tam āpatantaṃ saṃprekṣya rājānaṃ prati vegitam,
abhyadhāvañ jighāṃsantas tāvakā yuddha|dur|madāḥ.
tāla|mātrāṇi cāpāni vikarṣanto mahā|rathāḥ
tam ekam abhyadhāvanta nadantaḥ siṃha|saṅghavat.
ath' âinaṃ śara|varṣeṇa samantāt paryavākiran,
parvataṃ vāri|dhārābhiḥ śarad' îva balāhakāḥ.
93.5 sa gāḍha|viddho, vyathitas, tottr'|ârdita iva dvi|paḥ,
utpapāta tad" ākāśaṃ samantād Vainateyavat.
vyanadat su|mahā|nādaṃ jīmūta iva śāradaḥ,
diśaḥ, khaṃ, vidiśaś c' âiva nādayan bhairava|svanaḥ.

arrow with a semicircular head, the demon felled the banner of the king of the Sindhus—it was decorated in gold and emblazoned with a boar, great king—and with another he severed the king's bow. His eyes bloodshot with anger, 92.40
with four iron shafts Ghatótkacha killed four horses of the great-spirited prince of Avánti. He pierced Prince Brihad·bala with a sharpened copper arrow fired from his bow at full stretch, great king. The prince sank onto his chariot platform severely wounded, tormented with pain. Then the chief of demons, standing on his chariot, filled with rage, fired whetted and sharp-headed shafts that were like poisonous snakes; and those arrows, great king, injured Shalya skilled in warfare.

SÁNJAYA said:

HAVING FORCED all your troops to turn their backs in 93.1
battle, the demon charged against Duryódhana, best of the Bharatas, wanting to kill him. Seeing him advancing with great force toward the king, your warriors, ferocious in battle, rushed forward eager to kill the demon. Roaring like lions and drawing bows as big as palm trees, those great fighters assaulted the single warrior Ghatótkacha. They shrouded him all around with a rain of arrows, just as storm-clouds cover a mountain with torrents of rain in autumn. Seriously 93.5
wounded, tormented by pain like an elephant pricked with goads, the demon flew up into the sky just like Vínata's son Gáruda. Then he uttered a tremendous roar that was like the rumble of autumnal thunderclouds, and that terrible din resounded in the sky and in all the major and minor directions.

rākṣasasya tu taṃ śabdaṃ śrutvā rājā Yudhiṣṭhiraḥ
uvāca, Bharata|śreṣṭha, Bhīmasenam arin|damam:
«yudhyate rākṣaso nūnaṃ Dhārtarāṣṭrair mahā|rathaiḥ,
yath" âsya śrūyate śabdo nadato bhairavaṃ svanam.
ati|bhāraṃ ca paśyāmi tasmin rākṣasa|puṅgave.
pitā|mahaś ca saṃkruddhaḥ Pāñcālān hantum udyataḥ,
93.10 teṣāṃ ca rakṣaṇ'|ârthāya yudhyate Phālgunaḥ paraiḥ.
etaj jñātvā, mahā|bāho, kārya|dvayam upasthitam.
gaccha, rakṣasva Haiḍimbaṃ saṃśayaṃ paramaṃ gatam.»

bhrātur vacanam ājñāya tvaramāṇo Vṛkodaraḥ
prayayau siṃha|nādena trāsayan sarva|pārthivān,
vegena mahatā, rājan, parva|kāle yath" ôda|dhiḥ.
tam anvagāt Satyadhṛtiḥ, Saucittir yuddha|dur|madaḥ,
Śreṇimān, Vasudānaś ca putraḥ Kāśyasya c' âbhibhūḥ,
Abhimanyu|mukhāś c' âiva Draupadeyā mahā|rathāḥ,
Kṣatradevaś ca vikrāntaḥ, Kṣatradharmā tath" âiva ca,
93.15 Anūp'|âdhipatiś c' âiva Nīlaḥ sva|balam āsthitaḥ.
mahatā ratha|vaṃśena Haiḍimbaṃ paryavārayan.
kuñjaraiś ca sadā mattaiḥ ṣaṭ|sahasraiḥ prahāribhiḥ
abhyarakṣanta sahitā rākṣas'|êndraṃ Ghaṭotkacam.
siṃha|nādena mahatā, nemi|ghoṣeṇa c' âiva ha,
khura|śabda|ninādaiś ca kampayanto vasun|dharām.

teṣām āpatatāṃ śrutvā śabdaṃ taṃ tāvakaṃ balam
Bhīmasena|bhay'|ôdvignaṃ vivarṇa|vadanaṃ tathā
parivṛttaṃ, mahā|rāja, parityajya Ghaṭotkacam.

Hearing the demon's howl, best of the Bharatas, King
Yudhi·shthira spoke to Bhima·sena the tamer of enemies.
"Surely the demon is now fighting against Dhrita·rashtra's
great warriors, since we can hear the noise made by his
frightful war-cry. I fear that the burden may be too heavy for
that demon, though he is as mighty as a bull. But the furious
grandfather is intent on slaughtering the Panchálas, and in 93.10
order to protect them Phálguna is currently engaged with
the foe. Appreciating both of these pressing tasks, go and
protect the son of Hidímba, who is now in great danger!"

And on hearing his brother's words, Vrikódara, horrify-
ing all the kings with his lion-roar, rushed forward with
great vehemence, Your Majesty, like the ocean when the
moon changes. Satya·dhriti, Sauchítti ferocious in battle,
Shrénimat, the Kashi ruler's mighty son Vasu·dana, the
great warrior sons of Dráupadi led by Abhimányu, powerful Kshatra·deva, Kshatra·dharman, and Nila the ruler of 93.15
the Anúpas along with his force all followed him. They surrounded the son of Hidímba with a huge chariot division.
They started to protect that chief of demons Ghatótkacha
with the aid of six thousand maddened, violent elephants.
They made the earth quake with their tremendous lion-
roars, with the clatter of their chariot wheels, and with the
rumbling of their horses' hooves.

When they heard the noise of the attacking army, your troops were struck with terror and their faces became drained of color. Leaving Ghatótkacha, the Káuravas turned, great king.

tataḥ pravavṛte yuddhaṃ tatra tatra mah"|ātmanām
93.20 tāvakānāṃ pareṣāṃ ca saṃgrāmeṣv a|nivartinām.
nānā|rūpāṇi śastrāṇi visṛjanto mahā|rathāḥ
anyonyam abhidhāvantaḥ saṃprahāraṃ pracakrire.
vyatiṣaktaṃ mahā|raudraṃ yuddhaṃ bhīru|bhay'|āvaham.
hayā gajaiḥ samājagmuḥ, pādātā rathibhiḥ saha.
anyonyaṃ samare, rājan, prārthayānā samabhyayuḥ.
sahasā c' âbhavat tīvraṃ saṃnipātān mahad rajaḥ
gaj'|âśva|ratha|pattīnāṃ pada|nemi|samuddhatam.
dhūmr'|âruṇaṃ rajas tīvraṃ raṇa|bhūmiṃ samāvṛṇot.
n' âiva sve na pare, rājan, samajānan paras|param.
93.25 pitā putraṃ na jānīte, putro vā pitaraṃ tathā
nir|maryāde tathā|bhūte vaiśase loma|harṣaṇe.

śastrāṇāṃ, Bharata|śreṣtha, manuṣyāṇāṃ ca garjatām
su|mahān abhavac chabdo pretānām iva, Bhārata.
gaja|vāji|manuṣyāṇāṃ śoṇit'|ântra|taraṅgiṇī
prāvartata nadī tatra keśa|śaivala|śādvalā.
narāṇāṃ c' âiva kāyebhyaḥ śirasāṃ patatāṃ raṇe
śuśruve su|mahāñ śabdaḥ patatām aśmanām iva.
vi|śiraskair manuṣyaiś ca, cchinna|gātraiś ca vāraṇaiḥ,
aśvaiḥ saṃbhinna|dehaiś ca saṃkīrṇ" âbhūd vasun|dharā.
93.30 nānā|vidhāni śastrāṇi visṛjanto mahā|rathāḥ
anyonyam abhidhāvantaḥ saṃprahār'|ârtham udyatāḥ.
hayā hayān samāsādya preṣitā haya|sādibhiḥ
samāhatya raṇe 'nyonyaṃ nipetur gata|jīvitāḥ.
narā narān samāsādya krodha|rakt'|ēkṣaṇā bhṛśam
urāṃsy urobhir anyonyaṃ samāśliṣya nijaghnire.

Then a battle ensued between your and the enemy's great- 93.20
spirited warriors, who never flee in combat. Great warriors, hurling weapons of various types, charged and attacked each other. It was an immensely terrifying and chaotic battle, and it filled the timid with fear. Cavalry engaged in battle with elephants, and infantry with chariot warriors. They challenged and assaulted one another in that conflict. And as a result of that clash between elephants, horses, chariots, and foot soldiers, a thick cloud of dust appeared, raised by feet and by chariot wheels. Thick dust, colored black and red, enveloped the battlefield. Neither your troops nor the
enemy could tell each other apart, Your Majesty. During 93.25
this unrestrained and hair-raising massacre fathers could not recognize their sons, nor could sons recognize their fathers.

O best of the Bharatas, the clash of weapons and the shouts of men made a terrible noise, like the noise made by ghosts. O Bhárata, a surging river of the blood and entrails of elephants, horses, and men sprang up there; hair formed its moss and weeds. And the loud thud of the falling heads severed from men's bodies was heard in that battle, like the sound of stones dropping out of the sky. The earth was covered with headless human trunks, elephants with lacerated limbs, and horses with slashed bodies. Hurling vari- 93.30
ous weapons and charging against each other, great warriors were intent on striking each other down. Driven on by their riders, horses dashed in combat against horses, and smitten by one another they fell down lifeless. Their eyes bloodshot with violent rage, men barged against men and struck each other down with their chests.

preṣitāś ca mahā|mātrair vāraṇāḥ para|vāraṇāḥ
abhyaghnanta viṣāṇ'|âgrair vāraṇān eva saṃyuge.
te jāta|rudhir'|ôtpīḍāḥ, patākābhir alaṃ|kṛtāḥ
saṃsaktāḥ pratyadṛśyanta, meghā iva sa|vidyutaḥ.
93.35 ke cid bhinnā viṣāṇ'|âgrair, bhinna|kumbhāś ca tomaraiḥ
vinadanto 'bhyadhāvanta garjamānā ghanā iva.
ke cidd hastair dvidhā chinnaiś, chinna|gātrās tath" âpare
nipetus tumule tasmiṃś chinna|pakṣā iv' âdrayaḥ.
pārśvais tu dāritair anye vāraṇair vara|vāraṇāḥ
mumucuḥ śoṇitaṃ bhūri, dhātūn iva mahī|dharāḥ.
nārāc'|âbhihatās tv anye, tathā viddhāś ca tomaraiḥ
hat'|ārohā vyadṛśyanta, vi|śṛṅgā iva parvatāḥ.
ke cit krodha|samāviṣṭā mad'|ândhā, nir|avagrahāḥ
rathān, hayān, padātīṃś ca mamṛduḥ śataśo raṇe.
93.40 tathā hayā hay'|ārohais tāḍitāḥ prāsa|tomaraiḥ
tena ten' âbhyavartanta, kurvanto vyākulā diśaḥ.
rathino rathibhiḥ sārdhaṃ kula|putrās tanu|tyajaḥ
parāṃ śaktiṃ samāsthāya cakruḥ karmāṇy a|bhītavat.
svayaṃ|vara iv' āmarde prajahrur itar'|êtaram
prārthayānā yaśo, rājan, svargaṃ vā yuddha|śālinaḥ.
tasmiṃs tathā vartamāne saṃgrāme loma|harṣaṇe
Dhārtarāṣṭraṃ mahat sainyaṃ prāyaśo vimukhī|kṛtam.

Urged on by their riders, elephants clashed with hostile elephants, gashing them with the tips of their tusks in that conflict. Bleeding profusely and adorned with flags, they looked like clouds charged with lightning clashing against
each other. Some of them rampaged around, wounded by 93.35
tusks, their foreheads split open with spears, roaring like rumbling thunderclouds. Some collapsed in the mayhem with their trunks cut in two, and others with their limbs lacerated, just as the mountains did when they had their wings cut off. Other superb elephants, their sides ripped open by hostile tuskers, shed quantities of blood like mountains washed by streams mixed with red chalk and other minerals. Others, struck down with iron shafts and wounded with spears, their riders killed, looked like crestfallen mountains. Still others, filled with fury, blind with rut and frenzy, and free of the hook, crushed hundreds of chariots, horses, and
foot soldiers in that battle. And horses careered hither and 93.40
thither, wounded by cavalrymen with javelins and spears, creating confusion on all sides. Chariot warriors from noble families, ready to sacrifice their lives, fought fearlessly against enemy chariot warriors and performed feats of valor, applying themselves to the utmost of their power. Seeking heaven or glory the fighters smote each other in that violent carnage, your Majesty, as if they were competing for a bride. And in the course of that hair-raising battle, almost all of the mighty Dharta·rashtra troops were forced to turn tail.

SAÑJAYA uvāca:

94.1 SVA|SAINYAṂ nihataṃ dṛṣṭvā rājā Duryodhanaḥ svayam
abhyadhāvata saṃkruddho Bhīmasenam arin|damam;
pragṛhya su|mahac cāpam Indr'|âśani|sama|svanam
mahatā śara|varṣeṇa Pāṇḍavaṃ samavākirat;
ardha|candraṃ ca saṃdhāya su|tīkṣṇaṃ, loma|vāhinam,
Bhīmasenasya ciccheda cāpaṃ krodha|samanvitaḥ.
tad|antaraṃ ca saṃprekṣya tvaramāṇo mahā|rathaḥ
prasaṃdadhe śitaṃ bāṇaṃ girīṇām api dāraṇam;
94.5 ten' ôrasi mahā|bāhur Bhīmasenam atāḍayat.
sa gāḍha|viddho, vyathitaḥ, sṛkkiṇī parisaṃlihan
samālalambe tejasvī dhvajaṃ hema|pariṣkṛtam.
tathā vi|manasaṃ dṛṣṭvā Bhīmasenaṃ Ghaṭotkacaḥ
krodhen' âbhiprajajvāla, didhakṣann iva pāvakaḥ.
Abhimanyu|mukhāś c' âpi Pāṇḍavānāṃ mahā|rathāḥ
samabhyadhāvan krośanto
rājānaṃ jāta|saṃbhramāḥ.
saṃprekṣy' âitān saṃpatataḥ
saṃkruddhāñ jāta|saṃbhramān
Bhāradvājo 'bravīd vākyaṃ tāvakānāṃ mahā|rathān:
«kṣipraṃ gacchata, bhadraṃ vo, rājānaṃ parirakṣata
94.10 saṃśayaṃ paramaṃ prāptaṃ, majjantaṃ vyasan'|ârṇave.
ete kruddhā mah"|êṣv|āsāḥ Pāṇḍavānāṃ mahā|rathāḥ
Bhīmasenaṃ puras|kṛtya Duryodhanam upādravan
nānā|vidhāni śastrāṇi visṛjanto, jaye dhṛtāḥ,
nadanto bhairavān nādāṃs, trāsayantaś ca bhūmi|pān.»

SÁNJAYA said:

ON SEEING HIS troops slaughtered, Duryódhana him- 94.1
self, filled with rage, charged against Bhima·sena the tamer of enemies. Grabbing a huge bow that made a sound like Indra's thunderbolt, he shrouded the son of Pandu with a heavy rain of arrows. Excited with fury, he aimed an extremely sharp arrow with a semicircular head; and he severed Bhima·sena's bow with feathered shafts. Seeing his opportunity, the great warrior Duryódhana immediately aimed a sharp arrow that was even capable of splitting rocks;
and he struck Bhima·sena in the chest with it, great king. 94.5

Severely wounded and afflicted with pain, licking the corners of his mouth, the glorious hero remained standing only by leaning on his gilt-trimmed flagpole.

But seeing Bhima·sena dispirited, Ghatótkacha blazed up with fury like a fire that's about to burn everything down; and the Pándavas' great warriors, led by Abhimányu, agitated and shouting, charged against the king.

When he saw them advancing with force and fury, the son of Bharad·vaja addressed the great warriors of your host with these words:

"Blessings be to you! Go quickly and protect the king 94.10
who is now in great danger and sinking deep into an ocean of misfortune. These mighty archers, the great warriors of the Pándavas, filled with anger and led by Bhima·sena, are charging against Duryódhana, hurling weapons of various kinds and intent on victory. They are roaring fierce roars and terrifying the kings."

tad ācārya|vacaḥ śrutvā Saumadatti|puro|gamāḥ
tāvakāḥ samavartanta Pāṇḍavānām anīkinīm.
Kṛpo, Bhūriśravāḥ, Śalyo, Droṇa|putro, Viviṃśatiḥ,
Citraseno, Vikarṇaś ca, Saindhavo, 'tha Bṛhadbalaḥ,
Āvantyau ca mah"|êṣv|āsau Kauravaṃ paryavārayan.
94.15 te viṃśati|padaṃ gatvā saṃprahāraṃ pracakrire
Pāṇḍavā Dhārtarāṣṭrāś ca paras|para|jighāṃsavaḥ.
evam uktvā mahā|bāhur, mahad visphārya kārmukam,
Bhāradvājas tato Bhīmaṃ ṣaḍ|viṃśatyā samārpayat.
bhūyaś c' âinaṃ mahā|bāhuḥ śaraiḥ śīghram avākirat,
parvataṃ vāri|dhārābhiḥ śarad' îva balāhakaḥ.
taṃ pratyavidhyad daśabhir Bhīmasenaḥ śilīmukhaiḥ
tvaramāṇo mah"|êṣv|āsaḥ savye pārśve mahā|balaḥ.
sa gāḍha|viddho, vyathito, vayo|vṛddhaś ca, Bhārata,
pranaṣṭa|saṃjñaḥ sahasā rath'|ôpastha upāviśat.
94.20 guruṃ pravyathitaṃ dṛṣṭvā rājā Duryodhanaḥ svayam
Drauṇāyaniś ca saṃkruddhau Bhīmasenam abhidrutau.
tāv āpatantau saṃprekṣya kāl'|ântaka|Yam'|ôpamau
Bhīmaseno mahā|bāhur gadām ādāya sa|tvaraḥ
avaplutya rathāt tūrṇaṃ tasthau girir iv' â|calaḥ.
samudyamya gadāṃ gurvīṃ Yama|daṇḍ'|ôpamāṃ raṇe,
tam udyata|gadaṃ dṛṣṭvā, Kailāsam iva śṛṅgiṇam,
Kauravo Droṇa|putraś ca sahitāv abhyadhāvatām.
tāv āpatantau sahitau tvaritau balināṃ varau
abhyadhāvata vegena tvaramāṇo Vṛkodaraḥ.
94.25 tam āpatantaṃ saṃprekṣya

And when they heard the teacher Drona's words, your
fighters, led by the son of Soma·datta, attacked the Pándava
host. Kripa, Bhuri·shravas, Shalya, Drona's son, Vivímshati,
Chitra·sena, Vikárna, the king of the Sindhus, Brihad·bala,
and the two princes of Avánti supported the Kuru king.
Advancing by twenty steps, the Pándavas and the Dharta· 94.15
rashtras began to fight, trying to kill each other.

And the mighty-armed son of Bharad·vaja too, having
made his speech, drew his enormous bow and wounded
Bhima with twenty-six arrows. Then the mighty-armed hero
again immediately shrouded Bhima·sena with shafts once
again, just as a rain-cloud covers a mountain with torrents
of rain in the monsoon. In turn Bhima·sena the mighty
archer struck Drona in his left side with ten stone-whetted
arrows. Seriously wounded and racked with pain, the elderly teacher suddenly collapsed unconscious on the chariot platform, descendant of Bharata. At the sight of Drona 94.20
in the throes of agony, King Duryódhana and Drona's son,
full of anger, charged against Bhima·sena.

Seeing both of them advancing forward like Yama at the
end of an eon, mighty-armed Bhima·sena quickly seized a
mace and, jumping out of his chariot, stood still for battle like an immovable mountain, raising his heavy mace as
if it were Yama's staff. When the Kuru king and the son
of Drona saw him wielding his mace and looking like the
crested Mount Kailása, they both charged against him at the
same time. So Vrikódara too hurtled at speed and with great
force against those two champions of mighty men who were
bearing down upon him quickly, their forces united; and 94.25

samkruddham, bhīma|darśanam,
samabhyadhāvams tvaritāḥ
Kauravāṇām mahā|rathāḥ.
Bhāradvāja|mukhāḥ sarve Bhīmasena|jighāṃsayā
nānā|vidhāni śastrāṇi Bhīmasy' ôrasy apātayan,
sahitāḥ Pāṇḍavaṃ sarve pīḍayantaḥ samantataḥ.
taṃ dṛṣṭvā saṃśayaṃ prāptaṃ pīḍyamānaṃ mahā|ratham
Abhimanyu|prabhṛtayaḥ Pāṇḍavānāṃ mahā|rathāḥ
abhyadhāvan parīpsantaḥ, prāṇāṃs tyaktvā su|dus|tyajān.
Anūp'|âdhipatiḥ śūro
Bhīmasya dayitaḥ sakhā
Nīlo nīl'|âmbuda|prakhyaḥ
saṃkruddho Drauṇim abhyayāt.
94.30 spardhate hi mah"|êṣv|āso nityaṃ Droṇa|sutena saḥ.
sa visphārya mahac cāpaṃ Drauṇiṃ vivyādha patriṇā,
yathā Śakro, mahā|rāja, purā vivyādha dānavam
Vipracittiṃ dur|ādharṣaṃ devatānāṃ bhayaṅ|karam,
yena loka|trayaṃ krodhāt trāsitaṃ svena tejasā.
tathā Nīlena nirbhinnaḥ su|muktena patatriṇā
saṃjāta|rudhir'|ôtpīḍo Drauṇiḥ krodha|samanvitaḥ.
sa visphārya dhanuś citram Indr|āśani|sama|svanam
dadhre Nīla|vināśāya matiṃ matimatāṃ varaḥ.
tataḥ saṃdhāya vimalān bhallān karmāra|mārjitān,
94.35 jaghāna caturo vāhān, sārathiṃ, dhvajam eva ca;
saptamena ca bhallena Nīlaṃ vivyādha vakṣasi.
sa gāḍha|viddho, vyathito rath'|ôpastha upāviśat.

when they saw the fierce sight of furious Bhima·sena charging at them, the great warriors of the Káurava army advanced toward him even at greater pace. Led by the son of Bharad·vaja, they all wanted to kill Bhima·sena, and they hurled weapons of various types at his chest. Together they plagued the son of Pandu on every side. When, led by Abhimányu, the great warriors of the Pándava army saw that that mighty warrior was in danger, they came to his aid, ready to give up their own dear lives.

Heroic Nila the Anúpa king, who was Bhima's very dear friend, looking like a dark cloud, filled with anger, charged against Drona's son. That mighty archer had always sought 94.30
an encounter with the son of Drona. Drawing his large bow, he wounded Drona's son with a feathered arrow, great king, just as Shakra once injured the demon Vipra·chitti—who was fearful and difficult for the gods to conquer, and who in a fury had terrified the three worlds with his fiery power.

Wounded by Nila with his well-fired feathered arrow and bleeding copiously, the son of Drona became furious. He stretched his splendid bow, making a sound like that of Indra's thunderbolt; and that foremost of wise men set his mind on destroying Nila. He aimed gleaming, spear-headed shafts that had been polished by blacksmiths; he 94.35
felled Nila's four horses, his driver, and his banner, and with the seventh arrow he struck Nila in the chest. Severely wounded, Nila collapsed onto his chariot platform in distress.

mohitaṃ vīkṣya rājānaṃ Nīlam abhra|cay'|ôpamam,
Ghaṭotkaco 'bhisaṃkruddho jñātibhiḥ parivāritaḥ
abhidudrāva vegena Drauṇim āhava|śobhinam.
tath" êtare abhyadhāvan rākṣasā yuddha|dur|madāḥ.
tam āpatantaṃ saṃprekṣya rākṣasaṃ ghora|darśanam
abhyadhāvata tejasvī Bhāradvāj'|ātmajas tvaran,
nijaghāna ca saṃkruddho rākṣasān bhīma|darśanān
94.40 ye 'bhavann agrataḥ kruddhā rākṣasasya puraḥ|sarāḥ.
vimukhāṃś c' âiva tān dṛṣṭvā Drauṇi|cāpa|cyutaiḥ śaraiḥ,
akrudhyata mahā|kāyo Bhaimasenir Ghaṭotkacaḥ;
prāduś|cakre mahā|māyāṃ ghora|rūpāṃ, su|dāruṇām,
mohayan samare Drauṇiṃ māyāvī rākṣas'|âdhipaḥ.
tatas te tāvakāḥ sarve māyayā vimukhī|kṛtāḥ
anyonyaṃ samapaśyanta nikṛttā medinī|tale
viceṣṭamānāḥ, kṛpaṇāḥ, śoṇitena pariplutāḥ;
Droṇaṃ, Duryodhanaṃ, Śalyam, Aśvatthāmānam eva ca,
prāyaśaś ca mah"|êṣv|āsā ye pradhānāḥ sma Kauravāḥ;
94.45 vidhvastā rathinaḥ sarve, rājānaś ca nipātitāḥ,
hayāś ca sa|hay'|ārohā vinikṛttāḥ sahasraśaḥ.
tad dṛṣṭvā tāvakaṃ sainyaṃ vidrutaṃ śibiraṃ prati.
mama prākrośato, rājaṃs, tathā Devavratasya ca,
«yudhyadhvaṃ! mā palāyadhvaṃ! māy" âiṣā rākṣasī raṇe
Ghaṭotkaca|prayukt"!» êti n' âtiṣṭhanta vimohitāḥ.
n' âiva te śraddadhur bhītā vadator āvayor vacaḥ.

At the sight of King Nila, dark as a mass of storm-clouds, fallen senseless, Ghatótkacha was enraged, and surrounded by his relatives he charged with great force against Drona's son who was so brilliant in battle. And other demons ferocious in combat assailed Ashva·tthaman too.

When he saw that fierce-looking demon attacking him, Bharad·vaja's glorious grandson quickly charged against him; and full of anger, he struck down the fierce-looking and furious demon leaders who were in front of Ghatót- 94.40
kacha.

Seeing them turn their backs, shot by arrows fired from Drona's son's bow, Bhima·sena's huge-bodied son Ghatótkacha lost his temper; and that chief of demons, who was endowed with magical powers, displayed a hideous and horrible illusion and thus confounded the son of Drona in battle.

All your troops were put to flight by that illusion. They saw each other lying on the ground lacerated, writhing in agony, flooded with blood, in a pitiful state. They saw Drona, Duryódhana, Shalya, Ashva·tthaman, and other
prominent Káurava warriors in that condition. All the char- 94.45
iot warriors were crushed, the kings struck down, and the horses along with their riders were massacred in their thousands. At the sight of that scene your troops fled toward their camp, although Deva·vrata and I appealed to them, shouting "Fight on! Do not run away! It is merely a demonic illusion created by Ghatótkacha in battle!" They did

tāṃś ca pradravato dṛṣṭvā, jayaṃ prāptāś ca Pāṇḍavāḥ
Ghaṭotkacena sahitāḥ siṃha|nādān pracakrire.
śaṅkha|dundubhi|nirghoṣāḥ samantān nedire bhṛśam.
94.50 evaṃ tava balaṃ sarvaṃ Haiḍimbena dur|ātmanā
sūry'|âstamana|velāyāṃ prabhagnaṃ vidrutaṃ diśaḥ.

SAÑJAYA uvāca:

95.1 TASMIN MAHATI saṃkrande rājā Duryodhanas tadā
Gāṅgeyam upasaṃgamya, vinayen' âbhivādya ca,
tasya sarvaṃ yathā|vṛttam ākhyātum upacakrame.
Ghaṭotkacasya vijayam, ātmanaś ca parājayam
kathayām āsa dur|dharṣo viniḥśvasya punaḥ punaḥ.
abravīc ca tadā, rājan, Bhīṣmaṃ Kuru|pitāmaham:
«bhavantaṃ samupāśritya, Vāsudevaṃ yathā paraiḥ,
Pāṇḍavair vigraho ghoraḥ samārabdho mayā, prabho.
95.5 ekā|daśa samākhyātā akṣauhiṇyaś ca yā mama,
nideśe tava tiṣṭhanti mayā sārdhaṃ, paran|tapa.
so 'haṃ, Bharata|śārdūla, Bhīmasena|puro|gamaiḥ
Ghaṭotkacaṃ samāśritya Pāṇḍavair yudhi nirjitaḥ.
tan me dahati gātrāṇi, śuṣka|vṛkṣam iv' ânalaḥ,
yad icchāmi, mahā|bhāga, tvat|prasādāt, paran|tapa,
rākṣas'|âpasadaṃ hantuṃ svayam eva, pitā|maha,
tvāṃ samāśritya dur|dharṣaṃ. tan me kartuṃ tvam arhasi.»
etac chrutvā tu vacanaṃ rājño, Bharata|sattama,
Duryodhanam idaṃ vākyaṃ Bhīṣmaḥ Śāntanavo 'bravīt:
95.10 «śṛṇu, rājan, mama vaco yat tvā vakṣyāmi, Kaurava,
yathā tvayā, mahā|rāja, vartitavyaṃ, paran|tapa.
ātmā rakṣyo raṇe, tāta, sarv'|âvasthāsv, arin|dama.

not stop, for they were bewildered by that magic. Terror-stricken, they did not believe the words we spoke. And seeing the enemies fleeing, the Pándavas together with Ghatótkacha, winning the victory, uttered lion-roars. They filled
the air with the loud sound of conches and drums. And 94.50
so, as the day wore on, your whole army, routed by the ill-natured son of Hidímba, scattered in every direction.

SÁNJAYA said:

WHEN THAT GREAT episode was over, King Duryódhana 95.1
approached the son of Ganga, greeted him humbly, and started to describe to him everything that had occurred. Sighing deeply again and again, that unconquerable hero told Bhishma about Ghatótkacha's victory and his own defeat. Then, Your Majesty, he said to the Kuru grandfather Bhishma: "It is relying on you, my lord, just as our enemies the Pándavas rely on Krishna, that I have unleashed
this terrible war. My troops numbering eleven *akshäuhini* 95.5
divisions* are under your command, scorcher of enemies, as am I. And yet, tiger of the Bharatas, I have been vanquished in battle by the Pándavas led by Bhima·sena and relying on Ghatótkacha. This burns my limbs, like a fire burning up a dry tree, glorious enemy-taming grandfather, through your grace I long to kill that vile demon myself. I'm depending on you, the invincible; you must grant my wish."

Hearing King Duryódhana's words, best of the Bharatas, Bhishma the son of Shántanu made a speech in reply.
"Listen to what I have to say, Your Majesty, ruler of the 95.10
Kurus, about the way you should behave, great king, subduer of foes. Sir, you have to protect yourself under all cir-

Dharma|rājena saṃgrāmas tvayā kāryaḥ sad", ân|agha,
Arjunena, yamābhyāṃ vā, Bhīmasenena vā punaḥ.
rāja|dharmaṃ puras|kṛtya rājā rājānam ṛcchati.
ahaṃ, Droṇaḥ, Kṛpo, Drauṇiḥ, Kṛtavarmā ca Sātvataḥ,
Śalyaś ca, Saumadattiś ca, Vikarṇaś ca mahā|rathaḥ,
tava ca bhrātaraḥ śūrā Duḥśāsana|puro|gamāḥ—
tvad|arthaṃ pratiyotsyāmo rākṣasaṃ taṃ mahā|balam.
95.15 raudre tasmin rākṣas'|êndre yadi te 'nuśayo mahān,
ayaṃ vā gacchatu raṇe tasya yuddhāya dur|mateḥ
Bhagadatto mahī|pālaḥ Purandara|samo yudhi.»

etāvad uktvā rājānaṃ Bhagadattam ath' âbravīt
samakṣaṃ pārthiv'|êndrasya
vākyaṃ vākya|viśāradaḥ:
«gaccha śīghraṃ, mahā|rāja,
Haiḍimbaṃ yuddha|dur|madam
vārayasva raṇe yatto miṣatāṃ sarva|dhanvinām
rākṣasaṃ krūra|karmāṇaṃ, yath" Êndras Tārakaṃ purā.
tava divyāni c' âstrāṇi, vikramaś ca, paran|tapa,
samāgamaś ca bahubhiḥ pur" âbhūd amaraiḥ saha.
95.20 tvaṃ tasya, rāja|śārdūla, prati|yoddhā mah"|āhave.
sva|balena vṛto, rājan, jahi rākṣasa|puṅgavam.»

etac chrutvā tu vacanaṃ Bhīṣmasya pṛtanā|pateḥ
prayayau siṃha|nādena parān abhimukho drutam.
tam ādravantaṃ saṃpreksya, garjantam iva toya|dam,
abhyavartanta saṃkruddhāḥ Pāṇḍavānāṃ mahā|rathāḥ:
Bhimaseno, 'bhimanyuś ca, rākṣasaś ca Ghaṭotkacaḥ,

cumstances, tamer of enemies. And you should always engage in battle with the King of Righteousness, faultless one. Or else you should battle with Árjuna, the twins Nákula and Saha·deva, or Bhima·sena. Honoring the warrior code, a king encounters a king. Myself, Drona, Kripa, Drona's son, the Sátvata warrior Krita·varman, Shalya, the son of Soma·datta, Vikárna the great fighter, and your excellent brothers led by Duhshásana will fight for your sake against that powerful demon. Or, if you are filled with intense ha- 95.15
tred for that frightful chief of demons, let Bhaga·datta confront that evil-minded demon in battle. That protector of the earth is equal to Indra the destroyer of strongholds in combat."

After saying this, Bhishma, skilled in speech, addressed King Bhaga·datta in the presence of the king of kings:

"Great king, quickly proceed against the son of Hidímba who is ferocious in battle. Exert yourself in the fight, and in the sight of all the archers tame that demon of cruel deeds, just as Indra formerly checked the demon Táraka. Your weapons are divine, enemy-tamer, and so is your prowess; and you have had encounters with many demons in the past. O tiger-like king, you can oppose him in this great bat- 95.20
tle. Supported by your troops, slaughter that demon mighty as a bull!"

Hearing General Bhishma's words, Bhaga·datta with a lion-roar swiftly proceeded toward the enemies. When the great warriors of the Pándava army saw him rushing toward them like a rumbling thundercloud they advanced forward, full of anger. Bhima·sena, Abhimányu, the demon

Draupadeyāḥ, Satyadhṛtiḥ, Kṣatradevaś ca, māriṣa,
Cedi|po, Vasudānaś ca, Daśārṇ'|âdhipatis tathā.
Supratīkena tāṃś c' âpi Bhagadatto 'py upādravat.
95.25 tataḥ samabhavad yuddhaṃ ghora|rūpaṃ, bhayānakam
Pāṇḍūnāṃ Bhagadattena, Yama|rāṣṭra|vivardhanam.
prayuktā rathibhir bāṇā bhīma|vegāḥ, su|tejanāḥ;
te nipetur, mahā|rāja, nāgeṣu ca ratheṣu ca.
prabhinnāś ca mahā|nāgā vinītā hasti|sādibhiḥ
paras|paraṃ samāsādya saṃnipetur a|bhītavat.
mad'|ândhā, roṣa|saṃrabdhā viṣāṇ'|âgrair mah"|āhave
bibhidur danta|musalaiḥ samāsādya paras|param.
hayāś ca cāmar'|āpīḍāḥ prāsa|pāṇibhir āsthitāḥ
coditāḥ sādibhiḥ kṣipraṃ nipetur itar'|êtaram.
95.30 pādātāś ca padāty|oghais tāḍitāḥ śakti|tomaraiḥ
nyapatanta tadā bhūmau śataśo 'tha sahasraśaḥ.
rathinaś ca tathā, rājan, karṇi|nālīka|sāyakaiḥ
nihatya samare vīrān siṃha|nādān vinedire.

tasmiṃs tathā vartamāne saṃgrāme loma|harṣaṇe
Bhagadatto mah"|êṣv|āso Bhīmasenam ath' âdravat
kuñjareṇa prabhinnena saptadhā sravatā madam,
parvatena yathā toyaṃ sravamāṇena sarvataḥ,
kirañ śara|sahasrāṇi Supratīka|śiro|gataḥ,
Airāvata|stho Maghavān vāri|dhārā iv', ân|agha.
95.35 sa Bhīmaṃ śara|dhārābhis tāḍayām āsa pārthivaḥ,
parvataṃ vāri|dhārābhiḥ tap'|ânte jala|do yathā.

Ghatótkacha, the sons of Dráupadi, Satya·dhriti, Kshatra·deva, the Chedi king, Vasu·dana, and the ruler of the Dashárnas charged forward. Bhaga·datta attacked them on the elephant Supratíka.

Then a hideous and terrifying battle took place between 95.25
the Pándavas and Bhaga·datta, which increased the kingdom of Yama. Swift, well-sharpened arrows of fierce velocity were fired by chariot warriors and fell upon elephants and chariots, Your Majesty. Huge rutting elephants, tamed by their drivers, approached one another and pounced on each other without fear. Blind with rut and frenzy and excited with rage, they struck one another with their mace-like tusks in the great battle, piercing each other with their tips. Horses crested with yak tails and ridden by javelin-wielding warriors, urged on by their riders, dashed against each other at speed. Hundreds and thousands of foot sol- 95.30
diers were shot by other infantrymen with lances and spears and fell to the ground. Chariot warriors, Your Majesty, struck down hostile heroes in combat with their barbed shafts, darts, and arrows, and shouted lion-roars.

While that hair-raising battle was raging in this way, the mighty archer Bhaga·datta charged against Bhima·sena. He rode a rutting elephant secreting juices in seven rills, like a mountain covered all over with rivulets. He was scattering thousands of arrows from Supratíka's head, just as Mágha·vat, riding his elephant Airávata, pours torrents of rain, faultless one. That king struck Bhima with streams of ar- 95.35
rows, like a storm-cloud striking a mountain with torrents of water at the end of the summer. And with rains of shafts the wrathful Bhima·sena slaughtered hundreds of hostile

Bhīmasenas tu saṃkruddhaḥ pāda|rakṣān paraḥ|śatān
nijaghāna mah"|êṣv|āsaḥ saṃrabdhaḥ śara|vṛṣṭibhiḥ.
tān dṛṣṭvā nihatān kruddho Bhagadattaḥ pratāpavān
codayām āsa nāg'|êndraṃ Bhīmasena|rathaṃ prati.
sa nāgaḥ preṣitas tena, bāṇo jyā|codito yathā,
abhyadhāvata vegena Bhīmasenam arin|damam.

tam āpatantaṃ saṃpreksya Pāṇḍavānāṃ mahā|rathāḥ
abhyavartanta vegena Bhīmasena|puro|gamāḥ.
95.40 Kekayāś c', Âbhimanyuś ca, Draupadeyāś ca sarvaśaḥ,
Daśārṇ'|âdhipatiḥ śūraḥ, Kṣatradevaś ca, māriṣa,
Cedi|paś, Citraketuś ca saṃrabdhāḥ sarva eva te
uttam'|âstrāṇi divyāni darśayanto mahā|balāḥ
tam ekaṃ kuñjaraṃ kruddhāḥ samantāt paryavārayan.

sa viddho bahubhir bāṇair vyarocata mahā|dvipaḥ,
saṃjāta|rudhir'|ôtpīḍo dhātu|citra iv' âdri|rāṭ.
Daśārṇ'|âdhipatiś c' âpi gajaṃ bhūmi|dhar'|ôpamam
samāsthito 'bhidudrāva Bhagadattasya vāraṇam.
tam āpatantaṃ samare gajaṃ gaja|patiḥ sa ca
95.45 dadhāra Supratīko 'pi, vel" êva makar'|ālayam.
vāritaṃ prekṣya nāg'|êndraṃ Daśārṇasya mah"|ātmanaḥ,
«sādhu! sādhv!» iti sainyāni Pāṇḍaveyāny apūjayan.

tataḥ Prāgjyotiṣaḥ kruddhas tomarān vai catur|daśa
prāhiṇot tasya nāgasya pramukhe, nṛpa|sattama.
varma mukhyaṃ tanu|trāṇaṃ śātakumbha|pariṣkṛtam
vidārya prāviśan kṣipraṃ, valmīkam iva pannagāḥ.
sa gāḍha|viddho, vyathito nāgo, Bharata|sattama,

warriors who were guarding the elephant's legs. Vigorous Bhaga·datta became furious when he saw them killed, and he urged his mighty elephant on toward Bhima·sena's chariot. Driven on like an arrow released from a bowstring, the elephant charged with great force against Bhima·sena the tamer of enemies.

When the great warriors of the Pándavas, led by Bhima·sena, saw that attacking elephant, they charged forward
with vehemence. The Kékayas, Abhimányu, the sons of 95.40
Dráupadi, the valiant king of the Dashárnas, Kshatra·deva, the king of the Chedis, and Chitra·ketu, all of them furious and mighty, my lord, showed their excellent divine weapons and surrounded that lone elephant on all sides.

Wounded by numerous arrows, that huge elephant bled copiously, looking beautiful like the king of mountains washed with streams mixed with red chalk and other minerals. Then the ruler of the Dashárnas, riding his mountain-like elephant, charged against the elephant of Bhaga·datta.
That king of elephants Supratíka withheld the attacking en- 95.45
emy elephant in that battle, just as the shore withholds the ocean. As they watched the mighty elephant of the great-spirited king of the Dashárnas being repelled, the Pándava troops cheered Supratíka by exclaiming, "Excellent! Excellent!"

Then the king of the Prag·jyótishas, full of anger, hurled fourteen spears at the Dashárna king's elephant, best of kings. Tearing through fine armor trimmed with gold, the spears soon penetrated the elephant's body just as snakes enter an anthill. Severely wounded and tormented with pain, best of the Bharatas, its fury allayed, the elephant suddenly

upāvṛtta|madaḥ kṣipraṃ abhyavartata vegataḥ.
sa pradudrāva vegena praṇadan bhairavaṃ ravam,
95.50 saṃmardayānaḥ sva|balaṃ, vāyur vṛkṣān iv' âujasā.
tasmin parājite nāge Pāṇḍavānāṃ mahā|rathāḥ
siṃha|nādaṃ vinady' ôccair yuddhāy' âiv' âvatasthire.
tato Bhīmaṃ puras|kṛtya Bhagadattam upādravan,
kiranto vividhān bāṇāñ, śastrāṇi vividhāni ca.

teṣām āpatatāṃ, rājan, saṃkruddhānām, a|marṣiṇām
śrutvā sa ninadaṃ ghoram a|marṣād gata|sādhvasaḥ
Bhagadatto mah"|êṣv|āsaḥ sva|nāgaṃ pratyacodayat.
aṅkuś'|âṅguṣṭha|nuditaḥ sa gaja|pravaro yudhi
tasmin kṣaṇe samabhavat saṃvartaka iv' ânalaḥ.
95.55 ratha|saṅghāṃs, tathā nāgān, hayāṃś ca saha sādibhiḥ,
pādātāṃś ca su|saṃkruddhaḥ śataśo 'tha sahasraśaḥ
amṛdnāt samare nāgaḥ, saṃpradhāvaṃs tatas tataḥ.
tena saṃlodyamānaṃ tu Pāṇḍavānāṃ balaṃ mahat
saṃcukoca, mahā|rāja, carm' êv' âgnau samāhitam.

bhagnaṃ tu sva|balaṃ dṛṣṭvā Bhagadattena dhīmatā,
Ghaṭotkaco 'tha saṃkruddho Bhagadattam upādravat.
vikaṭaḥ puruṣo, rājan, dīpt'|āsyo, dīpta|locanaḥ,
rūpaṃ vibhīṣaṇaṃ kṛtvā, roṣeṇa prajvalann iva,
jagrāha vimalaṃ śūlaṃ girīṇām api dāraṇam,
95.60 nāgaṃ jighāṃsuḥ sahasā cikṣepa ca mahā|balaḥ.
sa visphuliṅga|jvālābhiḥ samantāt pariveṣṭitaḥ.
tam āpatantaṃ sahasā dṛṣṭvā Prāgjyotiṣo raṇe
cikṣepa ruciraṃ tīkṣṇam ardha|candraṃ su|dāruṇam;

turned around, and uttering fearful screams it ran away in haste, violently crushing its own troops as easily as a gale 95.50
blows down trees.

Though the Dashárna king's elephant had been defeated, the great warriors of the Pándavas, shouting loud lion-roars, stood ready for battle. Then, headed by Bhima, they charged against Bhaga·datta, scattering diverse arrows and various other weapons.

Hearing the terrifying roar of those enraged and frenzied assailants, the mighty archer Bhaga·datta, undaunted, furiously urged his elephant on against them. At that moment that supreme elephant, goaded by hooks and toes in battle, looked like the fire of the universal dissolution.
Rampaging hither and thither over the field of battle, the 95.55
elephant, filled with intense fury, crushed chariot divisions, elephants, horses and their riders, and hundreds and thousands of foot soldiers. And the great host of the Pándavas was thrown into disarray by that elephant and shrank, great king, as if a hide had been placed over a fire.

Seeing his army routed by wise Bhaga·datta, Ghatótkacha became filled with rage and charged against Bhaga·datta. Formidable and fierce, his face and eyes ablaze with anger, the mighty demon took on a frightful appearance, and burning with fury he seized a gleaming pike that was capable even of splitting rocks and hurled it powerfully, eager to 95.60
slaughter the hostile elephant. The pike was swathed all over in flickering flames. When the king of the Prag·jyótishas saw it flying toward him with great force, he shot a radiant, terrible, sharp arrow with a semicircular head; and with that arrow the vigorous king severed the mighty pike. Split

ciccheda tan mahac chūlaṃ tena bāṇena vegavat.
nipapāta dvidhā chinnaṃ śūlaṃ hema|pariṣkṛtam,
mah"|âśanir yathā bhraṣṭā Śakra|muktā nabho|gatā.

śūlaṃ nipatitaṃ dṛṣṭvā dvidhā kṛttaṃ sa pārthivaḥ
rukma|daṇḍāṃ mahā|śaktiṃ jagrāh' âgni|śikh"|ôpamām.
cikṣepa tāṃ rākṣasasya, «tiṣṭha! tiṣṭh'!» êti c' âbravīt.
95.65 tām āpatantīṃ saṃprekṣya, viyat|sthām aśanim iva,
utpatya rākṣasas tūrṇaṃ jagrāha ca nanāda ca;
babhañja c' âināṃ tvarito jānuny āropya, Bhārata,
paśyataḥ pārthiv'|êndrasya. tad adbhutam iv' âbhavat.
tad avekṣya kṛtaṃ karma rākṣasena balīyasā
divi devāḥ sa|gandharvā, munayaś c' âpi vismitāḥ.
Pāṇḍavāś ca mah"|êṣv|āsā Bhīmasena|puro|gamāḥ
«sādhu! sādhv!» iti nādena pṛthivīm anvanādayan.

taṃ tu śrutvā mahā|nādaṃ prahṛṣṭānāṃ mah"|ātmanām,
n' âmṛṣyata mah"|êṣv|āso Bhagadattaḥ pratāpavān.
95.70 sa visphārya mahac cāpam Indr'|âśani|sama|prabham,
tarjayām āsa vegena Pāṇḍavānāṃ mahā|rathān.
visṛjan vimalāṃs, tīkṣṇān nārācāñ jvalana|prabhān,
Bhīmam ekena vivyādha, rākṣasaṃ navabhiḥ śaraiḥ,
Abhimanyuṃ tribhiś c' âiva, Kekayān pañcabhis tathā.
pūrṇ'|āyata|visṛṣṭena svarṇa|puṅkhena patriṇā
bibheda dakṣiṇaṃ bāhuṃ Kṣatradevasya c' āhave.
papāta sahasā tasya sa|śaraṃ dhanur uttamam.
Draupadeyāṃs tataḥ pañca pañcabhiḥ samatāḍayat,
Bhīmasenasya ca krodhān nijaghāna turaṅ|gamān,

in two, the pike, dressed in gold, fell to the ground; like a mighty thunderbolt hurled by Shakra, it collapsed flashing through the sky.

When he saw the pike fallen, cut in two, King Bhaga·
datta seized a huge gold-shafted lance that gleamed like
flames of fire, and he hurled it at the demon, shouting: "Stay
still! Stay still!" Seeing that lance flying toward him through 95.65
the air, the demon leaped up, grabbed hold of it in a trice,
and roared. Then, wasting no time, he snapped it over his
knee, descendant of Bharata, under the eyes of that mighty
king. It was like a miracle. Watching that feat that that immensely powerful demon performed, even the gods, *gandhárvas*, and sages in heaven were filled with amazement.
And the Pándavas, led by Bhima·sena, great king, made the
earth resound with their shouts: "Superb! Superb!"

Vigorous Bhaga·datta, the mighty archer, could not endure those great-spirited heroes' loud shouts of rejoicing.
Stretching his large bow that was equal in radiance to In- 95.70
dra's thunderbolt, he threatened the Pándavas' great warriors with vehemence. Firing sharp iron arrows that shone
brightly as if they were burning, he pierced Bhima with one
shaft, the demon Ghatótkacha with nine, Abhimányu with
three, and the Kékayas with five. Then, with a straight arrow fired from his bow drawn at full stretch, he cut through
Kshatra·deva's right arm in battle; and the latter's fine bow
along with its shafts suddenly fell tumbling. After that,
Bhaga·datta struck the five sons of Dráupadi with five arrows, and, excited with anger, he killed Bhima·sena's horses.
With three arrows he severed Bhima's banner with its lion 95.75
emblem, and with another three feathered shafts he hit his

95.75 dhvajaṃ kesariṇaṃ c' âsya ciccheda viśikhais tribhiḥ,
nirbibheda tribhiś c' ânyaiḥ sārathiṃ c' âsya patribhiḥ.
sa gāḍha|viddho, vyathito rath'|ôpastha upāviśat
Viśoko, Bharata|śreṣṭha, Bhagadattena saṃyuge.

tato Bhīmo mahā|bāhur vi|ratho rathināṃ varaḥ
gadāṃ pragṛhya vegena pracaskanda rath'|ôttamāt.
tam udyata|gadaṃ dṛṣṭvā, sa|śṛṅgam iva parvatam,
tāvakānāṃ bhayaṃ ghoraṃ samapadyata, Bhārata.

etasminn eva kāle tu Pāṇḍavaḥ Kṛṣṇa|sārathiḥ
ājagāma, mahā|rāja, nighnañ śatrūn sahasraśaḥ,
95.80 yatra tau puruṣa|vyāghrau pitā|putrau paran|tapau
Prāgjyotiṣena saṃsaktau Bhīmasena|Ghaṭotkacau.
dṛṣṭvā ca Pāṇḍavo bhrātṝn yudhyamānān mahā|rathān,
tvarito, Bharata|śreṣṭha, tatr' āyudhyat kirañ śarān.
tato Duryodhano rājā tvaramāṇo mahā|rathaḥ
senām acodayat kṣipraṃ ratha|nāg'|âśva|saṃkulām.
tām āpatantīṃ sahasā Kauravāṇāṃ mahā|camūm
abhidudrāva vegena Pāṇḍavaḥ śveta|vāhanaḥ.
Bhagadattaś ca samare tena nāgena, Bhārata,
vimṛdnan Pāṇḍava|balaṃ Yudhiṣṭhiram upādravat.
95.85 tad" āsīt tumulaṃ yuddhaṃ Bhagadattasya, māriṣa,
Pañcālaiḥ, Sṛñjayaiś c' âiva, Kekayaiś c' ôdyat'|āyudhaiḥ.
Bhīmaseno 'pi samare tāv ubhau Keśav'|Ârjunau
aśrāvayad yathā|vṛttam Irāvad|vadham uttamam.

driver. Seriously wounded by Bhaga·datta in that combat and afflicted with pain, Vishóka sank onto the chariot platform, best of the Bharatas.

Then mighty-armed Bhima, that champion of chariot warriors, stripped of his vehicle, seized a mace and swiftly jumped out of the chariot. When they saw him wielding his mace and looking like a crested mountain, grave fear overwhelmed your troops, descendant of Bharata.

At that moment the Pándava Árjuna, with Krishna as
his chariot driver, striking down his enemies on all sides,
reached the place where the two mighty tiger-men Bhima· 95.80
sena and Ghatótkacha, father and son, were engaged in
combat with the king of the Prag·jyótishas. And the son
of Pandu, seeing his great warrior brothers battling away,
quickly began to fight, best of the Bharatas, scattering his
arrows. So King Duryódhana, that mighty warrior, immediately urged his army onwards with its chariots, elephants,
and horses. Seeing that large host assailing him, Árjuna Pándava of the white horses charged against it. Bhaga·datta
crushed the Pándava troops with his elephant in that battle,
and then he attacked Yudhi·shthira, descendant of Bharata.
And a huge battle ensued, my lord, between Bhaga·datta on 95.85
one side and the Panchálas, Srínjayas, and Kékayas, brandishing their weapons, on the other. And during that encounter Bhima·sena told both Késhava and Árjuna about
the awful slaying of Irávat, just as it had happened.

SAÑJAYA uvāca:

96.1 PUTRAṂ VINIHATAṂ śrutvā Irāvantaṃ Dhanañjayaḥ,
duḥkhena mahat" āviṣṭo niḥśvasan pannago yathā,
abravīt samare, rājan, Vāsudevam idaṃ vacaḥ:
«idaṃ nūnaṃ mahā|prājño Viduro dṛṣṭavān purā
Kurūṇāṃ Pāṇḍavānāṃ ca kṣayaṃ ghoraṃ mahā|matiḥ.
sa tato nivāritavān Dhṛtarāṣṭraṃ jan'|ēśvaram.
anye ca bahavo vīrāḥ saṃgrāme, Madhusūdana,
nihatāḥ Kauravaiḥ saṃkhye, tath" âsmābhiś ca Kauravāḥ.
96.5 artha|hetor, nara|śreṣṭha, kriyate karma kutsitam.
dhig arthān, yat|kṛte hy evaṃ kriyate jñāti|saṃkṣayaḥ.
a|dhanasya mṛtaṃ śreyo, na ca jñāti|vadhād dhanam.
kiṃ nu prāpsyāmahe, Kṛṣṇa, hatvā jñātīn samāgatān?
Duryodhan'|âparādhena, Śakuneḥ Saubalasya ca
kṣatriyā nidhanaṃ yānti, Karṇa|dur|mantritena ca.
idānīṃ ca vijānāmi su|kṛtaṃ, Madhusūdana,
kṛtaṃ rājñā, mahā|bāho, yācatā ca Suyodhanam.
rājy'|ârdhaṃ, pañca vā grāmān n' âkārṣit sa ca dur|matiḥ.
dṛṣṭvā hi kṣatriyāñ śūrāñ śayānān dharaṇī|tale,
96.10 nindāmi bhṛśam ātmānaṃ. dhig astu kṣatra|jīvikām!
a|śaktam iti mām ete jñāsyanti kṣatriyā raṇe.
yuddhaṃ tu me na rucitaṃ jñātibhir, Madhusūdana.

SÁNJAYA said:

WHEN DHANAN·JAYA heard about his son being slain, 96.1
he was overcome by grief and, sighing deeply like a snake, Your Majesty, he addressed Vásu·deva in combat with these words:

"Did not Vídura, endowed with great wisdom and intelligence, formerly foresee this terrible destruction of the Kurus and the Pándavas? That is why he tried to hold King Dhrita·rashtra back. Many of our heroes have been slain by the Káuravas in this war, and many of the Káuravas have
been slaughtered in battle by us, slayer of Madhu. It is for 96.5
the sake of wealth, best of men, that vile deeds are performed. Damn the riches for the sake of which this slaughter of kinsmen is being committed! For the man who has no wealth, death is better than acquiring wealth through the slaughter of kinsmen. What shall we gain, Krishna, by slaying the relatives assembled here? It is through the fault of Duryódhana and Shákuni the son of Súbala, and because of Karna's bad advice, that these warriors are being destroyed. Now I realize, mighty-armed slayer of Madhu, what a great act of virtue Yudhi·shthira performed by begging Suyódhana for either half of the kingdom or only five villages. But the evil-minded one did not heed his request.

Now that I see heroic warriors lying on the ground, I cen- 96.10
sure myself severely. Damn the life of a warrior! These warriors will deem me incapable in combat, but war between kinsmen is not agreeable to me, slayer of Madhu.

saṃcodaya hayān kṣipraṃ Dhārtarāṣṭra|camūṃ prati.
pratariṣye mahā|pāraṃ bhujābhyāṃ samar'|ôdadhim.
n' âyaṃ klībayituṃ kālo vidyate, Mādhava, kva cit.»
evam uktas tu Pārthena Keśavaḥ para|vīra|hā
codayām āsa tān aśvān pāṇḍurān, vāta|raṃhasaḥ.
atha śabdo mahān āsīt tava sainyasya, Bhārata,
mārut'|ôddhūta|vegasya sāgarasy' êva parvaṇi.
96.15 apar'|âhṇe, mahā|rāja, saṃgrāmaḥ samapadyata
parjanya|sama|nirghoṣo Bhīṣmasya saha Pāṇḍavaiḥ.
tato, rājaṃs, tava sutā Bhīmasenam upādravan
parivārya raṇe Droṇaṃ, Vasavo Vāsavaṃ yathā.
tataḥ Śāntanavo Bhīṣmaḥ, Kṛpaś ca rathināṃ varaḥ,
Bhagadattaḥ, Suśarmā ca Dhanañjayam upādravan.
Hārdikyo Bāhlikaś c' âiva Sātyakiṃ samabhidrutau.
Ambaṣṭhakas tu nṛ|patir Abhimanyum avārayat;
śeṣās tv anye, mahā|rāja, śeṣān eva mahā|rathān.
tataḥ pravavṛte yuddhaṃ ghora|rūpaṃ, bhay'|āvaham.
96.20 Bhīmasenas tu saṃprekṣya putrāṃs tava, jan'|ēśvara,
prajajvāla raṇe kruddho, haviṣā havya|vāḍ iva.
putrās tu tava Kaunteyaṃ chādayāṃ cakrire śaraiḥ,
prāvṛṣ' îva, mahā|rāja, jala|dā iva parvatam.
sa cchādyamāno bahudhā putrais tava, viśāṃ pate,
sṛkkiṇī saṃlihan vīraḥ, śārdūla iva darpitaḥ,
Vyūḍhoraskaṃ tato Bhīmaḥ pātayām āsa, pārthiva,
kṣurapreṇa su|tīkṣṇena. so 'bhavad gata|jīvitaḥ.
apareṇa tu bhallena pītena niśitena ca
apātayat Kuṇḍalinaṃ, siṃhaḥ kṣudra|mṛgaṃ yathā.

But quickly, drive the horses on toward the army of Dhrita·rashtra's son. With my two arms I shall cross this broad ocean of battle. There is no time to lose, Mádhava."

Addressed by the son of Pritha in this way, Késhava, the destroyer of enemy heroes, drove the white horses as swift as the wind. And a loud din rose among your troops, descendant of Bharata, like that of the sea tossed around by
a gale when the moon changes. The battle that took place 96.15
in the evening, great king, between Bhishma and the Pándavas, was accompanied by a thunderous racket. Your sons, Your Majesty, surrounding Drona in battle just as the Vasus surround Vásava, charged against Bhima·sena; Bhishma son of Shántanu, Kripa the best of chariot warriors, Bhaga·datta, and Sushárman attacked Dhanan·jaya; Hrídika's son and Báhlika rushed against Sátyaki; King Ambáshtha confronted Abhimányu; and the rest of your soldiers, great king, fought with the rest of the enemies. A hideous and horrific battle followed.

When Bhima·sena saw your sons, lord of the people, he 96.20
blazed up with battle-fury like a sacrificial fire fed with clarified butter. And your sons, great king, shrouded the son of Kunti with arrows just as storm-clouds cover a mountain with rains in the monsoon. Repeatedly covered with arrows by your sons, lord of the people, heroic Bhima, proud like a tiger, licking the corners of his mouth, struck down Vyudhoráska with a well-sharpened, razor-edged shaft; and the latter lost his life. With another sharp, copper, spear-headed arrow he felled Kúndalin just as a lion fells a young deer.

96.25 tataḥ su|niśitān, pītān samādatta śilīmukhān;
sasarja tvarayā yuktaḥ putrāṃs te prāpya, māriṣa.
preṣitā Bhīmasenena śarās te dṛḍha|dhanvanā
apātayanta putrāṃs te rathebhyaḥ su|mahā|rathān:
Anādhṛṣṭiṃ, Kuṇḍabhedaṃ, Vairāṭaṃ, Dīrghalocanam,
Dīrghabāhuṃ, Subāhuṃ ca, tath" âiva Kanakadhvajam.
prapatantaḥ sma vīrās te virejur, Bharata'|rṣabha,
vasante puṣpa|śabalāś cūtāḥ prapatitā iva.
tataḥ pradudruvuḥ śeṣāḥ putrās tava, viśāṃ pate,
taṃ Kālam iva manyanto Bhīmasenaṃ mahā|balam.
96.30 Droṇas tu samare vīraṃ nirdahantaṃ sutāṃs tava,
yath" âdriṃ vāri|dhārābhiḥ, samantād vyakirac charaiḥ.
 tatr' âdbhutam apaśyāma Kuntī|putrasya pauruṣam,
Droṇena vāryamāṇo 'pi nijaghne yat sutāṃs tava.
yathā go|vṛṣabho varṣaṃ saṃdhārayati khāt patat,
Bhīmas tathā Droṇa|muktaṃ śara|varṣam adīdharat.
adbhutaṃ ca, mahā|rāja, tatra cakre Vṛkodaraḥ,
yat putrāṃs te 'vadhīt saṃkhye, Droṇaṃ c' âiva nyavārayat.
putreṣu tava vīreṣu cikrīḍ' Ârjuna|pūrva|jaḥ,
mṛgeṣv iva, mahā|rāja, caran vyāghro mahā|balaḥ.
96.35 yathā hi paśu|madhya|stho drāvayeta paśūn vṛkaḥ,
Vṛkodaras tava sutāṃs tathā vyadrāvayad raṇe.
Gāṅgeyo, Bhagadattaś ca, Gautamaś ca mahā|rathaḥ
Pāṇḍavaṃ rabhasaṃ yuddhe vārayām āsur Arjunam.
astrair astrāṇi saṃvārya teṣāṃ so 'tiratho raṇe
pravīrāṃs tava sainyeṣu preṣayām āsa Mṛtyave.

Then he aimed well-sharpened, copper, stone-tipped arrows and quickly fired them at your sons, my lord. Shot by the mighty archer Bhima·sena, those arrows threw your great warrior sons down from their chariots. Bhima felled Anadhríshti, Kunda·bheda, Vairáta, Dirgha·lóchana, Dirgha·bahu, Subáhu, and Kánaka·dhvaja. As they were tumbling down those heroes looked beautiful, bull of the Bharatas, like mango trees fallen in full bloom in spring. The rest of your sons, considering immensely mighty Bhima·sena to be Death himself, fled away in that great bat- 96.25
tle. Then, just as a rain-cloud covers a mountain in torrents 96.30
of rain, Drona in that engagement completely covered in arrows the hero who had been incinerating your sons.

And we witnessed the wonderful manliness of Kunti's son, as he carried on striking your sons down even though he was being pelted by Drona. As a bull endures rain pouring from the sky, so did Bhima bear the shower of arrows released by Drona. Great king, Vrikódara performed a wondrous feat in battle as he continued to slaughter your sons and repel Drona at the same time. Árjuna's elder brother Bhima amused himself in the midst of your valiant sons,
great king, like a mighty tiger rampaging among deer. As 96.35
a wolf that gets among cattle tears and scatters them, so did wolf-bellied Bhima put your sons to flight in that combat. Ganga's son, Bhaga·datta, and Gótama's grandson the mighty warrior strenuously tried to check Árjuna Pándava in battle. But that warrior extraordinary in combat, thwarting their weapons with his, sent to Death many prominent heroes among your troops.

Abhimanyuś ca rājānam Ambaṣṭhaṃ loka|viśrutam
vi|rathaṃ rathināṃ śreṣṭhaṃ vārayām āsa sāyakaiḥ.
vi|ratho vadhyamānas tu Saubhadreṇa yaśasvinā
avaplutya rathāt tūrṇaṃ, Ambaṣṭho vasudh"|âdhipaḥ
96.40 asiṃ cikṣepa samare Saubhadrasya mah"|ātmanaḥ,
āruroha rathaṃ c' âiva Hārdikyasya mahā|balaḥ.
āpatantaṃ tu nistriṃśaṃ yuddha|mārga|viśāradaḥ
lāghavād vyaṃsayām āsa Saubhadraḥ para|vīra|hā.
vyaṃsitaṃ vīkṣya nistriṃśaṃ Saubhadreṇa raṇe tadā
«sādhu! sādhv!» iti sainyānāṃ praṇādo 'bhūd, viśāṃ pate.

Dhṛṣṭadyumna|mukhās tv anye tava sainyam ayodhayan;
tath" âiva tāvakāḥ sarve Pāṇḍu|sainyam ayodhayan.
tatr' ākrando mahān āsīt tava teṣāṃ ca, Bhārata,
nighnatāṃ dṛḍham anyonyaṃ, kurvatāṃ karma duṣ|karam.
96.45 anyonyaṃ hi raṇe śūrāḥ keśeṣv ākṣipya māninaḥ
nakhair, dantair ayudhyanta, muṣṭibhir, jānubhis tathā,
talaiś c' âiv', âtha nistriṃśair, bāhubhiś ca su|saṃsthitaiḥ.
vivaraṃ prāpya c' ânyonyam anayan Yama|sādanam.
nyahanac ca pitā putraṃ, putraś ca pitaraṃ tathā.
vyākulī|kṛta|sarv'|âṅgā yuyudhus tatra mānavāḥ.
raṇe cārūṇi cāpāni hema|pṛṣṭhāni, māriṣa,
hatānām apaviddhāni, kalāpāś ca mahā|dhanāḥ.
jātarūpamayaiḥ puṅkhai rājatair niśitāḥ śarāḥ
taila|dhautā vyarājanta nirmukta|bhujag'|ôpamāḥ.
96.50 hasti|danta|tsarūn khaḍgāñ jātarūpa|pariṣkṛtān,
carmāṇi c' âpaviddhāni rukma|citrāni dhanvinām,

And Abhimányu checked King Ambáshtha, that best of
chariot warriors, by depriving him of his chariot. Stripped
of his vehicle by the glorious son of Subhádra, the mighty
King Ambáshtha quickly leaped from the chariot, hurled 96.40
his sword at the great-spirited son of Subhádra in the fray,
and climbed onto the chariot of Hrídika's son. But the son
of Subhádra, that slayer of enemy heroes who was skilled
in all modes of battle, saw the sword flying toward him,
and foiled it with his dexterity. Seeing that sword foiled by
Abhimányu in battle, shouts of "Excellent! Excellent!" rose
among the troops, lord of the people.

Others, led by Dhrishta·dyumna, struggled against your
troops; and all your warriors fought against the Pándava
host. A great combat ensued between your warriors and
those of the enemy, descendant of Bharata, as they smashed
each other up severely, doing deeds that were difficult to
do. The proud heroes fought dragging one another by the 96.45
hair and using their fingernails, teeth, fists, knees, palms,
swords, and handsome arms. Finding each other's weak
spots, they sent one another to the realm of Yama. Father
struck down son, and son father. Men stunned in their every limb fought on there. Dropped by the slain warriors, my
lord, beautiful bows with golden staves, valuable quivers,
and sharpened arrows finished with nocks of gold and silver and cleansed with oil looked radiant on the battlefield,
like snakes that had cast off their sloughs. Fallen warriors 96.50
dropped their gold-adorned swords with ivory hilts, pierced
shields glistening with gold, gold-furnished javelins, gold-
decked spears, golden darts, lances of gold-like shine, glittering armor, heavy maces, iron clubs, sharp-edged spears

suvarṇa|vikṛta|prāsān paṭṭiśān hema|bhūṣitān,
jātarūpamayāś ca' rṣṭīḥ, śaktīś ca kanak'|ôjjvalāḥ,
su|saṃnāhāś ca patitā, musalāni gurūṇi ca,
parighān, paṭṭiśāṃś c' âiva, bhindipālāṃś ca, māriṣa,
patitāṃs tomarāṃś c' âpi citrā, hema|pariṣkṛtāḥ,
kuthā bahu|vidh'|ākārāś, cāmara|vyajanāni ca,
nānā|vidhāni śastrāṇi visṛjya patitā narāḥ
jīvanta iva dṛśyante gata|sattvā mahā|rathāḥ.
96.55 gadā|vimathitair gātrair, musalair bhinna|mastakāḥ,
gaja|vāji|ratha|kṣuṇṇāḥ śerate sma narāḥ kṣitau.
tath" âiv' âśva|nṛ|nāgānāṃ śarīrair vibabhau tadā
saṃchannā vasu|dhā, rājan, parvatair iva sarvaśaḥ.
samare patitaiś c' âiva śakty|ṛṣṭi|śara|tomaraiḥ,
nistriṃśaiḥ, paṭṭiśaiḥ, prāsair, ayas|kuntaiḥ, paraśvadhaiḥ,
parighair, bhindipālaiś ca, śata|ghnībhiś ca, māriṣa,
śarīraiḥ śastra|bhinnaiś ca samāstīryata medinī.
vi|śabdair, alpa|śabdaiś ca, śoṇit'|âugha|pariplutaiḥ,
gat'|âsubhir, amitra|ghna, vibabhau nicitā mahī.
96.60 sa|tala|traiḥ, sa|keyūrair bāhubhiś candan'|ôkṣitaiḥ,
hasti|hast'|ôpamaiś chinnair, ūrubhiś ca tarasvinām,
baddha|cūḍā|maṇi|varaiḥ śirobhiś ca sa|kuṇḍalaiḥ
pātitair vṛṣabh'|âkṣāṇāṃ babhau, Bhārata, medinī.
kavacaiḥ śoṇitā|digdhair viprakīrṇaiś ca kāñcanaiḥ
rarāja su|bhṛśaṃ bhūmiḥ śānt'|ârcirbhir iv' ânalaiḥ.
vipraviddhaiḥ kalāpaiś ca, patitaiś ca śar'|âsanaiḥ,
viprakīrṇaiḥ śaraiś c' âpi rukma|puṅkhaiḥ samantataḥ,
rathaiś ca sarvato bhagnaiḥ kiṅkiṇī|jāla|bhūṣitaiḥ,
vājibhiś ca hataiḥ kīrṇaiḥ, srasta|jihvaiḥ, sa|śoṇitaiḥ,

and small darts, various bows resplendent and adorned with
gold, elephants' housings of different shapes, yak tails and
fans, my lord.

Having dropped their diverse weapons, those mighty
men were lying on the ground lifeless, looking as if alive.
Men were lying on the ground, squashed by elephants, 96.55
horses and chariots, with their bodies crushed with maces
and their heads smashed with clubs. And the earth, covered
with the bodies of horses, men and elephants, appeared,
Your Majesty, as if it was covered with hills.

The battlefield was strewn with fallen lances, spears, arrows, javelins, swords, sharp-edged spears, darts, iron lances,
battle axes, iron clubs, small javelins, and *shata·ghni*
missiles,* my lord, as well as with dead bodies lacerated
by weapons. The earth was covered with warriors bathed
in blood, some in the silence of their death, others feebly
moaning, slayer of enemies. Strewn with the arms of mighty 96.60
bull-eyed combatants, smeared with sandal paste, furnished
with leather fences and bracelets, with their thighs like elephant trunks, and with their severed heads adorned with
earrings and crest-jewels, the field of action presented a
beautiful sight, descendant of Bharata.

Covered with blood-smeared golden armor scattered all
around, the earth glistened brightly as if it was overspread
with fires whose flames had died down. With dropped quivers, fallen bows, and gold-nocked arrows scattered on all
sides, with many broken chariots decorated with rows of
bells, with horses killed by arrows and soaked in blood with
their tongues lolling out, with axle-sets, flags, quivers, and 96.65
banners, with the great white conches of eminent heroes,

96.65 anukarṣaiḥ, patākābhir, upāsaṅgair, dhvajair api,
pravīrāṇāṃ mahā|śaṅkhair viprakīrṇaiś ca pāṇḍuraiḥ,
srasta|hastaiś ca mātaṅgaiḥ śayānair vibabhau mahī,
nānā|rūpair alaṃ|kāraiḥ pramad" êv' âbhyalaṃkṛtā.
dantibhiś c' âparais tatra sa|prāsair, gāḍha|vedanaiḥ,
karaiḥ śabdaṃ vimuñcadbhiḥ, śīkaraṃ ca muhur muhuḥ,
vibabhau tad raṇa|sthānaṃ syandamānair iv' â|calaiḥ.

nānā|rāgaiḥ kambalaiś ca, paristomaiś ca dantinām,
vaiḍūrya|maṇi|daṇḍaiś ca patitair aṅkuśaiḥ śubhaiḥ,
ghaṇṭābhiś ca gaj'|êndrāṇāṃ patitābhiḥ samantataḥ,
96.70 vipāṭita|vicitrābhiḥ kuthābhir, aṅkuśais tathā,
graiveyaiś citra|rūpaiś ca, rukma|kakṣyābhir eva ca,
yantraiś ca bahudhā chinnais, tomaraiś c' âpi kāñcanaiḥ,
aśvānāṃ reṇu|kapilai rukma|cchannair uraś|chadaiḥ,
sādināṃ ca bhujaiś chinnaiḥ patitaiḥ s'|âṅgadais tathā,
prāsaiś ca vimalais, tīkṣṇair, vimalābhis tatha" rṣṭibhiḥ,
uṣṇīṣaiś ca tathā citrair vipraviddhais tatas tataḥ,
vicitrair ardha|candraiś ca jātarūpa|pariṣkṛtaiḥ,
aśv'|āstara|paristomai, rāṅkavair mṛditais tathā,
nar'|êndra|cūḍā|maṇibhir vicitraiś ca mahā|dhanaiḥ,
96.75 chatrais tath" âpaviddhaiś ca, cāmara|vyajanair api,
padm'|êndu|dyutibhiś c' âiva vadanaiś cāru|kuṇḍalaiḥ,
kḷpta|śmaśrubhir atyarthaṃ vīrāṇāṃ samalaṃkṛtaiḥ,
apaviddhair, mahā|rāja, suvarṇ'|ôjjvala|kuṇḍalaiḥ
graha|nakṣatra|śabalā dyaur iv' āsīd vasun|dharā.

and with trunkless elephants, the earth looked like a young woman decorated with ornaments of various kinds. And with other elephants that had been pierced with javelins and severely wounded letting out groans and spraying here and there with their trunks, the battlefield looked as if it was covered in moving mountains.

Laden with multicolored blankets, elephants' caparisons, and nice lapis-handled hooks that had fallen to the ground,
with the bells from mighty elephants scattered about, with 96.70
diverse torn elephants' housings, goads, various neck-chains, and golden girths, with many broken appliances, with golden spears, with horses' gilt breastplates tawny from the dust, with horsemen's severed arms fallen down with bracelets on, with sharp gleaming javelins and resplendent spears, with colorful turbans dropped off here and there, with showers of diverse arrows decorated in gold, with the housings and caparisons of horses, with trampled deerskins,
with various precious royal crest-jewels, with scattered para- 96.75
sols, yak tails, and fans, with heroes' faces radiant as lotuses or the moon and graced with fine earrings and well-clipped beards, with glistening golden earrings dropped around, great king, the earth looked like the sky studded with planets and stars.

evam ete mahā|sene mṛdite tatra, Bhārata,
paras|paraṃ samāsādya tava teṣāṃ ca saṃyuge.
teṣu śrānteṣu, bhagneṣu, mṛditeṣu ca, Bhārata,
rātriḥ samabhavat tatra. n' âpaśyāma tato raṇam.
tato 'vahāraṃ sainyānāṃ pracakruḥ Kuru|Pāṇḍavāḥ.
96.80 rajanī|mukhe su|raudre vartamāne mahā|bhaye,
avahāraṃ tataḥ kṛtvā sahitāḥ Kuru|Pāṇḍavāḥ
nyaviśanta yathā|kālaṃ, gatvā sva|śibiraṃ tadā.

Thus the two huge armies, yours and the enemies', crushed one another there, descendant of Bharata, confronting each other in that combat. When the troops were exhausted, broken, and crushed, Bhárata, the night set in, and we could no longer make our companions out. Then
the Kurus and the Pándavas withdrew from action. As that 96.80
fierce-looking, frightful night was falling, the Kurus and the Pándavas, having withdrawn their troops, retired to their encampments and entered their respective tents.

Thus the two huge armies, yours and the enemy's, crushed one another there, descendant of Bharata, confronting each other in that combat. When the troops were exhausted, broken and crushed in battle, the night set in and we could no longer make out our opponents. Then the Kauravas and the Pāṇḍavas withdrew from action. As that fierce, terrifying, frightful night was falling, the Kurus and the Pāṇḍavas, having withdrawn their troops, returned to their encampments and entered their respective tents.

97–98
THE KÁURAVAS' CONSULTATIONS

SAÑJAYA uvāca:

97.1 TATO DURYODHANO rājā, Śakuniś c' âpi Saubalaḥ,
Duḥśāsanaś ca putras te, sūta|putraś ca dur|jayaḥ
samāgamya, mahā|rāja, mantraṃ cakrur vivakṣitam:
«kathaṃ Pāṇḍu|sutāḥ saṃkhye jetavyāḥ sa|gaṇā?» iti.
tato Duryodhano rājā sarvāṃs tān āha mantriṇaḥ,
sūta|putraṃ samābhāṣya, Saubalaṃ ca mahā|balam:
«Droṇo, Bhīṣmaḥ, Kṛpaḥ, Śalyaḥ, Saumadattiś ca saṃyuge
na Pārthān pratibādhante. na jāne tatra kāraṇam.
97.5 a|vadhyamānās te c' âpi kṣapayanti balaṃ mama.
so 'smi kṣīṇa|balaḥ, Karṇa, kṣīṇa|śastraś ca saṃyuge.
nikṛtaḥ Pāṇḍavaiḥ śūrair a|vadhyair daivatair api
so 'haṃ saṃśayam āpannaḥ: prahariṣye kathaṃ raṇe?»
tam abravīn, mahā|rāja, sūta|putro nar'|âdhipam.

KARṆA uvāca:

mā śuco, Bharata|śreṣṭha. kariṣye 'haṃ priyaṃ tava.
Bhīṣmaḥ Śāntanavas tūrṇam apayātu mahā|raṇāt.
nivṛtte yudhi Gāṅgeye nyasta|śastre ca, Bhārata,
ahaṃ Pārthān haniṣyāmi sahitān sarva|Somakaiḥ
paśyato yudhi Bhīṣmasya. śape satyena te, nṛ|pa!
97.10 Pāṇḍaveṣu dayāṃ, rājan, sa hi Bhīṣmaḥ karoti vai;
a|śaktaś ca raṇe Bhīṣmo jetum etān mahā|rathān.
abhimānī raṇe Bhīṣmo, nityaṃ c' âpi raṇa|priyaḥ.
sa kathaṃ Pāṇḍavān yuddhe jeṣyate, tāta, saṃgatān?
sa tvaṃ śīghram ito gatvā Bhīṣmasya śibiraṃ prati,
anumānya guruṃ vṛddhaṃ śastraṃ nyāsaya, Bhārata.

SÁNJAYA said:

THEN KING DURYÓDHANA, Shákuni the son of Súbala, 97.1
your son Duhshásana, and the charioteer's son Karna who is difficult to vanquish took counsel together as to how the sons of Pandu might be defeated in combat, great king. King Duryódhana, addressing the charioteer's son and the mighty son of Súbala, told all the counsellors: "Drona, Bhishma, Kripa, Shalya, and the son of Soma·datta cannot resist the sons of Pritha in battle. I do not know the
reason why not. Without having been killed, the Pándavas 97.5
have been destroying my forces. So I am growing weaker in power, Karna, and running out of weapons in combat. Humiliated by the heroic Pándavas, who cannot be slain even by the gods, I am doubtful how I ought to fight with them in battle." And the charioteer's son replied to the great king.

KARNA said:

Do not grieve, best of the Bharatas! I shall do what will please you. But the son of Shántanu should immediately be withdrawn from this great battle. When the son of Ganga lays down his arms and stops fighting, I will kill the sons of Pritha and all the Sómakas in battle while Bhishma looks
on. I swear to you on the truth, Your Majesty! Bhishma 97.10
always treats the Pándavas sympathetically; that's why he is not able to defeat these great warriors in battle. And anyway, Bhishma is proud in combat and is always fond of fighting. How then will he defeat the assembled Pándavas, dear sir, and put an end to the war? So go quickly to Bhishma's tent, and convince the revered teacher to lay down his arms, Bhárata. After Bhishma has laid down his

nyasta|śastre tato Bhīṣme nihatān paśya Pāṇḍavān
may" âikena raṇe, rājan, sa|suhṛd|gaṇa|bāndhavān.

SAÑJAYA uvāca:

evam uktas tu Karṇena putro Duryodhanas tava
abravīd bhrātaraṃ tatra Duḥśāsanam idaṃ vacaḥ:
97.15 «anuyātraṃ yathā sarvaṃ sajjī|bhavati sarvaśaḥ,
Duḥśāsana, tathā kṣipraṃ sarvam ev' ôpapādaya.»
evam uktvā tato, rājan, Karṇam āha jan'|ēśvaraḥ:
«anumānya raṇe Bhīṣmam eṣo 'haṃ dvi|padāṃ varam
āgamiṣye tataḥ kṣipraṃ tvat|sakāśam, arin|dama.
apakrānte tato Bhīṣme prahariṣyasi saṃyuge.»
niṣpapāta tatas tūrṇaṃ putras tava, viśāṃ pate,
sahito bhrātṛbhiḥ sarvair, devair iva Śatakratuḥ.
tatas taṃ nṛpa|śārdūlaṃ śārdūla|sama|vikramam
ārohayadd hayaṃ tūrṇaṃ bhrātā Duḥśāsanas tadā.
97.20 aṅgadī, baddha|mukuṭo, hast'|ābharaṇavān nṛ|paḥ
Dhārtarāṣṭro, mahā|rāja, vibabhau sa pathi vrajan.
bhaṇḍī|puṣpa|nikāśena tapanīya|nibhena ca
anuliptaḥ par'|ârdhyena candanena su|gandhinā,
a|rajo|'mbara|saṃvītaḥ, siṃha|khela|gatir nṛ|paḥ
śuśubhe vimal'|ârciṣman nabhas' îva divā|karaḥ.
taṃ prayāntaṃ nara|vyāghraṃ Bhīṣmasya śibiraṃ prati
anujagmur mah"|êṣv|āsāḥ sarva|lokasya dhanvinaḥ,
bhrātaraś ca mah"|êṣv|āsās, tri|daśā iva Vāsavam.
hayān anye samāruhya, gajān anye ca, Bhārata,

arms you will see the Pándavas slain in battle, with their friends and relatives, by me alone.

SÁNJAYA said:

Addressed in this way by Karna, your son Duryódhana then spoke to his brother Duhshásana. "Duhshásana, ar- 97.15
range for my retinue to be completely ready as soon as possible."

Having said this, Your Majesty, the lord of men spoke to Karna:

"After convincing Bhishma, that best of men, in debate, I shall immediately come to you, tamer of enemies. When Bhishma has withdrawn, you will smite the foes in combat." Then your son set out, lord of the people, surrounded by all his brothers like Shata·kratu surrounded by the gods. His brother Duhshásana quickly helped that tiger-like king, who was a tiger's equal in strength, to mount his horse.
Adorned with bracelets, with a diadem on his head, and 97.20
wearing ornaments on his arms, your son the king looked resplendent as he proceeded along the road, great king. Smeared with precious and fragrant sandal paste which was the color of *bhandi* flowers and had the luster of gold, dressed in dustless garments, and moving with the playful gait of a lion, Your Majesty, he shone like the pure-rayed sun in the sky. As that tiger-like man proceeded toward Bhishma's tent, mighty archers renowned all over the world followed him, armed with their bows; his brothers, those great bowmen, followed him just as the gods follow Vásava.
Some rode horses, others elephants, and still others rode on 97.25
chariots, descendant of Bharata. They surrounded that best

97.25 rathān anye nara|śreṣṭhāḥ parivavruḥ samantataḥ.
ātta|śastrāś ca su|hṛdo rakṣaṇ'|ârthaṃ mahī|pateḥ
prādur|babhūvuḥ sahitāḥ, Śakrasy' êv' âmarā divi.
sa pūjyamānaḥ Kurubhiḥ Kauravāṇāṃ mahā|balaḥ
prayayau sadanaṃ rājā Gāṅgeyasya yaśasvinaḥ,
anvīyamānaḥ satataṃ s'|ôdaraiḥ parivāritaḥ.
dakṣiṇaṃ dakṣiṇaḥ kāle saṃbhṛtya sva|bhujaṃ tadā
hasti|hast'|ôpamaṃ, śaikṣaṃ, sarva|śatru|nibarhaṇam,
pragṛhṇann añjalīn nṛṇām udyatān sarvato diśaḥ,
śuśrāva madhurā vāco nānā|deśa|nivāsinām,
97.30 saṃstūyamānaḥ sūtaiś ca māgadhaiś ca mahā|yaśāḥ,
pūjayānaś ca tān sarvān sarva|lok'|ēśvar'|ēśvaraḥ.
pradīpaiḥ kāñcanais tatra gandha|tail'|âvasecitaiḥ
parivavrur mah"|ātmānaṃ prajvaladbhiḥ samantataḥ.
sa taiḥ parivṛto rājā pradīpaiḥ kāñcanaiḥ śubhaiḥ
śuśubhe, candramā yukto dīptair iva mahā|grahaiḥ.
kāñcan'|ôṣṇīṣiṇas tatra vetra|jharjhara|pāṇayaḥ
protsārayantaḥ śanakais taṃ janaṃ sarvato|diśam.
saṃprāpya tu tato rājā Bhīṣmasya sadanaṃ śubham,
avatīrya hayāc c' âpi Bhīṣmaṃ prāpya jan'|ēśvaraḥ,
97.35 abhivādya tato Bhīṣmaṃ niṣaṇṇaḥ param'|āsane
kāñcane, sarvato|bhadre, spardhy'|āstaraṇa|saṃvṛte,
uvāca prāñjalir Bhīṣmaṃ bāṣpa|kaṇṭho 'śru|locanaḥ:
«tvāṃ vayaṃ hi samāśritya saṃyuge, śatru|sūdana,
utsahema raṇe jetuṃ s'|Êndrān api sur'|âsurān;
kim u Pāṇḍu|sutān vīrān sa|suhṛd|gaṇa|bāndhavān?
tasmād arhasi, Gāṅgeya, kṛpāṃ kartuṃ mayi, prabho.

of kings on all sides. Armed with weapons, his friends went along for the king's protection, accompanying him just as the gods accompany Shakra in heaven.

Revered by the Kurus, that powerful king of the Káuravas proceeded to the tent of the glorious son of Ganga,
followed all the way and surrounded by his brothers. Duly
raising his skillful right arm, which was as mighty as elephant's trunk and able to destroy all enemies, the dexterous king accepted the respects paid by men on every side
with their raised and folded hands, and heard the sweet
words of people from different countries. The glorious king 97.30
of the kings of all places, praised by bards and panegyrists,
honored all of them in turn. People surrounded the great
king on all sides with burning golden lamps filled with fragrant oil. And the king, illuminated by those golden lamps,
shone like the moon surrounded by the great shining planets. Then attendants wearing golden turbans, with canes
and drums in their hands, gradually dispersed the crowd in
all directions.

Reaching Bhishma's beautiful tent and descending from
his horse, the lord of men went up to Bhishma. Saluting 97.35
Bhishma, the king sat down on an exquisite symmetrical
golden seat overlaid with a fine coverlet. Folding his hands
in obeisance, with damp eyes and a tear-choked throat, he
spoke to Bhishma:

"Relying on you in battle, slayer of enemies, we could conquer even the gods and demons in battle, including Indra himself. What then of the Pándavas with their friends, allies, and relatives? Therefore, lord, son of Ganga, you must take pity on me. Slaughter the heroic sons of Pandu, like

jahi Pāṇḍu|sutān vīrān, mah"|Êndra iva dānavān.
‹ahaṃ sarvān, mahā|rāja, nihaniṣyāmi Somakān,
Pañcālān Kekayaiḥ sārdhaṃ, Karūṣāṃś c',› êti, Bhārata,
97.40 tvad|vacaḥ satyam ev' âstu! jahi Pārthān samāgatān,
Somakāṃś ca mah"|êṣv|āsān! satya|vāg bhava, Bhārata!
dayayā yadi vā, rājan, dveṣya|bhāvān mama, prabho,
manda|bhāgyatayā v" âpi mama rakṣasi Pāṇḍavān,
anujānīhi samare Karṇam āhava|śobhinam!
sa jeṣyati raṇe Pārthān sa|suhṛd|gaṇa|bāndhavān.»
etāvad uktvā nṛ|patiḥ putro Duryodhanas tava,
n' ôvāca vacanaṃ kiṃ cid Bhīṣmaṃ satya|parākramam.

SAÑJAYA uvāca:

98.1 VĀK|ŚALYAIS TAVA putreṇa so 'tividdho mahā|manāḥ
duḥkhena mahat" āviṣṭo n' ôvāc' â|priyam aṇv api.
sa dhyātvā su|ciraṃ kālaṃ duḥkha|roṣa|samanvitaḥ,
śvasamāno yathā nāgaḥ, praṇunno vāk|śalākayā,
udvṛtya cakṣuṣī kopān, nirdahann iva, Bhārata,
sa|dev'|âsura|gandharvaṃ lokaṃ loka|vidāṃ varaḥ,
abravīt tava putraṃ tu
sāma|pūrvam idaṃ vacaḥ:
«kiṃ tvaṃ, Duryodhan', âivaṃ māṃ
vāk|śalyair apakṛntasi
98.5 ghaṭamānaṃ yathā|śakti, kurvāṇaṃ ca tava priyam,
juhvānaṃ samare prāṇāṃs tava vai hita|kāmyayā?
yadā tu Pāṇḍavaḥ śūraḥ Khāṇḍave 'gnim atarpayat
parājitya raṇe Śakraṃ—paryāptaṃ tan nidarśanam.
yadā ca tvāṃ, mahā|bāho, gandharvair hṛtam ojasā

great Indra slaughtering demons. 'Great king, I will kill the Sómakas, the Panchálas, the Kékayas, and the Karúshas'— such were your words to me, Bhárata. May they come true! 97.40
Kill the assembled sons of Pritha, along with the Sómakas, those mighty archers! Be true to your word, descendant of Bharata! If you are sparing the Pándavas out of sympathy, or, unfortunately for me, out of hatred toward myself, then allow Karna, resplendent in battle, to fight! He will defeat the sons of Pritha with their friends, allies, and relatives." Your royal son Duryódhana said this to Bhishma, whose power is in truth; and he said nothing more.

SÁNJAYA said:

GREAT-SPIRITED Bhishma, hurt by the arrows of your 98.1
son's speech and overcome by deep sorrow, did not say even a single displeasing word in reply. Filled with grief and anger, he thought for a long time, hurt by those thorny words and sighing like an elephant goaded by a sharp stick. Then that best of experts in the ways of the world, raising his eyes as if he was about to burn down the entire world in his rage along with the gods, demons and *gandhárvas*, descendant of Bharata, calmly addressed your son as follows.

"Why are you afflicting me with these words like arrows,
Duryódhana? Being your well-wisher, I have been striving 98.5
to the best of my powers to do you good, ready to sacrifice my life in combat. Pandu's valiant son, having defeated Shakra himself in battle, gratified Agni by letting him consume the Khándava forest. That should suffice to show what Árjuna is like. That son of Pandu with his power rescued you, mighty-armed one, when you had been captured by

amocayat Pāṇḍu|sutaḥ—paryāptaṃ tan nidarśanam.
dravamāṇeṣu śūreṣu s'|ôdareṣu tava, prabho,
sūta|putre ca Rādheye—paryāptaṃ tan nidarśanam.

yac ca naḥ sahitān sarvān Virāṭa|nagare tadā
eka eva samudyātaḥ—paryāptaṃ tan nidarśanam.
98.10 Droṇaṃ ca yudhi saṃrabdhaṃ, māṃ ca nirjitya saṃyuge,
vāsāṃsi sa samādatta—paryāptaṃ tan nidarśanam.
tathā Drauniṃ mah"|êṣv|āsaṃ, Śāradvatam ath' âpi ca
go|grahe jitavān pūrvaṃ—paryāptaṃ tan nidarśanam.
vijitya ca yadā Karṇaṃ sadā puruṣa|māninam
Uttarāyai dadau vastraṃ—paryāptaṃ tan nidarśanam.
nivāta|kavacān yuddhe Vāsaven' âpi dur|jayān
jitavān samare Pārthaḥ—paryāptaṃ tan nidarśanam.
ko hi śakto raṇe jetuṃ Pāṇḍavaṃ rabhasaṃ tadā,
yasya goptā jagad|goptā śaṅkha|cakra|gadā|dharaḥ
98.15 Vāsudevo 'n|anta|śaktiḥ, sṛṣṭi|saṃhāra|kārakaḥ,
sarv'|ēśvaro, deva|devaḥ, param'|ātmā sanātanaḥ?

ukto 'si bahuśo, rājan, Nārad'|ādyair maha"|rṣibhiḥ;
tvaṃ tu mohān na jānīṣe vācy'|â|vācyaṃ, Suyodhana.
mumūrṣur hi naraḥ sarvān vṛkṣān paśyati kāñcanān,
tathā tvam api, Gāndhāre, viparītāni paśyasi.
svayaṃ vairaṃ mahat kṛtvā Pāṇḍavaiḥ saha|Sṛñjayaiḥ
yudhyasva tān! adya raṇe paśyāmaḥ. puruṣo bhava!

gandhárvas. That should suffice to show what he is like. O lord, at that time your heroic brothers and Karna, the son of Radha and the charioteer, had fled away, and Árjuna rescued you. That should suffice to show what he is like.

In Viráta's city Árjuna alone rose up against all our joint
troops. That should suffice to show what he is like. He 98.10
conquered Drona and myself in combat and took away our garments. That should suffice to show what he is like. Viráta's cattle had been stolen, and Árjuna defeated Drona's son, that mighty archer, and even the son of Sharádvat. That should suffice to show what he is like. After defeating Karna, who is always proud of his manliness, Árjuna gave Karna's garments to Princess Uttará. That should suffice to show what he is like. In battle the son of Pritha vanquished the demons whose armor is impenetrable, whom even Vásava found hard to vanquish. That should suffice to show what he is like. Who can defeat that mighty son of Pandu in combat, whose protector is the protector of the universe himself, the wielder of the conch, discus, and
mace—Vásu·deva endowed with limitless might, the cre- 98.15
ator and destroyer of the world, the lord of all, the god of gods, the supreme soul, the eternal one?

Your Majesty, you have been told again and again by Nárada and other sages, but out of delusion you do not know what should be said and what should not, Suyódhana. Just as a man on the verge of death sees all trees as made of gold, so you, son of Gandhári, see everything upside down. You yourself have stirred up this great feud with the Pándavas and the Srínjayas. Now fight with them! We'll

ahaṃ tu Somakān sarvān, Pañcālāṃś ca samāgatān
nihaniṣye, nara|vyāghra, varjayitvā Śikhaṇḍinam.
98.20 tair v" âhaṃ nihataḥ saṃkhye gamiṣye Yama|sādanam;
tān vā nihatya saṃgrāme prītiṃ dāsyāmy ahaṃ tava.
pūrvaṃ hi strī samutpannā Śikhaṇḍī rāja|veśmani;
vara|dānāt pumāñ jātaḥ. s" âiṣā vai strī Shikhaṇḍinī.
tām ahaṃ na haniṣyāmi prāṇa|tyāge 'pi, Bhārata;
y" âsau prāṅ nirmitā Dhātrā, s" âiṣā vai strī Shikhaṇḍinī.
sukhaṃ svapihi, Gāndhāre. śvo 'smi kartā mahā|raṇam,
yaṃ janāḥ kathayiṣyanti yāvat sthāsyati medinī.»

evam uktas tava suto nirjagāma, jan'|ēśvara;
abhivādya guruṃ mūrdhnā prayayau svaṃ niveśanam.
98.25 āgamya tu tato rājā, visṛjya ca mahā|janam,
praviveśa tatas tūrṇaṃ kṣayaṃ śatru|kṣayaṅ|karaḥ;
praviṣṭaḥ sa niśāṃ tāṃ ca gamayām āsa pārthivaḥ.

prabhātāyāṃ tu śarvaryāṃ prātar utthāya vai nṛ|paḥ
rājñaḥ samājñāpayata: «senāṃ yojayat'!» êti ha;
«adya Bhīṣmo raṇe kruddho nihaniṣyati Somakān!»

Duryodhanasya tac chrutvā rātrau vilapitaṃ bahu
manyamānaḥ sa taṃ, rājan, pratyādeśam iv' ātmanaḥ.
nirvedaṃ paramaṃ gatvā, vinindya para|vaśyatām,
dīrghaṃ dadhyau Śāntanavo yoddhu|kāmo 'rjunaṃ raṇe.
98.30 iṅgitena tu taj jñātvā Gāṅgeyena vicintitam
Duryodhano, mahā|rāja, Duḥśāsanam acodayat:

see you in battle. Be a man! As for me, I will kill all the mustered Sómakas and Panchálas except Shikhándin, tiger-like
man; I will either go to the realm of Yama, killed by them 98.20
in battle, or I will make you happy by killing them. First he was born in the royal palace as a female, Shikhándini; then, through a boon, she became a male. I'll not strike him even at the cost of my life, descendant of Bharata, for that one is the same woman Shikhándini as was originally made by the Creator. Sleep well, son of Gandhári. Tomorrow I shall fight a great battle, and people will speak of it as long as the earth lasts."

Addressed in this way, lord of men, your son honored the mentor with a bow of the head and went to his own tent.
Reaching it, the king, that destroyer of enemies, dismissed 98.25
his numerous attendants and quickly entered the tent; and after he had entered it the king spent the night in sleep.

At daybreak, when the night had passed, the king got up and commanded the kings: "Draw up the troops! Today Bhishma will slaughter the Sómakas in his battle-fury!"

After hearing Duryodhana's bitter lamentations the previous night, Bhishma considered them a command to himself, Your Majesty. The son of Shántanu felt deep distress, deplored his situation of dependence, and pondered for a long while, wanting to fight against Árjuna in battle.
Understanding the signs of what Ganga's son intended, 98.30
Your Majesty, Duryódhana gave Duhshásana his orders:

«Duḥśāsana, rathās tūrṇaṃ yujyantāṃ Bhīṣma|rakṣiṇaḥ.
dvā|triṃśatim anīkāni sarvāṇy ev' âbhicodaya.
idaṃ hi samanuprāptaṃ varṣa|pūg'|âbhicintitam
Pāṇḍavānāṃ sa|sainyānāṃ vadho, rājyasya c' āgamaḥ.
tatra kāryatamaṃ manye Bhīṣmasy' âiv' âbhirakṣaṇam.
sa no guptaḥ sahāyaḥ syādd, hanyāt Pārthāṃś ca saṃyuge.
abravīdd hi viśuddh'|ātmā: ‹n' âhaṃ hanyāṃ Śikhaṇḍinam.
strī|pūrvako hy asau jātas. tasmād varjyo raṇe mayā.
98.35 lokas tad veda, yad ahaṃ pituḥ priya|cikīrṣayā
rājyaṃ sphītaṃ, mahā|bāho, striyaś ca tyaktavān purā.
n' âiva c' âhaṃ striyaṃ jātu, na strī|pūrvaṃ kathaṃ cana
hanyāṃ yudhi, nara|śreṣṭha. satyam etad bravīmi te.
ayaṃ strī|pūrvako, rājañ, Śikhaṇḍī, yadi te śrutaḥ
udyoge kathitaṃ yat tat. tathā jātā Śikhaṇḍinī
kanyā bhūtvā pumāñ jātaḥ. sa ca yotsyati, Bhārata.
tasy' âhaṃ pramukhe bāṇān na muñceyaṃ kathaṃ cana.
yuddhe hi kṣatriyāṃs, tāta, Pāṇḍavānāṃ jay'|âiṣiṇaḥ
sarvān anyān haniṣyāmi saṃprāptān raṇa|mūrdhani.›
98.40 evaṃ māṃ Bharata|śreṣṭho Gāṅgeyaḥ prāha śāstra|vit.
tatra sarv'|ātmanā manye Gāṅgeyasy' âiva pālanam.
a|rakṣyamāṇaṃ hi vṛko hanyāt siṃhaṃ mah"|āhave.
mā vṛkeṇ' êva śārdūlaṃ ghātayema Śikhaṇḍinā.
mātulaḥ Śakuniḥ, Śalyaḥ, Kṛpo, Droṇo, Viviṃśatiḥ
yattā rakṣantu Gāṅgeyaṃ. tasmin gupte dhruvo jayaḥ.»

"Quickly, arrange chariots to protect Bhishma, Duhshásana. Invigorate each one of our twenty-two divisions. Now we have the opportunity for what we have sought all these years: the killing of the Pándavas and their troops, and the acquisition of the kingdom. As I see it, protecting Bhishma is our most important task. If we protect him, he will assist us by killing the sons of Pritha in battle. That pure-spirited hero told me: 'I will not strike Shikhándin. For he
was once female, so I must shun him in battle. The whole 98.35
world knows that in the past, wishing to do a favor for my father, I renounced the thriving kingdom and the company of women, mighty-armed hero. And I will never strike any female in battle, or anyone who was a female in the past, best of kings. I'm telling you the truth. Your Majesty, you have heard that first this Shikhándin was born as a female, and was called Shikhándini—I told you so myself, during the preparation for the war.* Born as a girl, he has become a man. He will fight with me, but I will not fire my arrows at him by any means. Yet in this war I will kill every other warrior who confronts me at the forefront of battle, desiring victory for the Pándavas.'

This is what the son of Ganga, that expert in advice, has 98.40
told me, best of the Bharatas. So I think we must protect Ganga's son wholeheartedly. Even a wolf can kill an unprotected lion in a great battle; so we should not let the son of Ganga be slain by Shikhándin. Our uncle Shákuni, Shalya, Kripa, Drona, and Vivímshati must protect the son of Ganga. If he is duly guarded, our victory is certain."

etac chrutvā tu te sarve Duryodhana|vacas tadā
sarvato ratha|vaṃśena Gāṅgeyaṃ paryavārayan.
putrāś ca tava Gāṅgeyaṃ parivārya yayur mudā
kampayanto bhuvaṃ dyāṃ ca, kṣobhayantaś ca Pāṇḍavān.
98.45 te rathaiś ca su|saṃyuktair, dantibhiś ca mahā|rathāḥ
parivārya raṇe Bhīṣmaṃ daṃśitāḥ samavasthitāḥ,
yathā dev'|âsure yuddhe tri|daśā vajra|dhāriṇam,
sarve te sma vyatiṣṭhanta rakṣantas taṃ mahā|ratham.
tato Duryodhano rājā punar bhrātaram abravīt:
«savyaṃ cakraṃ Yudhāmanyur, Uttamaujāś ca dakṣiṇam
goptārāv Arjunasy' âitāv; Arjuno 'pi Śikhaṇḍinaḥ.
sa rakṣyamāṇaḥ Pārthena, tath" âsmābhir vivarjitaḥ,
yathā Bhīṣmaṃ na no hanyād, Duḥśāsana tathā kuru.»
bhrātus tad vacanaṃ śrutvā putro Duḥśāsanas tava
98.50 Bhīṣmaṃ pramukhataḥ kṛtvā prayayau saha senayā.
Bhīṣmaṃ tu ratha|vaṃśena dṛṣṭvā samabhisaṃvṛtam
Arjuno rathināṃ śreṣṭho Dhṛṣṭadyumnam uvāca ha:
«Śikhaṇḍinaṃ, nara|vyāghra,
Bhīṣmasya pramukhe, 'n|agha,
sthāpayasv' âdya, Pāñcālya.
tasya gopt" âham» ity uta.

Hearing Duryódhana's instructions, all of your troops surrounded Ganga's son with hordes of chariots on every side; and your sons surrounded the son of Ganga too and advanced gladly, shaking the earth and sky and causing
some agitation among the Pándava troops. Those great war- 98.45
riors stood wearing their armor, surrounding Bhishma with well-equipped chariots and elephants. All of them stood ready to protect that mighty warrior, like the gods protecting thunderbolt-wielding Indra during the battle between the gods and demons.

Then King Duryódhana spoke to his brother once again:

"Yudha·manyu protects the left wheel of Árjuna's chariot, and Uttamáujas protects the right one. Protected by them, Árjuna is Shikhándin's protector. Protected by the son of Pritha, Shikhándin might be ignored by us and thus find himself in a position to kill our Bhishma; so make arrangements, Duhshásana, such that he is not."

Hearing his brother's words, your son Duhshásana, with 98.50
Bhishma before him, marched forward along with the troops.

And when he saw Bhishma surrounded by a chariot host, Árjuna, that best of chariot warriors, told Dhrishta·dyumna:

"Your Highness, prince of the Panchálas, place Shikhándin, that tiger-like man, opposite Bhishma. I shall be his protector."

99–106
DAY NINE

SAÑJAYA uvāca:

99.1 TATAḤ ŚĀNTANAVO Bhīṣmo niryayau saha senayā,
vyūhaṃ c' âvyūhata mahat sarvato|bhadram ātmanaḥ.
Kṛpaś ca, Kṛtavarmā ca, Śaibyaś c' âiva mahā|rathaḥ,
Śakuniḥ Saindhavaś c' âiva, Kāmbojaś ca Sudakṣiṇaḥ
Bhīṣmeṇa sahitāḥ sarve, putraiś ca tava, Bhārata,
agrataḥ sarva|sainyānāṃ vyūhasya pramukhe sthitāḥ.
Droṇo, Bhūriśravāḥ, Śalyo, Bhagadattaś ca, māriṣa,
dakṣiṇaṃ pakṣam āśritya sthitā vyūhasya daṃśitāḥ.
99.5 Aśvatthāmā, Somadatta, Āvantyau ca mahā|rathau
mahatyā senayā yuktā vāmaṃ pakṣam apālayan.
Duryodhano, mahā|rāja, Trigartaiḥ sarvato vṛtaḥ
vyūha|madhye sthito, rājan, Pāṇḍavān prati, Bhārata.
Alambuṣo ratha|śreṣṭhaḥ, Śrutāyuś ca mahā|rathaḥ
pṛṣṭhataḥ sarva|sainyānāṃ sthitau vyūhasya daṃśitau.
evaṃ ca taṃ tadā vyūhaṃ kṛtvā, Bhārata, tāvakāḥ
saṃnaddhāḥ samadṛśyanta, pratapanta iv' âgnayaḥ.
tathā Yudhiṣṭhiro rājā, Bhīmasenaś ca Pāṇḍavaḥ,
Nakulaḥ, Sahadevaś ca, Mādrī|putrāv ubhāv api
99.10 agrataḥ sarva|sainyānāṃ sthitā vyūhasya daṃśitāḥ.
Dhṛṣṭadyumno, Virāṭaś ca, Sātyakiś ca mahā|rathaḥ
sthitāḥ sainyena mahatā par'|ânīka|vināśanāḥ.
Śikhaṇḍī, Vijayaś c' âiva, rākṣasaś ca Ghaṭotkacaḥ,
Cekitāno mahā|bāhuḥ, Kuntibhojaś ca vīryavān
sthitā raṇe, mahā|rāja, mahatyā senayā vṛtāḥ.

SÁNJAYA said:

THEN BHISHMA THE son of Shántanu advanced with the army. He drew up his troops into the great symmetrical formation. Kripa, Krita·varman, the great warrior Shaibya, Shákuni, the king of the Sindhus, and Sudákshina the ruler of the Kambójas, all together, with Bhishma and your sons, descendant of Bharata, stood in the van of all the troops and at the head of that formation. Drona, Bhuri·shravas, Shalya, and Bhaga·datta, clad in armor, were stationed on the right flank of that formation, my lord. 99.1
Supported by a large division, Ashva·tthaman, Soma·datta, 99.5
and the two princes of Avánti, both of them great warriors, defended the left flank. Duryódhana, great king, surrounded on every side by the Tri·gartas, stood in the middle of that formation, facing the Pándavas, Your Majesty, descendant of Bharata. Wearing their armor, the supreme champion Alámbusha and the great warrior Shrutáyus were stationed in the rear of that formation, behind all the troops. After forming this array, your combatants, clad in armor, looked like blazing fires, descendant of Bharata.

King Yudhi·shthira, Bhima·sena Pándava, and Madri's
two sons Nákula and Saha·deva, wearing their armor, stood 99.10
in the front of their array and in the van of all the troops. Dhrishta·dyumna, Viráta, and the great warrior Sátyaki, destroyers of hostile divisions, stood there accompanied by a large force. Shikhándin, Víjaya, the demon Ghatótkacha, mighty-armed Chekitána, and vigorous Kunti·bhoja were stationed on the battlefield, surrounded by a large body of troops. The great archer Abhimányu, powerful Drúpada, the mighty archer Yuyudhána, vigorous Yudha·manyu, and

Abhimanyur mah"|êṣv|āso, Drupadaś ca mahā|balaḥ,
Yuyudhāno mah"|êṣv|āso, Yudhāmanyuś ca vīryavān,
Kekayā bhrātaraś c' âiva sthitā yuddhāya daṃśitāḥ.
evaṃ te 'pi mahā|vyūhaṃ prativyūhya su|durjayam
99.15 Pāṇḍavāḥ samare śūrāḥ sthitā yuddhāya daṃśitāḥ.
tāvakās tu raṇe yattāḥ saha|senā nar'|âdhipāḥ
abhyudyayū raṇe Pārthān, Bhīṣmaṃ kṛtv" âgrato, nṛ|pa.
tath" âiva Pāṇḍavā, rājan, Bhīmasena|puro|gamāḥ
Bhīṣmaṃ yoddhum abhīpsantaḥ, saṃgrāme vijay'|âiṣiṇaḥ,
kṣveḍāḥ, kilikilāḥ, śaṅkhān, krakacān, go|viṣāṇikāḥ,
bherī|mṛdaṅga|paṇavān nādayantaś ca puṣkarān,
Pāṇḍavā abhyavartanta nadanto bhairavān ravān.
bherī|mṛdaṅga|śaṅkhānāṃ, dundubhīnāṃ ca niḥsvanaiḥ,
utkruṣṭa|siṃha|nādaiś ca, valgitaiś ca pṛthag|vidhaiḥ
99.20 vayaṃ pratinadantas tān abhyagacchāma sa|tvarāḥ,
sahas" âiv' âbhisaṃkruddhās. tad" āsīt tumulaṃ mahat.
tato 'nyonyaṃ pradhāvantaḥ saṃprahāraṃ pracakrire.
tataḥ śabdena mahatā pracakampe vasun|dharā.
pakṣiṇaś ca mahā|ghoraṃ vyāharanto vibabhramuḥ.
sa|prabhaś c' ôditaḥ sūryo niṣ|prabhaḥ samapadyata.
vavuś ca tumulā vātāḥ śaṃsantaḥ su|mahad bhayam.
ghorāś ca ghora|nirhrādāḥ śivās tatra vavāśire
vedayantyo, mahā|rāja, mahad vaiśasam āgatam.
diśaḥ prajvalitā, rājan. pāṃsu|varṣaṃ papāta ca,
99.25 rudhireṇa samunmiśram asthi|varṣaṃ tath" âiva ca.
rudatāṃ vāhanānāṃ ca netrebhyaḥ prāpataj jalam.
susruvuś ca śakṛn|mūtraṃ pradhyāyanto, viśāṃ pate.
antar|hitā mahā|nādāḥ śrūyante, Bharata'|rṣabha,

the Kékaya brothers stood clad in their armor, ready for the fight.

Thus, forming a mighty counter-array which was extremely difficult to conquer, the valiant Pándavas stood clad 99.15
in armor, ready for battle.

Then, intent on battle, your kings and their armies, with Bhishma stationed at the front, attacked the sons of Pritha, Your Majesty. And the Pándavas charged forward led by Bhima·sena, eager to fight against Bhishma and desiring victory in battle. Making piercing noises, shouting cheers of joy, playing conches, cow-horns, cymbals, drums, kettle-drums, and tabors, and uttering fierce war-cries, the Pándavas assailed the enemy host. And we rushed against them 99.20
in rage and at speed, with sounds of kettle-drums, drums, conches, and tabors, with loud lion-roars, and with various jumps. Then a great tumult arose.

When both armies charged against each other and began to strike one another, the earth, affected by a huge noise, started to quake. Birds hovered above us, uttering terrible screams. The sun that had risen in full brightness lost its luster. Turbulent winds blew, striking terror into our hearts. Frightful jackals howled there in hideous fashion. The directions blazed up, Your Majesty, foreboding a great massacre. A shower of dust fell, great king, as well as a rain- 99.25
storm of bones mixed with blood. Tears fell from the eyes of weeping animals. Filled with anguish, the animals soiled themselves with feces and urine, lord of the people. Loud shouts were drowned out, bull of the Bharatas, by the horrible roars of man-eating demons. Jackals, cranes, crows, and

rakṣasāṃ puruṣ'|âdānāṃ, nadatāṃ bhairavān ravān.
saṃpatantaḥ sma dṛśyante gomāyu|baka|vāyasāḥ,
śvānaś ca vividhair nādair vāśantas tatra, māriṣa.
jvalitāś ca mah"|ôlkā vai samāhatya divā|karam
nipetuḥ sahasā bhūmau, vedayantyo mahad bhayam.
mahānty anīkāni mahā|samucchraye
tatas tayoḥ Pāṇḍava|Dhārtarāṣṭrayoḥ
cakampire śaṅkha|mṛdaṅga|nisvanaiḥ,
prakampitān' îva vanāni vāyunā.
99.30 nar'|êndra|nāg'|âśva|samākulānām
abhyāyatīnām a|śive muhūrte
babhūva ghoṣas tumulaś camūnāṃ,
vāt'|ôddhutānām iva sāgarāṇām.

SAÑJAYA uvāca:

100.1 ABHIMANYŪ RATH'|ôdāraḥ piśaṅgais turag'|ôttamaiḥ
abhidudrāva tejasvī Duryodhana|balaṃ mahat,
vikirañ śara|varṣāṇi vāri|dhārā iv' âmbu|daḥ.
na śekuḥ samare kruddhaṃ Saubhadram ari|sūdanam
śastr'|âughiṇaṃ gāhamānaṃ senā|sāgaram a|kṣayam
nivārayitum apy ājau tvadīyāḥ, Kuru|nandana.
tena muktā raṇe, rājañ, śarāḥ śatru|nibarhaṇāḥ
kṣatriyān anayañ śūrān preta|rāja|niveśanam.
100.5 Yama|daṇḍ'|ôpamān, ghorāñ, jvalan'|āśīviṣ'|ôpamān
Saubhadraḥ samare kruddhaḥ preṣayām āsa sāyakān.
sa|rathān rathinas tūrṇaṃ, hayāṃś c' âiva sa|sādinaḥ,
gaj'|ārohāṃś ca sa|gajān dārayām āsa Phālguniḥ.
tasya tat kurvataḥ karma mahat saṃkhye mahī|bhṛtaḥ
pūjayāṃ cakrire hṛṣṭāḥ, praśaśaṃsuś ca Phālgunim.

dogs were seen gathered there, uttering various cries, my lord.

Huge blazing meteors struck the solar disk and collapsed precipitously upon the earth, portending a great horror. And the mighty forces of the Pándavas and of the Dharta·rashtras trembled at the loud sounds of conches and drums, like groves shaken by a wind. As they confronted each other 99.30
in that inauspicious moment, the divisions teeming with kings, elephants, and horses made a tumultuous noise, like the roar of the ocean agitated by a storm.

SÁNJAYA said:

RIDING HIS FINE tawny horses, the noble and vigorous 100.1
warrior Abhimányu charged against Duryódhana's mighty host, scattering showers of arrows just as a storm-cloud pours torrents of rain. In that battle, delight of the Kurus, your troops could not restrain the enemy-slaying son of Subhádra, filled with battle-fury and armed with hordes of weapons, as he plunged into the boundless ocean of the enemy army. The enemy-killing arrows he released in that engagement, Your Majesty, sent many brave warriors to the abode of the king of the dead. Enraged in combat, 100.5
the son of Subhádra fired fearful arrows—arrows like staffs of Yama, arrows like blazing poisonous snakes. Phálguna's son quickly cut through chariot warriors and their chariots, horses and their riders, and elephant drivers and their elephants. As he performed that great feat in battle, the joyful kings honored and praised Phálguna's son.

tāny anīkāni Saubhadro drāvayām āsa, Bhārata,
tūla|rāśim iv' ādhūya mārutaḥ sarvato|diśam.
tena vidrāvyamāṇāni tava sainyāni, Bhārata,
trātāraṃ n' âdhyagacchanta, paṅke magnā iva dvi|pāḥ.
100.10 vidrāvya sarva|sainyāni tāvakāni, nar'|ôttama,
Abhimanyuḥ sthito, rājan, vi|dhūmo 'gnir iva jvalan.
na c' âinaṃ tāvakā, rājan, viṣehur ari|ghātinam,
pradīptaṃ pāvakaṃ yadvat pataṅgāḥ Kāla|coditāḥ.

praharan sarva|śatrubhyaḥ Pāṇḍavānāṃ mahā|rathaḥ
adṛśyata mah"|êṣv|āsaḥ, sa|vajra iva vajra|bhṛt.
hema|pṛṣṭhaṃ dhanuś c' âsya dadṛśe vicarad diśaḥ,
toya|deṣu yathā, rājan, rājamānā śata|hradā.
śarāś ca niśitāḥ pītā niścaranti sma saṃyuge,
vanāt phulla|drumād, rājan, bhramarāṇām iva vrajāḥ.
100.15 tath" âiva caratas tasya Saubhadrasya mah"|ātmanaḥ
rathena kañcan'|âṅgena dadṛśur n' ântaraṃ janāḥ.
mohayitvā Kṛpaṃ, Droṇaṃ, Drauṇiṃ ca sa|Bṛhadbalam,
Saindhavaṃ ca mah"|êṣv|āsaṃ, vyacaral laghu suṣṭhu ca.
maṇḍalī|kṛtam ev' âsya dhanuḥ paśyāma, māriṣa,
sūrya|maṇḍala|saṃkāśaṃ dahatas tava vāhinīm.
taṃ dṛṣṭvā kṣatriyāḥ śūrāḥ pratapantaṃ tarasvinam
dvi|Phālgunam imaṃ lokaṃ menire tasya karmabhiḥ.
ten' ârditā, mahā|rāja, Bhāratī sā mahā|camūḥ
babhrāma tatra tatr' âiva, yoṣin mada|vaśād iva.
100.20 drāvayitvā mahā|sainyaṃ, kampayitvā mahā|rathān,
nandayām āsa su|hṛdo, Mayaṃ jitv" êva Vāsavaḥ.

The son of Subhádra dispersed those divisions, descendant of Bharata, just as the wind scatters heaps of cotton in
all directions. Dispersed by him, Bhárata, your troops were
unable to find a protector, like elephants sunk in mud. And 100.10
having scattered all your troops, Your Majesty, Abhimányu
stood there like a blazing smokeless fire, best of kings. Your
combatants, Your Majesty, could not resist that slayer of
enemies, just as moths, prompted by Time, cannot resist a
burning flame.

That great warrior Abhimányu, the mighty archer of the
Pándavas, smiting all the enemies, looked like thunderbolt-
wielding Vásava. His gilt-edged bow, moving in all directions, looked like lightning flashing through the clouds,
Your Majesty. And the whetted copper arrows that that bow
discharged in that battle looked like swarms of bees coming out of a grove of blossoming trees. As the great-spirited 100.15
son of Subhádra rampaged around on his golden chariot,
his foes could not find any opportunity to strike at him.
Bewildering Kripa, Drona, Drona's son, Brihad·bala, and
the king of the Sindhus, the great archer careered around
skillfully and easily. When he was incinerating your host
we saw his bow stretched into a circle and looking like the
solar disk, descendant of Bharata. Seeing him forcefully attacking them, valiant warriors, judging by his feats, thought
that there were two Phálgunas in this world. Plagued by
him, the great army of the Bharatas reeled hither and thither
like a drunken woman. Routing the mighty host in this 100.20
way, making the great warriors tremble, he brought joy
to his friends just as Vásava did by defeating the demon

tena vidrāvyamāṇāni tava sainyāni saṃyuge
cakrur ārta|svaraṃ ghoraṃ Parjanya|ninad'|ôpamam.

tam śrutvā ninadaṃ ghoraṃ tava sainyasya, māriṣa,
mārut'|ôddhūta|vegasya samudrasy' êva parvaṇi,
Duryodhanas tadā rājā Ārṣyaśṛṅgim abhāṣata:

«eṣa Kārṣṇir mah"|êṣv|āso, dvitīya iva Phālgunaḥ,
camūṃ drāvayate krodhād, Vṛtro deva|camūm iva.
tasya n' ânyaṃ prapaśyāmi saṃyuge bheṣajaṃ mahat,
100.25 ṛte tvāṃ, rākṣasa|śreṣṭha, sarva|vidyāsu pāra|gam.
sa gatvā tvaritaṃ vīraṃ jahi Saubhadram āhave.
vayaṃ Pārthān haniṣyāmo Bhīṣma|Droṇa|puraḥ|sarāḥ.»

sa evam ukto balavān rākṣas'|êndraḥ pratāpavān
prayayau samare tūrṇaṃ tava putrasya śāsanāt,
nardamāno mahā|nādaṃ prāvṛṣ' îva balāhakaḥ.
tasya śabdena mahatā Pāṇḍavānāṃ mahad balam
prācalat sarvato, rājan, vāt'|ôddhūta iv' ârṇavaḥ.
bahavaś ca, mahā|rāja, tasya nādena bhīṣitāḥ
priyān prāṇān parityajya nipetur dharaṇī|tale.
100.30 Kārṣṇiś c' âpi mudā yuktaḥ pragṛhīta|śar'|âsanaḥ
nṛtyann iva rath'|ôpasthe tad rakṣaḥ samupādravat.
tataḥ sa rākṣasaḥ kruddhaḥ saṃprāpy' âiv' Ārjuniṃ raṇe
n' âtidūre sthitāṃ tasya drāvayām āsa vai camūm.
tāṃ vadhyamānāṃ ca tathā Pāṇḍavānāṃ mahā|camūm
pratyudyayau raṇe rakṣo, deva|senāṃ yathā Balaḥ.

Maya. Routed by him in combat, your troops uttered awful screams of anguish, making a sound like Parjánya's thunder.

On hearing the terrible wail of your troops—which was like the roar of the ocean when it's tossed about by a gale at the time of the moon's change, descendant of Bharata—Duryódhana spoke to the son of Rishya·shringa, Your Majesty.

"O mighty-armed hero, Krishna's nephew is indeed like another Phálguna. He is routing my army just as Vritra scattered the host of the gods. I can see no effective remedy for
him in battle except you, accomplished as you are in every 100.25
science, best of demons. So go immediately and slay the heroic son of Subhádra in combat; and we, led by Bhishma and Drona, shall slaughter the son of Pritha."

Addressed in this way, the mighty and vigorous chief of the demons went straight into battle at your son's command, bellowing fiercely like a thundercloud in the rainy season. The mighty host of the Pándavas was shaken by his tremendous roar, Your Majesty, like the ocean tossed by a storm. Frightened by his roar, many warriors fell to
the ground and gave up their lives, great king. Krishna's 100.30
nephew, filled with joy, seized his bow and arrows and, all but dancing on the chariot platform, he charged against the demon. The furious demon reached Árjuna's son in combat, and started to disperse the foe's troops which were stationed nearby. While the large Pándava army was being struck down in this way, the demon attacked it in battle just as the demon Bala had assaulted the host of the gods. When they were plagued by that fierce-looking demon in battle, my lord, there was a huge massacre of the troops.

vimardaḥ su|mahān āsīt tasya sainyasya, māriṣa,
rakṣasā ghora|rūpeṇa vadhyamānasya saṃyuge.
tataḥ śara|sahasrais tāṃ Pāṇḍavānāṃ mahā|camūm
vyadrāvayad raṇe rakṣo darśayan sva|parākramam.
100.35 sā vadhyamānā ca tathā Pāṇḍavānām anīkinī
rakṣasā ghora|rūpeṇa pradudrāva raṇe bhayāt.
pramṛdya ca raṇe senāṃ, padminīṃ vāraṇo yathā,
tato 'bhidudrāva raṇe Draupadeyān mahā|balān.
te tu kruddhā mah"|êṣv|āsā Draupadeyāḥ prahāriṇaḥ
rākṣasaṃ dudruvuḥ saṃkhye, grahāḥ pañca raviṃ yathā.
vīryavadbhis tatas tais tu pīḍito rākṣas'|ôttamaḥ,
yathā yuga|kṣaye ghore candramāḥ pañcabhir grahaiḥ.
Prativindhyas tato rakṣo bibheda niśitaiḥ śaraiḥ
sarva|pāraśavais tūrṇam a|kuṇṭh'|âgrair mahā|balaḥ.
100.40 sa tair bhinna|tanu|trāṇaḥ śuśubhe rākṣas'|ôttamaḥ,
marīcibhir iv' ârkasya saṃsyūto jala|do mahān.
viṣaktaiḥ sa śaraiś c' âpi tapanīya|paricchadaiḥ
Ārṣyaśṛṅgir babhau, rājan, dīpta|śṛṅga iv' â|calaḥ.
tatas te bhrātaraḥ pañca rākṣas'|êndraṃ mah"|āhave
vivyadhur niśitair bāṇais tapanīya|vibhūṣitaiḥ.
sa nirbhinnaḥ śarair ghorair, bhujagaiḥ kopitair iva,
Alambuṣo bhṛśaṃ, rājan, nāg'|êndra iva cukrudhe.
so 'tividdho, mahā|rāja, muhūrtam atha, māriṣa,
praviveśa tamo dīrghaṃ pīḍitas tair mahā|rathaiḥ.
100.45 pratilabhya tataḥ saṃjñāṃ, krodhena dvi|guṇī|kṛtaḥ,
ciccheda sāyakais teṣāṃ, dhvajāṃś c' âiva, dhanūṃṣi ca.
ek'|âikaṃ pañcabhir bāṇair ājaghāna smayann iva
Alambuṣo rath'|ôpasthe nṛtyann iva mahā|rathaḥ.

Demonstrating his courage, the demon routed that great army of the Pándavas with thousands of arrows on the field of battle; and the Pándava troops, being injured in combat 100.35
by the fierce-looking demon in this way, fled in fear.

Having crushed the hostile army in battle like an elephant trampling lotuses in a pond, the demon then charged against Dráupadi's mighty sons. The five sons of Dráupadi, those great archers skilled in warfare, rushed against the demon in that encounter, like five planets attacking the sun. And that foremost of demons was wounded by those valiant combatants, like the moon afflicted by five planets at the dissolution of an eon.

Prativíndhya, endowed with great strength, pierced the demon with whetted, sharp-headed arrows made entirely of iron. His armor torn through by those shafts, that foremost 100.40
of demons shone like a huge rain-cloud penetrated by sun-rays. With arrows covered in gold sticking into his body, the son of Rishya·shringa looked like a mountain with its crests ablaze, Your Majesty. The five brothers struck that chief of demons with sharpened arrows decorated in gold; and cut up by those horrible shafts like angry snakes, Alámbusha became immensely enraged like the king of elephants, Your Majesty. Tormented by those mighty warriors and severely wounded, great king, he fell into a swoon for quite some time, my lord.

Then he regained consciousness and, filled with a fury re- 100.45
doubled in intensity, he severed their arrows, banners, and bows. The great warrior Alámbusha, as if he were laughing and dancing on the chariot platform, shot them one by one with five arrows each. The powerful demon, excited with

tvaramāṇaḥ su|saṃrabdho hayāṃs teṣāṃ mah"|ātmanām
jaghāna rākṣasaḥ kruddhaḥ, sārathīṃś ca mahā|balaḥ,
bibheda ca su|saṃhṛṣṭaḥ punaś c' âinān su|saṃśitaiḥ
śarair bahu|vidh'|ākāraiḥ śataśo 'tha sahasraśaḥ.
vi|rathāṃś ca mah"|êṣv|āsān kṛtvā tatra sa rākṣasaḥ
abhidudrāva vegena hantu|kāmo niśā|caraḥ.
100.50 tān arditān raṇe tena rākṣasena dur|ātmanā
dṛṣṭv" Ârjuna|sutaḥ saṃkhye rākṣasaṃ samupādravat.
tayoḥ samabhavad yuddhaṃ Vṛtra|Vāsavayor iva.
dadṛśus tāvakāḥ sarve Pāṇḍavāś ca mahā|rathāḥ.
tau sametau mahā|yuddhe krodha|dīptau paras|param
mahā|balau, mahā|rāja, krodha|saṃrakta|locanau
paras|param avekṣetāṃ Kāl'|ânala|samau yudhi.
tayoḥ samāgamo ghoro babhūva kaṭuk'|ôdayaḥ,
yathā dev'|âsure yuddhe Śakra|Śambarayor iva.

DHṚTARĀṢTRA uvāca:

101.1 ĀRJUNIṂ SAMARE śūraṃ vinighnantaṃ mahā|rathān
Alambuṣaḥ kathaṃ yuddhe pratyayudhyata, Sañjaya?
Ārṣyaśṛṅgiṃ kathaṃ c' âiva Saubhadraḥ para|vīra|hā?
tan mam' ācakṣva tattvena, yathā|vṛttaṃ sma saṃyuge.
Dhanañjayaś ca kiṃ cakre mama sainyeṣu, Sañjaya,
Bhīmo vā balināṃ śreṣṭho, rākṣaso vā Ghaṭotkacaḥ,
Nakulaḥ, Sahadevo vā, Sātyakir vā mahā|rathaḥ?
etad ācakṣva me satyaṃ. kuśalo hy asi, Sañjaya.

anger, soon killed the horses of those great-spirited chariot warriors; and then, in his rage, he wounded them again with hundreds and thousands of well-whetted arrows of various types. After stripping the mighty archers of their chariots, the night-ranging demon, in his eagerness to slaughter the
Pándavas, assailed them with great force. Seeing them being 100.50
plagued by that ill-natured demon, Árjuna's son charged against him in that combat. The battle that then took place between them was like the one between Vritra and Vásava, and all the great warriors of your host and that of the Pándavas looked on. The two mighty heroes, inflamed with wrath, confronted each other in that great battle, great king, their eyes bloodshot with fury; and they glared at one another on the battlefield, both looking like the blazing fire of Time. The encounter between them was as terrible and as fraught with fateful consequences as Shakra's fight against Shámbara during the ancient war between the gods and demons.

DHRITA·RASHTRA said:

In that battle, how did Alámbusha counter Árjuna's 101.1
valiant son who had been slaughtering great warriors in combat, Sánjaya? And how did Subhádra's son, the destroyer of enemy heroes, fight against the son of Rishya·shringa? Tell it to me truthfully, exactly as it happened in that fight. What did Dhanan·jaya, Bhima the best of chariot warriors, the demon Ghatótkacha, Nákula, Saha·deva, and the mighty warrior Sátyaki do to my troops in that conflict? Tell me all this truly, Sánjaya, for you are skilled in speech.

SAÑJAYA uvāca:

101.5 hanta te 'haṃ pravakṣyāmi saṃgrāmaṃ loma|harṣaṇam
yath" âbhūd rākṣas'|êndrasya Saubhadrasya ca, māriṣa,
Arjunaś ca yathā saṃkhye, Bhīmasenaś ca Pāṇḍavaḥ,
Nakulaḥ, Sahadevaś ca raṇe cakruḥ parākramam.
tath" âiva tāvakāḥ sarve Bhīṣma|Droṇa|puraḥ|sarāḥ
adbhutāni vicitrāṇi cakruḥ karmāṇy a|bhītavat.

Alambusas tu samare Abhimanyuṃ mahā|ratham
vinadya su|mahā|nādaṃ, tarjayitvā muhur muhuḥ,
abhidudrāva vegena, «tiṣṭha! tiṣṭh'!» êti c' âbravīt;
Saubhadro 'pi raṇe, rājan, siṃhavad vinadan muhuḥ
101.10 Ārṣyaśṛṅgiṃ mah"|êṣv|āsaṃ pitur atyanta|vairiṇam.
tataḥ sameyatuḥ saṃkhye tvaritau nara|rākṣasau
rathābhyāṃ rathināṃ śreṣṭhau, yathā vai deva|dānavau:
māyāvī rākṣasa|śreṣṭho, divy'|âstra|jñaś ca Phālguniḥ.
tataḥ Kārṣṇir, mahā|rāja, niśitaiḥ sāyakais tribhiḥ
Ārṣyaśṛṅgiṃ raṇe viddhvā punar vivyādha pañcabhiḥ.
Alambuṣo 'pi saṃkruddhaḥ Kārṣṇiṃ navabhir āśu|gaiḥ
hṛdi vivyādha vegena, tottrair iva mahā|dvipam.
tataḥ śara|sahasreṇa kṣipra|kārī niśā|caraḥ
Arjunasya sutaṃ saṃkhye pīḍayām āsa, Bhārata.
101.15 Abhimanyus tataḥ kruddho navatiṃ nata|parvabhiḥ
cikṣepa niśitān bāṇān rākṣasasya mah"|ôrasi.
te tasya viviśus tūrṇaṃ kāyaṃ nirbhidya marmasu.

SÁNJAYA said:

Well, my lord, I shall describe the battle between the 101.5
chief of demons and the son of Subhádra to you in every
detail, just as it occurred. I shall also describe the valor with
which Árjuna, Bhima·sena Pándava, Nákula, and Saha·deva
fought in that encounter, and the various wondrous feats
that all your combatants fearlessly performed, led by Bhishma and Drona.

In that fight, Alámbusha, uttering terrible roars and
threatening the great warrior Abhimányu again and again,
attacked him with great force, exclaiming "Stay still! Stay
still!" And Abhimányu, roaring like a lion again and again,
charged vehemently against Rishya·shringa's son, that 101.10
mighty archer and avowed enemy of Abhimányu's father.
In that combat the man and the demon, both excellent
chariot warriors, soon confronted each other on their chariots, like a god and a demon. The best of demons was endowed with the power of illusion, whereas Phálguna's son
was skilled in the use of divine weapons. Krishna's nephew
pierced the son of Rishya·shringa in battle, great king, first
with three sharpened arrows, and then with five more. And
Alámbusha, enraged, violently wounded Krishna's nephew
in the chest with nine swift-flying shafts, as if he were piercing a mighty elephant with goads. Then, working with great
speed, the night-ranger pummeled the son of Árjuna with
a thousand arrows in that conflict, descendant of Bharata.
Infuriated Abhimányu then shot the chief of demons in his 101.15
broad chest with nine straight arrows. They cut through the
demon's body and quickly penetrated his vital organs.

sa tair vibhinna|sarv'|âṅgaḥ śuśubhe rākṣas'|ôttamaḥ,
puṣpitaiḥ kiṃśukai, rājan, saṃstīrṇa iva parvataḥ.
saṃdhārayañ śarān hema|puṅkhān api mahā|balaḥ
vibabhau rākṣasa|śreṣṭhaḥ sa|jvāla iva parvataḥ.
tataḥ kruddho, mahā|rāja, Ārṣyaśṛṅgir mahā|balaḥ
mah"|Êndra|pratimaṃ Kārṣṇiṃ chādayām āsa patribhiḥ.
tena te viśikhā muktā Yama|daṇḍ'|ôpamāḥ śitāḥ
101.20 Abhimanyuṃ vinirbhidya prāviśanta dharā|talam.
tath" âiv' Ārjuninā muktāḥ śarāḥ kanaka|bhūṣaṇāḥ
Alambuṣaṃ vinirbhidya prāviśanta dharā|talam.
Saubhadras tu raṇe rakṣaḥ śaraiḥ saṃnata|parvabhiḥ
cakre vimukham āsādya, Mayaṃ Śakra iv' āhave.
vimukhaṃ ca tato rakṣo vadhyamānaṃ raṇe 'riṇā
prāduś|cakre mahā|māyāṃ tāmasīṃ para|tāpanām.
tatas te tamasā sarve vṛtāś c' āsan, mahī|pate.
n' Âbhimanyum apaśyanta, n' âiva svān, na parān raṇe.
Abhimanyuś ca tad dṛṣṭvā ghora|rūpaṃ mahat tamaḥ
101.25 prāduś|cakre 'stram atyugraṃ bhāskaraṃ Kuru|nandanaḥ.
tataḥ prakāśam abhavaj jagat sarvaṃ, mahī|pate.
tāṃ c' âbhijaghnivān māyāṃ rākṣasasya dur|ātmanaḥ;
saṃkruddhaś ca mahā|vīryo rākṣas'|êndraṃ nar'|ôttamaḥ
chādayām āsa samare śaraiḥ saṃnata|parvabhiḥ;
bahvīs tath" ânyā māyāś ca prayuktās tena rakṣasā

With every part of his body cut up by those shafts, the foremost of demons looked resplendent, Your Majesty, like a mountain overgrown with flowering *kínshuka** trees. With those gold-nocked arrows sticking into his body, that supreme and hugely strong demon looked like a mountain ablaze.

Then, great king, the son of Rishya·shringa, intolerant and enraged, shrouded Krishna's nephew, who looked like great Indra himself, in feathered arrows. The sharp arrows
he released, each looking like the staff of Yama, pierced 101.20
through Abhimányu's body and entered the earth. And likewise the son of Árjuna fired shafts decorated in gold, which pierced through Alámbusha and penetrated the earth. Then Subhádra's son, besieging the enemy with his straight arrows, forced the demon to retreat from the encounter, just as Shakra once repelled the demon Maya in battle.

And when he had been plagued by his opponent and warded off in this way, the demon displayed a great enemy-scorching illusion of darkness. All the troops became enveloped in that darkness, protector of the earth; they could not discern Abhimányu, nor could they tell who were their friends and enemies in battle.

When he saw that terrible and utterly dense darkness,
Abhimányu, the delight of the Kurus, invoked the solar 101.25
weapon of utmost intensity; and the entire world became bright again, lord of the earth. Thus that best of men, endowed with great vigor, destroyed the illusion that the ill-natured demon had created; and then, filled with fury, he shrouded the chief of demons with straight arrows in the fray. After that the demon displayed many other illusions,

sarv'|âstra|vid, a|mey'|ātmā vārayām āsa Phālguniḥ.
hata|māyaṃ tato rakṣo, vadhyamānaṃ ca sāyakaiḥ,
rathaṃ tatr' âiva saṃtyajya prādravan mahato bhayāt.
tasmin vinirjite tūrṇaṃ kūṭa|yodhini rākṣase
101.30 Ārjuniḥ samare sainyaṃ tāvakaṃ saṃmamarda ha,
mad'|ândho gandha|nāg'|êndraḥ sa|padmāṃ padminīm iva.
tataḥ Śāntanavo Bhīṣmaḥ sainyaṃ dṛṣṭv" âbhividrutam,
mahatā śara|varṣeṇa Saubhadraṃ paryavārayat.
koṣṭhī|kṛtya ca taṃ vīraṃ Dhārtarāṣṭrā mahā|rathāḥ
ekaṃ su|bahavo yuddhe tatakṣuḥ sāyakair dṛḍham.
sa teṣāṃ rathināṃ vīraḥ, pitus tulya|parākramaḥ,
sadṛśo Vāsudevasya vikrameṇa balena ca,
ubhayoḥ sadṛśaṃ karma sa pitur mātulasya ca
raṇe bahu|vidhaṃ cakre sarva|śastra|bhṛtāṃ varaḥ.
101.35 tato Dhanañjayo, rājan, vinighnaṃs tava sainikān
āsasāda raṇe Bhīṣmaṃ putra|prepsur, a|marṣaṇaḥ.
tath" âiva samare, rājan, pitā Devavratas tava
āsasāda raṇe Pārthaṃ, Svarbhānur iva bhās|karam.
tataḥ sa|ratha|nāg'|âśvāḥ putrās tava, jan'|ēśvara,
parivavrū raṇe Bhīṣmaṃ, jugupuś ca samantataḥ.
tath" âiva Pāṇḍavā, rājan, parivārya Dhanañjayam
raṇāya mahate yuktā daṃśitā, Bharata'|rṣabha.
Śāradvatas tato, rājan, Bhīṣmasya pramukhe sthitam
Arjunaṃ pañca|viṃśatyā sāyakānāṃ samācinot.

but Phálguna's boundlessly spirited son, skilled in the use of all weapons, neutralized them all. The demon, pummeled with arrows, his illusions destroyed, left his chariot there and fled in great fear.

When that demon—who fought unfairly—had been defeated, Árjuna's son immediately began to crush your host 101.30
in that combat, just as a huge elephant, secreting juices and blind with rut and fury, tramples a lotus pond full of lotuses. And Bhishma son of Shántanu, seeing the troops routed, enveloped Subhádra's son in a heavy downpour of arrows. The mighty Dharta·rashtra warriors surrounded that hero and started to strike him violently with shafts, many against one. That champion of chariot warriors, who was equal to his father in bravery and to Vásu·deva in vigor and strength, was the best wielder of every weapon, and he performed numerous feats worthy of both his father and his uncle.

Then, Your Majesty, valiant Dhanan·jaya, filled with 101.35
anger, struck down your troops and assailed Bhishma in battle, eager to rescue his son. And your father Deva·vrata attacked the son of Pritha in that conflict too, Your Majesty, just as Svar·bhanu the eclipse demon attacks the sun. Your sons, lord of the people, surrounded Bhishma with their chariots, elephants, and horses in that battle, and started to protect him. And similarly the Pándavas, Your Majesty, clad in armor and surrounding Dhanan·jaya, were intent on a great battle, bull of the Bharatas. Then the son of Sharádvat struck Árjuna, who was stationed opposite Bhishma, with twenty-five arrows, Your Majesty.

101.40 pratyudgamy' âtha vivyādha Sātyakis taṃ śitaiḥ śaraiḥ
Pāṇḍava|priya|kām'|ârthaṃ, śārdūla iva kuñjaram.
Gautamo 'pi tvarā|yukto Mādhavaṃ navabhiḥ śaraiḥ
hṛdi vivyādha saṃkruddhaḥ kaṅka|patra|paricchadaiḥ.
Śaineyo 'pi tataḥ kruddho cāpam ānamya vegavān
Gautam'|ânta|karaṃ ghoraṃ samādhatta śilīmukham.
tam āpatantaṃ vegena Śakr'|âśani|sama|dyutim
dvidhā ciccheda saṃkruddho Drauṇiḥ parama|kopanaḥ.

samutsṛjy' âtha Śaineyo Gautamaṃ rathināṃ varam
abhyadravad raṇe Drauṇiṃ, Rāhuḥ khe śaśinaṃ yathā.
101.45 tasya Droṇa|sutaś cāpaṃ dvidhā ciccheda, Bhārata,
ath' âinaṃ chinna|dhanvānaṃ tāḍayām āsa sāyakaiḥ.
so 'nyat kārmukam ādāya śatru|ghnaṃ bhāra|sādhanam,
Drauṇiṃ ṣaṣṭyā, mahā|rāja, bāhvor urasi c' ārpayat.
sa viddho vyathitaś c' âiva muhūrtaṃ kaśmal'|āyutaḥ
niṣasāda rath'|ôpasthe dhvaja|yaṣṭim upāśritaḥ.
pratilabhya tataḥ saṃjñāṃ Droṇa|putraḥ pratāpavān
Vārṣṇeyaṃ samare kruddho nārācena samārpayat.
Śaineyaṃ sa tu nirbhidya prāviśad dharaṇī|talam,
vasanta|kāle balavān bilaṃ sarpa|śiśur yathā.
101.50 ath' âpareṇa bhallena Mādhavasya dhvaj'|ôttamam
ciccheda samare Drauṇiḥ, siṃha|nādaṃ mumoca ha.
punaś c' âinaṃ śarair ghoraiś chādayām āsa, Bhārata,
nidāgh'|ânte, mahā|rāja, yathā megho divā|karam.
Sātyakiś ca, mahā|rāja, śara|jālaṃ nihatya tat

Wanting to do the Pándava a favor, Sátyaki rose against 101.40
Kripa and wounded him with sharp arrows, charging at him as a tiger charges at an elephant; but with great expedition the grandson of Gótama furiously pierced Mádhava in the chest with nine heron-feathered arrows. Then Shini's grandson, excited with rage, drew his bow and quickly aimed a stone-tipped shaft at Gótama's grandson Kripa in order to kill him; but filled with violent rage the son of Drona, seeing that shaft as radiant as Indra's thunderbolt flying with great force, cut it in two.

Then Shini's grandson, that supreme chariot warrior, left the grandson of Gótama behind in the battle, and attacked the son of Drona just as Rahu the eclipse demon attacks
the moon in the sky. The son of Drona split Sátyaki's bow 101.45
in two, descendant of Bharata, and struck the bowless hero with many arrows; but seizing another accomplished bow that was fit for killing foes, Sátyaki wounded Drona's son in his arms and chest with sixty shafts, great king. Wounded and in distress, for a while he lost his senses and sank onto the chariot platform, leaning on the flagpole. But when he regained consciousness Drona's mighty son in his battle-fury struck the descendant of Vrishni with an iron shaft. Piercing through the body of Shini's grandson, the shaft entered the earth just as a powerful young snake enters its
hole in springtime. With a peerless spear-headed shaft the 101.50
son of Drona severed the Mádhava's superb banner in that fight, and let out a lion-roar. And once again he shrouded his opponent with hordes of arrows, great king, like a cloud shrouding the sun at the end of summer, descendant of Bharata. But Sátyaki destroyed that web of arrows, great

Drauṇim abhyakirat tūrṇaṃ śara|jālair an|ekadhā.
tāpayām āsa ca Drauṇiṃ Śaineyaḥ para|vīra|hā,
vimukto megha|jālena yath" âiva tapanas, tathā.
śarāṇāṃ ca sahasreṇa punar enaṃ samudyataḥ
Sātyakiś chādayām āsa, nanāda ca mahā|balaḥ.
101.55 dṛṣṭvā putraṃ tathā grastaṃ, Rāhuṇ" êva niśā|karam,
abhyadravata Śaineyaṃ Bhāradvājaḥ pratāpavān;
vivyādha ca pṛṣatkena su|tīkṣṇena mahā|mṛdhe,
parīpsan sva|sutaṃ, rājan, Vārṣṇeyen' âbhipīḍitam.
Sātyakis tu raṇe hitvā guru|putraṃ mahā|ratham,
Droṇaṃ vivyādha viṃśatyā sarva|pāraśavaiḥ śaraiḥ.
tad|antaram a|mey'|ātmā Kaunteyaḥ śveta|vāhanaḥ
abhyadravad raṇe kruddho Droṇaṃ prati mahā|rathaḥ.
tato Droṇaś ca Pārthaś ca sameyātāṃ mahā|mṛdhe,
yathā Budhaś ca Śukraś ca, mahā|rāja, nabhas|tale.

DHṚTARĀṢṬRA uvāca:

102.1 KATHAṂ DROṆO mah"|êṣv|āsaḥ
Pāṇḍavaś ca Dhanañjayaḥ
samīyatū raṇe yattau
tāv ubhau puruṣa'|rṣabhau?
priyo hi Pāṇḍavo nityaṃ Bhāradvājasya dhīmataḥ,
ācāryaś ca raṇe nityaṃ priyaḥ Pārthasya, Sañjaya.
tāv ubhau rathinau saṃkhye, hṛṣṭau siṃhāv iv' ôtkaṭau,
kathaṃ samīyatur yuddhe Bhāradvāja|Dhanañjayau?

king, and quickly spread nets of his own shafts around the son of Drona in various ways. Shini's grandson, the slayer of hostile heroes, freed from that web of shafts like the sun emerging from behind a mass of clouds, started to scorch Drona's son. Powerful Sátyaki, rising against his adversary once more, covered him with a thousand arrows and shouted out loud.

Seeing his son looking like the moon swallowed by Rahu, 101.55
the mighty son of Bharad·vaja charged against Shini's grandson; and Drona, eager to rescue his son who was being tormented by the descendant of Vrishni, pierced the latter with an immensely sharp arrow in that great battle, Your Majesty. So Sátyaki abandoned the teacher's son—that great warrior—and pierced Drona himself in battle, with twenty arrows made entirely of iron. At that moment Kunti's enemy-scorching and boundlessly spirited mighty warrior son, excited with rage, charged against Drona; and Drona and the son of Pritha encountered one another in that great battle, like the planets Mercury and Venus in the sky, great king.

DHRITA·RASHTRA said:

How DID THE mighty archer Drona and Dhanan·jaya 102.1
Pándava, two men like bulls, both eager to fight, confront each other in combat? For the Pándava is ever dear to the wise son of Bharad·vaja, and the teacher Drona is ever dear to the son of Pritha, Sánjaya. Those two chariot warriors, Bharad·vaja's son and Dhanan·jaya, excited like two frenzied lions on the battlefield—how did they treat each other in their duel?

SAÑJAYA uvāca:

na Droṇaḥ samare Pārthaṃ jānīte priyam ātmanaḥ
kṣatra|dharmaṃ puras|kṛtya, Pārtho vā gurum āhave.
102.5 na kṣatriyā raṇe, rājan, varjayanti paras|param;
nir|maryādaṃ hi yudhyante pitṛbhir bhrātṛbhiḥ saha.

raṇe, Bhārata, Pārthena Droṇo viddhas tribhiḥ śaraiḥ
n' âcintayac ca tān bāṇān Pārtha|cāpa|cyutān yudhi.
śara|vṛṣṭyā punaḥ Pārthaś chādayām āsa taṃ raṇe.
sa prajajvāla roṣeṇa, gahane 'gnir iv' ōrjitaḥ.
tato 'rjunaṃ raṇe Droṇaḥ śaraiḥ saṃnata|parvabhiḥ
chādayām āsa, rāj'|êndra, na|cirād iva, Bhārata.
tato Duryodhano rājā Suśarmāṇam acodayat
Droṇasya samare, rājan, pārṣṇi|grahaṇa|kāraṇāt.
102.10 Trigarta|rāḍ api kruddho bhṛśam āyamya kārmukam
chādayām āsa samare Pārthaṃ bāṇair ayo|mukhaiḥ.
tābhyāṃ muktāḥ śarā, rājann, antarikṣe virejire,
haṃsā iva, mahā|rāja, śarat|kāle nabhas|tale.
te śarāḥ prāpya Kaunteyaṃ samastā viviśuḥ, prabho,
phala|bhāra|nataṃ yadvat svādu|vṛkṣaṃ vihaṅ|gamāḥ.
Arjunas tu raṇe nādaṃ vinadya rathināṃ varaḥ
Trigarta|rājaṃ samare sa|putraṃ vivyadhe śaraiḥ.

te vadhyamānāḥ Pārthena, Kālen' êva yuga|kṣaye,
Pārtham ev' âbhyavartanta maraṇe kṛta|niścayāḥ,
102.15 mumucuḥ śara|vṛṣṭiṃ ca Pāṇḍavasya rathaṃ prati.
śara|vṛṣṭiṃ tatas tāṃ tu śara|varṣeṇa Pāṇḍavaḥ

SÁNJAYA said:

Making the warrior code their priority, in their battle Drona did not think of Pritha's son as someone dear to him, and nor the son of Pritha regarded the teacher in that way.
Warriors never avoid each other in combat, Your Majesty. 102.5
They fight without scruple, even against their fathers and brothers.

Drona was pierced by the son of Pritha with three arrows, but he paid no heed to those shafts that had been fired from the Partha's bow in that fight, descendant of Bharata. Then Pritha's son again covered his opponent with a downpour of arrows. And Drona blazed up with fury like a raging forest fire. Without wasting a moment Drona shrouded Árjuna with straight arrows in battle, descendant of Bharata. Then King Duryódhana commanded Sushárman to secure
Drona's rear, Your Majesty; and so the king of the Tri·gartas, 102.10
enraged, stretched his bow tightly and enveloped the son of Pritha with iron-tipped shafts in that contest. The arrows released by those two looked beautiful, Your Majesty, like geese in the sky in autumn, great king. Reaching the son of Kunti, those arrows penetrated his body all over, lord, just as birds take shelter in a tree that is bent down by the weight of sweet fruit. Then Árjuna, the best of chariot warriors, shouting out loud, pierced the king of the Tri·gartas and his son with countless arrows in that battle.

Tormented by Pritha's son, who looked like Time at the dissolution of an eon, the Tri·garta warriors, determined to
die in combat, rushed against the son of Pritha and poured a 102.15
heavy rain of arrows down on the Pándava's chariot. But the Pándava checked that downpour of arrows with a shower of

pratijagrāha, rāj'|êndra, toya|vṛṣṭim iv' â|calaḥ.
tatr' âdbhutam apaśyāma Bībhatsor hasta|lāghavam:
vimuktāṃ bahubhiḥ śūraiḥ śastra|vṛṣṭiṃ dur|āsadām
yad eko vārayām āsa, māruto 'bhra|gaṇān iva.
karmaṇā tena Pārthasya tutuṣur deva|dānavāḥ.

atha kruddho raṇe Pārthas Trigartān prati, Bhārata,
mumoc' âstraṃ, mahā|rāja, Vāyavyaṃ pṛtanā|mukhe.
prādur|āsīt tato vāyuḥ kṣobhayāṇo nabhas|talam,
102.20 pātayan vai taru|gaṇān, vinighnaṃś c' âiva sainikān.

tato Droṇo 'bhivīkṣy' âiva Vāyavy'|āstraṃ su|dāruṇam,
Śailam anyan, mahā|rāja, ghoram astraṃ mumoca ha.
Droṇena yudhi nirmukte tasminn astre, nar'|âdhipa,
praśaśāma tato vāyuḥ, prasannāś c' âbhavan diśaḥ.
tataḥ Pāṇḍu|suto vīras Trigartasya ratha|vrajān
nir|utsāhān raṇe cakre, vimukhān, vi|parākramān.

tato Duryodhano rājā, Kṛpaś ca rathināṃ varaḥ,
Aśvatthāmā, tataḥ Śalyaḥ, Kāmbojaś ca, Sudakṣiṇaḥ,
Vind'|Ânuvindāv Āvantyau, Bāhlikaś ca sa|Bāhlikaḥ
102.25 mahatā ratha|vaṃśena Pārthasy' âvārayan diśaḥ.
tath" âiva Bhagadattaś ca Śrutāyuś ca mahā|balaḥ
gaj'|ânīkena Bhīmasya tāv avārayatāṃ diśaḥ.
Bhūriśravāḥ, Śalaś c' âiva, Saubalaś ca, viśāṃ pate,
śar'|âughair vimalais tīkṣṇair Mādrī|putrāv avārayan.
Bhīṣmas tu saṃhataḥ saṃkhye Dhārtarāṣṭraiḥ sa|sainikaiḥ
Yudhiṣṭhiraṃ samāsādya sarvataḥ paryavārayat.

his own shafts, O king of kings, like a mountain receiving a shower of rain. It was marvelous for us to see Bibhátsu's dexterity as he single-handedly foiled that rainstorm of arrows, difficult to check as it was, like the wind dispersing a mass of clouds. Both the gods and the *dánavas* were thrilled by that feat of Pritha's son.

Then, descendant of Bharata, filled with battle-fury, the
son of Pritha fired Vayu's weapon at the Tri·garta warriors,
aiming at the front of their host, great king; and a gale arose,
shaking the sky, blowing down lots of trees, and killing 102.20
many troops.

When he saw Vayu's dreadful weapon, Drona let loose another frightful weapon named the Rock, great king. When that weapon had been discharged in the battle, Your Majesty, the tempest abated and the ten directions cleared up. So the valiant son of Pandu deprived the Tri·garta king's numerous warriors of their enthusiasm and courage and made them turn their backs on the fight.

Then Duryódhana, Kripa the best of chariot warriors,
Ashva·tthaman, Shalya, Kambója, Sudákshina, Vinda and
Anuvínda of Avánti, and King Báhlika and the Báhlikas
surrounded the son of Pritha on all sides with a large divi- 102.25
sion of chariots. Likewise Bhaga·datta and powerful Shrutáyus checked Bhima on every side with an elephant division;
and Bhuri·shravas, Shala, and the son of Súbala, lord of the
people, restrained the two sons of Madri with hordes of
sharp gleaming arrows. Bhishma, supported in that engagement by the Dharta·rashtras and their troops, approached
Yudhi·shthira and surrounded him on every side.

āpatantaṃ gaj'|ânīkaṃ dṛṣṭvā Pārtho Vṛkodaraḥ,
lelihan sṛkkiṇī vīro mṛga|rāḍ iva kānane.
Bhīmas tu rathināṃ śreṣṭho gadāṃ gṛhya mah"|āhave,
102.30 avaplutya rathāt tūrṇaṃ tava sainyāny abhīṣayat.
tam udvīkṣya gadā|hastaṃ tatas te gaja|sādinaḥ
parivavrū raṇe yattā Bhīmasenaṃ samantataḥ.

gaja|madhyam anuprāptaḥ Pāṇḍavaḥ sa vyarājata,
megha|jālasya mahato yathā madhya|gato raviḥ.
vyadhamat sa gaj'|ânīkaṃ gadayā Pāṇḍava'|rṣabhaḥ,
mah"|âbhra|jālam a|tulaṃ mātariśv" êva saṃtatam.
te vadhyamānā balinā Bhīmasenena dantinaḥ
ārta|nādaṃ raṇe cakrur, garjanto jala|dā iva.
bahudhā dāritaś c' âiva viṣāṇais tatra dantibhiḥ,
102.35 phull'|âśoka|nibhaḥ Pārthaḥ śuśubhe raṇa|mūrdhani.
viṣāṇe dantinaṃ gṛhya nir|viṣāṇam ath' âkarot,
viṣāṇena ca ten' âiva kumbhe 'bhyāhatya dantinam
pātayām āsa samare, daṇḍa|hasta iv' Ântakaḥ.
śoṇit'|âktāṃ gadāṃ bibhran, medo|majjā|kṛta|cchaviḥ,
kṛt'|âbhyaṅgaḥ śoṇitena Rudravat pratyadṛśyata.

evaṃ te vadhyamānāś ca hata|śeṣā mahā|gajāḥ
prādravanta diśo, rājan, vimṛdnantaḥ svakaṃ balam.
dravadbhis tair mahā|nāgaiḥ samantād, Bharata'|rṣabha,
Duryodhana|balaṃ sarvaṃ punar āsīt parāṅ|mukham.

Pritha's heroic son Vrikódara, seeing the elephant division attacking him, licked the corners of his mouth like a lion, the king of beasts, in the forest. Bhima, the best of chariot warriors, grabbed a mace in that fierce fight and
quickly jumped out of his chariot, terrifying your troops. 102.30
Then the elephant drivers, intent on battle, seeing Bhima·sena with mace in hand, surrounded him on all sides.

Standing amid the elephant division, the son of Pandu shone like the sun amid a huge mass of clouds. And that bull of the Pándavas began to scatter the elephant host with his mace, like a gale dispersing an immense web of mighty clouds that's spread across the sky. Pounded by powerful Bhima, the elephants let out screams of distress in the fight, like rumbling thunderclouds. Wounded in many parts of
his body by the tusks of those elephants, Pritha's son looked 102.35
beautiful at the front of the battle, like a blossoming *ashóka* tree with its red flowers. Seizing elephants by the tusks, he pulled those tusks out by the roots; and then he felled the elephants in that fight by smiting them on the forehead with their own tusks, like Death wielding his staff. Wielding his blood-smeared mace, bespattered with fat and marrow, and besmeared with blood, he looked like Rudra.

When they were destroyed in this way, the few huge elephants that survived ran away in all directions, Your Majesty, crushing their own troops. And with those mighty elephants fleeing everywhere, bull of the Bharatas, all of Duryódhana's troops turned tail once again.

SAÑJAYA uvāca:

103.1 MADHYAN|DINE, mahā|rāja, saṃgrāmaḥ samapadyata
loka|kṣaya|karo raudro Bhīṣmasya saha Somakaiḥ.
Gāṅgeyo rathināṃ śreṣṭhaḥ Pāṇḍavānām anīkinīm
vyadhaman niśitair bāṇaiḥ śataśo 'tha sahasraśaḥ.
saṃmamarda ca tat sainyaṃ pitā Devavratas tava,
dhānyānām iva lūnānāṃ prakaraṃ go|gaṇā iva.
Dhṛṣṭadyumnaḥ, Śikhaṇḍī ca, Virāṭo, Drupadas tathā
Bhīṣmam āsādya samare śarair jaghnur mahā|ratham.
103.5 Dhṛṣṭadyumnaṃ tato viddhvā, Virāṭaṃ ca tribhiḥ śaraiḥ,
Drupadasya ca nārācaṃ preṣayām āsa, Bhārata.
tena viddhā mah"|êṣv|āsā Bhīṣmeṇ' â|mitra|karṣiṇā
cukrudhuḥ samare, rājan, pāda|spṛṣṭā iv' ôragāḥ.
Śikhaṇḍī taṃ ca vivyādha Bharatānāṃ pitā|maham.
strīmayaṃ manasā dhyātvā n' âsmai prāharad a|cyutaḥ.
Dhṛṣṭadyumnas tu samare krodhen' âgnir iva jvalan
pitā|mahaṃ tribhir bāṇair bāhvor urasi c' ārpayat.
Drupadaḥ pañca|viṃśatyā, Virāṭo daśabhiḥ śaraiḥ,
Śikhaṇḍī pañca|viṃśatyā Bhīṣmaṃ vivyādha sāyakaiḥ.
103.10 so 'tividdho, mahā|rāja, śoṇit'|âugha|pariplutaḥ,
vasante puṣpa|śabalo rakt'|âśoka iv' ābabhau.
tān pratyavidhyad Gāṅgeyas tribhis tribhir a|jihma|gaiḥ,
Drupadasya ca bhallena dhanuś ciccheda, māriṣa.
so 'nyat kārmukam ādāya Bhīṣmaṃ vivyādha pañcabhiḥ,
sārathiṃ ca tribhir bāṇaiḥ su|śitai raṇa|mūrdhani.

SÁNJAYA said:

IN THE MIDDLE of the day, great king, a terrible battle 103.1
took place between Bhishma and the Sómakas, causing considerable loss of life. The son of Ganga, the best of chariot warriors, began to annihilate the army of the Pándavas with sharpened arrows fired by the hundreds and thousands. Your father Deva·vrata began to crush that host, just as herds of cows trample a stook of cut grain. Dhrishta·dyumna, Shikhándin, Viráta, and Drúpada confronted Bhishma and struck the mighty warrior with their shafts
in battle. Bhishma then hit Dhrishta·dyumna and Viráta 103.5
with three arrows, and shot an iron arrow at Drúpada, descendant of Bharata. Those great archers, wounded by Bhishma the tormentor of enemies, became enraged, Your Majesty, like snakes that have been trodden on. Shikhándin wounded the grandfather of the Bharatas, but, bearing in mind that adversary's female nature, the adamantine hero did not strike him back. Dhrishta·dyumna, blazing up with anger like a fire, struck the grandfather with three arrows in his arms and chest. Drúpada pierced Bhishma with twenty-five arrows, Viráta with ten, and Shikhándin
with twenty-five. Severely wounded and bathed in stream- 103.10
ing blood, Bhishma looked like a blossoming *ashóka* tree with its red flowers, great king. The son of Ganga then struck them in return with three straight-flying arrows, my lord, and severed Drúpada's bow with a spear-headed shaft. Drúpada, at the front of the battle, seized another bow, and he pierced Bhishma with five whetted arrows, and his driver with three.

tathā Bhīmo, mahā|rāja, Draupadyāḥ pañca c' ātma|jāḥ,
Kekayā bhrātaraḥ pañca, Sātyakiś c' âiva Sātvataḥ
abhyadravanta Gāṅgeyaṃ Yudhiṣṭhira|puro|gamāḥ,
rirakṣiṣantaḥ Pāñcālyaṃ Dhṛṣṭadyumna|puro|gamam.
103.15 tath" âiva tāvakāḥ sarve Bhīṣma|rakṣ"|ârtham udyatāḥ
pratyudyayuḥ Pāṇḍu|senāṃ saha|sainyā, nar'|âdhipa.
tatr' āsīt su|mahad yuddhaṃ tava teṣāṃ ca saṃkulam
nar'|âśva|ratha|nāgānāṃ, Yama|rāṣṭra|vivardhanam.
rathī rathinam āsādya prāhiṇod Yama|sādanam,
tath" êtarān samāsādya nara|nāg'|âśva|sādinaḥ
anayan para|lokāya śaraiḥ saṃnata|parvabhiḥ,
astraiś ca vividhair ghorais tatra tatra, viśāṃ pate.
rathās tu rathibhir hīnā, hata|sārathayas tathā,
vipradrut'|âśvāḥ samare diśo jagmuḥ samantataḥ.
103.20 mṛdnantas te narān, rājan, hayāṃś ca su|bahūn raṇe,
vātāyamānā dṛśyante gandharva|nagar'|ôpamāḥ.
rathinaś ca rathair hīnā, varmiṇas, tejasā yutāḥ,
kuṇḍal'|ôṣṇīṣiṇaḥ sarve, niṣk'|âṅgada|vibhūṣaṇāḥ,
deva|putra|samā rūpe, śaurye Śakra|samā yudhi,
ṛddhyā Vaiśravaṇaṃ c' âti, nayena ca Bṛhaspatim,
sarva|lok'|ēśvarāḥ śūrās tatra tatra, viśāṃ pate,
vipradrutā vyadṛśyanta prākṛtā iva mānavāḥ.

Then, great king, Bhima, the five sons of Dráupadi, the five Kékaya brothers, and Sátyaki the Sátvata, led by Yudhi·shthira, charged against the son of Ganga, eager to rescue the king of the Panchálas and his host led by Dhrishta·dyumna. Similarly, all your sons and their troops, intent 103.15
on protecting Bhishma, rose up against the Pándava army, lord of the people. A tremendous and chaotic battle followed between your troops and the enemy, both armies teeming with men, horses, chariots, and elephants. That battle swelled the kingdom of Yama considerably. Chariot warrior encountered chariot warriors and sent them to Yama's realm; and foot soldiers, horsemen, and elephant riders confronted each other, often dispatching one another to the other world with various fierce straight arrows, lord of the people. Deprived of their warriors or with their drivers killed, many chariots were dragged through the battle by horses that careered around all over the place. Crushing 103.20
countless men and horses on the battlefield, Your Majesty, those chariots were as swift as the wind and looked like *gandhárvas*' castles in the air.

The chariot warriors who had been stripped of their vehicles were all clad in armor, endowed with vigor, wearing earrings and turbans, and adorned with necklaces and bracelets. They looked like sons of the gods: they were equal to Shakra in battle prowess, and they surpassed Váishravana in wealth and Brihas·pati in political wisdom. The valiant rulers of all the world could be seen running hither and thither like ordinary men.

dantinaś ca, nara|śreṣṭha, vihīnā vara|sādibhiḥ
mṛdnantaḥ svāny anīkāni saṃpetuḥ sarva|śabda|gāḥ.
103.25 carmabhiś, cāmarair, dhvajaiḥ, patākābhiś ca, māriṣa,
chatraiḥ sitair hema|daṇḍais, tomaraiś ca samantataḥ
viśīrṇair vipradhāvanto dṛśyante sma diśo daśa
nava|megha|pratīkāśā, jalad'|ôdaya|niḥsvanāḥ.
tath" âiva dantibhir hīnā gaj'|ārohā, viśāṃ pate,
pradhāvanto 'nvyadṛśyanta tava teṣāṃ ca saṃkule.
nānā|deśa|samutthāṃś ca turagān hema|bhūṣitān
vātāyamānān adrākṣaṃ śataśo 'tha sahasraśaḥ.
aśv'|ārohān hatair aśvair, gṛhīt'|âsīn samantataḥ
dravamāṇān apaśyāma, drāvyamāṇāṃś ca saṃyuge.
103.30 gajo gajaṃ samāsādya dravamāṇaṃ mah"|āhave
yayau pramṛdnaṃs tarasā padātīn vājinas tathā.
tath" âiva ca rathān, rājan, saṃmamarda raṇe gajaḥ,
rathāś c' âiva samāsādya patitān turagān bhuvi.
vyamṛdnan samare, rājaṃs, turagāś ca narān raṇe.
evaṃ te bahudhā, rājan, pratyamṛdnan paras|param.

tasmin raudre tathā yuddhe vartamāne mahā|bhaye
prāvartata nadī ghorā, śoṇit'|āntra|taraṅgiṇī,
asthi|saṃghāta|saṃbādhā, keśa|śaivala|śādvalā,
ratha|hradā, śar'|āvartā, haya|mīnā, dur|āsadā,
103.35 śīrṣ'|ôpala|samākīrṇā, hasti|grāha|samākulā,
kavac'|ôṣṇīṣa|phen'|âughā, dhanur|dvīp", âsi|kacchapā,
patākā|dhvaja|vṛkṣ'|āḍhyā, martya|kūl'|âpahāriṇī,
kravy'|âda|haṃsa|saṃkīrṇā, Yama|rāṣṭra|vivardhinī.

O best of men, elephants, bereft of their superb riders, collapsed, crushing their own troops and uttering all kinds of screams. With their accoutrements—shields, yak tails, 103.25
various banners and flags, white parasols with gold staffs, and spears—all smashed up, my lord, elephants rumbling like looming clouds rushed around in all ten directions, looking like newly risen clouds. And likewise both your elephant riders and those of the enemy could be seen rushing about in confusion, deprived of their elephants, lord of the people. I saw hundreds and thousands of horses from all different countries, decorated in gold and as swift as the wind. And we saw horsemen whose horses had been killed, chasing and chased by each other on all sides in the fray. An 103.30
elephant met another fleeing elephant in that huge battle and quickly ran off, trampling foot soldiers and horses. Your Majesty, in that engagement one elephant crushed many chariots; chariots came across horses that had fallen to the ground and ran over them; and horses trampled foot soldiers on the field of battle, Your Majesty. Thus they crushed each other in various ways, Your Majesty.

During that hideous and terrifying battle, a dreadful surging river of blood and entrails appeared. It was choked by heaps of bones, and hair formed its moss and weeds. That rare river had chariots for its lakes, arrows for eddies, and horses for fish. It abounded in stones that were heads, 103.35
and it teemed with crocodiles in the form of elephants. It had armor and turbans for its copious froth, bows for its rapid current, and swords for tortoises. Its banks were overgrown with trees formed by flags and banners; it continually washed away its banks, which were constituted by

tāṃ nadīṃ kṣatriyāḥ śūrā haya|nāga|ratha|plavaiḥ
praterur bahavo, rājan, bhayaṃ tyaktvā mahā|rathāḥ.
apovāha raṇe bhīrūn kaśmalen' âbhisaṃvṛtān,
yathā Vaitaraṇī pretān preta|rāja|puraṃ prati.

prākrośan kṣatriyās tatra dṛṣṭvā tad vaiśasaṃ mahat:
«Duryodhan'|âparādhena kṣayaṃ gacchanti Kauravāḥ!
103.40 guṇavatsu kathaṃ dveṣaṃ Dhārtarāṣṭro jan'|ēśvaraḥ
kṛtavān Pāṇḍu|putreṣu pāp'|ātmā lobha|mohitaḥ?»
evaṃ bahuvidhā vācaḥ śrūyante sma paras|param
Pāṇḍava|stava|saṃyuktāḥ, putrāṇāṃ te su|dāruṇāḥ.
tā niśamya tadā vācaḥ sarva|yodhair udāhṛtāḥ
āgas|kṛt sarva|lokasya putro Duryodhanas tava
Bhīṣmaṃ, Droṇaṃ, Kṛpaṃ c' âiva,
Śalyaṃ c' ôvāca, Bhārata:
«yudhyadhvam an|ahaṅ|kārāḥ!
kiṃ ciraṃ kuruth'?» êti ca
tataḥ pravavṛte yuddhaṃ Kurūṇāṃ Pāṇḍavaiḥ saha
akṣa|dyūta|kṛtaṃ, rājan, su|ghoraṃ vaiśasaṃ tadā.
103.45 yat purā na nigṛhṇāsi vāryamāṇo mah"|ātmabhiḥ,
Vaicitravīrya, tasy' êdaṃ phalaṃ paśya tathā|vidham.
na hi Pāṇḍu|sutā, rājan, sa|sainyāḥ sa|pad'|ânugāḥ
rakṣanti samare prāṇān, Kauravā v" âpi saṃyuge.
etasmāt kāraṇād ghoro vartate sva|jana|kṣayaḥ,
daivād vā, puruṣa|vyāghra, tava c' âpanayān, nṛ|pa.

mortals; and it swarmed with geese in the form of carrion-eaters. That river swelled the kingdom of Yama considerably. Many valiant kshatriyas, the great warriors, giving up fear, crossed that river on their rafts in the form of horses, elephants and chariots. That river carried away the timid who had fainted, just as the River Váitarani conveys all departed spirits to the capital of the king of the dead.

At the sight of that terrible massacre, warriors exclaimed: "Because of Duryódhana's wrongdoing, warriors are being destroyed! Why did the evil-minded King Dhrita·rashtra, 103.40
bewildered by greed, develop such hatred for the virtuous sons of Pandu?" Many exclamations were heard from the warriors as they addressed each other, praising the Pándavas and bitterly censuring your sons in various ways. When he heard what all the soldiers were saying, your son Duryódhana, who had offended everyone, said to Bhishma, Drona, Kripa, and Shalya, descendant of Bharata: "Fight selflessly! Why do you linger?" Then an utterly terrifying battle took place between the Kurus and the Pándavas—butchery, caused by the game of dice. O son of Vichítra· 103.45
virya, see this horrible result of your former refusal to heed your great-spirited counsellors' admonitions! Neither the sons of Pandu nor the Káuravas spare their lives in battle, Your Majesty; and nor do their troops and followers. Hence this frightful destruction of kinsmen is taking place, tiger of a man, caused either by fate or by your bad policy, Your Majesty.

SAÑJAYA uvāca:

104.1 ARJUNAS TU NARA|vyāghraḥ Suśarma|pramukhān nṛ|pān
anayat preta|rājasya bhavanaṃ sāyakaiḥ śitaiḥ.
Suśarm" âpi tato bāṇaiḥ Pārthaṃ vivyādha saṃyuge,
Vāsudevaṃ ca saptatyā, Pārthaṃ ca navabhiḥ punaḥ.
tān nivārya śar'|âugheṇa Śakra|sūnur mahā|rathaḥ
Suśarmaṇo raṇe yodhān prāhiṇod Yama|sādanam.
te vadhyamānāḥ Pārthena, Kālen' êva yuga|kṣaye,
vyadravanta raṇe, rājan, bhaye jāte mahā|rathāḥ.
104.5 utsṛjya turagān ke cid, rathān ke cic ca, māriṣa,
gajān anye samutsṛjya prādravanta diśo daśa.
apare tu tad" ādāya vāji|nāga|rathān raṇāt
tvarayā parayā yuktāḥ prādravanta, viśāṃ pate.
pādātāś c' âpi śastrāṇi samutsṛjya mahā|raṇe
nir|apekṣā vyadhāvanta tena tena sma, Bhārata.
vāryamāṇāḥ sma bahuśas Traigartena Suśarmaṇā
tath" ânyaiḥ pārthiva|śreṣṭhair na vyatiṣṭhanta saṃyuge.
tad balaṃ pradrutaṃ dṛṣṭvā putro Duryodhanas tava
puras|kṛtya raṇe Bhīṣmaṃ sarva|sainya|puras|kṛtam,
104.10 sarv'|ôdyogena mahatā Dhanañjayam upādravat
Trigart'|âdhipater arthe jīvitasya, viśāṃ pate.
sa ekaḥ samare tasthau kiran bahu|vidhāñ śarān
bhrātṛbhiḥ sahitaḥ sarvaiḥ. śeṣā hi pradrutā narāḥ.
tath" âiva Pāṇḍavā, rājan, sarv'|ôdyogena daṃśitāḥ
prayayuḥ Phālgun'|ârthāya, yatra Bhīṣmo vyatiṣṭhata.

SÁNJAYA said:

WITH HIS SHARP arrows, the man-tiger Árjuna dispatched 104.1
the kings under Sushárman to the realm of the king of the dead. In that battle Sushárman hit the son of Pritha with numerous arrows, Vásu·deva with seventy, and then the son of Pritha again with nine more; but Shakra's mighty warrior son, repelling his opponent with a mass of arrows, sent Sushárman's soldiers to Yama's realm. Struck by the Partha as if by Time at the dissolution of an eon, Your Majesty, those great warriors fled terror-stricken from the battlefield.
They ran away in all directions, my lord, some of them 104.5
leaving their horses, others their chariots, still others their elephants. Others, on the contrary, took their horses, elephants, and chariots with them as they fled the field of battle in the utmost haste, lord of the people. And the foot soldiers, casting aside their weapons in that great battle, ran away here and there paying no heed to anyone, descendant of Bharata. Though Sushárman the king of the Tri·gartas and other excellent kings tried to restrain them, the troops would not stay in the battle.

Seeing that host routed, your son Duryódhana placed
Bhishma in the van and, leading all the troops, he assailed 104.10
Dhanan·jaya with all his might in order to save the life of the king of the Tri·gartas, lord of the people. Scattering arrows of various kinds, he and all his brothers stood alone in battle, the rest of the troops having fled. And the Pándavas, clad in armor, hurried to the place where Bhishma was, Your Majesty, in order to rescue Phálguna. Though they were aware of the fearsome valor of the wielder of the Gandíva bow, they ardently rushed against Bhishma

jñāyamānā raṇe vīryaṃ ghoraṃ Gāṇḍīva|dhanvanaḥ
hā|hā|kāra|kṛt'|ôtsāhā Bhīṣmaṃ jagmuḥ samantataḥ.
tatas tāla|dhvajaḥ śūraḥ Pāṇḍavānām varūthinīm
chādayām āsa samare śaraiḥ saṃnata|parvabhiḥ.
104.15 ekī|bhūtās tataḥ sarve Kuravaḥ saha Pāṇḍavaiḥ
ayudhyanta, mahā|rāja, madhyaṃ prāpte divā|kare.
Sātyakiḥ Kṛtavarmāṇaṃ viddhvā pañcabhir āśu|gaiḥ
atiṣṭhad āhave śūraḥ kiran bāṇān sahasraśaḥ.
tath" âiva Drupado rājā Droṇaṃ viddhvā śitaiḥ śaraiḥ
punar vivyādha saptatyā, sārathiṃ c' âsya pañcabhiḥ.
Bhīmasenas tu rājānaṃ Bāhlikaṃ prapitāmaham
viddhv" ânadan mahā|nādaṃ, śārdūla iva kānane.

Ārjuniś Citrasenena viddho bahubhir āśu|gaiḥ
atiṣṭhad āhave śūraḥ, kiran bāṇān sahasraśaḥ.
104.20 Citrasenaṃ tribhir bāṇair vivyādha samare bhṛśam.
samāgatau tau tu raṇe mahā|mātrau vyarocatām,
yathā divi mahā|ghorau, rājan, Budha|Śanaiścarau.
tasy' âśvāṃś caturo hatvā, sūtaṃ ca navabhiḥ śaraiḥ,
nanāda balavan nādaṃ Saubhadraḥ para|vīra|hā.
hat'|âśvāt tu rathāt tūrṇam so 'vaplutya mahā|rathaḥ
āruroha rathaṃ tūrṇaṃ Durmukhasya, viśāṃ pate.

Droṇaś ca Drupadaṃ viddhvā śaraiḥ saṃnata|parvabhiḥ
sārathiṃ c' âsya vivyādha tvaramāṇaḥ parākramī.
pīḍyamānas tato rājā Drupado vāhinī|mukhe
104.25 apāyāj javanair aśvaiḥ pūrva|vairam anusmaran.

from every side, shouting their war cries. Then the hero Bhishma, who had a palmyra tree on his banner, engulfed the Pándava army with straight arrows in the battle. When 104.15
the sun reached the meridian, all the Kurus and the Pándavas, enmeshed with each other, fought on, great king. Brave Sátyaki, piercing Krita·varman with five swift-flying shafts, stood in battle, scattering thousands of arrows. And King Drúpada, after striking Drona with several sharp arrows, pierced him with seventy more, and his driver with five. Bhima·sena struck his great-grandfather Báhlika and uttered a loud roar like a tiger in the forest.

Árjuna's valiant son, wounded by Chitra·sena with numerous swift-flying arrows, stood his ground, scattering thousands of arrows. He wounded Chitra·sena severely with 104.20
three shafts in that encounter. Confronting one another in combat, the two noble warriors shone like the awesome planets Venus and Saturn risen in the sky, Your Majesty. Killing with nine arrows his adversary's four horses and driver, Subhádra's son, the destroyer of enemy heroes, roared a loud roar. Jumping out of his horseless chariot, the great warrior Chitra·sena quickly climbed onto Dúrmukha's chariot, lord of the people.

Vigorous Drona tormented Drúpada with sharp arrows and had soon hit the latter's driver; wounded at the front of the army, King Drúpada then recalled their old enmity 104.25
and fled, carried away by his swift horses.

Bhīmasenas tu rājānaṃ muhūrtād iva Bāhlikam
vy|aśva|sūta|rathaṃ cakre sarva|sainyasya paśyataḥ.
sa|saṃbhramo, mahā|rāja, saṃśayaṃ paramaṃ gataḥ
avaplutya tato vāhād Bāhlikaḥ puruṣ'|ôttamaḥ
āruroha rathaṃ tūrṇaṃ Lakṣmaṇasya mahā|raṇe.

Sātyakiḥ Kṛtavarmāṇaṃ vārayitvā mahā|raṇe
śarair bahu|vidhai, rājann, āsasāda Pitāmaham.
sa viddhvā Bhārataṃ ṣaṣṭyā niśitair loma|vāhibhiḥ
nanart' êva rath'|ôpasthe, vidhunvāno mahad dhanuḥ.
104.30 tasy' āyasīṃ mahā|śaktiṃ cikṣep' âtha pitā|mahaḥ
hema|citrāṃ, mahā|vegāṃ, nāga|kany"|ôpamāṃ, śubhām.
tām āpatantīṃ sahasā Mṛtyu|kalpāṃ, su|tejanām
vyaṃsayām āsa Vārṣṇeyo lāghavena mahā|yaśāḥ.
an|āsādya tu Vārṣṇeyaṃ śaktiḥ parama|dāruṇā
nyapatad dharaṇī|pṛṣṭhe, mah"|ôlk" êva gata|prabhā.
Vārṣṇeyas tu tato, rājan, svāṃ śaktiṃ kanaka|prabhām
vegavad gṛhya cikṣepa pitā|maha|rathaṃ prati.
Vārṣṇeya|bhuja|vegena praṇunnā sā mah"|āhave
abhidudrāva vegena, Kāla|rātrir yathā naram.
104.35 tām āpatantīṃ sahasā dvidhā ciccheda, Bhārata,
kṣuraprābhyāṃ su|tīkṣṇābhyāṃ. sā vyaśīryata medinīm.
chittvā śaktiṃ tu Gāṅgeyaḥ Sātyakiṃ navabhiḥ śaraiḥ
ājaghān' ôrasi kruddhaḥ prahasañ śatru|karṣaṇaḥ.
tataḥ sa|ratha|nāg'|âśvāḥ Pāṇḍavāḥ, Pāṇḍu|pūrva|ja,
parivavrū raṇe Bhīṣmaṃ Mādhava|trāṇa|kāraṇāt.

In a trice Bhima·sena stripped King Báhlika of his horses, driver, and chariot while all the troops looked on. Báhlika, the foremost of men, finding himself in great danger and taking fright, great king, leaped down from his vehicle and quickly climbed onto Lákshmana's chariot in that vast battle.

Sátyaki held Krita·varman at bay in the great battle, and attacked grandfather Bhishma with arrows of various kinds, Your Majesty. When he struck the Bhárata hero with sixty sharpened and feathered arrows, Sátyaki appeared to dance on the chariot platform, brandishing his mighty bow. The 104.30
grandfather then hurled a mighty lance at him with great force; it was decorated with gold, and beautiful like a young *naga* woman. The glorious descendant of Vrishni, seeing that almost irresistible lance speeding toward him like Death, dexterously warded it off. Failing to reach the descendant of Vrishni, that frightful lance fell to the ground, like a huge meteor of great splendor. Then, Your Majesty, the descendant of Vrishni grabbed his spear that shone like gold, and hurled it at the grandfather's chariot. Propelled by the descendant of Vrishni's powerful throw, it flew speedily toward Bhishma in that great battle, like the fateful night of Time befalling a doomed man. But with two razor-edged 104.35
arrows the Bhárata hero split that swift-flying spear in two, and it collapsed to the ground. After severing that spear, the wrathful son of Ganga, that tormentor of his enemies, struck Sátyaki in the chest with nine arrows, laughing as he did so. Then the Pándavas, elder brother of Pandu, surrounded Bhishma with their chariots, elephants, and horses

tataḥ pravavṛte yuddhaṃ tumulaṃ, loma|harṣaṇam
Pāṇḍavānāṃ Kurūṇāṃ ca samare vijay'|âiṣiṇām.

SAÑJAYA uvāca:

105.1 DṚṢṬVĀ BHĪṢMAṂ raṇe kruddhaṃ
Pāṇḍavair abhisaṃvṛtam
yathā meghair, mahā|rāja,
tap'|ânte divi bhās|karam,
Duryodhano, mahā|rāja, Duḥśāsanam abhāṣata:
«eṣa śūro mah"|êṣv|āso Bhīṣmaḥ śatru|niṣūdanaḥ
chāditaḥ Pāṇḍavaiḥ śūraiḥ samantād, Bharata'|rṣabha.
tasya kāryaṃ tvayā, vīra, rakṣaṇaṃ su|mah"|ātmanaḥ.
rakṣyamāṇo hi samare Bhīṣmo 'smākaṃ pitā|mahaḥ
nihanyāt samare yattān Pañcālān Pāṇḍavaiḥ saha.
105.5 tatra kāryatamaṃ manye Bhīṣmasy' âiv' âbhirakṣaṇam.
goptā hy eṣa mah"|êṣv|āso Bhīṣmo 'smākaṃ mahā|vrataḥ.
sa bhavān sarva|sainyena parivārya pitā|maham
samare duṣ|karaṃ karma kurvāṇaṃ parirakṣatu.»
sa evam uktaḥ samare putro Duḥśāsanas tava
parivārya sthito Bhīṣmaṃ sainyena mahatā vṛtaḥ.
tataḥ śata|sahasreṇa hayānāṃ Subal'|ātmajaḥ
vimala|prāsa|hastānāṃ, ṛṣṭi|tomara|dhāriṇām,
darpitānāṃ, su|veśānāṃ, bala|sthānāṃ, patākinām
śikṣitair yuddha|kuśalair upetānāṃ nar'|ôttamaiḥ,
105.10 Nakulaṃ Sahadevaṃ ca, Dharma|rājaṃ ca Pāṇḍavam
nyavārayan nara|śreṣṭhān parivārya samantataḥ.

in that conflict, in order to rescue the Mádhava. And a tumultuous and hair-raising battle followed between the Pándavas and the Kurus, with both sides striving to gain the victory.

SÁNJAYA said:

SEEING BHISHMA filled with battle-fury, great king, and surrounded by the Pándavas like the sun surrounded in the sky by rain-clouds at the end of summer, Your Majesty, Duryódhana said to Duhshásana: 105.1

"This heroic Bhishma, the mighty archer and slayer of heroes, has been surrounded on all sides by the heroic Pándavas, bull of the Bharatas. It is your duty, hero, to protect that great-spirited warrior. For if he is protected in battle, our grandfather Bhishma will slaughter the Panchálas and the Pándavas, committed to battle as they are. I deem 105.5
protecting Bhishma to be our most important task, for this mighty archer Bhishma of rigid vows is our defender. So you must surround the grandfather with all of our troops, and protect that hero who performs feats that are so difficult to accomplish in battle."

Addressed in this way, your son Duhshásana stood with his mighty host surrounding Bhishma in that engagement.

Then the son of Súbala with a hundred thousand cavalrymen wielding radiant javelins, spears, and lances—all of them proud, well dressed, vigorous, bearing banners, and supported by trained infantrymen skilled in warfare—resisted Nákula, Saha·deva, and the Pándava King of Righ- 105.10
teousness, surrounding those best of men on every side. And King Duryódhana dispatched ten thousand horsemen

tato Duryodhano rājā śūrāṇāṃ haya|sādinām
ayutaṃ preṣayām āsa Pāṇḍavānāṃ nivāraṇe.
taiḥ praviṣṭair mahā|vegair, Garutmadbhir iv' āhave,
khur'|āhatā dharā, rājaṃś, cakampe ca nanāda ca.
khura|śabdaś ca su|mahān vājināṃ śuśruve tadā,
mahā|vaṃśa|vanasy' êva dahyamānasya parvate.
utpatadbhiś ca tais tatra samuddhūtaṃ mahad rajaḥ
divā|kara|rathaṃ prāpya cchādayām āsa bhās|karam.
105.15 vegavadbhir hayais tais tu kṣobhitā Pāṇḍavī camūḥ,
nipatadbhir mahā|vegair haṃsair iva mahat saraḥ.
hreṣatāṃ c' âiva śabdena na prājñāyata kiṃ cana.

tato Yudhiṣṭhiro rājā, Mādrī|putrau ca Pāṇḍavau
pratyaghnaṃs tarasā vegaṃ samare haya|sādinām,
udvṛttasya, mahā|rāja, prāvṛṭ|kālena pūryataḥ
paurṇamāsyām ambu|vegaṃ yathā velā mah"|ôdadheḥ.
tatas te rathino, rājañ, śaraiḥ saṃnata|parvabhiḥ
nyakṛntann uttam'|âṅgāni kāyebhyo haya|sādinām.
te nipetur, mahā|rāja, nihatā dṛḍha|dhanvibhiḥ,
105.20 nāgair iva mahā|nāgā yathāvad giri|gahvare.
te 'pi prāsaiḥ su|niśitaiḥ, śaraiḥ saṃnata|parvabhiḥ
nyakṛntann uttam'|âṅgāni vicaranto diśo daśa.

abhyāhatā hay'|ārohā ṛṣṭibhir, Bharata'|rṣabha,
atyajann uttam'|âṅgāni, phalān' îva mahā|drumāḥ.
sa|sādino hayā, rājaṃs, tatra tatra niṣūditāḥ
patitāḥ pātyamānāś ca śataśo 'tha sahasraśaḥ.
vadhyamānā hayāś c' âiva prādravanta bhay'|ârditāḥ,
yathā siṃhaṃ samāsādya mṛgāḥ prāṇa|parāyaṇāḥ.

to oppose the Pándavas. As those horses entered the battlefield, as impetuous as Gárudas, the earth, struck by their hooves, quaked and made a loud noise, Your Majesty. A tremendous clatter of hooves was heard, like the crackling of great bamboo grove burning on a mountainside. Charging forward, those horses raised a dense cloud of dust which reached the chariot of the sun and hid that sun from view.
And the Pándava army was thrown into disarray by those 105.15
impetuous horses, like a vast lake ruffled by a flight of geese suddenly alighting on its waters. Nothing could be heard there except their neighing.

King Yudhi·shthira and the Pándava sons of Madri promptly repulsed the onslaught of those horsemen, great king, just as the shore fends off the sea when it surges, swollen with the monsoon water, on the day of the full moon. Those chariot warriors chopped the horsemen's heads off from their bodies with straight arrows, Your Majesty; and the cavalrymen fell, killed by those mighty archers,
great king, like huge elephants, struck down by rival ele- 105.20
phants, falling into a mountain cave. The Pándava warriors rampaged every which way, slicing heads off enemy horsemen with straight and well-sharpened javelins.

Bull of the Bharatas, the cavalrymen, struck down by spears, dropped their heads like great trees dropping fruit. Horses and their riders, slain here and there, Your Majesty, were seen fallen and falling all over the place. And when they were struck down in this way, the terror-stricken horses bolted, just as deer run away at the sight of a lion, intent on saving their lives. Having defeated their enemies in

Pāṇḍavāś ca, mahā|rāja, jitvā śatrūn mah"|āhave
105.25 dadhmuḥ śaṅkhāṃś ca, bherīś ca tāḍayām āsur āhave.
tato Duryodhano dīno dṛṣṭvā sainyam parājitam
abravīd, Bharata|śreṣṭha, Madra|rājam idaṃ vacaḥ:
«eṣa Pāṇḍu|suto jyeṣṭho yamābhyāṃ sahito raṇe
paśyatāṃ no, mahā|bāho, senāṃ drāvayate, prabho.
taṃ vāraya, mahā|bāho, vel" êva makar'|ālayam.
tvaṃ hi saṃśrūyase 'tyartham a|sahya|bala|vikramaḥ.»
putrasya tava tad vākyaṃ śrutvā Śalyaḥ pratāpavān
prayayau ratha|vaṃśena, yatra rājā Yudhiṣṭhiraḥ.
tad āpatad vai sahasā Śalyasya su|mahad balam
105.30 mah"|âugha|vegaṃ samare vārayām āsa Pāṇḍavaḥ;
Madra|rājaṃ ca samare Dharma|rājo mahā|rathaḥ
daśabhiḥ sāyakais tūrṇam ājaghāna stan'|ântare;
Nakulaḥ Sahadevaś ca taṃ saptabhir a|jihma|gaiḥ.
Madra|rājo 'pi tān sarvān ājaghāna tribhis tribhiḥ;
Yudhiṣṭhiraṃ punaḥ ṣaṣṭyā vivyādha niśitaiḥ śaraiḥ;
Mādrī|putrau ca saṃbhrāntau
dvābhyāṃ dvābhyām atāḍayat.
tato Bhīmo mahā|bāhur
dṛṣṭvā rājānam āhave
Madra|rāja|rathaṃ prāptaṃ, Mṛtyor āsya|gataṃ yathā,
abhyapadyata saṃgrāme Yudhiṣṭhiram amitra|jit.
105.35 tato yuddhaṃ mahā|ghoraṃ prāvartata su|dāruṇam
aparāṃ diśam āsthāya patamāne divā|kare.

that great engagement, great king, the Pándavas blew their 105.25
conches and beat their kettle-drums on the battlefield.

Then Duryódhana, horrified to see his troops overpowered, addressed the king of the Madras with these words, best of the Bharatas.

"Look, mighty-armed lord! This eldest son of Pandu, supported by his twin brothers in battle, is routing our army. Keep him in check as the shore keeps the ocean in check, famous as you are for your irresistible strength and vigor."

And hearing your son's words, mighty Shalya advanced 105.30
with a chariot division to the place where King Yudhi·shthira was. The Pándava King of Righteousness, that great warrior, then repelled Shalya's mighty host in battle as it suddenly attacked him with the force of a powerful stream; he quickly struck the king of the Madras with ten arrows in the center of his chest. And Nákula and Saha·deva shot Shalya too, with seven straight-flying shafts. The king of the Madras in his turn struck all of them with three arrows each, and then he struck Yudhi·shthira again, with sixty sharpened arrows. He also hit the two bewildered sons of Madri with two shafts each.

At the sight of King Yudhi·shthira meeting the Madra king's chariot as if he were going into the jaws of Death, strong-armed conqueror of enemies Bhima rushed toward
him and into the fray. And as the sun was coursing toward 105.35
the west, a horrible and dreadful battle took place.

SAÑJAYA uvāca:

106.1 TATAḤ PITĀ TAVA kruddho niśitaiḥ sāyak'|ôttamaiḥ
ājaghāna raṇe Pārthān saha|senān samantataḥ.
Bhīmaṃ dvā|daśabhir viddhvā, Sātyakiṃ navabhiḥ śaraiḥ,
Nakulaṃ ca tribhir viddhvā, Sahadevaṃ ca saptabhiḥ,
Yudhiṣṭhiraṃ dvā|daśabhir bāhvor urasi c' ārpayat.
Dhṛṣṭadyumnaṃ tato viddhvā nanāda su|mahā|balaḥ.
taṃ dvā|daś'|ākhyair Nakulo, Mādhavaś ca tribhiḥ śaraiḥ,
Dhṛṣṭadyumnaś ca saptatyā, Bhīmasenaś ca saptabhiḥ,
106.5 Yudhiṣṭhiro dvā|daśabhiḥ pratyavidhyat pitā|maham.

Droṇas tu Sātyakiṃ viddhvā Bhīmasenam avidhyata
ek'|âikaṃ pañcabhir bāṇair Yama|daṇḍ'|ôpamaiḥ śitaiḥ.
tau ca taṃ pratyavidhyetāṃ tribhis tribhir a|jihma|gaiḥ,
tottrair iva mahā|nāgaṃ Droṇaṃ brāhmaṇa|puṅgavam.

Sauvīrāḥ, Kitavāḥ, Prācyāḥ, Pratīcy'|Ôdīcya|Mālavāḥ,
Abhīṣāhāḥ, Śūrasenāḥ, Śibayo, 'tha Vasātayaḥ
saṃgrāme na jahur Bhīṣmaṃ vadhyamānāḥ śitaiḥ śaraiḥ.
tath" âiv' ânye mahī|pālā nānā|deśa|samāgatāḥ
Pāṇḍavān abhyavartanta vividh'|āyudha|pāṇayaḥ.
106.10 tath" âiva Pāṇḍavā, rājan, parivavruḥ pitā|maham.

sa samantāt parivṛto rath'|âughair, a|parājitaḥ
gahane 'gnir iv' ôtsṛṣṭaḥ prajajvāla dahan parān.
rath'|âgny|agāraś, cāp'|ârcir, asi|śakti|gad"|êndhanaḥ,
śara|sphuliṅgo Bhīṣm'|âgnir dadāha kṣatriya'|rṣabhān.
suvarṇa|puṅkhair iṣubhir gārdhra|pakṣaiḥ, su|tejanaiḥ,

SÁNJAYA said:

THEN YOUR WRATHFUL father Bhishma began to strike Pritha's sons and their troops on all sides in battle with excellent sharpened arrows. He stung Bhima with twelve shafts, Sátyaki with nine, Nákula with three, and Saha·deva with seven; he wounded Yudhi·shthira in the arms and chest with twelve; and then that immensely mighty hero pierced Dhrishta·dyumna and shouted out loud. Nákula struck the grandfather back with twelve arrows, the Mádhava with three, Dhrishta·dyumna with seventy, Bhima·sena with seven, and Yudhi·shthira with twelve. 106.1

106.5

Drona then hit Sátyaki and Bhima·sena, each of them with five sharp arrows resembling the staff of Yama. But each of the two heroes pierced Drona, that bull of the brahmins, with three straight-flying shafts in return, as if they were tormenting a mighty elephant with goads.

The Sauvíras, the Kítavas, the Easterners, the Westerners, the Northerners, the Málavas, the Abhisháhas, the Shura·senas, the Shibis, and the Vasátis, though they were tormented by his sharp arrows, did not shun Bhishma. And likewise other kings, having come from different countries with diverse weapons in their hands, attacked the Pándavas. And the Pándavas, Your Majesty, surrounded the grandfather. 106.10

Surrounded on all sides by hordes of warriors, and yet undefeated, Bhishma blazed up and scorched his enemies, like a fire in a thicket. With his chariot for a fire sanctuary, his bow for flames, his swords, lances, and maces for fuel, and his arrows for sparks, Bhishma himself was the

karṇi|nālīka|nārācaiś chādayām āsa tad balam;
apātayad dhvajāṃś c' âiva rathinaś ca śitaiḥ śaraiḥ.
muṇḍa|tāla|vanān' îva cakāra sa ratha|vrajān.
nir|manuṣyān rathān, rājan, gajān, aśvāṃś ca saṃyuge
106.15 akarot sa mahā|bāhuḥ sarva|śastra|bhṛtāṃ varaḥ.
tasya jyā|tala|nirghoṣaṃ, visphūrjitam iv' âśaneḥ,
niśamya sarva|bhūtāni samakampanta, Bhārata.
a|moghā hy apatan bāṇāḥ pitus te, Bharata'|rṣabha;
n' âsajjanta tanu|treṣu Bhīṣma|cāpa|cyutāḥ śarāḥ.
hata|vīrān rathān, rājan, saṃyuktāñ javanair hayaiḥ
apaśyāma, mahā|rāja, hriyamāṇān raṇ|ājire.
Cedi|Kāśi|Karūṣāṇāṃ sahasrāṇi catur|daśa
mahā|rathāḥ samākhyātāḥ, kula|putrās, tanu|tyajaḥ,
a|parāvartinaḥ sarve, suvarṇa|vikṛta|dhvajāḥ
106.20 saṃgrāme Bhīṣmam āsādya, vyādit'|āsyam iv' Ântakam,
nimagnāḥ para|lokāya sa|vāji|ratha|kuñjarāḥ.
bhagn'|âkṣ'|ôpaskarān kāṃś cid,
bhagna|cakrāṃś ca sarvaśaḥ
apaśyāma rathān, rājañ,
śataśo 'tha sahasraśaḥ.
sa|varūthai rathair bhagnai, rathibhiś ca nipātitaiḥ,
śaraiḥ, su|kavacaiś chinnaiḥ, paṭṭiśaiś ca, viśāṃ pate,

fire incinerating those bull-like warriors. With his gold-nocked, vulture-feathered, well-sharpened arrows, barbed shafts, darts, and iron arrows, Bhishma shrouded the hostile force; and with sharp arrows he struck down the enemy's banners and chariot warriors. He made a large division of chariots look like a grove of palm trees stripped of their leafy tops. That strong-armed champion of all warriors deprived 106.15
chariots, elephants, and horses of their riders in that battle, Your Majesty.

On hearing the twang of his bow, which resembled the rumbling of thunder, all living beings trembled, descendant of Bharata. Your father's arrows hit their marks unfailingly, bull of the Bharatas; and the shafts discharged from Bhishma's bow were unimpeded by any armor. Your Majesty, great king, we saw umpteen chariots dragged over the battlefield by the swift horses to which they were yoked.

Fourteen thousand mighty warriors from among the Chedis, the Kashis, and the Karúshas, all of them illustrious combatants from noble families, ready to give up their lives, never retreating, bearing banners decorated with gold, confronted Bhishma; and he was like Death with his mouth 106.20
gaping in battle. They were sent to the other world, along with their horses, chariots, and elephants.

O mighty king, descendant of Bharata, we saw hundreds and thousands of chariots with their axles and poles shattered and their wheels broken. The earth was strewn with broken chariots and their shields, with fallen chariot warriors, with arrows, broken beautiful armor, and sharp-edged spears, lord of the people; with maces, small javelins, whetted stone-tipped shafts, axle-sets, quivers, and broken

gadābhir, bhindipālaiś ca, niśitaiś ca śilīmukhaiḥ,
anukarṣair, upāsaṅgaiś, cakrair bhagnaiś ca, māriṣa,
bāhubhiḥ, kārmukaiḥ, khaḍgaiḥ, śirobhiś ca sa|kuṇḍalaiḥ,
tala|trair, aṅguli|traiś, ca dhvajaiś ca vinipātitaiḥ,
106.25 cāpaiś ca bahudhā chinnaiḥ samāstīryata medinī.
hat'|ārohā gajā, rājan, hayāś ca hata|sādinaḥ
nyapatanta gata|prāṇāḥ śataśo 'tha sahasraśaḥ.
yatamānāś ca te vīrā dravamāṇān mahā|rathān
n' âśaknuvan vārayituṃ Bhīṣma|bāṇa|prapīḍitān.
mah"|Êndra|sama|vīryeṇa vadhyamānā mahā|camūḥ
abhajyata, mahā|rāja. na ca dvau saha dhāvataḥ.
āviddha|ratha|nāg'|âśvaṃ, patita|dhvaja|saṃkulam
anīkaṃ Pāṇḍu|putrāṇāṃ hā|hā|bhūtam, a|cetanam.
jaghān' âtra pitā putraṃ, putraś ca pitaraṃ tathā,
106.30 priyaṃ sakhāyaṃ c' ākrande sakhā daiva|balāt|kṛtaḥ.
vimucya kavacān anye Pāṇḍu|putrasya sainikāḥ,
prakīrya keśān dhāvantaḥ pratyadṛśyanta, Bhārata.
tad go|kulam iv' ôdbhrāntam udbhrānta|ratha|kūbaram
dadṛśe Pāṇḍu|putrasya sainyam ārta|svaraṃ tadā.
prabhajyamānaṃ sainyaṃ tu dṛṣṭvā Yādava|nandanaḥ
uvāca Pārthaṃ Bībhatsuṃ, nigṛhya ratham uttamam:
«ayaṃ sa kālaḥ samprāptaḥ, Pārtha, yaḥ kāṅkṣitas tava.
prahar' âsmin, nara|vyāghra, na cen mohād vimuhyase.
yat purā kathitaṃ, vīra, tvayā rājñāṃ samāgame
106.35 Virāṭa|nagare, Pārtha, Sañjayasya samīpataḥ,
‹Bhīṣma|Droṇa|mukhān sarvān Dhārtarāṣṭrasya sainikān
s'|ânubandhān haniṣyāmi, ye māṃ yotsyanti saṃgare,›
iti tat kuru, Kaunteya, satyaṃ vākyam, arin|dama.
kṣatra|dharmam anusmṛtya yudhyasva vigata|jvaraḥ.»

wheels, my lord; and with arms, bows, swords, heads offset with earrings, gloves, finger protectors, toppled banners, and bows cut into pieces. Hundreds and thousands of ele- 106.25
phants and horses were fallen and lifeless, and their riders had been killed too, Your Majesty.

And although they strove hard, the Pándava heroes were unable to rally the great warriors who fled away, tormented by Bhishma's arrows. Massacred by that hero who was the equal of great Indra in vigor, the large Pándava army was routed in such a way that no two men fled together, great king. The host of Pandu's sons screamed senselessly in their despair. Father killed son, and son killed father; and friend 106.30
struck down dear friend, compelled by fate. Some of the warriors of Pandu's son cast off their armor and were seen fleeing everywhere, their hair disheveled. The Pándava troops, uttering cries of pain, looked like panic-stricken bulls running away, unrestrained by the yoke.

Seeing the army broken, Krishna, the delight of the Yádavas, reined in their superb chariot and spoke to Pritha's son Bibhátsu.

"Partha, the moment for which you have longed has now come. Smite him, tiger-like man, unless you are confused by some delusion. Dear hero, once, in the assembly of kings in Viráta's city, and in Sánjaya's presence, you said 'I will 106.35
kill all of the Dharta·rashtra's warriors, and their followers, including Bhishma and Drona, and whoever will fight with me in battle!' enemy-taming son of Kunti, make your words come true! Keep the warrior code in mind, and fight free of anxiety!"

ity ukto Vāsudevena tiryag|dṛṣṭir, adho|mukhaḥ,
a|kāma iva Bībhatsur idaṃ vacanam abravīt:
«a|vadhyānāṃ vadhaṃ kṛtvā rājyaṃ vā narak'|ôttaram,
duḥkhāni vana|vāse vā—kiṃ nu me su|kṛtaṃ bhavet?
coday' âśvān, yato Bhīṣmaḥ. kariṣye vacanaṃ tava.
106.40 pātayiṣyāmi dur|dharṣaṃ vṛddhaṃ Kuru|pitāmaham.»
tato 'śvān rajata|prakhyāṃś codayām āsa Mādhavaḥ
yato Bhīṣmas, tato, rājan, duṣ|prekṣyo raśmivān iva.
tatas tat punar āvṛttaṃ Yudhiṣṭhira|balaṃ mahat
dṛṣṭvā Pārthaṃ mahā|bāhuṃ Bhīṣmāy' ôdyatam āhave.
tato Bhīṣmaḥ Kuru|śreṣṭhaḥ siṃhavad vinadan muhuḥ
Dhanañjaya|rathaṃ śīghraṃ śara|varṣair avākirat.
kṣaṇena sa rathas tasya sa|hayaḥ, saha|sārathiḥ
śara|varṣeṇa mahatā na prājñāyata, Bhārata.
Vāsudevas tv a|saṃbhrānto, dhairyam āsthāya sa|tvaraḥ
106.45 codayām āsa tān aśvān vinunnān Bhīṣma|sāyakaiḥ.
tataḥ Pārtho dhanur gṛhya divyaṃ jalada|niḥsvanam,
pātayām āsa Bhīṣmasya dhanuś chittvā śitaiḥ śaraiḥ.
sa cchinna|dhanvā Kauravyaḥ punar anyan mahad dhanuḥ
nimeṣ'|ântara|mātreṇa sa|jyaṃ cakre pitā tava.
cakarṣa ca tato dorbhyāṃ dhanur jalada|niḥsvanam.
ath' âsya tad api kruddhaś ciccheda dhanur Arjunaḥ.
tasya tat pūjayām āsa lāghavaṃ Śantanoḥ sutaḥ,
Gāṅgeyas tv abravīt Pārthaṃ dhanvi|śreṣṭhaṃ arin|damaḥ:
«sādhu, sādhu, mahā|bāho! sādhu, Kuntī|sut'!» êti ca.

Addressed by Vásu·deva in this way, lowering his head and looking askance, Bibhátsu spoke reluctantly.

"Either end up in hell and gain the kingdom by slaying those who are not to be slain, or suffer misfortunes in exile in the forest? What is the best thing for me to do? Drive the horses on to where Bhishma is. I will do as you say. I 106.40
will strike down unconquerable Bhishma, the grandfather of the Kurus."

And the Mádhava drove their silver-colored horses to the place where Bhishma was stationed, as dazzling as the very sun, Your Majesty.

Seeing the mighty-armed Partha rising against Bhishma in battle, Yudhi·shthira's mighty host rallied. Then Bhishma, the best of the Kurus, roaring like a lion again and again, immediately poured showers of arrows over Dhanan·jaya's chariot. In an instant Árjuna's chariot, with its horses and driver, became invisible due to that heavy rainstorm of shafts, descendant of Bharata. Yet without wavering Vásu·deva swiftly and patiently urged the horses, even though 106.45
they were pressed by Bhishma's arrows.

Then the son of Pritha, taking hold of his divine bow as loud as the rumbling of thunderclouds, struck Bhishma's bow down, severing it with sharp arrows. Stripped of his bow, your father the Káurava hero instantly strung another bow and stretched it with both arms, making a thunderous twang. But Árjuna, enraged, split that bow too. That tamer of enemies, the son of Shántanu and Ganga then praised his opponent's dexterity, saying to Pritha's son, the best of archers: "Excellent, excellent, mighty-armed hero! Well done, son of Kunti!"

106.50 samābhāṣy' âivam, aparaṃ pragṛhya ruciraṃ dhanuḥ,
mumoca samare Bhīṣmaḥ śarān Pārtha|rathaṃ prati.
adarśayad Vāsudevo haya|yāne paraṃ balam,
moghān kurvañ śarāṃs tasya, maṇḍalāni nidarśayan.
śuśubhāte nara|vyāghrau Bhīṣma|Pārthau śara|kṣatau,
go|vṛṣāv iva saṃrabdhau viṣāṇ'|ôllikhit'|âṅkitau.

Vāsudevas tu saṃprekṣya Pārthasya mṛdu|yuddhatām,
Bhīṣmaṃ ca śara|varṣāṇi sṛjantam a|niśaṃ yudhi,
pratapantam iv' ādityaṃ madhyam āsādya senayoḥ
varān varān vinighnantaṃ Pāṇḍu|putrasya sainikān,
106.55 yug'|ântam iva kurvāṇaṃ Bhīṣmaṃ Yaudhiṣṭhire bale,
n' âmṛṣyata mahā|bāhur Mādhavaḥ para|vīra|hā.
utsṛjya rajata|prakhyān hayān Pārthasya, māriṣa,
Vāsudevas tato yogī pracaskanda mahā|rathāt.
abhidudrāva Bhīṣmaṃ sa bhuja|praharaṇo, balī,
pratoda|pāṇis, tejasvī, siṃhavad vinadan muhuḥ,
dārayann iva padbhyāṃ sa jagatīṃ jagad|īśvaraḥ
krodha|tāmr'|ēkṣaṇaḥ Kṛṣṇo jighāṃsur a|mita|dyutiḥ.
grasann iva ca cetāṃsi tāvakānāṃ mah"|āhave
dṛṣṭvā Mādhavam ākrande Bhīṣmāy' ôdyantam āhave,
106.60 «hato Bhīṣmo! hato Bhīṣma!» iti tatra vaco mahat
aśrūyata, mahā|rāja, Vāsudeva|bhayāt tadā.

And having addressed him, Bhishma then seized another radiant bow and discharged numerous arrows at the Partha's chariot. Vásu·deva displayed his excellent skill at driving horses, as he foiled Bhishma's shafts, moving around in circles. Wounded with arrows, the two tiger-like men, Bhishma and the Partha, looked beautiful, like two infuriated bulls marked with scratches made by horns. 106.50

Vásu·deva saw that the son of Pritha was fighting mildly, whereas Bhishma, stationed between the two hosts, scorching his enemies like the sun and ceaselessly discharging downpours of arrows in battle, was slaughtering Pandu's
son's excellent warriors and producing in Yudhi·shthira's 106.55
army the kind of destruction that occurs at the end of an eon. And the mighty-armed Mádhava, that slayer of enemy heroes, could not bear it. Letting go of the reins of the Partha's silver-colored horses, my lord, Vásu·deva the yogin leaped down from the mighty chariot. Endowed with power and vigor, his bare arms his only weapon, and with his whip still in his hand, Krishna charged against Bhishma, roaring like a lion over and over. His eyes bloodshot with rage, Krishna, the lord of the universe, infinite in his splendor, was practically splitting the earth with his tread as he hurtled on, eager to slay the foe. Seeing that the Mádhava, devouring the minds of your combatants in that great battle, was nearing Bhishma and about to pounce on him
in the fray, loud shouts—"Bhishma is slain! Bhishma is 106.60
slain!"—were heard, great king, caused by the horror that Vásu·deva inspired.

pīta|kauśeya|saṃvīto, maṇi|śyāmo Janārdanaḥ
śuśubhe vidravan Bhīṣmaṃ, vidyun|mālī yath" âmbu|daḥ.
sa siṃha iva mātaṅgaṃ, yūtha'|rṣabha iva' rṣabham,
abhidudrāva tejasvī vinadan Yādava'|rṣabhaḥ.
tam āpatantaṃ saṃpreksya Puṇḍarīkākṣam āhave
a|saṃbhramaṃ raṇe Bhīṣmo vicakarṣa mahad dhanuḥ,
uvāca c' âiva Govindam a|saṃbhrāntena cetasā:
«ehy, ehi, Puṇḍarīkākṣa! deva|deva, namo 'stu te!
106.65 mām adya, Sātvata|śreṣṭha, pātayasva mah"|āhave!
tvayā hi, deva, saṃgrāme hatasy' âpi mam', ân|agha,
śreya eva paraṃ, Kṛṣṇa, loke bhavati sarvataḥ!
saṃbhāvito 'smi, Govinda, trailokyen' âdya saṃyuge!
praharasva yath"|êṣṭaṃ vai; dāso 'smi tava c', ân|agha!»
anvag eva tataḥ Pārthaḥ samabhidrutya Keśavam
nijagrāha mahā|bāhur bāhubhyāṃ parigṛhya vai.
nigṛhyamāṇaḥ Pārthena Kṛṣṇo rājīva|locanaḥ
jagām' âiv' âinam ādāya vegena Puruṣ'|ôttamaḥ.
Pārthas tu viṣṭabhya balāc caraṇau para|vīra|hā,
106.70 nijaghrāha Hṛṣīkeśaṃ kathaṃ cid daśame pade.
tata evam uvāc' ārtaḥ krodha|paryākul'|ēkṣaṇam,
niḥśvasantaṃ yathā nāgam Arjunaḥ praṇayāt sakhā:
«nivartasva, mahā|bāho! n' ân|ṛtaṃ kartum arhasi!
yat tvayā kathitaṃ pūrvaṃ, ‹na yotsyām'!› îti, Keśava,
mithyā|vād" îti lokas tvāṃ kathayiṣyati, Mādhava.
mam' âiṣa bhāraḥ sarvo hi. haniṣyāmi pitā|maham!

Dressed in yellow silk garments and as dark blue as a sapphire in complexion, Janárdana, as he was assailing Bhishma, looked resplendent like a rain-cloud garlanded with lightning. That bull of the Yádavas charged against Bhishma violently with a roar, as a lion attacks an elephant, or a leader of a herd of bulls attacks a lone bull. Seeing lotus-eyed Krishna advancing toward him in that fight, Bhishma, undaunted, began to draw his strong and mighty bow. He addressed Go·vinda with an intrepid heart.

"Come, come, Lotus-eyed god of gods! Obeisance to
you! Strike me down in this great battle today, best of the 106.65
Sátvatas! For if I am slain by you in this combat, faultless lord, I shall attain to the highest good in this world in every respect, Krishna! Today, in this battle, I have been honored by the three worlds, Go·vinda! Strike me as you please, sinless one, for I am your slave!"

But in the meantime the mighty-armed son of Pritha, running after Késhava, restrained him by clasping Krishna in his arms. Lotus-eyed Krishna, the Supreme Person, restrained by Pritha's son, carried on at some speed, carrying Árjuna along. Pritha's son, the slayer of enemy heroes, then
forcibly seized Krishna's legs and somehow stopped Hrishi· 106.70
kesha at the tenth step. Then Árjuna, his dear friend, deeply distressed, affectionately addressed Krishna, who was breathing like a snake and whose eyes were filled with fury.

"Stop, mighty-armed hero! You ought not to make your words false! Késhava, you've already said, 'I shall not fight!' —so people will call you a liar, Mádhava. All of this burden is on me. I will slay the grandfather! I swear by my weapons, by truth, and by my good deeds, that I will exterminate the

śape, Keśava, sakhyena, satyena, su|kṛtena ca,
antaṃ yathā gamiṣyāmi śatrūṇāṃ, śatru|sūdana.
ady' âiva paśya dur|dharṣaṃ pātyamānaṃ mahā|ratham,
106.75 tārā|patim iv' āpūrṇam anta|kāle yadṛcchayā.»
Mādhavas tu vacaḥ śrutvā Phālgunasya mah"|ātmanaḥ
na kiṃ cid uktvā sa|krodha āruroha rathaṃ punaḥ.
tau ratha|sthau nara|vyāghrau Bhīṣmaḥ Śāntanavaḥ punaḥ
vavarṣa śara|varṣeṇa, megho vṛṣṭyā yath" â|calau.
prāṇān ādatta yodhānāṃ pitā Devavratas tava,
gabhastibhir iv' ādityas tejasvī śiśir'|âtyaye.
yathā Kurūṇāṃ sainyāni babhañjur yudhi Pāṇḍavāḥ,
tathā Pāṇḍava|sainyāni babhañja yudhi te pitā.
hata|vidruta|sainyās tu, nir|utsāhā, vi|cetasaḥ
106.80 nirīkṣituṃ na śekus te Bhīṣmam a|pratimaṃ raṇe,
madhyaṃ gatam iv' ādityaṃ pratapantaṃ sva|tejasā.
te vadhyamānā Bhīṣmeṇa śataśo 'tha sahasraśaḥ,
kurvāṇaṃ samare karmāṇy ati|mānuṣa|vikramam
vīkṣāṃ cakrur, mahā|rāja, Pāṇḍavā bhaya|pīḍitāḥ.
tathā Pāṇḍava|sainyāni drāvyamāṇāni, Bhārata,
trātāraṃ n' âdhyagacchanta, gāvaḥ paṅka|gatā iva,
pipīlikā iva kṣuṇṇā dur|balā balinā raṇe.
mahā|rathaṃ, Bhārata, duṣ|prakampaṃ,
śar'|âughiṇaṃ, pratapantaṃ nar'|êndrān
Bhīṣmaṃ na śekuḥ prativīkṣituṃ te,
śar'|ârciṣaṃ sūryam iv' ātapantam.
106.85 vimṛdnatas tasya tu Pāṇḍu|senām
astaṃ jagām' âtha sahasra|raśmiḥ.
tato balānāṃ śrama|karśitānāṃ
mano 'vahāraṃ prati saṃbabhūva.

enemies, enemy-slayer! Even today you will see this unconquerable mighty warrior struck down by me with ease, like 106.75
the crescent moon at the end of the age!"

And hearing the words of great-spirited Phálguna, Mádhava, without saying a word, climbed onto the chariot once again. And Bhishma the son of Shántanu covered the two tiger-like men with a shower of arrows once more, like a storm-cloud pouring rain over two mountains.

Your father Deva·vrata, resplendent like the rousing sun at the end of winter, made enemy warriors' lives evaporate with his arrow-rays. As the Pándavas had broken the ranks of the Kurus, so your father broke the Pándava ranks in that combat.

The hostile warriors, wounded and routed, became cheerless and dispirited. They could not even look at Bhishma, 106.80
so incomparable was he in battle, blazing with his splendor like the midday sun. Pounded by Bhishma in their hundreds and thousands, the terror-stricken Pándava troops glanced timidly at Bhishma who was performing great feats in that combat, mighty king, endowed with superhuman vigor. And the Pándavas' routed troops, descendant of Bharata, could find no protector in that encounter, like cows sunk in mud, or like feeble ants trodden on by a strong man. O Bhárata, they were unable even to gaze at that mighty and unshakable warrior as he scorched the enemy kings with masses of shafts and blazed like the sun with with the radiance of his arrows. While Bhishma was pounding the 106.85
Pándava host the thousand-rayed sun was setting, and the troops, wasted from their exertions, wanted to withdraw.

enemies, enemy-slayer! Even today you will see this unconquerable mighty warrior struck down by [illegible] with ease, like the crescent moon at the end of the night.

And hearing the words of great-spirited [illegible], [illegible] without saying a word climbed onto the chariot once again. And Bhīshma the son of Shāntanu covered the two tiger-like men with a shower of arrows once more, like a storm-cloud pouring rain on a mountain.

Your father Devavrata, resplendent like the [illegible] at the end of winter, [illegible] enemy warriors [illegible] with his arrows. [illegible] the [illegible] of the [illegible] other [illegible] in that combat.

[illegible] the warriors [illegible] [illegible] they could not even [illegible] [illegible] like [illegible] [illegible] [illegible] hundreds and thousands [illegible] [illegible] [illegible] [illegible] [illegible] who was [illegible] [illegible] [illegible] with superhuman vigor, [illegible] [illegible] troops, descendant of Bharata, could find no [illegible] [illegible] [illegible] [illegible] like cows [illegible] [illegible] [illegible] only [illegible] O Bhārata, [illegible] [illegible] [illegible] [illegible] mighty [illegible] warrior as he scorched the enemy [illegible] with [illegible] [illegible] like the sun with the radiance of his arrows. While Bhīshma was pounding the [illegible] [illegible] [illegible] was setting, and the troops, [illegible] from their exhaustion, wanted to withdraw.

107

BHISHMA'S ADVICE TO THE PÁNDAVAS

SAÑJAYA uvāca:

107.1 YUDHYATĀM EVA teṣāṃ tu bhās|kare 'stam upāgate
saṃdhyā samabhavad ghorā. n' âpaśyāma tato raṇam.
tato Yudhiṣṭhiro rājā saṃdhyāṃ saṃdṛśya, Bhārata,
vadhyamānaṃ ca Bhīṣmeṇa tyakt'|âstraṃ, bhaya|vihvalam
sva|sainyaṃ ca parāvṛttaṃ, palāyana|parāyaṇam,
Bhīṣmaṃ ca yudhi saṃrabdham pīḍayantaṃ mahā|ratham,
Somakāṃś ca jitān dṛṣṭvā nir|utsāhān mahā|rathān,
cintayitvā tato rājā hy avahāram arocayat.
107.5 tato 'vahāraṃ sainyānāṃ cakre rājā Yudhiṣṭhiraḥ.
tath" âiva tava sainyānām avahāro hy abhūt tadā.

tato 'vahāraṃ sainyānāṃ kṛtvā tatra mahā|rathāḥ
nyaviśanta, Kuru|śreṣṭha, saṃgrāme kṣata|vikṣatāḥ.
Bhīṣmasya samare karma cintayānās tu Pāṇḍavāḥ
n' âlabhanta tadā śāntiṃ Bhīṣma|bāṇa|prapīḍitāḥ.
Bhīṣmo 'pi samare jitvā Pāṇḍavān saha|Sṛñjayān
pūjyamānas tava sutair vandyamānaś ca, Bhārata,
nyaviśat Kurubhiḥ sārdhaṃ hṛṣṭa|rūpaiḥ samantataḥ.

tato rātriḥ samabhavat sarva|bhūta|pramohinī.
107.10 tasmin rātri|mukhe ghore Pāṇḍavā Vṛṣṇibhiḥ saha,
Sṛñjayāś ca dur|ādharṣā mantrāya samupāviśan.
ātma|niḥśreyasaṃ sarve prāpta|kālaṃ mahā|balāḥ
mantrayām āsur a|vyagrā, mantra|niścaya|kovidāḥ.
tato Yudhiṣṭhiro rājā mantrayitvā ciraṃ, nṛ|pa,
Vāsudevaṃ samudvīkṣya vākyam etad uvāca ha:

SÁNJAYA said:

THE SUN HAD set while they were fighting, and a frightful twilight came; we could no longer see the battle. 107.1
Then, descendant of Bharata, King Yudhi·shthira saw that twilight had set in, and that his troops, crushed by Bhishma and overtaken by fear, had cast aside their weapons, turned tail, and sought shelter by fleeing, while the mighty warrior Bhishma, filled with battle-fury, was still tormenting them. Seeing the great Sómaka warriors were also vanquished and dejected, the king thought for a while and decided to withdraw the troops. So King Yudhi·shthira ordered the with- 107.5
drawal of his forces; and your troops were withdrawn too.

After withdrawing their forces, the great warriors, severely wounded by the day's fighting, entered their tents, best of the Kurus. But the Pándavas, pondering over Bhishma's feats in the battle, found no peace of mind, tormented as they were by Bhishma's arrows. Bhishma, having defeated the Pándavas and the Srínjayas in combat, was honored and praised by your sons, descendant of Bharata, and, accompanied by the joyful Kurus, he entered his encampment.

Then came night, bewildering all beings. And at grisly 107.10
nightfall the Pándavas, the Vrishnis, and the unconquerable Srínjayas met for a consultation. All those mighty heroes, skilled at reaching conclusions in council, calmly discussed what would be best for them to do in the present situation. After long deliberations, Your Majesty, King Yudhi·shthira looked over at Vásu·deva and addressed him with these words.

«Kṛṣṇa, paśya mah"|ātmānaṃ
 Bhīṣmaṃ Bhīma|parākramam,
gajaṃ nala|vanān' îva
 vimṛdnantaṃ balaṃ mama.
na c' âiv' âinaṃ mah"|ātmānam utsahāmo nirīkṣitum,
lelihyamānaṃ sainyeṣu pravṛddham iva pāvakam.
107.15 yathā ghoro mahā|nāgas Takṣako vai viṣ'|ôlbaṇaḥ,
tathā Bhīṣmo raṇe, Kṛṣṇa, tīkṣṇa|śastraḥ, pratāpavān,
gṛhīta|cāpaḥ samare pramuñcan niśitāñ śarān.
śakyo jetuṃ Yamaḥ kruddho, vajra|pāṇiś ca deva|rāṭ,
Varuṇaḥ pāśa|bhṛc c' âpi, sa|gado vā dhan'|ēśvaraḥ;
na tu Bhīṣmaḥ su|saṃkruddhaḥ śakyo jetuṃ mah"|āhave.
so 'ham evaṃ gate, Kṛṣṇa, nimagnaḥ śoka|sāgare
ātmano buddhi|daurbalyād Bhīṣmam āsādya saṃyuge,
vanaṃ yāsyāmi, dur|dharṣa. śreyo me tatra vai gatam.
na yuddhaṃ rocaye, Kṛṣṇa. hanti Bhīṣmo hi naḥ sadā.
107.20 yathā prajvalitaṃ vahniṃ pataṅgaḥ samabhidravan
ekato mṛtyum abhyeti, tath" âhaṃ Bhīṣmam īyivān.
kṣayaṃ nīto 'smi, Vārṣṇeya, rājya|hetoḥ parākramī.
bhrātaraś c' âiva me śūrāḥ sāyakair bhṛśa|pīḍitāḥ
mat|kṛte bhrātṛ|sauhārdād rājya|bhraṣṭā vanaṃ gatāḥ.
parikliṣṭā tathā Kṛṣṇā mat|kṛte, Madhu|sūdana.
jīvitaṃ bahu manye 'haṃ. jīvitaṃ hy adya dur|labham.
jīvitasy' âdya śeṣeṇa cariṣye dharmam uttamam.
yadi te 'ham anugrāhyo bhrātṛbhiḥ saha, Keśava,
sva|dharmasy' â|virodhena tad udāhara, Keśava.»

"You see, Krishna, Bhishma of great spirit and fearful
power crushes my host like an elephant trampling thick-
ets of reeds. And we can't even get a sight of that great-
spirited warrior when he licks our troops like flames of
raging fire. Immensely powerful Bhishma, filled with bat- 107.15
tle fury, armed with sharp weapons, wielding his bow and
releasing whetted arrows in combat, is like the fierce and
mighty serpent Tákshaka whose poison is so virulent.
Wrathful Yama, thunderbolt-wielding Indra the king of the
gods, Váruna with his noose, and Kubéra the lord of wealth
can be defeated, but Bhishma, filled with violent rage, can
never be conquered, even in a great war. In these circum-
stances, Krishna, having confronted Bhishma in combat, I
am plunged into a sea of grief, because of my own lack of
judgement. I shall go to the forest, invincible one. It will
be better for me there. I do not like this battle, Krishna, for
Bhishma constantly slaughters our troops. As a moth flying 107.20
into a blazing fire finds only its death, so do I by having
dared to take on Bhishma. I am led to destruction, vigorously struggling for the kingdom, descendant of Vrishni.
And my heroic brothers have been severely wounded with
arrows. Out of brotherly affection for me they went into
exile to the forest, robbed of their kingdom. And it was my
fault that Krishná was wronged, slayer of Madhu. Now I
value life highly, so difficult to save. For the rest of my life
I shall act with the utmost virtue. So if my brothers and I
deserve your grace, Késhava, then please advise me: what
will be beneficial for us but not incompatible with our own
propriety?"

107.25 evaṃ śrutvā vacas tasya kāruṇyād bahu|vistaram
pratyuvāca tataḥ Kṛṣṇaḥ sāntvayāno Yudhiṣṭhiram:
«Dharma|putra, viṣādaṃ tvaṃ mā kṛthāḥ, satya|saṃgara,
yasya te bhrātaraḥ śūrā dur|jayāḥ śatru|sūdanāḥ!
Arjuno Bhīmasenaś ca vāyv|agni|sama|tejasau;
Mādrī|putrau ca vikrāntau tri|daśānām iv' ēśvarau.
māṃ vā niyuṅkṣva sauhārdād. yotsye Bhīṣmeṇa, Pāṇḍava.
tvat|prayukto, mahā|rāja, kiṃ na kuryāṃ mah"|āhave?
haniṣyāmi raṇe Bhīṣmam āhūya puruṣa'|rṣabham
paśyatāṃ Dhārtarāṣṭrāṇāṃ, yadi n' êcchati Phālgunaḥ.
107.30 yadi Bhīṣme hate, rājañ, jayaṃ paśyasi, Pāṇḍava,
hant" âsmy eka|rathen' âdya Kuru|vṛddhaṃ pitā|maham.
paśya me vikramaṃ, rājan, mah"|Êndrasy' êva saṃyuge.
vimuñcantaṃ mah"|âstrāṇi pātayiṣyāmi taṃ rathāt.
yaḥ śatruḥ Pāṇḍu|putrāṇāṃ, mac|chatruḥ sa, na saṃśayaḥ.
mad|arthā bhavadīyā ye; ye madīyās tav' âiva te.
tava bhrātā mama sakhā, saṃbandhī, śiṣya eva ca.
māṃsāny utkṛttya dāsyāmi Phālgun'|ârthe, mahī|pate.
eṣa c' âpi nara|vyāghro mat|kṛte jīvitaṃ tyajet.
eṣa naḥ samayas, tāta: tārayema paras|param.
107.35 sa māṃ niyuṅkṣva, rāj'|êndra, yathā yoddhā bhavāmy aham.

pratijñātam Upaplavye yat tat Pārthena pūrvataḥ,
‹ghātayiṣyāmi Gāṅgeyam› iti lokasya saṃnidhau,
parirakṣyaṃ idaṃ tāvad vacaḥ Pārthasya dhīmataḥ.
anujñātaṃ tu Pārthena mayā kāryaṃ, na saṃśayaḥ;
atha vā Phālgunasy' âiṣa bhāraḥ parimito raṇe.

Having listened to that lengthy speech, Krishna replied 107.25
to Yudhi·shthira compassionately, to comfort him. "Son of Righteousness, do not give way to grief, true as you are to your word! Your enemy-slaying brothers are brave and invincible. Árjuna and Bhima·sena are as vigorous as the fire and the wind. And each of the two mighty sons of Madri is like the king of the gods. Or you can assign this task to me as your friend, and I will fight with Bhishma, Pándava. Commanded by you, what would I not accomplish in battle, great king! I will summon that bull-man Bhishma into combat and kill him while Dhrita·rashtra's troops look on,
if Phálguna doesn't want to do it himself. If you think that 107.30
victory will be certain once Bhishma is slain, Pándava, then I shall kill the old grandfather of the Kurus. You watch, Your Majesty; my vigor in battle is like that of great Indra himself. I will topple him from his chariot despite his firing mighty weapons. Whoever is an enemy of Pandu's sons is an enemy of mine too, no doubt about it. Your friends are my friends, and mine are yours. Your brother Árjuna is my friend, relative, and disciple. I would cut off and give away my own flesh for Phálguna's sake, Your Majesty. And this tiger-like man would give up his life for me. It is our agreement that we will protect one another. So command me, 107.35
king of kings, so that I may fight.

In the past, at Upaplávya, the son of Pritha made a vow in the presence of all: 'I will slay the son of Ganga!' The wise Partha's vow should be kept. If the son of Pritha will allow me, I will do it for him; have no doubt. Otherwise, it is no heavy burden for Phálguna in battle. Árjuna will kill Bhishma, that conqueror of enemy strongholds, in combat.

sa haniṣyati saṃgrāme Bhīṣmaṃ para|purañ|jayam!
a|śakyam api kuryādd hi raṇe Pārthaḥ samudyataḥ!
tri|daśān vā samudyuktān, sahitān daitya|dānavaiḥ
nihanyād Arjunaḥ saṃkhye! kim u Bhīṣmaṃ, nar'|âdhipa?
107.40 viparīto, mahā|vīryo, gata|sattvo, 'lpa|jīvanaḥ
Bhīṣmaḥ Śāntanavo nūnaṃ; kartavyaṃ n' âvabudhyate.»

YUDHIṢṬHIRA uvāca:

evam etan, mahā|bāho, yathā vadasi, Mādhava,
sarve hy ete na paryāptās tava vega|nivāraṇe.
niyataṃ samavāpsyāmi sarvam etad yath"|ēpsitam,
yasya me, puruṣa|vyāghra, bhavān pakṣe vyavasthitaḥ.
s'|Êndrān api raṇe devāñ jayeyaṃ, jayatāṃ vara,
tvayā nāthena, Govinda! kim u Bhīṣmaṃ mahā|ratham?
na tu tvām an|ṛtaṃ kartum utsahe sv'|ātma|gauravāt.
a|yudhyamānaḥ sāhāyyaṃ yath"|ôktaṃ kuru, Mādhava.
107.45 samayas tu kṛtaḥ kaś cid mama Bhīṣmeṇa saṃyuge:
«mantrayiṣye tav' ârthāya, na tu yotsye kathaṃ cana.
Duryodhan' ârthe yotsyāmi.» satyam etad iti, prabho.
sa hi rājyasya me dātā, mantrasy' âiva ca, Mādhava.
tasmād Devavrataṃ bhūyo vadh'|ôpāy'|ârtham ātmanaḥ
bhavatā sahitāḥ sarve prayāma, Madhusūdana.
tad vayaṃ sahitā gatvā Bhīṣmam āśu nar'|ôttamam
rucite tava, Vārṣṇeya, mantraṃ pṛcchāma Kauravam.
sa vakṣyati hitaṃ vākyaṃ tathyaṃ c' âiva, Janārdana;
yathā ca vakṣyate, Kṛṣṇa, tathā kart" âsmi saṃyuge.
107.50 sa no jayasya dātā ca mantrasya ca dṛḍha|vrataḥ.

Intent on fighting, the Partha could even do the impossible. He would even be able to slaughter the gods in battle, along with the *daityas* and the *dánavas*. What then of Bhishma,
king of kings? Powerful Bhishma the son of Shántanu, per- 107.40
verse, his energy gone, his life almost exhausted—well, he doesn't understand what he should do."

YUDHI·SHTHIRA said:

It is exactly as you say, mighty-armed Mádhava. Even all of them together could not bear the force of you. I will certainly obtain all that I wish for as long as you stay on my side, tiger-like man. With you as my protector, Go·vinda, champion of the victorious, I could conquer even the gods, including Indra. What then of the great warrior Bhishma? But I dare not let your words prove false, for my own self-respect. Go on giving us support without fighting, Mádhava, as you promised. An agreement was made between 107.45
Bhishma and myself. He said, "I will give you good advice in battle, but I shall by no means fight on your side. I shall fight for Duryódhana; that's the truth, my lord." He will grant me the kingdom through his counsel, Mádhava. So let all of us, including you, slayer of Madhu, go again to Deva·vrata and find out the means of his own death. Without delay, let's all quickly go together to that best of men, Bhishma the Káurava, and ask his advice, descendant of Vrishni. Truly, he will give us good counsel, Janárdana. I
will act in battle, Krishna, as he suggests. The observer of 107.50
rigid vows, he will grant us victory through his counsel.

bālāḥ pitrā vihīnāś ca tena saṃvardhitā vayam.
taṃ cet pitā|mahaṃ vṛddhaṃ hantum icchāmi, Mādhava,
pituḥ pitaram iṣṭaṃ ca: dhig astu kṣatra|jīvikām!

SAÑJAYA uvāca:

tato 'bravīn, mahā|rāja, Vārṣṇeyaḥ Kuru|nandanam:
«rocate me, mahā|prājña rāj'|êndra, tava bhāṣitam.
Devavrataḥ kṛtī Bhīṣmaḥ prekṣiten' âpi nirdahet.
gamyatāṃ sa vadh'|ôpāyaṃ praṣṭuṃ Sāgaragā|sutaḥ.
vaktum arhati satyaṃ sa tvayā pṛṣṭo viśeṣataḥ.
te vayaṃ tatra gacchāmaḥ praṣṭuṃ Kuru|pitāmaham.
107.55 gatvā Śāntanavaṃ vṛddhaṃ mantraṃ pṛcchāma, Bhārata.
sa no dāsyati yaṃ mantraṃ, tena yotsyāmahe parān.»
evaṃ āmantrya te vīrāḥ Pāṇḍavāḥ, Pāṇḍu|pūrva|ja,
jagmus te sahitāḥ sarve, Vāsudevaś ca vīryavān,
vimukta|śastra|kavacā Bhīṣmasya sadanaṃ prati.
praviśya ca tadā Bhīṣmaṃ śirobhiḥ praṇipedire.
pūjayanto, mahā|rāja, Pāṇḍavā Bharata'|rṣabham,
praṇamya śirasā c' âinaṃ Bhīṣmaṃ śaraṇam abhyayuḥ.
tān uvāca mahā|bāhur Bhīṣmaḥ Kuru|pitāmahaḥ:
«svāgataṃ tava, Vārṣṇeya! svāgataṃ te, Dhanañjaya!
107.60 svāgataṃ Dharma|putrāya, Bhīmāya, yamayos tathā!
kiṃ vā kāryaṃ karomy adya yuṣmākaṃ prīti|vardhanam?
sarv'|ātman" âpi kart" âsmi, yad api syāt su|duṣ|karam.»

When we lost our father as little children, it was Bhishma who brought us up. Damn the life of a warrior, Mádhava, since I wish to slay the venerable grandfather, who is our father's father and so dear to us!

SÁNJAYA said:

Then, great king, the descendant of Vrishni spoke to that delight of the Kurus.

"O wise king of kings, I like what you have said. Accomplished in warfare, Deva·vrata Bhishma can burn the enemy down with a mere glance. We should go to the son of the River Ganga and ask him about the means of his death. He must tell you the truth, especially if you ask him yourself. So let's go there and question the Kuru grandfather.
Coming to the elderly son of Shántanu, we shall seek his ad- 107.55
vice, descendant of Bharata. And following his counsel, we shall fight with our enemies." And having reached this conclusion, elder brother of Pandu, all of Pandu's heroic sons, accompanied by vigorous Vásu·deva, left their weapons behind and went to Bhishma's tent. Entering it, they bowed low before him. Honoring that bull-like man and bowing their heads to him, great king, they sought Bhishma's protection. Strong-armed Bhishma, the grandfather of the Kurus, addressed them.

"Welcome, descendant of Vrishni! Welcome, Dhanan·
jaya! Welcome, Son of Righteousness, Bhima, and the twins! 107.60
What can I do for you, to bring you joy? I will do it for you by all means, even if it is extremely difficult to accomplish."

tathā bruvāṇaṃ Gāṅgeyaṃ prīti|yuktaṃ punaḥ punaḥ
uvāca rājā dīn'|ātmā prīti|yuktam idaṃ vacaḥ:
«kathaṃ jayema, sarva|jña? kathaṃ rājyaṃ labhemahi?
prajānāṃ saṃkṣayo na syāt kathaṃ? tan me vada, prabho.
bhavān hi no vadh'|ôpāyaṃ bravītu svayam ātmanaḥ.
bhavantaṃ samare, rājan, viṣahema kathaṃ vayam?
na hi te sūkṣmam apy asti randhraṃ, Kuru|pitāmaha.
107.65 maṇḍalen' âiva dhanuṣā dṛśyase saṃyuge sadā;
ādadānaṃ, saṃdadhānaṃ, vikarṣantaṃ dhanur na ca
paśyāmas tvāṃ, mahā|bāho, rathe sūryam iv' âparam.
rath'|âśva|nara|nāgānāṃ hantāraṃ, para|vīra|han,
ko 'tha v" ôtsahate jetuṃ tvāṃ pumān, Bharata'|rṣabha?
varṣatā śara|varṣāṇi saṃyuge vaiśasaṃ kṛtam;
kṣayaṃ nītā hi pṛtanā bhavatā mahatī mama.
yathā yudhi jayema tvāṃ, yathā rājyaṃ bhaven mama,
mama sainyasya ca kṣemaṃ—tan me brūhi, pitā|maha.»
tato 'bravīc Chāntanavaḥ Pāṇḍavān, Pāṇḍu|pūrva|ja:
107.70 «na kathaṃ cana, Kaunteya, mayi jīvati saṃyuge
jayo bhavati, sarva|jña. satyam etad bravīmi vaḥ.
nirjite mayi yuddhe tu rane jeṣyatha, Pāṇḍavāḥ.
kṣipraṃ mayi praharadhvaṃ, yad' îcchatha raṇe jayam.
anujānāmi vaḥ, Pārthāḥ. praharadhvaṃ yathā|sukham.
evaṃ hi su|kṛtaṃ manye; bhavatāṃ vidito hy aham.
hate mayi hataṃ sarvaṃ. tasmād evaṃ vidhīyatām.»

And addressing the son of Ganga, who repeatedly spoke to them in such a friendly way, the dejected king said to him with fondness:

"All-knowing sir! How can we win? How can we obtain our kingdom? How can this extermination of creatures be prevented? Tell me that, lord. Tell us yourself about the means of your own death. How can we withstand you in combat, hero? There is not even the slightest weakness in
you, Kuru grandfather. You are always seen in battle with 107.65
your bow drawn into a circle. We can never see you taking your arrows, setting them, or drawing the bow. O mighty-armed slayer of enemy heroes, when you stand on your chariot and kill warriors, horses, and elephants, you look like another sun. Who would venture to defeat you, bull of the Bharatas? You have carried out a massacre by pouring rainstorms of arrows in combat. And my mighty army has been destroyed in this battle. How can we conquer you in battle? How can I gain the kingdom? How can my troops be safe? Tell me that, grandfather."

Then the son of Shántanu spoke to the Pándavas, younger
brother of Pandu. "O all-knowing son of Kunti, as long as 107.70
I am alive, you will not be able to win the victory. What I say to you is true. But after I am defeated in combat, you, the Pándavas, will surely be victorious in battle. Strike me down without delay, if you want victory in this war. I allow you, the sons of Pritha, to smite me down as you please; I consider it a good deed, you understand me. After I am slain, all the rest will be slain. So do as I say."

YUDHIṢṬHIRA uvāca:

brūhi tasmād upāyaṃ no, yathā yuddhe jayemahi
bhavantaṃ samare kruddhaṃ, daṇḍa|pāṇim iv' Ântakam.
śakyo vajra|dharo jetuṃ, Varuṇo, 'tha Yamas tathā;
107.75 na bhavān samare śakyaḥ s'|Êndrair api sur'|âsuraiḥ.

BHĪṢMA uvāca:

satyam etan, mahā|bāho, yathā vadasi, Pāṇḍava.
n' âhaṃ śakyo raṇe jetuṃ s'|Êndrair api sur'|âsuraiḥ
ātta|śastro, raṇe yatto, gṛhīta|vara|kārmukaḥ.
tato māṃ nyasta|śastraṃ tu ete hanyur mahā|rathāḥ.
nikṣipta|śastre, patite, vimukta|kavaca|dhvaje,
dravamāṇe ca, bhīte ca, «tav' âsm'» îti ca vādini,
striyām, strī|nāma|dheye ca, vikale c', âika|putrake,
a|praśaste nare c' âiva na yuddhaṃ rocate mama.
imaṃ me śṛṇu, rāj'|êndra, saṃkalpaṃ pūrva|cintitam.
107.80 a|maṅgalya|dhvajaṃ dṛṣṭvā na yudhyeyaṃ kathaṃ cana.
ya eṣa Draupado, rājaṃs, tava sainye mahā|rathaḥ
Śikhaṇḍī samar'|â|marṣī śūraś ca samitiñ|jayaḥ,
yath" âbhavac ca strī pūrvaṃ; paścāt puṃstvam samāgataḥ.
jānanti ca bhavanto 'pi sarvam etad yathā|tatham.
Arjunaḥ samare śūraḥ puras|kṛtya Śikhaṇḍinam
mām eva viśikhais tīkṣṇair abhidravatu daṃśitaḥ.
a|maṅgalya|dhvaje tasmin, strī|pūrve ca viśeṣataḥ,
na prahartum abhīpsāmi gṛhīt'|êṣuḥ kathaṃ cana.

YUDHI·SHTHIRA said:

Then tell us the means by which we can conquer you in combat, furious as you are in battle, like Death with his staff in hand. Thunderbolt-wielding Indra, Váruna, and Yama can be defeated in a fight; but you could never be van- 107.75
quished in battle even by the gods and demons combined, led by Indra himself.

BHISHMA said:

O mighty-armed Pándava, what you say is true. Armed with weapons, intent on fighting, and wielding my excellent bow, I could never be vanquished in battle even by the gods and demons combined, led by Indra himself. But if I lay aside my arms, these great warriors will be able to kill me. I do not like to fight with one who has cast aside his arms, who is fallen, whose armor and banner are shattered, who is fleeing, who is frightened, who says "I am yours," who is female, who bears a female name, who is disabled, who has only one son, or who is vile.

O king of kings, listen to the resolution I made in the past. I will never fight if I see any inauspicious sign. Drú- 107.80
pada's son Shikhándin, Your Majesty, the mighty warrior who fights in your ranks, and who is wrathful, brave, and victorious in combat, was once a female, and only later attained manhood. You all know how it happened. Let valiant Árjuna, clad in armor, place Shikhándin before him and assault me in battle with sharp arrows. Seeing an inauspicious sign, especially in the form of a man who used to be female, I will not strike, even if I am armed with arrows.

tad antaraṃ samāsādya Pāṇḍavo māṃ Dhanañjayaḥ
107.85 śarair ghātayatu kṣipraṃ samantād, Bharata'|rṣabha.
na taṃ paśyāmi lokeṣu yo māṃ hanyāt samudyatam,
ṛte Kṛṣṇān mahā|bhāgāt, Pāṇḍavād vā Dhanañjayāt.
eṣa tasmāt puro|dhāya kaṃ cid anyaṃ mam' âgrataḥ
ātta|śastro, raṇe yatto, gṛhīta|vara|kārmukaḥ
māṃ pātayatu Bībhatsur. evaṃ tava jayo dhruvam.
etat kuruṣva, Kaunteya, yath"|ôktaṃ mama, su|vrata.
saṃgrāme Dhārtarāṣṭrāṃś ca hanyāḥ sarvān samāgatān.

SAÑJAYA uvāca:

te tu jñātvā tataḥ Pārthā jagmuḥ sva|śibiraṃ prati,
abhivādya mah"|ātmānaṃ Bhīṣmaṃ Kuru|pitāmaham.
107.90 tath" ôktavati Gāṅgeye para|lokāya dīkṣite
Arjuno duḥkha|saṃtaptaḥ sa|vrīḍam idam abravīt:
«guruṇā, kula|vṛddhena, kṛta|prajñena, dhīmatā
pitā|mahena saṃgrāme kathaṃ yotsyāmi, Mādhava?
krīḍatā hi mayā bālye, Vāsudeva, mahā|manāḥ
pāṃsu|rūṣita|gātreṇa mah"|ātmā paruṣī|kṛtaḥ,
yasy' âham adhiruhy' âṅkaṃ bālaḥ kila, Gad'|âgra|ja,
‹tāt'!› êty avocaṃ pitaraṃ pituḥ Pāṇḍor mah"|ātmanaḥ,
‹n' âhaṃ tātas tava; pitus tāto 'smi tava, Bhārata›
iti mām abravīd bālye yaḥ, sa vadhyaḥ kathaṃ mayā?
107.95 kāmaṃ vadhyatu sainyaṃ me;
n' âhaṃ yotsye mah"|ātmanā;
jayo v" âstu vadho vā me!
kathaṃ vā, Kṛṣṇa, manyase?»

Taking his opportunity, Dhanan·jaya Pándava should 107.85
quickly shoot me all over with his arrows, bull of the Bharatas. In the three worlds I see no one who would be able to kill me when I rise up for battle, except glorious Krishna and Dhanan·jaya the Pándava. Let Bibhátsu, intent on the fight, armed with weapons and wielding his supreme bow, strike me down. Then your victory is certain. Do as I say, virtuous son of Kunti. Then you will be able to smash all of the Dharta·rashtras combined in the battle.

SÁNJAYA said:

Having learned this, the Parthas honored great-spirited Bhishma the grandfather of the Kurus, and headed toward
their camp. But after the son of Ganga had spoken as he 107.90
had, prepared to leave for the other world, Árjuna, tormented by suffering, said in shame:

"How shall I fight against the revered teacher in battle, the wise and intelligent grandfather of the Kurus, Mádhava? Vásu·deva, as a child I used to soil the garments of that noble-minded and great-spirited Bhishma when, while playing, covered in dust, I would climb onto his lap, elder brother of Gada, and say to that magnanimous father of my father Pandu, 'Father!' And he would say in reply, 'I am not your father, but your father's father, Bhárata.' How can he, who used to treat me like that when I was a child,
be slain by me? Let him slaughter my troops. Whether I 107.95
face victory or death, I will not fight against great-spirited Bhishma. What do you think, Krishna?"

VĀSUDEVA uvāca:

pratijñāya vadhaṃ, Jiṣṇo, purā Bhīṣmasya saṃyuge
kṣatra|dharme sthitaḥ, Pārtha, kathaṃ n' âinaṃ haniṣyasi?
pātay' âinaṃ rathāt, Pārtha, kṣatriyaṃ yuddha|dur|madam.
n' â|hatvā yudhi Gāṅgeyaṃ vijayas te bhaviṣyati.
diṣṭam etat purā devair: gamiṣyaty Yama|kṣayam.
yad diṣṭaṃ hi purā, Pārtha, tat tathā, na tad anyathā.
na hi Bhīṣmaṃ dur|ādharṣaṃ, vyātt'|ānanam iv' Ântakam,
tvad|anyaḥ śaknuyād yoddhum, api vajra|dharaḥ svayam.
107.100 jahi Bhīṣmaṃ, mahā|bāho! śṛṇu c' êdaṃ vaco mama,
yath" ôvāca purā Śakraṃ mahā|buddhir Bṛhaspatiḥ:
‹jyāyāṃsam api cec, Chakra, guṇair api samanvitam,
ātatāyinam āmantrya hanyād ghātakam ātmanaḥ.›
śāśvato 'yaṃ sthito dharmaḥ kṣatriyāṇāṃ, Dhanañjaya:
yoddhavyaṃ, rakṣitavyaṃ ca, yaṣṭavyaṃ c' ân|asūyubhiḥ.

ARJUNA uvāca:

Śikhaṇḍī nidhanaṃ, Kṛṣṇa, Bhīṣmasya bhavitā dhruvam.
dṛṣṭv" âiva hi sadā Bhīṣmaḥ Pāñcālyaṃ vinivartate.
te vayaṃ pramukhe tasya puras|kṛtya Śikhaṇḍinam
Gāṅgeyaṃ pātayiṣyāma upāyen', êti me matiḥ.
107.105 aham anyān mah"|êṣv|āsān vārayiṣyāmi sāyakaiḥ.
Śikhaṇḍy api yudhāṃ śreṣṭho Bhīṣmam ev' âbhiyodhayet.
śrutaṃ te Kuru|mukhyasya,
«n' âhaṃ hanyāṃ Śikhaṇḍinam.
kanyā hy eṣā purā bhūtvā
puruṣaḥ samapadyata.»

KRISHNA said:

O Pritha's son Jishnu, having formerly sworn to slay Bhishma in combat, how can you now refrain from killing him without violating the warrior code? Topple that warrior, ferocious in battle, from his chariot. If you do not strike down the son of Ganga in battle, you will not be victorious. It has been foreseen by the gods that he will go to Yama's realm. And whatever is foreseen, Partha, is as it is and not otherwise. No one except you would be able to battle with unconquerable Bhishma, who is like Death with his mouth gaping; not even thunderbolt-wielding Indra himself. Be firm, and kill Bhishma! Listen to my words—words 107.100
that immensely wise Brihas·pati once spoke to Indra. "One should slay even one's venerable elder, be he endowed with all virtues, if he comes intent upon killing one, Indra." This is the eternal duty of warriors, Dhanan·jaya: to fight, to protect the subjects, and to perform sacrifices without malevolence.

ÁRJUNA said:

Shikhándin is sure to become the cause of Bhishma's death; for at the sight of that prince of the Panchálas, Bhishma always desists from fighting. So I think we will strike the son of Ganga down by placing Shikhándin at our head, opposite Bhishma. I'll hold back the other mighty enemy 107.105
archers with my arrows; and Shikhándin must fight against Bhishma that best of fighters. We have heard that Kuru chief say, "I will not strike Shikhándin, for he was originally born as a girl, and became a man afterwards."

SAÑJAYA uvāca:

ity evaṃ niścayaṃ kṛtvā Pāṇḍavāḥ saha|Mādhavāḥ
anumānya mah"|ātmānaṃ prayayur hṛṣṭa|mānasāḥ;
śayanāni yathā|svāni bhejire puruṣa'|rṣabhāḥ.

SÁNJAYA said:

Having taken that decision and put their trust in the great-spirited Bhishma, those bull-like men, the Pándavas and Mádhava, went each to his own tent, rejoicing in their hearts.

108–119
DAY TEN

DHṚTARĀṢṬRA uvāca:

108.1 KATHAṂ ŚIKHAṆḌĪ Gāṅgeyam
abhyavartata saṃyuge,
Pāṇḍavāṃś ca kathaṃ Bhīṣmas?
tan mam' ācakṣva, Sañjaya.

SAÑJAYA uvāca:

tatas te Pāṇḍavāḥ sarve sūryasy' ôdayanaṃ prati
tāḍyamānāsu bherīṣu, mṛdaṅgeṣv, ānakeṣu ca,
dhmāyatsu dadhi|varṇeṣu jala|jeṣu samantataḥ,
Śikhaṇḍinaṃ puras|kṛtya niryātāḥ Pāṇḍavā yudhi
kṛtvā vyūhaṃ, mahā|rāja, sarva|śatru|nibarhaṇam.
Śikhaṇḍī sarva|sainyānām agra āsīd, viśāṃ pate.
108.5 cakra|rakṣau tatas tasya Bhīmasena|Dhanañjayau.
pṛṣṭhato Draupadeyāś ca, Saubhadraś c' âiva vīryavān,
Sātyakiś, Cekitānaś ca; teṣāṃ goptā mahā|rathaḥ
Dhṛṣṭadyumnas tataḥ paścāt Pañcālair abhirakṣitaḥ.
tato Yudhiṣṭhiro rājā yamābhyāṃ sahitaḥ prabhuḥ
prayayau siṃha|nādena nādayan, Bharata'|rṣabha.
Virāṭas tu tataḥ paścāt svena sainyena saṃvṛtaḥ,
Drupadaś ca, mahā|bāho, tataḥ paścād upādravat.
Kekayā bhrātaraḥ pañca, Dhṛṣṭaketuś ca vīryavān
jaghanaṃ pālayām āsuḥ Pāṇḍu|sainyasya, Bhārata.
108.10 evaṃ vyūhya mahā|sainyaṃ Pāṇḍavās tava vāhinīm
abhyadravanta saṃgrāme, tyaktvā jīvitam ātmanaḥ.
tath" âiva Kuravo, rājan, Bhīṣmaṃ kṛtvā mahā|ratham
agrataḥ sarva|sainyānāṃ prayayuḥ Pāṇḍavān prati.
putrais tava dur|ādharṣo rakṣitaḥ su|mahā|balaiḥ

DHRITA·RASHTRA said:

How did Shikhándin attack the son of Ganga in battle? How did Bhishma charge against the Pándavas? Tell me about it, Sánjaya. 108.1

SÁNJAYA said:

At sunrise, to the beat of kettle-drums, drums, and tabors, and with the blare of curd-colored conches resounding all around, the Pándavas advanced for battle, placing Shikhándin in the vanguard and drawing their troops into a formation that was able to destroy all enemies, great king.

Shikhándin was at the head of all the troops, lord of the people. Bhima·sena and Dhanan·jaya were to protect his 108.5
chariot's wheels. Dráupadi's sons and the vigorous son of Subhádra protected his rear. Sátyaki and Chekitána were there too; and behind them marched their protector, the great warrior Dhrishta·dyumna, protected by the Panchálas. Then came King Yudhi·shthira, that mighty lord, accompanied by his twin brothers and shouting out lion-roars, bull of the Bharatas. Behind him came Viráta, surrounded by his troops; and after him marched Drúpada, mighty-armed hero. The five Kékaya brothers and vigorous Dhrishta·ketu secured the rear of the Pándava army, descendant of Bharata. And having drawn their troops into such a forma- 108.10
tion, the Pándavas, ready to give up their lives in the battle, attacked your army. And the Kurus charged against the Pándavas, Your Majesty, placing the mighty warrior Bhishma at the head of all their troops. Protected by your immensely powerful sons, Bhishma the unconquerable son of Shántanu marched against the Pándava host. The great

prayayau Pāṇḍav'|ânīkaṃ Bhīṣmaḥ Śāntanu|nandanaḥ.
tato Droṇo mah"|êṣv|āsaḥ, putraś c' âsya mahā|balaḥ;
Bhagadattas tataḥ paścād gaj'|ânīkena saṃvṛtaḥ;
Kṛpaś ca Kṛtavarmā ca Bhagadattam anuvratau;
Kāmboja|rājo balavāṃs tataḥ paścāt Sudakṣiṇaḥ,
Māgadhaś ca Jayatsenaḥ, Saubalaś ca, Bṛhadbalaḥ.
108.15 tath" âiv' ânye mah"|êṣv|āsāḥ Suśarma|pramukhā nṛ|pāḥ
jaghanaṃ pālayām āsus tava sainyasya, Bhārata.

divase divase prāpte Bhīṣmaḥ Śāntanavo yudhi
āsurān akarod vyūhān, paiśācān, atha rākṣasān.
tataḥ pravavṛte yuddhaṃ tava teṣāṃ ca, Bhārata,
anyonyaṃ nighnatāṃ, rājan, Yama|rāṣṭra|vivardhanam.
Arjuna|pramukhāḥ Pārthāḥ puras|kṛtya Śikhaṇḍinam
Bhīṣmaṃ yuddhe 'bhyavartanta kiranto vividhāñ śarān.
tatra, Bhārata, Bhīmena pīḍitās tāvakāḥ śaraiḥ
rudhir'|âugha|pariklinnāḥ para|lokaṃ yayus tadā.
108.20 Nakulaḥ, Sahadevaś ca, Sātyakiś ca mahā|rathaḥ
tava sainyaṃ samāsādya pīḍayām āsur ojasā.

te vadhyamānāḥ samare tāvakā, Bharata'|rṣabha,
n' âśaknuvan vārayituṃ Pāṇḍavānāṃ mahad balam.
tatas tu tāvakaṃ sainyaṃ vadhyamānaṃ samantataḥ
su|samprāptaṃ daśa diśaḥ kālyamānaṃ mahā|rathaiḥ.
trātāraṃ n' âdhyagacchanta tāvakā, Bharata'|rṣabha,
vadhyamānāḥ śitair bāṇaiḥ Pāṇḍavaiḥ saha|Sṛñjayaiḥ.

archer Drona and his mighty son came after him. Behind them marched Bhaga·datta, surrounded by his elephant division. Kripa and Krita·varman followed Bhaga·datta, as did Sudákshina the powerful king of the Kambójas, the Mágadha ruler Jayat·sena, Súbala's son, and Brihad·bala. Other 108.15
great royal archers led by Susharman secured the rear of your army, descendant of Bharata.

Each day Bhishma son of Shántanu had drawn up his troops for battle using the formations of *ásuras*, *pisháchas*, or *rákshasas*. A battle then followed, Bhárata, between your troops and the enemy, and it augmented the kingdom of Yama. The Parthas, led by Árjuna, having placed Shikhándin before them, scattered various kinds of arrows and charged against Bhishma. And your troops, descendant of Bharata, shot by Bhima with his arrows and soaked in pools of blood, began to depart for the other world. Nákula, Saha· 108.20
deva, and the mighty warrior Sátyaki assaulted your army and tormented it vigorously.

As they were massacred in that conflict, bull of the Bharatas, your soldiers were unable to hold back the mighty host of the Pándavas; and your troops fled in every direction, slaughtered and crushed on all sides. Your warriors, bull of the Bharatas, afflicted by the sharp arrows of the Pándavas and the Srínjayas, could find no protector.

DHṚTARĀṢṬRA uvāca:

pīḍyamānaṃ balaṃ dṛṣṭvā Pārthair Bhīṣmaḥ parākramī
yad akārṣīd raṇe kruddhas, tan mam' ācakṣva, Sañjaya.
108.25 kathaṃ vā Pāṇḍavān yuddhe pratyudyātaḥ paran|tapaḥ
vinighnan Somakān vīras? tan mam' ācakṣva, Sañjaya.

SAÑJAYA uvāca:

ācakṣe te, mahā|rāja, yad akārṣīt pitā tava
pīḍite tava putrasya sainye Pāṇḍava|Sṛñjayaiḥ.
prahṛṣṭa|manasaḥ śūrāḥ Pāṇḍavāḥ, Pāṇḍu|pūrva|ja,
abhyavartanta nighnantas tava putrasya vāhinīm.
taṃ vināśaṃ, manuṣy'|êndra, nara|vāraṇa|vājinām
n' âmṛṣyata tadā Bhīṣmaḥ sainya|ghātaṃ raṇe paraiḥ.
sa Pāṇḍavān mah"|êṣv|āsaḥ, Pañcālāṃś c' âiva, Sṛñjayān
nārācair, vatsa|dantaiś ca, śitair añjalikais tathā
108.30 abhyavarṣata dur|dharṣas tyaktvā jīvitam ātmanaḥ.
sa Pāṇḍavānāṃ pravarān pañca, rājan, mahā|rathān
ātta|śastro raṇe yatnād vārayām āsa sāyakaiḥ.
nānā|śastr'|âstra|varṣais tān vīry'|â|marṣa|praveritaiḥ
nijaghne samare kruddho, hasty|aśvaṃ c' â|mitaṃ bahu.
rathino 'pātayad, rājan, rathebhyaḥ puruṣa'|rṣabhaḥ,
sādinaś c' âśva|pṛṣṭhebhyaḥ, pādātāṃś ca samāgatān,
gaj'|ārohān gajebhyaś ca pareṣāṃ jaya|kāriṇaḥ.
tam ekaṃ samare Bhīṣmaṃ tvaramāṇaṃ mahā|ratham
Pāṇḍavāḥ samavartanta, vajra|pāṇim iv' âsurāḥ.

DHRITA·RASHTRA said:

When he saw my troops tormented by the Parthas in such a fashion, what did mighty Bhishma do, wrathful in battle? Tell me about that, Sánjaya. Tell me, faultless one, 108.25
how that enemy-scorching hero rose up against the Pándavas and struck the Sómakas down.

SÁNJAYA said:

I'll tell you, great king, what your father did when your son's host was plagued by the Pándavas and the Sómakas. O elder brother of Pandu, the Pándava heroes, rejoicing, advanced, slaughtering your son's troops. O lord of men, Bhishma could not bear that massacre of your army's men, elephants, and horses by their foes in battle. That uncon- 108.30
querable and mighty archer, ready to give up his life, covered the Pándavas, the Panchálas, and the Srínjayas with iron shafts, calf-toothed arrows, and other whetted shafts. Wielding his weapons, Your Majesty, he strenuously repelled five of the Pándavas' most prominent and mighty warriors with his arrows in that encounter. And he harried them with rains of diverse weapons, propelled with vigor and wrath. Filled with battle-fury, he also killed numerous elephants and horses. Your Majesty, that bull-like man toppled enemy chariot warriors from their chariots, horsemen from the backs of their horses, and victorious elephant riders from their elephants; and he felled many of the foot soldiers that the enemy had assembled. The Pándavas attacked the mighty warrior Bhishma as he was whirring away on his own, just as the demons attacked the thunderbolt-wielding Indra.

108.35 Śakr'|âśani|sama|sparśān vimuñcan niśitāñ śarān
diksv adṛśyata sarvāsu ghoraṃ saṃdhārayan vapuḥ.
maṇḍalī|kṛtam ev' âsya nityaṃ dhanur adṛśyata
saṃgrāme yudhyamānasya Śakra|cāpa|nibhaṃ mahat.
tad dṛṣṭvā samare karma putrās tava, viśāṃ pate,
vismayaṃ paramaṃ gatvā pitā|maham apūjayan.
Pārthā vi|manaso bhūtvā praikṣanta pitaraṃ tava
yudhyamānaṃ raṇe śūraṃ, Vipracittim iv' âmarāḥ;
na c' âinaṃ vārayām āsur, vyātt'|ānanam iv' Ântakam.
108.40 daśame 'hani saṃprāpte rath'|ânīkaṃ Śikhaṇḍinaḥ
adahan niśitair bāṇaiḥ, kṛṣṇa|vartm" êva kānanam.

taṃ Śikhaṇḍī tribhir bāṇair abhyavidhyat stan'|ântare,
āśīviṣam iva kruddhaṃ, Kāla|sṛṣṭam iv' Ântakam.
sa ten' âtibhṛśaṃ viddhaḥ prekṣya Bhīṣmaḥ Śikhaṇḍinam
an|icchann api saṃkruddhaḥ prahasann idam abravīt:

«kāmam abhyasa vā, mā vā; na tvāṃ yotsye kathaṃ cana!
y" âiva hi tvam kṛtā Dhātrā, s" âiva hi tvaṃ Śikhaṇḍinī!»
tasya tad vacanaṃ śrutvā Śikhaṇḍī krodha|mūrchitaḥ
uvāc' âinaṃ tathā Bhīṣmaṃ sṛkkiṇī parisaṃlihan:

108.45 «jānāmi tvāṃ, mahā|bāho, kṣatriyāṇāṃ kṣayaṅ|kara.
mayā śrutaṃ ca te yuddhaṃ Jāmadagnyena vai saha.
divyaś ca te prabhāvo 'yaṃ mayā ca bahuśaḥ śrutaḥ.
jānann api prabhāvaṃ te yotsye 'dy' âhaṃ tvayā saha.
Pāṇḍavānāṃ priyaṃ kurvann, ātmanaś ca, nar'|ôttama,
adya tvā yodhayiṣyāmi raṇe, puruṣa|sattama.
dhruvaṃ ca tvā haniṣyāmi, śape satyena te 'grataḥ!

Firing sharpened arrows that crashed like Indra's thun- 108.35
derbolts, from every angle Bhishma looked as if he were assuming a fearsome form. As he battled away, his mighty bow always appeared circular, and looked like Indra's rainbow. Seeing that feat in combat, lord of the people, your sons were filled with the highest wonder and praised the grandfather. The dispirited Parthas looked at your valiant father fighting in that battle, just as the gods had looked at the demon Vipra·chitti. They could not check the demon
who was like Death with a gaping mouth. When the tenth 108.40
day of the war came, Bhishma began to scorch Shikhándin's chariot division with whetted shafts, like a fire burning up a grove.

Irate like a poisonous snake, Bhishma was like Death created by Time. Shikhándin hit him with three arrows to the center of the chest. Severely wounded by Shikhándin, Bhishma glared at him angrily, and though he didn't really want to, he said to him with a laugh:

"Whether you strike me or not, I will not fight with you, for you are the same Shikhándini as the Creator made you!" Hearing his words, Shikhándin, senseless with rage, licked the corners of his mouth and replied to Bhishma:

"I know you, strong-armed annihilator of warriors. I 108.45
have heard of the battle you waged with the son of Jamad·agni,* and I have also heard a lot about your divine powers. But though I am aware of your power, I will still fight with you today. Doing a favor to the Pándavas and to myself, I will fight with you in battle today, best and truest of men. I swear to you by the truth that I will surely slay you! Hear my words, then do what you must. Whether you strike me

etac chrutvā ca mad|vākyaṃ yat kṛtyaṃ, tat samācara.
kāmam abhyasa vā, mā vā; na me jīvan pramokṣyase.
su|dṛṣṭaḥ kriyatāṃ, Bhīṣma, loko 'yaṃ, samitiñ|jaya!»

SAÑJAYA uvāca:

108.50 evam uktvā tato Bhīṣmaṃ pañcabhir nata|parvabhiḥ
avidhyata raṇe, rājan, praṇunnaṃ vākya|sāyakaiḥ.
tasya tad vacanaṃ śrutvā Savyasācī paran|tapaḥ
«kālo 'yam» iti saṃcintya Śikhaṇḍinam acodayat:
«ahaṃ tvām anuyāsyāmi parān vidrāvayañ śaraiḥ.
abhidrava su|saṃrabdho Bhīṣmaṃ bhīma|parākramam.
na hi te saṃyuge pīḍāṃ śaktaḥ kartuṃ mahā|balaḥ.
tasmād adya, mahā|bāho, yatnād Bhīṣmam abhidrava.
a|hatvā samare Bhīṣmaṃ yadi yāsyasi, māriṣa,
avahāsyo 'sya lokasya bhaviṣyasi mayā saha.
108.55 n' âvahāsyā yathā, vīra, bhavema param'|āhave,
tathā kuru raṇe yatnaṃ; sādhayasva pitā|maham.
ahaṃ te rakṣaṇaṃ yuddhe kariṣyāmi, mahā|bala.
vārayan rathinaḥ sarvān sādhayasva pitā|maham.
Droṇaṃ ca, Droṇa|putraṃ ca,
Kṛpaṃ c', âtha Suyodhanam,
Citrasenaṃ, Vikarṇaṃ ca,
Saindhavaṃ ca Jayadratham,
Vind'|Ânuvindāv Āvantyau, Kāmbojaṃ ca Sudakṣiṇam,
Bhagadattaṃ tathā śūraṃ, Māgadhaṃ ca mahā|balam,
Saumadattiṃ tathā śūram, Ārṣyaśṛṅgiṃ ca rākṣasam,
Trigarta|rājaṃ ca raṇe saha sarvair mahā|rathaiḥ
aham āvārayiṣyāmi, vel" êva makar'|ālayam.
108.60 Kurūṃś ca sahitān sarvān yudhyamānān mahā|balān
nivārayiṣyāmi raṇe. sādhayasva pitā|maham.

or not, you shall not escape me with your life. Bhishma ever victorious in battle! Take a good look at this world!"

SÁNJAYA said:

Saying this, he struck Bhishma—who was already af- 108.50
flicted by the shafts of his enemy's words, Your Majesty—with five straight arrows. And hearing those words, the great warrior Savya·sachin, thinking the time to be right, urged Shikhándin on. "I shall follow you, routing the foe with my arrows. Work yourself up into a rage and attack Bhishma, whose power is awesome. Though immensely powerful, Bhishma cannot do you any harm in battle. So, mighty-armed hero, attack Bhishma, and spare no effort. If you return without killing Bhishma in this encounter, you, sir, along with me, will make yourself an object of the world's
derision. O hero, make every effort to slay the grandfather 108.55
in combat, so that we may not be held up for ridicule in this supreme battle.

I will protect you during this fight, powerful hero, by repelling all the chariot warriors. Slay the grandfather! I will restrain Drona, Drona's son, Kripa, Suyódhana, Chitra·sena, Vikárna, Jayad·ratha the king of the Sindhus, Vinda and Anuvínda of Avánti, Sudákshina the ruler of the Kambójas, valiant Bhaga·datta, the mighty king of the Mágadhas, the heroic son of Soma·datta, the demon Alámbusha 108.60
son of Rishya·shringa, and the king of the Tri·gartas along with all his great warriors, like a shore restraining the ocean. I will check the mighty Kurus and all those who are fighting against us in this battle. Just slay the grandfather!"

DHṚTARĀṢṬRA uvāca:

109.1 KATHAṂ ŚIKHAṆḌĪ Gāṅgeyam abhyadhāvat pitā|maham
Pāñcālyaḥ samare kruddho dharm'|ātmānaṃ yata|vratam?
ke 'rakṣan Pāṇḍav'|ānīke Śikhaṇḍinam ud|āyudham
tvaramāṇās tvarā|kāle jigīṣanto mahā|rathāḥ?
kathaṃ Śāntanavo Bhīṣmaḥ sa tasmin daśame 'hani
ayudhyata mahā|vīryaḥ Pāṇḍavaiḥ saha|Sṛñjayaiḥ?
na mṛṣyāmi raṇe Bhīṣmaṃ pratyudyātaṃ Śikhaṇḍinā.
kac cin na ratha|bhaṅgo 'sya? dhanur v" âśīryat' âsyataḥ?

SAÑJAYA uvāca:

109.5 n' âśīryata dhanus tasya, ratha|bhaṅgo na c' âpy abhūt
yudhyamānasya saṃgrāme Bhīṣmasya, Bharata'|ṛṣabha,
nighnataḥ samare śatrūñ śaraiḥ saṃnata|parvabhiḥ.
an|eka|śata|sāhasrās tāvakānāṃ mahā|rathāḥ,
tathā danti|gaṇā, rājan, hayāś c' âiva su|sajjitāḥ
abhyavartanta yuddhāya puras|kṛtya Pitāmaham.
yathā|pratijñaṃ, Kauravya, sa c' âpi samitiñ|jayaḥ
Pārthānām akarod Bhīṣmaḥ satataṃ samiti|kṣayam.
yudhyamānaṃ mah"|êṣv|āsaṃ vinighnantaṃ parāñ śaraiḥ
Pañcālāḥ Pāṇḍavaiḥ sārdhaṃ sarve te n' âbhyavārayan.
109.10 daśame 'hani saṃprāpte tatāpa ripu|vāhinīm
kīryamāṇāṃ śitair bāṇaiḥ śataśo 'tha sahasraśaḥ.
na hi Bhīṣmaṃ mah"|êṣv|āsaṃ Pāṇḍavāḥ, Pāṇḍu|pūrva|ja,
aśaknuvan raṇe jetuṃ, pāśa|hastam iv' Ântakam.

DHRITA·RASHTRA said:

HOW DID SHIKHÁNDIN, the prince of the Panchálas, furious in combat, charge against the grandfather, the virtuous son of Ganga, rigid in his vows? Which of the great warriors in the Pándava host protected Shikhándin, brandishing their weapons and making haste in their eagerness to win now that the time for such haste had come? How did vigorous Bhishma, the son of Shántanu, fight against the Pándavas and the Srínjayas on the tenth day of the war? I cannot bear the fact of Shikhándin' onslaught against Bhishma. Did Bhishma's chariot break down? Or was his bow shattered as he was fighting? 109.1

SÁNJAYA said:

While Bhishma was fighting in battle, striking down the enemies with straight arrows in that engagement, his bow did not get shattered, and nor did his chariot break down, bull of the Bharatas. Several hundred thousand of your great warriors as well as hosts of well-equipped elephants and horses, Your Majesty, rushed into the battle, placing Bhishma at their head. In accord with his vow, descendant of Kuru, Bhishma, ever victorious in combat, continued to destroy the Parthas' troops without a break. The Panchálas and the Pándavas were unable to resist that great archer with their combined efforts as he battled on, slaughtering 109.5
foes with his arrows. When the tenth day of the war came, 109.10
Bhishma began to scorch the enemy host, scattering hundreds and thousands of sharp arrows. O elder brother of Pandu, the Pándavas could not defeat Bhishma in battle, that mighty archer who was like noose-bearing Death.

ath' ôpāyān, mahā|rāja, Savyasācī paran|tapaḥ
trāsayan rathinaḥ sarvān Bībhatsur a|parājitaḥ
siṃhavad vinadann uccair, dhanur|jyāṃ vikṣipan muhuḥ,
śar'|âughān visṛjan Pārtho vyacarat Kālavad raṇe.
tasya śabdena vitrastās tāvakā, Bharata'|rṣabha,
siṃhasy' êva mṛgā, rājan, vyadravanta mahā|bhayāt.
109.15 jayantaṃ Pāṇḍavaṃ dṛṣṭvā, tvat|sainyaṃ c' âbhipīḍitam,
Duryodhanas tato Bhīṣmam abravīd bhṛśa|pīḍitaḥ:
«eṣa Pāṇḍu|sutas, tāta, śvet'|âśvaḥ kṛṣṇa|sārathiḥ
dahate māmakān sarvān, kṛṣṇa|vartm" êva kānanam.
paśya sainyāni, Gāṅgeya, dravamāṇāni sarvaśaḥ
Pāṇḍavena, yudhāṃ śreṣṭha, kālyamānāni saṃyuge.
yathā paśu|gaṇān pālaḥ saṃkālayati kānane,
tath" êdaṃ māmakaṃ sainyaṃ kālyate, śatru|tāpana.
Dhanañjaya|śarair bhagnaṃ dravamāṇam itas tataḥ
Bhīmo py eṣa dur|ādharṣo vidrāvayati me balam.
109.20 Sātyakiś, Cekitānaś ca, Mādrī|putrau ca Pāṇḍavau,
Abhimanyuḥ su|vikrānto vāhinīṃ dahate mama.
Dhṛṣṭadyumnas tathā śūro, rākṣasaś ca Ghaṭotkacaḥ
vyadrāvayetāṃ sahasā sainyaṃ mama mahā|balau.
vadhyamānasya sainyasya sarvair etair mahā|rathaiḥ
n' ânyāṃ gatiṃ prapaśyāmi sthāne yuddhe ca, Bhārata,
ṛte tvāṃ, puruṣa|vyāghra deva|tulya|parākrama.
paryāptas tu bhavāñ śīghraṃ pīḍitānāṃ gatir bhava.»

Then the undefeated Árjuna—also known as Dhanan·jaya, Savya·sachin, and Bibhátsu, great king—charged forward, striking terror into all the chariot warriors. The son of Pritha began to rampage in battle like Death himself, roaring loudly like a lion, stretching his bowstring and firing hordes of arrows over and over again. Horrified by his war-cries, Your Majesty, your combatants fled in great fear, like deer scared by the roar of a lion, bull of the Bharatas.
Seeing the Pándava in the ascendant and your troops being 109.15
hard pressed by him, Duryódhana, deeply distressed by it, spoke to Bhishma.

"Sir, this son of Pandu with his white horses and dark charioteer* is incinerating all my troops like a fire burning up a forest. Look, son of Ganga, best of warriors: my troops are being routed and crushed by the son of Pandu in this fight. He pummels my host just as a herdsman whips his herds, scorcher of enemies. And unconquerable Bhima is driving away my fleeing army that has already been broken by Dhanan·jaya's arrows. Sátyaki, Chekitána, the two 109.20
Pándava sons of Madri, and vigorous Abhimányu are also scorching my host. Valiant Dhrishta·dyumna and the demon Ghatótkacha have just routed my troops in this huge battle. O descendant of Bharata, I see no refuge for my army, to rally it and keep it in play as it is being massacred by all these great warriors, other than you, tiger-like man, endowed with the power of a god! You're capable of it, so hurry up and rally our tormented troops."

evam ukto, mahā|rāja, pitā Devavratas tava
cintayitvā muhūrtaṃ tu, kṛtvā niścayam ātmanaḥ,
109.25 tava saṃdhārayan putram abravīc Chāntanoḥ sutaḥ:
«Duryodhana, vijānīhi sthiro bhūtvā, viśāṃ pate.
pūrva|kālaṃ tava mayā pratijñātaṃ, mahā|bala:
«hatvā daśa|sahasrāṇi kṣatriyāṇāṃ mah"|ātmanām
saṃgrāmād vyapayātavyam. etat karma mam' āhnikam.»
iti tat kṛtavāṃś c' âhaṃ yath" ôktaṃ, Bharata'|rṣabha.
adya c' âpi mahat karma prakariṣye mah"|āhave:
ahaṃ v" âdya hataḥ śeṣye, haniṣye v" âdya Pāṇḍavān.
adya te, puruṣa|vyāghra, pratimokṣye ṛṇaṃ tava
bhartṛ|piṇḍa|kṛtaṃ, rājan, nihataḥ pṛtanā|mukhe.»
109.30 ity uktvā, Bharata|śreṣṭha, kṣatriyān pratapañ śaraiḥ
āsasāda dur|ādharṣaḥ Pāṇḍavānām anīkinīm.
anīka|madhye tiṣṭhantaṃ Gāṅgeyaṃ, Bharata'|rṣabha,
āśīviṣam iva kruddhaṃ Pāṇḍavāḥ paryavārayan.
daśame 'hani Bhīṣmas tu darśayañ śaktim ātmanaḥ,
rājañ, śata|sahasrāṇi so 'vadhīt, Kuru|nandana.
Pañcālānāṃ ca ye śreṣṭhā rāja|putrā mahā|rathāḥ,
teṣām ādatta tejāṃsi, jalaṃ sūrya iv' âṃśubhiḥ.
hatvā daśa sahasrāṇi kuñjarāṇāṃ tarasvinām
s'|ārohāṇāṃ, mahā|rāja, hayānāṃ c' âyutaṃ tathā,
109.35 pūrṇe śata|sahasre dve pādātānāṃ nar'|ôttamaḥ,
prajajvāla raṇe Bhīṣmo vi|dhūma iva pāvakaḥ.
na c' âinaṃ Pāṇḍaveyānāṃ ke cic chekur nirīkṣitum,
uttaraṃ mārgam āsthāya tapantam iva bhās|karam.
te Pāṇḍaveyāḥ saṃrabdhā mah"|êṣv|āsena pīḍitāḥ

Addressed in this way, great king, your father Deva·vrata
thought for a while and made a decision. Then the son of 109.25
Shántanu spoke to the king and encouraged him.

"O Duryódhana, lord of the people, hold firm and try
to understand. Formerly, powerful hero, I vowed to you
that I would desist from battle each day after having killed
ten thousand great-spirited warriors. So far I have kept my
promise; but today I will accomplish a great feat, mighty
hero. Today I will either lie down, slain, or I will slaughter the Pándavas. O tiger-like man, Your Majesty! Slain in
combat, today I will pay the debt I owe you for eating your
food."

And having said this, best of the Bharatas, that uncon- 109.30
querable hero assailed the army of the Pándavas, scattering
arrows and hitting enemy warriors with them. O bull of the
Bharatas, the Pándavas tried to repulse Ganga's furious son,
who was stationed amid his troops like a poisonous snake.
But on the tenth day of the war, Your Majesty, Bhishma,
displaying his might, slaughtered hundreds of thousands of
warriors, delight of the Kurus. And he stripped the Panchála
princes—those supreme warriors—of their energy, just as
the sun evaporates water by means of its rays.

He killed ten thousand swift elephants, ten thousand
horses along with their riders, and also two hundred thou- 109.35
sand foot soldiers; Bhishma, supreme among men, blazed
in battle like a smokeless fire. And not one of the Pándavas'
warriors could look at him, scorching as he was, like the sun
at the summer solstice. Tormented by that mighty archer,
the enraged Pándavas charged against Bhishma, trying to
kill him; and so did the great Srínjaya warriors. Bhishma

vadhāy' âbhyadravan Bhīṣmaṃ Sṛñjayāś ca mahā|rathāḥ.
sa yudhyamāno bahubhir Bhīṣmaḥ Śāntanavas tadā
avakīrṇo, mahā|Meruḥ śailo meghair iv' āvṛtaḥ.
putrās tu tava Gāṅgeyaṃ samantāt paryavārayan
mahatyā senayā sārdhaṃ. tato yuddham avartata.

SAÑJAYA uvāca:

110.1 ARJUNAS TU RAṆE, rājan, dṛṣṭvā Bhīṣmasya vikramam
Śikhaṇḍinam ath' ôvāca: «samabhyehi pitā|maham.
na c' âpi bhīs tvayā kāryā Bhīṣmād adya kathaṃ cana.
aham enaṃ śarais tīkṣṇaiḥ pātayiṣye rath'|ôttamāt.»
evam uktas tu Pārthena Śikhaṇḍī, Bharata'|rṣabha,
abhyadravata Gāṅgeyaṃ śrutvā Pārthasya bhāṣitam.
Dhṛṣṭadyumnas tathā, rājan, Saubhadraś ca mahā|rathaḥ
hṛṣṭāv ādravatāṃ Bhīṣmaṃ śrutvā Pārthasya bhāṣitam.
110.5 Virāṭa|Drupadau vṛddhau, Kuntibhojaś ca daṃśitaḥ
abhyadravanta Gāṅgeyaṃ putrasya tava paśyataḥ.
Nakulaḥ, Sahadevaś ca, Dharma|rājaś ca vīryavān,
tath" êtarāṇi sainyāni sarvāṇy eva, viśāṃ pate,
samādravanta Gāṅgeyaṃ śrutvā Pārthasya bhāṣitam.
pratyudyayus tāvakāś ca sametās tān mahā|rathān
yathā|śakti, yath"|ôtsāhaṃ. tan me nigadataḥ śṛṇu.

Citraseno, mahā|rāja, Cekitānaṃ samabhyayāt
Bhīṣma|prepsuṃ raṇe yāntaṃ, vṛṣaṃ vyāghra|śiśur yathā.
Dhṛṣṭadyumnaṃ, mahā|rāja, Bhīṣm'|ântikam upāgatam
110.10 tvaramāṇaṃ raṇe yattaṃ Kṛtavarmā nyavārayat.
Bhīmasenaṃ su|saṃkruddhaṃ Gāṅgeyasya vadh'|âiṣiṇam
tvaramāṇo, mahā|rāja, Saumadattir nyavārayat.

the son of Shántanu, battling against many, was shrouded by them just as great Mount Meru is covered by clouds. Your sons, supported by a large host, surrounded the son of Ganga on every side. Then a battle ensued!

SÁNJAYA said:

ÁRJUNA, YOUR MAJESTY, seeing Bhishma's vigor in that 110.1
battle, said to Shikhándin: "Attack the grandfather! You must have no fear of Bhishma today! I will topple him from his superb chariot with my sharp arrows." Addressed by the son of Pritha in this way, bull of the Bharatas, Shikhándin listened to the Partha's words, and then he charged against the son of Ganga. And Dhrishta·dyumna and Subhádra's mighty warrior son, delighted by what they had heard the
Partha say, assailed Bhishma, Your Majesty. The two el- 110.5
derly warriors Viráta and Drúpada, and Kunti·bhoja clad in armor, advanced against the son of Ganga under your son's very eyes. Nákula, Saha·deva, the vigorous King of Righteousness, and all the other combatants, lord of the people, charged against the son of Ganga when they heard the Partha's words. And your troops rose up against those united great enemy warriors, striving to the best of their power and enthusiasm. Listen to my report.

As a tiger cub attacks a bull, great king, so did Chitra·
sena attack Chekitána, who was advancing against Bhishma 110.10
in the fray. Krita·varman restrained Dhrishta·dyumna who, intent on combat, had quickly come close to Bhishma, great king. Without a moment's delay, the son of Soma·datta held Bhima·sena back—he was filled with violent rage and eager to slay the son of Ganga. Wanting to protect

tath" âiva Nakulam̄ vīram̄ kirantam̄ sāyakān bahūn
Vikarṇo vārayām āsa, icchan Bhīṣmasya jīvitam.
Sahadevam̄ tathā yāntam̄ yattam̄ Bhīṣma|ratham̄ prati
vārayām āsa saṃkruddhaḥ Kṛpaḥ Śāradvato yudhi.
rākṣasam̄ krūra|karmāṇam̄ Bhaimasenim̄ mahā|balam
Bhīṣmasya nidhanam̄ prepsum̄
Durmukho 'bhyadravad balī.
Sātyakim̄ samare yāntam
Ārṣyaśṛṅgir avārayat.
110.15 Abhimanyum̄, mahā|rāja, yāntam̄ Bhīṣma|ratham̄ prati
Sudakṣiṇo, mahā|rāja, Kāmbojaḥ pratyavārayat.
Virāṭa|Drupadau vṛddhau sametāv ari|mardanau
Aśvatthāmā tataḥ kruddho vārayām āsa, Bhārata.
tathā Pāṇḍu|sutam̄ jyeṣṭham̄ Bhīṣmasya vadha|kāṅkṣiṇam
Bhāradvājo raṇe yatto Dharma|putram avārayat.
Arjunam̄ rabhasam̄ yuddhe puras|kṛtya Śikhaṇḍinam
Bhīṣma|prepsum̄, mahā|rāja, bhāsayantam̄ diśo daśa
Duḥśāsano mah"|êṣv|āso vārayām āsa saṃyuge.
anye ca tāvakā yodhāḥ Pāṇḍavānām̄ mahā|rathān
110.20 Bhīṣmasy' âbhimukham̄ yātān vārayām āsur āhave.
Dhṛṣṭadyumnas tu sainyāni prākrośata punaḥ punaḥ:
«abhidravata saṃrabdhā Bhīṣmam ekam̄ mahā|balam!
eṣo 'rjuno raṇe Bhīṣmam̄ prayāti Kuru|nandanaḥ!
abhidravata! mā bhaiṣṭa! Bhīṣmo hi prāpsyate na vaḥ!
Arjunam̄ samare yoddhum̄ n' ôtsahet' âpi Vāsavaḥ!
kim u Bhīṣmo raṇe, vīrā, gata|sattvo, 'lpa|jīvitaḥ?»

Bhishma's life, Vikárna repelled brave Nákula who was scattering numerous arrows. Wrathful Kripa, the son of Sharádvat, repulsed Saha·deva in that conflict as he was rushing toward Bhishma's chariot, Your Majesty.

Mighty Dúrmukha charged against Bhima·sena's son, the immensely powerful demon whose deeds were so cruel and who desired Bhishma's death. Your son Duryódhana checked Sátyaki as he advanced into battle. Sudákshina the 110.15
ruler of the Kambójas resisted Abhimányu, who was advancing toward Bhishma's chariot, great king. Ashva·tthaman, enraged, warded off the two elderly enemy-crushing warriors Viráta and Drúpada both at once, descendant of Bharata. The son of Bharad·vaja, intent on battle, held back the Son of Righteousness, the eldest Pándava. In that encounter the mighty archer Duhshásana repelled violent Árjuna who, keeping Shikhándin before him, was rushing forward and lighting up all ten directions, eager as he was to slay Bhishma, great king. And your other combatants
checked any of the Pándavas' warriors who had advanced 110.20
toward Bhishma in battle. Dhrishta·dyumna appealed to the troops again and again:

"Charge furiously against mighty Bhishma alone! Árjuna, the delight of the Kurus, is proceeding against Bhishma in battle! Attack, do not fear! Bhishma will not be able to strike you. Even Vásava would not venture to fight against Árjuna; what then of Bhishma, who is running out of energy and has hardly any of his life left, heroes?"

iti senā|pateḥ śrutvā Pāṇḍavānāṃ mahā|rathāḥ
abhyadravanta saṃhṛṣṭā Gāṅgeyasya rathaṃ prati.
āgacchamānān samare vāry|oghān prabalān iva
110.25 avārayanta saṃhṛṣṭās tāvakāḥ puruṣa'|rṣabhāḥ.
Duḥśāsano, mahā|rāja, bhayaṃ tyaktvā mahā|rathaḥ
Bhīṣmasya jīvit'|ākāṅkṣī Dhanañjayam upādravat.
tath" âiva Pāṇḍavāḥ śūrā Gāṅgeyasya rathaṃ prati
abhyadravanta saṃgrāme tava putrān mahā|rathāḥ.

tatr' âdbhutam apaśyāma citra|rūpaṃ, viśāṃ pate,
Duḥśāsana|rathaṃ prāpya yat Pārtho n' âtyavartata.
yathā vārayate velā kṣubdha|toyaṃ mah"|ârṇavam,
tath" âiva Pāṇḍavaṃ kruddhaṃ tava putro nyavārayat.
ubhau tau rathināṃ śreṣṭhāv, ubhau, Bhārata, dur|jayau,
110.30 ubhau candr'|ârka|sadṛśau kāntyā dīptyā ca, Bhārata.
tathā tau jāta|saṃrambhāv anyonya|vadha|kāṅkṣiṇau
samīyatur mahā|saṃkhye Maya|Śakrau yathā purā.

Duḥśāsano, mahā|rāja, Pāṇḍavaṃ viśikhais tribhiḥ,
Vāsudevaṃ ca viṃśatyā tāḍayām āsa saṃyuge.
tato 'rjuno jāta|manyur Vārṣṇeyaṃ vīkṣya pīḍitam
Duḥśāsanaṃ śaten' ājau nārācānāṃ samārpayat.
te tasya kavacaṃ bhittvā papuḥ śoṇitam āhave.
Duḥśāsanas tataḥ kruddhaḥ Pārthaṃ vivyādha pañcabhiḥ
lalāṭe, Bharata|śreṣṭha, śaraiḥ saṃnata|parvabhiḥ.
110.35 lalāṭa|sthais tu tair bāṇaiḥ śuśubhe Pāṇḍavo raṇe

When they heard the general's words, the Pándavas' great warriors cheerfully charged toward the chariot of Ganga's son. And your fighters, those bull-like men, happily restrained the enemy forces as they were advancing like hugely powerful currents of water. The mighty warrior Duhshása- 110.25
na, great king, giving up all fear and wanting to protect Bhishma's life, charged against Dhanan·jaya. And likewise the valiant and mighty Pándava warriors advanced toward Ganga's son's chariot and attacked your sons in that engagement.

Then we witnessed an incredible and wonderful feat, lord of the people: the son of Pritha, on reaching Duhshásana's chariot, failed to proceed any further. As the shore holds the surging ocean back, so your son held the furious Pándava back. Descendant of Bharata, both of them were excellent chariot warriors, both were invincible, and both resem- 110.30
bled the moon and the sun in beauty and splendor, Bhárata. Filled with rage, and desiring to slaughter each other, they confronted one another just as Shakra and the demon Maya did in the past.

O great king, in that encounter Duhshásana struck the Pándava with three shafts and Vásu·deva with twenty. Then Árjuna, excited with fury, seeing that the descendant of Vrishni had been wounded, struck Duhshásana with a hundred iron arrows in the fray; and those arrows tore through Duhshásana's armor and drank his blood on the battlefield. Enraged, Duhshásana then pierced the son of Pritha with feathered straight arrows in the forehead, descendant of Bharata; and the Pándava looked resplendent with those 110.35
arrows stuck in his forehead, great king, like Mount Meru

yathā Merur, mahā|rāja, śṛṅgair atyartham ucchritaiḥ.
so 'tividdho mah"|êṣv|āsaḥ putreṇa tava dhanvinā
vyarājata raṇe Pārthaḥ, kiṃśukaḥ puṣpavān iva.
Duḥśāsanaṃ tataḥ kruddhaḥ pīḍayām āsa Pāṇḍavaḥ,
parvaṇ' îva su|saṃkruddho Rāhur pūrṇaṃ niśā|karam.
pīḍyamāno balavatā putras tava, viśāṃ pate,
vivyādha samare Pārthaṃ kaṅka|patraiḥ śilā|śitaiḥ.
tasya Pārtho dhanuś chittvā, rathaṃ c' âsya tribhiḥ śaraiḥ,
ājaghāna tataḥ paścāt putraṃ te niśitaiḥ śaraiḥ.
110.40 so 'nyat kārmukam ādāya Bhīṣmasya pramukhe sthitaḥ
Arjunaṃ pañca|viṃśatyā bāhvor urasi c' ārpayat.
tasya kruddho, mahā|rāja, Pāṇḍavaḥ śatru|tāpanaḥ
apraiṣīd viśikhān ghorān Yama|daṇḍ'|ôpamān bahūn.
a|prāptān eva tān bāṇāṃś ciccheda tanayas tava
yatamānasya Pārthasya. tad adbhutam iv' âbhavat.
Pārthaṃ ca niśitair bāṇair avidhyat tanayas tava.
tataḥ kruddho raṇe Pārthaḥ śarān saṃdhāya kārmuke
preṣayām āsa samare svarṇa|puṅkhāñ śilā|śitān.
nyamajjaṃs te, mahā|rāja, tasya kāye mah"|ātmanaḥ,
110.45 yathā haṃsā, mahā|rāja, taḍāgaṃ prāpya, Bhārata.
pīḍitaś c' âiva putras te Pāṇḍavena mah"|ātmanā
hitvā Pārthaṃ raṇe tūrṇaṃ Bhīṣmasya ratham āvrajat.
a|gādhe majjatas tasya dvīpo Bhīṣmo 'bhavat tadā.
pratilabhya tataḥ saṃjñāṃ putras tava, viśāṃ pate,
avārayat tataḥ śūro bhūya eva parākramī
śaraiḥ su|niśitaiḥ Pārthaṃ, yathā Vṛtraḥ Purandaram.

shining with its lofty peaks. Severely wounded by your bow-wielding son, the Partha, that mighty archer, looked handsome like a blossoming *kínshuka* tree.

The furious Pándava then afflicted Duhshásana just as Rahu, filled with intense rage, afflicts the full moon during an eclipse. But your son, tormented by mighty Árjuna, wounded the Partha in that combat with stone-whetted and heron-feathered arrows, lord of the people. The son of Pritha then shattered his enemy's bow and chariot with three shafts, and struck your son with several sharpened arrows. But Duhshásana took another bow and, standing 110.40
before Bhishma, he hit Árjuna in his arms and chest with twenty-five arrows. The wrathful and enemy-scorching Pándava then fired many terrible shafts at his adversary, great king, each of them looking like the staff of Yama; but before they could reach him your son split the shafts of the Partha, who was struggling hard against him. It was like a miracle. Your son then injured the Partha with sharpened arrows. The son of Pritha, filled with battle-fury, strung several gold-nocked and stone-whetted shafts and discharged them in the contest; and they plunged into great-spirited Duhshásana's body, great king, like geese diving into a lake, 110.45
Your Majesty.

And so your son, wounded by the great-spirited Pándava, descendant of Bharata, abandoned the Partha in battle and swiftly made for Bhishma's chariot; and Bhishma then became an island for him as he was sinking in that fathomless sea. And when he came round, lord of the people, your valiant and vigorous son once again restrained the son of Pritha, just as Indra the crusher of enemy strongholds

nirbibheda mahā|kāyo; vivyathe n' âiva c' Ârjunaḥ.

SAÑJAYA uvāca:

111.1 SĀTYAKIṂ DAṂŚITAṂ yuddhe
Bhīṣmāy' âbhyudyataṃ tadā
Ārṣyaśṛṅgir mah"|êṣv|āso
vārayām āsa saṃyuge.
Mādhavas tu su|saṃkruddho rākṣasaṃ navabhiḥ śaraiḥ
ājaghāna raṇe, rājan, prahasann iva, Bhārata.
tath" âiva rākṣaso, rājan, Mādhavaṃ navabhiḥ śaraiḥ
ardayām āsa, rāj'|êndra, saṃkruddhaḥ Śini|puṅgavam.
Śaineyaḥ śara|saṅghaṃ tu preṣayām āsa saṃyuge
rākṣasāya su|saṃkruddho Mādhavaḥ para|vīra|hā.
111.5 tato rakṣo mahā|bāhuṃ Sātyakiṃ satya|vikramam
vivyādha viśikhais tīkṣṇaiḥ, siṃha|nādaṃ nanāda ca.
Mādhavas tu bhṛśaṃ viddho rākṣasena raṇe tadā,
vāryamāṇaś ca tejasvī jahāsa ca nanāda ca.
Bhagadattas tataḥ kruddho Mādhavaṃ niśitaiḥ śaraiḥ
tāḍayām āsa samare, tottrair iva mahā|gajam.
vihāya rākṣasaṃ yuddhe Śaineyo rathināṃ varaḥ
Prāgjyotiṣāya cikṣepa śarān saṃnata|parvaṇaḥ.
tasya Prāgjyotiṣo rājā Mādhavasya mahad dhanuḥ
ciccheda śita|dhāreṇa bhallena kṛta|hastavat.
111.10 ath' ânyad dhanur ādāya vegavat para|vīra|hā
Bhagadattaṃ raṇe kruddhaṃ vivyādha niśitaiḥ śaraiḥ.

restrained Vritra. But although huge-bodied Duhshásana pierced him all over, Árjuna did not waver.

SÁNJAYA said:

111.1 IN THAT ENCOUNTER the great archer son of Rishya·shringa repelled Sátyaki who, clad in armor, was charging across the battlefield toward Bhishma. Filled with intense fury, Your Majesty, the Mádhava struck the demon with nine arrows in battle, almost laughing as he did so, descendant of Bharata. And, Your Majesty, the demon also shot that Mádhava hero, the grandson of Shini, with nine arrows, king of kings. The Mádhava warrior, Shini's grandson, that slayer of enemy heroes, immensely enraged amid
111.5 the fray, discharged a swarm of arrows at the demon. Then the demon wounded Sátyaki, whose power is in truth, with sharp arrows, and roared the roar of a lion. But though he was seriously injured by the demon and had been checked by him in that play, the vigorous Mádhava laughed and let out a roar of his own.

Then Bhaga·datta lost his temper and struck the Mádhava with whetted shafts in the fight, as if he were hitting a massive elephant with goads. Leaving the demon aside, Shini's grandson, that best of chariot warriors, shot many straight arrows at the king of the Prag·jyótishas in battle. The king of the Prag·jyótishas then dexterously severed the Mádhava's mighty bow with a sharp spear-headed shaft.
111.10 But that slayer of enemy heroes quickly seized another bow and pierced Bhaga·datta, who was filled with battle-fury, with sharpened arrows.

so 'tividdho mah"|êṣv|āsaḥ sṛkkiṇī parisaṃlihan
śaktiṃ kanaka|vaiḍūrya|bhūṣitām, āyasīṃ, dṛḍhām,
Yama|daṇḍ'|ôpamāṃ, ghorāṃ cikṣepa param'|āhave.
tām āpatantīṃ sahasā tasya bāhu|bal'|ēritām
Sātyakiḥ samare, rājaṃs, tridhā ciccheda sāyakaiḥ.
tataḥ papāta sahasā, mah"|ôlk" êva hata|prabhā.
śaktiṃ vinihatāṃ dṛṣṭvā putras tava, viśāṃ pate,
mahatā ratha|vaṃśena vārayām āsa Mādhavam.
111.15 tathā parivṛtaṃ dṛṣṭvā Vārṣṇeyānāṃ mahā|ratham
Duryodhano bhṛśaṃ kruddho bhrātṝn sarvān uvāca ha:
«tathā kuruta, Kauravyā, yathā vaḥ Sātyako yudhi
na jīvan pratiniryāti mahato 'smād ratha|vrajāt.
tasmin hate hataṃ manye Pāṇḍavānāṃ mahad balam.»
«tath"!» êti ca vacas tasya parigṛhya mahā|rathāḥ
Śaineyaṃ yodhayām āsur Bhīṣmāy' âbhyudyataṃ raṇe.
Abhimanyuṃ tad" āyāntaṃ Bhīṣmāy' âbhyudyataṃ mṛdhe
Kāmboja|rājo balavān vārayām āsa saṃyuge.
Ārjunir nṛ|patiṃ viddhvā śaraiḥ saṃnata|parvabhiḥ
punar eva catuḥ|ṣaṣṭyā, rājan, vivyādha taṃ nṛ|pam.
111.20 Sudakṣiṇas tu samare Kārṣṇiṃ vivyādha pañcabhiḥ,
sārathiṃ c' âsya navabhir, icchan Bhīṣmasya jīvitam.
tad yuddham āsīt su|mahat tayos tatra samāgame,

Severely wounded, the great archer licked the corners of his mouth, and in that utterly fierce war he hurled a strong and frightful iron spear that was decorated with gold and lapis lazuli and looked like the staff of Yama. As it was flying toward him with great force, propelled by Bhaga·datta's powerful throw, Sátyaki, in his play, split the spear in two with his arrows. The spear fell forcefully to the ground, like a huge meteor deprived of its radiance. Seeing that spear cut down, lord of the people, your son cut the Mádhava off with a large column of chariots.

Then, seeing the great warrior of the Vrishnis isolated by 111.15
that host, Duryódhana, filled with a violent rage, addressed all of his brothers. "O Káuravas, strive to your utmost, so that Sátyaki may not escape with his life from our large chariot host. If he were to be killed, I would consider the entire mighty force of the Pándavas to be destroyed."

"All right!" replied the great warriors, accepting his commission; and they engaged in a fight with Shini's grandson, who was trying to get across the battlefield to Bhishma. Then the mighty king of the Kambójas restrained Abhimányu, who was also racing across the battlefield toward Bhishma. He pierced Árjuna's son Abhimányu with many straight shafts, Your Majesty, and then struck him again, with sixty-
four arrows. Willing to protect Bhishma's life in battle, 111.20
Sudákshina pierced Abhimányu with five arrows, and his driver with nine. And some extremely fierce fighting ensued in that engagement between those two warriors.

yad" âbhyadhāvad Gāṅgeyaṃ Śikhaṇḍī śatru|karṣaṇaḥ.
Virāṭa|Drupadau vṛddhau vārayantau mahā|camūm,
Bhīṣmaṃ ca yudhi saṃrabdhāv ādravantau mahā|rathau.
Aśvatthāmā tataḥ kruddhaḥ samāyād ratha|sattamaḥ.
tataḥ pravavṛte yuddhaṃ tava teṣāṃ ca, Bhārata.
Virāṭo daśabhir bhallair ājaghāna, paran|tapa,
yatamānaṃ mah"|êṣv|āsaṃ Drauṇim āhava|śobhinam.
111.25 Drupadaś ca tribhir bāṇair vivyādha niśitais tathā
guru|putraṃ samāsādya praharantau mahā|balau.
Aśvatthāmā tatas tau tu vivyādha daśabhiḥ śaraiḥ
Virāṭa|Drupadau vṛddhau, Bhīṣmaṃ prati samudyatau.
tatr' âdbhutam apaśyāma vṛddhayoś caritaṃ mahat,
yad Drauṇeḥ sāyakān ghorān pratyavārayatāṃ yudhi.
Sahadevaṃ tathā yāntaṃ Kṛpaḥ Śāradvato 'bhyayāt,
yathā nāgo vane nāgaṃ matto mattam upādravat.
Kṛpaś ca samare śūro Mādrī|putraṃ mahā|ratham
ājaghāna śarais tūrṇaṃ saptatyā rukma|bhūṣaṇaiḥ.
111.30 tasya Mādrī|sutaś cāpaṃ dvidhā ciccheda sāyakaiḥ;
ath' âinaṃ chinna|dhanvānaṃ vivyādha navabhiḥ śaraiḥ.
so 'nyat kārmukam ādāya samare bhāra|sādhanam
Mādrī|putraṃ su|saṃhṛṣṭo daśabhir niśitaiḥ śaraiḥ
ājaghān' ôrasi kruddha, icchan Bhīṣmasya jīvitam.
tath" âiva Pāṇḍavo, rājan, Śāradvatam a|marṣaṇam
ājaghān' ôrasi kruddho Bhīṣmasya vadha|kāṅkṣayā.
tayor yuddhaṃ samabhavad ghora|rūpaṃ, bhay'|āvaham.

The enemy-tormentor Shikhándin charged toward the son of Ganga. The two great elderly warriors, Viráta and Drúpada, infuriated, checked the large Káurava host and advanced to battle with Bhishma. The excellent warrior Ashva·tthaman, filled with battle-fury, opposed them. Then a fight took place between him and those two heroes. With ten spear-headed arrows Viráta struck Drona's mighty archer son, who was radiant in battle, and was exerting himself in that encounter, scorcher of enemies; and Drú- 111.25
pada pierced the teacher's son with three sharpened arrows. Attacking those two powerful combatants, Ashva·tthaman pierced both heroes, Viráta and Drúpada, who had been charging against Bhishma. And it was a wonder for us to see the great feat the two old heroes performed, as they thwarted the fierce arrows of Drona's son in battle.

Kripa, the son of Sharádvat, charged against the advancing Saha·deva, just as a maddened elephant charges against a maddened elephant in the forest. In that encounter, valiant Kripa swiftly wounded Madri's great archer son with seventy arrows that were decorated with gold. The son of 111.30
Madri then split Kripa's bow in two with his arrows, and hit the bowless hero with nine shafts. Seizing another bow that was accomplished in battle, Kripa, immensely delighted in his rage, and willing to save Bhishma's life, struck Madri's son in the chest with sharpened arrows in the fray. And the Pándava, Your Majesty, in his eagerness to kill Bhishma, struck the wrathful son of Sharádvat in the chest. And a hideous and terrifying battle ensued between the two heroes.

Nakulaṃ tu raṇe kruddhaṃ Vikarṇaḥ śatru|tāpanaḥ
vivyādha sāyakaiḥ ṣaṣṭyā, rakṣan Bhīṣmaṃ mahā|balam.

111.35 Nakulo 'pi bhṛśaṃ viddhas tava putreṇa dhanvinā,
Vikarṇaṃ sapta|saptatyā nirbibheda śilīmukhaiḥ.
tatra tau nara|śārdūlau Bhīṣma|hetoḥ paran|tapau
anyonyaṃ jaghnatur vīrau, goṣṭhe go|vṛṣabhāv iva.

Ghaṭotkacaṃ raṇe yāntaṃ nighnantaṃ tava vāhinīm
Durmukhaḥ samare prāyād Bhīṣma|hetoḥ parākramī.
Haiḍimbas tu tato, rājan, Durmukhaṃ śatru|tāpanam
ājaghān' ôrasi kruddhaḥ śareṇ' ānata|parvaṇā.
Bhīmasena|sutaṃ c' âpi Durmukhaḥ su|mukhaiḥ śaraiḥ
ṣaṣṭyā vīro nadan hṛṣṭo vivyādha raṇa|mūrdhani.

111.40 Dhṛṣṭadyumnaṃ tathā yāntaṃ
Bhīṣmasya vadha|kāṅkṣiṇam
Hārdikyo vārayām āsa
ratha|śreṣṭhaṃ mahā|rathaḥ.
Ājaghāna mahā|bāhuḥ Pārṣataṃ taṃ mahā|ratham.
punaḥ pañcāśatā tūrṇam, «tiṣṭha! tiṣṭh'!» êti c' âbravīt.
Hārdikyaḥ Pārṣataṃ c' âpi viddhvā pañcabhir āyasaiḥ
taṃ c' âiva Pārṣato, rājan, Hārdikyaṃ navabhiḥ śaraiḥ
vivyādha niśitais tīkṣṇaiḥ kaṅka|patrair a|jihma|gaiḥ.
tayoḥ samabhavad yuddhaṃ Bhīṣma|hetor mahā|raṇe
anyony'|âtiśaye yuktaṃ, yathā Vṛtra|mah"|Êndrayoḥ.
Bhīmasenam tath" āyāntaṃ Bhīṣmaṃ prati mahā|balam

Enemy-scorching Vikárna, filled with battle-fury, busy protecting mighty Bhishma, pierced Nákula with sixty arrows. But though he was severely wounded by your wise 111.35
son, Nákula shot him back with seventy-seven stone-tipped arrows. And the two enemy-scorching heroes, those tiger-like men, began to smite each other like two bulls in a cowshed.

Courageous Dúrmukha, advancing to defend Bhishma in battle, encountered Ghatótkacha, who was pressing forward in the fray, slaughtering your troops. And in a rage the son of Hidímba, Your Majesty, struck enemy-scorching Dúrmukha in the chest with a straight arrow in that fight. Heroic Dúrmukha pierced the son of Bhima·sena too with sixty sharp-pointed arrows, roaring with joy at the forefront of the battle as he did so.

Hrídika's son, the great warrior, opposed that superb 111.40
combatant Dhrishta·dyumna, who was charging forward in his eagerness to slay Bhishma. The son of Hrídika, after piercing Príshata's grandson with five iron shafts, struck him straight away with fifty more, and yelled "Stay still! Stay still!" Thus strong-armed Krita·varman wounded Príshata's great warrior grandson. And the grandson of Príshata, Your Majesty, afflicted Hrídika's son in turn with nine whetted, sharp, heron-feathered, and straight-flying arrows. In that fight that occurred between them for Bhishma's sake in the vast war, each of them strove to overcome the other, just as in the fight between Vritra and great Indra. Bhuri·shravas soon attacked Bhima·sena, who was charging toward the mighty warrior Bhishma, and shouted "Stand still! 111.45
Stand still!" In his attack the son of Soma·datta then struck

111.45 Bhūriśrav" âbhyayāt tūrṇaṃ, «tiṣṭha! tiṣṭh'!» êti c' âbravīt.
Saumadattir atho Bhīmam ājaghāna stan'|ântare
nārācena su|tīkṣṇena rukma|puṅkhena saṃyuge.
uraḥ|sthena babhau tena Bhīmasenaḥ pratāpavān,
Skanda|śaktyā yathā Krauñcaḥ purā, nṛ|pati|sattama.
tau śarān sūrya|saṃkāśān karmāra|parimārjitān
anyonyasya raṇe kruddhau cikṣipāte nara'|rṣabhau.
Bhīmo Bhīṣma|vadh'|ākāṅkṣī Saumadattiṃ mahā|ratham,
tathā Bhīṣma|jaye gṛdhnuḥ Saumadattiś ca Pāṇḍavam
kṛta|pratikṛte yattau yodhayām āsatū raṇe.

111.50 Yudhiṣṭhiraṃ tu Kaunteyaṃ mahatyā senayā vṛtam
Bhīṣm'|âbhimukham āyāntaṃ Bhāradvājo nyavārayat.
Droṇasya ratha|nirghoṣaṃ Parjanya|ninad'|ôpamam
śrutvā Prabhadrakā, rājan, samakampanta, māriṣa.
sā senā mahatī, rājan, Pāṇḍu|putrasya saṃyuge
Droṇena vāritā yattā na cacāla padāt padam.

Cekitānaṃ raṇe kruddhaṃ Bhīṣmaṃ prati, jan'|ēśvara,
Citrasenas tava sutaḥ kruddha|rūpam avārayat.
Bhīṣma|hetoḥ parākrāntaś Citrasenaḥ parākramī
Cekitānaṃ paraṃ śaktyā yodhayām āsa, Bhārata.
111.55 tath" âiva Cekitāno 'pi Citrasenam avārayat.
tad yuddham āsīt su|mahat tayos tatra samāgame.

Arjuno vāryamāṇas tu bahuśas tatra, Bhārata,
vimukhī|kṛtya putraṃ te senāṃ tava mamarda ha.
Duḥśāsano 'pi parayā śaktyā Pārtham avārayat,
«kathaṃ Bhīṣmaṃ paro hanyād?» iti niścitya, Bhārata.

Bhima in the middle of the chest with a very sharp gold-nocked iron arrow. With that arrow stuck in his chest, mighty Bhima·sena looked like Mount Kráuncha when it was struck by Skanda's spear way back then, best of kings. Those two bull-like men, filled with battle-fury, fired on one another with arrows radiant as the sun and polished by blacksmiths. Bhima, wanting to kill Bhishma, shot Soma·datta's great warrior son; and the son of Soma·datta, greedy for Bhishma's triumph, struck the Pándava in turn. Thus they fought, countering each other in their combat.

The son of Bharad·vaja repelled Kunti's son Yudhi· 111.50
shthira, who, surrounded by his mighty host, was making an attempt on Bhishma. When they heard the rattle of Drona's chariot resounding like Parjánya's thunder, the Prabhádrakas trembled, my lord. That mighty division of Pandu's son, Your Majesty, checked by Drona in that encounter, could not take a single step forward no matter how hard they strove.

O lord of the people, your son Chitra·sena restrained fierce-looking Chekitána who, intent on battle, was advancing toward Bhishma. Vigorous and powerful Chitra·sena fought against Chekitána to the best of his ability, descendant of Bharata; and Chekitána resisted Chitra·sena as hard 111.55
as he could. That was a really great fight, that one, between those two, both going at it.

Árjuna kept on forcing your son to retreat and began to crush your troops, Bhárata; but Duhshásana, having resolved to prevent Árjuna from slaying Bhishma, tried his utmost to resist the son of Pritha, descendant of Bharata. Your

sā vadhyamānā samare putrasya tava vāhinī
loḍyate rathibhiḥ śreṣṭhais tatra tatr' âiva, Bhārata.

SAÑJAYA uvāca:

112.1 ATHA VĪRO MAH"|êṣv|āso matta|vāraṇa|vikramaḥ
samādāya mahac cāpaṃ matta|vāraṇa|vāraṇam,
vidhunvāno dhanuḥ śreṣṭhaṃ, drāvayāṇo varūthinīm,
pṛtanāṃ Pāṇḍaveyānāṃ gāhamāno mahā|balaḥ,
nimittāni nimitta|jñaḥ sarvato vīkṣya vīryavān
pratapantam anīkāni Droṇaḥ putram abhāṣata:
«ayaṃ hi divasas, tāta, yatra Pārtho mahā|rathaḥ
jighāṃsuḥ samare Bhīṣmaṃ paraṃ yatnaṃ kariṣyati.
112.5 utpatanti hi me bāṇā; dhanuḥ prasphurat' îva me;
yogam astrāṇi gacchanti; krūre me vartate matiḥ.
dikṣv a|śāntāni ghorāṇi vyāharanti mṛga|dvijāḥ.
nīcair gṛdhrā nilīyante Bhāratānāṃ camūṃ prati.
naṣṭa|prabha iv' ādityaḥ. sarvato lohitā diśaḥ.
rasate, vyathate bhūmir, kampat' îva ca sarvaśaḥ.
kaṅkā gṛdhrā balākāś ca vyāharanti muhur muhuḥ,
śivāś c' âiv' â|śivā ghorā vedayantyo mahad bhayam.
papāta mahatī c' ôlkā madhyen' āditya|maṇḍalāt.
sa|kabandhaś ca parigho bhānum āvṛtya tiṣṭhati.
112.10 pariveṣas tathā ghoraś candra|bhāskarayor abhūt
vedayāno bhayaṃ ghoraṃ rājñāṃ deh'|âvakartanam.
devat"|āyatana|sthāś ca Kaurav'|êndrasya devatāḥ
kampante ca, hasante ca, nṛtyanti ca, rudanti ca.

son's army was taking a battering, and it was shaken here and there by that best of enemy chariot warriors, Bhárata.

SÁNJAYA said:

THEN THE HEROIC mighty archer Drona, the best of men, 112.1
endowed with great strength, as vigorous as a maddened elephant, seizing and shaking his mighty bow that could even have restrained a maddened elephant, penetrated the Pándava ranks and began to drive back the enemy host. That powerful warrior, who was familiar with all omens, saw various omens all around and spoke to his son, who was scorching the hostile troops.

"This is the day, my son, that the immensely powerful Partha will try his hardest, eager to slay Bhishma in battle. My arrows are coming out of the quiver by themselves, 112.5
and my bow seems to be vibrating. My weapons are setting themselves on the bowstring, and my thoughts are engaged in cruel matters. Animals and birds are uttering restless and fierce cries on all sides; and vultures are swooping down on the army of the Bháratas. The sun is as if devoid of its radiance; all the directions have turned red; and the earth seems to be screaming, suffering, and quaking all over. Herons, vultures, and cranes are crying non-stop, and jackals are making hideous and inauspicious howls, foreboding great horror. A huge meteor has fallen from the middle of the solar disk, and a line of clouds in the shape of headless bodies has covered the sun. A frightful halo has en- 112.10
veloped the moon and the sun, portending a great horror: the cutting down of kings' bodies. The images of deities in the temples of the Káurava king are trembling, laughing,

apasavyaṃ grahāś cakrur a|lakṣmāṇaṃ divā|karam.
avāk|śirāś ca bhagavān udatiṣṭhata candramāḥ.
vapūṃṣi ca nar'|êndrāṇāṃ vigat'|ābhāni lakṣaye.
Dhārtarāṣṭrasya sainyeṣu na ca bhrājanti daṃśitāḥ.
senayor ubhayoś c' âpi samantāc chrūyate mahān
Pāñcajanyasya nirghoṣo Gāṇḍīvasya ca niḥsvanaḥ.

112.15 dhruvam āsthāya Bībhatsur uttam'|âstrāṇi saṃyuge
apāsy' ânyān raṇe yodhān abhyeṣyati pitā|maham.
hṛṣyanti roma|kūpāni, sīdat' îva ca me manaḥ
cintayitvā, mahā|bāho, Bhīṣm'|Ârjuna|samāgamam.
taṃ c' êha nikṛti|prajñaṃ Pāñcālyaṃ pāpa|cetasam
puras|kṛtya raṇe Pārtho Bhīṣmasy' āyodhanaṃ gataḥ.

abravīc ca purā Bhīṣmo, ‹n' âhaṃ hanyāṃ Śikhaṇḍinam.
strī hy eṣā vihitā Dhātrā; daivāc ca sa punaḥ pumān.›
a|maṅgalya|dhvajaś c' âiva Yājñasenir mahā|balaḥ.
na c' â|māṅgalike tasmin prahared āpagā|sutaḥ.

112.20 etad vicintayānasya prajñā sīdati me bhṛśam.
abhyudyato raṇe Pārthaḥ Kuru|vṛddham upādravat.
Yudhiṣṭhirasya ca krodho, Bhīṣm'|Ârjuna|samāgamaḥ,
mama c' âstra|samārambhaḥ prajānām a|śivaṃ dhruvam.

dancing, and weeping. The planets are revolving, keeping the inauspicious sun on their right. The divine moon has risen with its horns turned downward. I perceive the bodies of the kings in the Dharta·rashtra ranks as if they were devoid of splendor; though they are wearing armor, they are not gleaming. The loud blare of the Pancha·janya conch and the twang of the Gandíva bow are to be heard on every side of both armies.

Surely Bibhátsu will use his excellent weapons, abandon 112.15
the battle's other combatants, and attack the grandfather. My hair is standing on end and my heart is sinking at the very thought of an encounter between Bhishma and Árjuna, mighty-armed hero. The son of Pritha is advancing to fight against Bhishma with the evil-minded and cheating prince of the Panchálas placed in front of him.

Formerly, Bhishma said, 'I will not strike Shikhándin, for he was made female by the Creator, and it is only by chance that he has become a male.' The powerful son of Yajna·sena is considered to be an inauspicious sign. The son of the River Ganga will never strike that inauspicious one.

As I am pondering over all this, my mind is becoming 112.20
very ill at ease. The Partha, intent on battle, is charging in combat against the old grandfather of the Kurus. Yudhi·shthira's wrath, the encounter between Bhishma and Árjuna, and my intensive use of weapons: all these are sure to show creatures no mercy.

manasvī, balavāñ, śūraḥ, kṛt'|âstro, dṛḍha|vikramaḥ,
dūra|pātī, dṛḍh'|êṣuś ca, nimitta|jñaś ca Pāṇḍavaḥ;
a|jeyaḥ samare c' âpi devair api sa|Vāsavaiḥ,
balavān, buddhimāṃś c' âiva, jita|kleśo yudhāṃ varaḥ.
vijayī ca raṇe nityaṃ, bhairav'|âstraś ca Pāṇḍavaḥ.
tasya mārgaṃ pariharan drutaṃ gaccha yata|vratam.
112.25 paśya c' âitan mahā|ghore saṃyuge vaiśasaṃ mahat.
hema|citrāṇi śūrāṇāṃ mahānti ca śubhāni ca
kavacāny avadīryante śaraiḥ saṃnata|parvabhiḥ;
chidyante ca dhvaj'|âgrāṇi, tomarāś ca, dhanūṃṣi ca,
prāsāś ca vimalās tīkṣṇāḥ, śaktyaś ca kanak'|ôjjvalāḥ,
vaijayantyaś ca nāgānāṃ saṃkruddhena Kirīṭinā.
n' âyaṃ saṃrakṣituṃ kālaḥ prāṇān putr'|ôpajīvibhiḥ.
yāhi svargaṃ puras|kṛtya yaśase vijayāya ca.
ratha|nāga|hay'|āvartāṃ mahā|ghorāṃ, su|dus|tarām
rathena saṃgrāma|nadīṃ taraty eṣa kapi|dhvajaḥ.
112.30 brahmaṇyatā, damo, dānaṃ, tapaś ca, caritaṃ mahat
ih' âiva dṛśyate Pārthe, bhrātā yasya Dhanañjayaḥ,
Bhīmasenaś ca balavān, Mādrī|putrau ca Pāṇḍavau;
Vāsudevaś ca Vārṣṇeyo yasya nātho vyavasthitaḥ.
tasy' âiṣa manyu|prabhavo Dhārtarāṣṭrasya dur|mateḥ
tapo|dagdha|śarīrasya kopo dahati Bhāratīm.
eṣa saṃdṛśyate Pārtho Vāsudeva|vyapāśrayaḥ
dārayan sarva|sainyāni Dhārtarāṣṭrāṇi sarvaśaḥ.

Pandu's son Árjuna is intelligent, powerful, courageous, accomplished in weaponry, solid of stride, able to hit his marks from afar, armed with strong arrows, and familiar with omens. He is invincible in combat even by the gods led by Vásava. That champion of warriors is endowed with strength and wisdom and withstands all pain. That son of Pandu is always armed with frightful weapons; he is always victorious in battle. Avoiding his path, quickly proceed toward Bhishma, the observer of rigid vows. Look what a 112.25
huge massacre is happening in this horrible war. The strong and glinting armor of the heroes, embellished in gold, is being torn through by straight arrows. Tops of standards are being chopped off; spears and bows are being severed; sharp gleaming javelins, lances glittering with gold, and flags on the backs of elephants are all being cut down by diadem-adorned Árjuna in his rage.

Son, this is no time for dependents to spare their own lives. Making heaven your goal, press forward to win glory and victory. Monkey-bannered Árjuna, riding his chariot, is crossing the dreadful river of battle; the river which has chariots, elephants, and horses for its eddies, and which
is extremely difficult to cross. Piety, self-restraint, generos- 112.30
ity, asceticism, and virtuous conduct are to be observed in Pritha's eldest son, whose brothers are Dhanan·jaya, mighty Bhima·sena, and the two Pándava sons of Madri, and whose constant protector is Vásu·deva the descendant of Vrishni. It is the wrath of Yudhi·shthira, whose body was purified in the fire of austerities, that, born of hardships, has been incinerating the Bhárata host of Dhrita·rashtra's evil-minded son. Here is Pritha's son Árjuna, who, with Vásu·deva for

etad ālokyate sainyaṃ kṣobhyamāṇaṃ Kirīṭinā,
mah"|ōrmi|naddhaṃ su|mahat timin" êva nadī|mukham.
112.35 hā|hā|kilakilā|śabdāḥ śrūyante ca camū|mukhe.
yāhi Pāñcāla|dāy'|ādam; ahaṃ yāsye Yudhiṣṭhiram.
dur|gamaṃ hy antaraṃ rājño vyūhasy' â|mita|tejasaḥ
samudra|kukṣi|pratimaṃ, sarvato 'tirathaiḥ sthitaiḥ.
Sātyakiś c', Âbhimanyuś ca, Dhṛṣṭadyumna|Vṛkodarau
paryarakṣanta rājānaṃ, yamau ca manuj'|ēśvaram.
Upendra|sadṛśaḥ, śyāmo, mahā|śāla iv' ôdgataḥ
eṣa gacchaty anīkāni dvitīya iva Phālgunaḥ.
uttam'|âstrāṇi c' ādhatsva, gṛhītvā ca mahad dhanuḥ
Pārṣataṃ yāhi rājānaṃ, yudhyasva ca Vṛkodaram.
112.40 ko hi n' êcchet priyaṃ putraṃ jīvantaṃ śāśvatīḥ samāḥ?
kṣatra|dharmaṃ puras|kṛtya tatas tvā niyunajmy aham.
eṣa c' âtiraṇe Bhīṣmo dahate vai mahā|camūm
yuddheṣu sadṛśas, tāta, Yamasya Varuṇasya ca.»

SAÑJAYA uvāca:

113.1 BHAGADATTAḤ, KṚPAḤ, Śalyaḥ, Kṛtavarmā tath" âiva ca,
Vind'|Ânuvindāv Āvantyau, Saindhavaś ca Jayadrathaḥ,
Citraseno, Vikarṇaś ca, tathā Durmarṣaṇ'|ādayaḥ—
daś' âite tāvakā yodhā Bhīmasenam atāḍayan
mahatyā senayā yuktā nānā|deśa|samutthayā
Bhīṣmasya samare, rājan, prārthayānā mahad yaśaḥ.

his refuge, has been destroying all Dhrita·rashtra's troops completely.

The Káurava army is being thrown into disarray by diadem-adorned Árjuna, like a vast and billowing ocean thrown into disarray by a whale. Cries of distress and cheers 112.35
of joy can both be heard at the front of the division.

You go and confront the prince of the Panchálas, and I shall advance against Yudhi·shthira. The core of that limitlessly splendid king's array is guarded on every side by superior warriors; it is as difficult to get to as the belly of the ocean. Sátyaki, Abhimányu, Dhrishta·dyumna, Vrikódara, and the twins are protecting the king. As dark as Indra's younger brother Vishnu and as tall as a big *shala* tree, Abhimányu is advancing at the head of the troops, like another Phálguna. Take your excellent weapons, grab hold of your mighty bow, charge against the grandson of Príshata, and
fight with Vrikódara. Who would not wish his beloved son 112.40
to live for many years? And yet, observing the warrior code, I am assigning this task to you. Here is Bhishma, the equal of Yama and Váruna in combat, scorching the great host of the enemy in this supreme battle, my son."

SÁNJAYA said:

BHAGA·DATTA, KRIPA, Shalya, Krita·varman, Vinda and 113.1
Anuvínda of Avánti, Jayad·ratha the king of the Sindhus, Chitra·sena, Vikárna, and Durmárshana—these ten of your warriors fought against Bhima·sena. Supported by a mighty division of troops from different countries, Your Majesty, they sought great fame fighting for Bhishma's sake. Shalya shot Bhima·sena with nine arrows; Krita·varman struck him

Śalyas tu navabhir bāṇair Bhīmasenam atāḍayat;
Kṛtavarmā tribhir bāṇaiḥ; Kṛpaś ca navabhiḥ śaraiḥ.
113.5 Citraseno, Vikarṇaś ca, Bhagadattaś ca, māriṣa,
daśabhir daśabhir bhallair Bhīmasenam atāḍayan.
Saindhavaś ca tribhir bāṇair jatru|deśe 'bhyatāḍayat;
Vind'|Ânuvindāv Āvantyau pañcabhiḥ pañcabhiḥ śaraiḥ;
Durmarṣaṇaś ca viṃśatyā Pāṇḍavaṃ niśitaiḥ śaraiḥ.
sa tān sarvān, mahā|rāja, rājamānān pṛthak pṛthak,
pravīrān sarva|lokasya Dhārtarāṣṭrān mahā|rathān
jaghāna samare vīraḥ Pāṇḍavaḥ para|vīra|hā.
saptabhiḥ Śalyam āvidhyat, Kṛtavarmāṇam aṣṭabhiḥ,
Kṛpasya sa|śaraṃ cāpaṃ madhye ciccheda, Bhārata.
113.10 ath' âinaṃ chinna|dhanvānaṃ punar vivyādha pañcabhiḥ,
Vind'|Ânuvindau ca tathā tribhis tribhir atāḍayat.
Durmarṣaṇaṃ ca viṃśatyā, Citrasenaṃ ca pañcabhiḥ,
Vikarṇaṃ daśabhir bāṇaiḥ, pañcabhiś ca Jayadratham
viddhvā Bhīmo 'nadadd hṛṣṭaḥ,
Saindhavaṃ ca punas tribhiḥ.
ath' ânyad dhanur ādāya
Gautamo rathināṃ varaḥ
Bhīmaṃ vivyādha saṃrabdho daśabhir niśitaiḥ śaraiḥ.
sa viddho bahubhir bāṇais, tottrair iva mahā|dvipaḥ,
tataḥ kruddho, mahā|rāja, Bhīmasenaḥ pratāpavān
Gautamaṃ tāḍayām āsa śarair bahubhir āhave,
113.15 Saindhavasya tath" âśvāṃś ca sārathiṃ ca tribhiḥ śaraiḥ
prāhiṇon Mṛtyu|lokāya Kāl'|Ântaka|sama|dyutiḥ.
hat'|âśvāt tu rathāt tūrṇam avaplutya mahā|rathaḥ
śarāṃś cikṣepa niśitān Bhīmasenasya saṃyuge.

with three, and Kripa with nine. Chitra·sena, Vikárna, and 113.5
Bhaga·datta, my lord, each hit Bhima·sena with ten shafts. The king of the Sindhus pierced Bhima·sena with three arrows. Vinda and Anuvínda of Avánti shot him with five arrows each. Durmárshana struck the son of Pandu with twenty whetted shafts.

In that encounter, the heroic Pándava, that slayer of enemy heroes, great king, wounded all those glorious, prominent, and world-famous mighty warriors of Dhrita·rashtra's army in turn, one by one. He pierced Shalya with seven shafts and Krita·varman with eight, and he split Kripa's arrow-bearing bow down the middle, descendant of Bharata. Then he struck bowless Kripa with seven more shafts 113.10
and hit Vinda and Anuvínda with three arrows each. Then, having pierced Durmárshana with twenty arrows, Chitra·sena with five, Vikárna with ten, and Jayad·ratha with five, Bhima, filled with delight, let out a roar and shot the king of the Sindhus again, with three shafts.

Gótama's grandson, that best of chariot warriors, seized another bow, and in a rage he cut Bhima with ten sharpened arrows. Wounded by those ten shafts like a mighty elephant struck with goads, powerful Bhima·sena, excited with fury, shot Gótama's grandson with many arrows in that contest, great king. Endowed with the brilliance of Time the 113.15
Destroyer, with three shafts Bhima sent the Sindhu king's horses and chariot driver to the realm of Death. The great warrior Jayad·ratha quickly leaped down from his horseless chariot and fired numerous sharpened arrows at Bhima·sena in the fray. Then, my lord, Bhima split the great-spirited Sindhu ruler's bow down the middle with two

tasya Bhīmo dhanur madhye dvābhyāṃ ciccheda, māriṣa,
bhallābhyāṃ, Bharata|śreṣṭha, Saindhavasya mah"|ātmanaḥ.
sa cchinna|dhanvā, vi|ratho, hat'|âśvo, hata|sārathiḥ
Citrasena|rathaṃ, rājann, āruroha tvar"|ânvitaḥ.

aty|adbhutaṃ raṇe karma kṛtavāṃs tatra Pāṇḍavaḥ:
mahā|rathāñ śarair viddhvā, vārayitvā ca, māriṣa,
113.20 vi|rathaṃ Saindhavaṃ cakre sarva|lokasya paśyataḥ.
tadā na mamṛṣe Śalyo Bhīmasenasya vikramam.
sa saṃdhāya śarāṃs tīkṣṇān, karmāra|parimārjitān,
Bhīmaṃ vivyādha samare, «tiṣṭha! tiṣṭh'!» êti c' âbravīt.

Kṛpaś ca, Kṛtavarmā ca, Bhagadattaś ca, māriṣa,
Vind'|Ânuvindāv Āvantyau, Citrasenaś ca saṃyuge,
Durmarṣaṇo, Vikarṇaś ca, Sindhu|rājaś ca vīryavān—
Bhīmaṃ te vivyadhus tūrṇaṃ Śalya|hetor arin|damāḥ.
sa ca tān prativivyādha pañcabhiḥ pañcabhiḥ śaraiḥ.
Śalyaṃ vivyādha saptatyā, punaś ca daśabhiḥ śaraiḥ.
113.25 taṃ Śalyo navabhir bhittvā punar vivyādha pañcabhiḥ,
sārathiṃ c' âsya bhallena gāḍhaṃ vivyādha marmaṇi.

Viśokaṃ prekṣya nirbhinnaṃ Bhīmasenaḥ pratāpavān
Madra|rājaṃ tribhir bāṇair bāhvor urasi c' ārpayat.
tath" êtarān mah"|êṣv|āsāṃs tribhis tribhir a|jihma|gaiḥ
tāḍayām āsa samare, siṃhavad vinanāda ca.
te hi yattā mah"|êṣv|āsāḥ Pāṇḍavaṃ yuddha|kovidam
tribhis tribhir a|kuṇṭh'|âgrair bhṛśaṃ marmasv atāḍayan.
so 'tividdho mah"|êṣv|āso Bhīmaseno na vivyathe,

spear-headed shafts, best of the Bharatas. Bereft of his chariot, with his bow split and his horses and driver killed, Jayad·ratha hurriedly climbed onto Chitra·sena's chariot, Your Majesty.

The Pándava performed an utterly amazing feat in that encounter, my lord: while piercing those mighty warriors and thus holding them back them with his arrows, he 113.20
stripped the king of the Sindhus of his chariot while the whole world was watching. And Shalya could not bear Bhima·sena's vigor; he strung sharp arrows polished by blacksmiths, and fired on Bhima in that battle, shouting "Stay still! Stay still!" Kripa, Krita·varman, powerful Bhaga·datta, Vinda and Anuvínda of Avánti, Chitra·sena, Durmárshana, Vikárna, and the mighty king of the Sindhus—all those enemy-tamers quickly struck Bhima in the hope of rescuing Shalya. But Bhima shot them in return with five arrows each; and he also struck Shalya with seventy shafts, and then with ten more. Shalya opened Bhima up with 113.25
nine arrows, cut him with another five, and then severely wounded Bhima's driver in his vital organs with a spear-headed shaft.

Seeing Vishóka injured, powerful Bhima·sena afflicted the king of the Madras with three arrows in his arms and chest; and he also struck the other great archers in the battle with three straight-flying arrows each, and roared like a lion. Fighting strenuously, each of those mighty bowmen then seriously wounded that Pándava war veteran in his vital parts with three sharp-pointed arrows. Though he was

parvato vāri|dhārābhir varṣamāṇair iv' âmbu|daiḥ.
113.30 sa tu krodha|samāviṣṭaḥ Pāṇḍavānāṃ mahā|rathaḥ
Madr'|ēśvaraṃ tribhir bāṇair bhṛśaṃ viddhvā mahā|yaśāḥ,
Kṛpaṃ ca navabhir bāṇair bhṛśaṃ viddhvā samantataḥ,
Prāgjyotiṣaṃ śatair ājau, rājan, vivyādha sāyakaiḥ.
tatas tu sa|śaraṃ cāpaṃ Sātvatasya mah"|ātmanaḥ
kṣurapreṇa su|tīkṣṇena ciccheda kṛta|hastavat.
ath' ânyad dhanur ādāya Kṛtavarmā Vṛkodaram
ājaghāna bhruvor madhye nārācena paran|tapaḥ.
Bhīmas tu samare viddhvā Śalyaṃ navabhir āyasaiḥ,
Bhagadattaṃ tribhiś c' âiva, Kṛtavarmāṇam aṣṭabhiḥ,
113.35 dvābhyāṃ dvābhyāṃ ca vivyādha
Gautama|prabhṛtīn rathān.
te 'pi taṃ samare, rājan,
vivyadhur niśitaiḥ śaraiḥ.
sa tathā pīḍyamāno 'pi sarva|śastrair mahā|rathaiḥ,
matvā tṛṇena tāṃs tulyān vicacāra gata|vyathaḥ.
te c' âpi rathināṃ śreṣṭhā Bhīmāya niśitāñ śarān
preṣayām āsur a|vyagrāḥ śataśo 'tha sahasraśaḥ.
tasya śaktiṃ mahā|vegāṃ Bhagadatto mahā|rathaḥ
cikṣepa samare vīraḥ svarṇa|daṇḍāṃ, mahā|mate.
tomaraṃ Saindhavo rājā paṭṭiśaṃ ca mahā|bhujaḥ,
śata|ghnīṃ ca Kṛpo, rājañ, śaraṃ Śalyaś ca saṃyuge,
113.40 ath' êtare mah"|êṣv|āsāḥ pañca pañca śilīmukhān
Bhīmasenaṃ samuddiśya preṣayām āsur ojasā.

severely wounded, the great archer Bhima·sena did not waver; he was like a mountain being bombarded by storm-
clouds pouring down their torrents of rain. Excited with 113.30
rage, that glorious and mighty Pándava warrior cut the lord of the Madras deeply with three arrows, seriously wounded Kripa all over with nine shafts, and afflicted the king of the Prag·jyótishas with a hundred arrows in battle, Your Majesty.

Then, with a razor-edged shaft, Bhima skillfully sliced through the great-spirited Sátvata warrior's arrow-bearing bow. Krita·varman, the tamer of enemies, took up another bow and shot Vrikódara between the eyebrows with an iron shaft. Bhima, having struck Shalya in combat with nine iron arrows, Bhaga·datta with three, and Krita·varman with
eight, pierced the other warriors led by Gótama's grand- 113.35
son with two arrows each. And they shot him with whetted shafts in return.

Though he was cut up by those great warriors with all types of weapons, Bhima regarded them as mere straw, and he careered around free of pain. Those supreme chariot warriors calmly discharged hundreds and thousands of sharpened arrows at Bhima. The heroic and mighty warrior Bhaga·datta hurled a gold-staffed spear at him with great velocity in that encounter, high-minded lord. The strong-armed king of the Sindhus threw a lance and a sharp-edged spear for his play, Kripa hurled a *shata·ghni* missile, Your
Majesty, and Shalya shot an arrow; and each of the other 113.40
great archers vigorously released five stone-whetted arrows, aimed at Bhima·sena.

tomaraṃ sa dvidhā cakre kṣurapreṇ' Ânil'|ātmajaḥ,
paṭṭiśaṃ ca tribhir bāṇaiś ciccheda tila|kāṇḍavat.
sa bibheda śata|ghnīṃ ca navabhiḥ kaṅka|patribhiḥ,
Madra|rāja|prayuktaṃ ca śaraṃ chittvā mahā|balaḥ,
śaktiṃ ciccheda sahasā Bhagadatt'|ēritāṃ raṇe.
tath" êtarāñ śarān ghorāñ śaraiḥ saṃnata|parvabhiḥ
Bhīmaseno raṇa|ślāghī tridh" âik'|âikaṃ samācchinat;
tāṃś ca sarvān mah"|êṣv|āsāṃs tribhis tribhir atāḍayat.
113.45 tato Dhanañjayas tatra vartamāne mahā|raṇe
ājagāma rathen' ājau Bhīmaṃ dṛṣṭvā mahā|ratham
nighnantaṃ samare śatrūn, yodhayānaṃ ca sāyakaiḥ.
tau tu tatra mah"|ātmānau sametau vīkṣya Pāṇḍavau
n' āśaśaṃsur jayaṃ tatra tāvakāḥ puruṣa'|rṣabhāḥ.
ath' Ârjuno raṇe Bhīmaṃ yodhayantaṃ mahā|ratham,
Bhīṣmasya nidhan'|ākāṅkṣī, puras|kṛtya Śikhaṇḍinam
āsasāda raṇe vīrāṃs tāvakān daśa, Bhārata.
ye sma Bhīmaṃ raṇe, rājan, yodhayanto vyavasthitāḥ,
Bībhatsus tān ath' âvidhyad Bhīmasya priya|kāmyayā.
113.50 tato Duryodhano rājā Suśarmāṇam acodayat
Arjunasya vadh'|ârthāya Bhīmasenasya c' ôbhayoḥ:
«Suśarman, gaccha śīghraṃ tvaṃ bal'|âughaiḥ parivāritaḥ;
jahi Pāṇḍu|sutāv etau Dhanañjaya|Vṛkodarau!»
tac chrutvā śāsanaṃ tasya Trigartaḥ Prasthal"|âdhipaḥ
abhidrutya raṇe Bhīmam Arjunaṃ c' âiva dhanvinau,
rathair an|eka|sāhasraiḥ samantāt paryavārayat.
tataḥ pravavṛte yuddham Arjunasya paraiḥ saha.

Bhima, son of the god Wind,* cut the lance in two with a razor-edged arrow, and with three shafts he smashed the sharp-edged spear as if it were a sesame stalk. With nine heron-feathered arrows that mighty warrior broke the *shata·ghni* missile, cut down the arrow shot by the king of the Madras, and forcibly sliced through the spear that Bhaga·datta had hurled in battle; and with his straight arrows Bhima·sena, proud in battle, chopped the other terrible shafts, one by one, into three pieces each. He then wounded those mighty archers with three arrows each.

As that huge battle was raging, Dhanan·jaya, seeing the 113.45
great warrior Bhima fighting against his foes in battle and striking them down with his arrows, arrived there on his chariot. And when they saw those two great-spirited sons of Pandu fighting together, your bulls of men abandoned their hopes of victory. Árjuna, longing to slay Bhishma, and with Shikhándin placed before him, approached Bhima who was battling away against those great enemy warriors; and he encountered those ten of your heroic combatants in battle, descendant of Bharata. Wanting to do Bhima a favor, Bibhátsu wounded the warriors; but they carried on fighting
against Bhima, Your Majesty. Then King Duryódhana sent 113.50
Sushárman to kill both Árjuna and Bhima·sena. "Sushárman, surround yourself with masses of troops, and go and kill these two sons of Pandu—Dhanan·jaya and Vrikódara!" And when they heard the king's command, the king of the Tri·gartas, the ruler of Prásthala, attacked the two bowmen Bhima and Árjuna in that engagement, surrounding them on every side with several thousand warriors. Then a battle took place between Árjuna and his foes!

SAÑJAYA uvāca:

114.1 ARJUNAS TU RAṆE Śalyaṃ yatamānaṃ mahā|ratham
chādayām āsa samare śaraiḥ saṃnata|parvabhiḥ.
Suśarmāṇaṃ Kṛpaṃ c' âiva tribhis tribhir avidhyata,
Prāgjyotiṣaṃ ca samare, Saindhavaṃ ca Jayadratham,
Citrasenaṃ, Vikarṇaṃ ca, Kṛtavarmāṇam eva ca,
Durmarṣaṇaṃ ca, rāj'|êndra, Āvantyau ca mahā|rathau
ek'|âikaṃ tribhir ānarchat kaṅka|barhiṇa|vājitaiḥ.
śarair ati|ratho yuddhe pīḍayan vāhinīṃ tava
114.5 Jayadratho raṇe Pārthaṃ viddhvā, Bhārata, sāyakaiḥ
Bhīmaṃ vivyādha tarasā Citrasena|rathe sthitaḥ.
Śalyaś ca samare Jiṣṇuṃ Kṛpaś ca rathināṃ varaḥ
vivyadhāte mahā|bāhuṃ bahudhā marma|bhedibhiḥ.
Citrasen'|ādayaś c' âiva putrās tava, viśāṃ pate,
pañcabhiḥ pañcabhis tūrṇaṃ saṃyuge niśitaiḥ śaraiḥ
ājaghnur Arjunaṃ saṃkhye Bhīmasenaṃ ca, māriṣa.
tau tatra rathināṃ śreṣṭhau Kaunteyau Bharata'|rṣabhau
apīḍayetāṃ samare Trigartānāṃ mahad balam.
Suśarm" âpi raṇe Pārthaṃ śarair navabhir āśu|gaiḥ;
114.10 nanāda balavan nādaṃ trāsayāno mahad balam.
anye ca rathinaḥ śūrā Bhīmasena|Dhanañjayau
vivyadhur niśitair bāṇai rukma|puṅkhair a|jihma|gaiḥ.

SÁNJAYA said:

IN THAT EXCHANGE, Árjuna shrouded the great warrior Shalya, who was fighting strenuously on the battlefield, with his straight arrows. In that exchange Árjuna struck Susharman and Kripa with three shafts each, and he also pierced Prag·jyótisha, Jayad·ratha the king of the Sindhus, Chitra·sena, Vikárna, Krita·varman, Durmárshana, and the two great warriors of Avánti, one by one, with three arrows each—arrows with heron and peacock feathers. That supreme warrior oppressed your host with arrows in that
114.1
exchange. Then Jayad·ratha, descendant of Bharata, stand- 114.5
ing on Chitra·sena's chariot, cut the son of Pritha smartly in that fight with numerous arrows; and he afflicted Bhima·sena as well. In that contest, Shalya and that best of chariot warriors Kripa struck Jishnu with many shafts that were able to penetrate the vital organs, great king. And your sons too, led by Chitra·sena, each firing five sharpened arrows, soon pierced Árjuna and Bhima·sena in battle, lord of the people.

My lord, those two sons of Kunti, the best of chariot warriors, the bulls of the Bharatas, plagued the mighty force of the Tri·gartas in the fray. Susharman then hit the son
of Pritha in battle with nine swift-flying shafts and let out 114.10
a loud roar, terrifying the large enemy host. Other valiant chariot warriors shot Bhima·sena and Dhanan·jaya with sharpened and gold-nocked arrows that flew true.

teṣāṃ tu rathināṃ madhye Kaunteyau rathināṃ varau
krīḍamānau rath'|ôdārau citra|rūpau vyadṛśyatām,
āmiṣ'|ēpsū gavāṃ madhye siṃhāv iva bal'|ôtkaṭau.
chittvā dhanūṃṣi śūrāṇāṃ, śarāṃś ca bahudhā raṇe,
pātayām āsatur vīrau śirāṃsi śataśo nṛṇām.
rathāś ca bahavo bhagnā, hayāś ca śataśo hatāḥ,
gajāś ca sa|gaj'|ārohāḥ petur urvyāṃ mah"|āhave.
114.15 rathinaḥ sādinaś c' âpi tatra tatra niṣūditāḥ
dṛśyante bahavo, rājan, vepamānāḥ samantataḥ.
hatair gaja|padāty|oghair, vājibhiś ca niṣūditaiḥ,
rathaiś ca bahudhā bhagnaiḥ samāstīryata medinī.
chatraiś ca bahudhā chinnair, dhvajaiś ca vinipātitaiḥ,
aṅkuśair apaviddhaiś ca, paristomaiś ca, Bhārata,
keyūrair, aṅgadair, hārai, rāṅkavair mṛditais tathā,
uṣṇīṣair, ṛṣṭibhiś c' âiva, cāmara|vyajanair api,
tatra tatr' âpaviddhaiś ca bāhubhiś candan'|ôkṣitaiḥ,
ūrubhiś ca nar'|êndrāṇāṃ samāstīryata medinī.
114.20 tatr' âdbhutam apaśyāma raṇe Pārthasya vikramam,
śaraiḥ saṃvārya tān vīrān yaj jaghāna mahā|balaḥ.
putras tu tava taṃ dṛṣṭvā Bhīm'|Ârjuna|samāgamam
Gāṅgeyasya rath'|âbhyāśam upajagme mahā|balaḥ.
Kṛpaś ca, Kṛtavarmā ca, Saindhavaś ca Jayadrathaḥ,
Vind'|Ânuvindāv Āvantyāu na jahuḥ saṃyugaṃ tadā.
tato Bhīmo mah"|êṣv|āsaḥ Phālgunaś ca mahā|rathaḥ
Kauravāṇāṃ camūṃ ghorāṃ bhṛśaṃ dudruvatū raṇe
tato barhiṇa|vājānām ayutāny arbudāni ca

Those two sons of Kunti, bulls of the Bharatas and noble warriors, looked wonderful as they were playing in the midst of the chariot warriors, like two lions, hugely strong and hungry for meat, amid a herd of cows. Having cut down the bows and arrows of the hostile heroes in various ways in battle, those two heroes chopped off hundreds of human heads.

Many broken chariots and hundreds of slain horses fell to the ground in that huge contest, as did elephants and their riders. Many maimed chariot warriors and cavalrymen 114.15
were seen all around, struck down here and there in their hundreds and writhing in agony, Your Majesty.

The earth was strewn with hordes of killed elephants and foot soldiers, slain horses, shattered chariots, parasols torn into many pieces, felled banners, and scattered hooks and caparisons, descendant of Bharata; and with armlets, bracelets, necklaces, trampled woolen under-saddles, turbans, darts, yak tails, and fans. The earth was covered all over with the fallen thighs and sandalwood-smeared arms of great men. In that battle we witnessed the powerful Partha's 114.20
incredible courage, as he held those heroes back and smote them with his arrows.

Your mighty son Duryódhana saw Bhima and Árjuna united, and pressed on toward the chariot of Ganga's son; but Kripa, Krita·varman, Jayad·ratha the king of the Sindhus, and Vinda and Anuvínda of Avánti did not flee from combat. Then the mighty archer Bhima and the great warrior Phálguna began a massive assault upon the terrible Káurava army in battle. The hostile kings immediately fired tens of thousands and millions of peacock-feathered arrows

Dhanañjaya|rathe tūrṇaṃ pātayanti sma bhūmi|pāḥ.
114.25 tatas tāñ śara|jālena saṃnivārya mahā|rathān
Pārthaḥ samantāt samare preṣayām āsa Mṛtyave.
Śalyas tu samare Jiṣṇuṃ krīḍann iva mahā|rathaḥ
ājaghān' ôrasi kruddho bhallaiḥ saṃnata|parvabhiḥ.
tasya Pārtho dhanuś chittvā, hast'|āvāpaṃ ca pañcabhiḥ,
ath' âinaṃ sāyakais tīkṣṇair bhṛśaṃ vivyādha marmaṇi.
ath' ânyad dhanur ādāya samare bhāra|sādhanam
Madr'|ēśvaro raṇe Jiṣṇuṃ tāḍayām āsa roṣitaḥ
tribhiḥ śarair, mahā|rāja, Vāsudevaṃ ca pañcabhiḥ,
Bhīmasenaṃ ca navabhir bāhvor urasi c' ārpayat.
114.30 tato Droṇo, mahā|rāja, Māgadhaś ca mahā|rathaḥ
Duryodhana|samādiṣṭau taṃ deśam upajagmatuḥ,
yatra Pārtho, mahā|rāja, Bhīmasenaś ca Pāṇḍavaḥ
Kauravyasya mahā|senāṃ jaghnatus tau mahā|rathau.
Jayatsenas tu samare Bhīmaṃ bhīm'|āyudhaṃ yudhi
vivyādha niśitair bāṇair aṣṭabhir, Bharata'|rṣabha.
taṃ Bhīmo daśabhir viddhvā punar vivyādha pañcabhiḥ,
sārathiṃ c' âsya bhallena ratha|nīḍād apāharat.
udbhrāntais turagaiḥ so 'tha dravamāṇaiḥ samantataḥ
Māgadho 'pahṛto rājā sarva|sainyasya paśyataḥ.
114.35 Droṇaś ca vivaraṃ dṛṣṭvā Bhīmasenaṃ śilīmukhaiḥ
vivyādha bāṇair niśitaiḥ pañca|ṣaṣṭibhir āyasaiḥ.
taṃ Bhīmaḥ samara|ślāghī guruṃ pitṛsamaṃ raṇe
vivyādha navabhir bhallais tathā ṣaṣṭyā ca, Bhārata.

at Dhanan·jaya's chariot; but the son of Pritha repelled those 114.25
great warriors with a web of arrows and began to send them from all over the battlefield to Death. Then the enraged mighty warrior Shalya shot Jishnu in the chest with straight spear-headed shafts as if the war was a game to him. And the son of Pritha cut through Shalya's bow and his hand guard with five arrows, and with a number of sharp arrows he wounded his opponent in his vitals. The lord of the Madras then took hold of another bow that was fit for the task, and, filled with fury, he struck Jishnu in battle with three shafts and Vásu·deva with five, and pierced Bhima·sena in the chest with nine arrows, great king.

Then, great king, having been commanded by Duryó- 114.30
dhana, Drona and the mighty warrior king of the Mágadhas reached the spot where the two extremely powerful warriors Árjuna Partha and Bhima·sena Pándava had been crushing the large Káurava host. And Jayat·sena pierced Bhima the wielder of terrifying weapons in combat with eight whetted arrows, bull of the Bharatas. But Bhima shot Jayat·sena back with ten shafts, cut him with five more, and toppled his driver from the chariot platform with a spear-headed arrow. While all the troops were looking on, the king of the Mágadhas was carried away by his frightened horses,
careering every which way. Taking his opportunity, Drona 114.35
struck Bhima·sena with sixty-five sharpened iron arrows with stone tips; and in that fight Bhima, famed for his fighting, afflicted the teacher, who was like a father to him, with sixty-five spear-headed shafts in return, descendant of Bharata.

Arjunas tu Suśarmāṇaṃ viddhvā bahubhir āyasaiḥ
vyadhamat tasya tat sainyaṃ, mah"|âbhrāṇi yath" ânilaḥ.
tato Bhīṣmaś ca, rājā ca, Kauśalaś ca Bṛhadbalaḥ
samavartata saṃkruddhā Bhīmasena|Dhanañjayau.
tath" âiva Pāṇḍavāḥ śūrā Dhṛṣṭadyumnaś ca Pārṣataḥ
abhyadravan raṇe Bhīṣmaṃ vyādit'|āsyam iv' Ântakam.

114.40 Śikhaṇḍī tu samāsādya Bhāratānāṃ pitā|maham
abhyadravata saṃhṛṣṭo, bhayaṃ tyaktvā mahā|rathāt.
Yudhiṣṭhira|mukhāḥ Pārthāḥ puras|kṛtya Śikhaṇḍinam
ayodhayan raṇe Bhīṣmaṃ sahitāḥ sarva|Sṛñjayaiḥ.
tath" âiva tāvakāḥ sarve puras|kṛtya yata|vratam
Śikhaṇḍi|pramukhān Pārthān yodhayanti sma saṃyuge.
tataḥ pravavṛte yuddhaṃ Kauravāṇāṃ bhay'|āvaham
tatra Pāṇḍu|sutaiḥ sārdhaṃ Bhīṣmasya vijayaṃ prati.
tāvakānāṃ raṇe Bhīṣmo glaha āsīd, viśāṃ pate.
tatra hi dyūtam āyātaṃ vijayāy' êtarāya vā.

114.45 Dhṛṣṭadyumnas tu, rāj'|êndra, sarva|sainyāny acodayat:
«abhidravata Gāṅgeyaṃ! mā bhaiṣṭa, nara|sattamāḥ!»
senā|pati|vacaḥ śrutvā
    Pāṇḍavānāṃ varūthinī
Bhīṣmam ev' âbhyayāt tūrṇaṃ
    prāṇāṃs tyaktvā mah"|āhave.
Bhīṣmo 'pi rathināṃ śreṣṭhaḥ pratijagrāha tāṃ camūm
āpatantīṃ, mahā|rāja, velām iva mah"|ôdadhiḥ.

Meanwhile Árjuna pierced Sushárman with many iron arrows and dispersed his troops just as the wind disperses huge clouds. Now Bhishma, King Duryódhana, and Brihad·bala the ruler of the Kósalas attacked Bhima·sena and Dhanan·jaya with a fury. At the same time, the brave Pándavas and Príshata's grandson Dhrishta·dyumna charged against Bhishma, who was like Death with his mouth gaping in
battle; and Shikhándin, reaching the grandfather of the 114.40
Bharatas, overcame his fear of that mighty warrior and attacked him, delighted. In combination with all the Sríñjayas, the Parthas, led by Yudhi·shthira, placed Shikhándin at their forefront and began to fight against Bhishma. Likewise all your warriors, placing Bhishma the observer of rigid vows at their head, engaged in combat with the Parthas who were headed by Shikhándin. And a dreadful battle followed, between the Káuravas and the sons of Pandu, for the sake of Bhishma's victory or defeat. It was like a game of dice, played to win or played to lose, lord of the people;
and Bhishma was your warriors' stake. Dhrishta·dyumna 114.45
urged all the troops on, king of kings: "Attack the son of Ganga! Do not fear, foremost of warriors!" And when they heard their general's order the Pándava troops were willing to sacrifice their lives in that fierce battle, and they swiftly charged against Bhishma. But Bhishma, the best of chariot warriors, restrained that host that was charging him, just as the shore restrains the surging ocean, great king.

DHṚTARĀṢṬRA uvāca:

115.1 KATHAM Śāntanavo Bhīṣmo daśame 'hani, Sañjaya,
ayudhyata mahā|vīryaiḥ Pāṇḍavaiḥ saha|Sṛñjayaiḥ?
Kuravaś ca katham yuddhe Pāṇḍavān pratyavārayan?
ācakṣva me mahā|yuddhaṃ Bhīṣmasy' āhava|śobhinaḥ.

SAÑJAYA uvāca:

Kuravaḥ Pāṇḍavaiḥ sārdhaṃ yad ayudhyanta, Bhārata,
yathā ca tad abhūd yuddhaṃ, tat te vakṣyāmi sāmpratam.
gamitāḥ para|lokāya param'|âstraiḥ Kirīṭinā
ahany ahani saṃkruddhās tāvakānāṃ mahā|rathāḥ.
115.5 yathā|pratijñaṃ Kauravyaḥ sa c' âpi samitiñ|jayaḥ
Pārthānām akarod Bhīṣmaḥ satataṃ samiti|kṣayam.
Kurubhiḥ sahitaṃ Bhīṣmaṃ yudhyamānaṃ mahā|ratham
Arjunaṃ ca sa|Pāñcālyaṃ dṛṣṭvā saṃśayitā janāḥ.
daśame 'hani tasmiṃs tu Bhīṣm'|Ârjuna|samāgame
avartata mahā|raudraḥ satataṃ samiti|kṣayaḥ.
tasminn ayutaśo, rājan, bhūyaśaś ca paran|tapaḥ
Bhīṣmaḥ Śāntanavo yodhāñ jaghāna param'|âstra|vit.
yeṣām a|jñāta|kalpāni nāma|gotrāṇi, pārthiva,
te hatās tatra Bhīṣmeṇa śūrāḥ sarve '|nivartinaḥ
115.10 daś' âhāni tatas taptvā Bhīṣmaḥ Pāṇḍava|vāhinīm
niravidyata dharm'|ātmā jīvitena paran|tapaḥ.
sa kṣipraṃ vadham anvicchann ātmano 'bhimukho raṇe,
«na hanyāṃ mānava|śreṣṭhān saṃgrāme su|bahūn,» iti

DHRITA·RASHTRA said:

HOW DID THE immensely powerful Bhishma fight on the tenth day, Sánjaya, against the Pándavas and the Srínjayas? How did the Kurus oppose the Pándavas in that encounter? Tell me about the great war-deeds of Bhishma so splendid in battle. 115.1

SÁNJAYA said:

I will now tell you of the battle that the Kurus fought against the Pándavas and how it unfolded, descendant of Bharata. Day by day your host's mighty warriors, full of fury, were sent to the other world by diadem-adorned Árjuna wielding his superior weapons. The Káurava hero 115.5
Bhishma, ever victorious in battle, kept on destroying the Parthas' troops in accordance with his vow. At the sight of that mighty warrior Bhishma battling away at the head of the Kurus, and Árjuna supported by the Panchálas, people weren't sure of the outcome.

And on the tenth day of the war, in the course of an encounter between Bhishma and Árjuna, a horrible and continuous massacre took place. Your Majesty, Shántanu's son Bhishma, the tormentor of his foes and an expert in superior weapons, slaughtered tens of thousands of hostile warriors. All those valiant combatants, who refused to retreat and whose names and surnames were unknown, were killed there by Bhishma, Your Majesty.

Having afflicted the Pándava host for ten days, Bhishma, 115.10
righteous in spirit, became disgusted with his life that scorcher of enemies. Wanting to be killed at the front of the battle, and thinking "I shall no longer kill so many excellent

cintayitvā mahā|bāhuḥ pitā Devavratas tava
abhyāśa|sthaṃ, mahā|rāja, Pāṇḍavaṃ vākyam abravīt:
«Yudhiṣṭhira mahā|prājña, sarva|śāstra|viśārada,
śṛṇu me vacanaṃ, tāta, dharmyaṃ svargyaṃ ca jalpataḥ.
nirviṇṇo 'smi bhṛśaṃ, tāta, dehen' ânena, Bhārata.
ghnataś ca me gataḥ kālaḥ su|bahūn prāṇino raṇe.
115.15 tasmāt Pārthaṃ puro|dhāya, Pañcālān Sṛñjayāṃs tathā,
mad|vadhe kriyatāṃ yatno, mama ced icchasi priyam.»
tasya tan matam ājñāya Pāṇḍavaḥ satya|darśanaḥ
Bhīṣmaṃ prati yayau yattaḥ saṃgrāme saha Sṛñjayaiḥ.
Dhṛṣṭadyumnas tato, rājan, Pāṇḍavaś ca Yudhiṣṭhiraḥ
śrutvā Bhīṣmasya tāṃ vācaṃ codayām āsatur balam:
«abhidravata! yudhyadhvaṃ! Bhīṣmaṃ jayata saṃyuge
rakṣitāḥ satya|saṃdhena Jiṣṇunā ripu|jiṣṇunā!
ayaṃ c' âpi mah"|êṣv|āsaḥ Pārṣato vāhinī|patiḥ,
Bhīmasenaś ca samare pālayiṣyati vo dhruvam.
115.20 mā vo Bhīṣmād bhayaṃ kiṃ cid astv adya yudhi, Sṛñjayāḥ.
dhruvaṃ Bhīṣmaṃ vijeṣyāmaḥ puras|kṛtya Śikhaṇḍinam.»
te tathā samayaṃ kṛtvā daśame 'hani Pāṇḍavāḥ
Brahma|loka|parā bhūtvā saṃjagmuḥ krodha|mūrchitāḥ.
Śikhaṇḍinaṃ puras|kṛtya, Pāṇḍavaṃ ca Dhanañjayam,
Bhīṣmasya pātane yatnaṃ paramaṃ te samāsthitāḥ.

warriors in combat," your strong-armed father Deva·vrata, great king, addressed the eldest son of Pandu as follows.

"O Yudhi·shthira of great wisdom, expert in all fields of knowledge, listen to my virtuous words that can lead to heaven. I am sick of this body of mine, descendant of Bharata, sir. I am slaughtering countless creatures in battle, but
my time has come. So if you wish to do me a favor, make 115.15
an effort to kill me by placing the Partha in your vanguard, with the Panchálas and the Srínjayas."

When he had discovered Bhishma's intentions, the Pándava king, that exponent of truth, advanced against him, together with the Srínjayas. And having heard Bhishma's words, Yudhi·shthira Pándava and Dhrishta·dyumna urged their troops on, Your Majesty.

"Attack! Fight! Defeat Bhishma in combat! You are protected by the enemy-conqueror Jishnu who is true to his vows; and Bhima·sena and this general, Príshata's grandson the mighty archer, will surely protect you in battle too.
During today's fight you must have no fear of Bhishma, 115.20
Srínjayas! We will defeat Bhishma for sure, by placing Shikhándin at the head!"

The Pándavas made this agreement on the tenth day. Intent on attaining the world of Brahma and senseless with fury, they placed Shikhándin and Dhanan·jaya Pándava at the forefront, and acting as one they strove to their utmost to strike Bhishma down.

tatas tava sut'|ādiṣṭā nānā|jana|pad'|ēśvarāḥ,
Droṇena saha|putreṇa saha|senā mahā|balāḥ,
Duḥśāsanaś ca balavān saha sarvaiḥ sah'|ôdaraiḥ
Bhīṣmaṃ samara|madhya|sthaṃ pālayāṃ cakrire tadā.
115.25 tatas tu tāvakāḥ śūrāḥ puras|kṛtya yata|vratam
Śikhaṇḍi|pramukhān Pārthān yodhayanti sma saṃyuge.
Cedibhiś ca sa|Pañcālaiḥ sahito vānara|dhvajaḥ
yayau Śāntanavaṃ Bhīṣmaṃ puras|kṛtya Śikhaṇḍinam.
Droṇa|putraṃ Śiner naptā, Dhṛṣṭaketus tu Pauravam,
Yudhāmanyuḥ sah'|âmātyaṃ Duryodhanam ayodhayat.
Virāṭas tu sah'|ânīkaḥ saha|senaṃ Jayadratham
Vṛddhakṣatrasya dāy'|ādam āsasāda paran|tapaḥ.
Madra|rājaṃ mah"|êṣv|āsaṃ saha|sainyaṃ Yudhiṣṭhiraḥ,
Bhīmaseno 'bhiguptaś ca nāg'|ânīkam upādravat.
115.30 a|pradhṛṣyam, an|āvāryaṃ, sarva|śastra|bhṛtāṃ varam
Drauṇiṃ prati yayau yattaḥ Pāñcālyaḥ saha s'|ôdaraiḥ.
karṇikāra|dhvajaṃ c' âiva siṃha|ketur arin|damaḥ
pratyujjagāma Saubhadraṃ rāja|putro Bṛhadbalaḥ.
Śikhaṇḍinaṃ ca putrās te Pāṇḍavaṃ ca Dhanañjayam
rājabhiḥ samare sārdham abhipetur jighāṃsavaḥ.

tasminn ati|mahā|bhīme senayor vai parākrame
saṃpradhāvatsv anīkeṣu medinī samakampata.
tāny anīkāny anīkeṣu samasajjanta, Bhārata,
tāvakānāṃ pareṣāṃ ca dṛṣṭvā Śāntanavaṃ raṇe.
115.35 tatas teṣāṃ prataptānām anyonyam abhidhāvatām
prādur|āsīn mahāñ śabdo dikṣu sarvāsu, Bhārata.

At your son's command, many powerful kings from various countries, along with their troops, and Drona and his son, and also mighty Duhshásana with all his brothers, began to protect Bhishma who stood in the middle of the battlefield. With Bhishma the observer of great vows 115.25
placed before them, your heroes started to fight against the Párthas headed by Shikhándin. Monkey-bannered Árjuna, joined by the Chedis and the Panchálas, charged against Bhishma the son of Shántanu. Shini's grandson fought with the son of Drona; Dhrishta·ketu fought with the Páurava; and Abhimányu fought with Duryódhana and his companions. The enemy-scorcher Viráta and his division encountered Jayad·ratha the heir of Vriddha·kshatra. Yudhi·shthira confronted the king of the Madras, that mighty archer, and his troops. Well-protected Bhima·sena attacked the enemy's elephant division. The prince of the Panchálas and 115.30
his brothers advanced vigorously against the irresistible and unconquerable son of Drona, that champion of all warriors. The enemy-taming Prince Brihad·bala, who had a lion on his banner, assailed the son of Subhádra, who had a *karnikára** on his. Supported by many kings, your sons flew at Shikhándin and Pritha's son Dhanan·jaya in the fray, desiring to kill them both.

And as the forces rushed against each other in that utterly terrifying battle waged by the two armies, the earth quaked. Having caught sight of Shántanu's son on the battlefield, the divisions of your host clashed with those of the enemy, descendant of Bharata. As the fighters charged against each 115.35
other in fury, a horrible noise rose up on all sides, Bhárata. The blare of conches, the beat of drums, the trumpeting

śaṅkha|dundubhi|ghoṣaiś ca, vāraṇānāṃ ca bṛṃhitaiḥ,
siṃha|nādaś ca sainyānāṃ dāruṇaḥ samapadyata.
sā ca sarva|nar'|êndrāṇāṃ candr'|ârka|sadṛśī prabhā
vīr'|âṅgada|kirīṭeṣu niṣ|prabhā samapadyata.
rajo|meghās tu saṃjajñuḥ śastra|vidyudbhir āvṛtāḥ.
dhanuṣāṃ c' âiva nirghoṣo dāruṇaḥ samapadyata.
bāṇa|śaṅkha|praṇādāś ca, bherīṇāṃ ca mahā|svanāḥ,
ratha|ghoṣāś ca saṃjagmuḥ senayor ubhayor api.
115.40 prāsa|śakty|ṛṣṭi|saṅghaiś ca, bāṇ'|âughaiś ca samākulam
niṣ|prakāśam iv' ākāśaṃ senayoḥ samapadyata.
anyonyaṃ rathinaḥ petur, vājinaś ca mah"|āhave,
kuñjarāḥ kuñjarāñ jaghnuḥ, padātīṃś ca padātayaḥ.
tatr' āsīt su|mahad yuddhaṃ Kurūṇāṃ Pāṇḍavaiḥ saha
Bhīṣma|hetor, nara|vyāghra, śyenayor āmiṣe yathā.
teṣāṃ samāgamo ghoro babhūva yudhi, Bhārata,
anyonyasya vadh'|ârthāya jigīṣūṇāṃ raṇ'|âjire.

SAÑJAYA uvāca:

116.1 ABHIMANYUR, mahā|rāja, tava putram ayodhayat
mahatyā senayā yukto Bhīṣma|hetoḥ parākramī.
Duryodhano raṇe Kārṣṇiṃ navabhir nata|parvabhiḥ
ājaghān' ôrasi kruddhaḥ punaś c' âinaṃ tribhiḥ śaraiḥ.
tasya śaktiṃ raṇe Kārṣṇir, Mṛtyor ghorām iva svasām,
preṣayām āsa saṃkruddho Duryodhana|rathaṃ prati.
tām āpatantīṃ sahasā ghora|rūpāṃ, viśāṃ pate,
dvidhā ciccheda te putraḥ kṣurapreṇa mahā|rathaḥ
116.5 tāṃ śaktiṃ patitāṃ dṛṣṭvā Kārṣṇiḥ parama|kopanaḥ

of elephants, and the lion-roar of the combatants mingled together to make a tremendous din.

The gleam of all the heroic kings' bracelets and diadems grew dim; clouds of dust were stirred up, with weapons flashing within them like lightning. The twang of bows was terrible. From both armies the whizz of arrows, the blare of conches, the loud beating of kettle-drums, and the rattle of chariots spread out all around. The sky was obscured, 115.40
as it was filled with hordes of javelins, lances, spears, and masses of arrows from both hosts. In that fierce battle chariot warriors encountered chariot warriors, horsemen confronted horsemen, elephants crushed elephants, and foot soldiers killed foot soldiers. There was a huge battle between the Kurus and the Pándavas, for Bhishma; they were like two hawks competing for a piece of meat, tiger-like man. In the course of the great war between those troops eager to vanquish and slay one another, the battle that took place next was a terrible one indeed.

SÁNJAYA said:

SUPPORTED BY a large host and heading for Bhishma, vig- 116.1
orous Abhimányu encountered your son, great king. Duryódhana, enraged, struck Krishna's nephew in the chest with nine straight shafts in the contest, and then with three more. In turn Krishna's nephew furiously hurled a dreadful spear at Duryódhana's chariot—a spear that looked like the sister of Death. But as it flew toward him with great force, lord of people, your great warrior son cut that horrible spear
in two with a razor-edged arrow. Seeing that spear fallen, 116.5
Krishna's nephew was filled with a violent rage; he injured

Duryodhanaṃ tribhir bāṇair bāhvor urasi c' ārpayat.
punaś c' âinaṃ śarair ghorair ājaghāna stan'|ântare
daśabhir, Bharata|śreṣṭha, Bharatānāṃ mahā|rathaḥ.
tad yuddham abhavad ghoraṃ citra|rūpaṃ ca, Bhārata,
indriya|prīti|jananaṃ sarva|pārthiva|pūjitam.
Bhīṣmasya nidhan'|ârthāya Pārthasya vijayāya ca
yuyudhāte raṇe vīrau Saubhadra|Kuru|puṅgavau.

Sātyakiṃ rabhasaṃ yuddhe
Drauṇir brāhmaṇa|puṅgavaḥ
ājaghān' ôrasi kruddho
nārācena paran|tapaḥ.

116.10 Śaineyo 'pi guroḥ putraṃ sarva|marmasu, Bhārata,
atāḍayad a|mey'|ātmā navabhiḥ kaṅka|vājitaiḥ.
Aśvatthāmā tu samare Sātyakiṃ navabhiḥ śaraiḥ,
triṃśatā ca punas tūrṇaṃ bāhvor urasi c' ārpayat.
so 'tividdho mah"|êṣv|āso Droṇa|putreṇa Sātvataḥ
Droṇa|putraṃ tribhir bāṇair ājaghāna mahā|yaśāḥ.

Pauravo Dhṛṣṭaketuṃ ca śarair ācchādya saṃyuge
bahudhā dārayāṃ cakre mah"|êṣv|āsaṃ mahā|ratham.
tath" âiva Pauravaṃ yuddhe Dhṛṣṭaketur mahā|rathaḥ
triṃśatā niśitair bāṇair vivyādha su|mahā|balaḥ.
116.15 Pauravas tu dhanuś chittvā Dhṛṣṭaketor mahā|rathaḥ
nanāda balavan nādaṃ, vivyādha ca śitaiḥ śaraiḥ.
so 'nyat kārmukam ādāya Pauravaṃ niśitaiḥ śaraiḥ
ājaghāna, mahā|rāja, tri|saptatyā śilīmukhaiḥ.
tau tu tatra mah"|êṣv|āsau mahā|mātrau mahā|rathau
mahatā śara|varṣeṇa paras|param avidhyatām.

Duryódhana with three arrows in the arms and chest, and then that mighty Bhárata warrior shot your son in the center of his chest with ten fearful shafts, best of the Bharatas. The battle between them was fearsome and wonderful; a delight for the senses, it was praised by all the kings. Subhádra's son and the bull-like lord of the Kurus both fought heroically, one aiming to slay Bhishma, the other aiming to vanquishing the son of Pritha.

Drona's irate son, that enemy-scorching brahmin bull, struck Sátyaki violently in the chest with an iron arrow
in their encounter. And Shini's boundlessly spirited grand- 116.10
son shot the teacher's son in all his vulnerable spots with nine heron-feathered shafts, descendant of Bharata. In return Ashva·tthaman pierced Sátyaki with nine arrows in the fray, and then he quickly struck him in the arms and chest with thirty more. The glorious Sátvata, that mighty archer, was heavily wounded by the son of Drona, but he shot him back with three arrows.

The great warrior Páurava shrouded the mighty archer Dhrishta·ketu with arrows in battle, injuring him in various ways; and the great and strong-armed warrior Dhrishta·ketu immediately struck the Páurava back with thirty whetted shafts in that fight. Then the Páurava, the great war- 116.15
rior, severed Dhrishta·ketu's bow, let out a loud roar, and pierced his opponent with sharp arrows. Seizing another bow, Dhrishta·ketu hit the Páurava with seventy-three sharp and stone-whetted shafts, great king. The two mighty archers—great fighters with massive bodies—struck one another with heavy downpours of arrows; and after they had severed each other's bows and killed each other's horses

anyonyasya dhanuś chittvā, hayān hatvā ca, Bhārata,
vi|rathāv asi|yuddhāya samīyatur a|marṣanau.
ārṣabhe carmaṇī citre, śata|candra|pariṣ|kṛte,
tārakā|śata|citre ca nistriṃśau su|mahā|prabhau
116.20 pragṛhya vimalau, rājaṃs, tāv anyonyam abhidrutau,
vāśitā|saṃgame yattau siṃhāv iva mahā|vane.
maṇḍalāni vicitrāṇi, gata|pratyāgatāni ca
ceratur darśayantau ca, prārthayantau paras|param.
Pauravo Dhṛṣṭaketuṃ tu śaṅkha|deśe mah"|âsinā
tāḍayām āsa saṃkruddhas, «tiṣṭha! tiṣṭh'!» êti c' âbravīt.
Cedi|rājo 'pi samare Pauravaṃ puruṣa'|rṣabham
ājaghāna śit'|âgreṇa jatru|deśe mah"|âsinā.
tāv anyonyaṃ, mahā|rāja, samāsādya mah"|āhave
anyonya|veg'|âbhihatau nipetatur arin|damau.
116.25 tataḥ sva|ratham āropya Pauravaṃ tanayas tava
Jayatseno rathen' ājāv apovāha raṇ'|âjirāt.
Dhṛṣṭaketuṃ ca samare Mādrī|putraḥ paran|tapaḥ
apovāha raṇe, rājan, Sahadevaḥ parākramī.

Citrasenaḥ Suśarmāṇaṃ viddhvā navabhir āyasaiḥ,
punar vivyādha taṃ ṣaṣṭyā, punaś ca navabhiḥ śaraiḥ.
Suśarmā tu raṇe kruddhas tava putraṃ, viśāṃ pate,
daśabhir daśabhiś c' âiva vivyādha niśitaiḥ śaraiḥ.
Citrasenaś ca taṃ, rājaṃs, triṃśatā nata|parvabhiḥ
ājaghāna raṇe kruddhaḥ; sa ca taṃ pratyavidhyata.

they confronted each other in a rage, stripped of their chariots, to fight with swords, descendant of Bharata. Picking up their bright and gleaming swords, and their splendid shields that were made of bull hide and decorated with a hundred moons and a hundred stars, Your Majesty, they 116.20
charged against one another, like two lions in a big forest competing over a lioness on heat. They busied themselves in displaying wondrous circular movements, advancing, retreating, and seeking to smite each other. The furious Páurava struck Dhrishta·ketu on the forehead with his massive sword and shouted "Stand still! Stand still!" Then the king of the Chedis hit the Páurava, that bull-like man, in the shoulder with his large and keen-edged sword. And having met each other in that great duel, great king, those two enemy-tamers fell down, toppled by one another's impetuosity. Then your son Jayat·sena, lifting the Páurava onto his 116.25
chariot, took him away from the battlefield. And Madri's powerful and courageous son Saha·deva, furious in battle, carried Dhrishta·ketu away from the field of play.

Chitra·sena, having pierced Sushárman with nine iron arrows, struck him with sixty shafts and then with nine more. Sushárman, filled with battle-fury, shot your son back with successive volleys of ten whetted shafts each, lord of the people. In his battle-rage Chitra·sena struck his opponent with thirty straight arrows, Your Majesty; and Sushárman shot him again in return.

116.30 Bhīṣmasya samare, rājan, yaśo mānaṃ ca vardhayan.
Saubhadro rāja|putraṃ tu Bṛhadbalam ayodhayat,
Pārtha|hetoḥ parākrānto Bhīṣmasy' āyodhanaṃ prati.
Ārjuniṃ Kosal'|êndras tu viddhvā pañcabhir āyasaiḥ
punar vivyādha viṃśatyā śaraiḥ saṃnata|parvabhiḥ.
Saubhadraḥ Kosal'|êndraṃ tu vivyādh' âṣṭabhir āyasaiḥ;
n' âkampayata saṃgrāme; vivyādha ca punaḥ śaraiḥ.
Kausalyasya dhanuś c' âpi punaś ciccheda Phālguṇiḥ,
ājaghāna śaraiś c' âiva triṃśatā kaṅka|patribhiḥ.
so 'nyat kārmukam ādāya rāja|putro Bṛhadbalaḥ
116.35 Phālguniṃ samare kruddho vivyādha bahubhiḥ śaraiḥ.

tayor yuddhaṃ samabhavad Bhīṣma|hetoḥ, paran|tapa,
saṃrabdhayor, mahā|rāja, samare citra|yodhinoḥ,
yathā dev'|âsure yuddhe Bali|Vāsavayor abhūt.

Bhīmaseno gaj'|ânīkaṃ yodhayan bahv aśobhata,
yathā Śakro vajra|pāṇir dārayan parvat'|ôttamān.
te vadhyamānā Bhīmena mātaṅgā giri|saṃnibhāḥ
nipetur urvyāṃ sahitā, nādayanto vasun|dharām.
giri|mātrā hi te nāgā bhinn'|âñjana|cay'|ôpamāḥ
virejur vasu|dhāṃ prāpya, vikīrṇā iva parvatāḥ.
116.40 Yudhiṣṭhiro mah"|êṣv|āso Madra|rājānam āhave
mahatyā senayā guptaṃ pīḍayām āsa saṃgatam.
Madr'|ēśvaraś ca samare Dharma|putraṃ mahā|ratham
pīḍayām āsa saṃrabdho Bhīṣma|hetoḥ parākramī.

In that battle for Bhishma, Subhádra's son, enhancing his glory and honor, fought against Prince Brihad·bala, Your Majesty, and demonstrated his valor as he helped the Partha in his onslaught on Bhishma. The king of the Kósalas cut Árjuna's son with five iron arrows, and then struck him with twenty straight shafts. Subhádra's son shot the king of the Kósalas with eight iron arrows, but failed to shake him; so he pierced Brihad·bala again in the battle, with many shafts. Phálguna's son then severed the Kósala ruler's bow and hit him with thirty heron-feathered arrows. Taking up another bow, Prince Brihad·bala, filled with battle-fury, pierced the son of Phálguna with many shafts. 116.30 116.35

O scorcher of enemies, the fight for Bhishma which took place between those two irate warriors, both of whom were skilled in diverse modes of battle, was like the fight between Bali and Vásava during the war the gods waged against the demons, great king.

Bhima·sena, fighting against the elephant division, looked as beautiful as thunderbolt-wielding Shakra when he split the highest mountains. Slain by Bhima, those mountainous elephants collapsed all at once to the ground, making the earth resound with their screams. Those mountainous elephants were like heaps of broken antimony; they were like mountains scattered over the earth.

The mighty archer Yudhi·shthira confronted the king of the Madras, who was protected by a mighty force; and he wounded him in that encounter. And the powerful lord of the Madras, excited with rage, began to harass the Son of Righteousness in order to rescue Bhishma. 116.40

Virāṭaṃ Saindhavo rājā viddhvā saṃnata|parvabhiḥ,
navabhiḥ sāyakais tīkṣṇais triṃśatā punar ārpayat.
Virāṭaś ca, mahā|rāja, Saindhavaṃ vāhinī|patiḥ
triṃśatā niśitair bāṇair ājaghāna stan'|ântare.
citra|kārmuka|nistriṃśau, citra|varm'|āyudha|dhvajau
rejatuś citra|rūpau tau saṃgrāme Matsya|Saindhavau.
116.45 Droṇaḥ Pāñcāla|putreṇa samāgamya mahā|raṇe,
mahā|samudayaṃ cakre śaraiḥ saṃnata|parvabhiḥ.
tato Droṇo, mahā|rāja, Pārṣatasya mahad dhanuḥ
chittvā pañcāśat" êṣūṇāṃ, Pārṣataṃ samavidhyata.
so 'nyat kārmukam ādāya Pārṣataḥ para|vīra|hā
Droṇasya miṣato yuddhe preṣayām āsa sāyakān.
tāñ śarāñ śara|ghātena ciccheda sa mahā|rathaḥ.
Droṇo Drupada|putrāya prāhiṇot pañca sāyakān.
tataḥ kruddho, mahā|rāja, Pārṣataḥ para|vīra|hā
Droṇāya cikṣepa gadāṃ Yama|daṇḍ'|ôpamāṃ raṇe.
116.50 tām āpatantīṃ sahasā hema|paṭṭa|vibhūṣitām
śaraiḥ pañcāśatā Droṇo vārayām āsa saṃyuge.
sā chinnā bahudhā, rājan, Droṇa|cāpa|cyutaiḥ śaraiḥ,
cūrṇī|kṛtā, viśīryantī papāta vasudhā|tale.
gadāṃ vinihatāṃ dṛṣṭvā Pārṣataḥ śatru|tāpanaḥ
Droṇāya śaktiṃ cikṣepa sarva|pāraśavīṃ śubhām.
tāṃ Droṇo navabhir bāṇaiś ciccheda yudhi, Bhārata,
Pārṣataṃ ca mah"|êṣv|āsaṃ pīḍayām āsa saṃyuge.

The king of the Sindhus pierced Viráta with nine straight and sharp arrows, and then afflicted him with thirty more. Viráta, the commander of a large division, struck the king of the Sindhus in return, with thirty whetted shafts in the center of his chest, great king. The king of the Matsyas and the ruler of the Sindhus both shone brightly in that engagement: both were armed with glistening bows and swords, and equipped with glittering armor, weapons, and banners.

In that great war Drona confronted the prince of the 116.45
Panchálas and waged fierce battle, shooting numerous straight arrows. Drona severed Príshata's grandson's mighty bow, great king, and then pierced him with fifty shafts; but in that encounter Príshata's grandson, the destroyer of enemy heroes, took up another bow and started firing arrows again before Drona could blink. Then the mighty warrior Drona cut through those arrows with a volley of his shafts, and fired five arrows at the son of Drúpada. Príshata's grandson, the slayer of enemy heroes, enraged, hurled a mace at Drona in the fray—a mace that looked
like the staff of Yama, great king, and was decorated with 116.50
golden cloth. And as that mace swiftly flew toward him in battle, Drona warded it off with fifty arrows. Splintered into many pieces by the shafts fired from Drona's bow, Your Majesty, the mace fell pulverized to the ground. The enemy-scorching grandson of Príshata, seeing his mace struck down, hurled at Drona a beautiful spear made entirely of iron; but Drona's move was to split it with nine arrows, descendant of Bharata, and then he fired again at Príshata's grandson and wounded that mighty archer. That is how the great, frightful, and terrifying battle for Bhishma

evam etan mahad yuddhaṃ Droṇa|Pārṣatayor abhūt
Bhīṣmaṃ prati, mahā|rāja, ghora|rūpaṃ bhayānakam.
116.55 Arjunaḥ prāpya Gāṅgeyaṃ, pīḍayan niśitaiḥ śaraiḥ,
abhyadravata saṃyatto, vane mattam iva dvi|pam.
pratyudyayau ca taṃ Pārthaṃ Bhagadattaḥ pratāpavān
tridhā bhinnena nāgena mad'|ândhena mahā|balaḥ.
tam āpatantaṃ sahasā mah"|Êndra|gaja|saṃnibham,
paraṃ yatnaṃ samāsthāya Bībhatsuḥ pratyapadyata.
tato gaja|gato rājā Bhagadattaḥ pratāpavān
Arjunaṃ śara|varṣeṇa vārayām āsa saṃyuge.
Arjunas tu tato nāgam āyāntaṃ rajat'|ôpamam
vimalair āyasais tīkṣṇair avidhyata mahā|raṇe.
116.60 Śikhaṇḍinaṃ ca Kaunteyo «yāhi! yāh'!» îty acodayat
Bhīṣmaṃ prati, mahā|rāja, «jahy enam!» iti c' âbravīt.

Prāgjyotiṣas tato hitvā Pāṇḍavaṃ, Pāṇḍu|pūrva|ja,
prayayau tvarito, rājan, Drupadasya rathaṃ prati.
tato 'rjuno, mahā|rāja, Bhīṣmam abhyadravad drutam
Śikhaṇḍinaṃ puras|kṛtya. tato yuddham avartata.
tatas te tāvakāḥ śūrāḥ Pāṇḍavaṃ rabhasaṃ raṇe
sarve 'bhyadhāvan krośantas. tad adbhutam iv' âbhavat.
nānā|vidhāny anīkāni putrāṇāṃ te, jan'|âdhipa,
Arjuno vyadhamat kāle, div' îv' âbhrāṇi mārutaḥ.
116.65 Śikhaṇḍī tu samāsādya Bharatānāṃ pitā|maham
iṣubhis tūrṇam a|vyagro bahubhiḥ sa samācinot.

continued, mighty king, between Drona and the grandson of Príshata.

Árjuna got close to the son of Ganga, vexed him with 116.55
many sharpened arrows, and strenuously charged forward as if he was attacking a maddened elephant in a forest. But the valiant King Bhaga·datta, riding his elephant that was blind with rut, its temples oozing in three lines, rose against Árjuna. Bibhátsu exerted himself fully and confronted that elephant as it charged forcefully against him looking like the elephant of great Indra. With a rainstorm of arrows the courageous, elephant-riding King Bhaga·datta held Árjuna off in that great battle; but Árjuna afflicted the charging elephant with whetted iron shafts that gleamed like silver. The 116.60
son of Kunti urged Shikhándin on, shouting "Go ahead, great king! Advance toward Bhishma and kill him!"

Then, forsaking the Pándava, elder brother of Pandu, the king of the Prag·jyótishas set off at speed toward Drúpada's chariot, Your Majesty; and Árjuna, keeping Shikhándin in front of him, immediately charged against Bhishma, great king. Then a battle ensued! Your heroic warriors furiously assailed the Pándava, shouting their war cries on the battlefield. It was like a miracle. But Árjuna duly scattered your sons' various forces, lord of the people, as the wind disperses clouds in the sky. Meanwhile, Shikhándin reached 116.65
the Bhárata grandfather and, quickly but calmly, he struck him with many arrows.

rath'|âgny|agāraś, cāp'|ârcir, asi|śakti|gad"|êndhanaḥ,
śara|saṅgha|mahā|jvālaḥ kṣatriyān samare 'dahat.
Somakāṃś ca raṇe Bhīṣmo jaghne Pārtha|pad'|ânugān,
nyavārayata sainyaṃ ca Pāṇḍavānāṃ mahā|rathaḥ.
yath"|âgniḥ su|mahān iddhaḥ kakṣe carati s'|ânilaḥ,
tathā jajvāla Bhīṣmo 'pi divyāny astrāṇy udīrayan.
suvarṇa|puṅkhair iṣubhiḥ śitaiḥ saṃnata|parvabhiḥ
nādayan sa diśo Bhīṣmaḥ pradiśaś ca mah"|āhave,
116.70 pātayan rathino, rājan, hayāṃś ca saha sādibhiḥ,
muṇḍa|tāla|vanān' îva cakāra sa ratha|vrajān.
nir|manuṣyān rathān, rājan, gajān, aśvāṃś ca saṃyuge
cakāra sa tadā Bhīṣmaḥ sarva|śastra|bhṛtāṃ varaḥ.
tasya jyā|tala|nirghoṣaṃ visphūrjitam iv' âśaneḥ
niśamya sarvato, rājan, samakampanta sainikāḥ.
a|moghā nyapatan bāṇāḥ pitus te, manuj'|ēśvara;
n' âsajjanta śarīreṣu Bhīṣma|cāpa|cyutāḥ śarāḥ.
nir|manuṣyān rathān, rājan, su|yuktāñ javanair hayaiḥ,
vātāyamānān adrākṣam hriyamāṇān, viśāṃ pate.
116.75 Cedi|Kāśi|Karūṣāṇāṃ sahasrāṇi catur|daśa
mahā|rathāḥ samākhyātāḥ, kula|putrās, tanu|tyajaḥ,
a|parāvartinaḥ, śūrāḥ, suvarṇa|vikṛta|dhvajāḥ
saṃgrāme Bhīṣmam āsādya sa|vāji|ratha|kuñjarāḥ
jagmus te para|lokāya, vyādit'|āsyam iv' Ântakam.

With his chariot for a fire sanctuary, his bow for flames, his swords, spears, and maces for fuel, and his masses of arrows for an intense blaze, Bhishma himself was a fire, scorching the enemy warriors in battle. Just as a huge conflagration, fed with fuel and supported by the wind, spreads across a dry forest, so Bhishma blazed up, using his divine weapons. In that encounter the mighty warrior Bhishma crushed the Sómakas who followed the Partha; and he repelled the Pándava's host with his sharp, straight, gold-nocked arrows, making the major and minor directions resound with his roar in that great war. Toppling chariot 116.70
warriors and striking down horses and their riders, Your Majesty, he made hosts of warriors look like groves of palm trees stripped of their leafy tops. Bhishma, the best of all warriors, deprived chariots, elephants, and horses of their riders in that battle, Your Majesty. Combatants all around trembled when they heard the twang of his bowstring like rumbling thunder, Your Majesty. Your father's arrows hit their targets unfailingly, lord of the people; and shafts fired from Bhishma's bow did not just hit the bodies they were aimed at, but pierced them right through. Your Majesty, I watched well-yoked but driverless chariots being carried around by their swift horses, lord of the people.

Fourteen thousand renowned, noble, and mighty war- 116.75
riors from among the Chedis, the Kashis, and the Karúshas—all of them ready to give up their lives, never turning tail, valiant, and equipped with banners decorated in gold—encountered Bhishma who was like Death with his mouth gaping in battle, and went to the other world along with their horses, chariots, and elephants.

na tatr' āsīd raṇe, rājan, Somakānāṃ mahā|rathaḥ,
yaḥ saṃprāpya raṇe Bhīṣmaṃ jīvite sma mano dadhe.
tāṃś ca sarvān raṇe yodhān preta|rāja|puraṃ prati
nītān amanyanta janā, dṛṣṭvā Bhīṣmasya vikramam.
na kaś cid enaṃ samare pratyudyāti mahā|rathaḥ,
116.80 ṛte Pāṇḍu|sutaṃ vīraṃ śvet'|âśvaṃ, kṛṣṇa|sārathim,
Śikhaṇḍinaṃ ca samare Pāñcālyam a|mit'|âujasam.

SAÑJAYA uvāca:

117.1 ŚIKHAṆḌĪ TU raṇe Bhīṣmam āsādya puruṣa'|rṣabham
daśabhir daśabhir bhallair ājaghāna stan'|ântare.
Śikhaṇḍinaṃ tu Gāṅgeyaḥ krodha|dīptena cakṣuṣā
saṃpraikṣata kaṭ'|âkṣeṇa nirdahann iva, Bhārata.
strītvaṃ tasya smaran, rājan, sarva|lokasya paśyataḥ
n' ājaghāna raṇe Bhīṣmaḥ. sa ca taṃ n' âvabuddhavān.
Arjunas tu, mahā|rāja, Śikhaṇḍinam abhāṣata:
«abhidravasva tvarito! jahi c' âinaṃ pitā|maham!
117.5 kiṃ te vivakṣayā, vīra? jahi Bhīṣmaṃ mahā|ratham.
na hy anyam anupaśyāmi kaṃ cid Yaudhiṣṭhire bale,
yaḥ śaktaḥ samare Bhīṣmaṃ pratiyoddhum ih' āhave,
ṛte tvāṃ, puruṣa|vyāghra. satyam etad bravīmi te.»
evam uktas tu Pārthena Śikhaṇḍī, Bharata'|rṣabha,
śarair nānā|vidhais tūrṇaṃ pitā|maham upādravat.
a|cintayitvā tān bāṇān pitā Devavratas tava
Arjunaṃ samare kruddhaṃ vārayām āsa sāyakaiḥ.

Your Majesty, in that battle there was not a single mighty Sómaka warrior who hoped to survive his encounter with Bhishma; for once they saw Bhishma's courage, people considered all his foes to be as good as sent to the city of the king of the dead. No great warrior stood up to Bhishma in battle
except Pandu's heroic son with his white horses and black 116.80
chariot driver,* and Prince Shikhándin of the Panchálas, limitless in vigor.

SÁNJAYA said:

CONFRONTING THAT tiger of a man Bhishma in battle, 117.1
Shikhándin struck him in the middle of his chest with ten whetted and spear-headed arrows. The son of Ganga then cast a sidelong glance at Shikhándin, as if to incinerate him with his eyes ablaze with anger, descendant of Bharata; but as the whole world looked on, Your Majesty, Bhishma did not shoot back at him in battle, for he was conscious of his adversary's female nature. Shikhándin, however, did not realize this.

Árjuna then told Shikhándin, great king: "Quickly, advance and kill the grandfather! Why are you hesitating, 117.5
hero? Slay that mighty warrior Bhishma! I can see no other combatant in Yudhi·shthira's host who would be able to counter Bhishma in battle except you, tiger-like man. I am telling you the truth!" Addressed by the son of Pritha in this way, bull of the Bharatas, Shikhándin quickly sprayed the grandfather with arrows of various kinds. Ignoring those arrows, your father Deva·vrata held Árjuna, who was filled with battle-fury, at bay with his shafts; and with sharp arrows that mighty warrior sent one of the Pándavas' divisions

tath" âiva ca camūṃ sarvāṃ Pāṇḍavānāṃ mahā|rathaḥ
apraiṣīt samare tīkṣṇaiḥ para|lokāya, māriṣa.
117.10 tath" âiva Pāṇḍavā, rājan, sainyena mahatā vṛtāḥ
Bhīṣmaṃ saṃchādayām āsur, meghā iva divā|karam.
sa samantāt parivṛto Bhārato, Bharata'|ṛṣabha,
nirdadāha raṇe śūrān, vanaṃ vahnir iva jvalan.

tatr' âdbhutam apaśyāma tava putrasya pauruṣam,
ayodhayac ca yat Pārthaṃ, jugopa ca pitā|maham.
karmaṇā tena samare tava putrasya dhanvinaḥ
Duḥśāsanasya tutuṣuḥ sarve lokā mah"|ātmanaḥ.
yad ekaḥ samare Pārthān s'|ânugān samayodhayat,
na c' âinaṃ Pāṇḍavā yuddhe vārayām āsur ulbaṇam.
117.15 Duḥśāsanena samare rathino vi|rathī|kṛtāḥ;
sādinaś ca mah"|êṣv|āsā, hastinaś ca mahā|balāḥ
vinirbhinnāḥ śarais tīkṣṇair nipetur vasudhā|tale;
śar'|āturās tath" âiv' ânye dantino vidrutā diśaḥ.
yath" âgnir indhanaṃ prāpya jvaled dīpt'|ârcir ulbaṇaḥ,
tathā jajvāla putras te Pāṇḍu|senāṃ vinirdahan.
taṃ Bhārata|mahā|mātraṃ Pāṇḍavānāṃ mahā|rathaḥ
jetuṃ n' ôtsahate kaś cin n' âbhyudyātuṃ kathaṃ cana,
ṛte mah"|Êndra|tanayāc chvet'|âśvāt kṛṣṇa|sāratheḥ.

sa hi taṃ samare, rājan, nirjitya Vijayo 'rjunaḥ
117.20 Bhīṣmam ev' âbhidudrāva sarva|sainyasya paśyataḥ.
vijitas tava putro 'pi Bhīṣma|bāhu|vyapāśrayaḥ
punaḥ punaḥ samāśvasya prāyudhyata mad'|ôtkaṭaḥ.
Arjunas tu raṇe, rājan, yodhayan saṃvyarājata.

to the next world in its entirety, my lord. But the Pándavas, 117.10
surrounded as they were by a great force, Your Majesty, enveloped Bhishma just as clouds envelop the sun. Totally surrounded by them, bull of the Bharatas, the Bhárata warrior began to scorch the hostile heroes like a fire burning up a forest.

Then we witnessed the incredible courage of your son, as he fought against Pritha's son and protected the grandfather at the same time. All the people were pleased with that feat of Duhshásana, your bow-wielding and great-spirited son; for he single-handedly battled with all the Parthas, including Árjuna, and the Pándavas could not check that powerful
fighter in the fray. In that battle, chariot warriors stripped of 117.15
their chariots by Duhshásana, horsemen armed with their mighty bows, and immensely powerful elephants were all pierced through with sharp arrows and felled to the ground; and other elephants, plagued by arrows, ran away in all directions. Just as a fire, when supplied with fuel, blazes up intensely with a bright glow, so your son was inflamed; and he scorched the Pándava troops. None of the Pándavas' great warriors had the power to overcome or even to attack that Bhárata with his massive body by any means at all, except the son of great Indra with his white horses and his black chariot driver.*

Árjuna, also known as Víjaya, conquered Duhshásana in
combat, and then charged against Bhishma in the sight of 117.20
the entire troops. But even though he had been defeated, your son placed his trust in the power of Bhishma's arms; excited with fury, he composed himself and kept joining the

Śikhaṇḍī tu raṇe, rājan, vivyādh' âiva pitā|maham
śarair aśani|saṃsparśais tathā sarpa|viṣ'|ôpamaiḥ.
na ca sma te rujaṃ cakruḥ pitus tava, jan'|eśvara.
smayamānas tu Gāṅgeyas tān bāṇāñ jagṛhe tadā.
uṣṇ'|ārto hi naro yadvaj jala|dhārāḥ pratīcchati,
tathā jagrāha Gāṅgeyaḥ śara|dhārāḥ Śikhaṇḍinaḥ.
117.25 taṃ kṣatriyā, mahā|rāja, dadṛśur ghoram āhave,
Bhīṣmaṃ dahantaṃ sainyāni Pāṇḍavānāṃ mah"|ātmanām.
tato 'bravīt tava sutaḥ sarva|sainyāni, māriṣa:
«abhidravata saṃgrāme Phālgunaṃ sarvato raṇe!
Bhīṣmo vaḥ samare sarvān pālayiṣyati dharma|vit.
te bhayaṃ su|mahat tyaktvā Pāṇḍavān pratiyudhyata.
hema|tālena mahatā Bhīṣmas tiṣṭhati pālayan
sarveṣāṃ Dhārtarāṣṭrāṇāṃ samare śarma varma ca.
tridaś" âpi samudyuktā n' âlaṃ Bhīṣmaṃ samāsitum!
kim u Pārthā mah"|ātmānaṃ martya|bhūtā mahā|balāḥ?
117.30 tasmād dravata mā, yodhāḥ, Phālgunaṃ prāpya saṃyuge.
aham adya raṇe yatto yodhayiṣyāmi Pāṇḍavam
sahitaḥ sarvato yattair bhavadbhir vasudh"|âdhipaiḥ.»
tac chrutvā tu vaco, rājaṃs, tava putrasya dhanvinaḥ,
sarve yoddhāḥ su|saṃrabdhā, balavanto, mahā|balāḥ,
te Videhāḥ, Kaliṅgāś ca, Dāśeraka|gaṇāś ca ha
abhipetur; Niṣādāś ca, Sauvīrāś ca mahā|raṇe,
Bāhlikā, Daradāś c' âiva, prācy'|ôdīcyāś ca, Mālavāḥ,
Abhīṣāhāḥ, Śūrasenāḥ, Śibayo, 'tha Vasātayaḥ,

fray again and again. Árjuna looked splendid as he fought in that battle, Your Majesty.

Then Shikhándin cut the grandfather in combat with his shafts, Your Majesty. But those shafts did not inflict any pain on your father, lord of the people; the son of Ganga received them with a smile. As a man who is tormented by heat welcomes torrents of rain, so the son of Ganga received
the torrents of Shikhándin's arrows. Great king, the warriors 117.25
saw how terrifying Bhishma was in battle, as he incinerated the host of the great-spirited Pándavas.

Then, my lord, your son addressed all his troops:

"Attack Phálguna from all sides in battle! Bhishma knows what is right, and he will fight to protect you all. Give up the fear that's afflicting you so badly, and fight against the Pándavas! With the emblem of a golden palmyra on his banner, Bhishma is still standing, providing shelter and protection to all of Dhrita·rashtra's warriors. Even the gods, striving hard, would be unable to overpower the great-spirited Bhishma! What then of the Parthas, who are just powerful mortals? So do not flee, warriors, when you confront 117.30
Phálguna on the battlefield. I will fight with you against the Pándava today, and I will exert myself fully in the fight, just as you are all trying your very best."

When they heard the words of your bow-wielding son, Your Majesty, all the mighty warriors, immensely strong, filled with violent rage, and drawn from the Vidéhas, the Kalíngas, the Dashéraka tribes, the Nishádas, the Sauvíras, the Báhlikas, the Dáradas, the westerners, the northerners, the Málavas, the Abhisháhas, the Shura·senas, the Shibis,

Śālvāḥ, Śakās, Trigartāś ca, Ambaṣṭhāḥ Kekayaiḥ saha
117.35 abhipetū raṇe Pārthaṃ pataṅgā iva pāvakam;
śalabhā iva, rāj'|êndra, Pārtham a|pratimaṃ raṇe.
etān sarvān sah'|ânīkān, mahā|rāja, mahā|rathān
divyāny astrāṇi saṃcintya, prasaṃdhāya Dhanañjayaḥ
sa tair astrair mahā|vegair dadāha su|mahā|balaḥ
śara|pratāpair Bībhatsuḥ, pataṅgān iva pāvakaḥ.
tasya bāṇa|sahasrāṇi sṛjato dṛḍha|dhanvinaḥ
dīpyamānam iv' ākāśe Gāṇḍīvaṃ samadṛśyata.
te śar'|ārtā, mahā|rāja, viprakīrṇa|ratha|dhvajāḥ
n' âbhyavartanta rājānaḥ sahitā vānara|dhvajam.
sa|dhvajā rathinaḥ petur, hay'|ārohā hayaiḥ saha,
117.40 sa|gajāś ca gaj'|ārohāḥ Kirīṭi|śara|tāḍitāḥ.

tato 'rjuna|bhuj'|ôtsṛṣṭair āvṛt" āsīd vasun|dharā,
vidravadbhiś ca bahudhā balai rājñāṃ samantataḥ.
atha Pārtho, mahā|rāja, drāvayitvā varūthinīm
Duḥśāsanāya su|bahūn preṣayām āsa sāyakān.
te tu bhittvā tava sutaṃ Duḥśāsanam ayo|mukhāḥ
dharaṇīṃ viviśuḥ sarve, valmīkam iva pannagāḥ.
hayāṃś c' âsya tato jaghne, sārathiṃ ca nyapātayat;

Viviṃśatiṃ ca viṃśatyā virathaṃ kṛtavān prabhuḥ,
ājaghāna bhṛśaṃ c' âiva pañcabhir nata|parvabhiḥ.
117.45 Kṛpaṃ, Vikarṇaṃ, Śalyaṃ ca viddhvā bahubhir āyasaiḥ
cakāra vi|rathāṃś c' âiva Kaunteyaḥ śveta|vāhanaḥ.

the Vasátis, the Shalvas, the Shakas, the Tri·gartas, the Ambáshthas, and the Kékayas, pounced on the son of Pritha 117.35
in battle, like moths flying into the fire. They attacked Pritha's peerless son like hordes of locusts in that contest, king of kings. The immensely powerful Dhanan·jaya, who is known as Bibhátsu, invoked and aimed his divine weapons, great king; and with those powerful weapons, and with the force of his shafts, he incinerated all those mighty warriors and their troops just as a fire consumes moths. As that mighty archer was firing his thousands of shafts, his Gandíva bow practically shone in the sky. Tormented by his arrows, those kings, their large banners torn and scattered all over, could not assail monkey-bannered Árjuna even with their forces combined, great king. Struck by the shafts of that diadem-decorated hero, chariot warriors fell
down with their banners, horsemen with their horses, and 117.40
elephant riders with their elephants.

And soon the earth was covered everywhere by the troops of those kings as they fled in droves from the arrows Árjuna's arms had released. And when he had routed the enemy army, great king, Pritha's son shot countless arrows at your son Duhshásana; and all those iron-tipped shafts cut through Duhshásana's body and entered the earth, like snakes entering an anthill. Árjuna then killed his opponent's horses and toppled his chariot driver.

After that, the lord deprived Vivímshati of his chariot with twenty arrows, and seriously wounded him with five
straight shafts. Then Kunti's son, the man with the white 117.45
horses, pierced Kripa, Vikárna, and Shalya with many iron arrows and stripped them of their chariots; and all those

evaṃ te vi|rathāḥ pañca—Kṛpaḥ, Śalyaś ca, māriṣa,
Duḥśāsano, Vikarṇaś ca, tath" âiva ca Viviṃśatiḥ—
saṃprādravanta samare nirjitāḥ Savyasācinā.

pūrv'|âhṇe, Bharata|śreṣṭha, parājitya mahā|rathān
prajajvāla raṇe Pārtho, vi|dhūma iva pāvakaḥ.
tath" âiva śara|varṣeṇa bhās|karo raśmivān iva
anyān api, mahā|rāja, tāpayām āsa pārthivān.
parāṅ|mukhī|kṛtya tadā śara|varṣair mahā|rathān
117.50 prāvartayata saṃgrāme śoṇit'|ôdāṃ mahā|nadīm
madhyena Kuru|sainyānāṃ Pāṇḍavānāṃ ca, Bhārata.
gajāś ca ratha|saṅghāś ca bahudhā rathibhir hatāḥ,
rathāś ca nihatā nāgair, hayāś c' âiva padātibhiḥ.
antar" ācchidhyamānāni śarīrāṇi śirāṃsi ca
nipetur dikṣu sarvāsu gaj'|âśva|ratha|yodhinām.

channam āyodhanaṃ reje kuṇḍal'|âṅgada|dhāribhiḥ
patitaiḥ pātyamānaiś ca rāja|putrair mahā|rathaiḥ,
ratha|nemi|nikṛttaiś ca, gajaiś c' âiv' âvapothitaiḥ.
pādātāś c' âpy adhāvanta, s'|âśvāś ca haya|yodhinaḥ.
117.55 gajāś ca ratha|yodhāś ca paripetuḥ samantataḥ,
vikīrṇāś ca rathā bhūmau bhagna|cakra|yuga|dhvajāḥ.

tad gaj'|âśva|rath'|âughānāṃ rudhireṇa samukṣitam
channam āyodhanaṃ reje, rakt'|âbhram iva śāradam.
śvānaḥ, kākāś ca, gṛdhrāś ca, vṛkā gomāyubhiḥ saha
praṇedur bhakṣyam āsādya, vikṛtāś ca mṛga|dvijāḥ.
vavur bahu|vidhāś c' âiva dikṣu sarvāsu mārutāḥ

chariotless heroes—Kripa, Shalya, Duhshásana, Vikárna, and Vivímshati, my lord—ran away, defeated by Savya·sachin in that encounter.

And when he conquered those great warriors in the morning, best of the Bharatas, the son of Pritha blazed in 117.50
battle like a fire without smoke. In the same way he began to scorch other kings with volleys of arrows, great king, like the sun sending forth its rays. Forcing those mighty warriors to retreat by firing volleys of shafts, he made a large river of blood flow through the battlefield, between the armies of the Kurus and the Pándavas, descendant of Bharata. Elephants and fleets of chariots were smashed up by chariot warriors in great numbers; chariots were struck down by elephants, and horses by foot soldiers. Chopped to the innards, the bodies and the heads of those who fought on elephants, horses, and chariots fell in all directions.

The field of play was strewn with the fallen and falling bodies of princes and great warriors, graced with earrings and bracelets, Your Majesty; and those bodies were crushed by chariot wheels and trampled by elephants. Foot soldiers took flight, and so did horsemen and their horses.
Elephants and chariot warriors fell down all around. Char- 117.55
iots were scattered on the ground, their wheels, yokes, and banners broken.

Drenched in the blood of elephants, horses, and chariot warriors, the battlefield looked resplendent, like a red autumnal cloud. Dogs, crows, vultures, wolves, jackals, and other fierce animals and birds let out loud screams as they took their food. Various winds blew, in every direction. Roaring demons and evil spirits came into view. Golden

dṛśyamāneṣu rakṣaḥsu, bhūteṣu vinadatsu ca.
kāñcanāni ca dāmāni, patākāś ca mahā|dhanāḥ
dhūyamānā vyadṛśyanta sahasā mārut'|ēritāḥ.
117.60 śveta|cchatra|sahasrāṇi, sa|dhvajāś ca mahā|rathāḥ
vikīrṇāḥ samadṛśyanta śataśo 'tha sahasraśaḥ.
sa|patākāś ca mātaṅgā diśo jagmuḥ śar'|āturāḥ,
kṣatriyāś ca, manuṣy'|êndra, gadā|śakti|dhanur|dharāḥ
samantato vyadṛśyanta patitā dharaṇī|tale.

tato Bhīṣmo, mahā|rāja, divyam astram udīrayan
abhyadhāvata Kaunteyaṃ miṣatāṃ sarva|dhanvinām.
taṃ Śikhaṇḍī raṇe yāntam abhyadravata daṃśitaḥ.
saṃjahāra tato Bhīṣmas tad astraṃ pāvak'|ôpamam.
tvarito Pāṇḍavo, rājan, madhyamaḥ śveta|vāhanaḥ
nijaghne tāvakaṃ sainyaṃ, mohayitvā pitā|maham.

SAÑJAYA uvāca:

118.1 SAMAṂ VYŪḌHEṢV anīkeṣu bhūyiṣṭheṣv a|nivartinaḥ
Brahma|loka|parāḥ sarve samapadyanta, Bhārata.
na hy anīkam anīkena samasajjata saṃkule:
rathā na rathibhiḥ sārdhaṃ, padātā na padātibhiḥ,
aśvā n' âśvair ayudhyanta, gajā na gaja|yodhibhiḥ.
unmattavan, mahā|rāja, yudhyante tatra, Bhārata.
mahān vyatikaro raudraḥ senayoḥ samapadyata
nara|nāga|gaṇeṣv evaṃ vyavakīrṇeṣu sarvaśaḥ.
118.5 kṣaye tasmin mahā|raudre nir|viśeṣam ajāyata.

strings and valuable flags were suddenly seen, flapping in the wind. Thousands of white parasols and hundreds and 117.60
thousands of great chariots furnished with banners could be seen, scattered about. Elephants with banners on their backs, plagued by arrows, ran away in all directions. Lord of men, warriors armed with maces, spears, and bows were seen, fallen to the ground on all sides.

Then, great king, Bhishma invoked a divine weapon and charged against the son of Kunti while all the archers looked on. Shikhándin, clad in armor, attacked Bhishma as the latter was advancing in battle; and Bhishma withdrew that fiery weapon. And in the meantime Pandu's middle son, carried by his white horses, confounded the grandfather and continued to massacre your host, Your Majesty.

SÁNJAYA said:

ALL THE NUMEROUS troops of both armies were in the 118.1
same fix: they refused to retreat, intent as they were on attaining the world of Brahma, and they charged forward, descendant of Bharata. In that chaotic clash, no similar divisions confronted each other: chariots did not fight with chariots, nor infantry with infantry, nor cavalry with cavalry, nor elephants with elephants. They battled in a frenzy, great Bhárata king. A great and terrible confusion spread among both hosts, and men and elephants lay scattered everywhere. That's what it was like. In that terrifying battle 118.5
there was indiscriminate carnage.

tataḥ Śalyaḥ, Kṛpaś c' âiva, Citrasenaś ca, Bhārata,
Duḥśāsano, Vikarṇaś ca rathān āsthāya bhāsvarān
Pāṇḍavānāṃ raṇe śūrā dhvajinīṃ samakampayan.
sā vadhyamānā samare Pāṇḍu|senā mah"|ātmabhiḥ
bhrāmyate bahudhā, rājan, māruten' âva naur jale.
yathā hi śaiśiraḥ kālo gavāṃ marmāṇi kṛntati,
tathā Pāṇḍu|sutānāṃ vai Bhīṣmo marmāṇy akṛntata.
at' îva tava sainyasya Pārthena ca mah"|ātmanā
nava|megha|pratīkāśāḥ pātitā bahudhā gajāḥ
118.10 mṛdyamānāś ca dṛśyante Pārthena nara|yūtha|pāḥ.
iṣubhis tāḍyamānāś ca nārācaiś ca sahasraśaḥ
petur ārta|svaraṃ kṛtvā tatra tatra mahā|gajāḥ.
ānaddh'|ābharaṇaiḥ kāyair nihatānāṃ mah"|ātmanām
channam āyodhanaṃ reje śirobhiś ca sa|kuṇḍalaiḥ.

tasminn eva, mahā|rāja, mahā|vīra|vara|kṣaye,
Bhīṣme ca yudhi vikrānte, Pāṇḍave ca Dhanañjaye,
te parākrāntam ālokya, rājan, yudhi pitā|maham
ayabhyavartanta te putrā Brahma|loka|puras|kṛtāḥ.
icchanto nidhanaṃ yuddhe, svargaṃ kṛtvā parāyaṇam,
118.15 Pāṇḍavān abhyavartanta tasmin vīra|vara|kṣaye.

Pāṇḍavāś ca, mahā|rāja, smaranto vividhān bahūn
kleśān kṛtān sa|putreṇa tvayā pūrvaṃ, nar'|âdhipa,
bhayaṃ tyaktvā raṇe śūrā Brahma|lokāya tat|parāḥ
tāvakāṃs tava putrāṃś ca yodhayanti sma hṛṣṭavat.

Then, descendant of Bharata, the heroes Shalya, Kripa, Chitra·sena, Duhshásana, and Vikárna, mounted on their splendid chariots, began an offensive that shook the Pándava army. The Pándava host, hard pressed by those great-spirited fighters in that battle, Your Majesty, reeled in various ways, like a boat being tipped around on the water by the wind. Just as the wintry cold pierces cows to the marrow, so Bhishma cut the sons of Pandu to the quick. Likewise numerous elephants of your army, looking like newly arisen clouds, were killed by the great-spirited Partha.
Leaders of troops of men were seen crushed by the son of 118.10
Pritha. Struck by thousands of his arrows and iron shafts, huge elephants collapsed there, letting out screams of agony. Covered with the ornamented bodies of illustrious slain fighters, and with their heads complete with earrings, the battlefield looked splendid.

During that battle so fraught with the destruction of great heroes, while Bhishma and Dhanan·jaya were displaying their courage, all your sons, Your Majesty, watching the
grandfather battle vigorously in that engagement, advanced 118.15
at the head of their troops against the Pándavas and into a massacre of superb heroes; they wanted to die in battle and had made heaven their goal.

And the Pándavas, great king, valiant in combat, keeping in their minds the many different misfortunes caused to them by you and your sons, lord of the people, gave up all fear and, intent on attaining the world of Brahma, fought zestfully against your sons.

senā|patis tu samare prāha senāṃ mahā|rathaḥ:
«abhidravata Gāṅgeyaṃ, Somakāḥ, Sṛñjayaiḥ saha!»
senā|pati|vacaḥ śrutvā Somakāḥ Sṛñjayāś ca te
abhyadravanta Gāṅgeyaṃ śastra|vṛṣṭyā samantataḥ.
vadhyamānas tato, rājan, pitā Śāntanavas tava
118.20 a|marṣa|vaśam āpanno yodhayām āsa Sṛñjayān.
tasya kīrtimatas, tāta, purā Rāmeṇa dhīmatā
saṃpradatt" âstra|śikṣā vai par'|ânīka|vināśinī.
sa tāṃ śikṣām adhiṣṭhāya, kṛtvā para|bala|kṣayam,
ahany ahani Pārthānāṃ vṛddhaḥ Kuru|pitāmahaḥ
Bhīṣmo daśa sahasrāṇi jaghāna para|vīra|hā.
tasmiṃs tu daśame prāpte divase, Bharata'|rṣabha,
Bhīṣmeṇ' âikena Matsyeṣu Pañcāleṣu ca saṃyuge
gaj'|âśvam a|mitaṃ hatvā hatāḥ sapta mahā|rathāḥ.
hatvā pañca sahasrāṇi rathināṃ prapitāmahaḥ,
118.25 narāṇāṃ ca mahā|yuddhe sahasrāṇi catur|daśa,
dantināṃ ca sahasrāṇi, hayānām ayutaṃ punaḥ
śikṣā|balena nihataṃ pitrā tava, viśāṃ pate.
tataḥ sarva|mahī|pānāṃ kṣobhayitvā varūthinīm
Virāṭasya priyo bhrātā Śatāniko nipātitaḥ.
Śatānīkaṃ ca samare hatvā Bhīṣmaḥ pratāpavān
sahasrāṇi, mahā|rāja, rājñāṃ bhallair apātayat.

Then the general of the Pándava army, the great warrior Dhrishta·dyumna, commanded his troops in battle. "Sómakas, charge together with the Srínjayas against the son of Ganga!"

Hearing the general's order, the Sómakas and the Srínjayas, even though they had been struck by a very deluge of arrows, attacked the son of Ganga. Besieged by them, Your
Majesty, your father the son of Shántanu, overpowered by 118.20
wrath, began to fight with the Srínjayas.

Formerly, my lord, wise Rama had given your glorious father some instructions about how to use weapons to exterminate hostile troops. Relying on those instructions and carrying out the destruction of the enemy forces, Bhishma, the venerable grandfather of the Kurus, that annihilator of hostile heroes, slaughtered ten thousand of the Parthas' soldiers every day. When the tenth day of the war came, bull of the Bharatas, Bhishma single-handedly killed innumerable elephants and horses belonging to the Matsyas and the Panchálas in combat, and also seven of their great warriors. Then the great-grandfather, laying waste to five thousand
chariot-riding warriors and fourteen thousand foot soldiers 118.25
in that huge battle, killed several thousand elephants and ten thousand horses. It is due to those instructions, lord of the people, that they were massacred by your father.

Having destroyed the host of all those kings, he struck down Viráta's beloved brother Shataníka. After slaying Shataníka in that fight, mighty Bhishma cut down thousands of kings with spear-headed arrows, Your Majesty.

udvignāḥ samare yodhā vikrośanti Dhanañjayam.
ye ca ke cana Pārthānām abhiyātā Dhanañjayam
rājāno, Bhīṣmam āsādya gatās te Yama|sādanam.
118.30 evaṃ daśa diśo Bhīṣmaḥ śara|jālaiḥ samantataḥ
atītya senāṃ Pārthānām avatasthe camū|mukhe.
sa kṛtvā su|mahat karma tasmin vai daśame 'hani,
senayor antare 'tiṣṭhat pragṛhīta|śar'|âsanaḥ.
na c' âinaṃ pārthivā ke cic chaktā, rājan, nirīkṣitum
madhyaṃ prāptaṃ yathā grīṣme tapantaṃ bhās|karaṃ divi.
yathā daitya|camūṃ Śakras tāpayām āsa saṃyuge,
tathā Bhīṣmaḥ Pāṇḍaveyāṃs tāpayām āsa, Bhārata.

tathā c' âinaṃ parākrāntam ālokya Madhu|sūdanaḥ
uvāca Devakī|putraḥ prīyamāṇo Dhanañjayam:
118.35 «eṣa Śāntanavo Bhīṣmaḥ senayor antare sthitaḥ.
saṃnihatya balād enaṃ vijayas te bhaviṣyati.
balāt saṃstambhayasv' âinaṃ, yatr' âiṣā bhidyate camūḥ.
na hi Bhīṣma|śarān anyaḥ soḍhum utsahate, vibho.
tatas tasmin kṣaṇe, rājaṃś,
codito vānara|dhvajaḥ
sa|dhvajaṃ, sa|rathaṃ, s'|âśvaṃ
Bhīṣmam antar|dadhe śaraiḥ.
sa c' âpi Kuru|mukhyānām ṛṣabhaḥ Pāṇḍav'|ēritān
śara|vrātaiḥ śara|vrātān bahudhā vidudhāva tān.

The dejected Pándava warriors appealed to Dhanan·jaya. The royal combatants of the Parthas' host who accompanied Dhanan·jaya were sent to Yama's realm the moment they confronted Bhishma. And so, enveloping all ten direc- 118.30
tions with webs of his shafts and overcoming the army of the Parthas every which way, Bhishma stayed at the front of his army. On the tenth day he stood between the two hosts, wielding his bow and performing the greatest feats. And none of the enemy kings could really look at him; he was like the scorching midday sun in the sky in summer. As Shakra once scorched the host of demons in battle, so Bhishma scorched the Pándavas, descendant of Bharata.

And seeing Bhishma so vigorous in battle, the slayer of Madhu and the son of Dévaki, delighted, said to Dhanan·jaya: "Here is Bhishma the son of Shántanu, stationed be- 118.35
tween the two armies. If you strike him down violently, victory will be yours! Forcibly block him off there, where he is breaking our ranks! Nobody else is able to withstand Bhishma's arrows, lord." And at that very moment, Your Majesty, monkey-bannered Árjuna, urged on by Krishna, shrouded Bhishma, along with his banner, chariot, and horses, in his arrows. But with many volleys of shafts the bull of the Kuru leaders dispersed those swarms of arrows fired by the Pándava.

tataḥ Pañcāla|rājaś ca, Dhṛṣṭaketuś ca vīryavān,
Pāṇḍavo Bhīmasenaś ca, Dhṛṣṭadyumnaś ca Pārṣataḥ,
118.40 yamau ca, Cekitānaś ca, Kekayāḥ pañca c' âiva ha,
Sātyakiś ca mahā|bāhuḥ, Saubhadro, 'tha Ghaṭotkacaḥ,
Draupadeyāḥ, Śikhaṇḍī ca, Kuntibhojaś ca vīryavān,
Suśarmā ca, Virāṭaś ca—Pāṇḍaveyā mahā|balāḥ
ete c' ânye ca bahavaḥ pīḍitā Bhīṣma|sāyakaiḥ
samuddhṛtāḥ Phālgunena nimagnāḥ śoka|sāgare.
tataḥ Śikhaṇḍī vegena pragṛhya param'|āyudham
Bhīṣmam ev' âbhidudrāva rakṣyamāṇaḥ Kirīṭinā.
tato 'sy' ânucarān hatvā sarvān raṇa|vibhāga|vit
Bhīṣmam ev' âbhidudrāva Bībhatsur a|parājitaḥ.
118.45 Sātyakiś, Cekitānaś ca, Dhṛṣṭadyumnaś ca Pārṣataḥ,
Virāṭo, Drupadaś c' âiva, Mādrī|putrau ca Pāṇḍavau
dudruvur Bhīṣmam ev' ājau rakṣitā dṛḍha|dhanvanā.
Abhimanyuś ca samare, Draupadyāḥ pañca c' ātma|jāḥ
dudruvuḥ samare Bhīṣmaṃ samudyata|mah"|āyudhāḥ.
te sarve dṛḍha|dhanvānaḥ, saṃyugeṣv a|palāyinaḥ
bahudhā Bhīṣmam ānarchan mārgaṇaiḥ kṣata|mārgaṇāḥ.
vidhūya tān bāṇa|gaṇān ye muktāḥ pārthiv'|ôttamaiḥ,
Pāṇḍavānām a|dīn'|ātmā vyagāhata varūthinīm.
cakre śara|vighātaṃ ca krīḍann iva pitā|mahaḥ.
118.50 n' âbhisaṃdhatta Pāñcālye smayamāno muhur muhuḥ,
strītvaṃ tasy' ânusaṃsmṛtya Bhīṣmo bāṇāñ Shikhaṇḍine.
jaghāna Drupad'|ânīke rathān sapta mahā|rathaḥ.
tataḥ kilakilā|śabdaḥ kṣaṇena samapadyata

Then the king of the Panchálas, vigorous Dhrishta·ketu,
Bhima·sena Pándava, Príshata's grandson Dhrishta·dyumna,
the twins Nákula and Saha·deva, Chekitána, the five Kékaya 118.40
brothers, strong-armed Sátyaki, Subhádra's son, Ghatótkacha, the sons of Dráupadi, Shikhándin, vigorous Kunti·bhoja, Susharman, Viráta—these and many other mighty Pándava combatants, wounded by Bhishma's arrows and sunk into a sea of grief, were rescued by Phálguna. And, protected by diadem-adorned Árjuna, Shikhándin grabbed a superb weapon and charged against Bhishma with great force. Undefeated Bibhátsu, who knew all about battle tactics, killed Bhishma's followers and then attacked the man
himself. Sátyaki, Chekitána, Príshata's grandson Dhrishta· 118.45
dyumna, Viráta, Drúpada, and the two Pándava sons of Madri advanced against Bhishma in that engagement, with the mighty archer Árjuna providing cover for them. Brandishing their weapons, Abhimányu and the five sons of Dráupadi also charged against Bhishma in that encounter. All those powerful bowmen, never fleeing in combat, afflicted Bhishma in many ways with their wound-seeking arrows.

But Bhishma, buoyant within himself, repelled the hordes of shafts those supreme kings released, and penetrated the Pándava host. The grandfather warded off the enemy arrows as if he was doing if for fun. Bhishma did not 118.50
aim a single arrow at Prince Shikhándin of the Panchálas, but thinking about his female nature he laughed over and over again. The great warrior Bhishma then smashed up seven chariots in Drúpada's division, after which loud shouts were heard from the Matsyas, the Panchálas, and the Chedis,

Matsya|Pāñcāla|Cedīnāṃ tam ekam abhidhāvatām.
te nar'|âśva|ratha|vrātair, mārgaṇaiś ca, paran|tapa,
tam ekaṃ chādayām āsur, meghā iva divā|karam,
Bhīṣmaṃ Bhāgīrathī|putraṃ pratapantaṃ raṇe ripūn.
tatas tasya ca teṣāṃ ca yuddhe dev'|âsur|ôpame
Kirīṭī Bhīṣmam ānarchat puras|kṛtya Śikhaṇḍinam.

SAÑJAYA uvāca:

119.1 EVAṂ TE PĀṆḌAVĀḤ sarve puras|kṛtya Śikhaṇḍinam
vivyadhuḥ samare Bhīṣmaṃ parivārya samantataḥ.
śata|ghnībhiḥ su|ghorābhiḥ, paṭṭiśaiḥ sa|paraśvadhaiḥ,
mudgarair, musalaiḥ, prāsaiḥ, kṣepaṇīyaiś ca sarvaśaḥ,
śaraiḥ kanaka|puṅkhaiś ca, śakti|tomara|kampanaiḥ,
nārācair, vatsa|dantaiś ca, bhuśuṇḍībhiś ca sarvaśaḥ
atāḍayan raṇe Bhīṣmaṃ sahitāḥ sarva|Sṛñjayāḥ.
sa viśīrṇa|tanu|trāṇaḥ, pīḍito bahubhis tadā
119.5 na vivyathe tadā Bhīṣmo bhidyamāneṣu marmasu.
saṃdīpta|śara|cāp'|âgnir, astra|prasṛta|mārutaḥ,
nemi|nirhrāda|saṃnādo, mah"|âstr'|ôdaya|pāvakaḥ,
citra|cāpa|mahā|jvālo, vīra|kṣaya|mah"|êndhanaḥ
yug'|ânt'|âgni|sama|prakhyaḥ pareṣāṃ samapadyata.
vivṛtya ratha|saṅghānām antareṇa viniḥsṛtaḥ
dṛśyate sma nar'|êndrāṇāṃ punar madhya|gataś caran.

and they assailed that lone warrior. Just as clouds shroud the sun, scorcher of foes, so with multitudes of men, horses, and chariots, and also with masses of shafts, they enveloped the son of Bhagi·ratha's daughter Ganga, that singular hero Bhishma, who was scorching enemies in battle. Then, during the combat between him and them, which was like the battle between the gods and demons, diadem-adorned Árjuna placed Shikhándin before him and began to strike at Bhishma.

SÁNJAYA said:

So ALL THE PÁNDAVAS placed Shikhándin before them, 119.1
surrounded Bhishma on all sides, and began to strike him in the battle. And all the Srínjayas joined together and started to bombard Bhishma in that encounter with utterly frightful *shata·ghni* missiles, iron clubs, battle-axes, mallets, maces, javelins, and all kinds of other missiles: gold-nocked arrows, spears, lances, darts, iron shafts, calf-toothed arrows, and slings.

But though he was being wounded by many adversaries
and having his armor torn through and his vitals pierced, 119.5
Bhishma was unperturbed. With his bow and arrows for its blazing fire, the impetus of his weapons for its wind, the rattle of chariot wheels for its heat, the flight of his mighty weapons for its glow, the resplendent bow for its huge blaze, and the destruction of heroes for its fuel, Bhishma appeared to the enemies like the fire that comes at the end of the age. He was seen rampaging through the hostile kings' chariot divisions, then coming out of their ranks and penetrating them again.

tataḥ Pañcāla|rājaṃ ca Dhṛṣṭaketum a|cintya ca
Pāṇḍav'|ânīkinī|madhyam āsasāda, viśāṃ pate.
tataḥ Sātyaki|Bhīmau ca, Pāṇḍavaṃ ca Dhanañjayam,
119.10 Drupadaṃ ca, Virāṭaṃ ca, Dhṛṣṭadyumnaṃ ca Pārṣatam
bhīma|ghoṣair mahā|vegair marm'|āvaraṇa|bhedibhiḥ
ṣaḍ etān niśitair Bhīṣmaḥ pravivyādh' ôttamaiḥ śaraiḥ.
tasya te niśitān bāṇān saṃnivārya mahā|rathāḥ
daśabhir daśabhir Bhīṣmam ardayām āsur ojasā.
Śikhaṇḍī tu raṇe bāṇān yān mumoca mahā|vrate,
na cakrus te rujaṃ tasya svarṇa|puṅkhāḥ śilā|śitāḥ.
tataḥ Kirīṭī saṃrabdho Bhīṣmam ev' âbhyavartata
Śikhaṇḍinaṃ puras|kṛtya, dhanuś c' âsya samācchinat.
Bhīṣmasya dhanuṣaś chedaṃ n' âmṛṣyanta mahā|rathāḥ:
119.15 Droṇaś ca, Kṛtavarmā ca, Saindhavaś ca Jayadrathaḥ,
Bhūriśravāḥ, Śalaḥ, Śalyo, Bhagadattas tath" âiva ca.
sapt' âite parama|kruddhāḥ Kirīṭinam abhidrutāḥ.
tatra śastrāṇi divyāni darśayanto mahā|rathāḥ
abhipetur bhṛśaṃ kruddhāś, chādayantaś ca Pāṇḍavam.
teṣām āpatatāṃ śabdaḥ śuśruve Phālgunaṃ prati,
udvṛttānāṃ yathā śabdaḥ samudrāṇāṃ yuga|kṣaye.
«ghnat'! ānayata! gṛhṇīta! yudhyat'!» âpi ca «kṛntata!»
ity āsīt tumulaḥ śabdaḥ Phālgunasya rathaṃ prati.
tam śabdaṃ tumulaṃ śrutvā Pāṇḍavānāṃ mahā|rathāḥ
119.20 abhyadhāvan parīpsantaḥ Phālgunaṃ, Bharata'|rṣabha.
Sātyakir, Bhīmasenaś ca, Dhṛṣṭadyumnaś ca Pārṣataḥ,
Virāṭa|Drupadau c' ôbhau,

Taking no notice of Dhrishta·ketu and the king of the Panchálas, Bhishma reached the center of the Pándava host, lord of the people. Then he pierced these six great warriors—Sátyaki, Bhima, Pandu's son Dhanan·jaya, Drúpada, 119.10
Viráta, and Dhrishta·dyumna the grandson of Príshata—with fiercely whizzing, speedy, sharpened, excellent arrows that could cut through armor and penetrate the very vitals. And those mighty warriors warded off his sharp arrows and vigorously struck Bhishma, each of them firing ten shafts. But the gold-nocked and stone-whetted arrows discharged by the great warrior Shikhándin inflicted no damage upon Bhishma. So diadem-adorned Árjuna, in a rage, with Shikhándin before him, charged against Bhishma and severed the latter's bow.

Unable to put up with Bhishma having his bow severed, seven mighty warriors, namely Drona, Krita·varman, 119.15
Jayad·ratha the king of the Sindhus, Bhuri·shravas, Shala, Shalya, and Bhaga·datta, filled with intense fury, attacked diadem-adorned Árjuna, displaying their divine weapons. They pounced on the Pándava in their violent rage, enveloping him with their shafts. As they advanced toward Phálguna, the noise they made sounded like the roar of the surging oceans at the end of the age. "Strike! Bring it on! Seize! Pierce! Chop off!"—such were the shouts that made that tumultuous din near Phálguna's chariot.

And hearing that tremendous noise, the great warriors of the Pándava army rushed there, eager to rescue Phálguna, 119.20
bull of the Bharatas. Sátyaki, Bhima·sena, Príshata's grandson Dhrishta·dyumna, the two heroes Viráta and Drúpada, the demon Ghatótkacha, and irate Abhimányu—these

rākṣasaś ca Ghaṭotkacaḥ,
Abhimanyuś ca saṃkruddhaḥ—
sapt' âite krodha|mūrchitāḥ
samabhyadhāvaṃs tvaritāś citra|kārmuka|dhāriṇaḥ.
teṣāṃ samabhavad yuddhaṃ tumulaṃ, loma|harṣaṇam
saṃgrāme, Bharata|śreṣtha, devānāṃ dānavair iva.
Śikhaṇḍī tu raṇe śrestho rakṣyamāṇaḥ Kirīṭinā
avidhyad daśabhir Bhīṣmaṃ chinna|dhanvānam āhave,
sārathiṃ daśabhiś c' âsya, dhvajaṃ c' âikena cicchide.
119.25 so 'nyat kārmukam ādadau Gāṅgeyo vegavattaram.
tad apy asya śitair bhallais tribhiś ciccheda Phālgunaḥ.
evaṃ sa Pāṇḍavaḥ kruddha āttam āttaṃ punaḥ punaḥ
dhanur Bhīṣmasya ciccheda Savyasācī paran|tapaḥ.
sa cchinna|dhanvā, saṃkruddhaḥ, sṛkkiṇī parisaṃlihan
śaktiṃ jagrāha saṃkruddho, girīṇām api dāraṇīm.
tāṃ ca cikṣepa saṃkruddhaḥ Phālgunasya rathaṃ prati.
tām āpatantīṃ saṃprekṣya, jvalantīm aśanīm iva,
samādatta śitān bhallān pañca Pāṇḍava|nandanaḥ;
tasya ciccheda tāṃ śaktiṃ pañcadhā pañcabhiḥ śaraiḥ
119.30 saṃkruddho, Bharata|śreṣtha, Bhīṣma|bāhu|bal'|ēritām.
sā papāta tathā chinnā saṃkruddhena Kirīṭinā,
megha|vṛnda|paribhraṣṭā vichinn" êva śata|hradā.
chinnāṃ tāṃ śaktim ālokya Bhīṣmaḥ krodha|samanvitaḥ
acintayad raṇe vīro buddhyā para|purañ|jayaḥ:
«śakto 'haṃ dhanuṣ" âikena nihantuṃ sarva|Pāṇḍavān,
yady eṣāṃ na bhaved goptā Viṣvakseno mahā|balaḥ.
kāraṇa|dvayam āsthāya n' âhaṃ yotsyāmi Pāṇḍavān:
a|vadhyatvāc ca Pāṇḍūnāṃ, strī|bhāvāc ca Śikhaṇḍinaḥ.

seven combatants, senseless with fury, charged forward at the double, armed with their splendid bows. Then a tumultuous and hair-raising battle took place between them, like the war between the gods and demons, best of the Bharatas.

Shikhándin, an excellent fighter, protected by diadem-decorated Árjuna, pierced bowless Bhishma with ten arrows in that conflict, wounded his chariot driver with another ten, and cut down his banner with one more. And when 119.25 the son of Ganga seized another, swifter bow, Phálguna instantly sliced through that one as well. In his fury the Pándava Savya·sachin, that scorcher of enemies, cut through every bow that Bhishma picked up, again and again. Then Bhishma, his bows useless, filled with anger, licking the corners of his mouth, swiftly grabbed a lance that could even split rocks. Enraged, he hurled it at Phálguna's chariot. Seeing that lance flying toward him like a blazing thunderbolt, Árjuna, the delight of the Pándavas, excited with wrath, 119.30 drew five sharp, spear-headed shafts, and with those five shafts he chopped that lance that Bhishma's arm had propelled into five pieces, best of the Bharata. It fell, severed by the irate diadem-decorated Árjuna, just as lightning falls, discharged from a cluster of thunderclouds. When he saw his lance severed, brave Bhishma, the conqueror of hostile strongholds, though he was filled with fury, applied his intelligence and began to reflect.

"I could have slaughtered all the Pándavas with just one bow if mighty Vishvak·sena* himself had not been their protector. I shall not fight with the Pándavas for two reasons: the inviolability of Pandu's sons, and the female nature of Shikhándin. In the past, when I arranged my father's

pitrā tuṣṭena me pūrvaṃ yadā Kālīm udāvaham,
119.35 sva|cchanda|maraṇaṃ dattam, a|vadhyatvaṃ raṇe tathā.
tasmān mṛtyum ahaṃ manye prāpta|kālam iv' ātmanaḥ.»
evaṃ jñātvā vyavasitaṃ Bhīṣmasy' â|mita|tejasaḥ
ṛṣayo Vasavaś c' âiva viyat|sthā Bhīṣmam abruvan:
«yat te vyavasitaṃ, tāta, tad asmākam api priyam.
tat kuruṣva, mah"|êṣv|āsa. yuddhād buddhiṃ nivartaya.»
tasya vākyasya nidhane prādur|āsīc chivo 'nilaḥ
anulomaḥ, su|gandhī ca, pṛṣataiś ca samanvitaḥ.
deva|dundubhayaś c' âiva saṃpraṇedur mahā|svanāḥ,
papāta puṣpa|vṛṣṭiś ca Bhīṣmasy' ôpari, māriṣa.
119.40 na ca tac chuśruve kaś cit teṣāṃ saṃvadatāṃ, nṛ|pa,
ṛte Bhīṣmaṃ mahā|bāhuṃ, māṃ c' âpi muni|tejasā.
saṃbhramaś ca mahān āsīt tri|daśānāṃ, viśāṃ pate,
patiṣyati rathād Bhīṣme sarva|loka|priye tadā.
iti deva|gaṇānāṃ ca śrutvā vākyaṃ, mahā|tapāḥ
tataḥ Śāntanavo Bhīṣmo Bībhatsuṃ n' âbhyavartata
bhidyamānaḥ śitair bāṇaiḥ sarv'|āvaraṇa|bhedibhiḥ.
Śikhaṇḍī tu, mahā|rāja, Bharatānāṃ pitā|maham
ājaghān' ôrasi kruddho navabhir niśitaiḥ śaraiḥ.
sa ten' âbhihataḥ saṃkhye Bhīṣmaḥ Kuru|pitāmahaḥ
119.45 n' âkampata, mahā|rāja, kṣiti|kampe yath" â|calaḥ.
tataḥ prahasya Bībhatsur vyākṣipan Gāṇḍivaṃ dhanuḥ
Gāṅgeyaṃ pañca|viṃśatyā kṣudrakāṇāṃ samārpayat.

marriage with Kali,* my father, pleased with me, granted 119.35
me two boons: my own choice of when I die, and my inviolability in battle. I think that the proper time for my death has now come."

Learning of the limitlessly vigorous Bhishma's decision, *rishis** and Vasus stationed in the sky said to him: "Sir, the resolution that you have made is agreeable to us! Do as you have resolved, great king! Withdraw your mind from the battle!" At the conclusion of these words an auspicious, gentle, and fragrant breeze came up, filled with fine droplets of water. Thunderous heavenly drums resounded, and a shower of flowers poured upon Bhishma, my lord.
No one heard the words uttered by the celestials, Your 119.40
Majesty, except strong-armed Bhishma, and also myself through the power of the sage.* Great perplexity spread among the gods, lord of the people, when they thought that Bhishma, beloved in all the worlds, was going to fall from his chariot.

Hearing the words of the celestials, the great ascetic Bhishma, the son of Shántanu, though he was afflicted by sharp arrows that could tear through any armor, did not attack Bibhátsu.

Meanwhile, great king, Shikhándin, enraged, wounded the grandfather of the Bharatas in the chest with nine whetted shafts. Struck by him in that encounter, the Kuru grandfather Bhishma stood unwaveringly like an immovable 119.45
mountain during an earthquake, great king. Bibhátsu, stretching his Gandíva bow, shot the son of Ganga with

punaḥ śara|śaten' âinaṃ tvaramāṇo Dhanañjayaḥ
sarva|gātreṣu saṃkruddhaḥ sarva|marmasv atāḍayat.
evam anyair api bhṛśaṃ vidhyamāno mahā|raṇe
tān apy āśu śarair Bhīṣmaḥ pravivyādha mahā|rathaḥ.
taiś ca muktāñ śarān Bhīṣmo yudhi satya|parākramaḥ
nivārayām āsa śaraiḥ samaṃ saṃnata|parvabhiḥ.
Śikhaṇḍī tu raṇe bāṇān yān mumoca mahā|rathaḥ,
119.50 na cakrus te rujaṃ tasya rukma|puṅkhāḥ śilā|śitāḥ.
tataḥ Kirīṭī saṃrabdho Bhīṣmam ev' âbhyavartata
Śikhaṇḍinaṃ puras|kṛtya, dhanuś c' âsya samācchinat.
ath' âinaṃ navabhir viddhvā, dhvajam ekena cicchide,
sārathiṃ viśikhaiś c' âsya daśabhiḥ samakampayat.
so 'nyat kārmukam ādāya Gāṅgeyo balavattaram,
tad apy asya śitair bhallais tridhā tribhir aghātayat.
nimeṣ'|ârdhena Kaunteya āttam āttaṃ mahā|raṇe
evam asya dhanūṃṣy ājau ciccheda su|bahūny api.
tataḥ Śāntanavo Bhīṣmo Bībhatsuṃ n' âtyavartata.
119.55 ath' âinaṃ pañca|viṃśatyā kṣudrakāṇāṃ samārpayat.
so 'tividdho mah"|êṣv|āso Duḥśāsanam abhāṣata:
«eṣa Pārtho raṇe kruddhaḥ Pāṇḍavānāṃ mahā|rathaḥ
śarair an|eka|sāhasrair mām ev' âbhyahanad raṇe.
na c' âiṣa samare śakyo jetuṃ vajra|bhṛtā hy api;
na c' âpi sahitā vīrā deva|dānava|rākṣasāḥ
māṃ c' âpi śaktā nirjetuṃ. kim u martyā mahā|rathāḥ?»

twenty-five short arrows. And again and again Dhanan·jaya, excited with fury, struck him in haste with hundreds of shafts in every part of his body, wherever he was exposed.

Heavily pelted by other combatants with thousands of arrows, the mighty warrior Bhishma instantly shot them back with his shafts. Bhishma, whose power is in truth, took out their arrows the moment they were released with his straight shafts. But the gold-nocked and stone-whetted arrows fired by the great warrior Shikhándin inflicted no 119.50
wound upon Bhishma.

Then diadem-adorned Árjuna, with Shikhándin before him, charged furiously against Bhishma and severed his bow. Piercing Bhishma with nine arrows, he cut down his opponent's banner with one more; and he shook Bhishma's chariot driver with ten shafts. The son of Ganga then seized another, stronger bow, but Árjuna chopped it into three pieces with his sharp, spear-headed arrows. And so, in half the twinkling of an eye the son of Kunti sliced through innumerable bows picked up by Bhishma in that great war. And after that, Bhishma the son of Shántanu attacked Bibhátsu no more. And yet again Árjuna hammered his adver- 119.55
sary, with twenty-five short arrows.

Terribly wounded, the great archer said to Duhshásana: "This Partha, the mighty warrior of the Pándavas, filled with battle-fury, has struck me with many thousands of arrows in this battle. He is invincible even by thunderbolt-wielding Indra in battle. As for myself, even all the heroic gods, *dánavas*, and *rákshasas*, united together, would be unable to defeat me. What then of human warriors?"

evaṃ tayoḥ saṃvadatoḥ Phālguno niśitaiḥ śaraiḥ
Śikhaṇḍinaṃ puras|kṛtya Bhīṣmaṃ vivyādha saṃyuge.
tato Duḥśāsanaṃ bhūyaḥ smayamāna iv' âbravīt
119.60 ati|viddhaḥ śitair bāṇair bhṛśaṃ Gāṇḍīva|dhanvanā:
«vajr'|âśani|sama|sparśā Arjunena śarā yudhi
muktāḥ sarve '|vyavacchinnā. n' ême bāṇāḥ Śikhaṇḍinaḥ.
nikṛntamānā marmāṇi, dṛḍh'|āvaraṇa|bhedinaḥ,
musalā īva me ghnanti. n' ême bāṇāḥ Śikhaṇḍinaḥ.
Brahma|daṇḍa|sama|sparśā, vajra|vegā, dur|āsadāḥ,
mama prāṇān ārujanti. n' ême bāṇāḥ Śikhaṇḍinaḥ.
nāśayant' îva me prāṇān, Yama|dūtā iv' āhitāḥ,
gadā|parigha|saṃsparśā. n' ême bāṇāḥ Śikhaṇḍinaḥ.
bhujagā iva saṃkruddhā, lelihānā, viṣ'|ôlbaṇāḥ
119.65 samāviśanti marmāṇi. n' ême bāṇāḥ Śikhaṇḍinaḥ.
Arjunasya ime bāṇā; n' ême bāṇāḥ Śikhaṇḍinaḥ.
kṛntanti mama gātrāṇi, māghamāṃ segavā iva.
sarve hy api na me duḥkhaṃ kuryur anye nar'|âdhipāḥ,
vīraṃ Gaṇḍīva|dhanvānam ṛte Jiṣṇuṃ kapi|dhvajam.»
iti bruvañ Śāntanavo, didhakṣur iva Pāṇḍavam,
śaktiṃ Bhīṣmaḥ sa Pārthāya tataś cikṣepa, Bhārata.
tām asya viśikhaiś chittvā tridhā tribhir apātayat.
paśyatāṃ Kuru|vīrāṇāṃ sarveṣāṃ tava, Bhārata,
carm' âth' ādatta Gāṅgeyo jātarūpa|pariṣkṛtam,
119.70 khaḍgaṃ c' ânyatara|prepsur mṛtyor agre jayāya vā.
tasya tac chatadhā carma vyadhamat sāyakais tathā

While they were talking like this, Phálguna, keeping 119.60
Shikhándin before him, fired on Bhishma and stuck him with sharpened arrows. Then Bhishma, smiling slightly, deeply pierced as he was by the sharp arrows of the wielder of the Gandíva bow, spoke to Duhshásana again:

"These shafts, crashing like thunderbolts, have been released non-stop in battle by Árjuna. These arrows are not Shikhándin's. These arrows, that tear through my strong armor and cut me to the quick, pounding my body, are not Shikhándin's. These arrows, crashing and irresistible like impetuous thunderbolts, affecting my very breath of life, are not Shikhándin's. These arrows, destroying my breath
of life as if they were messengers sent by Yama, are not 119.65
Shikhándin's; they smash home like maces and clubs. These arrows, penetrating my vital organs like this, like raging and virulently poisonous snakes licking their tongues, are not Shikhándin's. These are Árjuna's arrows, not Shikhándin's. They cut through my limbs just as newly born crabs cut through the mother crab. Apart from monkey-bannered Jishnu the wielder of the Gandíva bow, none of the other princes can inflict pain on me, even if they're all rolled into one."

After saying these words, Bhishma the son of Shántanu, as if he wanted to incinerate the Pándava, hurled a spear at the son of Pritha, descendant of Bharata. But Árjuna struck it down by slicing it into three pieces with three shafts. Then, while all your Kuru heroes looked on, Bhárata, the
son of Ganga picked up a gilt-edged shield and a sword in 119.70
his eagerness to achieve either death or victory. But just as

rathād an|avarūḍhasya. tad adbhutam iv' âbhavat.
tato Yudhiṣṭhiro rājā svāny anīkāny acodayat:
«abhidravata Gāṅgeyam! mā vo 'stu bhayam aṇv api!»
atha te tomaraiḥ, prāsair, bāṇ'|âughaiś ca samantataḥ,
paṭṭiśaiś ca sa|nistriṃśair, nārācair niśitais tathā,
vatsa|dantaiś ca, bhallaiś ca tam ekam abhidudruvuḥ.
siṃha|nādas tato ghoraḥ Pāṇḍavānām abhūt tadā.
tath" âiva tava putrāś ca, rājan, Bhīṣma|jay'|âiṣiṇaḥ
119.75 tam ekam abhyavartanta, siṃha|nādāṃś ca nedire.
tatr' āsīt tumulaṃ yuddhaṃ tāvakānāṃ paraiḥ saha.
daśame 'hani, rāj'|êndra, Bhīṣm'|Ârjuna|samāgame,
āsīd Gaṅga iv' āvarto muhūrtam uda|dher iva.
sainyānāṃ yudhyamānānāṃ, nighnatām itar'|êtaram
a|gamya|rūpā pṛthivī śoṇit'|âktā tad" âbhavat.
samaṃ ca viṣamaṃ c' âiva na prājñāyata kiṃ cana.
yodhānām ayutaṃ hatvā tasmin sa daśame 'hani
atiṣṭhad āhave Bhīṣmo bhidyamāneṣu marmasu.
tataḥ senā|mukhe tasmin sthitaḥ Pārtho Dhanañjayaḥ
119.80 madhyena Kuru|sainyānāṃ drāvayām āsa vāhinīm.
vayaṃ śveta|hayād bhītāḥ Kuntī|putrād Dhanañjayāt,
pīḍyamānāḥ śitaiḥ śastraiḥ prādravāma raṇe tadā.
Sauvīrāḥ, Kitavāḥ, prācyāḥ, pratīcy'|ôdīcya|Mālavāḥ,
Abhīṣāhāḥ, Śūrasenāḥ, Śibayo, 'tha Vasātayaḥ,
Śālv'|āśrayās Trigartāś ca Ambaṣṭhāḥ Kekayaiḥ saha,

Bhishma was alighting from his chariot, Árjuna smashed his shield into a hundred fragments. It was like a miracle.

King Yudhi·shthira urged his troops on. "Attack the son of Ganga without even the slightest fear!" And they charged against Bhishma, that lone fighter, from all sides with their lances, javelins, masses of arrows, sharp-edged spears, fine swords, sharp iron shafts, calf-toothed arrows, and spear-headed shafts. A fierce lion-roar rose among the Pándavas; and your sons shouted too, desiring Bhishma's victory. They 119.75
surrounded that single warrior and let out their lion-roars; and a tumultuous battle then ensued, between your troops and the enemy.

On the tenth day, king of kings, when Bhishma and Árjuna engaged in combat, the battlefield looked for a while like a whirlpool at the spot where Ganga falls into the ocean. As the battling troops were slaying each other, the earth, drenched in blood, looked unsightly. The even and uneven parts of its surface could no longer be discerned. On the tenth day, having slaughtered ten thousand combatants, Bhishma stood in battle, being broken just where he was vulnerable.

The bow-wielding Partha, stationed at the front of his
army, broke through the middle of the Kuru ranks and 119.80
began to rout the hostile troops. Terrified by Dhanan·jaya the white-horsed son of Kunti, pressed by his sharp arrows, we ran from the battlefield. The Sauvíras, the Kítavas, the easterners, the westerners, the northerners, the Málavas, the Abhisháhas, the Shura·senas, the Shibis, the

sarva ete mah"|ātmānaḥ śar'|ārtā, vraṇa|pīḍitāḥ
saṃgrāme na jahur Bhīṣmaṃ yudhyamānaṃ Kirīṭinā.
tatas tam ekaṃ bahavaḥ parivārya samantataḥ
parikālya Kurūn sarvāñ śara|varṣair avākiran.
119.85 «nipātayata! gṛhṇīta! yudhyadhvam! avakṛnta!»
ity āsīt tumulaḥ śabdo, rājan, Bhīṣma|rathaṃ prati.
nihatya samare rājañ śataśo 'tha sahasraśaḥ
na tasy' āsīd a|nirbhinnaṃ gātre dvy|aṅgulam antaram.
evaṃ|bhūtas tava pitā śarair viśakalī|kṛtaḥ
śit'|âgraiḥ Phālgunen' ājau prāk|śirāḥ prāpatad rathāt
kiṃ cic cheṣe dina|kare, putrāṇāṃ tava paśyatām.
«hā, h"!» êti divi devānāṃ pārthivānāṃ ca, Bhārata,
patamāne rathād Bhīṣme babhūva su|mahā|svanaḥ.
taṃ patantam abhiprekṣya mah"|ātmānaṃ pitā|maham
119.90 saha Bhīṣmeṇa sarveṣāṃ prāpatan hṛdayāni naḥ.
sa papāta mahā|bāhur vasu|dhām anunādayan,
Indra|dhvaja iv' ôtsṛṣṭaḥ ketuḥ sarva|dhanuṣmatām.
dharaṇīṃ na sa pasparśa śara|saṅghaiḥ samāvṛtaḥ.
śara|talpe mah"|êṣv|āsaṃ śayānaṃ puruṣa'|rṣabham
rathāt prapatitaṃ c' âinaṃ divyo bhāvaḥ samāviśat.
abhyavarṣata Parjanyaḥ; prākampata ca medinī.

Vasátis, the Tri·gartas together with the Shalvas, the Ambáshthas, and the Kékayas —all these great-spirited warriors, though they were plagued by arrows and tormented by their wounds, did not forsake Bhishma, who was fighting with diadem-adorned Árjuna in that engagement. Then the Pándava combatants, surrounding Bhishma on all sides many against one, and pushing all the Kurus aside, spat at
him with downpours of shafts. "Strike it down! Catch it! 119.85
Fight! Cut it off!"—such were the tumultuous shouts near Bhishma's chariot.

In that conflict Bhishma slaughtered hundreds and thousands of enemy warriors. But over his entire body there was not even a space two fingers wide that was not pierced by arrows. And your father, lacerated in battle in this way by Phálguna with his sharp-pointed arrows, fell down from his chariot with his head toward the east, a little before sunset, under your sons' very eyes. As Bhishma fell down from the chariot, both the gods and the terrestrial kings screamed out loud in distress, descendant of Bharata. Seeing the great-spirited grandfather fall, we all lost heart. That 119.90
mighty-armed hero, the banner of all archers, collapsed to the ground like an uprooted standard of Indra, making a noise to fill the earth. Yet as he was pierced all over with hordes of arrows, Bhishma could not actually touch the earth.

As soon as that mighty archer, that bull-like man, fallen from his chariot, lay down on the bed of arrows, his divine nature took possession of him. Parjánya poured a hard rain, and the earth quaked.

patan sa dadṛśe c' âpi dakṣiṇena divā|karam.
saṃjñāṃ c' ôpālabhad vīraḥ kālaṃ saṃcintya, Bhārata,
antarikṣe ca śuśrāva divyāṃ vācaṃ samantataḥ:
119.95 «kathaṃ mah"|ātmā Gāṅgeyaḥ sarva|śastra|bhṛtāṃ varaḥ
kāla|kartā nara|vyāghraḥ saṃprāpte dakṣiṇ'|âyane?»
«sthito 'sm'» îti ca Gāṅgeyas tac chrutvā vākyam abravīt,
dhārayām āsa ca prāṇān patito 'pi mahī|tale,
uttar'|âyaṇam anvicchan Bhīṣmaḥ Kuru|pitāmahaḥ.
tasya tan matam ājñāya Gaṅgā Himavataḥ sutā
maha'|rṣīn haṃsa|rūpeṇa preṣayām āsa tatra vai.
tataḥ saṃpātino haṃsās tvaritā Mānas'|âukasaḥ
ājagmuḥ sahitā draṣṭuṃ Bhīṣmaṃ Kuru|pitāmaham,
yatra śete nara|śreṣṭhaḥ śara|talpe pitā|mahaḥ.
119.100 te tu Bhīṣmaṃ samāsādya munayo haṃsa|rūpiṇaḥ
apaśyañ śara|talpa|sthaṃ Bhīṣmaṃ Kuru|kul'|ôdbhavam.
te taṃ dṛṣṭvā mah"|ātmānaṃ, kṛtvā c' âpi pradakṣiṇam
Gāṅgeyaṃ Bharata|śreṣṭhaṃ; dakṣiṇena ca bhās|karam,
itar'|êtaram āmantrya prāhus tatra manīṣiṇaḥ:
«Bhīṣmaḥ kathaṃ mah"|ātmā san saṃsthātā dakṣiṇ'|âyane?»
ity uktvā prasthitā haṃsā dakṣiṇām abhito diśam.

While he was falling, Bhishma noticed that the sun was in the southern part of the ecliptic; and considering this to be an inauspicious time to die,* Bhárata, the hero retained his consciousness. And he heard divine words uttered in
the sky all around: "How can Ganga's great-spirited son, 119.95
the best of all warriors, the tiger-like man, depart this life when the sun is heading southward?" And when he heard that, the son of Ganga said, "I am still alive." Though he had fallen to the ground, the Kuru grandfather Bhishma held on to his life-breaths, waiting for the sun to begin its journey north.

Ganga, the daughter of Hímavat, aware of his intentions, sent great sages to Bhishma in the form of geese. Assuming the form of geese, those sages, the dwellers of the Mánasa lake, flew swiftly in formation to see the Kuru grandfather Bhishma; and they reached the place where that best
of men, the grandsire, lay on the bed of arrows. Coming to 119.100
Bhishma, the sages in the form of geese saw that prosperer of the Kuru lineage lying on his bed of shafts. On seeing the great-spirited hero they respectfully circled that best of the Bharatas, the son of Ganga, keeping him on their right. Knowing the sun to be in the southern part of the ecliptic, the sages addressed each other, wondering "How can Bhishma, being so great a soul, pass away when the sun is heading southward?" Saying this, the geese were about to head off to the south.

saṃprekṣya vai mahā|buddhiś, cintayitvā ca, Bhārata,
tān abravīc Chāntanavo: «n' âhaṃ gantā kathaṃ cana
dakṣiṇ'|āvarta āditye. etan me manasi sthitam.
119.105 gamiṣyāmi svakaṃ sthānam, āsīd yan me purātanam,
udag'|āvṛtta āditye. haṃsāḥ, satyaṃ bravīmi vaḥ.
dhārayiṣyāmy ahaṃ prāṇān uttar'|âyaṇa|kāṅkṣayā
aiśvarya|bhūtaḥ prāṇānām, utsargo hi yato mama.
tasmāt prāṇān dhārayiṣye mumūrṣur udag'|âyane.
yaś ca datto varo mahyaṃ pitrā tena mah"|ātmanā,
chandato mṛtyur, ity evaṃ tasya c' âstu varas tathā.
dhārayiṣye tataḥ prāṇān utsarge niyate sati.»
ity uktvā tāṃs tadā haṃsān aśeta śara|talpa|gaḥ.
evaṃ Kurūṇāṃ patite śṛṅge Bhīṣme mah"|âujasi
119.110 Pāṇḍavāḥ Sṛñjayāś c' âiva siṃha|nādaṃ pracakrire.
tasmin hate mahā|sattve Bharatānām pitā|mahe
na kiṃ cit pratyapadyanta putrās te, Bharata'|rṣabha.
saṃmohaś c' âiva tumulaḥ Kurūṇām abhavat tadā.
Kṛpa|Duryodhana|mukhā niḥśvasya rurudus tataḥ,
viṣādāc ca ciraṃ kālam atiṣṭhan vigat'|êndriyāḥ;
dadhyuś c' âiva, mahā|rāja, na yuddhe dadhire manaḥ.
ūru|grāha|gṛhītāś ca n' âbhyadhāvanta Pāṇḍavān.

Then, descendant of Bharata, the greatly intelligent son of Shántanu, looking at the geese, pondered for a while and told them: "I will by no means depart as long as the sun
is declining southward. I have set my mind on departing 119.105
for my primordial abode when the sun is heading north. Geese, I am telling you the truth. As my time of passing away is under my control, I will hold on to my life-breaths, waiting for the sun to progress toward the north. Wishing to die during the sun's passage northward, I will retain my life-breaths until then. May the boon of dying at will, that was granted to me by my great-spirited father, hold true. Since the time of my departure is totally up to me, I will hold my life-breath till then." And having said that to the geese, he remained lying on the bed of arrows.

When Bhishma, that pinnacle of the Kurus, endowed
with great energy, fell, the Pándavas and the Srínjayas 119.110
shouted a lion-roar.

When the immensely powerful grandfather of the Bharatas was struck down, your sons did not know what to do, bull of the Bharatas. Tremendous bewilderment spread among the Kurus. Beginning with Kripa and Duryódhana, they all began to sob violently. For a long time they remained senseless with distress. Lost in thought, they could not set their hearts on battle, great king. They were unable to advance against the Pándavas; it was as if their thighs were paralyzed.

a|vadhye Śantanoḥ putre hate Bhīṣme mah"|âujasi
a|bhāvaḥ sahasā, rājan, Kuru|rājasya tarkitaḥ.
119.115 hata|pravīrās tu vayaṃ, nikṛttāś ca śitaiḥ śaraiḥ,
kartavyaṃ n' âbhijānīmo nirjitāḥ Savyasācinā.

Pāṇḍavās tu jayaṃ labdhvā, paratra ca parāṃ gatim,
sarve dadhmur mahā|śaṅkhāñ śūrāḥ parigha|bāhavaḥ.
Somakāś ca sa|Pañcālāḥ prāhṛṣyanta, jan'|ēśvara.
tatas tūrya|sahasreṣu nadatsu sa mahā|balaḥ
āsphoṭayām āsa bhṛśaṃ Bhīmaseno, nanāda ca.

senayor ubhayoś c' âpi Gāṅgeye nihate vibhau
saṃnyasya vīrāḥ śastrāṇi prādhyāyanta samantataḥ.
prākrośan, prādravaṃś c' ânye, jagmur mohaṃ tath" âpare,
119.120 kṣatraṃ c' ânye 'bhyanindanta,
Bhīṣmaṃ c' ânye 'bhyapūjayan.
ṛṣayaḥ pitaraś c' âiva
praśaśaṃsur mahā|vratam;
Bharatānāṃ ca ye pūrve, te c' âinaṃ praśaśaṃsire.

mah"|ôpaniṣadaṃ c' âiva yogam āsthāya vīryavān
japañ Śāntanavo dhīmān kāl'|ākāṅkṣī sthito 'bhavat.

Since Shántanu's inviolable son Bhishma, endowed with great energy, had been struck down, the imminent destruction of the Kuru king suddenly began to seem quite reasonable, Your Majesty. Our prominent heroes slain, and our- 119.115
selves lacerated with sharp arrows and defeated by Savya·sachin, we did not know what to do.

And all the valiant Pándavas, their arms like iron bars, winning both victory here and the highest state in the next world, blew their great conches. The Sómakas and the Panchálas were filled with joy, lord of the people. As thousands of musical instruments blared out, mighty Bhima·sena slapped his arms and roared loudly.

After the mighty son of Ganga had been struck down, all the heroic combatants in both armies lay down their weapons and became thoughtful. Some of them howled, some
fled, some fainted, some blamed the warrior code, and some 119.120
simply extolled Bhishma. Sages and ancestors praised that man of great vows, and the forebears of the Bharatas also eulogized him.

And the manly and wise son of Shántanu, resorting to yoga as expounded in the great Upanishads,* lay still, repeating his prayers, waiting for his last hour.

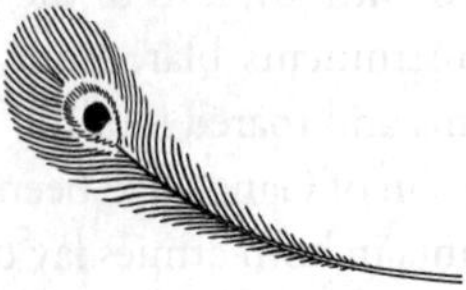

120–122

BHISHMA ON THE BED OF ARROWS

DHṚTARĀṢṬRA uvāca:

120.1 KATHAM ĀSAṂS tadā yodhā hīnā Bhīṣmeṇa, Sañjaya,
balinā deva|kalpena, gurv|arthe brahma|cāriṇā?
tad" âiva nihatān manye Kurūn, anyāṃś ca pārthivān,
na prāharad yadā Bhīṣmo ghṛṇitvād Drupad'|ātmaje.
tato duḥkhataraṃ, manye, kim anyat prabhaviṣyati,
ady' âhaṃ pitaraṃ śrutvā nihataṃ sma su|durmatiḥ?
aśma|sāra|mayaṃ nūnaṃ hṛdayaṃ mama, Sañjaya,
śrutvā vinihataṃ Bhīṣmaṃ śatadhā yan na dīryate.
120.5 yad anyan nihaten' ājau Bhīṣmeṇa jayam icchatā
ceṣṭitaṃ Kuru|siṃhena, tan me kathaya, Sañjaya.
punaḥ punar na mṛṣyāmi hataṃ Devavrataṃ raṇe.
na hato Jāmadagnyena divyair astraiḥ sma yaḥ purā,
sa hato Draupadeyena Pāñcālyena Śikhaṇḍinā.

SAÑJAYA uvāca:

sāy'|âhne nyapatad bhūmau Dhārtarāṣṭrān viṣādayan,
Pāñcālānāṃ dadadd harṣaṃ Kuru|vṛddhaḥ pitā|mahaḥ.
sa śete śara|talpa|stho, medinīm a|spṛśaṃs tadā.
Bhīṣme rathāt prapatite pracyute dharaṇī|tale
«hā, h"!» êti tumulaḥ śabdo bhūtānāṃ samapadyata.
120.10 sīmā|vṛkṣe nipatite Kurūṇāṃ samiti|kṣaye
ubhayoḥ senayo, rājan, kṣatriyān bhayam āviśat.
Bhīṣmaṃ Śāntanavaṃ dṛṣṭvā viśīrṇa|kavaca|dhvajam
Kuravaḥ paryavartanta, Pāṇḍavāś ca, viśāṃ pate.

DHRITA·RASHTRA said:

SÁNJAYA, WHAT WAS the state of my warriors, deprived of 120.1
the powerful, god-like Bhishma, who had taken a vow of chastity for the sake of his father? Since Bhishma, out of his abhorrence, refused to strike the son of Drúpada, I consider the Kurus and all the others to be already as good as slaughtered by the Pándavas. Dim-witted as I am, I hear today that my father has been struck down. What greater pain can there be than this? My heart must be made of stone, Sánjaya, that it does not shatter into a hundred pieces when
I hear that Bhishma has been struck down. What else did 120.5
Bhishma do, that lion of the Kurus, desiring victory, after he was struck down in combat? Tell me that, observer of rigid vows. I cannot bear the thought of Deva·vrata being slain in battle. He, whom the son of Jamad·agni with his divine weapons was not able to kill in former days,* has now been slaughtered by the prince of the Panchálas, Shikhándin son of Drúpada!

SÁNJAYA said:

Coming down to earth in the evening, the Kuru grandfather Bhishma brought despair to the Dharta·rashtras and joy to the Panchálas. He lay on the bed of arrows, not touching the ground. As Bhishma toppled from his chariot and fell to the ground, living beings cried out loud in
distress. When that boundary-tree of the Kurus fell, that 120.10
hero ever victorious in battle, terror struck the warriors of both armies, Your Majesty. At the sight of Bhishma with his armor and banner cut to pieces, both the Kurus and the Pándavas surrounded him, lord of the people. When

khaṃ tamaḥ|saṃvṛtam abhūd, āsīd bhānur gata|prabhaḥ,
rarāsa pṛthivī c' âiva Bhīṣme Śāntanave hate.
«ayaṃ brahma|vidāṃ śreṣṭho hy;
ayaṃ brahma|vidāṃ varaḥ!»
ity abhāṣanta bhūtāni
śayānaṃ Bharata'|rṣabham.
«ayaṃ pitaram ājñāya kām'|ārtaṃ Śāntanuṃ purā,
ūrdhva|retasam ātmānaṃ cakāra puruṣa'|rṣabhaḥ.»
120.15 iti sma śara|talpa|sthaṃ Bharatānām mahattamam
ṛṣayas tv abhyabhāṣanta sahitāḥ siddha|cāraṇaiḥ.
hate Śāntanave Bhīṣme Bharatānāṃ pitā|mahe
na kiṃ cit pratyapadyanta putrās tava hi, māriṣa,
vivarṇa|vadanāś c' āsan, gata|śrīkāś ca, Bhārata;
atiṣṭhan vrīḍitāś c' âiva, hriyā yuktā hy, adho|mukhāḥ.
Pāṇḍavāś ca jayaṃ labdhvā saṃgrāma|śirasi sthitāḥ
sarve dadhmur mahā|śaṅkhān hema|jāla|pariṣkṛtān.
harṣāt tūrya|sahasreṣu vādyamāneṣu c', ân|agha,
apaśyāma raṇe, rājan, Bhīmasenaṃ mahā|balam
120.20 vikrīḍamānaṃ Kaunteyaṃ harṣeṇa mahatā yutam,
nihatya samare śatrūn mahā|bala|samanvitān.
saṃmohaś c' âpi tumulaḥ Kurūṇām abhavat tadā.
Karṇa|Duryodhanau c' âpi niḥśvasetāṃ muhur muhuḥ.
tathā nipatite Bhīṣme Kauravāṇāṃ pitā|mahe
hā|hā|kṛtam abhūt sarvaṃ; nir|maryādam avartata.
dṛṣṭvā ca patitaṃ Bhīṣmaṃ putro Duḥśāsanas tava
uttamaṃ javam āsthāya Droṇ'|ânīkaṃ upādravat.
bhrātrā prasthāpito vīraḥ sven' ânīkena daṃśitaḥ
prayayau puruṣa|vyāghraḥ sva|sainyam sa viṣādayan.

Bhishma the son of Shántanu was struck down, the sky became shrouded in darkness, the sun lost its radiance, and the earth produced fierce sounds. Living creatures spoke of that bull-like man as he lay there: "He is the best of the men who know Brahman! He is the foremost of the men who know Brahman!" "This bull-like man once, coming to know that his father Shántanu had become lovesick, made
the vow of permanent celibacy."* These were the words that 120.15
sages together with *siddhas* and *chāranas** said about that greatest man of the Bharatas as he lay on his bed of arrows.

When Bhishma son of Shántanu, the grandfather of the Bharatas, was struck down, your sons did not know what to do, my lord. They stood downcast, with sad faces, bereft of glory, ashamed, and overcome with remorse, descendant of Bharata. And having gained their victory, all the Pándavas, stationed at the front of the battle, blew their great conches adorned with gold. As thousands of musical instruments sounded with joy, great and faultless king, we saw powerful Bhima·sena, the son of Kunti, cavorting, filled as he was 120.20
with intense delight at their having struck down the enemy endowed with great might. Tremendous confusion spread among the Kurus. Karna and Duryódhana sighed heavy sighs, over and over. When Bhishma the Káurava grandfather fell down, there was crying in distress all around; all proprieties were broken.

Having seen Bhishma fall, your son Duhshásana went off at top speed toward Drona's division. Sent by his elder brother, that heroic, tiger-like man, clad in armor and accompanied by his own contingent, advanced forward, to

120.25 tam āyāntam abhiprekṣya Kuravaḥ paryavārayan
Duḥśāsanaṃ, mahā|rāja, «kim ayaṃ vakṣyat'?» îti ca.
tato Droṇāya nihataṃ Bhīṣmam ācaṣṭa Kauravaḥ.
Droṇas tatr' â|priyaṃ śrutvā mumoha, Bharata'|rṣabha.
sa saṃjñām upalabhy' āśu Bhāradvājaḥ pratāpavān
nivārayām āsa tadā svāny anīkāni, māriṣa.
vinivṛttān Kurūn dṛṣṭvā Pāṇḍavāś ca sva|sainikān
dūtaiḥ śīghr'|âśva|saṃyuktair avahāram akārayan.
vinivṛtteṣu sainyeṣu pāramparyeṇa sarvaśaḥ
vimukta|kavacāḥ sarve Bhīṣmam īyur nar'|âdhipāḥ.
120.30 vyuparamya tato yuddhād yodhāḥ śata|sahasraśaḥ
upatasthur mah"|ātmānaṃ, Prajāpatim iv' âmarāḥ.
te tu Bhīṣmaṃ samāsādya śayānaṃ Bharata'|rṣabham
abhivādy' âvatiṣṭhanta Pāṇḍavāḥ Kurubhiḥ saha.
atha Pāṇḍūn Kurūṃś c' âiva praṇipaty' âgrataḥ sthitān
abhyabhāṣata dharm'|ātmā Bhīṣmaḥ Śāntanavas tadā:
«svāgataṃ vo, mahā|bhāgāḥ! svāgataṃ vo, mahā|rathāḥ!
tuṣyāmi darśanāc c' âhaṃ yuṣmākam, amar'|ôpamāḥ!»
abhinandya sa tān evaṃ śirasā lambat" âbravīt:
«śiro me lambate 'tyartham. upadhānaṃ pradīyatām.»
120.35 tato nṛ|pāḥ samājahrus tanūni ca mṛdūni ca
upadhānāni mukhyāni. n' âicchat tāni pitā|mahaḥ.
ath' âbravīn nara|vyāghraḥ prahasann iva tān nṛ|pān:
«n' âitāni vīra|śayyāsu yukta|rūpāṇi, pārthivāḥ.»

the distress of his troops. Looking at Duhshásana as he ap- 120.25
proached them, the Káuravas surrounded him, great king, wondering what he had to say. The Káurava prince informed Drona that Bhishma had been struck down; and when he heard the sorrowful news, bull of the Bharatas, Drona lost his senses. After regaining control of himself, the powerful son of Bharad·vaja immediately restrained his troops from further fighting, my lord. And the Pándavas, seeing that the Kurus had stopped fighting, made their forces desist from battle too, on all parts of the field, through swift-horsed messengers.

When one by one all the divisions had stopped fighting, all the kings cast off their armor and went up to Bhishma.
After they had stopped fighting, hundreds of thousands of 120.30
warriors came up to that eminent Bhishma to pay their respects, just as the gods come to honor Praja·pati. Approaching Bhishma the bull of the Bharatas lying supine on his bed of arrows, both the Pándavas and the Kurus stood and saluted him together. And Shántanu's son Bhishma, righteous in spirit, addressed the Kurus and Pándavas standing reverently before him. "Welcome, fortunate, god-like, mighty warriors! I am pleased to see you!"

Addressing them with his head hanging down, he said "My head is hanging down too much. Please give me a pillow." So the kings brought many fine, soft, and superb pil- 120.35
lows, but the grandfather did not like them. The tiger-like hero said to the kings with a chuckle, "These pillows do not fit a hero's bed, kings." Then, looking at the long-armed

tato vīkṣya nara|śreṣṭham abhyabhāṣata Pāṇḍavam
Dhanañjayaṃ dīrgha|bāhuṃ sarva|loka|mahā|ratham:
«Dhanañjaya mahā|bāho, śiro me, tāta, lambate.
dīyatām upadhānaṃ vai, yad yuktam iha manyase.»

SAÑJAYA uvāca:

samāropya mahac cāpam, abhivādya pitā|maham,
netrābhyām aśru|pūrṇābhyām idaṃ vacanam abravīt:
120.40 «ājñāpaya, Kuru|śreṣṭha, sarva|śastra|bhṛtāṃ vara!
preṣyo 'haṃ tava, dur|dharṣa. kriyatāṃ kiṃ, pitā|maha?»
tam abravīc Chāntanavaḥ: «śiro me, tāta, lambate.
upadhānaṃ, Kuruśreṣṭha Phālgun', ôpadadhatsva me.
śayanasy' ânurūpaṃ hi śīghraṃ, vīra, prayaccha me.
tvaṃ hi, Pārtha, samartho vai, śreṣṭhaḥ sarva|dhanuṣmatām,
kṣatra|dharmasya vettā ca, buddhi|sattva|guṇ'|ânvitaḥ.»
Phālguno 'pi «tath"» êty uktvā vyavasāyam arocayat.
pragṛhy' āmantrya Gāṇḍīvaṃ śarān saṃnata|parvaṇaḥ,
anumānya mah"|ātmānaṃ Bharatānām a|madhyamam,
120.45 tribhis tīkṣṇair mahā|vegair anvagṛhṇāc chiraḥ śaraiḥ.
abhiprāye tu vidite dharm"|ātmā Savyasācinā
atuṣyad Bharata|śreṣṭho Bhīṣmo dharm'|ârtha|tattva|vit.
upadhānena dattena pratyanandad Dhanañjayam;
prāha sarvān samudvīkṣya
Bharatān Bhārataṃ prati
Kuntī|putraṃ, yudhāṃ śreṣṭhaṃ,
su|hṛdāṃ prīti|vardhanam:

Pándava Dhanan·jaya, the best of men and the greatest warrior in all the worlds, Bhishma said to him: "O mighty-armed Dhanan·jaya, my head is hanging down. Son, please give me a pillow that you consider suitable."

SÁNJAYA said:

Stringing his mighty bow and honoring the grandfather, Árjuna, his eyes full of tears, addressed Bhishma with these
words. "O best of the Kurus, foremost of all warriors, com- 120.40
mand me! I am your servant, unconquerable hero; what shall I do for you, grandfather?" The son of Shántanu replied to him, "Son, my head is hanging down. Phálguna, best of the Kurus, get me a pillow suitable for my bed, and give it to me quickly. For being the foremost of all archers and knowing the warrior code, you are capable of it, endowed as you are with intelligence and pure goodness."

"So be it!" said Phálguna, and he complied with Bhishma's intentions. He consecrated his Gandíva bow and straight arrows with mantras, and, having received the permission of that great-spirited mighty warrior of the Bharatas, with three sharp and very swift arrows he made a sup- 120.45
port for his head.

Righteous Bhishma, the best of the Bharatas, truly knowing the meaning of virtue, was pleased with Savya·sachin, who had understood what he had been implying. He praised Dhanan·jaya for giving him the pillow and, looking at all the Bharatas, he spoke to that Bhárata son of Kunti, that foremost of warriors, who inspired his friends with delight.

«śayanasy' ânurūpaṃ me, Pāṇḍav', ôpahitaṃ tvayā.
yady anyathā prapadyethāḥ, śapeyaṃ tvām ahaṃ ruṣā.
evam eva, mahā|bāho, dharmeṣu pariniṣṭhitā
svaptavyaṃ kṣatriyeṇ' ājau śara|talpa|gatena vai.»
120.50 evam uktvā tu Bībhatsuṃ sarvāṃs tān abravīd vacaḥ
rājñaś ca rāja|putrāṃś ca Pāṇḍaven' âbhisaṃsthitān:
«paśyadhvam upadhānaṃ me Pāṇḍaven' âbhisaṃdhitam.
śeṣye 'ham asyāṃ śayyāyāṃ yāvad āvartanaṃ raveḥ.
ye tadā māṃ gamiṣyanti, te ca prekṣyanti māṃ nṛ|pāḥ.
diśaṃ Vaiśravaṇ'|ākrāntāṃ yadā gantā divā|karaḥ
arciṣmān, pratapal lokān rathen' ôttama|tejasā,
vimokṣye 'haṃ tadā prāṇān, su|hṛdaḥ su|priyān api.
parikhā khanyatām atra mam' âvasadane, nṛ|pāḥ.
upāsiṣye Vivasvantam evaṃ śara|śat'|ācitaḥ.
120.55 upāramadhvaṃ saṃgrāmād vairāṇy utsṛjya, pārthivāḥ.»

SAÑJAYA uvāca:

upātiṣṭhann atho vaidyāḥ śaly'|ôddharaṇa|kovidāḥ,
sarv'|ôpakaraṇair yuktāḥ, kuśalaiḥ sādhu śikṣitāḥ.
tān dṛṣṭvā Jāhnavī|putraḥ provāca tanayaṃ tava:
«dhanaṃ dattvā visṛjyantāṃ pūjayitvā cikitsakāḥ.
evaṃ|gate may" êdānīṃ vaidyaiḥ kāryam ih' âsti kim?
kṣatra|dharme praśastāṃ hi prāpto 'smi paramāṃ gatim.
n' âiṣa dharmo, mahī|pālāḥ, śara|talpa|gatasya me.
etair eva śaraiś c' âhaṃ dagdhavyo 'smi, nar'|âdhipāḥ.»

"Had you acted otherwise, I would have cursed you in a rage. It is on a bed of arrows on the battlefield that a warrior who abides strictly by the warrior code should sleep."

And saying that to Bibhátsu, he addressed all the kings 120.50
and princes present there with these words. "Look at the pillow that the Pándava provided me with. I shall lie on this bed until the sun turns toward the north. The kings who come to me then, will see me depart. It is when the sun, on its exceedingly splendid chariot yoked to seven horses, reaches the quarter occupied by Váishravana* that I shall give up my life-breaths that are like dear friends to me. Dig a trench around this place of mine, kings. Covered with
hundreds of arrows, I will worship the sun. Renounce your 120.55
animosity and desist from war, kings!"

SÁNJAYA said:

Then well-trained healers, skilled in extracting arrows, came to him with all the effective implements. But when the son of Jahnu's daughter saw them he said to your son Duryódhana, "Honor these physicians, pay them their reward, and dismiss them. Now that I am in this condition, what is the use of these healers? I have reached the highest state, as extolled by the warrior code. Now that I lie on this bed of arrows, lords of the earth, being cured does not accord with my duty. I should be burnt with these arrows in my body, kings."

tac chrutvā vacanaṃ tasya putro Duryodhanas tava
120.60 vaidyān visarjayām āsa, pūjayitvā yath" ârhataḥ.
tatas te vismayaṃ jagmur nānā|jana|pad'|ēśvarāḥ,
sthitiṃ dharme parāṃ dṛṣṭvā Bhīṣmasy' â|mita|tejasaḥ.
upadhānaṃ tato dattvā pitus te manuj'|ēśvarāḥ,
sahitāḥ Pāṇḍavāḥ sarve Kuravaś ca mahā|rathāḥ
upagamya mah"|ātmānaṃ śayānaṃ śayane śubhe,
te 'bhivādya tato Bhīṣmaṃ, kṛtvā ca triḥ pradakṣiṇam,
vidhāya rakṣāṃ Bhīṣmasya sarva eva samantataḥ,
vīrāḥ sva|śibirāṇy eva dhyāyantaḥ param'|āturāḥ
niveśāy' âbhyupāgacchan sāy'|âhne rudhir'|ôkṣitāḥ.
120.65 niviṣṭān Pāṇḍavāṃś c' âpi prīyamāṇān mahā|rathān
Bhīṣmasya patanādd hṛṣṭān upagamya mahā|balān
uvāca Mādhavaḥ kāle Dharma|putraṃ Yudhiṣṭhiram:
«diṣṭyā jayasi, Kauravya! diṣṭyā Bhīṣmo nipātitaḥ
a|vadhyo mānuṣair eṣa satya|saṃdho mahā|rathaḥ,
atha vā daivataiḥ, Pārtha, sarva|śastr'|âstra|pāra|gaḥ
tvāṃ tu cakṣur|haṇaṃ prāpya dagdho ghoreṇa cakṣuṣā!»
evam ukto Dharma|rājaḥ pratyuvāca Janārdanam:
«tava prasādād vijayaḥ; krodhāt tava parājayaḥ.
tvaṃ hi naḥ śaraṇaṃ, Kṛṣṇa, bhaktānām a|bhayaṅ|karaḥ.
120.70 an|āścaryo jayas teṣāṃ, yeṣāṃ tvam asi, Keśava,
rakṣitā samare nityaṃ, nityaṃ c' âpi hite rataḥ.
sarvathā tvāṃ samāsādya n' āścaryam, iti me matiḥ.»

Hearing Bhishma's words, your son Duryódhana dismissed the healers, after duly honoring them. 120.60

The kings of various countries, witnessing the firmness in virtue displayed by Bhishma so infinite in splendor, were filled with amazement. After your father had been given his pillow, all those leaders of men, including the notable Pándava and Kuru warriors, came together to approach Bhishma, that great character, lying on his fine bed of arrows. They paid Bhishma their respects, circled him three times keeping him on their right, and made arrangements to protect him on all sides. And in the evening all those heroes, drenched in blood, thoughtful and extremely anguished, went to the camps and entered their tents.

A while later the powerful Mádhava joined the joyful 120.65
Pándavas, who were sitting together, delighted at Bhishma's fall, and said to Yudhi·shthira the Son of Righteousness:

"What fortune it is that you are victorious, Káurava! What fortune it is that Bhishma has been struck down! That mighty warrior, true to his vows, who has complete knowledge of all teachings and secret weapons, cannot be slain by men or by gods. But confronting you who can kill with your eyes, he has been incinerated by your fierce glare."

Addressed in this way, the King of Righteousness replied to Janárdana:

"Victory comes by your grace, and defeat comes from your wrath. You are our only refuge, Krishna, the granter of safety to your devotees as you are. Victory is no wonder 120.70
for those whom you, Késhava, constantly protect in battle and for whose well-being you are always concerned. I believe nothing to be extraordinary for those who have found

evam uktaḥ pratyuvāca smayamāno Janārdanaḥ:
«tvayy ev' âitad yukta|rūpaṃ vacanaṃ, pārthiv'|ôttama.»

SAÑJAYA uvāca:

121.1 VYUṢṬĀYĀṂ TU, mahā|rāja, śarvaryāṃ sarva|pārthivāḥ
Pāṇḍavā Dhārtarāṣṭrāś ca abhijagmuḥ pitā|maham.
taṃ vīra|śayane vīraṃ śayānaṃ Kuru|sattamam
abhivādy' ôpatasthur vai kṣatriyāḥ kṣatriya'|rṣabham.
kanyāś candana|cūrṇaiś ca, lājair, mālyaiś ca sarvaśaḥ
avākirañ Śāntanavaṃ tatra gatvā sahasraśaḥ.
striyo, vṛddhās, tathā bālāḥ, prekṣakāś ca pṛthag|janāḥ
samabhyayuḥ Śāntanavaṃ, bhūtān' îva tamo|nudam.
121.5 tūryāṇi śata|saṃkhyāni, tath" âiva naṭa|nartakāḥ
upānṛtyañ, jaguś c' âiva vṛddhaṃ Kuru|pitāmaham.
śilpinaś ca tath" ājagmuḥ Kuru|vṛddhaṃ pitā|maham.
upāramya ca yuddhebhyaḥ, saṃnāhān vipramucya ca,
āyudhāni ca nikṣipya sahitāḥ Kuru|Pāṇḍavāḥ
anvāsata dur|ādharṣaṃ Devavratam arin|damam,
anyonyaṃ prītimantas te yathā|pūrvaṃ, yathā|vayaḥ.
sā pārthiva|śat'|ākīrṇā samitir Bhīṣma|śobhitā
śuśubhe Bhāratī dīptā div' îv' āditya|maṇḍalam.
vibabhau ca nṛ|pāṇāṃ sā Gaṅgā|sutam upāsatām,
devānām iva dev'|ēśaṃ Pitāmaham upāsatām.
121.10 Bhīṣmas tu vedanāṃ dhairyān nigṛhya, Bharata'|rṣabha,
abhitaptaḥ śaraiś c' âiva, n'|âtihṛṣṭa|man" âbravīt:
«śar'|âbhitapta|kāyo 'haṃ, śastra|saṃpāta|mūrchitaḥ,
pānīyam abhikāṅkṣe 'haṃ» rājñas tān praty abhāṣata.
tatas te kṣatriyā, rājann, upājahruḥ samantataḥ

shelter in you in every way." And in response to his words Janárdana said with a smile, "These words are indeed worthy of you, foremost of kings."

SÁNJAYA said:

AFTER THE NIGHT had passed, great king, all the kings 121.1
who fought for the Pándavas and for the sons of Dhrita·rashtra approached the grandfather. Making obeisance to that hero, who lay on his heroic bed, the warriors stood by that bull-like warrior, best of the Kurus. Thousands of girls spread sandal powder, grains of rice, and garlands of flowers over the body of Shántanu's son. Women, old men, children, and ordinary spectators came to see the son of Shántanu, just as creatures welcome the rising sun. Hundreds of 121.5
musicians, actors, and dancers came and played before the venerable Kuru grandfather. Having stopped fighting, having cast off their armor and thrown down their arms, the Kurus and the Pándavas all together came up to the unconquerable enemy-tamer Deva·vrata. They were friendly and duly respectful toward each other, as in former times. That assembly of the Bharatas, joined by hundreds of kings and set off by Bhishma, looked resplendent like the disk of the sun shining in the sky. And the assembly of kings honoring the son of Ganga looked like that of the gods honoring their lord Grandsire Brahma.

Bhishma, tormented by arrows, yet subduing his pain 121.10
through fortitude, bull of the Bharatas, said without much excitement, addressing those kings: "My body is scorched by the arrows and I am nearly senseless from the strokes of weapons. I am thirsting for water." Then, Your Majesty,

bhakṣyān ucc'|âvacāṃs tatra, vāri|kumbhāṃś ca śītalān.

upānītaṃ ca tad dṛṣṭvā Bhīṣmaḥ Śāntanavo 'bravīt:

«n' âdya tāta mayā śakyaṃ bhogān kāṃś cana mānuṣān

upabhoktuṃ manuṣyebhyaḥ; śara|śayyā|gato hy ahaṃ

pratīkṣamāṇas tiṣṭhāmi nivṛttiṃ śaśi|sūryayoḥ.»

121.15   evam uktvā Śāntanavo, nindan vākyena pārthivān,

«Arjunaṃ draṣṭum icchām'» îty abhyabhāṣata, Bhārata.

ath' ôpetya mahā|bāhur, abhivādya pitā|maham,

atiṣṭhat prāñjaliḥ, prahvaḥ, «kiṃ karom'?» îti c' âbravīt.

taṃ dṛṣṭvā Pāṇḍavaṃ, rājann, abhivādy' âgrataḥ sthitam

abhyabhāṣata dharm'|âtmā Bhīṣmaḥ prīto Dhanañjayam:

«dahyate 'daḥ śarīraṃ me saṃvṛtasya tav' êṣubhiḥ,

marmāṇi paridūyante, mukhaṃ ca pariśuṣyati.

vedan"|ârta|śarīrasya prayacch' āpo mam', Ârjuna.

tvaṃ hi śakto, mah"|êṣv|āsa, dātum āpo yathā|vidhi.»

121.20   Arjunas tu «tath"» êty uktvā, ratham āruhya vīryavān,

adhijyaṃ balavat kṛtvā Gāṇḍīvaṃ, vyākṣipad dhanuḥ.

tasya jyā|tala|nirghoṣaṃ, visphūrjitam iv' âśaneḥ,

vitresuḥ sarva|bhūtāni śrutvā, sarve ca pārthivāḥ.

tataḥ pradakṣiṇaṃ kṛtvā rathena rathināṃ varaḥ

śayānaṃ Bharata|śreṣṭhaṃ sarva|śastra|bhṛtāṃ varam,

saṃdhāya ca śaraṃ dīptam, abhimantrya sa Pāṇḍavaḥ,

Parjany'|âstreṇa saṃyojya sarva|lokasya paśyataḥ,

avidhyat pṛthivīṃ Pārthaḥ pārśve Bhīṣmasya dakṣiṇe.

those warriors brought various viands and jars of cold water from every side. But the son of Shántanu looked at the water that had been brought for him, and said:

"My son, it is no longer possible for me to accept any human sustenance from humans. Now that I lie on the bed of arrows, I have renounced the society of men. I am staying here, waiting for the moon and the sun to return."

Scorning the kings with these words, descendant of Bha- 121.15
rata, the son of Shántanu said, "I wish to see Árjuna." And that strong-armed hero, approaching and honoring the grandfather, stood there humbly with his hands folded in respect and asked, "What can I do?" At the sight of the Pándava standing reverently before him, Bhishma, righteous in spirit, was pleased with Dhanan·jaya and spoke to him. "Covered all over as I am with your arrows, my body is burning, my vital organs are afflicted with pain, and my mouth is parched. Give me water to drink, Árjuna, for my body is tormented by pain. Mighty archer, only you can give me water in the proper fashion."

"So be it!" replied vigorous Árjuna, and ascended his 121.20
chariot. Then he strung the Gandíva bow tightly, and he began to draw it. All living creatures and all the kings trembled when they heard the terrible noise of his bowstring and palms, which sounded like a roll of thunder. The Pándava, the champion of chariot warriors, respectfully circled that best of the Bharatas, the foremost of all warriors, who was lying supine. Then, aiming a gleaming arrow, consecrating it with mantras, and furnishing it with Parjánya's weapon, the Pártha shot it into the ground to Bhishma's right; and a

utpapāta tato dhārā vāriṇo vimalā, śubhā,
121.25 śītasy' âmṛta|kalpasya, divya|gandha|rasasya ca.
atarpayat tataḥ Pārthaḥ śītayā jala|dhārayā
Bhīṣmaṃ Kurūṇām ṛṣabhaṃ divya|karma|parākramam.
karmaṇā tena Pārthasya, Śakrasy' êva vikurvataḥ,
vismayaṃ paramaṃ jagmus tatas te vasudh"|âdhipāḥ.
tat karma prekṣya Bībhatsor ati|mānuṣa|vikramam,
saṃprāvepanta Kuravo, gāvaḥ śīt'|ârditā iva.
vismayāc c' ôttarīyāṇi vyāvidhyan sarvato nṛ|pāḥ.
śaṅkha|dundubhi|nirghoṣais tumulaṃ sarvato 'bhavat.
tṛptaḥ Śāntanavaś c' âpi, rājan, Bībhatsum abravīt
121.30 sarva|pārthiva|vīrāṇāṃ saṃnidhau pūjayann iva:
«n' âitac citraṃ, mahā|bāho, tvayi, Kaurava|nandana.
kathito Nāraden' âsi pūrva'|ṛṣir, a|mita|dyute;
Vāsudeva|sahāyas tvaṃ mahat karma kariṣyasi,
yan n' ôtsahati dev'|Êndraḥ saha devair api dhruvam.
vidus tvāṃ nidhanaṃ, Pārtha, sarva|kṣatrasya tad|vidaḥ.
dhanur|dharāṇām ekas tvaṃ pṛthivyāṃ pravaro nṛṣu.
manuṣyā jagati śreṣṭhāḥ, pakṣiṇāṃ Garuḍo varaḥ,
sarasāṃ sāgaraḥ śreṣṭho, gaur variṣṭhā catuṣ|padām,
121.35 ādityas tejasāṃ śreṣṭho, giriṇāṃ Himavān varaḥ,
jātīnāṃ brāhmaṇaḥ śreṣṭhaḥ; śreṣṭhas tvam asi dhanvinām.
na vai śrutaṃ Dhārtarāṣṭreṇa vākyaṃ
may" ôcyamānaṃ, Vidureṇa c' âiva,
Droṇena, Rāmeṇa, Janārdanena,

spurt of pure, fine, cool, ambrosial water, water with a di- 121.25
vine fragrance and taste, gushed from that spot. With that cool spurt of water the son of Pritha gratified Bhishma, that Kuru bull of divine exploits and might.

And all those lords of earth were filled with utter amazement at that feat accomplished by the Partha, who was acting like Shakra himself. Seeing Bibhátsu's feat, which bespoke superhuman capabilities, the Kurus trembled like cows shivering all over with cold. The kings all around began to wave their capes in wonder, and a tremendous sound of conches and kettle-drums spread around.

His thirst slaked, the son of Shántanu addressed Bibhátsu, Your Majesty, praising him in the presence of all the 121.30
royal heroes.

"This feat is no miracle for you, mighty-armed hero, delight of the Kurus. Nárada spoke of you as a primordial sage, you who are infinite in splendor. Vásu·deva being your helper, you will perform great exploits such as even Indra, the king of the gods, with all the deities together, does not venture to accomplish. Those who know recognize you, Partha, as the exterminator of all kshatriyas. You are the foremost of all archers on earth, and the best of men. Just as men are the best of all worldly beings, and as Gáruda is the foremost of birds, as the ocean is the best of all bodies of water, and a cow is the foremost of all four-footed creatures,
as the sun is the best of all luminaries, and Hímavat is the 121.35
foremost of all mountains, and as a brahmin is the best of all classes, just so are you the best of all archers. Dhrita·rashtra's son paid no heed to the words spoken repeatedly by myself, Vídura, Drona, Rama, Janárdana, and Sánjaya. His mind

muhur muhuḥ Sañjayen' âpi c' ôktam.
parīta|buddhir hi vi|saṃjña|kalpo
Duryodhano na ca tac chraddadhāti.
sa śeṣyate vai nihataś cirāya
śāstr'|âtigo Bhīma|bal'|âbhibhūtaḥ.»
etac chrutvā tad|vacaḥ Kaurav'|êndro
Duryodhano dīna|manā babhūva.
tam abravīc Chāntanavo 'bhivīkṣya:
«nibodha, rājan, bhava vīta|manyuḥ.
dṛṣṭaṃ, Duryodhan', âitat te, yathā Pārthena dhīmatā
jalasya dhārā janitā śītasy' âmṛta|gandhinaḥ.
121.40 etasya kartā loke 'smin
n' ânyaḥ kaś cana vidyate.
Āgneyaṃ, Vāruṇaṃ, Saumyaṃ,
Vāyavyam, atha Vaiṣṇavam,
Aindraṃ, Pāśupataṃ, Brāhmaṃ,
Pārameṣṭhyaṃ, Prajāpateḥ,
Dhātus, Tvaṣṭuś ca, Savitur,
Vaivasvataṃ tath" âpi vā
sarvasmin mānuṣe loke vetty eko hi Dhanañjayaḥ,
Kṛṣṇo vā Devakī|putro. n' ânyo ved' êha kaś cana.
a|śakyaḥ Pāṇḍavas, tāta, yuddhe jetuṃ kathaṃ cana.
a|mānuṣāṇi karmāṇi yasy' âitāni mah"|ātmanaḥ,
tena sattvavatā saṃkhye śūreṇ' āhava|śobhinā,
kṛtinā samare, rājan, saṃdhir bhavatu mā ciram.
121.45 yāvat Kṛṣṇo mahā|bāhuḥ sv'|âdhīnaḥ, Kuru|sattama,
tāvat Pārthena śūreṇa saṃdhis te, tāta, yujyatām.
yāvan na te camūḥ sarvāḥ śaraiḥ saṃnata|parvabhiḥ
nāśayaty Arjunas, tāvat saṃdhis te, tāta, yujyatām.
yāvat tiṣṭhanti samare hata|śeṣāḥ sah'|ôdarāḥ

possessed as if he was wanting in his faculties, Duryódhana did not believe what we told him. Having spurned what he was taught, he will be overpowered by Bhima's might and will lie crushed on the battlefield for quite some time."

Duryódhana, the king of the Káuravas, became dispirited when he heard Bhishma's words. And the son of Shántanu looked at him and spoke.

"Listen, Your Majesty. Give up your anger. Duryódhana, you have just seen how the wise son of Pritha created that spurt of cool water that smelled like nectar. Nobody else in 121.40
the world is able to accomplish such a feat.

The weapons which belong to Agni, Váruna, Soma, Vayu, Vishnu, Indra, Pashu·pati, Brahma, Paraméshthin, Praja·pati, Dhatri, Tvashtri, Sávitri, and Vivásvat are known in the entire human world only to Dhanan·jaya and Krishna the son of Dévaki. No one else here knows them. This great-spirited Pándava, who is capable of such superhuman exploits, sir, cannot be vanquished in combat by any means, even by the gods. Peace should be made immediately, Your Majesty, with that powerful hero resplendent in battle, that skilled expert in matters of war.

O best of the Kurus, As long as mighty-armed Krishna 121.45
restrains himself, you should make peace with the valiant son of Pritha, sir. As long as Árjuna has not annihilated all your divisions with his straight arrows, you should make peace with the Parthas, sir. As long as your surviving brothers and many kings are alive, Your Majesty, you should make peace with the Pándavas. As long as Yudhi·shthira

nṛ|pāś ca bahavo, rājaṃs, tāvat saṃdhiḥ prayujyatām.
na nirdahati te yāvat krodha|dīpt'|ēkṣaṇaś camūm
Yudhiṣṭhiro raṇe, tāvat saṃdhis te, tāta, yujyatām.
Nakulaḥ, Sahadevaś ca, Bhīmasenaś ca Pāṇḍavaḥ
yāvac camūṃ, mahā|rāja, nāśayanti na sarvaśaḥ,
121.50 tāvat te Pāṇḍavair vīraiḥ sauhārdaṃ mama rocate.
yuddhaṃ mad|antam ev' âstu. tāta, saṃśāmya Pāṇḍavaiḥ.
etat te rocatāṃ vākyaṃ yad ukto 'si may", ân|agha.
etat kṣemam ahaṃ manye tava c' âiva kulasya ca.
tyaktvā manyum upaśāmyasva Pārthaiḥ.
paryāptam etad yat kṛtaṃ Phālgunena.
Bhīṣmasy' ântād astu vaḥ sauhṛdaṃ ca;
jīvantu śeṣāḥ. sādhu, rājan, prasīda.
rājyasy' ârdhaṃ dīyatāṃ Pāṇḍavānām.
Indraprasthaṃ Dharma|rājo 'bhiyātu.
mā mitra|dhruk pārthivānāṃ jaghanyaḥ
pāpāṃ kīrtiṃ prāpsyase, Kaurav'|êndra.
mam' âvasānāc chāntir astu prajānāṃ.
saṃgacchantāṃ pārthivāḥ prītimantaḥ.
pitā putraṃ, mātulaṃ bhāgineyo,
bhrātā c' âiva bhrātaraṃ praitu, rājan.
121.55 na ced evaṃ prāpta|kālaṃ vaco me
moh'|āviṣṭaḥ pratipatsyasy a|buddhyā,
tapsyasy ante; etad|antāḥ stha sarve.
satyām etāṃ bhāratīm īrayāmi.»
etad vākyaṃ sauhṛdād Āpageyo
madhye rājñāṃ bhārataṃ śrāvayitvā,
tūṣṇīm āsīc chalya|saṃtapta|marmā,
yojy' ātmānaṃ, vedanāṃ saṃniyamya.

has not incinerated your host in battle with his eyes blazing with wrath, you should make peace with the Pándavas, sir. As long as Nákula, Saha·deva, and Bhima·sena Pándava have not completely destroyed your army, Your Majesty, I would like friendship to be established between you and 121.50
the heroic sons of Pandu. Let this war end with my death. Make peace with the Pándavas, sir. Be favorable to what I have told you, faultless one. I believe this solution is beneficial to both you and the Kuru lineage.

Give up your anger, and make peace with the Parthas. What Phálguna has already done is enough. Through Bhishma's death, let friendship be established between you; and may the survivors live happily. Relent, Your Majesty. Give half of the kingdom to the Pándavas and let the King of Righteousness go to Indra·prastha, lest you should achieve the ill fame of being the vilest of kings and a traitor to your friends, lord of the Káuravas. Let peace come to the people with my death. Let kings meet with each other joyfully. Let father be reunited with son, nephew with uncle, and brother with brothers, Your Majesty. If, possessed by 121.55
folly, you do not consent to my timely words through lack of judgement, in the end you will repent, and all of you will perish in this war. I am telling you the truth."

The son of the River Ganga said these words to the Bhárata chief out of fondness, and then he became silent. And despite the fact that his vitals were tormented by arrows, he overcame his pain and applied himself to yoga.

SAÑJAYA uvāca:

dharm'|ârtha|sahitaṃ vākyaṃ śrutvā hitam, an|āmayam,
n' ârocayata putras te, mumūrṣur iva bheṣajam.

SAÑJAYA uvāca:

122.1 TATAS TE PĀRTHIVĀḤ sarve jagmuḥ svān ālayān punaḥ
tūṣṇīm|bhūte, mahārāja, Bhīṣme Śāntanu|nandane.
śrutvā tu nihataṃ Bhīṣmaṃ Rādheyaḥ puruṣa'|rṣabhaḥ
īṣad āgata|saṃtrāsaḥ tvaray" ôpajagāma ha.
sa dadarśa mah"|ātmānaṃ śara|talpa|gataṃ tadā
janma|śayyā|gataṃ devaṃ Kārtikeyam iva prabhum.
nimīlit'|âkṣaṃ taṃ vīraṃ s'|âśru|kaṇṭhas tadā Vṛṣaḥ:
«Bhīṣma Bhīṣma mahābāha!» ity uvāca mahā|dyutiḥ.
122.5 «Rādheyo 'haṃ, Kuru|śreṣṭha, nityaṃ c' âkṣi|gatas tava
dveṣyo 'tyantam, an|āgāḥ sann» iti c' âinam uvāca ha.
tac chrutvā Kuru|vṛddho hi balī, saṃvṛta|locanaḥ,
śanair udvīkṣya sa|sneham idaṃ vacanam abravīt,
rahitaṃ dhiṣṇyam ālokya, samutsārya ca rakṣiṇaḥ,
pit" êva putraṃ Gāṅgeyaḥ pariṣvajy' âika|bāhunā:
«ehy, ehi, me vipratīpa! spardhase tvaṃ mayā saha.
yadi māṃ n' âbhigacchethā, na te śreyo dhruvaṃ bhavet!
Kaunteyas tvaṃ; na Rādheyo. na tav' Âdhirathaḥ pitā.
Sūrya|jas tvaṃ, mahā|bāho, vidito Nāradān mayā,

SÁNJAYA said:

After hearing those beneficial and salutary words that were charged with virtue and profit, your son rejected them, just as a dying man rejects medicine.

SÁNJAYA said:

WHEN BHISHMA the son of Shántanu had become silent, 122.1
great king, all those lords of the earth went to their respective quarters. Hearing that Bhishma had been struck down, Radha's son, that bull-like man, came to him in haste, and not without some apprehension. He saw the great-spirited warrior lying supine on his bed of arrows, just as the heroic lord Kartikéya had lain on his bed of reeds after his birth. Then, his voiced choked with tears, the immensely glorious Vrisha spoke to that hero, who lay there with his eyes closed:

"Bhishma, strong-armed Bhishma! I am Radha's son, 122.5
best of the Kurus, who was always looked upon with distaste whenever he came into your sight."

Hearing Karna's words, the mighty and revered Kuru warrior son of Ganga, who was lying with his eyes shut, slowly lifted his eyelids and, seeing that everybody had left that place, dismissed the guards. Embracing Karna with one arm as a father embraces his son, he spoke to him with fondness.

"Come, come, my rival! You have been competing with me, but it would surely have done you no good had you failed to come to see me. You are Kunti's son, not Radha's; and Ádhiratha is not your father! Mighty-armed hero, you were born of the Sun god.* I learned about you from

122.10 Kṛṣṇa|Dvaipāyanāc c' âiva, Keśavāc ca, na saṃśayaḥ.
na ca dveṣo 'sti me, tāta, tvayi. satyaṃ bravīmi te.
tejo|vadha|nimittaṃ tu paruṣam tv aham abruvam.
a|kasmāt Pāṇḍavān sarvān avākṣipasi, su|vrata,
yen' âsi bahuśo rājñā coditaḥ, sūta|nandana.
jāto 'si dharma|lopena; tatas te buddhir īdṛśī,
nīc'|āśrayān matsareṇa dveṣiṇī guṇinām api;
ten' âsi bahuśo rūkṣaṃ śrāvitaḥ Kuru|saṃsadi.

jānāmi samare vīryaṃ śatrubhir duḥ|sahaṃ bhuvi,
brahmaṇyatāṃ ca, śauryaṃ ca, dāne ca paramāṃ sthitim.
122.15 na tvayā sadṛśaḥ kaś cit puruṣeṣv, amar'|ôpama,
kula|bheda|bhayāc c' âhaṃ sadā paruṣam uktavān.
iṣv|astre c', âstra|saṃdhāne, lāghave, 'stra|bale tathā
sadṛśaḥ Phālgunen' âsi, Kṛṣṇena ca mah"|ātmanā.
Karṇa, Kāśi|puraṃ gatvā tvay" âikena dhanuṣmatā
kany" ârthe Kuru|rājasya rājāno mṛditā yudhi.
tathā ca balavān rājā Jarāsandho dur|āsadaḥ
samare samara|ślāghī tvayā na sadṛśo 'bhavat.
brahmaṇyaḥ, sattva|yodhī ca, tejasā ca balena ca,
deva|garbho, 'jitaḥ saṃkhye; manuṣyair adhiko yudhi.

Nárada, and also from Krishna Dvaipáyana. It is undoubtedly true. I feel no hatred for you, son; and I am telling you the truth. I used to address you with harsh words, but it was only in order to reduce your blazing potency. Incited by the king, man of rigid vows, you have often reviled the Pándavas without justification, son of a charioteer. But you were born through a violation of law; and that is why your mind, by way of envy and the company of the mean, became so malicious even toward the virtuous. That is why I often said harsh words to you in the Kuru assembly. 122.10

I know that your prowess in combat cannot be matched by any terrestrial rivals; and nor can your devotion to brahmins, your valor, or your supreme dedication to charity.
Among men there is no one like you, god-like hero. I al- 122.15
ways spoke harsh words to you, but it was only for fear of family discord. In bowmanship, in the dexterity with which you set your missiles upon the string, and in the power of those missiles, you are the equal of Phálguna and of great-spirited Krishna. When you went to the city of Kashi, you alone, Karna, wielding your bow, routed the kings in battle in order to win the bride for the Kuru king. And the mighty King Jara·sandha, though so difficult to conquer, was no match for you in combat, hero ever proud in battle. You are devoted to brahmins, and you fight fairly. Endowed with glory and power, the child of a god, you are invincible on the battlefield; you are far superior to men in war.

122.20 vyapanīto 'dya manyur me, yas tvāṃ prati purā kṛtaḥ.
daivaṃ puruṣa|kāreṇa na śakyam ativartitum.
s'|ôdaryāḥ Pāṇḍavā vīrā bhrātaras te, 'ri|sūdana.
saṃgaccha tair, mahā|bāho, mama ced icchasi priyam.
mayā bhavatu nirvṛttaṃ vairam, āditya|nandana!
pṛthivyāṃ sarva|rājāno bhavantv adya nir|āmayāḥ!»

KARṆA uvāca:

jānāmy ahaṃ, mahā|prājña, sarvam etan, na saṃśayaḥ,
yathā vadasi, dur|dharṣa. Kaunteyo 'haṃ, na sūta|jaḥ.
avakīrṇas tv ahaṃ Kuntyā, sūtena ca vivardhitaḥ.
bhuktvā Duryodhan'|âiśvaryaṃ na mithyā kartum utsahe.
122.25 Vasudeva|suto yadvat Pāṇḍavāya dṛḍha|vrataḥ,
vasu c' âiva, śarīraṃ ca, putra|dāraṃ, tathā yaśaḥ
sarvaṃ Duryodhanasy' ârthe tyaktaṃ me, bhūri|dakṣiṇa.
mā c' âitad vyādhi|maraṇaṃ kṣatraṃ syād iti, Kaurava,
kopitāḥ Pāṇḍavā nityaṃ may" āśritya Suyodhanam.
avaśyabhāvī vai yo 'rtho na sa śakyo nivartitum.
daivaṃ puruṣa|kāreṇa ko nivartitum utsahet?
pṛthivī|kṣaya|śaṃsīni nimittāni, pitā|maha,
bhavadbhir upalabdhāni, kathitāni ca saṃsadi.
Pāṇḍavā Vāsudevaś ca viditā mama sarvaśaḥ
122.30 a|jeyāḥ puruṣair anyair; iti tāṃś c' ôtsahāmahe.
vijayiṣye raṇe Pāṇḍūn, iti me niścitaṃ manaḥ.
na ca śakyam avasraṣṭuṃ vairam etat su|dāruṇam.
Dhanañjayena yotsye 'haṃ sva|dharma|prīta|mānasaḥ.

The grudge I nursed against you in the past has now 122.20
gone. But one cannot overcome fate by human efforts. The heroic Pándavas are your uterine brothers, slayer of enemies. Unite with them, mighty-armed hero, if you wish to do me good. O son of the Sun god, may this enmity cease with my death, and may all the kings on earth be free from distress."

KARNA said:

Mighty-armed hero, I do know all this. It is undoubtedly true: as you have said, Bhishma, I am a son of Kunti, and I am not born of a charioteer; but I was forsaken by Kunti and brought up by a charioteer. And having enjoyed Duryódhana's patronage, I couldn't bear to play him false.
Just as the son of Vasu·deva is firm in his vows toward 122.25
the Pándavas, so I have renounced everything for Duryódhana's sake: my wealth, my body, my sons, my wife, and my honor, bestower of rich gifts. Death from disease should not befall a warrior, Káurava; so I have sided with Suyódhana, and I have always irritated the Pándavas.

This conflict is inevitable and cannot be averted. Who would venture to overcome fate by means of human effort? Grandfather, various portents foreboding the earth's destruction were observed and announced by you in the assembly. I know perfectly well that the Pándavas and Vásu·
deva are invincible by other men; and yet we dare to fight 122.30
with them. I will defeat them in combat; such is my firm decision. This ferocious enmity between us cannot be given up. I will fight with Dhanan·jaya with a joyful heart, and in accordance with my own duty. I have made up my mind,

anujānīṣva māṃ, tāta, yuddhāya kṛta|niścayam.
anujñātas tvayā, vīra, yudhyeyam iti me matiḥ.
dur|uktaṃ vi|pratīpaṃ vā saṃrambhāc cāpalāt tathā
yan may" âpakṛtaṃ kiṃ cit, tad anukṣantum arhasi.

BHĪṢMA uvāca:

na cec chakyam ath' ôtsraṣṭuṃ vairam etat su|dāruṇam,
anujānāmi, Karṇa, tvāṃ. yudhyasva svarga|kāmyayā
122.35 nir|manyur, gata|saṃrambhaḥ, kṛta|karmā nṛ|pasya hi,
yathā|śakti, yath"|ôtsāhaṃ, satāṃ vṛtteṣu vṛttavān!
ahaṃ tvām anujānāmi. yad icchasi, tad āpnuhi.
kṣatra|dharma|jitāl̐ lokān avāpsyasi Dhanañjayāt.
yudhyasva nir|ahaṃ|kāro, bala|vīrya|vyapāśrayaḥ!
dharmyādd hi yuddhāc chreyo 'nyat kṣatriyasya na vidyate.
praśame hi kṛto yatnaḥ su|mahān su|ciraṃ mayā;
na c' âiva śakitaḥ kartuṃ. Karṇa, satyaṃ bravīmi te.

SAÑJAYA uvāca:

ity uktavati Gāṅgeye, abhivādy' ôpamantrya ca,
Rādheyo ratham āruhya prāyāt tava sutaṃ prati.

iti Śrī|Mahābhārate Bhīṣma|parva samāptam.

sir; grant me permission to join the battle. I would like to fight with your approval, hero. If out of impetuosity and insolence I have offended you in any way with my rogue speeches or my obstinacy, then please forgive me.

BHISHMA said:

If you are unable to renounce this bitter enmity, Karna, then I grant you my permission. Fight, driven by the desire
for heaven! Perform your duty in battle to the best of your 122.35
power and vigor, free of fury and arrogance and abiding by the conduct of the virtuous. I grant you my permission; may you attain what it is you desire. On Dhanan·jaya's account you will attain the realms that are won through the righteous deeds of the warrior class. Give up your pride, rely on your strength and valor, and fight. For there is nothing better for a warrior than a righteous battle! For such a long long time I made great efforts to achieve peace. It could not be done. Karna, I am telling you the truth.

SÁNJAYA said:

When the son of Ganga had said this, Radha's son, having honored and pleased Bhishma, ascended his chariot and moved off toward your son.

Thus in the glorious "Maha·bhárata"
the Book of Bhishma is completed.

ŚRAVAṆA|MAHIMĀ:

VAIŚAMPĀYANA uvāca:

122.40 ity etad bahu|vṛttāntaṃ Bhīṣma|parv' âkhilaṃ mayā
śṛṇvate te, mahā|rāja, proktaṃ pāpa|haraṃ, śubham.
yaḥ śrāvayet sadā, rājan, brāhmaṇān veda|pāra|gān,
śraddhāvantaś ca ye c' âpi śroṣyanti manujā bhuvi,
vidhūya sarva|pāpāni, vihāy' ânte kalevaram,
prayānti tat padaṃ Viṣṇor, yat prāpya na nivartate.
tasmāt sarva|prayatnena, Bhārata Bharata'|rṣabha,
śṛṇuyāt siddhim anvicchann iha v" âmutra mānavaḥ.
bhojanaṃ bhojayed viprān gandha|mālyair alaṃ|kṛtān;
Bhīṣma|parvaṇi, rāj|êndra, dadyāt pānīyam uttamam.

THE GLORY OF LISTENING:

VAISHAMPÁYANA said:

To you, the listener, great king, I have related the entire Book of "Bhishma" which is auspicious, abounds in events, and removes evil. Your Majesty, the man who retells it to brahmins perfectly versed in the Vedas, and the men who listen to it on earth with devotion, are freed from all sins; and when their lives come to an end and they give up their bodies, they attain the realm of Vishnu, from where one never returns. So a man who seeks accomplishment in this world or in the other should listen to the "Maha·bhárata," bull of the Bharatas; and at the close of the Book of "Bhishma" he should adorn the brahmins with fragrant garlands and give them food and pure water, king of kings. 122.40

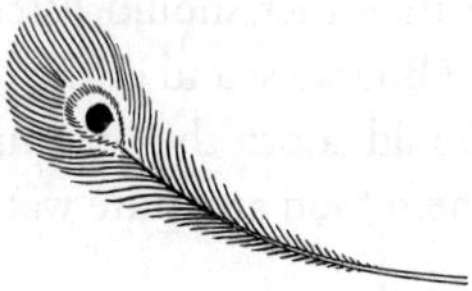

NOTES

Bold *references are to the English text;* ***bold italic*** *references are to the Sanskrit text. An asterisk (*) in the body of the text marks the word or passage being annotated.*

65.3 **Vídura's words**: Vídura warned Dhrita·rashtra a number of times against indulging Duryódhana in the latter's evil plots against the sons of Pandu, and advised him to put an end to the game of dice lest it should lead to disastrous consequences. See 'The Great Hall' (*Sabhāparvan*), CSL edition (CSL) cantos 62, 63, 66 = Critical Edition (CE) 55, 56, 59.

65.52 See note to 67.17. Also note the play on the word Hari, one of Vishnu's names.

65.54 **Brahman** is the impersonal Absolute, the unmanifested source of emanation of the universe.

65.58 **Lotus-naveled powerful god**: see 67.12.

65.64 **Gandhárvas** are celestial musicians. **Yakshas** are semi-divine attendants on god Kubéra, and guardians of his riches. **Rákshasas** are cannibal demons that attack in the dark. **Pisháchas** are a class of demons feeding on corpses.

66.9 **Daityas** and **dánavas** are classes of demons who warred against the gods.

66.11 **Nara** (Man) and **Naráyana** (Vishnu) are two gods often coupled together and are identified with Árjuna and Krishna respectively.

66.21 **Shri**, or Lakshmi, the goddess of prosperity, is Vishnu's consort, who rests on his chest. The curl on Vishnu's chest is a sign of good fortune.

66.22 **Káustubha** is a magic jewel obtained at the churning of the ocean and worn by Vishnu/Krishna on his bosom.

66.25 **Ápsarases** are heavenly nymphs.

66.39 **Brahmins** are priests, **kshatriyas** are warriors, **vaishyas** are engaged in agriculture, cattle breeding, and trade, whereas **shudras** are to serve the three superior orders.

66.40 **Dvápara** is the third and **kali** is the fourth of the four yugas, or ages (the first two being krita and treta). Dharma, or righteousness, degrades by one fourth with each age.

67.3 **Markandéya describes**: see the vision of Markandéya in 'The Forest' (*Āraṇyakaparvan*) CE.III.186.79–129.

67.12 **The Grandsire**: Brahma.

67.17 **The Boar, the Lion, and the Lord of Three Strides**: these are three of the ten avatars of Vishnu. Assuming the form of a boar (*varāha*), he raised the earth from the ocean, into which it had been plunged by a demon Hiranyáksha. Vishnu assumed the form of a man-lion (*nara/siṃha*) in order to deliver the world from the tyranny of a demon king Hiránya·káshipu, who was secure from the gods, men and animals. The three strides of Vishnu are first mentioned in "Rig Veda" 1.154. In his incarnation as a dwarf (*vāmana*), Vishnu, granted three steps of land by the demon king Bali, grew in size to measure the entire earth with his first step, the entire heaven with the second, and with the third he pushed Bali down into hell.

67.19 **Kshatriyas** are warriors, **vaishyas** are engaged in agriculture, cattle breeding, and trade; **shudras** are the servants of the three superior orders, of which the **brahmins**, or priests, are the highest. On their mythical origin and status see "The Laws of Manu," chapter 1.

68.4 **Puránas** are compendia of myths, legends and religious instructions of Hinduism. There are eighteen chief Puránas, of which the *Viṣṇupurāṇa* is one of the most important.

68.19 **Your father**: Bhishma.

72.32 **The slayer of Vritra**: Indra.

72.32 **Ásuras** are ancient deities, anti-gods.

73.12 **The two Krishnas**: Krishna and Árjuna.

73.15 **Bibhátsu**: Árjuna.

75.8 **King of Righteousness**: Yudhi·shthira

76.12 **World-guardians**: eight *lokapāla* deities protecting eight directions.

81.40 See note to 73.12

84.3 **Son of Righteousness**: Yudhi·shthira.

85.3 **The son of Shakra**: Árjuna was born from Indra.

87.19 **Árjuna with his white horses and dark charioteer**: note the contrast of colors, as Krishna's name literally means "dark," or "black."

88.30 **What Bhima had said in the assembly-hall**: Bhima·sena made a pledge to send Duryódhana and his followers to the abode of Yama. See 'The Great Hall,' CSL.II.77.16–29 (CE.II.68.16–29).

88.33 **Words that Kshattri Vídura ... had spoken**: see note to 65.3.

95.5 An **aksháuhini** is a large army consisting of 21,870 chariots, as many elephants, 65,610 horsemen and 109,350 foot soldiers.

96.58 **Shata·ghni missiles**: "hundred-killer" is a kind of weapon, presumably a studded log meant for throwing down from the city walls on the attacking enemy. See *Arthaśāstra*.

98.37 For Bhishma's recount of **Shikhándin's birth**, see 'Preparations for War' (*Udyogaparvan*) CSL.V.187–91 (CE.V.188–192).

101.17 **Kínshuka** trees have red blossoms.

108.45 **Rama the son of Jamad·agni**: a famous brahmin warrior, also known as Párashu·rama, or Rama-with-the-axe, who slaughtered the entire warrior caste twenty-one times and gave the earth to the brahmins. He fought a battle with Bhishma, but failed to defeat him. On the duel between Bhishma and Párashu·rama and its cause see 'Preparations for War' CSL.V.178–184.

109.16 See note to 87.19.

113.41 **Son of the god Wind**: Bhima·sena is the son of Kunti by the Wind god Vayu.

115.31 **Karnikára** is a tree with red, orange or yellow flowers.

116.80 See note to 87.19.

117.19 See note to 87.19.

119.33 **Vishvak·sena**: Krishna.

119.34 **When I arranged my father's marriage with Kali**: Bhishma arranged his father Shántanu's marriage with a fisherman's daughter Kali and agreed to the condition that the son born from her would be given the right of kingship. In order to avoid further feud between the descendants in future, Bhishma took a vow of celibacy. Then grateful Shántanu granted him the two boons. See 'The Beginning' (*Ádiparvan*) CE.I.100.

119.36 **Rishis** are seers, sages, saints.

119.40 **Through the power of the sage**: The sage Vyasa granted Sánjaya divine vision that enabled him to witness the entire events of the great battle and to narrate them to king Dhrita·rashtra. See 'Bhishma' CSL.VI.2.4–12.

119.94 **An inauspicious time to die**: dying during the six months of the sun's northward course i.e. between the winter and the summer solstices was considered auspicious. See 'Bhishma' CSL.VI.32.23–28.

119.121 **Upanishads**: a class of philosophical texts concerning the relationship of the human soul with the supreme reality.

120.6 **He, whom the son of Jamad·agni with his divine weapons was not able to kill**: see 108.45.

120.14 **Coming to know that his father Shántanu had become lovesick...** See 119.34.

120.15 **Siddhas** are semi-divine beings that have reached the state of great perfection; **cháranas** are celestial singers.

120.52 **The quarter occupied by Váishravana**: the north.

122.9 **You were born of the Sun god**: Karna was the eldest, illegitimate, son of Kunti by the Sun god Surya, born before Kunti married Pandu.

PROPER NAMES AND EPITHETS

ABHIMÁNYU Son of Árjuna and Subhádra.

ABHISHÁHA Name of a people fighting for the Káuravas.

ÁCHYUTA A name for Krishna. Also used of many others in the epic. Literally, "unfallen," "imperishable."

ÁDHIRATHA A charioteer. Adoptive father of Karna.

ADÍTYA·KETU A son of Dhrita·rashtra.

AGNI The god of fire.

AIRÁVATA Elephant of Indra.

AJÁTA·SHATRU A name for Yudhi·shthira. Literally, "he whose enemy is not born."

ALÁMBUSHA A demon that fights on the side of the Káuravas.

AMBÁSHTHA Name of a people fighting for the Káuravas.

ANADHRÍSHTI A son of Dhrita·rashtra.

ANÁNTA A name of the cosmic serpent Shesha. Literally, "infinite."

ÁNGIRAS An ancient seer.

ANIRÚDDHA Son of Pradyúmna. Grandson of Krishna.

ANÚPA Name of a people fighting on the side of the Pándavas.

ANUVÍNDA Prince of Avánti. Brother of Vinda. Fights for the Káuravas.

APARÁJITA A son of Dhrita·rashtra.

ARÁTTA An ancient name of Punjab.

ÁRJAVA A son of Súbala; brother of Shákuni.

ÁRJUNA The third of the five Pándava brothers. The son of Pandu and Kunti. Also known as Bibhátsu, Dhanan·jaya, Jishnu, Pándava, Partha, Phálguna, Savya·sachin, Víjaya. Literally, "white," "bright."

ASHVA·TTHAMAN Son of Drona and Kripi. Fights for the Káuravas.

ASHVINS Twin gods associated with the morning and evening twilights; healers; fathers of the twin brothers Nákula and Saha·deva. Literally, "horsemen."

ÁSITA DÉVALA A sage.

AVÁNTI Name of a country in West India.

BÁHLIKA Father of Soma·datta. Brother of Shántanu. Fights for the Káuravas. Also name of a people fighting on the side of the Káuravas.

BAHVÁSHIN A son of Dhrita·rashtra.

BHAGA·DATTA King of Prag·jyótisha. Fights for the Káuravas.

BHARAD·VAJA An ancient seer. Father of Drona. Grandfather of Ashva·tthaman.

BHARATA A famous king of the Lunar dynasty who ruled in North India. Son of Duhshánta and Shakúntala. Ancestor of most of the characters in the "Maha·bhárata." In the plural, the Bharatas are the descendants of Bharata.

BHÁRATA Descendant of Bharata. Common in the epic.

BHIMA The second of the five Pándava brothers. Son of Pandu and Kunti. Literally, "terrifying." Also known as Bhima·sena, Pándava, Partha, Vrikódara.

BHIMA·SENA Name for Bhima. Literally, "he who has a terrifying army."

BHISHMA Son of Shántanu and Ganga. Literally, "frightful." Also known as Deva·vrata. Fights for the Káuravas.

BHRIGU An ancient seer.

BHURI·SHRAVAS Son of Soma·datta. Grandson of Báhlika. Fights for the Káuravas.

BIBHÁTSU A name for Árjuna. Literally, "the tormentor."

BRAHMA The progenitor of all creatures; the personification of the universal absolute.

BRIHAD·BALA King of Kósala. Fights for the Káuravas.

CHÁRMAVAT A son of Súbala; brother of Shákuni.

CHARU·CHITRA A son of Dhrita·rashtra.

CHEDI Name of a people fighting for the Pándavas.

CHEKITÁNA A Vrishni warrior. Ally of the Pándavas.

CHITRA·DÁRSHANA A son of Dhrita·rashtra.

CHITRA·KETU A son of Dhrita·rashtra.

CHITRÁNGA A son of Dhrita·rashtra.

CHITRA·SENA A son of Dhrita·rashtra.

DAITYA Class of demons, sons of Diti and the sage Káshyapa.

DAKSHA A son of Brahma.

DÁNAVA Class of demons, sons of Danu and the sage Káshyapa.

DÁRADA Name of a people fighting for the Káuravas.

DASHÁRHA Name of a people. Krishna is their chief.

DASHÁRNA Name of a people fighting for the Pándavas.

DÉVAKI Wife of Vasu·deva. Mother of Krishna.

DEVA·VRATA Bhishma's original name. Literally, "he whose vows are divine."

DHANAN·JAYA A name for Árjuna. Literally, "the wealth-conqueror."

DHARTA·RASHTRA Descendant of Dhrita·rashtra. Refers to Duryódhana and his brothers.

DHATRI Deity associated with Brahma. Literally, "arranger," "establisher."

DHRISHTA·DYUMNA Son of the Panchála king Drúpada, brother of Dráupadi. Born from a sacrificial fire. Fights for the Pándavas.

DHRISHTA·KETU A warrior that fights on the side of the Pándavas.

DHRITA·RASHTRA King of the Kurus. Son of Krishna Dvaipáyana and Ámbika. Father of Duryódhana and 99 other sons.

DIRGHA·BAHU A son of Dhrita·rashtra.

DIRGHA·LÓCHANA A son of Dhrita·rashtra.

DRÁUPADI Daughter of Drúpada. Wife of the five Pándava brothers. Also known as Krishna. She has five sons: Prativíndhya, Suta·soma, Shruta·kirti, Shataníka and Shruta·sena.

DRONA Son of Bharad·vaja. Husband of Kripi. Father of Ashva·tthaman. Preceptor of the sons of Pandu and the sons of Dhrita·rashtra. Fights for the Káuravas.

DRÚPADA King of the Panchálas. Son of Príshata. Fights for the Pándavas.

DÚHSAHA A son of Dhrita·rashtra.

DUHSHÁSANA A son of Dhrita·rashtra.

DÚRJAYA A son of Dhrita·rashtra.

DÚRMADA A son of Dhrita·rashtra.

DURMÁRSHANA A son of Dhrita·rashtra.

DÚRMUKHA A son of Dhrita·rashtra.

DÚRVISHAHA A son of Dhrita·rashtra.

DURYÓDHANA Eldest son of Dhrita·rashtra and Gandhári. Literally, "he who is difficult to fight." Also known as Suyódhana.

DUSHKÁRNA A son of Dhrita·rashtra.

DVAIPÁYANA see Krishna Dvaipáyana.

DVÁRAKA Capital of Krishna. Literally, "city of gates."

GAJA A son of Súbala; brother of Shákuni.

GANDHA·MÁDANA Name of a mountain in the Himalayas.

GANDHÁRA Name of a country and its people. Shákuni is their chief.

GANDHÁRI Wife of Dhrita·rashtra. Mother of Duryódhana and 99 other sons. Daughter of Súbala. Literally, "princess of Gandhára."

GANDÍVA The bow of Árjuna.

GANGA The river Ganges personified as a goddess and the mother of Bhishma.

GÁRUDA Son of seer Káshyapa by Vínata. King of birds. Vehicle of Vishnu. Enemy of snakes.

GAVÁKSHA A son of Súbala; brother of Shákuni.

GHATÓTKACHA Son of Bhima and Hidímba. A *rákshasa* demon. Fights on the side of the Pándavas.

GÓTAMA An ancient seer. Father of Sharádvat. Grandfather of Kripa.

GO·VINDA A name for Krishna. Literally, "cowherd."

HARI A name for Krishna.

HIDÍMBA A *rákshasa* demoness. Mother of Ghatótkacha.

HRÍDIKA Father of Krita·varman.

HRISHI·KESHA A name for Krishna. Literally, "he whose hair is splendid."

INDRA King of the gods (devas). Also known as Mághavat, Shakra, Vásava.

IRÁVAT Son of Árjuna by his *naga* wife Ulúpi.

INDRA·PRASTHA Capital of the Pándavas (identified with Delhi). Literally, "Indra's plain."

JAHNU A sage who drank up the Ganges and then issued its stream from his ear.

JAMAD·AGNI A seer. Father of Párashu·rama.

JANÁRDANA A name for Krishna. Literally, "people-agitator."

JARA·SANDHA King of Mágadha, son of Brihad·ratha. Krishna's enemy. Fights for the Káuravas.

JAYA A son of Dhrita·rashtra.

JAYAD·RATHA King of the Sindhus. Fights for the Káuravas.

JAYAT·SENA A son of Dhrita·rashtra.

JISHNU A name for Árjuna. Literally, "victorious."

KAILÁSA A sacred mountain in the Himalayas.

KALI Name for Sátyavati. Literally, "the black one."

KALÍNGA Name of a people fighting on the side of the Káuravas.

KAMBÓJA Name of a people fighting for the Káuravas. Sudákshina is their king.

KÁNAKA·DHVAJA A son of Dhrita·rashtra.

KARA·KARSHA A warrior that fights for the Pándavas.

KARNA The eldest (illegitimate) son of Kunti by the Sun god Surya. Adopted by the charioteer Ádhiratha and his wife Radha. Often known as "the charioteer's son." Sworn enemy of the Pándavas. Fights for the Káuravas.

KARTIKÉYA A name for Shiva's son Skanda, god of war. Was fostered by Kríttika (the Pleiades), hence his name.

KASHI Name of a people fighting on the side of the Pándavas.

KÁURAVA Descendant of Kuru. Often refers to Dhrita·rashtra's sons and followers, but the Pándavas are also sometimes called Káurava (since they too are descendants of Kuru).

KÉKAYA Name of a people. Also refers to five princes of the Kékayas that joined Yudhi·shthira.

KÉSHAVA A name for Krishna. Literally, "he who has fine hair."

KHÁNDAVA Name of a forest that Árjuna, after conquering Indra, let Agni consume.

KING OF RIGHTEOUSNESS (DHARMA) Yudhi·shthira.

KÍTAVA Name of a people fighting for the Káuravas.

KÓSALA Name of a people fighting on the side of the Káuravas.

KRÁUNCHA A mountain.

KRIPA Son of Sharádvat. Grandson of Gótama. Brother of Kripi. Fights for the Káuravas.

KRISHNA Son of Vasu·deva and Dévaki. Also identified with Vishnu/ Naráyana, the supreme god. Also known as Áchyuta, Go·vinda, Hari, Hrishi·kesha, Janárdana, Késhava, Vásu·deva. Árjuna's charioteer. Literally, "black," "dark." The "two Krishnas" are Krishna and Árjuna.

KRISHNA DVAIPÁYANA Son of Sátyavati and the seer Paráshara. Father of Dhrita·rashtra, Pandu, and Vídura. Also known as Vyasa. His name derives from the fact that he was of black complexion and was abandoned on an island (*dvīpa*).

KRITA·VARMAN A Vrishni ruler. Son of Hrídika. Fights for the Káuravas.

KSHATRA·DEVA A warrior fighting for the Pándavas.

KSHATRA·DHARMAN A warrior that fights for the Pándavas.

KSHATTRI A name for Vídura. A term referring to the fact that he was born from a low-caste shudra woman; also meaning "steward."

KUNDA·BHEDA A son of Dhrita·rashtra.

KUNDA·DHARA A son of Dhrita·rashtra.

KÚNDALIN A warrior fighting for the Káuravas.

KURU Ancestor of the Bharatas. "The Kurus" are the descendants of Kuru and include both the Káuravas and the Pándavas, although it often refers only to Dhrita·rashtra's sons and their followers.

KUBÉRA The god of riches.

KUNTI Wife of Pandu. Mother of Karna by the god Surya (the Sun), and mother of Yudhi·shthira, Bhima and Árjuna by Pandu (through the gods Dharma, Vayu, and Indra respectively). Also known as Pritha.

KUNTI·BHOJA Adoptive father of Kunti. Fights for the Pándavas.

KARÚSHA Name of a people.

KURU·VINDA Name of a people fighting for the Káuravas.

LÁKSHMANA Son of Duryódhana.

MÁDHAVA A name of a people. Descendant of Madhu. A name for Krishna, Sátyaki, and Krita·varman.

MADHU A demon killed by Vishnu/Krishna.

MADRA Name of a people fighting for the Káuravas. Shalya is their king.

MADRI Second wife of Pandu. A princess of the Madras. Mother of the twins Nákula and Saha·deva by the two Ashvins.

MÁGADHA Name of a people fighting on the side of the Káuravas.

MÁGHAVAT A name for Indra. Literally, "bountiful."

MAHA·RAUDRA A demon.

MAHI Name of a country.

MAHÓDARA A son of Dhrita·rashtra.

MAINÁKA A mountain.

MÁLAVA Name of a people fighting for the Káuravas.

MARKANDÉYA An ancient seer.

MATSYA Name of a people fighting on the side of the Pándavas.

MAYA A demon defeated by Indra.

MÉKALA Name of a people fighting for the Káuravas.

MERU A mountain at the center of the cosmos.

NAGA serpents; serpent-like demons of the underworld.

NÁKULA One of the Pándava brothers. Twin brother of Saha·deva. Son of Pandu and Madri (by one of the Ashvin gods).

NÁMUCHI A demon killed by Indra.

NANDA A son of Dhrita·rashtra.

NARA Primeval Man. Often considered a god and coupled with Naráyana. Identified with Árjuna.

NÁRADA A seer.

NARÁYANA Name of the god Vishnu. Often coupled with Nara. Identified with Krishna.

NILA King of the Anúpas. Fights for the Pándavas.

NISHÁDA Name of a people supporting the Káuravas.

PANCHA·JANYA The conch of Krishna.

PANCHÁLA Name of a people fighting on the side of the Pándavas. Drúpada is their king.

PÁNDAVA Son of Pandu = Yudhi·shthira, Bhima, Árjuna, Nákula and Saha·deva. Often refers to the followers of the sons of Pandu.

PÁNDITAKA A son of Dhrita·rashtra.

PANDU Son of Krishna Dvaipáyana. Half-brother of Dhrita·rashtra and Vídura. Father of the Pándavas. Husband of Kunti and Madri.

PARÁSHARA A seer. Father of Krishna Dvaipáyana.

PÁRASHU·RAMA Son of Jamad·agni. Literally, "Rama with the axe." Destroyer of kshatriyas. Failed to defeat Bhishma.

PARJÁNYA God of rain, often identified with Indra.

PARTHA Son of Pritha = Yudhi·shthira, Bhima, Árjuna, Nákula and Saha·deva. Often refers to the followers of the sons of Pritha.

PASHU·PATI God associated and often identified with Shiva. Literally, "lord of creatures."

PÁURAVA Descendant of Puru. Name of a people.

PHÁLGUNA A name for Árjuna. Literally, "born under the constellation Phálguni."

PRABHÁDRAKA A division of the Panchálas.

PRADYÚMNA Son of Krishna by Rúkmini. Father of Anirúddha.

PRAG·JYÓTISHA Name of a people fighting on the side of the Káuravas.

PRAJA·PATI A name for Brahma. Literally, "lord of creatures."

PRAMÁTHIN A demon.

PRÁSTHALA A country of the Tri·gartas.

PRATIVÍNDHYA A warrior fighting for the Pándavas.

PRÍSHATA Father of Drúpada. Grandfather of Dhrishta·dyumna.

PRITHA A name for Kunti.

PURU·MITRA A warrior that fights on the side of the Káuravas.

RADHA Adoptive mother of Karna. Wife of the charioteer Ádhiratha.

RAHU A planet; the demon of eclipse.

RAMA see Párashu·rama.

RISHYA·SHRINGA A sage

RUDRA A god. Associated with Shiva.

SAHA·DEVA One of the Pándava brothers. Twin brother of Nákula. Son of Pandu and Madri (by one of Ashvin gods).

SANAT·KUMÁRA A sage. A mental son of Brahma.

SÁNJAYA Son of charioteer Gaválgana. Royal herald or bard at the Káurava court. Narrates the events of the great battle to the blind king Dhrita·rashtra.

SANKÁRSHANA Elder brother of Krishna.

SARÁSVATI Name of a river and the goddess associated with speech and learning.

SÁTVATA Name of a people belonging to the Yádavas. Used of Krishna, Krita·varman and Sátyaki.

SATYA·DHRITI A warrior that fights for the Pándavas.

SÁTYAKI A Vrishni. Also called Yuyudhána. Means "son of Sátyaka." Grandson of Shini. Fights for the Pándavas.

SÁTYAVATI Daughter of a fisherman. Second wife of Shántanu. Mother of Chitrángada and Vichítra·virya by Shántanu. Mother of Vyasa by Paráshara.

SATYA·VRATA A warrior fighting on the side the Káuravas.

SAUCHÍTTI see Satya·dhriti.

SAUVÍRA Name of a people fighting for the Káuravas.

SÁVITRI A solar god.

SAVYA·SACHIN A name for Árjuna. Literally, "he who draws (a bow) with his left hand."

SHAKA Name of a people fighting on the side of the Káuravas.

SHAKRA Name of Indra. Literally, "mighty."

SHÁKUNI Son of the Gandhára king Súbala. Father of Ulúka.

SHALA A warrior that fights for the Káuravas.

SHALVA Name of a people and their king fighting for the Káuravas.

SHALYA King of the Madras. Brother of Madri. Fights on the side of the Káuravas.

SHANKHA A son of Viráta. Fights for the Pándavas.

SHÁNTANU Father of Bhishma by Ganga.

SHARÁDVAT Father of Kripa.

SHARNGA The bow of Vishnu/Krishna.

SHATANÍKA Son of Nákula and Dráupadi. Fights for the Pándavas.

SHATÁYUS A warrior that fights for the Káuravas.

SHESHA Thousand-headed cosmic serpent forming the couch of Vishnu and supporting the world.

SHIBI Name of a people fighting for the Káuravas.

SHIKHÁNDIN Son (originally daughter) of Drúpada. Fights for the Pándavas and is instrumental in Árjuna's slaughter of Bhishma.

SHINI Father of Sátyaka. Grandfather of Sátyaki.

SHIVA A god.

SHRÉNIMAT A warrior that fights for the Pándavas.

SHRI The goddess of prosperity who is incarnate in Dráupadi.

SHRUTÁYUS A warrior that fights for the Káuravas.

SHUKA A son of Súbala; brother of Shákuni.

SHURA·SENA Name of a people fighting for the Káuravas.

SINDHU Name of the river Indus and a people dwelling in its valley, who are allied to the Káuravas.

SKANDA Son of Shiva. God of war and commander of the military forces of the gods. Also known as Kartikéya.

SOMA The Moon god.

SOMA·DATTA Father of Bhuri·shravas. Fights for the Káuravas.

SÓMAKA Name of a people. Often grouped with the Panchálas.

SON OF RIGHTEOUSNESS (DHARMA) Yudhi·shthira.

SRÍNJAYA Name of a people. Often grouped with the Panchálas.

SUBÁHU King of the Chedis. Fights for the Pándavas.

SÚBALA King of Gandhára. Father of Shákuni and Gandhári.

SUBHÁDRA Younger sister of Krishna. Mother of Abhimányu by Árjuna.

SUCHÁRU A son of Dhrita·rashtra.

SUCHÍTRA A son of Dhrita·rashtra.

SUDÁKSHINA King of the Kambójas. Fights for the Káuravas.

SUDÁRSHANA A son of Dhrita·rashtra.

SUNÁBHA A son of Dhrita·rashtra.

SUPÁRNA A name for Gáruda.

SUPRATÍKA One of the elephants guarding the eight cardinal points.

SUYÓDHANA Name for Duryódhana. Literally, "good fighter."

SUSHÁRMAN King of the Tri·gartas. Fights for the Káuravas.

SUVÁRMAN A warrior that fights for the Káuravas.

TÁRAKA Name of a demon.

TRI·GARTA Name of a people fighting on the side of the Káuravas.

TRI·PURA Name of a people who fight for the Káuravas.

TUKHÁRA Name of a people.

TVASHTRI Divine craftsman of weapons such as thunderbolt.

UPANÁNDA A son of Dhrita·rashtra.

UTTAMÁUJAS A Panchála warrior fighting on the side of the Pándavas. Brother of Yudha·manyu.

ULÚKA Son of Shákuni. Fights for the Káuravas.

UPANÁNDA A son of Dhrita·rashtra.

UPÉNDRA A name for Vishnu; literally, "younger brother of Indra."

UTTARÁ Princess of the Matsyas. Daughter of Viráta. Wife of Abhimányu.

VAIRÁTA A son of Dhrita·rashtra.

VÁITARANI Name of the river of hell.

VAISHAMPÁYANA Disciple of Krishna Dvaipáyana. Recited the "Maha·bhárata" at Janam·éjaya's snake sacrifice.

VÁISHRAVANA Name of Kubéra.

VANÁYU A country.

VANGA Name of a people.

VÁRUNA A god associated with waters.

VASÁTI Name of a people fighting for the Káuravas.

VÁSAVA A name for Indra. Literally, "the lord of the Vasus."

VASU A class of deities. Indra is their chief.

VASU·DANA A warrior fighting for the Pándavas.

VÁSU·DEVA Name of Krishna. Means "son of Vasu·deva."

VAYU The god of wind.

VÉGAVAT Name of a *rákshasa* demon that fights for the Káuravas.

VICHÍTRA·VIRYA Son of Shántanu by Sátyavati through Krishna Dvaipáyana. Father of Dhrita·rashtra, Pandu and Vídura.

VIDÉHA Name of a people fighting on the side of the Káuravas.

VÍDURA Son of Krishna Dvaipáyana and a low-caste shudra woman. Uncle of the Pándavas and sons of Dhrita·rashtra.

VIDYUJ·JIHVA A demon.

VÍJAYA A name for Árjuna. Literally, "victory."

VIKÁRNA A son of Dhrita·rashtra.

VÍNATA Mother of Gáruda.

VINDA Prince of Avánti. Brother of Anuvínda Fights for the Káuravas.

VIPRA·CHITTI A *rákshasa* demon fighting for the Káuravas.

VIRÁTA King of the Matsyas, at whose court the Pándavas lived in disguise during the thirteenth year of their exile, as recounted in 'Viráta' (*Virāṭaparvan*).

VISHALÁKSHA A son of Dhrita·rashtra.

VISHNU A god. Preserver of the universe. The supreme god in the "Maha·bhárata."

VISHÓKA Driver of Bhima's chariot.

VISHVA·KARMAN A deity. Divine architect. Literally, "all-maker."

VISHVAK·SENA A name for Vishnu. Literally, "he whose hosts are everywhere."

VIVÁSVAT Father of Yama. A solar god.

VRIKÓDARA A name for Bhima. Literally, "wolf-bellied."

VRISHA A name for Karna. Means "bull."

VRÍSHABHA A son of Súbala; brother of Shákuni.

VRISHNI Name of a Yádava people. Krishna, Sátyaki and Krita·varman belong to this clan.

VRITRA Name of a demon slain by Indra.

VYASA Name of Krishna Dvaipáyana. Traditionally considered to be the arranger of the Vedas and the author of the "Maha·bhárata."

VYUDHORÁSKA A warrior fighting for the Káuravas.

YÁDAVA Name of a people. Descendant of Yadu. Used of Krishna.

YADU Son of Yayáti, ancestor of the Yadus (Yádavas). The Yadus are often synonymous with the Vrishnis.

YAMA The god of the dead. Son of Vivásvat.

YÁVANA Name of a people. Connected with the Greeks (Ionians).

YUDHA·MANYU A Panchála warrior fighting for the Pándavas. Brother of Uttamáujas.

YUDHI·SHTHIRA Eldest of the five Pándava brothers. Son of Pandu and Kunti (by the god Dharma). Also known as the Son of Righteousness (Dharma), the King of Righteousness, and Ajáta·shatru.

YUYUDHÁNA Sátyaki's proper name.

THE CLAY SANSKRIT LIBRARY

The volumes in the series are listed here in order of publication.
Titles marked with an asterisk* are also available in the
Digital Clay Sanskrit Library (eCSL).
For further information visit www.claysanskritlibrary.org

1. The Emperor of the Sorcerers (*Bṛhatkathāślokasaṃgraha*) (vol. 1 of 2) by *Budhasvāmin*. SIR JAMES MALLINSON
2. Heavenly Exploits (*Divyāvadāna*). JOEL TATELMAN
3. Maha·bhárata III: The Forest (*Vanaparvan*) (vol. 4 of 4)* WILLIAM J. JOHNSON
4. Much Ado about Religion (*Āgamaḍambara*) by *Bhaṭṭa Jayanta*. CSABA DEZSŐ
5. The Birth of Kumára (*Kumārasaṃbhava*) by *Kālidāsa*. DAVID SMITH
6. Ramáyana I: Boyhood (*Bālakāṇḍa*) by *Vālmīki*. ROBERT P. GOLDMAN
7. The Epitome of Queen Lilávati (*Līlāvatīsāra*) (vol. 1 of 2) by *Jinaratna*. R.C.C. FYNES
8. Ramáyana II: Ayódhya (*Ayodhyākāṇḍa*) by *Vālmīki*. SHELDON I. POLLOCK
9. Love Lyrics (*Amaruśataka, Śatakatraya & Caurapañcāśikā*) by *Amaru, Bhartṛhari & Bilhaṇa*. GREG BAILEY & RICHARD GOMBRICH
10. What Ten Young Men Did (*Daśakumāracarita*) by *Daṇḍin*. ISABELLE ONIANS
11. Three Satires (*Kaliviḍambana, Kalāvilāsa & Bhallaṭaśataka*) by *Nīlakaṇṭha, Kṣemendra & Bhallaṭa*. SOMADEVA VASUDEVA
12. Ramáyana IV: Kishkíndha (*Kiṣkindhākāṇḍa*) by *Vālmīki*. ROSALIND LEFEBER
13. The Emperor of the Sorcerers (*Bṛhatkathāślokasaṃgraha*) (vol. 2 of 2) by *Budhasvāmin*. SIR JAMES MALLINSON
14. Maha·bhárata IX: Shalya (*Śalyaparvan*) (vol. 1 of 2)* JUSTIN MEILAND

15. Rákshasa's Ring (*Mudrārākṣasa*)*
by *Viśākhadatta*. Michael Coulson
16. Messenger Poems (*Meghadūta, Pavanadūta & Haṃsadūta*)
by *Kālidāsa, Dhoyī & Rūpa Gosvāmin*. Sir James Mallinson
17. Ramáyana III: The Forest (*Aranyakāṇḍa*)
by *Vālmīki*. Sheldon I. Pollock
18. The Epitome of Queen Lilávati (*Līlāvatīsāra*) (vol. 2 of 2)
by *Jinaratna*. R.C.C. Fynes
19. Five Discourses on Worldly Wisdom (*Pañcatantra*)*
by *Viṣṇuśarman*. Patrick Olivelle
20. Ramáyana V: Súndara (*Sundarakāṇḍa*) by *Vālmīki*.
Robert P. Goldman & Sally J. Sutherland Goldman
21. Maha·bhárata II: The Great Hall (*Sabhāparvan*)
Paul Wilmot
22. The Recognition of Shakúntala (*Abhijñānaśākuntala*) (Kashmir Recension) by *Kālidāsa*. Somadeva Vasudeva
23. Maha·bhárata VII: Drona (*Droṇaparvan*) (vol. 1 of 4)*
Vaughan Pilikian
24. Rama Beyond Price (*Anargharāghava*)
by *Murāri*. Judit Törzsök
25. Maha·bhárata IV: Viráta (*Virāṭaparvan*)
Kathleen Garbutt
26. Maha·bhárata VIII: Karna (*Karṇaparvan*) (vol. 1 of 2)
Adam Bowles
27. "The Lady of the Jewel Necklace" & "The Lady who Shows her Love" (*Ratnāvalī & Priyadarśikā*) by *Harṣa*.*
Wendy Doniger
28. The Ocean of the Rivers of Story (*Kathāsaritsāgara*) (vol. 1 of 7)
by *Somadeva*. Sir James Mallinson
29. Handsome Nanda (*Saundarananda*)*
by *Aśvaghoṣa*. Linda Covill
30. Maha·bhárata IX: Shalya (*Śalyaparvan*) (vol. 2 of 2)*
Justin Meiland
31. Rama's Last Act (*Uttararāmacarita*) by *Bhavabhūti*.
Sheldon Pollock. Foreword by Girish Karnad

32. "Friendly Advice" (*Hitopadeśa*) by *Nārāyaṇa* &
"King Víkrama's Adventures" (*Vikramacarita*). JUDIT TÖRZSÖK

33. Life of the Buddha (*Buddhacarita*)
by *Aśvaghoṣa*. PATRICK OLIVELLE

34. Maha·bhárata V: Preparations for War (*Udyogaparvan*) (vol. 1 of 2)
KATHLEEN GARBUTT. Foreword by GURCHARAN DAS

35. Maha·bhárata VIII: Karna (*Karṇaparvan*) (vol. 2 of 2)
ADAM BOWLES

36. Maha·bhárata V: Preparations for War (*Udyogaparvan*) (vol. 2 of 2)
KATHLEEN GARBUTT

37. Maha·bhárata VI: Bhishma (*Bhīṣmaparvan*) (vol. 1 of 2)*
Including the "Bhagavad Gita" in Context
ALEX CHERNIAK. Foreword by RANAJIT GUHA

38. The Ocean of the Rivers of Story (*Kathāsaritsāgara*) (vol. 2 of 7)
by *Somadeva*. SIR JAMES MALLINSON

39. "How the Nagas were Pleased" (*Nāgānanda*) by *Harṣa* &
"The Shattered Thighs" (*Ūrubhaṅga*) by *Bhāsa*.*
ANDREW SKILTON

40. Gita·govínda: Love Songs of Radha and Krishna (*Gītagovinda*)*
by *Jayadeva*. LEE SIEGEL. Foreword by SUDIPTA KAVIRAJ

41. "Bouquet of Rasa" & "River of Rasa" (*Rasamañjarī & Rasataraṅgiṇī*) by *Bhānudatta*. SHELDON POLLOCK

42. Garland of the Buddha's Past Lives (*Jātakamālā*) (vol. 1 of 2)*
by *Āryaśūra*. JUSTIN MEILAND

43. Maha·bhárata XII: Peace (*Śāntiparvan*) (vol. 3 of 5)*
"The Book of Liberation" (*Mokṣadharma*). ALEXANDER WYNNE

44. The Little Clay Cart (*Mṛcchakaṭikā*) by *Śūdraka*.
DIWAKAR ACHARYA. Foreword by PARTHA CHATTERJEE

45. Bhatti's Poem: The Death of Rávana (*Bhaṭṭikāvya*)*
by *Bhaṭṭi*. OLIVER FALLON

46. "Self-Surrender," "Peace," "Compassion," and "The Mission of the Goose": Poems and Prayers from South India (*Ātmārpaṇastuti, Śāntivilāsa, Dayāśataka & Haṃsasaṃdeśa*) by *Appayya Dīkṣita, Nīlakaṇṭha Dīkṣita & Vedānta Deśika.* Yigal Bronner & David Shulman
Foreword by Gieve Patel

47. Maha·bhárata VI: Bhishma (*Bhīṣmaparvan*) (vol. 2 of 2)* Alex Cherniak

48. How Úrvashi Was Won (*Vikramorvaśīya*) by *Kālidāsa* Velcheru Narayana Rao & David Shulman

49. The Quartet of Causeries (*Caturbhāṇī*) by *Śūdraka, Śyāmilaka, Vararuci & Īśvaradatta.* Csaba Dezső & Somadeva Vasudeva

50. Garland of the Buddha's Past Lives (*Jātakamālā*) (vol. 2 of 2)* by *Āryaśūra.* Justin Meiland

51. Princess Kadámbari (*Kādambarī*) (vol. 1 of 3) by *Bāṇa.* David Smith

52. The Rise of Wisdom Moon (*Prabodhacandrodaya*)* by *Kṛṣṇamiśra.* Matthew T. Kapstein
Foreword by J.N. Mohanty

53. Maha·bhárata VII: Drona (*Droṇaparvan*) (vol. 2 of 4)* Vaughan Pilikian

54. Maha·bhárata X & XI: Dead of Night & The Women (*Sauptikaparvan & Strīparvan*).* Kate Crosby

55. Seven Hundred Elegant Verses (*Āryāsaptaśatī*)* by *Govardhana.* Friedhelm Hardy

56. Málavika and Agni·mitra (*Mālavikāgnimitram*) by *Kālidāsa.* Dániel Balogh & Eszter Somogyi